Historical Adventures: 2

Historical Adventures: 2

The Virgin and the Sun
★
Fair Margaret

H. Rider Haggard

LEONAUR

Historical Adventures: 2
The Virgin and the Sun & Fair Margaret
by H. Rider Haggard

Leonaur is an imprint of Oakpast Ltd

Material original to this edition and
presentation of text in this form
copyright © 2009 Oakpast Ltd

ISBN: 978-1-84677-996-1 (hardcover)
ISBN: 978-1-84677-995-4 (softcover)

http://www.leonaur.com

Publisher's Notes

Contents

The Virgin
and the Sun

Dedication

My Dear Little,
Some five-and-thirty years ago it was our custom to discuss many matters, among them, I think, the history and romance of the vanished empires of Central America.

In memory of those far-off days will you accept a tale that deals with one of them, that of the marvellous Incas of Peru; with the legend also that, long before the Spanish conquerors entered on their mission of robbery and ruin, there in that undiscovered land lived and died a white God risen from the sea?
Ever sincerely yours,
H. Rider Haggard
Ditchingham
Oct. 24, 1921
James Stanley Little, Esq.

Introductory

There are some who find great interest, and even consolation, amid the worries and anxieties of life in the collection of relics of the past, drift or long-sunk treasures that the sea of time has washed up upon our modern shore. The great collectors are not of this class. Having large sums at their disposal, these acquire any rarity that comes upon the market and add it to their store which in due course, perhaps immediately upon their deaths, also will be put upon the market and pass to the possession of other connoisseurs. Nor are the dealers who buy to sell again and thus grow wealthy. Nor are the agents of museums in many lands, who purchase for the national benefit things that are gathered together in certain great public buildings which perhaps, some day, though the thought makes one shiver, will be looted or given to the flames by enemies or by furious, thieving mobs.

Those that this Editor has in mind, from one of whom indeed he obtained the history printed in these pages, belong to a quite different category, men of small means often, who collect old things, for the most part at out-of-the-way sales or privately, because they love them, and sometimes sell them again because they must. Frequently these old things appeal, not because of any intrinsic value that they may have, not even for their beauty, for they may be quite unattractive even to the cultivated eye, but rather for their associations. Such folk love to reflect upon and to speculate about the long-dead individuals who have owned the relics, who have supped their soup from the worn Elizabethan spoon, who have sat at the rickety oak table found in a kitchen or an out-house, or upon the broken, ancient chair. They love to think of the little children whose skilful, tired hands wrought the faded sampler and whose bright eyes smarted over its innumerable stitches.

Who, for instance, was the May Shore ("Fairy" broidered in a bracket underneath, was her pet name), who finished yonder elaborate example on her tenth birthday, the 1st of May—doubtless that is where she got her name—in the year 1702, and on what far shore does she keep her birthdays now? None will ever know. She has vanished into the great sea of mystery whence she came, and there she lives and has her being, forgotten upon earth, or sleeps and sleeps and sleeps. Did she die young or old, married or single? Did she ever set *her* children to work other samplers, or had she none? was she happy or unhappy, was she homely or beautiful? Was she a sinner or a saint? Again none will ever know. She was born on the 1st of May, 1692, and certainly she died on some date unrecorded. So far as human knowledge goes that is all her history, just as much or as little as will be left of most of us who breathe to-day when this earth has completed two hundred and eighteen more revolutions round the sun.

But the kind of collector alluded to can best be exemplified in the individual instance of him from whom the manuscript was obtained, of which a somewhat modernized version is printed on these pages. He has been dead some years, leaving no kin; and under his will, such of his motley treasures as it cared to accept went to a local museum, while the rest and his other property were sold for the benefit of a mystical brotherhood, for the old fellow was a kind of spiritualist. Therefore, there is no harm in giving his plebeian name, which was Potts. Mr. Potts had a small draper's shop in an undistinguished and rarely visited country town in the east of England, which shop he ran with the help of an assistant almost as old and peculiar as himself. Whether he made anything out of it or whether he lived upon private means is now unknown and does not matter. Anyway, when there was something of antiquarian interest or value to be bought, generally he had the money to pay for it, though at times, in order to do so, he was forced to sell something else. Indeed these were the only occasions when it was possible to purchase anything, indifferent hosiery excepted, from Mr. Potts.

Now, I, the Editor, who also love old things, and to whom therefore Mr. Potts was a sympathetic soul, was aware of this fact and entered into an arrangement with the peculiar assistant to whom I have alluded, to advise me of such crises which arose whenever the local bank called Mr. Potts's attention to the state of his account. Thus it came about that one day I received the following letter:

Sir,

The Guv'nor has gone a bust upon some cracked china, the ugliest that ever I saw though no judge. So if you want to get that old

tall clock at the first price or any other of his rubbish, I think now
is your chance. Anyhow, keep this dark as per agreement.
Your obedient,
Tom

(He always signed himself Tom, I suppose to mystify, although I
believe his real name was Betterly.)

The result of this epistle was a long and disagreeable bicycle ride
in wet autumn weather, and a visit to the shop of Mr. Potts. Tom, alias
Betterly, who was trying to sell some mysterious undergarments to a
fat old woman, caught sight of me, the Editor aforesaid, and winked.
In a shadowed corner of the shop sat Mr. Potts himself upon a high
stool, a wizened little old man with a bent back, a bald head, and a
hooked nose upon which were set a pair of enormous horn-rimmed
spectacles that accentuated his general resemblance to an owl perched
upon the edge of its nest-hole. He was busily engaged in doing nothing, and in staring into nothingness as, according to Tom, was his habit
when communing with what he, Tom, called his "dratted speerits."

"Customer!" said Tom in a harsh voice. "Sorry to disturb you at
your prayers, Guv'nor, but not having two pair of hands I can't serve a
crowd," meaning the old woman of the undergarments and myself.

Mr. Potts slid off his stool and prepared for action. When he saw,
however, who the customer was he bristled—that is the only word for
it. The truth is that although between us there was an inward and spiritual sympathy, there was also an outward and visible hostility. Twice I
had outbid Mr. Potts at a local auction for articles which he desired.
Moreover, after the fashion of every good collector he felt it to be his
duty to hate me as another collector. Lastly, several times I had offered
him smaller sums for antiques upon which he set a certain monetary
value. It is true that long ago I had given up this bargaining for the
reason that Mr. Potts would never take less than he asked. Indeed he
followed the example of the vendor of the Sibylline books in ancient
Rome. He did not destroy the goods indeed after the fashion of that
person and demand the price of all of them for the one that remained,
but invariably he put up his figure by 10 per cent. and nothing would
induce him to take off one farthing.

"What do *you* want, sir?" he said grumpily. "Vests, hose, collars,
or socks?"

"Oh, socks, I think," I replied at hazard, thinking that they would
be easiest to carry, whereupon Mr. Potts produced some peculiarly
objectionable and shapeless woollen articles which he almost threw

13

at me, saying that they were all he had in stock. Now I detest woollen socks and never wear them. Still, I made a purchase, thinking with sympathy of my old gardener whose feet they would soon be scratching, and while the parcel was being tied up, said in an insinuating voice, "Anything fresh upstairs, Mr. Potts?"

"No, sir," he answered shortly, "at least, not much, and if there were what's the use of showing them to you after the business about that clock?"

"It was £15 you wanted for it, Mr. Potts?" I asked.

"No, sir, it was £17 and now it's 10 per cent. on to that; you can work out the sum for yourself."

"Well, let's have another look at it, Mr. Potts," I replied humbly, whereon with a grunt and a muttered injunction to Tom to mind the shop, he led the way upstairs.

Now the house in which Mr. Potts dwelt had once been of considerable pretensions and was very, very old, Elizabethan, I should think, although it had been refronted with a horrible stucco to suit modern tastes. The oak staircase was good though narrow, and led to numerous small rooms upon two floors above, some of which rooms were panelled and had oak beams, now whitewashed like the panelling—at least they had once been whitewashed, probably in the last generation.

These rooms were literally crammed with every sort of old furniture, most of it decrepit, though for many of the articles dealers would have given a good price. But at dealers Mr. Potts drew the line; not one of them had ever set a foot upon that oaken stair. To the attics the place was filled with this furniture and other articles such as books, china, samplers with the glass broken, and I know not what besides, piled in heaps upon the floor. Indeed where Mr. Potts slept was a mystery; either it must have been under the counter in his shop, or perhaps at nights he inhabited a worm-eaten Jacobean bedstead which stood in an attic, for I observed a kind of pathway to it running through a number of legless chairs, also some dirty blankets between the moth-riddled curtains.

Not far from this bedstead, propped in an intoxicated way against the sloping wall of the old house, stood the clock which I desired. It was one of the first "regulator" clocks with a wooden pendulum, used by the maker himself to check the time-keeping of all his other clocks, and enclosed in a chaste and perfect mahogany case of the very best style of its period. So beautiful was it, indeed, that it had been an instance of "love at first sight" between us, and although

14

there was an estrangement on the matter of settlements, or in other words over the question of price, now I felt that never more could that clock and I be parted.

So I agreed to give old Potts the £20 or, to be accurate, £18 14s. which he asked on the 10 per cent. rise principle, thankful in my heart that he had not made it more, and prepared to go. As I turned, however, my eye fell upon a large chest of the almost indestructible yellow cypress wood of which were made, it is said, the doors of St. Peter's at Rome that stood for eight hundred years and, for aught I know, are still standing, as good as on the day when they were put up.

"Marriage coffer," said Potts, answering my unspoken question.

"Italian, about 1600?" I suggested.

"May be so, or perhaps Dutch made by Italian artists; but older than that, for somebody has burnt 1597 on the lid with a hot iron. Not for sale, not for sale at all, much too good to sell. Just you look inside it, the old key is tied to the spring lock. Never saw such poker-work in my life. Gods and goddesses and I don't know what; and Venus sitting in the middle in a wreath of flowers with nothing on, and holding two hearts in her hands, which shows that it was a marriage chest. Once it was full of some bride's outfit, sheets and linen and clothes, and God knows what. I wonder where she has got to to-day. Some place where the moth don't eat clothes, I hope. Bought it at the break-up of an ancient family who fled to Norfolk on the revocation of the Edict of Nantes—Huguenot, of course. Years ago, years ago! Haven't looked into it for many years, indeed, but think there's nothing there but rubbish now."

Thus he mumbled on while he found and untied the old key. The spring lock had grown stiff from disuse and want of oil, but at length it turned and reopened the chest revealing the poker-work glories on the inner side of the lid and elsewhere. Glories they were indeed, never had I seen such artistry of the sort.

"Can't see it properly," muttered Potts, "windows want washing, haven't been done since my wife died, and that's twenty years ago. Miss her very much, of course, but thank God there's no spring-cleaning now. The things I've seen broken in spring-cleaning! yes, and lost, too. It was after one of them that I told my wife that now I understood why the Mahomedans declare that women have no souls. When she came to understand what I meant, which it took her a long time to do, we had a row, a regular row, and she threw a Dresden figure at my head. Luckily I caught it, having been a cricketer when young. Well, she's gone now, and no doubt heaven's a tidier place than it used to be—that is, if they will stand her rummagings there, which I doubt. Look at that Venus, ain't she a beauty? Might have been done by Titian when his paints ran out, and he had to take to a hot iron to express his art. What, you can't see her well? Wait a bit and I'll get a lantern. Can't have a naked candle here—things too valuable; no money could buy them again. My wife and I had another row about naked candles, or it may have been a paraffin lamp. You sit in that old prayer-stool and look at the work."

Off he went crawling down the dusky stairs and leaving me wondering what Mrs. Potts, of whom now I heard for the first time, could have been like. An aggravating woman, I felt sure, for upon whatever points men differ, as to "spring-cleaning" they are all of one mind. No doubt he was better without her, for what did that dried-up old artist want with a wife?

Dismissing Mrs. Potts from my mind, which, to tell the truth, seemed to have no room for her shadowy and hypothetical entity, I fell to examining the chest. Oh! it was lovely. In two minutes the clock was deposed and that chest became the sultana in my seraglio of beauteous things. The clock had only been the light love of an hour. Here was the eternal queen, that is, unless there existed a still better chest somewhere else, and I should happen to find it. Meanwhile, whatever price that old slave-dealer Potts wanted for it, must be paid to him even if I had to overdraw my somewhat slender account. Seraglios, of whatever sort, it must be remembered, are expensive luxuries of the rich indeed, though, if of antiques, they can be sold again, which cannot be said of the human kind for who wants to buy a lot of antique frumps?

There were plenty of things in the chest, such as some odds and ends of tapestry and old clothes of a Queen Anne character, put here, no doubt, for preservation, as moth does not like this cypress wood. Also there were some books and a mysterious bundle tied up in a curious shawl with stripes of colour running through it. That bundle excited me, and I drew the fringes of the shawl apart and looked in. So far as I could see it contained another dress of rich colours, also a thick packet of what looked like parchment, badly prepared and much rotted upon one side as though by damp, which parchment appeared to be covered with faint black-letter writing, done by some careless scribe with poor ink that had faded very much. There were other things, too, within the shawl, such as a box made of some red foreign wood, but I had not time to investigate further for just then I heard old Potts's foot upon the stair, and thought it best to replace the bundle. He arrived with the lantern and by its light we examined the chest and the poker work.

"Very nice," I said, "very nice, though a good deal knocked about."

"Yes, sir," he replied with sarcasm, "I suppose you'd like to see it neat and new after four hundred years of wear, and if so, I think I can tell you where you can get one to your liking. I made the designs for it myself five years ago for a fellow who wanted to learn how to manufacture antiques. He's in quod now and his antiques are for sale cheap. I helped to put him there to get him out of the way as a danger to Society."

"What's the price?" I asked with airy detachment.

"Haven't I told you it ain't for sale. Wait till I'm dead and come and buy it at my auction. No, you won't, though, for it's going somewhere else."

I made no answer but continued my examination while Potts took his seat on the prayer-stool and seemed to go off into one of his fits of abstraction.

"Well," I said at length when decency told me that I could remain no longer, "if you won't sell it's no use my looking. No doubt you want to keep it for a richer man, and of course you are quite right. Will you arrange with the carrier about sending the clock, Mr. Potts, and I will let you have a cheque. Now I must be off, as I've ten miles to ride and it will be dark in an hour."

"Stop where you are," said Potts in a hollow voice. "What's a ride in the dark compared with a matter like this, even if you haven't a lamp and get hauled before your own bench? Stop where you are, I'm listening to something."

So I stopped and began to fill my pipe.

"Put that pipe away," said Potts, coming out of his reverie, "pipes mean matches; no matches here."

I obeyed, and he went on thinking till at last what between the chest and the worm-eaten Jacobean bed and old Potts on the prayer-stool, I began to feel as if I were being mesmerized. At length he rose and said in the same hollow voice:

"Young man, you may have that chest, and the price is £50. Now for heaven's sake don't offer me £40, or it will be £100 before you leave this room."

"With the contents?" I said casually.

"Yes, with the contents. It's the contents I'm told you are to have."

"Look here, Potts," I said, exasperated, "what the devil do you mean? There's no one in this room except you and me, so who can have told you anything unless it was old Tom downstairs."

"Tom," he said with unutterable sarcasm, "Tom! Perhaps you mean the mawkin that was put up to scare birds from the peas in the garden, for it has more in its head than Tom. No one here? Oh! what fools some men are. Why, the place is thick with them."

"Thick with whom?"

"Who? why, ghosts, of course, as you would call them in your ignorance. Spirits of the dead I name them. Beautiful enough, too, some of them. Look at that one there," and he lifted the lantern and pointed to a pile of old bed posts of Chippendale design.

"Good day, Potts," I said hastily.

"Stop where you are," repeated Potts. "You don't believe me yet, but when you are as old as I am you will remember my words and believe—more than I do and see—clearer than I do, because it's in your soul, yes, the seed is in your soul, though as yet it is choked by the world, the flesh, and the devil. Wait till your sins have brought you trouble; wait till the fires of trouble have burned the flesh away; wait till you have sought Light and found Light and live in Light, then you will believe; *then* you will see."

All this he said very solemnly, and standing there in that dusky room surrounded by the wreck of things that once had been dear to dead men and women, waving the lantern in his hand and staring—at what was he staring?—really old Potts looked most impressive. His twisted shape and ugly countenance became spiritual; he was one who had "found Light and lived in Light."

"You won't believe me," he went on, "but I pass on to you what a woman has been telling me. She's a queer sort of woman; I never saw her like before, a foreigner and dark-hued with strange rich garments and something on her head. There, that, *that*," and he pointed through the dirty window-place to the crescent of a young moon which appeared in the sky. "A fine figure of a woman," he went on, "and oh! heaven, what eyes—I never saw such eyes before. Big and tender, something like those of the deer in the park yonder. Proud, too, she is, one who has ruled, and a lady, though foreign. Well, I never fell in love before, but I feel like it now, and so would you, young man, if you could see her, and so I think did someone else in his day."

"What did she say to you?" I asked, for by now I was interested enough. Who wouldn't be when old Potts took to describing beautiful women?

"It's a little difficult to tell you for she spoke in a strange tongue, and I had to translate it in my head, as it were. But this is the gist of it. That you were to have that chest and what was in it. There's a writing there, she says, or part of a writing for some has gone—rotted away.

You are to read that writing or to get it read and to print it so that the world may read it also. She said that 'Hubert' wishes you to do so. I am sure the name was Hubert, though she also spoke of him with some other title which I do not understand. That's all I can remember, except something about a city, yes, a City of Gold and a last great battle in which Hubert fell, covered with glory and conquering. I understood that she wanted to talk about that because it isn't in the writing, but you interrupted and of course she's gone. Yes, the price is £50 and not a farthing less, but you can pay it when you like for I know you're as honest as most, and whether you pay it or not, you must have that chest and what's in it and no one else."

"All right," I said, "but don't trust it to the carrier. I'll send a cart for it to-morrow morning. Lock it now and give me the key."

****

In due course the chest arrived, and I examined the bundle for the other contents do not matter, although some of them were interesting. Pinned inside the shawl I found a paper, undated and unsigned, but which from the character and style of the writing was, I should say, penned by a lady about sixty years ago. It ran thus:—

"My late father, who was such a great traveller in his young days and so fond of exploring strange places, brought these things home from one of his journeys before his marriage, I think from South America. He told me once that the dress was found upon the body of a woman in a tomb and that she must have been a great lady, for she was surrounded by a number of other women, perhaps her servants who were brought to be buried with her here when they died. They were all seated about a stone table at the end of which were the remains of a man. My father saw the bodies near the ruins of some forest city, in the tomb over which was heaped a great mound of earth. That of the lady, which had a kind of shroud made of the skins of long-wooled sheep wrapped about it as though to preserve the dress beneath, had been embalmed in some way, which the natives of the place, wherever it was, told him showed that she was royal. The others were mere skeletons, held together by the skin, but the man had a long fair beard and hair still hanging to his skull, and by his side was a great cross-hilted sword that crumbled to fragments when it was touched, except the hilt and the knob of amber upon it which had turned almost black with age. I think my father said that the packet of skins or parchment of which the underside is badly rotted with damp was set under the feet of the man. He told me that he gave those who

19

found the tomb a great deal of money for the dress, gold ornaments, and emerald necklace, as nothing so perfect had been found before, and the cloth is all worked with gold thread. My father told me, too, that he did not wish the things to be sold."

This was the end of the writing.

Having read it I examined the dress. It was of a sort that I had never seen before, though experts to whom I have shown it say that it is certainly South American of a very early date, and like the ornaments, probably pre-Inca Peruvian. It is full of rich colours such as I have seen in old Indian shawls which give a general effect of crimson. This crimson robe clearly was worn over a skirt of linen that had a purple border. In the box that I have spoken of were the ornaments, all of plain dull gold: a waist-band; a circlet of gold for the head from which rose the crescent of the young moon and a necklace of emeralds, uncut stones now much flawed, for what reason I do not know, but polished and set rather roughly in red gold. Also there were two rings. Round one of these a bit of paper was wrapped upon which was written, in another hand, probably that of the father of the writer of the memorandum:—

"Taken from the first finger of the right hand of a lady's mummy which I am sorry, in our circumstances, it was quite impossible to carry away."

This ring is a broad band of gold with a flat bezel upon which something was once engraved that owing to long and hard wear now cannot be distinguished. In short, it appears to be a signet of old European make but of what age and from what country it is impossible to determine. The other ring was in a small leathery pouch, elaborately embroidered in gold thread or very thin wire, which I suppose was part of the lady's costume. It is like a very massive wedding ring, but six or eight times as thick, and engraved all over with an embossed conventional design of what look like stars with rays round them, or possibly petalled flowers. Lastly there was the sword-hilt, of which presently.

Such were the trinkets, if so they may be called. They are of little value intrinsically except for their weight in gold, because, as I have said, the emeralds are flawed as though they have been through a fire or some other unknown cause. Moreover, there is about them nothing of the grace and charm of ancient Egyptian jewellery; evidently they belonged to a ruder age and civilization. Yet they had, and still have, to my imagining, a certain dignity of their own.

Also—here I became infected with the spirit of the peculiar Potts—without doubt these things were rich in human associations.

Who had worn that dress of crimson with the crosses worked on it in gold wire (they cannot have been Christian crosses), and the purple-bordered skirt underneath, and the emerald necklace and the golden circlet from which rose the crescent of the young moon? Apparently a mummy in a tomb, the mummy of some long-dead lady of a strange and alien race. Was she such a one as that old lunatic Potts had dreamed he saw standing before him in the filthy, cumbered upper-chamber of a ruinous house in an England market town, I wondered, one with great eyes like to those of a doe and a regal bearing?

No, that was nonsense. Potts had lived with shadows until he believed in shadows that came out of his own imagination and into it returned again. Still, she was a woman of some sort, and apparently she had a lover or a husband, a man with a great fair beard. How at this date, which must have been remote, did a golden-bearded man come to foregather with a woman who wore such robes and ornaments as these? And that sword hilt, worn smooth by handling and with an amber knob? Whence came it? To my mind—this was before expert examination confirmed my view—it looked very Norse. I had read the Sagas and I remembered a tale recovered in them of some bold Norsemen who about the years eight or nine hundred had wandered to the coast of what is known now to be America—I think a certain Eric was their captain. Could the fair-haired man in the grave have been one of these?

Thus I speculated before I looked at the pile of parchments so evidently prepared from sheep skins by one who had only a very rudimentary knowledge of how to work such stuff, not knowing that in those parchments was hid the answer to many of my questions. To these I turned last of all, for we all shrink from parchments; their contents are generally so dull. There was a great bundle of them that had been lashed together with a kind of straw rope, fine straw that reminded me of that used to make Panama hats. But this had rotted underneath together with all the bottom part of the parchments, many sheets of them, of which only fragments remained, covered with dry mould and crumbling. Therefore the rope was easy to remove and beneath it, holding the sheets in place, was only some stout and comparatively modern string—it had a red thread in it that marked it as navy cord of an old pattern.

I slipped these fastenings off and lifted a blank piece of skin set upon the top. Beneath appeared the first sheet of parchment, closely, very closely covered with small "black-letter" writing, so faint and faded that even if I were able to read black-letter, which I cannot, of

21

it I could have made nothing at all. The thing was hopeless. Doubt-less in that writing lay the key to the mystery, but it could never be deciphered by me or any one else. The lady with the eyes like a deer had appeared to old Potts in vain; in vain had she bidden him to hand over this manuscript to me.

So I thought at the time, not knowing the resources of science. Afterwards, however, I took that huge bundle to a friend, a learned friend whose business in life it was and is, to deal with and to decipher old manuscripts.

"Looks pretty hopeless," he said, after staring at these. "Still, let's have a try; one never knows till one tries."

Then he went to a cupboard in his muniment room and pro-duced a bottle full of some straw-coloured fluid into which he dipped an ordinary painting brush. This charged brush he rubbed backwards and forwards over the first lines of the writing and waited. Within a minute, before my astonished eyes, that faint, indistinguishable script turned coal-black, as black as though it had been written with the best modern ink yesterday.

"It's all right," he said triumphantly, "it's vegetable ink, and this stuff has the power to bring it up as it was on the day when it was used. It will stay like that for a fortnight and then fade away again. Your manu-script is pretty ancient, my friend, time of Richard II, I should say, but I can read it easily enough. Look, it begins, 'I, Hubert de Hastings, write this in the land of Tavantinsuyu, far from England where I was born, whither I shall never more return, being a wanderer as the rune upon the sword of my ancestor, Thorgrimmer, foretold that I should be, which sword my mother gave me on the day of the burning of Hastings by the French,' and so on." Here he stopped.

"Then for heaven's sake, do read it," I said.

"My dear friend," he answered, "it looks to me as though it would mean several months' work, and forgive me for saying that I am paid a salary for my time. Now I'll tell you what you have to do. All this stuff must be treated, sheet by sheet, and when it turns black it must be photographed before the writing fades once more. Then a skilled person—so-and-so, or so-and-so, are two names that occur to me—must be employed to decipher it again, sheet by sheet. It will cost you money, but I should say that it was worth while. Where the devil is, or was, the land of Tavantinsuyu?"

"I know," I answered, glad to be able to show myself superior to my learned friend in one humble instance. "Tavantinsuyu was the na-tive name for the Empire of Peru before the Spanish Invasion. But how did this Hubert get there in the time of Richard II? That is some centuries earlier than Pizarro set foot upon its shores."

"Go and find out," he answered. "It will amuse you for quite a long while and perhaps the results may meet the expenses of decipherment, if they are worth publishing. I expect they are not, but then, I have read so many old manuscripts and found most of them so jolly dull."

Well, that business was accomplished at a cost that I do not like to record, and here are the results, more or less modernised, since often Hubert of Hastings expressed himself in a queer and archaic fashion. Also sometimes he used Indian words as though he had talked the tongue of these Peruvians, or rather the *Chanca* variety of it, so long that he had begun to forget his own language. Myself I have found his story very romantic and interesting, and I hope that some others will be of the same opinion. Let them judge.

But oh, I do wonder what was the end of it, some of which doubtless was recorded on the rotted sheets though of course there can have been no account of the great battle in which he fell, since Quilla could not write at all, least of all in English, though I suppose she survived it and him.

The only hint of that end is to be found in old Potts's dream or vision, and what is the worth of dreams and visions?

Book 1

CHAPTER 1

The Sword and the Ring

I, Hubert of Hastings, write this in the land of Tavantinsuyu, far from England, where I was born, whither I shall never more return, being a wanderer as the rune upon the sword of my ancestor, Thorgrimmer, foretold that I should be, which sword my mother gave me on the day of the burning of Hastings by the French. I write it with a pen that I have shaped from a wing feather of the great eagle of the mountains, with ink that I have made from the juices of certain herbs which I discovered, and on parchment that I have split from the skins of native sheep, with my own hands, but badly I fear, though I have seen that art practised when I was a merchant of the Cheap in London Town.

I will begin at the beginning.

I am the son of a fishing-boat owner and was a trader in the ancient town of Hastings, and my father was drowned while following his trade at sea. Afterwards, being the only child left of his, I took on his business, and on a certain day went out to sea to net fish with two of my serving men. I was then a young man of about three and twenty years of age and not uncomely. My hair, which I wore long, was fair in colour and curled. My eyes, set wide apart, were and still are large and blue, although they have darkened somewhat and sunk into the head in this land of heat and sunshine. My nose was wide-nostrilled and large, my mouth also was over-large, although my mother and some others used to think it well-shaped. In truth, I was large all over though not so tall, being burly, with a great breadth of chest and uncommon thickness through the body, and very strong; so strong that there were few who could throw me when I was young.

For the rest, like King David, I, who am now so tanned and weather worn that at a little distance were my hair and beard hidden I might almost be taken for one of the Indian chiefs about me, was of a ruddy and a pleasant countenance, perhaps because of my wonderful health, who had never known a day of sickness, and of an easy nature that often goes with health. I will add this, for why should I not—that I was no fool, but one of those who succeed in that upon which they set their minds. Had I been a fool I should not to-day be the king of a great people and the husband of their queen; indeed, I should not be alive.

But enough of myself and my appearance in those years that seem as far off as though they had never been save in the land of dreams.

Now I and my two serving men, sailors both of them like myself and most of the folk of Hastings set out upon a summer eve, purposing to fish all night and return at dawn. We came to our chosen ground and cast out the net, meeting with wonderful fortune since by three in the morning the big boat was full of every kind of fish. Never before, indeed, had we made so large a haul.

Looking back at that great catch, as here in this far land it is my habit to do upon everything, however small, that happened to me in my youth before I became a wanderer and an exile, I seem to see in it an omen. For has it not always been my lot in life to be kissed of fortune and to gather great store, and then of a sudden to lose it all as I was to lose that rich multitude of fishes?

To-day, when I write this, once more I have great wealth of pomp and love and power, of gold also, more than I can count. When I go forth, my armies, who still look on me as half a god, shout their welcome and kiss the air after their heathen fashion. My beauteous queen bows down to me and the women of my household abase themselves into the dust. The people of the Ancient City of Gold turn their faces to the wall and the children cover their eyes with their hands that they may not look upon my splendour as I pass, while maidens throw flowers for my feet to tread. Upon my judgment hangs life or death, and my lightest word is as though it were spoken from heaven. These and many other things are mine, the trappings of power, the prerogative of the Lord-from-the-Sea who brought victory to the Chanca people and led them back to their ancient home where they might live safe, far from the Inca's rage.

And yet often, as I sit alone in my splendour upon the roof of the ancient halls or wander through the starlit palace gardens, I call to mind that great catch of fishes in the English sea and of what followed after. I call to mind also my prosperity and wealth as one of the first merchants of London Town and what followed after. I call to mind, too, the winning of Blanche Aleys, the lady so far above me in rank and station and what followed after. Then it is that I grow afraid of what may follow after this present hour of peace and love and plenty.

Certainly one thing will follow, and that is death. It may come late or it may come soon. But yesterday a rumour reached me through my spies that Kari Upanqui, the Inca of Tavantinsuyu, he who once was as my brother, but who now hates me because of his superstitions, and because I took a Virgin of the Sun to be my wife, gathers a great host to follow on the path we trod many years ago when the Chancas fled from the Inca tyranny back to their home in the ancient City of Gold and to smite us here. That host, said the rumours, cannot march till next year, and then will be another year upon its journey. Still, know-ing Kari, I am sure that it will march, yes, and arrive, after which must befall the great battle in the mountain passes wherein, as of old, I shall lead the Chanca armies.

Perchance I am doomed to fall in that battle. Does not the rune upon Wave-Flame, the sword of Thorgrimmer my ancestor, say of him that holds it that,

Conquering, conquered shall he be,
And far away shall sleep with me?

Well, if the Chancas conquer, what care I if I am conquered? 'Twould be a good death and a clean, to fall by Kari's spear, if I knew that Kari and his host fell also, as I swear that fall they shall, St. Hubert helping me. Then at least Quilla and her children would live on in peace and greatness since they can have no other foe to fear.

Death, what is death? I say that it is the hope of every one of us and most of all the exile and the wanderer. At the best it may be glory; at the worst it must be sleep. Moreover, am I so happy that I should fear to die? Quilla cannot read this writing, and therefore I will an-swer, No. I am a Christian, but she and those about her, aye, my own children with them, worship the moon and the host of heaven. I am white-skinned, they are the hue of copper, though it is true that my little daughter, Gudruda, whom I named so after my mother, is almost white. There are secrets in their hearts that I shall never learn and there are secrets in mine from which they cannot draw the veil because our bloods are different. Yet God knows, I love them well enough, and most of all that greatest of women, Quilla.

Oh! the truth is that here on earth there is no happiness for man.

It is because of this rumour of the coming of Kari with his host that I set myself to this task, that I have long had in my mind, to write down something of my history, both in England and in this land which, at any rate for hundreds of years, mine is the first white foot to press. It seems a foolish thing to do since when I have written who will read, and what will chance to that which I have written? I shall leave orders that it be placed beneath my feet in the tomb, but who will ever find that tomb again? Still I write because something in my heart urges me to the task.

****

I return to the far-off days. Our boat being full with merry hearts we set sail before a faint wind for Hastings beach. As yet there was little light and much fog, still the landward breeze was enough to draw us forward. Then of a sudden we heard sounds as of men talking upon ships and the clank of spars and blocks. Presently came a puff of air lifting the fog for a little and we saw that we were in the midst of a great fleet, a French fleet, for the Lilies of France flew at their mastheads, saw, too, that their prows were set for Hastings, though for the while they were becalmed, since the wind that was enough for our light, large-sailed fishing-boat could not stir their bulk. Moreover, they saw us, for the men-at-arms on the nearest ship shouted threats and curses at us and followed the shouts with arrows that almost hit us.

Then the fog closed down again, and in it we slipped through the French fleet.

It may have been the best part of an hour later that we reached Hastings. Before the boat was made fast to the jetty, I sprang to it shouting:

"Stir! stir! the French are upon you! To arms! We have slipped through a whole fleet of them in the mist."

Instantly the sleepy quay seemed to awaken. From the neighbouring fish market, from everywhere sailormen and others came running, followed by children with gaping mouths, while from the doors of houses far away shot women with scared faces, like ferreted rabbits from their burrows. In a minute the crowd had surrounded me, all asking questions at once in such a fashion that I could only answer them with my cry of:

"Stir! the French are upon you. To arms, I say. To arms!"

Presently through the throng advanced an old white-bearded man who wore a badge of office, crying as he came, "Make way for the bailiff!"

The crowd obeyed, opening a path, and soon we were face to face.

"What is it, Hubert of Hastings?" he asked. "Is there fire that you shout so loudly?"

"Aye, Worship," I answered. "Fire and murder and all the gifts that the French have for England. The Fleet of France is beating up for Hastings, fifty sail of them or more. We crept through them in the fog, for the wind which would scarce move them served our turn and beyond an arrow or two, they took no note of a fishing-boat."

"Whence come they?" asked the bailiff, bewildered.

"I know not, but those in another boat we passed in the midst shouted that these French were ravaging the coast and heading for Hastings to put it to fire and sword. Then that boat vanished away, I know not where, and that is all I have to tell save that the French will be here within an hour."

Without staying to ask more questions, the bailiff turned and ran towards the town, and presently the alarm bells rang out from the towers of All Saints and St. Clement's, while criers summoned all men to the market-place. Meanwhile I, not without a sad look at my boat and the rich catch within, made my way into the town, followed by my two men.

Presently I reached an ancient, timbered house, long, low, and rambling, with a yard by its side full of barrels, anchors, and other marine stores such as rope, that had to do with the trade I carried on at this place.

I, Hubert, with a mind full of fears, though not for myself, and a stirring of the blood such as was natural to my age at the approach of my first taste of battle, ran fast up to that house which I have described, and paused for a moment by the big elm tree that grew in front of the door, of which the lower boughs were sawn off because they shut out the light from the windows. I remember that elm tree very well, first because when I was a child starlings nested in a hole in the trunk, and I reared one in a wicker cage and made a talking bird of it which I kept for several years. It was so tame that it used to go about sitting on my shoulder, till at last, outside the town a cat frightened it thence, and before I could recapture it, it was taken by a hawk, which hawk I shot afterwards with an arrow out of revenge.

Also this elm is impressed upon me by the fact that on that morning when I halted by it, I noted how green and full of leaf it was. Next morning, after the fire, I saw it again, all charred and blackened, with its beautiful foliage withered by the heat. This contrast remained upon my memory, and whenever I see any great change of fortune from prosperity to ruin, or from life to death, always I bethink me of that elm. For it is by little things which we ourselves have seen and not by those written of or told by others, that we measure and compare events.

The reason that I ran so hard and then paused by the elm, was because my widowed mother lived in that house. Knowing that the French meant mischief for a good reason, because one of their arrows, or perhaps a quarrel from a cross-bow, whistled just past my head out there upon the sea, my first thought was to get her away to some place of safety, no easy task seeing that she was infirm with age. My second, that which caused me to pause by the tree, was how I should break the news to her in such a fashion that she would not be over-frightened. Having thought this over I went on into the house.

The door opened into the sitting-room that had a low roof of plaster and big oak beams. There I found my mother kneeling by the table upon which food was set for breakfast: fried herrings, cold meat, and a jug of ale. She was saying her prayers after her custom, being very religious though in a new fashion, since she was a follower of a preacher called Wycliffe, who troubled the Church in those days. She seemed to have gone to sleep at her prayers, and I watched her for a moment, hesitating to waken her. My mother, as even then I noted, was a very handsome woman, though old, for I was born when she had been married twenty years or more, with white hair and well-cut features that showed the good blood of which she came, for she was better bred than my father and quarrelled with her kin to marry him.

At the sound of my footsteps she woke up and saw me.

"Strange," she said, "I slept at my prayers who did so little last night, as has become a habit with me when you are out a-fishing, for which God forgive me, and dreamed that there was some trouble forward. Scold me not, Hubert, for when the sea has taken the father and two sons, it is scarcely wonderful that I should be fearful for the last of my blood. Help me to rise, Hubert, for this water seems to gather in my limbs and makes them heavy. One day, the leech says, it will get to the heart and then all will be over."

I obeyed, first kissing her on the brow, and when she was seated in her armed chair by the table, I said,

"You dream too well, Mother. There is trouble. Hark! St. Clement's bells are talking of it. The French come to visit Hastings. I know for I sailed through their fleet just after dawn."

"Is it so?" she asked quietly. "I feared worse. I feared lest the dream meant that you had gone to join your brothers in the deep. Well, the French are not here yet, as thank God you are. So eat and drink, for we of England fight best on full bellies."

Again I obeyed who was very hungry after that long night and needed food and ale, and as I swallowed them we heard the sound of folk shouting and running.

"You are in haste, Hubert, to join the others on the quay and send a Frenchman or two to hell with that big bow of yours?" she said inquiringly.

"Nay," I answered, "I am in haste to get you out of this town, which I fear may be burnt. There is a certain cave up yonder by the Minnes Rock where I think you might lie safe, Mother."

"It has come down to me from my fathers, Hubert, that it was never the fashion of the women of the north to keep their men to shield them when duty called them otherwise. I am helpless in my limbs and heavy, and cannot climb, or be borne up yonder hill to any cave. Here I stop where I have dwelt these five-and-forty years, to live or die as God pleases. Get you to your duty, man. Stay. Call those wenches and bid them fly inland to their folk, out Burwash way. They are young and fleet of foot, and no Frenchman will catch them."

I summoned the girls who were staring, white-faced, from the attic window-place. In three minutes they were gone, though it is true that one of them, the braver, wished to bide with her mistress.

I watched them start up the street with other fugitives who were pouring out of Hastings, and came back to my mother. As I did so a great shout told me that the French fleet had been sighted.

"Hubert," she said, "take this key and go to the oak chest in my sleeping room, lift out the linen at the top and bring me that which lies wrapped in cloth beneath."

I did so, returning with a bundle that was long and thin. With a knife she cut the string that tied it. Within were a bag of money and a sword in an ancient scabbard covered with a rough skin which I took to be that of a shark, which scabbard in parts was inlaid with gold.

"Draw it," said my mother.

I did so, and there came to light a two-edged blade of blue steel, such as I had never seen before, for on the blade were engraved strange characters whereof I could make nothing, although as it chanced I could read and write, having been taught by the monks in my child-hood. The hilt, also, that was in the form of a cross, had gold inlaid upon it; at the top of it, a large knob or apple of amber, much worn by handling. For the rest it was a beauteous weapon and well balanced.

"What of this sword?" I asked.

"This, Son. With the black bow that you have," and she pointed to the case that leaned against the table, "it has come down in my family for many generations. My father told me that it was the sword of one Thorgrimmer, his ancestor, a Norseman, a Viking he called him, who came with those who took England before the Norman time; which

I can well believe since my father's name, like mine, till I married, was Grimmer. This sword, also, has a name and it is Wave-Flame. With it, the tale tells, Thorgrimmer did great deeds, slaying many after their heathen fashion in his battles by land and sea. For he was a wanderer, and it is said of him that once he sailed to a new land far across the ocean, and won home again after many strange adventures, to die at last here in England in some fray. That is all I know, save that a learned man from the north once told my father's father that the writing on the sword means:

"He who lifts Wave-Flame on high In love shall live and in battle die; Storm-tossed o'er wide seas shall roam And in strange lands shall make his home. Conquering, conquered shall he be, And far away shall sleep with me.

"Those were the words which I remember because of the jingle of them; also because such seems to have been the fate of Thorgrimmer and the sword that his grandson took from his tomb."

Here I would have asked about this grandson and the tomb, but having no time, held my peace.

"All my life have I kept that sword," went on my mother, "not giving it to your father or brothers, lest the fate written on it should befall them, for those old wizards of the north, who fashioned such weapons with toil and skill, could foresee the future—as at times I can, for it is in my blood. Yet now I am moved to bid you take it, Hubert, and go where its flame leads you and dree your gloom, whatever it may be, for I know you will use it like Thorgrimmer's self."

She paused for a moment, then went on:

"Hubert, perhaps we part for the last time, for I think that my hour is at hand. But let not that trouble you, since I am glad to go to join those who went before, and others with them, perchance Thorgrimmer's self. Hearken, Hubert. If aught befalls me, or this place, stay not here. Go to London town and seek out John Grimmer, my brother, the rich merchant and goldsmith who dwells in the place called Cheap. He knew you as a child and loved you, and lacking offspring of his own will welcome you for both our sakes. My father would not give John the sword lest its fate should be on him, but I say that John will be glad to welcome one of our race who holds it in his hand. Take it then, and with it that bag of gold, which may prove of service ere all be done.

"Aye, and there is one more thing—this ring which, so says the tale, came down with the sword and the bow, and once had writing on it like the sword, though that is long since rubbed away. Take it and wear it till perchance, in some day to come, you give it to another as I did."

Wondering at all this tale which, after her secret fashion, my mother had kept from me till that hour, I set the ring upon my finger.

"I gave yonder ring to your father on the day that we were betrothed," went on my mother, "and I took it back again from his corpse after he had been found floating in the sea. Now I pass it on to you who soon will be all that is left of both of us."

"Hark!" she continued, "the crier summons all men with their arms to the market-place to fight England's foes. Therefore one word more while I buckle the sword Wave-Flame on to you, as doubtless his women folk did on to Thorgrimmer, your ancestor. My blessing on you, Hubert. Be you such a one as Thorgrimmer was, for we of the Norse blood desire that our loves and sons should prove not backward when swords are aloft and arrows fly. But be you more than he, be you a Christian also, remembering that however long you live, and the Battle-maidens have not marked you yet, at last you must die and give account.

"Hubert, you are such a one as women will love; one, too, who, I fear me, will be a lover of women, for that weakness goes with strength and manhood by Nature's laws. Be careful of women, Hubert, and if you may, choose those who are not false and cling to her who is most true. Oh, you will wander far; I read it in your eyes that you will wander far, yet shall your heart stay English. Kiss me and begone! Lad, are you forgetting your spare arrows and the bull-hide jerkin that was your father's? You will want them both to-day. Farewell, farewell! God and His Christ be with you—and shoot you straight and smite you hard. Nay, no tears, lest my eyes should be dimmed, for I'll climb to the attic and watch you fight."

CHAPTER 2

The Lady Blanche

So I went, with a sore heart, for I remembered that when my father and brothers were drowned, although I was then but a little one, my mother had foreseen it, and I feared much lest it might be thus in her own case also. I loved my mother. She was a stern woman, it was true, with little softness about her, which I think came with her blood, but she had a high heart, and oh! her last words were noble. Yet through it all I was pleased, as any young man would have been, with the gift of the wonderful sword which once had been that of Thorgrimmer, the sea-rover, whose blood ran in my body against which it lay, and I hoped that this day I might have chance to use it worthily as Thorgrimmer did in forgotten battles. Having imagination, I wondered also whether the sword knew that after its long sleep it had come forth again to drink the blood of foes.

Also I was pleased with another thing, namely, that my mother had told me that I should live my life and not die that day by the hand of Frenchmen; and that in my life I should find love, of which to tell truth already I knew a little of a humble sort, for I was a comely youth, and women did not run away from me, or if they did, soon they stopped. I wanted to live my life, I wanted to see great adventures and to win great love. The only part of the business which was not to my taste was that command of my mother's, that I should go to London to sit in a goldsmith's shop. Still, I had heard that there was much to be seen in London, and at least it would be different from Hastings.

The street outside our doors was crowded with folk, some of the men making their way to the market-place, about whom hung women and children weeping; others, old people, wives and girls and little ones fleeing from the town. I found the two sailormen who had been with me on the boat, waiting for me. They were brawny fellows named Jack Grieves and William Bull, who had been in our service since my childhood, good fishermen and fighters both; indeed one of them, William Bull, had served in the French wars.

"We knew that you were coming, Master, so we bided here for you," said William, who having once been an archer was armed with a bow and a short sword, whereas Jack had only an axe, also a knife such as we used on the smacks for cleaning fish.

I nodded, and we went on to the market-place and joined the throng of men, a vast number of them, who were gathered there to defend Hastings and their homes. Nor were we too soon, for the French ships were already beaching within a few yards of the shore or on it, their draught being but small, while the sailors and men-at-arms were pushing off in small boats or wading to the strand.

There was great confusion in the market-place, for as is common in England, no preparation had been made against attack though such was always to be feared.

The bailiff ran about shouting orders, as did others, but proper officers were lacking, so that in the end men acted as the fancy took them. Some went down towards the beach and shot with arrows at the Frenchmen. Others took refuge in houses, others stood irresolute, waiting, knowing not which way to turn. I and my two men were with those who went on to the beach where I loosed some arrows from my big black bow, and saw a man fall before one of them.

But we could do little or nothing, for these Frenchmen were trained soldiers under proper command. They formed themselves into companies and advanced, and we were driven back. I stopped as long as I dared, and drawing the sword, Wave-Flame, fought with a French-man who was in advance of the others. What is more, making a great blow at his head which I missed, I struck him on the arm and cut it off, for I saw it fall to the ground. Then others rushed up at me and I fled to save my life.

Somehow I found myself being pressed up the steep Castle Hill with a number of Hastings folk, followed by the French. We reached the Castle and got into it, but the old portcullis would not close, and in sundry places the walls were broken down. Here we found a number of women who had climbed for refuge, thinking that the place would be safe. Among these was a beautiful and high-born maiden whom I knew by sight. Her father was Sir Robert Aleys who, I believe, was then the Warden of the Castle of Pevensey, and she was named the lady Blanche. Once, indeed, I had spoken with her on an occasion too long to tell. Then her large blue eyes, which she knew well how to use, had left me with a swimming head, for she was very fair and very sweet and gracious, with a most soft voice, and quite unlike any other woman I had ever seen, nor did she seem at all proud. Soon her father, an old knight, who had no name for gentleness in the countryside, but was said to be a great lover of gold, had come up and swept her away, asking her what she did, talking with a common fishing churl. This had happened some months before.

Well, there I found her in the Castle, alone it seemed, and knowing me again, which I thought strange, she ran to me, praying me to protect her. More, she began to tell me some long tale, to which I had not time to listen, of how she had come to Hastings with her father, Sir Robert, and a young lord named Deleroy, who, I understood, was some kinsman of hers, and slept there. How, too, she had been separated from them in the throng when they were attempting to return to Pevensey which her father must go to guard, because her horse was frightened and ran away, and of how finally men took her by the arm and brought her to this castle, saying that it was the safest place.

"Then here you must bide, Lady Blanche," I answered, cutting her short. "Cling to me and I will save you if I can, even if it costs me my life."

Certainly she did cling to me for all the rest of that terrible day, as will be seen.

From this height we saw Hastings beginning to burn, for the Frenchmen had fired the town in sundry places, and being built of wood, it burnt furiously. Also we saw and heard horrible scenes and sounds of rapine, such as chance in this Christian world of ours where a savage foe finds peaceful folk of another race at his mercy. In the houses people were burnt; in the streets they were being murdered, or worse. Yes, even children were murdered, for afterwards I saw the bodies of some of them.

Awhile later through the wreaths of smoke we perceived companies of the French advancing to attack the Castle. There may have been three hundred of them in all, and we did not count more than fifty men, some of us ill-armed, together with a mob of aged people and many women and children. What had become of the other men I do not know, but orders had been shouted from all quarters, and some had gone this way and some that. Some, too, I think, had fled, lacking leaders.

The French having climbed the hill, began to attack our ill-fenced gateways, bringing up beams of timber to force them in. Those of us who had bows shot some of them, though, their armour being good, for the most part the arrows glanced. But few had bows.

Moreover, whenever we showed ourselves they poured such a rain of quarrels and other shafts upon us that we could not face it, lacking mail as we did, and a number of us were killed or wounded. At last they forced the easternmost gate which was the weakest, and got in there and over a place in the wall were it was broken. We fought them as well as we could; myself I cut down two with the sword, Wave-Flame, hewing right through the helm of one, for the steel of that sword was good. Here, too, Jack Grieves was killed by my side by a pike thrust, and died calling to me to fight on for old England and Hastings town; after which he said something about beer and breathed his last.

The end of it was that those who were left were driven out of the Castle together with the women and children, the murdering French killing every man who fell wounded where he lay, and trying to make prisoner any women they thought young and fair enough. Especially did they seek to capture the lady Blanche because they saw that she was beautiful and of high station. But by good fortune more than aught else, I saved her from this fate.

As it chanced we were among the last to leave the Castle, whence, to tell the truth, I was loath to go, for by now my blood was up, and with a few others fought till I was driven out. I prayed the lady Blanche to run forward with the other women. But she would not, answering that she trusted no one else, but would stay to die with me, as though that would help either of us.

Thus it came about that a tall French knight who had set his eyes on her, out-climbed his fellows upon the slope of the hill, for they were weary and gathering to re-form, and catching her round the middle, strove to drag her away. I fell on him and we fought. He had fine armour and a shield while I had none, but I held the long sword while he only wielded a battle-axe. I knew that if he could get in a blow with that battle-axe, I was sped, since the bull's hide of my jerkin would never stand against it. Therefore it was my business to keep out of his reach. This, being young and active, for the most part I made shift to do, especially as he could not move very quickly in his mail. The end of it was that I cut him on the arm through a joint in his harness, whereon he rushed at me, swearing French oaths.

I leapt on one side and as he passed, smote with all my strength. The blow fell between neck and shoulder, from behind as it were, and such was the temper of that sword named Wave-Flame that it shore through his mail deep into the flesh beneath, to the backbone as I believe. At least he went down in a heap—I remember the rattle of his armour as he fell, and there lay still. Then we fled on down the steep path, I holding the bloody sword with one hand and Lady Blanche with the other, while she thanked me with her eyes.

At length we were in the town again, running up my own street. On either side of us the houses burned, and behind us came another body of the French. The reek got into our eyes and we stumbled over dead or fainting people.

Looking to the left I caught sight of the elm tree of which I have spoken, that grew in front of our door, and saw that the house behind it was burning. Yes, and I saw more, for at the attic window, which was open, the flames making an arch round her, sat my mother. Moreover, she was singing for I heard her voice and the wild words she sang, though this was a strange thing for a woman to do in the hour of such a death. Further, she saw and knew me, for she waved her hands to me, then pointed towards the sea, why, I did not guess at the time. I stopped, purposing to try to rescue her though the front of the house was flaming, and the attempt must have ended in my death. But at that moment the roof fell in, causing the fire to spout upwards and out-wards. This was the last that I saw of my mother, though afterwards we found her body and gave it burial with those of many other victims.

There was no time to stay, for the conquering French were pour-ing up the street behind us, shooting as they came and murdering any laggards whom they could catch. On we went up the steep slope of the Minnes Rock. I would have fled on into the open country, but the lady Blanche had no strength left. Twice she sank to the ground, stricken with terror and weariness, and each time prayed me not to leave her; nor indeed did I wish to do so. The end of it was that William Bull and I between us half carried her with much toil to the cave of which I had spoken to my mother. The task was heavy and slow, since always we must scramble over sheer ground. What is more, a party of the French, seeing our plight, followed us. Perhaps some of them guessed who the lady was, for there were many spies in Hastings who might have told them, and desired to capture and hold her to ransom.

At the least they came on after us and a few others, women all of them, who had joined our company, being unable to travel further, or trusting to William Bull and myself to protect them.

We reached the cave, and thrusting the women along it, William and I stood in the mouth and waited. He had no bow and all my arrows were gone save three, but of these I, who was noted for my archery, determined to make the best use I could. So I drew them out, and having strung the bow, sat down to get my breath. On came the

French, shouting and jabbering at us to the effect that they would cut our throats and carry off *la belle dame* to be their sport.

"She shall be mine!" yelled a big fellow with a flattened nose and a wide mouth who was ahead of the others, and not more than fifty yards away.

I rose, and praying my patron, good St. Hubert after whom I was named because I first saw light upon his day, the 23rd of November, to give me skill, I drew the great bow to my ear, aimed, and loosed. Nor did St. Hubert, a lover of fine shooting, fail me in my need, for that arrow rushed out and found its home in the big mouth of the Frenchman, through which it passed, pinning his foul tongue to his neck bone.

Down he went, and cheered by the sight I refitted and loosed at the next. Him, too, the arrow caught, so that he fell almost on the other.

I set the third and last arrow on the string and waited a space. Behind these two was a squat, broad man, a knight I suppose, for he wore armour, and had a shield with a cock painted on it. This man, frightened by the fate of his companions, yet not minded to give up the venture for those in rear of him urged him on, bent himself almost double, and holding the shield over his helm which was closed, so as to protect his head and body, came on at a good pace.

I waited till he was within five-and-twenty yards or so, hoping that the roughness of the ground would cause him to stumble and the shield to shift so that I could get a chance at him behind it. But I did not, so at last, again praying to St. Hubert, I drew the big bow till the string touched my ear, and let drive. The shaft, pointed with tempered steel, struck the shield full in the centre, and by Heaven, pierced it, aye, and the mail behind, aye, and the flesh it covered, so that he, too, got his death.

"A great shot, Master," said William, "that no other bow in Hastings could have sped."

"Not so ill," I answered, "but it is my last. Now we must fight as we can with sword and axe until we be sped."

William nodded, and the women in the cave began to wail while I unstrung my bow and set it in its case, from habit I think, seeing that I never hoped to look upon it again. Just then from the French ships in the harbour there came a great blaring of trumpets giving some alarm, and the Frenchmen of a sudden, ceasing from their attack, turned and ran towards the shore. I stepped out of the cave with William and looked. There on the sea, drawing near from the east before a good wind, I saw ships, and saw, too, that from their masts flew the pennons of England, for the golden leopards gleamed in the sun.

"It is our fleet, William," I said, "come to talk with these French."

"Then I would that it had come sooner," answered William. "Still, better now than not at all."

****

Thus were we saved, through Hamo de Offyngton, the Abbot of Battle Abbey, or so I was told afterwards, who collected a force by land and sea and drove off the French after they had ravaged the Isle of Wight, attacked Winchelsea, and burned the greater part of Hastings. So it came about that in the end these pirates took little benefit by their wickedness, since they lost sundry ships with all on board, and others left in such haste that their people remained on shore where they were slain by the mob that gathered as soon as it was seen that they were deserted, helped by a company of the Abbot's men who had marched from Battle. But with all this I had nothing to do who now that the fight was over, felt weak as a child and could think of little save that I had seen my mother burning.

Presently, however, that happened which woke me from my grief and caused my blood which had grown sluggish to run again. For when she knew that she was safe the lady Blanche came out of the cave and addressed me as I stood there leaning against the rock with the red sword Wave-Flame in my hand, as I had drawn it to make ready for the last fight to the death. All sorts of sweet names she called me—a hero, her deliverer, and I know not what besides.

In the end, as I made no answer, being dazed, also hurt by an axe blow on the breast which I had not felt before, dealt by that Frenchman whom I slew near the Castle, she did more. Throwing her arms about me she kissed me thrice, on either cheek and on the lips, doubtless because she was overwrought, and in her thankfulness forgot her maidenly reserve, though as William Bull said afterwards, this forgetfulness did not cause her to kiss him who had also helped her up the hill.

Those kisses were like wine to me, for it is strange how, if we love her, by the decree of Nature the touch of a beautiful woman's lips, felt for the first time, affects us in our youth. Whatever else we forget, that we always remember, however false those lips afterwards be proved. For then the wax is soft and the die sinks deep, so deep that no after-heats can melt its stamp and no fretting wear it out while we live beneath the sun.

Now my young blood being awakened, I was minded to return those kisses, and began to do so with a Jew's interest, when I heard a rough voice swearing many strange oaths, and heard also the other women who had sheltered with us in the cave begin to titter, for the moment forgetting all their private woes, as those of their sex will do when there is kissing in the wind.

"God's blood!" said the rough voice, "who is this that handles my daughter as though they had been but an hour wed? Take those lips of yours from her, fellow, or I'll cut them from your chops."

I looked round astonished, to see Sir Robert Aleys mounted on a grey horse, and followed by a company of men-at-arms who appeared to be under the command of a well-favoured, dark-eyed young captain with long hair, and dressed more wondrously than any man I had ever seen before. Had he put on Joseph's coat over his mail, he could not have worn more colours, and I noted that the toes of his shoes curled up so high that I wondered however he worked them through his stirrups, and what would happen to him if by chance he were unhorsed.

Being taken aback I made no answer, but William Bull, who, if a rough fellow, had a tongue in his head and a ready wit, spoke up for me.

"If you want to know," he said in his Sussex drawl, "I'll tell you who he is, Sir Robert Aleys. He is my worshipful master, Hubert of Hastings, ship-owner, householder, and trader of this town. Or at least he was these things, but now it seems that his ships and house are burnt and his mother with them; also that there will be no trade in Hastings for many a day."

"Mayhap," answered Sir Robert, adding other oaths, "but why does he buss my daughter?"

"Perchance because he must give as good as he got, which is a law among honest merchants, noble Sir Robert. Or perchance because he has a better right to buss her than any man alive, seeing that but for him, by now she would be but stinking clay, or a Frenchman's leman."

Here the fine young captain cut in, saying,

"Whatever else this worshipful trader may need, he does not lack a trumpeter."

"That is so, my Lord Deleroy," replied William, unmoved, "for when I find a good song I like to sing it. Go now and look at those three men who lie yonder on the slope, and see whether the arrows in them bear my master's mark. Go also and look upon the Castle hill and find a knight with his head well-nigh hewn from his shoulders, and see whether yonder sword fits into the cut. Aye, and at others that I could tell you of, slain, every one of them, to save this fair lady. Aye, go you whose garments are so fine and unstained, and then come back and talk of trumpeters."

"Pish!" said my Lord Deleroy with a shrug of his shoulders, "a lady

who is over-wrought and hangs to some common fellow, like one who kisses the feet of a wooden saint that she thinks has saved her from calamity!"

At these words I, who had been listening like a man in a dream, awoke, as it were, for they stung me. Moreover, I had heard that this fine Deleroy was one of those who owed his place and rank to the King's favour, as he did his high name, being, it was reported, by birth but a prince's bastard sprung from some relative of Sir Robert whom therefore he called cousin.

"Sir," I said, "you know best whether I am more common than you are. Let that be. At least I hold in my hand the sword of one who begat my forefather hundreds of years ago, a certain Thorgrimmer who was great in his time. Now I have had my fill of fighting to-day, and you, doubtless through no fault of your own, have had none; you also are clad in mail and I, a common fellow, have none. Deign then to descend from that horse and take a turn with me though I be tired, and thus prove my commonness upon my body. Of your nobility do this, seeing that after all we are of one flesh."

Now, stung in his turn, he made as though he would do what I prayed, when for the first time, after glancing at her father who sat still—puzzled, it would seem—the lady Blanche spoke.

"Be not mad, Cousin," she said. "I tell you that this gentleman has saved my life and honour, twice at least to-day. Is it wonderful, then, if I thanked him in the best fashion that a woman can, and thus brought your insults on him?"

He hesitated, though one of his curled-up shoes was out of the stirrup, when suddenly Sir Robert broke in in his big voice, saying:

"God's truth, Cousin, I think that you will do well to leave this young cock alone, since I like not the look of that red spur of his," and he glanced at the sword Wave-Flame. "Though he be weary, he may have a kick or two in him yet." hen he turned to me and added: "Sir, you have fought well; many a man has earned knighthood for less, and if a fair maid thanked you in her own fashion, you are not to blame. I, her father, also thank you and wish you all good fortune till we meet again. Farewell. Daughter, make shift to share this horse with me, and let us away out of this stricken town to Pevensey, where perchance it will please those French to call to-morrow."

A minute later they were gone, and I noted with a pang that as they went the lady Blanche, having waved her good-bye to me, talked fast to her cousin Deleroy and that he held her hand to steady her upon her father's horse.

44

CHAPTER 3

Hubert Comes to London

When the lady Blanche was out of sight, followed by the women who had sheltered with us in the cave, William and I went to a stream we knew of not far away and drank our fill. Then we walked to the three whom I had shot with my big bow, hoping to regain the arrows, for I had none left. This, however, could not be done though all the men were dead, for one of the shafts, the last, was broken, and the other two were so fixed in flesh and bone that only a surgeon's saw would loose them.

So we left them where they were, and before the men were buried many came to marvel at the sight, thinking it a wonderful thing that I should have killed these three with three arrows, and that any bow which arm might bend could have driven the last of them through an iron shield and a breastplate behind it.

This armour, I should tell, William took for himself, since it was of his size. Also on the morrow, returning to the Castle Hill, I stripped the knight whom I had slain with the sword, Wave-Flame, of his splendid Milan mail, whereof the *plastron*, or breast-plate, was inlaid with gold, having over it a *camail* of chain to cover the joints, through which my good sword had shorn into his neck. The cognizance on his shield strangely enough was three barbed arrows, but what was the name of the knight who bore it I never learned. This mail, which must have cost a great sum, the Bailiff of Hastings granted me to keep, since I had slain its wearer and borne myself well in the fight. Moreover, I took the three arrows for my own cognizance, though in truth I had no right to any, being in those days but a trader. (Little did I know then how well this mail was to serve me in the after years.)

By now night was coming on, and as we could see from the cave mouth that the part of Hastings which lies towards the village of St. Leonards seemed to have escaped the fire, thitherward we went by the beach to avoid the heat and falling timbers in the burning town. On our way we met others and from them heard all that had befallen. It would seem that the French loss in life was heavier than our own, since many of them were cut off when they tried to fly to their ships, and some of these could not be floated from the beach or were rammed and sunk with all aboard by the English vessels. But the damage done to Hastings was as much as could scarcely be made good in a generation, for the most of it was burnt or burning. Also many, like my own mother, had perished in the fire, being sick or aged or in childbed, or for this reason and that forgotten and unable to move. Indeed on the beach were hundreds of folk in despair, nor was it only the women and children who wept that evening.

For my part, with William I went beyond the burning to the house of a certain old priest who was my confessor, and the friend of my father before me, and there we found food and slept, he returning thanks to God for my escape and offering me consolation for the loss of my mother and goods.

I rested but ill that night, as those do who are over-weary. Moreover, this had been my first taste of battle, and again and again I saw those men falling before my sword and arrows. Very proud was I to have slain them, wicked ravishers as they were, and very glad that from my boyhood I had practised myself with sword and bow till I could fence with any, and was perhaps the most skilled marksman in Hastings, having won the silver arrow at the butts at the last meeting, and from archers of all ages. Yet the sight of their deaths haunted me who remembered how well their fate might have been my own, had they got in the first shot or blow.

Where had they gone to, I wondered? To the priest's Heaven or Hell? Were they now telling their sins to some hard-faced angel while he checked the count from his book, reminding them of many that they had forgotten? Or were they fast asleep for ever and ever as a shrewd thinker whom I knew had told me secretly he was sure would be the fate of all of us, whatever the priests might teach and believe. And where was my mother whom I had loved and who loved me well, although outwardly she was so stern a woman, my mother whom I had seen burned alive, singing as she burned? Oh! it was a vile world, and it seemed strange that God should cause men and women to be born that they might come to such cruel ends. Yet who were we to question His decrees of which we knew neither the beginning nor the finish?

Anyway, I was glad I was not dead, for now that all was over I trembled and felt afraid, which I had never done during the fighting, even when my hour seemed very near.

Lastly there was this high-born lady, Blanche Aleys, with whom fortune had thrown me so strangely that day. Those blue eyes of hers had pierced my heart like darts, and do what I would I might not rid my mind of the thought of her, or my ears of the sound of her soft voice, while her kisses seemed still to burn upon my lips. It wrung me to think that perhaps I should never see her again, or that if I did I might not speak with her, being so far beneath her in condition, and having already earned the wrath of her father, and, as I guessed, the jealousy of that scented cousin of hers whom they said the King loved like a brother.

What had my mother told me? To leave this place and go to London, there to find my uncle, John Grimmer, goldsmith and merchant, who was my godfather, and to ask him to take me into his business. I remembered this uncle of mine, for some seven or eight years before, when I was a growing lad, because there was a plague in London he had come down to Hastings to visit us. He only stayed a week, however, because he said that the sea air tied up his stomach and that he would rather risk the plague with a good stomach than leave it behind him with a bad one—though I think it was his business he thought of, not his stomach.

He was a strange old man, not unlike my mother, but with a nose more hooked, small dark eyes, and a bald head on which he set a cap of velvet. Even in the heat of summer he was always cold and wore a frayed fur robe, complaining much if he came into a draught of air. Indeed he looked like a Jew, though a good Christian enough, and laughed about it, because he said that this appearance of his served him well in his trade, since Jews were always feared, and it was held to be impossible to overreach them.

For the rest I only recalled that he examined me as to my book learning which did not satisfy him, and went about valuing all our goods and fishing-boats, showing my mother how we were being cheated and might earn more than we did. When he departed he gave me a gold piece and said that Life was nothing but vanity, and that I must pray for his soul when he was dead as he was sure it would need such help, also that I ought to put the gold piece out to interest. This I did by buying with it a certain fierce mastiff dog I coveted that had been brought on a ship from Norway, which dog bit some great man in our town, who hauled my mother before the bailiff about it and caused the poor beast to be killed, to my great wrath.

Now that I came to think of it, I had liked my Uncle John well enough although he was so different from others. Why should I not go to him? Because I did not wish to sit in a shop in London, I who loved the sea and the open air; also because I feared he might ask me what I had done with that gold piece and make a mock of me about the dog. Yet my mother had bidden me go, and it was her last command to me, her dying words which it would be unlucky to disobey. Moreover, our boats and house were burnt and I must work hard and long before these could be replaced. Lastly, in London I should see no more of the lady Blanche Aleys, and there could learn to forget the lights in her blue eyes. So I determined that I would go, and at last fell asleep.

Next morning I made my confession to the old priest that, amongst other matters, he might shrive me of the blood which I had shed, though this he said needed no forgiveness from God or man, being, as I think, a stout Englishman at heart. Also I took counsel with him as to what I should do, and he told me it was my duty to obey my mother's wishes, since such last words were often inspired from on high and declared the will of Heaven. Further he pointed out that I should do well to avoid the lady Blanche Aleys who was one far above me in degree, the following of whom might bring me to trouble, or even to death; moreover, that I might mend my broken fortunes through the help of my uncle, a very rich man as he had heard, to whom he would write a letter about me.

Thus this matter was settled.

Still some days went by before I left Hastings, since first I must wait until the ashes of our house were cool enough to search in them for my mother's body. Those who found her at length said that she was not so much burned as might have been expected, but as to this I am uncertain, since I could not bring myself to look upon her who desired to remember her as she had been in life. She was buried by the side of my father, who was drowned, in the churchyard of St. Clement's, and when all had gone away I wept a little on her grave.

The rest of that day I spent making ready for my journey. As it chanced when the house was burnt the outbuildings which lay on the farther side of the yard behind escaped the fire, and in the stable were two good horses, one a grey riding-gelding and the other a mare that used to drag the nets to the quay and bring back the fish, which horses, although frightened and alarmed, were unharmed. Also there was a quantity of stores, nets, salt, dried fish in barrels, and I know not what besides. The horses I kept, but all the rest of the gear, together with the premises, the ground on which the house had stood, and the other property I made over to William, my man, who promised me to pay me their value when he could earn it in better times.

Next morning I rode away for London upon the grey horse, loading the armour of the knight I had killed and such other possessions as remained to me upon the mare which I led with a rope. Save William there was none to say me good-bye, for the misery in Hastings was so great that all were concerned with their own affairs or in mourning their dead. I was not sorry that it fell out thus, since I was so full of sadness at leaving the place where I was born and had lived all my life, that I think I should have shed tears if any who had been my friends had spoken kind words to me, which would have been unmanly. Never had I felt so lonely as when from the high ground I gazed back to the ruins of Hastings over which still hung a thin pall of smoke. My courage seemed to fail me altogether; I looked forward to the future with fear, believing that I had been born unlucky, that it held no good for me who probably should end my days as a common soldier or a fisherman, or mayhap in prison or on the gallows. From childhood I had suffered these fits of gloom, but as yet this was the blackest of them that I had known.

At length, the sun that had been hidden shone out and with its coming my temper changed. I remembered that I who might so easily have been dead, was sound, young, and healthy, that I had sword, bow, and armour of the best, also twenty or more of gold pieces, for I had not counted them, in the bag which my mother gave me with Wave-Flame. Further, I hoped that my uncle would befriend me, and if he did not, there were plenty of captains engaged in the wars who might be glad of a squire, one who could shoot against any man and handle a sword as well as most.

So putting up a prayer to St. Hubert after my simple fashion, I pushed on blithely to the crest of a long rise and there came face to face with a gay company who, hawk on wrist and hound at heel, were, I guessed, on their way to hunt in the Pevensey marshes. While they were still a little way off I knew these to be no other than Sir Robert Aleys, his daughter Blanche, and the King's favourite, young Lord Deleroy, with their servants, and was minded to turn aside to avoid them. Then I remembered that I had as much right to the King's Highway as they, and my pride aiding me, determined to ride on taking no note of them, unless first they took note of me. Also they knew me, for my ears being very sharp, I heard Sir Robert say in his big voice:

"Here comes that young fisherman again. Pass him in silence,

Daughter"; heard, too, Lord Deleroy drawl it, "It seems that he has been gathering gear from the slain, and like a good chapman bears it away for secret sale."

Only the lady Blanche answered neither the one nor the other, but rode forward with her eyes fixed before her, pretending to talk to the hawk upon her wrist, and now that she was rested and at ease, looking even more beautiful than she had done on the day of the burning.

So we met and passed, I glancing at them idly and guiding my horses to the side of the road. When there were perhaps ten yards between us I heard Lady Blanche cry:

"Oh, my hawk!" I looked round to see that the falcon on her wrist had in some way loosed itself, or been loosed, and being hooded, had fallen to the ground where one of the dogs was trying to catch and kill it. Now there was great confusion, the eyes of all being fixed upon the hawk and the dog, in the midst of which the lady Blanche very quietly turned her head, and lifting her hand as though to see how the hawk had fallen from it, with a swift movement laid her fingers against her lips and threw a kiss to me.

As swiftly I bowed back and went on my way with a beating heart. For a few moments I was filled with joy, since I could not mistake the meaning of this signalled kiss. Then came sorrow like an April cloud, since my wound which was in the way of healing was all re-opened. I had begun to forget the lady Blanche, or rather by an effort of the will, to thrust her from my thought, as my confessor had bidden me. But now on the wings of that blown kiss thither she had flown back again, not to be frighted out for many a day.

That night I slept at an inn at Tonbridge, a comfortable place where the host stared at the gold piece from the bag which I tendered in payment, and at first would not take what was due to him out of it, because it bore the head of some ancient king. However, in the end a merchant of Tonbridge who came in for his morning ale showed him that it was good, so that trouble passed.

About two in the afternoon I came to Southwark, a town that to me seemed as big as Hastings before it was burned, where was a fine inn called the Tabard at which I stopped to bait my horses and to take a bite and drink of ale. Then I rode on over the great Thames where floated a multitude of ships and boats, crossing it by London Bridge, a work so wonderful that I marvelled that it could be made by the hand of man, and so broad that it had shops on either side of the roadway, in which were sold all sorts of merchandise. Thence I inquired my way to Cheapside, and came there at last thrusting a path through a roaring multitude of people, or so it seemed to me who never before had seen so many men and women gathered together, all going on their way and, it would appear, ignorant of each other.

Here I found a long and crowded thoroughfare with gabled houses on either side in which all kinds of trades were carried on. Down this I wandered, being cursed at more than once because my pack mare, growing frightened, dragged away from me and crossed the path of carts which had to stop till I could pull her free. After the third of these tangles I halted by the side of the footway behind a wain with barrels on it, and looked about me bewildered.

To my left was a house somewhat set back from the general line that had a little patch of garden ground in front of it in which grew some untended and thriftless-looking shrubs. This house seemed to be a place of business because from an iron fastened to the front of it hung a board on which was painted an open boat, high at the prow and stern, with a tall beak fashioned to the likeness of a dragon's head and round shields all down the rail.

While I was staring at this sign and wondering emptily what kind of a boat it was and of what nation were the folk who had sailed in her, a man came down the garden path and leaned upon the gate, staring in turn at me. He was old and strange-looking, being clad in a rusty gown with a hood to it that was pulled over his head, so that I could only see a white, peaked beard and a pair of brilliant black eyes which seemed to pierce me as a shoemaker's awl pierces leather.

"What do you, young man," he asked in a high thin voice, "cumbering my gate with those nags of yours? Would you sell that mail you have on the pack-horse? If so I do not deal in such stuff, though it seems good of its kind. So get on with it elsewhere."

"Nay, sir," I answered, "I have naught to sell who in this hive of traders seek one bee and cannot find him."

"Hive of traders! Truly the great merchants of the Cheap would be honoured. Have they stung you, then, already, young bumpkin from the countryside, for such I write you down? But what bee do you seek? Stay, now, let me guess. Is it a certain old knave named John Grimmer, who trades in gold and jewels and other precious things and who, if he had his deserts, should be jail?"

"Aye, aye, that's the man," I said.

"Surely he also will be honoured," exclaimed the old fellow with a cackle. "He's a friend of mine and I will tell him the jest."

"If you would tell me where to find him it would be more seasonable."

"All in good time. But first, young sir, where did you get that fine armour? If you stole it, it should be better hid."

"Stole it!" I began in wrath. "Am I a London chapman—?"

"I think not, though you may be before all is done, for who knows what vile tricks Fortune will play us? Well, if you did not steal it, mayhap you slew the wearer and are a murderer, for I see black blood on the steel."

"Murderer!" I gasped.

"Aye, just as you say John Grimmer is a knave. But if not, then perchance you slew the French knight who wore it on Hastings Hill, ere you loosed the three arrows at the mouth of the cave near Minnes Rock."

Now I gaped at him.

"Shut your mouth, young man, lest those teeth of yours should fall out. You wonder how I know? Well, my friend John Grimmer, the goldsmith knave, has a magic crystal which he purchased from one who brought it from the East, and I saw it in that crystal."

As he spoke, as though by chance he pushed back the hood that covered his head, revealing a wrinkled old face with a mocking mouth which drooped at one corner, a mouth that I knew again, although many years had passed since I looked upon it as a boy.

"You are John Grimmer!" I muttered.

"Yes, Hubert of Hastings, I am that knave himself. And now tell me, what did you do with the gold piece I gave you some twelve summers gone?"

Then I was minded to lie, for I feared this old man. But thinking better of it, I answered that I had spent it on a dog. He laughed outright and said:

"Pray that it is not an omen and that you may not follow the gold piece to the dogs. Well, I like you for speaking the truth when you are tempted to do otherwise. Will you be pleased to shelter for a while beneath the roof of John Grimmer, the merchant knave?"

"You mock me, sir," I stammered.

"Perhaps, perhaps! But there's many a true word spoken in jest; for if you do not know it now you will learn it afterwards that we are all knaves, each in his own fashion, who if we do not deceive others, at least deceive ourselves, and I perhaps more than most. Vanity of vanities! All is vanity."

Then, waiting for no reply, he drew a silver whistle from under his dusty robe and blew it, whereon—so swiftly that I marvelled whether he were waiting—a stout-built serving man appeared to whom he said:

"Take these horses to the stable and treat them as though they were my own. Unload the pack beast, and when it has been cleaned, set the mail and the other gear upon it in the room that has been made ready for this young master, Hubert of Hastings, my nephew."

Without a word the man led off the horses.

"Be not afraid," chuckled John Grimmer, "for though I am a knave, dog does not eat dog and what is yours is safe with me and those who serve me. Now enter," and he led the way into the house, opening the iron-studded oak door with a key from his pouch.

Within was a shop where I saw precious things such as furs and gold ornaments lying about.

"The crumbs to catch the birds, especially the ladybirds," he said with a sweep of his hand, then took me through the shop into a passage and thence to a room on the right. It was not a large room but more wonderfully furnished than any I had ever seen. In the centre was a table of black oak with cunningly carved legs, on which stood cups of silver and a noble centre piece that seemed to be of gold. From the ceiling, too, hung silver lamps that already had been lit, for the evening was closing in, and gave a sweet smell. There was a hearth also with what was rare, a chimney, upon which burned a little fire of logs, while the walls were hung with tapestries and broidered silks.

Whilst I stared about me, my uncle took off his cloak beneath which he was clothed in some rich but rather threadbare stuff, only retaining the velvet skullcap that he wore. Then he bade me do the same, and when I had laid my outer garment aside, looked me all over in the lamplight.

"A proper young man," he muttered to himself, "and I'd give all I have to be his age and like him. I suppose those limbs and sinews of his came from his father, for I was ever thin and spare, as was my father before me. Nephew Hubert, I have heard all the tale of your dealings with the Frenchmen, on whom be God's curse, at Hastings yonder; and I say that I am proud of you, though whether I shall stay so is another matter. Come hither."

I obeyed, and taking me by my curling hair with his delicate hand, he drew down my head and kissed me on the brow, muttering, "Neither chick nor child for me and only this one left of the ancient blood. May he do it honour."

Then he motioned to me to be seated and rang a little silver bell that stood upon the table. As in the case of the man without, it was answered instantly from which I judged that Master Grimmer was well served. Before the echoes of the bell died away a door opened, the tapestry swung aside, and there appeared two most comely serving maids, tall and well-shaped both of them, bearing food.

"Pretty women, Nephew, no wonder that you look at them," he said when they had gone away to fetch other things, "such as I like to have about me although I am old. Women for within and men for without, that is Nature's law, and ill will be the day when it is changed. Yet beware of pretty women, Nephew, and I pray you kiss not those as you did the lady Blanche Aleys at Hastings, lest it should upset my household and turn servants into mistresses."

I made no answer, being confounded by the knowledge that my uncle showed of me and my affairs, which afterwards I discovered he had, in part at any rate, from the old priest, my confessor, who had written to commend me to him, telling my story and sending the letter by a King's messenger, who left for London on the morrow of the Burning. Nor did he wait for any, for he bade me sit down and eat, plying me with more meats than I could swallow, all most delicately dressed, also with rare wines such as I had never tasted, which he took from a cupboard where they were kept in curious flasks of glass. Yet as I noted, himself he ate but little, only picking at the breast of a fowl and drinking but the half of a small silver goblet filled with wine.

"Appetite, like all other good things, for the young," he said with a sigh as he watched my hearty feasting. "Yet remember, Nephew, that if you live to reach it, a day will come when yours will be as mine is. Vanity of vanities, saith the preacher, all is vanity!"

At length, when I could eat no more, again he rang the silver bell and those fair waiting girls dressed alike in green appeared and cleared away the broken meats. After they were gone he crouched over the fire rubbing his thin hands to warm them, and said suddenly:

"Now tell me of my sister's death and all the rest of your tale."

So as well as I was able I told him everything from the hour when I had first sighted the French fleet on board my fishing-boat to the end.

"You are no fool," he said when I had finished, "who can talk like any clerk and bring things that have happened clearly to the listener's eye, which I have noted few are able to do. So that's the story. Well, your mother had a great heart, and she made a great end, such an one as was loved of our northern race, and that even I, the old merchant knave, desire and shall not win, who doubtless am doomed to die a cow's death in the straw. Pray the All-Father Odin—nay, that is heresy for which I might burn if you or the wenches told it to the priests—pray God, I mean, that He may grant you a better, as He did to old Thorgrimmer, if the tale be true,

54

Thorgrimmer whose sword you wear and have wielded shrewdly, as that French knight knows in hell to-day."

"Who was Odin?" I asked.

"The great god of the North. Did not your mother tell you of him? Nay, doubtless she was too good a Christian. Yet he lives on, Nephew. I say that Odin lives in the blood of every fighting man, as Freya lives in the heart of every lad and girl who loves. The gods change their names, but hush! hush! talk not of Odin and of Freya, for I say that it is heresy, or pagan, which is worse. What would you do now? Why came you to London?"

"Because my mother bade me and to seek my fortune."

"Fortune—what is fortune? Youth and health are the best fortune, though, if they know how to use it, those who have wealth as well may go further than the rest. Also beauteous things are pleasant to the sight and there is joy in gathering them. Yet at the last they mean nothing, for naked we came out of the blackness and naked we return there. Vanity of vanities, all is vanity!"

CHAPTER 4

Kari

Thus began my life in London in the house of my uncle, John Grimmer, who was called the Goldsmith. In truth, however, he was more than this, since not only did he fashion and trade in costly things; he lent out moneys to interest upon security to great people who needed it, and even to the king Richard and his Court. Also he owned ships and did much commerce with Holland, France, yes, and with Spain and Italy. Indeed, although he appeared so humble, his wealth was very large and always increased, like a snowball rolling down a hill; moreover, he owned much land, especially in the neighbourhood of London where it was likely to grow in value.

"Money melts," he would say, "furs corrupt with moth and time, and thieves break in and steal. But land—if the title be good—remains. Therefore buy land, which none can carry away, near to a market or a growing town if may be, and hire it out to fools to farm, or sell it to other fools who wish to build great houses and spend their goods in feeding a multitude of idle servants. Houses eat, Hubert, and the larger they are, the more they eat."

No word did he say to me as to my dwelling on with him, yet there I remained, by common consent, as it were. Indeed on the morrow of my coming a tailor appeared to measure me for such garments as he thought I should wear, by his command, I suppose, as I was never asked for payment, and he bade me furnish my chamber to my own liking, also another room at the back of the house that was much larger than it seemed, which he told me was to be mine to work in, though at what I was to work he did not say.

For a day or two I remained idle, staring at the sights of London and only meeting my uncle at meals which sometimes we ate alone and sometimes in the company of sea-captains and learned clerks or of other merchants, all of whom treated him with great deference and as I soon guessed, were in truth his servants. At night, however, we were always alone and then he would pour out his wisdom on me while I listened, saying little. On the sixth day, growing weary of this idleness, I made bold to ask him if there was aught that I could do.

"Aye, plenty if you have a mind to work," he answered. "Sit down now, and take pen and paper and write what I shall tell you."

Then he dictated a short letter to me as to shipping wine from Spain, and when it was sanded, read it carefully.

"You have it right," he said, seeming pleased, "and your script is clear if boyish. They taught you none so ill yonder at Hastings where I thought you had only learned to handle ropes and arrows. Work? Yes, there is plenty of it of the more private sort which I do not give to this scribe or to that who might betray my secrets. For know," he went on in a stern voice, "there is one thing which I never pardon, and it is betrayal. Remember that, nephew Hubert, even in the arms of your loves, if you should be fool enough to seek them, or in your cups."

So he talked on, and while he did so went to an iron chest that he unlocked, and thence drew out a parchment roll which he bade me take to my workroom and copy there. I did so, and found that it was an inventory of his goods and estates, and oh! before I had done I wished that there were fewer of them. All the long day I laboured, only stopping for a bite at noon, till my head swam and my fingers ached. Yet as I did so I felt proud, for I guessed that my uncle had set me this task for two reasons: first, to show his trust in me, and, secondly, to acquaint me with the state of his possessions, but as it were in the way of business. By nightfall I had finished and checked the copy which with the original I hid in my robe when the green-robed waiting maid summoned me to eat.

At our meal my uncle asked me what I had seen that day and I replied—naught but figures and crabbed writing—and handed him the parchments which he compared item by item.

"I am pleased with you," he said at last, "for heresofar I find but a single error and that is my fault, not yours; also you have done two days' work in one. Still, it is not fit that you who are accustomed to the open air should bend continually over deeds and inventories. Therefore, to-morrow I shall have another task for you, for like yourself your horse needs exercise."

And so he had, for with two stout servants riding with me and guiding me, he sent me out of London to view a fair estate of his upon the borders of the Thames and to visit his tenants there and make report of their husbandry, also of certain woods where he proposed to fell oak for shipbuilding. This I did, for the servants made me known to the tenants, and got back at night-fall, able to tell him all which he was glad to learn, since it seemed that he had not seen this estate for five long years.

On another day he sent me to visit ships in which goods of his were being laden at the wharf, and on another took me with him to a sale of furs that came from the far north where I was told the snow never melts and there is always ice in the sea.

Also he made me known to merchants with whom he traded, and to his agents who were many, though for the most part secret, together with other goldsmiths who held moneys of his, and in a sense were partners, forming a kind of company so that they could find great sums in sudden need. Lastly, his clerks and dependents were made to understand that if I gave an order it must be obeyed, though this did not happen until I had been with him for some time.

Thus it came about that within a year I knew all the threads of John Grimmer's great business, and within two it drifted more and more into my hands. The last part of it with which he made me acquainted was that of lending money to those in high places, and even to the State itself, but at length I was taught this also and came to know sundry of these men, who in private were humble borrowers, but if they met us in the street passed us with the nod that the great give to their inferiors. Then my uncle would bow low, keeping his eyes fixed upon the ground and bid me do the same. But when they were out of hearing he would chuckle and say,

"Fish in my net, goldfish in my net! See how they shine who presently must wriggle on the shore. Vanity of vanities! All is vanity, and doubtless Solomon knew such in his day."

Hard I worked, and ever harder, toiling at the mill of all these large affairs and keeping myself in health during such time as I could spare by shooting at the butts with my big bow where I found that none could beat me, or practising sword play in a school of arms that was kept by a master of the craft from Italy. Also on holidays and on Sundays after mass I rode out of London to visit my uncle's estates where sometimes I slept a night, and once or twice sailed to Holland or to Calais with his cargoes.

One day, it was when I had been with him about eighteen months, he said to me suddenly.

"You plough the field, Hubert, and do not tithe the crop, but live upon the bounty of the husbandman. Henceforward take as much of it as you will. I ask no account."

So I found myself rich, though in truth I spent but little, both because my tastes were simple and it was part of my uncle's policy to make no show which he said would bring envy on us. From this time forward he began to withdraw himself from business, the truth being that age took hold of him and he grew feeble. The highest of the affairs he left to me, only inquiring of them and giving his counsel from time to time. Still, because he must do something, he busied himself in the shop which, as he said, he kept as a trap for the birds, chaffering in ornaments and furs as though his bread depended upon his earning a gold piece, and directing the manufacture of beautiful jewels and cups which he, who was an artist, designed to be made by his skilled and highly paid workmen, some of whom were foreigners.

"We end where we began," he would say. "A smith was I from my childhood and a smith I shall die. What a fate for one of the blood of Thorgrimmer! Yet I am selling you into the same bondage, or so it would seem. But who knows? Who knows? We design, but God decrees."

It is to be noted that when old men cease from the occupation of their lives, often enough within a very little time they also cease from life itself. So it was with my uncle. Day by day he faded till at last at the beginning of the third winter after I came to him he took to his bed where he lay growing ever weaker till at length he died in the hour of the birth of the new year.

To the last his mind remained clear and strong, and never more so than on the night of his death. That evening after I had eaten I went to his room as usual and found him reading a beautiful manuscript of the book of the Wisdom of Solomon that is called Ecclesiastes, a work which he preferred to all others, since its thoughts were his. "I gathered me also silver and gold and the peculiar treasures of kings," he read aloud, whether to himself or to me I knew not, and went on, "So I was great, and increased more than all that were before me. . . . Then I looked on all the works that my hands had wrought, and on the labour that I had laboured to do; and behold all was vanity and vexation of spirit, and there was no profit under the sun."

He closed the book, saying,

"So shall you find, Nephew, you, and every man in the evil days of age when you shall say, 'I have no pleasure in them.' Hubert, I am going to my long home, nor do I grieve. In youth I met with sorrow, for though I have never told you, I was married then and had one son, a bright boy, and oh! I loved him and his mother. Then came the plague and took them both. So having naught left and being by nature one of those who could wean himself from women, which I fear that you are not, Hubert, noting all the misery there is in the world and how those who are called noble whom I hate, grind down the humble and the poor, I turned myself to good works. Half of all my gains I have given and still give to those who minister to poverty and sickness; you will find a list of them when I am gone should you wish to continue the bounty, as to which I do not desire to bind you in any way. For know, Hubert, that I have left you all that is mine; the gold and the ships with the movables and chattels to be your own, but the lands which are the main wealth, for life and afterwards to be your children's, or if you should die childless, then to go to certain hospitals where the sick are tended."

Now I would have thanked him, but he waved my words aside and went on:

"You will be a very rich man, Hubert, one of the richest in all London; yet set not your heart on wealth, and above all do not ape nobility or strive to climb from the honest class of which you come into the ranks of those idle and dissolute cut-throats and pick-brains who are called the great. Lighten their pockets if you will, but do not seek to wear their silken, scented garments. That is my counsel to you." He paused a while, picking at the bedclothes as the dying do, and continued: "You told me that your mother thought you would be a wanderer, and it is strange that now my mind should be as hers was in this matter. For I seem to see you far away amidst war and love and splendour, holding Wave-Flame aloft as did that Thorgrimmer who begat us. Well, go where you are called or as occasion drives, though you have much to keep you at home. I would that you were wed, since marriage is an anchor that few ships can drag. Yet I am not sure, for how know I whom you should wed, and once that anchor is down no windlass will wind it up and death alone can cut its chain. One word more. Though you are so young and strong remember that as I am, so shall you be. To-day for me, to-morrow for thee, said the wise old man, and thus it ever was and is.

"Hubert, I do not know why we are born to struggle and to suffer and at last be noosed with the rope of Doom. Yet I hope the priests are right and that we live again, though Solomon thought not so; that is, if we live where there is neither sin nor sorrow nor fear of death. If so, be sure that in some new land we shall meet afresh, and there I shall ask account of you of the wealth I entrusted to your keeping. Think of me kindly at times, for I have learned to love you who are of my blood, and while we live on in the hearts of those we love, we are not truly dead. Come hither that I may bless you in your coming in and going out while you still look upon the sun."

So he blessed me in beautiful and tender words, and kissed me on the brow, after which he bade me leave him and send the woman to watch him, because he desired to sleep.

When she looked at him at midnight just as the bells rang in the new year, he was dead.

According to his wish John Grimmer, the last of that name, was buried by the bones of his forgotten wife and child, who had left the world over fifty years before, in the chancel of that church in the Cheap which was within a stone's throw of his dwelling house. By his desire also the funeral was without pomp, yet many came to it, some of them of high distinction, although the day was cold and snowy. I noted, moreover, the deference they showed to me who by now was known to be his heir, even if they had never spoken with me before, as was the case with certain of them, taking occasion to draw me aside and say that they trusted that their ancient friendship with my honoured uncle would be continued by myself.

Afterwards I looked up their names in his private book and found that one and all of those who had spoken thus owed moneys to his estate.

When the will was sworn and I found myself the master of many legions, or rather of more money, land, and other wealth than I had ever dreamed of, at first I was minded to be rid of trade and to take up my abode upon one or other of my manors, where I might live in plenty for the rest of my days. In the end, however, I did not do so, partly because I shrank from new faces and surroundings, and partly because I was sure that such would not have been my uncle's wish.

Instead I set myself to play and outpass his game. He had died very rich; I determined that I would die five or ten times richer; the richest man in England if I could, not because I cared for money, of which indeed I spent but little upon myself, but because the getting of it and the power that it brought, seemed to me the highest kind of sport. So bending my mind to the matter I doubled and trebled his enterprises on this line and on that, and won and won again, for even where skill and foresight failed, Fortune stood my friend with a such strange persistence that at length I became superstitious and grew frightened of her gifts. Also I took pains to hide my great riches from the public eye, placing much of them in the names of others whom I could trust, and living most modestly in the same old house, lest I should become a man envied by the hungry and marked for plunder by the spendthrift great.

****

It was during the summer following my uncle's death that I went to the wharves to see to the unloading of a ship that came in from Venice, bearing many goods from the East on my account, such as ivory, silks, spices, glass, carpets, and I know not what. Having finished my business and seen these precious things warehoused, I handed over the checking of a list of them to another and turned to seek my horse.

Then it was that I saw a number of half-grown lads and other idlers mobbing a man who stood among them wrapped in a robe of what looked like tattered sheepskin, yet was not because the wool on it was of a reddish hue and very long and soft, which robe was thrown over his head hiding his face. At this man—a tall figure who stood there patiently like a martyr at the stake—these lewd fellows were hurling offal, such as fishes' heads and rotted fruits that lay in plenty on the quay, together with coarse words. "Blackamoor" was one I caught.

Such sights were common enough, but there was a quiet dignity of bearing about this victim which moved me, so that I went to the rabble commanding them to desist. One of them, a rough bumpkin, not knowing who I was, pushed me aside, bidding me mind my own business, whereupon, being very strong, I dealt him such a blow between the eyes that he went down like a felled ox and lay there half stunned. His companions beginning to threaten me, I blew upon my whistle, whereon two of my serving-men, without whom I seldom rode in those troublous times, ran up from behind a shed, laying hands upon their short swords, on seeing which the idlers took to their heels.

When they had gone I turned to look at the stranger, whose hood had fallen back in the hustling, and saw that he was about thirty years of age, and of a dark and noble countenance, beardless, but with straight black hair, black flashing eyes, and an aquiline nose. Another thing I noted about him was that the lobe of his ear was pierced and in a strange fashion, since the gristle was stretched to such a size that a small apple could have been placed within its ring. For the rest the man's limbs were so thin as though from hunger, that everywhere his bones showed, while his skin was scarred with cuts and scratches, and on his forehead was a large bruise. He seemed bewildered also and very weak, yet I think he understood that I was playing a friend's part to him, for he bowed towards me in a stately, courteous way and kissed the air thrice, but what this meant at the time I did not know.

I spoke to him in English, but he shook his head gently to show that he did not understand. Then, as though by an afterthought, he touched his breast several times, and after each touch, said in a voice of strange softness, "Kari," which I took it he meant was his name. At any rate, from that time forward I called him Kari.

Now the question was how to deal with him. Leave him there to be mocked or to perish I could not, nor was there anywhere whither I could send him. Therefore it seemed the only thing to do was to take him home with me. So grasping his arm gently I led him off the quay where our horses were and motioned to him to mount one that had been ridden by a servant whom I bade to walk. At the sight of these horses, however, a great terror took hold of him for he trembled all over, a sweat bursting out upon his face, and clung to me as though for protection, making it evident that he had never seen such an animal before. Indeed, nothing would persuade him to go near them, for he shook his head and pointed to his feet, thus showing me that he preferred to walk, however weak his state.

The end of it was that walk he did and I with him from Thames side to the Cheap, since I dared not leave him alone for fear lest he should run away. A strange sight we presented, I leading this dusky wanderer through the streets, and glad was I that night was falling so that few saw us and those who did thought, I believe, that I was bringing some foreign thief to jail.

At length we reached the Boat House as my dwelling was called, from the image of the old Viking vessel that my uncle had carved and set above the door, and I led him in staring about him with all his eyes, which in his thin face looked large as those of an owl, taking him up the stairs, which seemed to puzzle him much, for at every step he lifted his leg high into the air, to an empty guest room.

Here besides the bed and other furniture was a silver basin with its jug, one of the beautiful things that John Grimmer had brought I know not whence. On these Kari fixed his eyes at once, staring at them in the light of the candles that I had lit, as though they were familiar to him. Indeed, after glancing at me as though for permission, he went to the jug that was kept full of water in case of visitors of whom I had many on business, lifted it, and after pouring a few drops of the water on to the floor as though he made some offering, drank deeply, thus showing that he was parched with thirst.

Then without more ado he filled the basin and throwing off his tattered robe began to wash himself to the waist, round which he wore another garment, of dirty cotton I thought, which looked like a woman's petticoat. Watching him I noted two things, that his poor body was as scratched and scarred as though by old thorn wounds, as were his face and hands, also marked with great bruises as though from kicks and blows, and secondly that hung about his neck was a wondrous golden image about four inches in length. It was of rude workmanship with knees bent up under the chin, but the face, in which little emeralds were set for eyes, was of a great and solemn dignity.

This image Kari washed before he touched himself with water, bowing to it the while, and when he saw me observing him, looked upwards to the sky and said a word that sounded like *Pachacamac*, from which I took it to be some idol that the poor man worshipped. Lastly, tied about his middle was a hide bag filled with I knew not what.

Now I found a washball made of oil of olives mixed with beech ash and showed him the use of it. At first he shrank from this strange thing, but coming to understand its office, served himself of it readily, smiling when he saw how well it cleansed his flesh. Further, I fetched a shirt of silk with a pair of easy shoes and a fur-lined robe that had belonged to my uncle, also hosen, and showed him how to put them on, which he learned quickly enough. A comb and a brush that were on the table he seemed to understand already, for with them he dressed his tangled hair.

When all was finished in a fashion, I led him down the stairs again to the eating-room where supper was waiting, and offered him food, at the sight of which his eyes glistened, for clearly he was well-nigh starving. The chair I gave him he would not sit on, whether from respect for me or because it was strange to him, I do not know, but seeing a low stool of tapestry which my uncle had used to rest his feet, he crouched upon this, and thus ate of whatever I gave him, very delicately though he was so hungry. Then I poured wine from Portugal into a goblet and drank some myself to show him that it was harmless, which, after tasting it, he swallowed to the last drop.

The meal being finished which I thought it was well to shorten lest he should eat too much who was so weak, again he lifted up his eyes as though in gratitude, and as a sign of thankfulness, or so I suppose, knelt before me, took my hand, and pressed it against his forehead, thereby, although I did not know it at the time, vowing himself to my service. Then seeing how weary he was I conducted him back to the chamber and pointed out the bed to him, shutting my eyes to show that he should sleep there. But this he would not do until he had dragged the bedding on to the floor, from which I gathered that his people, whoever they might be, had the habit of sleeping on the ground.

Greatly did I wonder who this man was and from what race he sprang, since never had I seen any human being who resembled him at all. Of one thing only was I certain, namely, that his rank was high, since no noble of the countries that I knew had a bearing so gentle or manners so fine. Of black men I had seen several, who were called negroes, and others of a higher sort called Moors; gross, vulgar fellows for the most part and cut-throats if in an ill-humour, but never a one of them like this Kari.

It was long before my curiosity was satisfied, and even then I did not gather much. By slow degrees Kari learned English, or something of it, though never enough to talk fluently in that tongue into which he always seemed to translate in his mind from another full of strange figures of thought and speech. When after many months he had mastered sufficient of our language, I asked him to tell me his story which he tried to do. All I could make of it, however, came to this.

He was, he said, the son of a king who ruled over a mighty empire far far away, across thousands of miles of sea towards that part of the sky where the sun sank. He declared that he was the eldest lawful son, born of the King's sister, which seemed dreadful to my ideas though perhaps he meant cousin or relative, but that there were scores of other children of his father, which, if true, showed that this king must be a very loose-living man who resembled in his domesticities the wise Solomon of whom my uncle was so fond.

It appeared, further, according to the tale, that this king, his father, had another son born of a different mother, and that of this son he was fonder than of my guest, Kari. His name was Urco, and he was jealous of and hated Kari the lawful heir. Moreover, as is common, a woman came into the business, since Kari had a wife, the loveliest lady in all the land, though as I understood, not of the same tribe or blood as himself, and with this wife of his Urco fell in love. So greatly did he desire her, although he had plenty of wives of his own, that being the general of the King's troops, he sent Kari, with the consent of their father, to command an army that was to fight a distant savage nation, hoping that he would be killed, much as David did in the matter of Uriah and Bathsheba, of whom the Bible tells the story. But as it happened, instead of being killed like Uriah, Kari conquered the distant nation, and after two years returned to the King's court, where he found that his brother Urco had led astray his wife whom he had taken into his household. Being very angry, Kari recovered his wife by command of the King, and put her to death because of her faithlessness.

Thereon the King, his father, a stern man, ordered him into banishment because he had broken the laws of the land, which did not permit of private vengeance over a matter of a woman who was not even of the royal blood, however fair she might be. Before he went, however, Urco, who was mad at the loss of his love, caused some kind of poison to be given to Kari, which although it does not kill, for he dared not kill him because of his station, deprives him who takes it of his reason, sometimes for ever and sometimes for a year or more. After this, said Kari, he remembered little or nothing, save long travellings in boats and through forests, and then again upon a raft or boat on which he was driven alone, for many, many days, drinking a jar of water which he had with him, and eating some dried flesh and with it a marvellous drug of his people, some of which remained to him in the leathern bag that has power to keep the life in a man for weeks, even if he is labouring hard.

At last, he declared, he was picked up by a great ship such as he had never seen before, though of this ship he recalled little. Indeed he remembered nothing more until he found himself upon the quay where I discovered him, and of a sudden his mind seemed to return but he said he believed that he had come ashore in a boat in which were fishermen, having been thrown into it by the people on the ship which went on elsewhere, and that he had walked up the shores of a river. This story the bruises on his forehead and body seemed to bear out, but it was far from clear, and by the time I learned it months afterwards of course no traces of the fishermen or their boat could be found. I asked him the name of the country from which he came. He answered that it was called *Tavantinsuyu.* He added that it was a wonderful country in which were cities and churches and great snow-clad mountains and fertile valleys and high plains and hot forests through which ran wide rivers.

From all the learned men whom I could meet, especially those who had travelled far, I made inquiries concerning this country called Tavantinsuyu, but none of them had so much as heard its name. Indeed, they declared that my brown man must have come from Africa, and that his mind being disordered, he had invented this wondrous land which he said lay far away to the west where the sun sank.

So there I must leave this matter, though for my part I was sure that Kari was not mad, whatever he might have been in the past. A great dreamer he was, it is true, who declared that the poison which his brother had given him had "eaten a hole in his mind" through which he could see and hear things which others could not. Thus he was able to read the secret motives of men and women with wonderful clearness, so much so that sometimes I asked him, laughing, if he could not give me some of that poison that I might see into the hearts of those with whom I dealt. Of another thing, too, he was always certain, namely, that he would return to his country Tavantinsuyu of which he thought day and night, and that *I should accompany him*. At this I laughed again and said that if so it would be after we were both dead.

By degrees he learned English quite well and even how to read and write it, teaching me in return much of his own language which he called *Quichua*, a soft and beautiful tongue, though he said that there were also many others in his country, including one that was secret to the King and his family, which he was not allowed to reveal although he knew it. In time I mastered enough of this Quichua to be able to talk to Kari in brief sentences of it when I did not wish others to understand what I said.

To tell the truth, while I studied thus and listened to his marvellous tales, a great desire arose in me to see this land of his and to open up a trade with it, since there he declared gold was as plentiful as was iron with us. I thought even of making a voyage of discovery to the west, but when I spoke of it to certain sea-captains, even the most venturesome mocked at me and said that they would wait for that journey till they "went west" themselves, by which in their sea parlance that they had learned in the Mediterranean, they meant until they died.[1] When I told Kari this he smiled in his mysterious way and answered that all the same, I and he should make that journey together and this before we died, a thing that came about, indeed, though, not by my own will or his.

For the rest when Kari saw my workmen fashioning gold and setting jewels in it for sale to the nobles and ladies of the Court, he was much interested and asked if he might be allowed to follow this craft, of which he said he understood something, and thus earn the bread he ate. I answered, yes, for I knew that it irked his proud nature to be dependent on me, and gave him gold and silver with a little room having a furnace in it where he could labour. The first thing he made was an object about two inches across, round and with a groove at the back of it, on the front of which he fashioned an image of the sun having a human face and rays of light projecting all about. I asked him what was its purpose, whereon he took the piece and thrust it into the lobe of his ear where the gristle had been stretched in the fashion that I have described, which it fitted exactly. Then he told me that in his country all the nobles wore such ornaments and that those who did so were called "ear-men" to distinguish them from the common

---

1. Of late there has been much dispute as to the origin of the phrase "to go west," or in other words, to die. Surely it arises from the custom of the Ancient Egyptians who, after death, were ferried across the Nile and entombed upon the western shore.—Ed.

people. Also he told me many other things too long to set out, which made me desire more than ever to see this empire with my eyes, for an empire and no less he declared it to be.

Afterwards Kari made many such ornaments which I sold for brooches with a pin set at the back of them. Also he shaped other things, for his skill as a goldsmith was wonderful, such as cups and platters of strange design and rich ornamentation which commanded a great price. But on every one of them, in the centre or some other part of the embossment, appeared this image of the sun. I asked him why. He answered because the sun was his god and his people were Sun-worshippers. I reminded him that he had said that a certain Pachacamac whose image he wore about his neck was his god. To this he replied:

"Yes, Pachacamac is the god above gods, the Creator, the Spirit of the World, but the Sun is his visible house and raiment that all may see and worship," a saying that I thought had truth in it, seeing that all Nature is the raiment of God.

I tried to instruct him in our faith, but although he listened patiently and I think understood, he would not become a Christian, making it very plain to me that he thought that a man should live and die in the religion in which he was born and that from what he saw in London he did not hold that Christians were any better than those who worshipped the sun and the great spirit, Pachacamac. So I abandoned this attempt, although there was danger to him while he remained a heathen. Indeed twice or thrice the priests made inquiry concerning his faith, being curious as to all that had to do with him. However, I silenced them by pretending that I was instructing him as well as I was able and that as yet he did not know enough English to hearken to their holy expositions. Also when they became persistent I made gifts to the monasteries to which they belonged, or if they were parish priests, then to their *curés* or churches.

Still I was troubled about this matter, for some of these priests were very fierce and intolerant, and I was sure that in time they would push the business further.

One more thing I noticed about Kari, namely, that he shrank from women and indeed seemed to hate them. The maids who had remained with me since my uncle's death noticed this, by nature as it were, and in revenge would not serve him. The end of it was that, fearing lest they should do him some evil turn with the priests or otherwise, I sent them away and hired men to take their place. This distaste of Kari for women I set down to all that he had suffered at the hands of his false and beautiful wife not wrongly as I think.

CHAPTER 5

The Coming of Blanche

One day, it was the last of the year, the anniversary of the death of my uncle whose goodness and wisdom I pondered on more and more as time went by, having a little time to spare from larger affairs, I chanced to be in the shop in the front of the house, which, as John Grimmer had said, he kept as a trap to "snare the ladybirds," and I continued, because I knew that he would not wish that anything should be changed. Here I was pleasing myself by looking over such pieces as we had to sell which the head craftsman was showing to me, since myself I knew little of them, except as a matter of account.

Whilst I was thus engaged there entered the shop a very fine lady accompanied by a still finer lordling arrayed so similarly that, at first sight, in their hooded ermine cloaks it was difficult to know which was man and which was woman. When they threw these aside, however, for the shop was warm after the open air, I knew more than that, since with a sudden stoppage of the heart I saw before me none other than the lady Blanche Aleys and her relative, the lord Deleroy.

She, who in the old days of the Hastings burnings had been but a lily bud, was now an open flower and beautiful exceedingly; indeed in her own fashion the most beautiful woman that ever I beheld. Tall she was and stately as a lily bloom, white as a lily also, save for those wondrous blue eyes over which curled the dark lashes. In shape, too, she was perfect, full-breasted, yet not too full, small-waisted, and with delicate limbs, a very Venus, such an one as I had seen in ancient marble brought in a ship from Italy and given, as I believe, to the King, who loved such things, to be set up in his palace.

My lord also was yet handsomer than he had been, more set and manly, though still he affected his coxcomb party-coloured dress with the turned-up shoes of which the points were fastened by little golden chains beneath the knee. Still he was a fine man with his roving black eyes, his loose mouth and little pointed beard from which, as from his hair, came an odour of scents. Seeing me in my merchant's gown, for I remained mindful of my uncle's advice as regards attire, he spoke to me as great men do to shop-keepers.

"Well met, Goldsmith," he said in his round, well-trained voice, "I would make a new-year gift to the lady here, and I am told that you have plate-wares of the best; gold cups and jewels of rich and rare design, stamped all of them with the image of the sun which one would wish to remember on such a day as this. But hearken, let John Grimmer himself come to serve me for I would treat with no underlings, or take me to him where he is."

Now I bowed before him, rubbing my hands, and answered, for so the humour led me: "Then I fear that I must take my lord farther than my lord would wish to travel just at present, though who knows? Perchance, like the rest of us, he may take that journey sooner than he thinks."

Now at the sound of my voice I saw the lady Blanche stare at me, trying to catch sight of my face beneath the hood which I wore on this cold day, while Deleroy started and said briefly:

"Your meaning?"

"It is plain, my lord. John Grimmer is dead and I know not where he dwells at present since he took that secret with him. But I, who unworthily carry on his trade, am at your lordship's service."

Then I turned and bade the shopman command Kari to come hither and bring with him the choicest of our cups and jewels.

He went and I busied myself in setting stools for these noble customers to rest on before the fire. As I did so by chance my hand touched that of the lady Blanche, whereat once more she strove to peer beneath my hood. It was as though the nature in her knew that touch again, as by some instinct every woman does, if once the toucher's lips have been near her own, though it be long ago. But I only turned my head away and drew that hood the closer.

Now Kari came and with him the shopman, bearing the precious wares. Kari wore a wool-lined robe, very plain, which yet became him so well that with his fine-cut face and flashing eyes he looked like an Eastern prince disguised. At him this fine pair stared, for never had they seen such a man, but taking no note, with many bows he showed the jewels one by one. Among these was a gem of great value, a large, heart-shaped ruby that Kari had set in a surround of twisted golden serpents with heads raised to strike and little eyes of diamonds. Upon this brooch the lady Blanche fixed her gaze and discarding all others, began to play with it, till at length the lord Deleroy asked the price. I consulted with Kari, explaining that myself I did not handle this branch of my business, then named it carelessly; it was a great sum.

"God's truth! Blanche," said Deleroy, "this merchant thinks I am made of gold. You must choose a cheaper ornament for your new year's gift, or he will have to wait for payment."

"Which mayhap I should be willing to do from one of your quality, my lord," I interrupted, bowing.

He looked at me and said:

"Can I have a word apart with you, merchant?"

Again I bowed and led him to the eating-room where he gazed about him, amazed at the richness of the furnishings. He sat him down upon a carven chair while I stood before him humbly and waited.

"I am told," he said at length, "that John Grimmer did other business besides that of selling jewels."

"Yes, my lord, some foreign trade."

"And some home trade also. I mean that he lent money."

"At times, my lord, and on good security, if he chanced to have any at command, and at a certain interest. Perhaps my lord will come to his point."

"It is short and clear. Those of us who are at Court always want money where it is needful if we would have advancement and earn the royal favour of one who does not pay, at least in gold."

"Be pleased to state the amount and the security offered, my lord."

He did so. The sum was high and the security was bad.

"Are there any who would stand surety for my lord?"

"Yes, one of great estate, Sir Robert Aleys, who has wide lands in Sussex."

"I have heard the name, and if my lord will bid his lawyers put the matter in writing, I will cause the lands to be valued and give an answer as quickly as may be."

"For a young man you are careful, merchant."

"Alas! such as I need to be who must guard our small earnings in these troublous times of war and tumult. Such a sum as you speak of would take all that John Grimmer and I have laid by after years of toil."

Again he looked at the furnishings of the room and shrugged his shoulders, then said:

"Good, it shall be done for the need is urgent. To whom is the letter to be sent?"

"To John Grimmer, at the Boat House, Cheapside."

"But you told me that John Grimmer was dead."

"And so he is, my lord, but his name remains."

Then we returned to the sop and as we went I said,

"If your lordship's lady should set her heart upon the ruby the cost of it can stand over a while, since I know that it is hard for a husband to disappoint a wife of what she desires."

"Man, she is my distant cousin, not my wife. I would she were, but how can two high-placed paupers wed?"

"Perhaps it is for this reason that my lord wishes to borrow money."

Again he shrugged his shoulders, and as we entered the shop I threw back the hood from off my head upon which I wore a merchant's cap of velvet. The lady Blanche caught sight of me and started.

"Surely, surely," she began, "you are he who shot the three arrows at the cave's mouth at Hastings."

"Yes, my lady, and did your hawk escape the dogs upon the London road?"

"Nay, it was crippled and died, which was the first of many troubles, for I think my luck rode away with you that day, Master Hubert of Hastings," she added with a sigh.

"There are other hawks and luck returns," I replied, bowing. "Perhaps this trinket will bring it back to you, my lady," and taking the snake-surrounded ruby heart, I proffered it to her with another bow.

"Oh!" she said, her blue eyes shining with pleasure, "oh! it is beautiful, but whence is the price to come for so costly a thing?"

"I think the matter is one that can wait."

At that moment the lord Deleroy broke in, saying,

"So you are the man who slew the French knight with an ancient sword, and afterwards shot three other Frenchmen with three shafts, sending one of them through shield and mail and body, a tale that was spoken of afterwards, even in London. God's truth! you should be serving the King in the wars, not yourself behind the counter."

"There are many ways of serving, my lord," I answered, "by pen and merchandise as well as by steel and shafts. Now with me it is the turn of the former, though perhaps the ancient sword and the great black bow wait till their time comes again."

He stared at me and muttered, half to himself:

"A strange merchant and a grim, as those dead Frenchmen may have thought. I tell you, Sir Trader, that your talk and the eyes of that tall Moor of yours turn my back cold; it is as though someone walked over my grave. Come, Blanche, let us begone ere our horses be chilled as I am. Master Grimmer, or Hastings, you shall hear from me, unless I can do my business otherwise, and for the trinket send me a note at your leisure."

Then they went, but as the lady Blanche left the shop she caught her robe and turned to free it, while she did so flashing at me one of her sweet looks such as I remembered well.

Kari followed to the door and watched them mount their horses at the gate, then he searched the ground with his eyes.

"What was it hooked her cloak?" I asked.

"A dream, or the air, Master, for there is nothing else to which it could have hung. Those who would throw spears behind them must first turn round."

"What think you of those two, Kari?"

"I think that they will not pay for your jewel, but perhaps this was but a bait upon the hook."

"And what more, Kari?"

"I think that the lady is very fair and false, and that the great lord's heart is as black as are his eyes. Also I think that they are dear to each other and well matched. But it seems that you have met them both before, Master, so you will know better about them than your slave."

"Yes, I have met them," I answered sharply, for his words about Blanche angered me, adding, "I have noted, Kari, that you have never a good word for any one whom I favour. You are jealous-natured, Kari, especially of women."

"You ask, I answer," he replied, falling into broken English, as was his fashion when moved, "and it is true that those who have much love, are much jealous. That is a fault in my people. Also I love not women. Now I go make another piece for that which Master give the lady. Only this time it all snake and no heart."

He went, taking the tray of jewels with him, and I, too, went to the eating-room to think.

How strange was this meeting. I had never forgotten the lady Blanche, but in a sense I had lived her memory down and mindful of my uncle's counsel, had not sought to look upon her again, for which reason I kept away from Hastings where I thought that I should find her. And now here she was in London and in my house, brought thither by fate. Nor was that all, since those blue eyes of hers had re-lighted the dead fires in my heart and, seated there alone, I knew that I loved her; indeed had never ceased to love her. She was more to me than all my wealth, more than anything, and alas! between us there was still a great gulf fixed.

She was not wed, it was true, but she was a highly placed lady, and I but a merchant who could not even call myself a squire, or by law wear garments made of certain stuffs which I handled daily in my trade. How might that gulf be crossed?

Then as I mused there rose in my mind a memory of certain sayings of my wise old uncle, and with it an answer to the question. Gold would bridge the widest streams of human difference. These fine folk for all their flauntings were poor. They came to me to borrow money wherewith to gild their coronets and satisfy the importunate creditors at their door, lest they should be pulled from their high place and forced back into the number of the common herd as those who could no longer either give or pay.

And after all, was this difference between them and me so wide? The grandsire of Sir Robert Aleys, I had been told, gathered his wealth by trade and usury in the old wars; indeed, it was said that he was one who dealt in cattle, while Lord Deleroy was reported to be a bastard, if of the bluest blood, so blue that it ran nigh to the royal purple. Well, what was mine? On the father's side, Saxon descended from that of Thanes who went down before the Normans and thereafter became humble landed folk of the lesser sort. On the mother's, of the race of the old sea-kings who slew and conquered through all the world they knew. Was I then so far beneath these others? Nay, but like my father and my uncle I was one who bought and sold and the hand of the dyer was stained to the colour of his vat.

Thus stood the business. I, a stubborn man, not ill-favoured, to whom Fortune had given wealth, was determined to win this woman who, it seemed to me, looked upon me with no unkind eye since I had saved her from certain perils. To myself then and there I swore I would win her. The question was—how could it be done? I might enter the service of the King and fight his battles and doubtless win myself a knighthood, or more, which would open the closed gate.

Nay, it would take too long, and something warned me that time pressed. That strange foreign man, Kari, said that Blanche was enamoured of this Deleroy, and although I was wrath with him, setting his words down to jealousy of any on whom I looked with kindness, I knew well that Kari saw far. If I tarried, this rare white bird would slip from my hand into another's cage. I must stir at once or let the matter be. Well, I had wealth, so let wealth be my friend. Time enough to try war when it failed me.

****

On the third day of the new year, which at this time of Court revelry showed that the matter must indeed be pressing, I received those particulars for which I had asked, together with a list of the lands and tenements that Sir Robert Aleys was ready to put in pawn on behalf of his friend and relative, the lord Deleroy. Why should he do this, I wondered? There could only be one answer: because he and not Deleroy was to receive the money, or most of it.

Nay, another came into my mind as probable. Because he looked upon Deleroy as his heir, which, should he marry the lady Blanche, he would become. If this were so I must act, and quickly, that is, if I would ever see more of the lady Blanche, as perchance I might do by treading this gold-paved road, but not otherwise. I studied the list of lands. As it chanced I knew most of them, for they lay about Pevensey and Hastings, and saw that they were scarcely worth the moneys which were asked of me. Well, what of it? This matter was not one of trade and large as the sum might be, I would risk it for the chance of winning Blanche.

The end of it was that waiting for no valuings I wrote that on proof of title clean and unencumbered and completion of all deeds, I would pay over the gold to whoever might be appointed to receive it.

This letter of mine proved to be but the beginning of a long business whereof the details may be left untold. On the very next day indeed I was summoned to the house of Sir Robert Aleys which was near to the palace and abbey of Westminster. Here I found the gruff old knight grown greyer and having, as it seemed to me, a hunted air, and with him the lord Deleroy and two foxy lawyers of whom I did not like the look. Indeed, for the first, I suspected that I was being tricked and had it not been for the lady Blanche, would have broken off the loan. Because of her, however, this I did not do, but having stated my terms anew, and the rate and dates of interest, sat for a long while saying as little as possible, while the others unfolded parchments and talked and talked, telling tales that often contradicted each other, till at length the lord Deleroy, who seemed ill at ease, grew weary and left the chamber. At last all was done that could be done at that sitting and it being past the hour of dinner, I was taken in to eat, consenting, because I hoped that I should see the lady Blanche.

A butler, or chamber-groom, led me to the dining-hall and sat me with the lawyers at a table beneath the dais. Presently on this dais appeared Sir Robert Aleys, his daughter Blanche, the lord Deleroy, and perhaps eight or ten other fine folk whom I had never seen. She, looking about her, saw me seated at the lower table, and spoke to her father and Deleroy, reasoning with the latter, as it would appear. Indeed, in a sudden hush I caught some of her words. They were, "If you are not ashamed to take his money, you should not be ashamed to sit at meat with him."

Deleroy stamped his foot, but the end of it was that I was summoned to the high table where the lady Blanche made place for me beside her, while Deleroy sat himself down between two splendid dames at the other end of the board.

Here, then, I stayed by Blanche who, I noted, wore the ruby heart encircled by serpents. Indeed, this was the first thing of which she spoke to me, saying,

"It looks well upon my robe, does it not, and I thank you for it, Master Hubert, who know surely that it is not my cousin Deleroy's gift, but yours, since for it you will never see your money."

By way of answer I looked at the sumptuous plate and furnishings, the profusion of the viands, and the number of the serving-men. Reading my thought, she replied,

"Aye, but pledged, all of it. I tell you, Master Hubert, that we are starved hounds, though we live in a kennel with golden bars. And now they would pawn you that kennel also."

Then, while I wondered what to say, she began to talk of our great adventure in bygone years, recalling every tiny thing that had happened and every word that had been spoken between us, some of which I had forgotten. Of one thing only she said nothing—the kisses with which we parted. Amongst much else, she spoke of how the ancient sword had shorn through the armour of the French knight, and I told her that the sword was named Wave-Flame and that it had come down to me from my ancestor, Thorgrimmer the Viking, and of what was written on its blade, to all of which she listened greedily.

"And they thought you not fit to sit at meat with them, you whose race is so old and who are so great a warrior, as you showed that day. And it is to you that I owe my life and more than life, to you and not to them."

So saying she shot a glance at me that pierced me through and through, as my arrows had pierced the Frenchmen, and what is more beneath the cover of the board for a moment let her slim hand rest upon my own.

After this for a while we were silent, for indeed I could not speak. Then we talked on as we could do well enough, since there was no one on my left where the board ended, and on Blanche's right was a fat old lord who seemed to be deaf and occupied himself in drinking more than he should have done. I told her much about myself, also what my mother had said to me on the day of the Burning, and of how she had prophesied that I should be a wanderer, words at which Blanche sighed and answered:

"Yet you seem to be well planted in London and in rich soil, Master Hubert."

"Aye, Lady, but it is not my native soil and for the rest we go where Fate leads us."

"Fate! What does that word bring to my mind? I have it; yonder Moor of yours who makes those jewels. He has the very eyes of Fate and I fear him."

"That is strange, Lady, and yet not so strange, for about this man there is something fateful. Ever he swears to me that I shall accompany him to some dim land where he was born, of which land he is a prince."

Then I told her all the story of Kari, to which she listened open-eyed and wondering, saying when I had finished,

"So you saved this poor wanderer also, and doubtless he loves you well."

"Yes, Lady, almost too well, seeing that at times he is jealous of me, though God knows I did little for him save pick him from a crowd upon the quay."

"Ah! I guess it, who saw him watching you the other day. Yet it is strange, for I thought that only women could be jealous of men, and men of women. Hush! they are mocking us because we talk so friendly."

I looked up, following her glance, and saw that Deleroy and the two fine ladies between whom he sat, all of whom appeared to have had enough of wine, were pointing at us. Indeed, in a silence, such as now and again happens at feasts, I heard one of them say,

"You had best beware lest that fair white dove of yours does not slip your hand and begin to coo in another's ear, my Lord Deleroy," and heard his answer,

"Nay, I have her too fast, and who cares for a pining dove whereof the feathers adorn another's cap?"

Whilst I was wondering what this dark talk might mean the company broke up, the lady Blanche gliding away through a door at the back of the dais, followed, as I noted, by Deleroy who seemed flushed and angry.

Many times I visited that prodigal house which seemed to me to be the haunt of folk who, however highly placed and greatly favoured at Court, were as loose in their lives as they were in their talk. Indeed, although I was no saint, I liked them not at all, especially the men with their scented hair, turned-up shoes, and party-coloured clothes. Nor as I thought, did Sir Robert Aleys like them, who, whatever his faults, was a bluff knight of the older sort, who had fought with credit in the French wars. Yet I noted that he seemed to be helpless in their hands, or rather in those of Deleroy, the King's favourite, who was the chief of all the gang. It was as though that gay and handsome young man had some hold over the old soldier, yes, and over his daughter also, though what this might be I could not guess.

Now I will move on with the tale. In due course the parchments were signed and delivered, and the money in good gold was paid over on my behalf, after which the great household at Westminster became more prodigal than before. But when the time came for the discharge of the interest due not a groat was forthcoming. Then afterwards there was talk of my taking over certain of the pledged lands in lieu of this interest. Sir Robert suggested this and I assented, because Blanche had told me that it would help her father. Only when the matter was set on foot by my lawyers was it found that these lands were not his to transfer, inasmuch as they had been already mortgaged to their value.

Then there was a fierce quarrel between Sir Robert Aleys and the lord Deleroy, at which I was present. Sir Robert with many oaths accused his cousin of having forged his name when he was absent in France, while Deleroy declared that what he did was done with due authority. Almost they drew swords on each other, till at length Deleroy took Aleys aside and with a fierce grin whispered something into his ear which caused the old knight to sink down on a stool and call out,

"Get you gone, you false rogue! Get out of this house, aye, and out of England. If I meet you again, by God's Blood I swear that King's favourite or no King's favourite, I'll throat you like a hog!"

To which Deleroy mocked in answer:

"Good! I'll go, my gentle cousin, which it suits me well to do who have certain business of the King's awaiting me in France. Aye, I'll go and leave you to settle with this worthy trader who may hold that you have duped him. Do it as you will, except in one fashion, of which you know. Now a word with my cousin Blanche and another at the Palace and I ride for Dover. Farewell, Cousin Aleys. Farewell, worthy merchant for whose loss I should grieve, did I not know that soon you will recoup yourself out of gentle pockets. Mourn not over me over much, either of you, since doubtless ere so very long I shall return."

Now my blood flamed up and I answered:

"I pray you do not hurry, my lord, lest you should find me waiting for you with a shield and a sword in place of a warrant and a pen."

He heard and called out, "Fore God, this chapman thinks himself a knight!"

Then with a mocking laugh he went.

CHAPTER 6

Marriage—and After

Sir Robert and I stood facing each other speechless with rage, both of us. At length he said in a hoarse voice:

"Your pardon, Master Hastings, for the affronts that this bastard lordling has put upon you, an honest man. I tell you that he is a loose-living knave, as you would agree if you knew all his story, a cockatrice that for my sins I have nurtured in my bosom. 'Tis he that has wasted all my substance; 'tis he that has made free of my name, so that I fear me you are defrauded. 'Tis he that uses my house as though it were his own, bringing into it vile women of the Court, and men that are viler still, however high their names and gaudy their attire," and he choked with his wrath and stopped.

"Why do you suffer these things, sir?" I asked.

"Forsooth because I must," he answered sullenly, "for he has me and mine by the throat. This Deleroy is very powerful, Master Hastings. At a word from him whispered in the King's ear, I, or you, or any man might find ourselves in the Tower accused of treason, whence we should appear no more."

Then, as though he wished to get away from the subject of Deleroy and his hold upon him, he went on:

"I fear me that your money, or much of it, is in danger for Deleroy's bond is worthless, and since the land is already pledged without my knowledge, I have nowhere to turn for gold. I tell you that I am an honest man if one who has fallen into ill company, and this wickedness cuts me deep, for I know not how you will be repaid."

Now a thought came to me, and as was my bold fashion in all business, I acted on it instantly.

"Sir Robert Aleys," I said, "should it be pleasing to you and another, I can see a way in which this debt may be cancelled without shame to you and yet to my profit."

"Then in God's name speak it! For I see none."

"Sir, in bygone time, as it chanced I was able yonder at Hastings to do some service to your daughter and in that hour she took my heart."

He started but motioned to me to continue.

"Sir, I love her truly and desire more than anything to make her my wife. I know she is far above me in station, still although but a merchant, I am of good descent as I can prove to you. Moreover, I am rich, for this money that I have advanced to you, or to the lord Deleroy, is but a small part of my wealth which grows day by day through honest trade. Sir, if my suit were accepted I should be ready, not only to help you further on certain terms, but by deed and will to settle most of it upon the lady Blanche and upon our children. Sir, what say you?"

Sir Robert tugged at his red beard and stared down at the floor. Presently he lifted his head and I saw that his face was troubled, the face of a man, indeed, who is struggling with himself, or, as I thought, with his pride.

"A fair offer fairly put," he said, "but the question is, not what I say, but what says Blanche."

"Sir, I do not know who have never asked her. Yet at times I have thought that her mind towards me is not unkind."

"Is it so? Well, perhaps now that he—well, let that lie. Master Hastings, you have my leave to try your fortune and I tell you straight that I hope it will be good. With your wealth your rank may be soon mended and you are an honest man whom I should be glad to welcome as a son, for I have had enough of these Court knaves and painted Jezebels. But if such is your fancy towards Blanche, my counsel to you is that you put it quickly to the proof—aye, man, at once. Mark my words, for such a swan as she is many snares are set beneath the dirty waters of this Court."

"The sooner the better, sir."

"Good. I'll send her to you and, one word more—be not over shy, or ready to take the first 'no' for an answer, or to listen to the tale of bygone fancies, such as all women have."

Then suddenly he went, leaving me there wondering at his words and manner, which I did not understand. This I understood, however, that he desired that I should marry Blanche, which considering all things I held somewhat strange, although I had the wealth she lacked. Doubtless, I thought, it must be because his honour had been touched on the matter of the trick that had been played upon him without his knowledge. Then I ceased from these wonderings and gave my thought to what I should say to Blanche.

I waited a long while and still she did not come, till at last I believed that she was away from the house, or guessing my business, had refused to see me. At length, however, she entered the room, so silently that I who was staring at the great abbey through a window-place never heard the door open or close. I think that some sense of her presence must have drawn me, since suddenly I turned to see her standing before me. She was clad all in white, having a round cap or coronet upon her head beneath which her shining fair hair was looped in braids. Her little coat, trimmed with ermine, was fastened with a single jewel, that ruby heart embraced by serpents which I had given her. She wore no other ornament. Thus seen she looked most lovely and most sweet and all my heart went out in yearning for her.

"My father tells me that you wish to speak with me, so I have come," she said in her low clear voice, searching my face curiously with her large eyes.

I bowed my head and paused, not knowing how to begin.

"How can I serve you, who, I fear, have been ill served?" she went on with a little smile as though she found amusement in my confusion.

"In one way only," I exclaimed, "by giving yourself in marriage to me. For that I seek, no less."

Now her fair face that had been pale became stained with red and she let her eyes fall as though she were searching for something among the rushes that strewed the floor.

"Hearken before you answer," I continued. "When first I spoke with you on that bloody day at Hastings and you had but just come to womanhood, I loved you and swore to myself that I would die to save you. I saved you and we kissed and were parted. Afterwards I tried to put you out of my heart, knowing that you were set far above me and no meat for such as I, though still for your sake I wooed no other woman in marriage. The years went by and fortune brought us together again, and lo! the old love was stronger than before. I know that I am not worthy of you who are so high and good and pure. Still—" and I stopped, lacking words.

She moved uneasily and the red colour left her cheeks as though she had been suddenly pained.

"Bethink you," she said with a touch of hardness in her voice, "can one who lives the life I live and keeps my company, remain as holy and unstained as you believe? If you would gather such a lily, surely you should seek it in a country garden, not in the reek of London."

"I neither know nor care," I answered, whose blood was all afire. "I know only that wherever you grow and from whatever soil, you are the flower I would pluck."

"Bethink you again; an ugly slug might have smeared my whiteness."

"If so the honest sun and rain will recover and wash it and I am a gardener who scatters lime to shrivel slugs."

"If to this one you will not listen, then hear another argument. Perchance I do not love you. Would you win a loveless bride?"

"Perchance you can learn of love, or if not, I have enough for two."

"By my faith! it should not be difficult with a man so honest and so well favoured. And yet—a further plea. My cousin Deleroy has cheated you" (here her face hardened), "and I think I am offered to you by my father in satisfaction of his honour, as men who have no gold offer a house or a horse to close a debt."

"It is not so. I prayed you of your father. The loss, if loss there be, is but a chance of trade, such as I face every day. Still, I will be plain and tell you that I risked it with open eyes, expecting nothing less, that I might come near to you."

Now she sat herself down in a chair, covering her face with her hands, and I saw from the trembling of her body that she was sobbing. While I wondered what to do, for the sight wrung me, she let fall her hands and there were tears upon her face.

"Shall I tell you all my story, you good, simple gentleman?" she asked.

"Nay, only two things. Are you the wife of some other man?"

"Not so, though perhaps—once I went near to it. What is the other question?"

"Do you love some other man so that your heart tells you it is not possible that you should ever love me?"

"No, I do not," she answered almost fiercely, "but by the Rood! I hate one."

"Which is no affair of mine," I said, laughing. "For the rest, let it sleep. Few are they that know life's wars who have no scar to hide, and I am not one of them, though in truth your lips made the deepest yonder by the cave at Hastings."

When she heard this she coloured to her brow and forgetting her tears, laughed outright, while I went on:

"Therefore let the past be and if it is your will, let us set our eyes upon the future. Only one promise would I ask of you, that never again will you be alone with the lord Deleroy, since one so light-fingered with a pen would, I think, steal other things."

"By my soul! the last thing I desire is to be alone with my cousin Deleroy."

Now she rose from the chair and for a little while we stood facing each other. Then she very slightly opened her arms and lifted her face towards me.

Thus did Blanche Aleys and I become affianced, though afterwards, when I thought the business over, I remembered that never once did she say that she would marry me. This, however, troubled me little, since in such matters it is what women do that weighs, not what they say. For the rest I was mad with love of her, also both then and as the days went by, more and more did she seem to be travelling on this same road of Love. If not, indeed she acted well.

Within a month we were wed on a certain October day in the church of St. Margaret's at Westminster. Once it was agreed all desired to push on this marriage, and not least Blanche herself. Sir Robert Aleys said that he wished to be gone from London to his estates in Sussex, having had enough of the Court and its ways, desiring there to live quietly till the end; I, being so much in love, was on fire for my bride, and Blanche herself vowed that she was eager to become my wife, saying that our courtship, which began on Hastings Hill, had lasted long enough. For the rest, there was nothing to cause delay. I cancelled Sir Robert's debt to me and signed a deed in favour of his daughter and her offspring, whereof I gave a copy to his lawyer and there was nought else to be done except to prepare my house for her which, with money at command, was easy.

No great business was made of this marriage, since neither his kin nor Sir Robert himself wished to noise it about that his only child, the last of his House, was taking a merchant for her husband to save her and him from wreck. Nor did I, the merchant, wish to provoke talk amongst those of my own station, especially as it was known that I had advanced moneys to these fine folks of the Court. So it came about that few were asked to the ceremony that was fixed for an early hour, and of these not many came, because on that day, although it was but October, a great gale with storms of rain began to blow, the greatest indeed that I had known in my life.

Thus it chanced that we were wed in an almost empty church while the fierce wind, thundering against the windows, overcame the feeble voice of the old priest, so that he looked like one acting in a show without words. The darkness caused by the thick rain was so deep, also, that scarce could I see my bride's lovely face or find the finger upon which I must set the ring.

At length it was done and we went down the aisle to find our horses whereon we must ride to my house in Cheapside, where there was to be a feast for my dependents and such of my few friends as cared to come, among whom were not numbered any grand folk from Westminster. As we drew near the church door I noted among those who were present those two gaudy ladies between whom Deleroy had sat at that meal after the business of the loan was settled. Moreover, I heard one of them say:

"What will Deleroy do when he comes back to find his darling gone?" and the other answer with a high laugh:

"Seek another, doubtless, or borrow more money from the merchant, and—" Here I lost their talk in the rush of the wind through the opened door.

In the porch was old Sir Robert Aleys.

"Mother of God!" he shouted, "may the rest of the lives of you two be smoother than your nuptials. No Cheapside feast for me, I'm for home in such fiend's weather. Farewell, son Hubert, and all joy to you. Farewell, Blanche. Learn to be obedient as a wife and keep your eyes for your husband's face, that is my counsel to you. Till we meet again at Christmastide in Sussex, whither I ride to-morrow, farewell to both of you."

Farewell, it was indeed, for never did either of us look on him again.

Wrapped close in our cloaks we battled through the storm and at length, somewhat breathless, reached my house in the Cheap where the garlands of autumn flowers and greenery that I had caused to be wreathed from posts before the door were all torn away by the gale. Here I welcomed my wife as best I could, kissing her as she crossed the threshold and saying certain sweet words that I had prepared, to which she smiled an answer. Then the women took her to her chamber to make herself ready and afterwards came the feast, which was sumptuous of its sort, though the evil weather kept some of the guests away.

Scarcely had it begun when Kari, who of late had been sad-faced and brooding, and who did not eat with us, entered and whispered to me that my Master of Lading from the docks prayed to see me at once on a matter which would brook no delay. Making excuse to Blanche and the company, I went out to see him in the shop and found the man much disturbed. It seemed that a certain vessel of mine that I had rechristened *Blanche* in honour of my wife, which lay in the stream ready to sail, was in great danger because of the tempest. Indeed, she was dragging at her anchor, and it was feared that unless more anchors could be let down she would come ashore and be wrecked against the jetty-heads or otherwise. The reason why this had not been done, was that only the master and one sailor were on board the vessel; the rest were feasting ashore in honour of my marriage, and refused to row out to her, saying that the boat would be swamped in the gale.

Now this ship, although not very large, was the best and staunchest that I owned, being almost new; moreover, the cargo on board of her, laden for the Mediterranean, was of great value, so great indeed that its loss would have been very grievous to me. Therefore, it was plain that I must see to the matter without delay, since from my servant's account there was no hope that these rebellious sailors would listen to any lesser man than myself. So, if I would save the ship and her cargo, I must ride for the docks at once.

Going back to the eating-chamber, in a few words I told my wife and the guests how the matter stood, praying the oldest man among the latter to take my place by the bride, which he did unwillingly, muttering that this was an unlucky marriage feast.

Then it was that Blanche rose, beseeching me earnestly and almost with tears that I would take her with me to the docks. I laughed at her, as did the company, but still she besought with much persistence, till I began to believe that she must be afraid of something, though the others cried that it was but love and fear lest I should come to harm.

In the end I made her drink a cup of wine with me, but her hand shook so much that she spilled the cup and the rich red wine ran down her breast, staining the whiteness of her robe, whereat some women among the company murmured, thinking it a bad omen. At length with a kiss I tore myself away, for I could bide no longer and the horses were waiting presently. So I was riding for the docks as fast as the storm would suffer, with tiles from the roofs, and when we were clear of these the torn-off limbs of trees hurtling round me. Kari, I should say, would have accompanied me, but I took a serving-man, bidding Kari bide where he was in the house in case he might be of service.

At last we came safely to the docks where I found all as my cargo-master had described. The ship *Blanche* was in great peril and dragging every minute towards a pier-head, which, if she struck, would stave her in and make an end of her. The men, too, were still feasting in the inn with their wharf-side trollops, and some of them half drunk. I spoke to them, showing them their shame, and saying that if they would not come, I and my man would take a boat and get aboard alone and this upon my wedding day. Then they hung their heads and came.

We won to the ship safely though with much toil and danger, and there found the master almost crazed with fear and doubt of the issue, and the man with him injured by a falling block. Indeed, this poor captain clung to the rail, watching the cable as it dragged the anchor and fearing every moment lest it should part.

The rest is soon told. We got out two more anchors and did other things such as sailors know, to help in such a case. When all was as safe as it could be made, I and my man and four sailors started for the quay, telling the master that I would return upon the morrow. The wind and current aiding us, we landed safe and sound and at once I rode back to Cheapside.

Now, though it is short to tell, all this had taken a long while, also the way was far to ride in such a storm. Thus it came about that it was nigh to ten o'clock at night when, thanking God, I dismounted at the gate of my house and bade the servant take the horses to the stable. As I drew near the door, it opened, which astonished me and, as the light within showed, there stood Kari. What astonished me still more, he had the great sword, Wave-Flame, in his hand, though not drawn, which sword he must have fetched from where it was kept with the French knight's armour and the shield that bore three arrows as a cognizance.

Laying his finger on his lips he shut the door softly, then said in a low voice:

"Master, there is a man up yonder with the lady."

"What man?" I asked.

"That same lord, Master, who came here with her once before to buy jewels and borrow gold. Hearken. The feast being finished the guests went away at fall of night, but the wife-lady withdrew herself into the chamber that is called sun-room (the solar), that up the stairs, which looks out on the street. About one hour gone there came a knock at the door. I who was watching, opened, thinking it was you returned, and there stood that lord. He spoke to me, saying:

"'Moor-man, I know that your master is from home, but that the lady is here. I would speak with her.'

"Now I would have turned him away, but at that moment the lady herself, who it seemed was watching, came down the stairs, looking very white, and said:

"'Kari, let the lord come in. I have matters of your master's business about which I must talk with him.' So, Master, knowing that you had lent money to this lord, I obeyed, though I liked it not, and having fetched the sword which I thought perchance might be needed, I waited."

This was the substance of what he said, though his talk was more broken since he never learned to speak English well and helped it out with words of his own tongue, of which, as I have told, he had taught me something.

"I do not understand," I exclaimed, when he had finished. "Doubtless it is little or nothing. Yet give me the sword, for who knows? and come with me."

Kari obeyed, and as I went up the stairs I buckled Wave-Flame about me. Also Kari brought two candles of Italian wax lighted upon their stands. Coming to the door of the solar I tried to open it, but it was bolted.

"God's truth!" I said, "this is strange," and hammered on the panel with my fist.

Presently it opened, but before entering it, for I feared some trick, I stood without and looked in. The room was lit by a hanging lamp and a fire burned brightly on the hearth, for the night was cold. In an oak chair by the fire and staring into it sat Blanche still as any statue. She glanced round and saw me in the light of the candles that Kari held, and again stared into the fire. Half-way between her and the door stood Deleroy, dressed as ever in fine clothes, though I noted that his cape was off and hung over a stool near the fire as though to dry. I noted also that he wore a sword and a dagger. I entered the room, followed by Kari, shut the door behind me and shot the bolt. Then I spoke, asking:

"Why are you here with my wife, Lord Deleroy?"

"It is strange, Master merchant," he answered, "but I was about to put much the same question to you: namely, why is *my* wife in your house?"

Now, while I reeled beneath these words, without turning her head, Blanche by the fire said:

"He lies, Hubert. I am not his wife."

"Why are you here, my Lord Deleroy?" I repeated.

"Well, if you would know, Master merchant, I bring a paper for you, or rather a copy of it, for the writ itself will be served on you to-morrow by the King's officers. It commits you to the Tower under the royal seal for trading with the King's enemies, a treason that can be proved against you, of which as you know, or will shortly learn, the punishment is death," and as he spoke he threw a writing down upon a side table.

"I see the plot," I answered coldly. "The King's unworthy favourite, forger and thief, uses the King's authority to try to bring the King's honest subject to bonds and death by a false accusation. It is a common trick in these days. But let that be. For the third time I ask you—why are you here with my new-wed wife and at this hour of the night?"

"So courteous a question demands a courteous answer, Master merchant, but to give it I must trouble you to listen to a tale."

"Then let it be like my patience, brief," I replied.

"It shall," he said with a mocking bow.

Then very clearly and quietly he set out a dreadful story, giving dates and circumstances. Let that story be. The substance of it was that he had married Blanche soon after she reached womanhood and that she had borne him a child which died.

"Blanche," I said when he had done, "you have heard. Is this true?"

"Much of it is true," she answered in that strange, cold voice, still staring at the fire. "Only the marriage was a false one by which I was deceived. He who celebrated it was a companion of the Lord Deleroy tricked out as a priest."

"Do not let us wrangle of this matter," said Deleroy. "A man who mixes with the world like yourself, Master merchant, will know that women in a trap rarely lack excuses. Still if it be admitted that this marriage did not fulfil all formalities, then so much the better for Blanche and myself. If she be your lawful wife and not mine, you, I learn, have signed a writing in her favour under which she will inherit your great wealth. That indenture I think you can find no opportunity to dispute, and if you do I have a promise that the property of a certain traitor shall pass to me, the revealer of his treachery. Let it console you in your last moments, Master merchant, to remember that the lady whom you have honoured with your fancy will pass her days in wealth and comfort in the company of him whom she has honoured with her love."

"Draw!" I said briefly as I unsheathed my sword.

"Why should I fight with a base, trading usurer?" he asked, still mocking me, though I thought that there was doubt in his voice.

"Answer your own question, thief. Fight if you will, or die without fighting if you will not. For know that until I am dead you do not leave this room living."

"Until I dead too, O Lord," broke in Kari in his gentle voice, bowing in his courteous foreign fashion.

As he did so with a sudden motion Kari shook the cloak back from his body and for the first time I saw that thrust through his leathern belt was a long weapon, half sword and half dagger, also that its sharpened steel was bare.

"Oh!" exclaimed Deleroy, "now I understand that I am trapped and that when you told me, Blanche, that this man would not return to-night and that therefore we were safe together, you lied. Well, my Lady Blanche, you shall pay for this trick later."

Whilst he spoke thus, slowly, as though to gain time, he was looking about him, and as the last word left his lips, knowing that the door was locked, he dashed for the window, hoping, I suppose, to leap through the casement, or if that failed, to shout for help. But Kari, who had set the candles he bore on a side table, that where the writing lay, read his mind. With a movement more swift than that of a polecat leaping on its prey, the swiftest indeed that ever I saw, he sprang between him and the casement, so that Deleroy scarce escaped pinning himself upon the steel that he held in his long, outstretched arm. Indeed, I think it pricked his throat, for he checked himself with an oath and drew his sword, a double-edged weapon with a sharp point, as long as mine perhaps, but not so heavy.

"I see that I must finish the pair of you. Perchance, Blanche, you will protect my back as a loving wife should do, until this lout is done with," he said, swaggering to the last.

"Kari," I commanded, "hold the candles aloft that the light may be good, and leave this man to me."

Kari bowed and took the copper taper stands, one in either hand, and held them aloft. But first he placed his long dagger, not back in his belt, but between his teeth with the handle towards his right hand. Even then in some strange fashion I noted how terrible looked this grim dark man holding the candles high with the knife gripped between his white teeth.

Deleroy and I faced each other in the open space between the fire and the door. Blanche turned round upon her stool and watched, uttering no sound. But I laughed aloud for of the end I had no doubt. Had there been ten Deleroys I would have slain them all. Still presently I found there was cause to doubt, for when, parrying his first thrust, I drove at him with all my strength, instead of piercing him through and through the ancient sword, Wave-Flame, bent in my hand like a bow as it is strung, telling me that beneath his Joseph's coat of silk Deleroy wore a shirt of mail.

Then I cried: "*A-hoi!*" as Thorgrimmer my ancestor may have done when he wielded this same sword, and while Deleroy still staggered beneath my thrust I grasped Wave-Flame with both hands, wheeled it aloft, and smote. He lifted his arm round which he had wound his cloak, to protect his head, but the sword shore through cloak and arm, so that his hand with the glittering rings upon it fell to the floor.

Again I smote for, as both of us knew, this business was to the death, and Deleroy fell down dead, smitten through the brain.

Kari smiled gently, and lifting the cloak, shook it out and threw it over what had been Deleroy. Then he took my sword and while I watched him idly, cleansed it with rushes from the floor.

Next I heard a sound from the neighbourhood of the fire, and bethinking me of Blanche turned to speak to her, though what I was going to say God knows for I do not.

A terrible sight met my eyes and burned itself into my very soul so that it could never be forgot. Blanche was leaning back in the oak chair over which flowed her long, fair locks, and the front of her robe was red. I remembered how she had spilt the wine at the feast and thought I saw its stain, till presently, still staring, I noted that it grew and knew it to be caused by another wine, that of her blood. Also I noted that from the midst of it seen in the lamplight, just beneath the snake-encircled ruby heart, appeared the little handle of a dagger.

I sprang to her, but she lifted her hand and waved me back.

"Touch me not," she whispered, "I am not fit, also the thrust is mortal. If you draw the knife I shall die at once, and first I would speak. I would have you know that I love you and hoped to be a good wife to you. What I said was true. That dead man tricked me with a false marriage when I was scarcely more than a child, and afterwards he would not mend it with an honest. Perchance he himself was wed, or he had other reasons, I do not know. My father guessed much but not all. I tried to warn you when you offered yourself, but you were deaf and blind and would not see or listen. Then I gave way, liking you well and thinking that I should find rest, as indeed I do; thinking also that I should be wealthy and able to shut that villain's mouth with gold. I never knew he was coming here or even that he had sailed home from France, but he broke in upon me, having learned that you were away, and was about to leave when you returned. He came for money for which he believed that I had wed, and thinking to win me back from one doomed by his lies to a traitor's death. You know the rest, and for me there was but one thing to do. Be glad that you are no longer burdened with me and go find happiness in the arms of a more fortunate or a better woman. Fly, and swiftly, for Deleroy had many friends and the King himself loved him as a brother—as well he may. Fly, I say, and forgive—forgive! Hubert, farewell!"

Thus she spoke, ever more slowly and lower, till with the last word her life left her lips.

****

Thus ended the story of my marriage with Blanche Aleys.

Book 2

CHAPTER 1

The New World

They were forever silent now, who, but a breath before, had been so full of life and the stir of mortal passion; Deleroy dead beneath the cloak upon the floor, Blanche dead in the oaken chair. We who remained alive were silent also. I glanced at Kari's face; it was as that of a stone statue on a tomb, only in it his large eyes shone, noting all things and, as I imagined in my distraught fancy, filled with triumph and foreknowledge. Considering it in that strange calm of the spirit which sometimes supervenes on great and terrible events that for a while crush its mortality from the soul and set it free to marvel at the temporal pettiness of all we consider immediate and mighty, I wondered what was the aspect of my own.

At the moment, I, who on this day had passed the portals of so many emotions: that of the lover's longing for his bride won at last, only to be lost again, that of acute and necessary business, that of the ancient joy of battle and vengeance wreaked upon an evil man; that of the unshuttering of my own eyes to the flame of a hellish truth, that of the self-murder and turning to cold clay before those same eyes of her whom I had hoped to clasp in honest love—I, I say, felt as though I, too, were dead. Indeed all within was dead, only the shell of flesh remained alive, and in my heart I echoed the words of my old uncle and of a wiser than he who went before him—"Vanity of vanities! All is vanity!"

It was Kari who spoke first, Kari as ever calm and even-voiced, saying in his broken English of which but the substance is recorded:

"Things have happened, good things I hold, though you, Master, may think otherwise for a little while. Yet in this rough land of savages and small justice these things may bring trouble. That lord brought a writing," and he nodded towards the document on the table, "and talked of death for *you*, Master—not for himself. And the lady, while she still lived, she say—'Fly, fly or die!' And now?" and he glanced at the two bodies.

I looked at him vacantly for the numbness following the first shock was passing away and all the eating agony of my loss began to fix its fangs upon my heart.

"Whither can I fly?" I asked. "And why should I fly? I am an innocent man and for the rest, the sooner I am dead the better."

"My Master must fly," answered Kari in swift, broken words, "because he still live and is free. Also sorrow behind, joy before. Kari, who hate women and read heart, Kari who drink this same bitter water long ago, guess these things coming and think and think. No need that Master trouble, Kari settle all and tell Master that if he do what he say, everything come right."

"What am I to do?" I asked with a groan.

"Ship *Blanche* on great river ready for sea. Master and Kari sail in her before daybreak. Here leave everything: much land, much wealth— what matter? Life more than these things which can get again. Come. No, one minute, wait."

Then he went to the body of Deleroy and with wonderful swiftness took off it the chain coat he wore beneath his tunic, which he put on his own body. Also he took his sword and buckled it about him, while the parchment writ he threw upon the fire. Then he extinguished the hanging lamp and gave me one of the candles, taking the other himself.

At the door I held up my candle and by the light of it looked my last upon the ashen face of Blanche, which face I knew must go with me through all my life's days.

Kari locked the stout oaken door of the solar from the outside and took me into my chamber, where was the armour of the knight whom I had killed on Hastings Hill, which armour I had caused to be altered to fit myself. Swiftly he buckled it on to me, throwing over all a long, dark robe such as merchants wear. From the cupboard, too, he brought the big black bow and a sheath of arrows, also a purseful of gold pieces from where they were kept, and with them the leathern bag which he had worn when I found him on the quay.

We went into the room where the feast had been held and there drank some wine, though eat I could not. The cup from which I drank was, as it chanced, the same in which I had pledged Blanche at the bride feast. Now I pledged her spirit whereon I prayed God's mercy.

We left the house and in the stable saddled two horses, strong, quiet beasts. Then by way of the back yard we rode out into the night, none seeing us, for by now all were asleep, and in that weather the streets were empty, even of such as walked them in darkness.

We reached the quay I know not how long afterwards whose mind was full of thoughts that blotted out all else. How strange had been my life—that was one of them. Within a few years I had risen to great wealth, and won the woman I desired. And now where was the wealth and where was the woman, and what was I? One flying his native land by night with blood upon his hands, the blood of a King's favourite that, if he were taken, would bring him to the noose. Oh! how great was the contrast between the morn and the midnight of that day for me! "Vanity of vanities. All is vanity!"

I think that my mind must have wandered, for when my soul was swallowed in this deepest pit of hell, it seemed to me that he whom I had worshipped as a heavenly patron, St. Hubert, appeared striding by my horse with a shining countenance and said to me:

"Have good courage, Godson, and remember your mother's words—a wanderer shall you be, but where'er you go the good bow and the good sword shall keep you safe and I wander with you. Nor does all love die with one woman's passing breath."

This fantasy, as it were, lanced the abscess of my pain and for a while I was easier. Also something of hope came back to me. I no longer desired to die but rather to live and in life, not in the tomb, to find forgetfulness.

We reached the quay and placed the horses in a shed that served as stables there, ridding them of their bits and saddles that they might eat of the hay in the racks. The thought to do this came to me, which showed that my mind was working again since still I could attend to the wants of other creatures. Then we went to the quayside where was made fast that boat in which I had come ashore some hours gone. There was a moon which now and again showed between the drifting clouds, and by the light of it I saw that the *Blanche* lay safe at her anchors not a bowshot away. The gale had fallen much with the rising of the moon, as it often does, and so it came about that although the boat was over-large for two men to handle rightly, Kari and I, by watching our chance, were able to row it to the ship, on to which we climbed by the ladder.

Here we found a sailor on watch who was amazed to see us, and with his help, made the boat fast by the tow rope to the stern of the ship.

This done I caused the captain to be awakened and told him briefly that as the gale had abated and tide and wind served, I desired to sail at once. He stared at me, thinking me mad, whom he knew to have been married but that day.

Surely, he said, I should wait for the light and to gather up those of the ship's company who were still ashore. I answered that I would wait for nothing, and when he asked why, was inspired to tell him that it was because I went about the King's business, having letters from his Grace to deliver to his Envoys in the South Seas that brooked of no delay, since on them hung peace or war.

"Beware," I said to him, "how you, or any of you, dare to disobey the King's orders, for you know that the fate of such is a short shrift and a long rope."

Then that captain grew frightened and summoned the sailors, who by now had slept off their drink, and to them he told my commands. They murmured, pointing to the sky, but when they saw me standing there, wearing a knight's armour and looking very stern with my hand upon my sword, when also through Kari I promised them double pay for the voyage, they, too, grew frightened, and having set some small sails, got up the anchors.

So it came about that within little more than an hour of our boarding of that ship she was running out towards the sea as fast as tide and wind could drive her. I think that it was not too soon, for as the quay vanished in the gloom I saw men with lanterns moving on it, and thought to myself that perhaps an alarm had been given and they were come to take me.

This captain was one who knew the river well, and with the help of another sailor he steered us down its reaches safely. By dawn we had passed Tilbury and at full light were off Gravesend racing for the open sea. Now it was that behind us we perceived from the rushing clouds that the gale, which had lulled during the night, was coming up more strongly than ever and still easterly. The sailors grew afraid again and together with the captain vowed that it was madness to face the sea in such weather, and that we must anchor, or make the shore if we could.

I refused to listen to them, whereat they seemed to give way.

At that moment Kari, who had gone forward, called to me. I went to him and he pointed out to me men galloping along the bank and waving kerchiefs, as though to signal to us to stop.

"I think, Master," said Kari, "that some have entered the sun-room at your house."

I nodded and watched the men who galloped and waved. For some minutes I watched them till suddenly I saw that the ship was altering her course so that her bow pointed first one way and then another, as though she were no longer being steered. We ran aft to learn the cause, and found this.

That crew of dastards, every man of them and the captain with them, had drawn up the boat in which Kari and I came aboard, that was still tied to the ship's stern, and slid down the rope into her, purposing to win ashore before it was too late. Kari smiled as though he were not astonished, but in my rage I shouted at them, calling them curs and traitors. I think that the captain heard my words for I saw him turn his head and look away as though in shame, but not the others. They were engaged in hunting for the oars, only to find them gone, for it would seem that they had been washed or had fallen overboard.

Then they tried to set some kind of sail by aid of a boathook, but while they were doing this, the boat, which had drifted side on to the great waves raised by the gale upon the face of the broad river, overturned. I saw some of the men clinging to the boat and one or two scrambling on to her keel, but what chanced to them and the others I do not know, who had rushed to the steering gear to set the ship upon her course again, lest her fate should be that of the boat, or we should go ashore and be captured by those who galloped on the bank, or be drowned. This was the last I ever saw or heard of the crew of the *Blanche*.

The ship's bow came round and, driven by the ever-increasing gale, she rushed on her course towards the sea, bearing us with her, two weak and lonely men.

"Kari," I said, "what shall we do? Try to run ashore, or sail on?"

He thought awhile then answered, pointing to those who galloped, now but tiny figures on the distant bank:

"Master, yonder is death, sure death; and yonder," here he pointed to the sea, "is death—perhaps. Master, you have a God, and I, Kari, have another God, mayhap same God with different name. I say— Trust our Gods and sail on, for Gods better than men. If we die in water, what matter? Water softer than rope, but I think not die."

I nodded, for the reasoning seemed good. Rather would I be drowned than fall into the hands of those who were galloping on the shore, to be dragged back to London and a felon's doom.

So I pressed upon the tiller to bring the *Blanche* more into mid-channel, and headed for the sea. Wider and wider grew the estuary and farther and farther away the shores as the *Blanche* scudded on beneath her small sails with the weight of the gale behind her, till at last there was the open sea.

Within a few feet of the tiller was a deck-house, in which the crew ate, built of solid oak and clamped with iron. Here was food in plenty, ale, too, and with these we filled ourselves. Also, leaving Kari to hold the tiller, I took off my armour and in place of it clothed myself in the rough sea garments that lay about with tall greased boots, and then sent him to do likewise.

Soon we lost sight of land and were climbing the great ocean billows, whose foamy crests rolled and spurted wherever the eye fell. We could set no course but must go where the gale drove us, away, away we knew not whither. As I have said, the *Blanche* was new and strong and the best ship that ever I had sailed in upon a heavy sea. Moreover, her hatches were closed down, for this the sailors had done after we weighed, so she rode the waters like a duck, taking no harm. Oh! well it was for me that from my childhood I had had to do with ships and the sailing of them, and flying from the following waves thus was able to steer and keep the *Blanche*'s poop right in the wind, which seemed to blow first from one quarter and then from that.

****

Now over my memory of these events there comes a great confusion and sense of amazement. All became fragmentary and disjointed, separated also by what seemed to be considerable periods of time—days or weeks perhaps. There was a sense of endless roaring seas before which the ship fled on and on, driven by a screaming gale that I noted dimly seemed to blow first from the northwest and then steadily from the east.

I see myself, very distinctly, lashing the tiller to iron rings that were screwed in the deck beams, and know that I did this because I was too weak to hold it any longer and desired to set it so that the *Blanche* should continue to drive straight before the gale. I see myself lying in the deck-house of which I have spoken, while Kari fed me with food and water and sometimes thrust into my mouth little pellets of I knew not what, which he took from the leathern bag he wore about him. I remembered that bag. It had been on his person when I rescued him at the quay, for I had seen it first as he washed himself afterwards, half full of something, and wondered what it contained. Later, I had seen it in his hand again when we left my house after the death of Blanche. I noted that whenever he gave me one of these pellets I seemed to grow strong for a while, and then to fall into sleep, deep and prolonged.

After more days—or weeks, I began to behold marvels and to hear strange voices. I thought that I was talking with my mother and with my patron, St. Hubert; also that Blanche came to me and explained everything, showing how little she had been to blame for all that had happened to me and her. These things made me certain that I was dead and I was glad to be dead, since now I knew there would be no more pain or strivings; that the endeavours which make up life from hour to hour had ceased and that rest was won. Only then appeared my uncle, John Grimmer, who kept quoting his favourite text at me— "Vanity of vanities. All is vanity," he said, adding: "Did I not tell you that it was thus years ago? Now you have learned it for yourself. Only, Nephew Hubert, don't think that you have finished with vanities yet, as I have, for I say that there are plenty more to come for you."

Thus he seemed to talk on about this and other matters, such as what would happen to his wealth and whether the hospitals would be quick to seize the lands to which he had given it the reversion, till I grew quite tired of him and wished that he would go away.

Then at length there was a great crash that I think disturbed him, for he did go, saying that it was only another "vanity," after which I seemed to fall asleep for weeks and weeks.

I woke up again for a warmth and brightness on my face caused me to open my eyes. I lifted my hand to shield them from the brightness and noted with a kind of wonder that it was so thin that the light shone through it as it does through parchment, and that the bones were visible beneath the skin. I let it fall from weakness, and it dropped on to hair which I knew must be that of a beard, which set me wondering, for it had been my fashion to go clean-shaven. How, then, did I come by a beard? I looked about me and saw that I was lying on the deck of a ship, yes, of the *Blanche* itself, for I knew the shape of her stern, also certain knots in one of the uprights of the deck-house that formed a rude resemblance to a human face. Nothing of this deck-house was left now, except the corner posts between which I lay, and to the tops of these was lashed a piece of canvas as though to keep off the sun and the weather.

With difficulty I lifted my head a little and looked about me. The bulwarks of the ship had gone, but some of the uprights to which the planks had been nailed remained, and between them I perceived tall-stemmed trees with tufts of great leaves at the top of them, which trees seemed to be within a few yards of me. Bright-winged birds flew about them and in their crowns I saw apes such as the sailors used to bring home from Barbary. It would seem, then, that I must be in a river (in fact, it was a little bay or creek, on either side of which these trees appeared).

Noting these and the creeping plants with beautiful flowers, such as I had never seen, that climbed up them, and the sweet scents that floated on the air, and the clear light, now I grew sure that I was dead and had reached Paradise. Only then how came it that I still lay on the ship, for never had I heard that such things also went to Paradise?

Nay, I must dream; it was nothing but a dream that I wished were true, remembering as I did the terrors of that gale-tossed sea. Or, if I did not dream, then I was in some new world.

While I mused thus I heard a sound of soft footsteps and presently saw a figure bending over me. It was Kari, very thin and hollow-eyed, much, indeed, as he had been when I found him on the quay in London, but still Kari without doubt. He looked at me in his grave fashion, then said softly:

"Master awake?"

"Yes, Kari," I said, "but tell me, where am I?"

He did not answer at once but went away and returned presently with a bowl from which he bade me drink, holding it to my lips. I did so, swallowing what seemed to be broth though I thought it strangely flavoured, after which I felt much stronger, for whatever was in that broth ran through my veins like wine. At last he spoke in his queer English.

"Master," he said, "when we still in Thames River, you ask me whether we should run ashore into the hands of the hunters who try to catch us, or sail on. I answer, 'You have God and I have God and better fall into hands of gods than into hands of men.' So we sail on into the big storm. For long we sail, and though once it turn, always the great wind blew, behind us. You grow weak and your mind leave you, but I keep you alive with medicine that I have and for many days I stay awake and steer. Then at last my mind leave me, too, and I know no more. Three days ago I wake up and find the ship in this place. Then I eat more medicine and get strength, also food from people on the shore who think us gods. That all the story, except that you live, not die. Your God and my God bring us here safe."

"Yes, Kari, but where are we?"

"Master, I think in that country from which I come; not in my own land which is still far away, but still in that country. You remember," he added with a flash of his dark eyes, "I always say that you and I go there together one day."

"But what is the country, Kari?"

"Master, not know its name. It big and have many names, but you first white man who ever come here, that why people think you God. Now you go sleep again; to-morrow we talk."

I shut my eyes, being so very tired, and as I learned afterwards, slept for twelve hours or more, to awake on the morning of the following day, feeling wonderfully stronger and able to eat with appetite. Also Kari brought me water and washed me, and clean clothes which he had found in the ship that I put on.

Thus it went on for a long while and day by day I recovered strength till at length I was almost as I had been when I married Blanche Aleys in the church of St. Margaret at Westminster. Only now sorrow had changed me within and without my face had grown more serious, while to it hung a short yellow beard, which, when I looked at my reflection, seemed to become me well enough. That beard puzzled me much, since such are not grown in a day, although it is true that as yet it was not over-long. Weeks must have passed since it began to sprout upon my chin and as we had been but three days in this place when I woke up, those weeks without doubt were spent upon the sea.

Whither, then, had we come? Driving all the while before a great gale, that for most of our voyage had blown from the east, as, if Kari were right, we had done, this country must be very far away from England. That it was so, indeed there could be no doubt, since here everything was different. For example, having been a mariner from my childhood, I had been taught and observed something of the stars, and noted that the constellations had changed their places in the heavens, also that some with which I was familiar were missing, while other new ones had appeared. Further, the heat was great and constant, even at night being more than that of our hottest summer day, and the air was full of stinging insects, which at first troubled me much, though afterwards I grew hardened to them. In short, everything was changed, and I was indeed in a new world that was not told of in Europe, but what world? What world? At least the sea joined it to the old, for beneath me was still the *Blanche*, which timber by timber I had seen built up upon the shores of Thames from oaks cut in my own woods.

As soon as I was strong enough, I went over the ship, or what was left of her. It was a marvel that she had floated for so long, since her hull was shattered. Indeed, I do not think she could have done so, save for the fine wool that was packed into the lower part of her, which wool seemed to have swollen when it grew wet and to have kept the water out. For the rest she was but a hulk, since both her masts were gone, and much of the deck with them. Still she had kept afloat and driving into this creek, had beached herself upon the mud as though it were the harbour that she sought.

How had we lived through such a journey? The answer seemed to be, after we were too weak to find or take food, by means of the drug that Kari cherished in his skin bag, and water of which there was plenty left at hand in barrels, since the *Blanche* had been provisioned for a long voyage to Italy and farther. At least we had lived for weeks, and weeks, being still young and very strong, and not having been called upon to suffer great cold, since it would appear that although the gale continued after the first few days of our flight before it, the weather had turned warm.

During this time of my recovery, every morning Kari would go ashore, which he did by means of planks set upon the mud, since we were within a few feet of the bank of the creek into which a streamlet ran. Later he would return, bringing with him fish and wildfowl, and corn of a sort that I did not know, for its grains were a dozen times the size of wheat, flat-sided, and if ripe, of a yellow colour, which he said he had purchased from those who dwelt upon the land. On this good food I feasted, washing it down with ale and wine from the ship's stores; indeed never before did I eat so much, not even when I was a boy.

At length, one morning Kari made me put on my armour, the same which I had taken from the French knight, and fled in from London, that he had burnished till it shone like silver, and seat myself in a chair upon what remained of the poop of the ship. When I asked him why, he answered in order that he might show me to the inhabitants of that land. In this chair he bade me sit and wait, holding the shield upon my arm and the bare sword in my right hand.

As I had come to know that Kari never did anything without a reason and remembered that I was in a strange country where, lacking him, I should not have lived or could continue to do so, I fell into his humour. Moreover, I promised that I would remain still and neither speak, nor smile, nor rise from my chair unless he bade me. So there I sat glittering in the hot sunshine which burned me through the armour.

Then Kari went ashore and was absent for some time. At length among the trees and undergrowth I heard the sound of people talking in a strange tongue. Presently they appeared on the bank of the creek, a great number of them, very curious people, brown-skinned with long, lank black hair and large eyes, but not over-tall in stature; men, women and children together.

Among them were some who wore white robes whom I took to be their gentlefolk, but the most of them had only cloths or girdles about their middles. Leading the throng was Kari, who, as it appeared from the bushes, waved his hand and pointed me out seated in the shining armour on the ship, the visor up to show my face and the long sword in my hand. They stared, then, with a low, sighing exclamation, one and all fell upon their faces and rubbed their brows upon the ground.

As they lay there Kari addressed them, waving his arms and pointing towards me from time to time. Afterwards I learned that he was telling them I was a god, for which lie may his soul be forgiven.

The end of it was that he bade them rise and led certain of them who wore the white robes across the planks to the ship. Here, while they hung back, he advanced towards me, bowing and kissing the air till he drew near, then he went upon his knees and laid his hands upon my steel-clad feet. More, from the bosom of his robe he drew out flowers which he placed upon my knees as though in offering.

"Now, Master," he whispered to me, "rise and wave your sword and shout aloud, to show that you are alive and not an image."

So up I sprang, circling Wave-Flame about my head and roaring like any bull of Bashan, for my voice was always loud and carried far. When they saw the bright sword whirling through the air and heard these bellowings, uttering cries of fear, those poor folk fled. Indeed most of them fell from the plank into the mud, where one stuck fast and was like to drown, had not Kari rescued him, which his brethren were in too great haste to do.

After they had gone Kari came and said that everything went well and that henceforward I was not a man but the Spirit of the Sea come to earth, such a spirit as had never been dreamed of even by the wizards.

****

Thus then did Hubert of Hastings become a god among those simple people, who had never before so much as heard of a white man, or seen armour or a sword of steel.

CHAPTER 2

The Rocky Isle

For another week or more I remained upon the *Blanche* waiting till my full strength returned, also because Kari said I must do so. When I asked him why, he replied for the reason that he wished news of my coming to spread far and wide throughout the land from one tribe to another, which it would do with great swiftness, flying, as he put it, like a bird. Meanwhile, every day I sat upon the poop in the armour for an hour or more, and both these people and others from afar came to look at me, bringing me presents in such quantity that we knew not what to do with them. Indeed, they built an altar and sacrificed wild creatures to me, and birds, burning them with fire. Both those that I had seen and the other folk from a long way off made this offering.

At last one night, when, having eaten, Kari and I were seated together in the moonshine before we slept, I turned on him suddenly, hoping thus to surprise the truth out of his secret heart, and said:

"What is your plan, Kari? For, know, I weary of this life."

"I was waiting for the Master to ask that question," he replied with his gentle smile. (Again, I give not the very words he spoke in his bad English, but the substance of them.) "Now will the Master be pleased to listen? As I have told the Master, I believe that the gods, his God and my God, have brought me back to that part of the world which is unknown to the Master, where I was born. I believed this from the first hour that my eyes opened on it after our swoon, for I knew the trees and the flowers and the smell of the earth, and saw that the stars in the heavens stood where I used to see them. When I went ashore and mingled with the natives, I discovered that this belief was right, since I could understand something of their talk and they could understand something of mine. Moreover, among them was a man who came from far away, who said that he had seen me in past years, wandering like one mad, only that this man whom he had seen wore the image of a certain god about his neck, whose name was too high for him to mention. Then I opened my robe and showed him that which I wear about my neck, and he fell down and worshipped it, crying out that I was the very man."

"If so, it is marvellous," I said. "But what shall we do?"

"The Master can do one of two things. He can stop here, where these simple people will make him their king and give him wives and all that he desires, and so live out his life, since of return to the land whence he came there is no hope."

"And if there were I would not go," I interrupted.

"Or," went on Kari, "he can try to travel to my country. But that is very far away. Something of the journey which I made when I was mad comes back and tells me that it is very, very far away. First, yonder mountains must be crossed till another sea is reached, which is no great journey, though rough. Then the coast of that sea must be followed southward, for I know not how far, but, as I think, for months or years of journeying, till at length the country of my people is reached. Moreover, that journeying is hard and terrible, since the road runs through forests and deserts where dwell savage tribes and huge snakes and wild beasts, like those planted on the flag of your country, and where famine and sicknesses are common. Therefore my counsel to the Master is that he should leave it unattempted."

Now I thought awhile, and asked what he meant to do if I took this counsel of his. To which he replied:

"I shall wait here awhile till I see the Master made a king among these people and established in his rule. Then I shall start on that journey alone, hoping that what I could do when I was mad I shall be able to do again when I am not mad."

"I thought it," I said. "But tell me, Kari, if we were to make this journey and perchance live to reach your people, how would they welcome us?"

"I do not know, Master; but I think that of the master they would make a god, as will all the other people of this country. Perhaps, too, they will sacrifice this god that his strength and beauty may enter into them. As for me, some of them will try to kill me and others will cling to me. Who will conquer I do not know, and to me it matters little. I go to take my own and to be avenged, and if in seeking vengeance I die—well, I die in honour."

"I understand," I said. "And now, Kari, let us start as soon as possible before I become as mad from staring at those trees and flowers and those big-eyed natives, that you say would make me a king, as you tell me you were when you left your country. Whether we shall ever find that country I cannot say. But at least we shall have done our best and, if we fail, shall perish seeking, as in this way or in that it is the lot of all brave men to do."

"The Master has spoken," said Kari, even more quietly than usual, though as he spoke I saw his dark eyes flash and a trembling as of joy run down his body. "Knowing all, he has made his choice, and whatever happens, being what it is, he will not blame me. Yet because the Master has thus chosen, I say this—that if we reach my country, and if, perchance, I become a king there, even more than before I shall be the Master's servant."

"That is easy to promise now, Kari, but it will be time to talk of it when we do reach your land," I said, laughing, and asked him when we were to start.

He replied not yet awhile, as he must make plans, and that in the meantime I must walk upon the shore so that my legs might grow strong again. So there every day I walked in the cool of the morning and in the evening, not going out of sight of the wreck. I went armed and carrying my big bow, but saw no one, since the natives had been warned that I should walk and must not be looked upon while I did so. Therefore, even when I passed through one of their villages of huts built of mud and thatched with leaves, it seemed to be deserted.

Still, in the end the bow did not come amiss, for one evening, hearing a little noise in a big tree under which I was about to pass that reminded me of the purring of a cat, I looked up and saw a great beast of the tiger sort lying on the bough of the tree and watching me. Then I drew the bow and sent an arrow through that beast, piercing it from side to side, and down it came roaring and writhing, and biting at the arrow till it died.

After this I returned to the ship and told Kari what had happened. He said it was fortunate I had killed the beast, which was of a very fierce kind, and if I had not seen it, would have leapt on me as I passed under the tree. Also he sent natives to skin it who when they saw that it was pierced through and through by the arrow, were amazed and thought me an even greater god than before, their own bows being but feeble and their arrows tipped with bone.

****

Three days after the killing of this beast we started on our journey into a land unknown. For a long while before Kari and I had been engaged in collecting all the knives we could find in the ship, also arrows, nails, axes, tools of carpentering, clothes, and I know not what else besides, which goods we tied up in bundles wrapped in sailcloth, each bundle weighing from thirty to forty pounds, to serve as presents to natives or to trade away with them. When I asked who would carry them, Kari answered that I should see. This I did at dawn on the following morning when there arrived upon the shore a great number of men, quite a hundred indeed, who brought with them two litters made of light wood jointed like reeds, only harder, in which Kari said he and I were to be carried. Among these men he parcelled out the loads which they were to bear upon their heads, and then said that it was time for us to start in the litters.

So we started, but first I went down into a cabin and kneeling on my knees, thanked God for having brought me safe so far, and prayed Him and St. Hubert to protect me on my further wanderings, and if I died, to receive my soul. This done I left the ship and while the natives bowed themselves about me, entered my litter, which was comfortable enough, having grass mats to lie on and other mats for curtains, very finely woven, so that they would turn even the heaviest rain.

Then away we went, eight men bearing the pole to which each litter was slung on their shoulders, while others carried the bundles upon their heads. Our road ran through forest uphill, and on the crest of the first hill I descended from the litter and looked back.

There in the creek below lay the wreck of the *Blanche*, now but a small black blot showing against the water, and beyond it the great sea over which we had travelled. Yonder broken hulk was the last link which bound me to my distant home thousands of miles across the ocean, that home, which my heart told me I should never see again, for how could I win back from a land that no white foot had ever trod?

On the deck of this ship Blanche herself had stood and smiled and talked, for once we visited it together shortly before our marriage, and I remembered how I had kissed her in its cabin. Now Blanche was dead by her own hand and I, the great London merchant, was an outcast among savages in a country of which I did not even know the name, where everything was new and different. And there the ship with her rich cargo, after bearing us so bravely through weeks of tempest, must lie until she rotted in the sun and rain and never again would my eyes behold her. Oh! then it was that a sense of all my misery and loneliness gripped my heart as it had not done before since I rode away after killing Deleroy with the sword Wave-Flame, and I wondered why I had been born, and almost hoped that soon I might die and go to seek the reason.

Back into the litter I crept and there hid my face and wept like a child. Truly I, the prosperous merchant of London town who might have lived to become its mayor and magistrate and win nobility, was now an outcast adventurer of the humblest. Well, so God had decreed, and there was no more to say.

That night we encamped upon a hilltop past which rushed a river in the vale below and were troubled with heat and insects that hummed and bit, for to these as yet I was not accustomed, and ate of the food that we had brought with us, dried flesh and corn.

Next morning with the light we started on again, up and down mountains and through more forests, following the course of the river and the shores of a lake. So it went on until on the third evening from high land we saw the sea beneath us, a different sea from that which we had left, for it seemed that we had been crossing an isthmus, not so wide but that if any had the skill, a canal might be cut across it joining those two great seas.

Now it was that our real travels began, for here, after staring at the stars and brooding apart for a long while, Kari turned southwards. With this I had nothing to do who did not greatly care which way he turned. Nor did he speak to me of the matter, except to say that his god and such memory as remained to him through his time of madness told him that the land of his people lay towards the south, though very far away.

So southwards we went, following paths through the forests with the ocean on our right hand. After a week of this wearisome marching we came to another tribe of natives of whose talk those with us could understand enough to tell them our story. Indeed the rumour that a white god had appeared in the land out of the sea had already reached them, and therefore they were prepared to worship me. Here our people left us, saying that they dared not go further from their own country.

The scene of the departure was strange, since every one of them came and rubbed his forehead in the dust before me and then went away, walking backwards and bowing. Still their going did not make a great difference to us, since the new tribe was much as the old one, though if anything, rather less clothed and more dirty. Also it accepted me as a god without question and gave us all the food we needed. Moreover, when we left their land men were provided to carry the litters and the loads.

Thus, then, passing from tribe to tribe, we travelled on southward, ever southwards, finding always that the rumour of the coming of "the god" had gone before us. So gentle were all these people, that not once did we meet with any who tried to harm us or to steal our

110

goods, or who refused us the best of what they had. Our adventures, it is true, were many. Thus, twice we came to tribes that were at war with other tribes, though on my appearance they laid down their arms, at any rate, for a time, and bore our litters forward.

Again, sometimes we met tribes who were cannibals and then we suffered much from want of meat, since we dared not touch their food unless it were grain. In the town of the first of these cannibal people, being moved with fury, I killed a man whom I found about to murder a child and eat her, sweeping off his head with my sword. For this deed I expected that they would murder us, but they did not. They only shrugged their shoulders and saying that a god can do as he pleases, took away the slain man and ate him.

Sometimes our road ran through terrible forests where the great trees shut out the light of day, and a path must be hacked through the undergrowth. Sometimes it was haunted by tigers or tree lions such as I have spoken of, against which we must watch continuously, especially at night, keeping the brutes off by means of fires. Sometimes we were forced to wade great rivers, or worse still, to walk over them on swaying bridges made of cables of twisted reeds that until I grew accustomed to them caused my head to swim, though never did I permit myself to show fear before the natives. Again, once we came to swampy lands that were full of snakes which terrified me much, especially after I had seen some natives whom they bit, die within a few minutes.

Other snakes there were also, as thick as a man's body, and four or five paces in length, which lived in trees and killed their food by coiling round it and pressing it to death. These snakes, it was said, would take men in this fashion, though I never saw one of them do so. At any rate, they were terrible to look on, and reminded me of their forefather through whose mouth Satan talked with Mother Eve in the Garden of Eden, and thus brought us all to woe.

Once, too, on the bank of a great river, I saw such a snake that at the sight of it my knees knocked together. By St. Hubert, the beast was sixty feet or more in length; its head was of the bigness of a barrel, and its skin was of all the colours of the rainbow. Moreover, it seemed to hold me with its eyes, for till it slipped away into the river I could not move a foot.

Month after month we travelled thus, covering a matter of perhaps five miles a day, since sometimes the country was open and we crossed it with speed. Yet although our dangers were so many, strangely enough, during all this time, even in that heat neither of us fell sick, as I think because of the herb which Kari carried in his bag, that I

111

found was named *Coca*, whereof we obtained more as we went and ate from time to time. Nor did we ever really suffer from starvation, since when we were hungry we took more of this herb which supported us until we could find food. These mercies I set down to the good offices of St. Hubert watching from Heaven over me, his poor namesake and godson, though perhaps the skill and courage of Kari which provided against everything had something to do with them.

At length, in the ninth month of our travelling, as Kari reckoned it by means of knots which he tied on pieces of native string, for I had long lost count of time, we came to the borders of a great desert that the natives said stretched southwards for a hundred leagues and more and was without water. Moreover, to the east of this desert rose a chain of mountains bordered by precipices up which no man could climb. Here, therefore, it seemed as though our journey must end, since Kari had no knowledge of how he crossed or went round this desert in his madness of bygone years, if indeed he ever travelled that road at all, a matter of which I was not certain.

For a week or more we remained among the tribe that lived in a beautiful watered valley upon the borders of this desert, wondering what we should do. For my part I was by now so tired of travelling upon an endless quest that I should have been glad to stay among that tribe, a very gentle and friendly people, who like all the rest believed me to be a god, and make my home there till I died. But this was not Kari's mind, which was set fiercely upon winning back to his own country that he believed to lie towards the south.

Day by day we sat there regaining our strength upon the good food of that valley, and staring first at the desert to the south, then at the precipices on our left hand, and lastly at the ocean upon our right. Now this people, I should say, drew their wealth from the sea as well as from the land, since they were great fishermen and went out upon it in rude boats or rafts made of a wooden frame to which were lashed blown-up skins and bundles of dried reeds. Upon these boats, frail as they seemed, such as further south were called *balsas*, they made considerable journeys to distant islands where they caught vast quantities of fish, some of which they used to manure their land. Moreover, besides the oars, they rigged a square cotton sail upon the *balsas* which enabled them to run before the wind without labour, steering the craft by means of a paddle at the stern.

While we were there I observed that on the springing up of a wind from the north, although it was of no great strength, the *balsas* all came to shore and were drawn up out of reach of the waves. When

I inquired why through Kari, the answer given was because the fishing season was over, since that wind from the north would blow for a long time without changing and those who went out in it upon the sea might be driven southwards to return no more. They stated, indeed, that often this had happened to venturesome men who had vanished away and been lost.

"If you wish to travel south, there is a way of doing so," I said to Kari.

At the time he made no answer, but on the following day asked me suddenly if I dared attempt such a journey.

"Why not?" I answered. "It is as easy to die in the water as on land and I weary of journeying through endless swamps and forests or of crossing torrents and climbing mountain ridges."

The end of it was that for a knife and a few nails Kari purchased the largest *balsa* that these people had, provisioning it with as much dried fish, corn and water in earthenware jars as it would carry together with ourselves, and such of our remaining goods as we wished to take with us. Then we announced that I, the god who had come out of the sea, desired to return into the sea with himself, my servant.

So on a certain fine morning when the wind was blowing steadily but not too strongly from the north, we embarked upon that *balsa* while the simple savages made obeisance with wonder in their eyes, hoisted the square canvas, and sailed away upon what I suppose was one of the maddest voyages ever made by man.

Although it was so clumsy the *balsa* moved through the water at a good rate, covering quite two leagues the hour, I should say, before that strong and steady wind. Soon the village that we had left vanished; then the mountains behind it grew dim and in time vanished also, and there remained nothing but the great wilderness upon our left and the vast sea around. Steering clear of the land so as to avoid sunken rocks, we sailed on all that day and all the night that followed, and when the light came again perceived that we were running past a coastline that was backed by high mountains on some of which lay snow. By the second evening these mountains had become tremendous, and between them I saw valleys down which ran streams of water.

Thus we went on for three days and nights, the wind from the north blowing all the while and the *balsa* taking no hurt, by the end of which time I reckon that we had travelled as far along the coast as we had done in six months when we journeyed over land, at which I rejoiced. Kari rejoiced also, because he said that the shape and greatness of the mountains we were passing reminded him of those of his own country, to which he believed that we were drawing near.

On the fourth morning, however, our troubles began, since the friendly wind from the north grew steadily stronger, till at length it rose to a gale. Soon our little rag of canvas was torn away, but still we rushed on before the following seas at a very great speed.

Now I thought of trying to make the land, but found that we could not do so with the oars, because of the current that set out towards the ocean against which it was impossible to urge our clumsy craft. Therefore we must content ourselves with trying to keep her head straight with the steering oar, but even then we were often whirled round and round.

About two hours after noon the sky clouded over, and there burst upon us a great thunder-storm with torrents of rain; also the wind grew stronger and stronger.

Now we could no longer steer or do anything except lie flat upon the bottom of the *balsa*, gripping the cords with which it was tied together, to save ourselves from being washed overboard, since often the foaming crests of the waves broke upon us. Indeed, it was marvellous that this frail craft should hang together at all, but owing to the lightness of the reeds and the blown-up skins that were tied in them, still she floated and, whirling round and round, sped upon her southward path. Yet I knew that this could not endure for very long, and committed my soul to God as well as I was able in my half-drowned state, wishing that my miseries were ended.

The darkness came down, but still the thunder roared and the lightning blazed, and by the flare of it I caught sight of snow-capped mountains far away upon the coast, also of Kari clinging to the reeds of the *balsa* at my side, and from time to time kissing the golden image of Pachacamac which hung about his neck. Presently he set his lips against my ear and shouted:

"Be bold! Our gods are still with us in storm."

"Yes," I answered, "and soon we shall be with our gods—in peace."

After this I heard no more of him, and fell to thinking with such wits as were left to me of how many perils we had passed since we saw the shores of Thames, and that it seemed sad that all should have been for nothing, since it would have been better to die at the beginning than now at the end, after so much misery. Then the glare of the lightning shone upon the handle of the sword Wave-Flame, which was still strapped about me, and I remembered the rune written upon it which my mother had rendered to me upon the morning of the fight against the Frenchmen. How did it run?

He who lifts Wave-Flame on high In love shall live and in battle die. Storm-tossed o'er wide seas shall roam And in strange lands shall make his home. Conquering, conquered shall he be And far away shall sleep with me.

It fitted well, though of the love I had known little and that most unhappy, and the battle in which I must die was one with water. Also, I had conquered nothing who myself was conquered by Fate. In short, the thing could be read two ways, like all prophecies, and only one line of it was true beyond a doubt—namely, that Wave-Flame and I should sleep together.

Awhile later the lightning shone awesomely, like to the swords of a whole army of destroying angels, so that the sky became alive with fire. In its light for an instant I saw ahead of us great breakers, and beyond them what looked like a dark mass of land. Now we were in them, for the first of those hungry, curling waves got a hold of the *balsa* and tossed it up dizzily, then flung it down into a deep valley of water. Another came and another, till my senses reeled and went. I cried to St. Hubert, but he was a land saint and could not help me; so I cried to Another greater than he.

My last vision was of myself riding a huge breaker as though it were a horse. Then there came a crash and darkness.

****

Lo! it seemed to me as though one were calling me back from the depths of sleep. With trouble I opened my eyes only to shut them again because of the glare of the light. Then after a while I sat up, which gave me pain, for I felt as if I had been beaten all over, and looked once more. Above me shone the sun in a sky of deepest blue; before me was the sea almost calm, while around were rocks and sand, among which crawled great reptiles that I knew for turtles, as I had seen many of them in our wanderings. Moreover, kneeling at my side, with the sword that he had taken from the body of Deleroy still strapped about him, was Kari, who bled from some wound and was almost white with encrusted salt, but otherwise seemed unharmed. I stared at him, unable to open my mouth from amazement, so it was he who spoke the first, saying, in a voice that had a note of triumph in it:

"Did I not tell you that the gods were with us? Where is your faith, O White Man! Look! They have brought me back to the land of which I am Prince."

Now there was that in Kari's tone which in my weak state angered me. Why did he scold me about faith? Why did he address me as "White Man" instead of "Master"? Was it because he had reached

115

a country where he was great and I was nothing? I supposed so, and answered: "And are these your subjects, O noble Kari?" and I pointed to the crawling turtles. "And is this the rich and wondrous land where gold and silver are as mud?" and I pointed to the barren rocks and sand around.

He smiled at my jest, and answered more humbly:

"Nay, Master, yonder is my land."

Then I looked, following his glance, and saw many leagues way across the water two snow-clad peaks rising above a bank of clouds.

"I know those mountains," he went on; "without doubt they are one of the gateways of my land."

"Then we might as well be in London for all the hope we have of passing that gate, Kari. But tell me what has chanced."

"This, I think. A very great wave caught us and threw us right over those rocks on to the shore. Look—there is the *balsa*," and he pointed to a broken heap of reeds and pierced skins.

With his help I rose and went to it. Now none could know that it had been a boat. Still, the *balsa* it was and nothing else, and tied in its tangled mass still remained those things which we had brought with us, such as my black bow and armour, though all the jars were broken.

"It has borne us well, but will never bear us again," I said.

"That is so, Master. But if we were in my own country yonder I would set its fragments in a case of gold and place them in the Temple of the Sun as a memorial."

Then we went to a pool of rainwater that lay in a hollow rock near by, and drank our fill, for we were very thirsty. Also among the ruins of the *balsa* we found some of the dried fish that was left to us, and having washed it, filled ourselves. After this we limped to the crest of the land behind and perceived that we were on a little island, perhaps two hundred English acres in extent, whereon nothing grew except some coarse grass. This island, however, was the haunt of great numbers of seafowl which nested there, also of the turtles that I have mentioned, and of certain beasts like seals or otters.

"At least we shall not starve," I said, "though in the dry season we may die of thirst."

****

Now there on that island we remained for four long months. For food we ate the turtles, which we cooked over fires that Kari made by cunningly twirling a pointed piece of driftwood in the hollow of another piece that he filled with the dust of dried grass. Had he lacked that knowledge we must have starved or lived on raw flesh. As it was, we had plenty with this meat and that of birds and their eggs, also of fish that we caught in the pools when the tide was down. From the shells of the turtles, by the help of stones, we built us a kind of hut to keep off the sun and the rain, which in that hot place was sufficient shelter; also, when the stench was out of them, we used other shells in which to catch rainwater that we stored as best we could against seasons of drought. Lastly, with my big bow which was saved with the armour, I shot sea-otters, and from their pelts we made us garments after rubbing the skins with turtle fat and handling them to make them soft.

Thus, then, we lived from moon to moon upon that desert place, till I thought I should go mad with loneliness and despair, for no help came near us. There were the mountains of the mainland far away, but between them and us stretched leagues of sea that we could not swim, nor had we anything of which to make a boat.

"Here we must remain until we die!" at last I cried in my wretchedness.

"Nay," answered Kari, "our gods are still with us and will save us in their season."

****

This, indeed, they did in a strange fashion.

CHAPTER 3

The Daughter of the Moon

For the fourth time since we were cast away on this island the huge full moon shone in a sky of wondrous blue. Kari and I watched it rise between the two snow-clad peaks far away that he had called a gateway to his land, which was so near to us and yet it would seem more distant than Heaven itself. Heaven we might hope to reach upon the wings of spirit when we died, but to that country how could we come?

We watched that great moon climb higher and higher up a ladder of little bar-like clouds, till wearying we let our eyes fall upon the glittering pathway which its light made upon the bosom of the placid sea. Suddenly Kari stared and stared.

"What is it?" I asked idly.

"I thought I saw something yonder far away where Quilla's footsteps make the waters bright," he said, speaking in his own language in which now we often talked together.

"Quilla's?" I exclaimed. "Oh! I forgot: that is the lady moon's name in your tongue, is it not? Well, come, Quilla, and I will wed and worship you, as 'tis said the ancients did, and never turn to look upon another, be she woman, or goddess, or both. Only come and take me from this accursed isle and in payment I'll die for you, if need be, when first I've taught you how to love as star or woman never loved before."

"Hush!" said Kari in a grave voice, when he had listened to this mad stuff that burst through my lips from the spring of a mind distraught by misery and despair.

"Why should I hush?" I asked. "Is it not pleasant to think of the moon wearing a lovely woman's shape and descending to give a lonely mortal love and comfort?"

"Because, Master, to me and my people the moon is a goddess who hears prayer and answers it. Suppose, then, that she heard you and answered you and came to you and claimed your love, what then?"

"Why, then, friend Kari," I raved on, "then I should welcome her, for love goes a begging, ready as ripe fruit to be plucked by the first hand if it be fair enough, ready to melt beneath the first lips if they be warm enough. 'Tis said that it is the man who loves and the woman who accepts the love. But that is not true. It is the man, Kari, who waits to be loved and pays back just as much as is given to him, and no more, like an honest merchant; for if he does otherwise, then he suffers for it, as I have learned. Therefore, come, Quilla, and love as a Celestial can and I swear that step by step I'll keep pace with you in flesh and spirit through Heaven, or through Hell, since love I must have, or death."

"I pray you, talk not so," said Kari again, in a frightened voice, "since those words of yours come from the heart and will be heard. The goddess is a woman, too, and what woman will turn from such a bait?"

"Let her take it, then. Why not?"

"Because, O friend, because *Quilla* is wed to *Yuti*; the Moon is the Sun's wife, and if the Sun grows jealous what will happen to the man who has robbed the greatest of the world's gods?"

"I do not know and I do not care. If Quilla would but come and love me, I'd take my chance of Yuti whom as a Christian I defy."

Kari shuddered at this blasphemy, then having once more scanned that silver pathway on the waters, but without avail for the great fish or drifting tree or whatever he had seen, was gone, prayed after his fashion at night, to Pachacamac, Spirit of the Universe, or to the Sun his servant, god of the world, I know not which, and rolling himself in his rug of skins, crept into our little hut to sleep.

But as yet I did not sleep, for though Kari hated both, this talk of love and women had stirred my blood and made me wakeful. So I took a rough comb that I had fashioned from the shell of a turtle, and dragged it through my long fair beard, which, growing fast, now hung down far upon my breast, and through the curling hair that lay upon my shoulders, for I had become as other wild men are, and sang to myself there by the little fire which we kept burning day and night and tried to think of happy things that never should I know again.

At length the fit passed and I grew weary and laid myself down by the fire, for the night being so fine and warm I would not go into the hut, and there sleep found me.

I dreamed in my sleep. I dreamed that a very beautiful woman who wore upon her naked breast the emblem of the moon fashioned in crystal, stood over me, looking down upon me with large dark eyes. And as she looked she sighed. Thrice she sighed, each time more deeply than the last. Then she knelt down by me—or so it seemed in my dream, and laid a tress of her long dark hair against my yellow locks, as though she would match them together. She did more, indeed—in my dream—for lifting that tress of fragrant hair, she let it fall like thistledown across my face and mouth, and then kissed the hair, for I felt her breath reach me through its strands.

The dream ended thus, though I wished very much that it would go on, and I felt as though it had gone away as such visions do. Awhile later, as I suppose, I awoke quite suddenly, and opened my eyes. There, near to me, glittering in the full light of the brilliant moon, stood the woman of my dream, only now her naked breast was covered with a splendid cloak broidered with silver, and on her dark locks was a feathered headdress in front of which rose the crescent of the moon, likewise fashioned in silver. Also in her hand she held a little silver spear.

I stared at her, for move I could not. Then remembering my crazy talk with Kari, uttered one word, only one. It was—*Quilla*.

She bowed her head and answered in a voice soft as the murmur of the wind through rushes, speaking in the rich language called Quichua that Kari had taught me. In this tongue, as I have told, we talked together for practice during our journeys and on the island. So that now I knew it well.

"So indeed am I named after my mother, the 'Moon,'" she said. "But how did you know it, O Wanderer, whose skin is white as the foam of the sea and whose hair is yellow as the fine gold in the temples?"

"I think you must have told me when you knelt over me just now," I said.

I saw the red blood run to her brow, but she only shook her head, and answered:

"Nay, my mother, the Moon, must have told you; or perchance you learned it in the spirit. At least, Quilla am I named and you called me aright."

Now I stood up and stared at her, overcome by the strangeness of the business, and she stared at me. A marvellously beautiful woman she was in her dazzling robe and headdress, and lighter coloured than any native I had seen, almost white, indeed, in the moonlight save for the copper tinge that marked her race; tall, too, yet not over-tall; slim and straight as an arrow, but high-breasted and round-limbed, and with a wild grace in her movements like to that of a hawk upon the wing. Also to my fancy in her face there was something more than common youthful beauty, something spiritual, such as great artists show upon the carven countenances of saints.

120

Indeed she might well have been one whose human blood was mixed with some other alien strain—as she had called herself, a daughter of the Moon.

A question rose to my lips and burst from them; it was:

"Tell me, O Quilla, are you wife or maid?"

"Maid am I," she answered, "yet one who is promised as a wife," and she sighed, then went on quickly as though this matter were something of which she did not wish to talk, "And tell me, O Wanderer, are you god or man?"

Now I grew cunning and answered,

"I am a Son of the Sea as you are a Daughter of the Moon."

She turned her head and glanced at the radiance which lay upon the face of the deep, then said as though to herself:

"The moon shines upon the sea and the sea mirrors back the moon, yet they are far apart and never may draw near."

"Not so, O Quilla. Out of the sea does the moon rise and, her course run, into the sea's white arms she sinks to sleep at last."

Again the red blood ran to her brow and her great eyes fell, those eyes of which never before had I seen the like.

"It seems that they speak our tongue in the sea, and prettily," she murmured, adding, "But is it not from and into Heaven that the Moon rises and departs?"

At that moment to my grief our talk came to an end, for out of the hut crept Kari. He rose to his feet and stood there as ever calm and dignified, looking first at Quilla and then at me.

"What did I tell you, Master?" he said in English. "Did I not say that prayers such as yours are answered? Lo! here is that Child of the Moon for whom you sought, clothed in beauty and bringing her gifts of love and woe."

"Yes," I exclaimed, "and I am glad that she is here. For the rest, were she but mine, I think I should not grudge her price whate'er it be."

Quilla looked at Kari frowning over the spear that when he appeared she had lifted, as though to defend herself, which in my case she had not thought needful.

"So the sea breeds men of my own race also," she said, addressing him. "Tell me, O Stranger, how did you and yonder white god come to this isle?"

"Riding on the ocean billows, riding for thousands of leagues," he answered. "And you, O Lady, how did you come to this isle?"

"Riding on the moonbeams," she replied, smiling, "I, the daughter of the Moon, who am named Moon and wear her symbol on my brow."

"Did I not tell you so?" exclaimed Kari to me with a gloomy air. Then Quilla went on:

"Strangers, I was out fishing with two of my maidens and we had drifted far from land. As the sun sank I caught sight of the smoke of your fire, and having been told that this isle was desert, my heart drew me to discover who had lit it. So, though my maidens were afraid, hither I sailed and paddled, and the rest you know. Hearken! I will declare myself. I am the only child of Huaracha, King of the People of the Chancas, born of his wife, a princess of the Inca blood who now has been gathered to her Father, the Sun. I am here on a visit to my mother's kinsman, Quismancu, the Chief of the Yuncas of the Coastlands, to whom my father, the King, has sent an embassy on matters of which I know nothing. Behind yonder rock is my *balsa* and with it are the two maidens. Say, is it your wish to bide here upon this isle, or to return into the sea, or to accompany me back to the town of Quismancu? If so, we must sail ere the weather breaks, lest we should be drowned."

"Certainly it is my wish to accompany you, Lady, though a god of the sea cannot be drowned," I said quickly before Kari could speak. Indeed, he did not speak at all, he only shrugged his shoulders and sighed, like one who accepts some evil gift from Fate because he must.

"So be it!" exclaimed Quilla. "Now I go to make ready the *balsa* and to warn the maidens lest they be frightened. When you are prepared you will find us yonder behind the rock."

Then she bowed in a stately fashion an departed, walking with the proud, light step of a deer.

From our little hut I took out my armour and with Kari's help, put it on, because he declared that thus it would be more easily carried, though I think he had other reasons in his mind.

"Yes," I answered, "unless the *balsa* oversets, when I shall find mail hard to swim in."

"The *balsa* will not overset, sailing beneath the moon with that Moon-lady for a pilot," he replied heavily. "Had the sun been up, it might have been different. Moreover, the path into a net is always wide and easy."

"What net?" I asked.

"One that is woven of women's hair, I think. Already, if I mistake not, such a net has been about your throat, Master, and next time it will stay there. Hearken now to me. The gods thrust us into high matters. The Yuncas of whose chief this lady is a guest are a great people whom my people have conquered in war, but who wait the opportunity to rebel, if they have not already done so. The Chancas, of those king she is the daughter, are a still greater people who for years have threatened war upon my people."

"Well, what of it, Kari? With such questions this lady will have nothing to do."

"I think she has much to do with them. I think that she knows more than she seems to know, and that she is an envoy from the Chancas to the Yuncas. To whom is she affianced, I wonder? Some Great One, doubtless. Well, we shall learn in time; and meanwhile, I pray you, Master, remember that she says she *is* affianced, and that in this land men are very jealous even of a white god who rises from the sea."

"Of course I shall remember," I answered sharply. "Have I not had enough of women who are affianced?"

"By your prayer of the moon this night, which the moon answered so well and quickly, one might think not. Also this daughter of hers is fair, and perchance when she gave her hand she kept her heart. Listen again, Master. Of me and of whom I am, say nothing, save that you found me on this island where I dwelt a hermit when you rose from the sea. As for my name, why, it is Zapana. Remember that if you breathe my rank and history, however much sweet lips may try to cozen them out of you, you bring me to my death, who now do not wish to die, having a vengeance to accomplish and a throne to win. Therefore treat me as a dog, as one of no account, and be silent even in your sleep."

"I will remember, Kari."

"That is not enough—swear it."

"Good. I swear it—by the moon."

"Nay, not by the moon, for the moon is woman and changes. Swear it by this," and from beneath his skin robe he drew out the golden image of Pachacamac. "Swear it by the Spirit of the Universe, of whom Sun and Moon and Stars are but servants, the Spirit whom all men worship in this shape or in that."

So to please him I laid my hand upon the golden symbol and swore. Then, very hurriedly, we made up a tale of how, clad in my armour, I had risen from the sea and found him on the island, and how knowing me for a white god who once in ages past had visited that land and who, as prophecy foretold, should return to it in days to come, he had worshipped me and become my slave.

This done we went down to the rock, Kari walking after me and bearing all our small possessions and with them Deleroy's sword. Passing round the rock we saw the *balsa* drawn up to the sand, and by it the lady Quilla, who now had put off her fine robes and again was attired as a fishing-girl as I had seen her in my dream, and with her two tall girls in the same scanty garments. When these saw me in the glittering armour, which in our long idle hours we had polished till it shone like silver, with the shield upon my arm and the *casque* upon my head and the great sword girded about my middle and the black bow in my hand, they screamed with fear and fell upon their faces, while even Quilla started back and glanced towards the boat.

"Fear not," I said. "The gods are kind to those who do them service, though to those who would harm them they are terrible."

Kari also went to them and whispered in their ears what tale I know not. In the end they rose trembling, and having motioned to me to be seated in it, with the help of Kari pushed the *balsa*, which I noted with joy was large and well made, down into the sea. Then one by one they climbed in, Quilla taking the steering-oar, while Kari and the two maidens hoisted the little sail and paddled till we were clear of the island, where the gentle wind caught the *balsa*. Then they shipped the paddles, and although full laden, we sailed quietly towards the mainland.

Now I was at the bow of the *balsa* and Quilla was at its stern, and between us were the others, so that during all that long night's journey I had no speech with her and must content myself with gazing over my shoulder at her beauty as best I could, which was not well, because of Kari, who ever seemed to come between my eyes and hers.

Thus the long hours went by till at length when we were near the land the moon sank, and we sailed on through the twilight. Then came the dawn, and there in front of us we saw the lovely strand green with palms within a ring of snow-clad mountains, two of them the great peaks that we had seen from our isle.

On the shore was a city of white, flat-roofed houses, and rising above it, perchance the half of a mile from the sea, a hill four or five hundred feet in height and terraced. On the top of the hill stood a mighty building, painted red, that from the look of it I took to be one of the churches of these people, in the centre of which gleamed great doors that, as I found afterwards, were covered with plates of gold.

"Behold the temple of Pachacamac, Master," whispered Kari, bowing his head and kissing the air in token of reverence.

By this time watchmen, who had been set there to search the sea or the boat of Quilla, had noted our approach. They shouted and pointed to me who sat in the prow clad in my armour upon which the sun glittered, then began to run to and fro as though in fear or excitement, so that ere we reached the shore a great crowd had gathered. Meanwhile, Quilla had put on her silver-broidered mantle and her head-dress of feathers, crowned with the crescent of the moon. As we touched the beach she came forward, and for the first time during that night spoke to me saying:

"Remain here in the *balsa*, Lord, while I talk with these people, and when I summon you be pleased to come. Fear not—none will harm you."

Then she sprang from the prow of the *balsa* to the shore, followed by her two maidens, who dragged it further up the beach, and went forward to talk with certain white-robed men in the crowd. For a long while she talked, turning now and again to point at me. At length these men, accompanied by a number of others, ran forward. At first I thought they meant mischief and grasped my sword-hilt, then, remembering what Quilla had said, remained seated and silent.

Indeed, there was no cause for fear, for when the white-robed chiefs or priests and their following were close to me, suddenly they prostrated themselves and beat their heads upon the sand, from which I learned that they, too, believed me to be a god. Thereon I bowed to them and, drawing my sword—at the sight of which I saw them stare and shiver, for to these people steel was unknown—held it straight up in front of me in my right hand, the shield with the cognizance of the three arrows being on my left arm.

Now all the men rose, and some of them of the humbler sort, creeping to the *balsa*, suddenly seized it and lifted it on to their shoulders, which, being but a light thing of reeds and blown-out skins, they could do easily enough. Then, preceded by the chiefs, they advanced up the beach into the town, I still remaining seated in the boat with Kari crouching behind me. So strange was the business that almost I laughed aloud, wondering what those grave merchants of the Cheap whom I had known in London would think if they could see me thus.

"Kari," I said, without turning my head, "what are they going to do with us? Set us in yonder temple to be worshipped with nothing to eat?"

"I think not, Master," answered Kari, "since there the lady Quilla could not come to speak with you if she would. I think that they will take you to the house of the king of this country where, I understand, she is dwelling."

This, indeed, proved to be the case, for we were borne solemnly up the main street of the town, that now was packed with thousands of people, some of whom threw flowers before the feet of the bearers, bowing and staring till I thought that their eyes would fall out, to a large, flat-roofed house set in a walled courtyard. Passing through the gates the bearers placed the *balsa* on the ground and fell back. Then from out of the door of the house appeared Quilla, accompanied by a tall, stately looking man who wore a fine robe, and a woman of middle age also gorgeously apparelled.

"O Lord," said Quilla, bowing, "behold my kinsman the *Caraca*" (which is the name for a lesser sort of king) "of the Yuncas, named Quismancu, and his wife, Mira."

"Hail, Lord Risen from the Sea!" cried Quismancu. "Hail, White God clothed in silver! Hail, *Hurachi*!"

Why he called me "Hurachi" at the time I could not guess, but afterwards I learned that it was because of the arrows painted on my shield, *hurachi* being their name for arrows. At any rate, thenceforth by this name of Hurachi I was known throughout the land, though when addressed for the most part I was called "Lord-from-the-Sea" or "God-of-the-Sea."

Then Quilla and the lady Mira came forward and, placing their hands beneath my elbows, assisted me to climb out of that *balsa*, which I think was the strangest way that ever a shipwrecked wanderer came to land.

They led me into a large room with a flat roof that was being hastily prepared for me by the hanging of beautiful broideries on the walls, and sat me on a carven stool, where presently Quilla and other ladies brought me food and a kind of intoxicating drink which they called *chicha*, that after so many months of water drinking I found cheering and pleasant to the taste. This food, I noted, was served to me on platters of gold and silver, and the cups also were of gold strangely fashioned, by which I knew that I had come to a very rich land. Afterwards I learned, however, that in it there was no money, all the gold and silver that it produced being used for ornament or to decorate the temples and the palaces of the *Incas*, as they called their kings, and other great lords.

CHAPTER 4

The Oracle of Rimac

In this town of Quismancu I remained for seven days, going abroad but little, for when I did so the people pressed about me and stared me out of countenance. There was a garden at the back of the hose surrounded by a wall built of mud bricks. Here for the most part I sat and here the great ones of the place came to visit me, bringing me offerings of robes and golden vessels and I know not what besides. To all of them I told the same story—or, rather, Kari told it for me—namely, that I had risen out of the sea and found him a hermit, named Zapana, on the desert island. What is more, they believed it and, indeed, it was true, for had I not risen out of the sea?

From time to time Quilla came to see me also in this garden, bearing gifts of flowers, and with her I talked alone. She would sit upon a low stool, considering me with her beautiful eyes, as though she would search out my soul. One day she said to me:

"Tell me, Lord, are you a god or a man?"

"What is a god?" I asked.

"A god is that which is adored and loved."

"And is a man never adored and loved, Quilla? For instance, I understand that you are to be married, and doubtless you adore and love him who will be your husband."

She shivered a little and answered: "It is not so. I hate him."

"Then why are you going to marry him? Are you forced to do so, Quilla?"

"No, Lord. I marry him for my people's sake. He desires me for my inheritance and my beauty, and by my beauty I may lead him down that road on which my people wish that he should go."

"An old story, Quilla, but will you be happy thus?"

"No, Lord, I shall be very unhappy. But what does it matter? I am only a woman, and such is the lot of women."

"Women, like gods and men, are also sometimes loved and adored, Quilla."

She flushed at the words and answered:

"Ah! if that were so life might be different. But even if it were so and I found the man who could love and adore even for a year, for me it is now too late. I am sworn away by an oath that may not be broken, for to break it might bring death upon my people."

"To whom are you sworn?"

"To the Child of the Sun, no less a man; to the god who will be Inca of all this land."

"And what is this god like?"

"They say that he is huge and swarthy, with a large mouth, and I know that he has the heart of a brute. He is cruel and false also, and he counts his women by the score. Yet his father, the Inca, loves him more than any of his children, and ere long he will be king after him."

"And would you, who are sweet and lovely as the moon after which you are named, give yourself body and soul to such a one?"

Again she flushed.

"Do my own ears hear the White-God-from-the-Sea call me sweet and lovely as the moon? If so, I thank him, and pray him to remember that the perfect and lovely are always chosen to be the sacrifice of gods."

"But, Quilla, the sacrifice may be all in vain. How long will you hold the fancy of this loose-living prince?"

"Long enough to serve my purpose, Lord—or, at least," she added with flashing eyes, "long enough to kill him if he will not go my country's road. Oh! ask me no more, for your words stir something in my breast, a new spirit of which I never dreamed. Had I heard them but three moons gone, it might have been otherwise. Why did you not appear sooner from the sea, my lord Hurachi, be you god or man?"

Then, with something like a sob, she rose, made obeisance, and fled away.

****

That evening, when we were alone in my chamber where none could hear us, I told Kari that Quilla was promised in marriage to a prince who would be Inca of all the land.

"Is it so?" said Kari. "Well, learn, Master, that this prince is my brother, he whom I hate, he who has done me bitter wrong, he who stole away my wife and poisoned me. Urco is his name. Does this lady Quilla love him?"

"I think not. I think that like you she hates him, yet will marry him for reasons of policy."

"Doubtless she hates him now, whatever she did a week ago," said Kari in a dry voice. "But what fruit will this tree bear? Master, are you minded to come with me to-morrow to visit the temple of Pachacamac in the inner sanctuary of which sits the god Rimac who speaks oracles?"

"For what purpose, Kari?" I answered moodily.

"That we may hear oracles, Master. I think that if you choose to go the lady Quilla would come with us, since perhaps she would like also to hear oracles."

"I will go if it can be done in secret, say at night, for I weary of being stared at by these people."

This I said because I desired to learn of the religion of this nation and to see new things.

"Perhaps it can be so ordered, Master. I will ask of the matter."

It seemed that Kari did ask, perhaps of the high priest of Pachacamac, for between all the worshippers of this god there was a brotherhood; perhaps of the lord Quismancu, or perhaps of Quilla herself—I do not know. At least, on this same day Quismancu inquired whether it would please me to visit the temple that night, and so the matter was settled.

Accordingly, after the darkness had fallen, two litters were brought into which we entered, Quilla and a waiting woman seating themselves in one of them and Kari and I in the other, for Quismancu and his wife did not come—why I cannot say. Then, preceded by another litter in which was a priest of the god, and surrounded by a guard of soldiers, through a rain-storm we were borne up the hill—it was but a little way—to the temple.

Here, before the golden doors on which the lightning glimmered fitfully, we descended and were led by white-robed men bearing lanterns, through various courts to the inner sanctuary of the god, on the threshold of which I crossed myself, not loving the company of heathen idols. So far as I could see by the lamplight it was a great and glorious place, and everywhere that the eye fell was gold—places of gold on the walls, offerings of gold upon the floor, stars of gold upon the roof. The strange thing about this holy place, however, was that it seemed to be quite empty except for the aforesaid gold. There was neither altar nor image—nothing but a lamp-lit void.

Here all prostrated themselves, save I alone, and prayed in silence. When they rose again, in a whisper I asked of Kari where was the god.

To which he answered: "Nowhere, yet everywhere." This I thought a true saying, and indeed so solemn was that place that I felt as though I were surrounded by that which is divine.

After a while the priests, who were gorgeously apparelled, led us across the sanctuary to a door that opened upon some stairs. Down these stairs we went into a long passage that seemed to run beneath the earth, for the air in it was heavy. When we had walked a hundred paces or more in this narrow place, we came to other steps and another door, passing through which we found ourselves in a second temple, smaller than that which we had visited, but like to it rich with gold. In the centre of this temple sat the image of a man rudely fashioned of gold.

"Behold Rimac the Speaker!" whispered Kari.

"How can gold speak?" I asked.

Kari made no answer.

Presently the priests began to mutter prayers and incantations that I thought unholy, after which they laid offerings of what looked like raw flesh set in cups of gold before the idol, that I thought unholier still. Lastly they drew back and asked of what we would learn.

I made no answer who did not like the business. Nor did Kari say anything, but Quilla spoke out boldly, saying that we would learn of the future and what would befall us.

Now there was a long silence, and I confess that fear got hold of me, for it seemed to me as though spirits were moving in the air and through the darkness behind us—yes, as though I could hear their whisperings and the rustle of their wings. Suddenly, at the end of this silence, the golden image in front of us began to glow as though it were molten, and the emerald eyes that were set in its head to sparkle terribly, which frightened me so much that had it not been for shame's sake I would have run away, but because of this stood still and prayed to St. Hubert to protect me from the devil and his works. Presently I prayed still harder, for the image began to speak—yes, in a horrid, whistling voice it spoke, although no one was near to it. These were the words it said:

"Who is this clad in silver whose skin is white and whose hair is yellow? Such an one I have not seen for a thousand years, and such as he it is that shall possess themselves of the Land of Tavantinsuyu, shall steal its wealth, shall slay its people, and shall cast down its gods. But not yet, not yet! Therefore this is the command of Pachacamac, uttered by the voice of Rimac the Speaker, that none do harm to or cross the will of this mighty seaborn lord, since he shall be as a strong wall to many and his sword shall be red with the blood of the wicked."

The whistling voice ceased while the priests and all there stared at me, for they seemed to think its words fateful. Then suddenly it began again:

"And who is this that came out of the sea with the Shining One, having wandered further than any of his ancient blood? I know. I know, yet I may not say, since the Spirit of spirits whose image he wears upon his heart bids me be silent. Be bold! Be bold! Prosper and grow great, Child of Pachacamac, for thy wanderings are not yet done. Still there is a mountain to be climbed, and on the crest of it hangs a fringe of Heaven's gold."

Again the voice ceased, while this time all stared at Kari, who shook his head humbly as though bewildered by what he could not understand. Once more the image spoke:

"Who is this daughter of the Sun, in whose veins play moonbeams and who is fairer than the evening star? One, I think, whom men shall desire and because of whom shall flow the blood of the great. One whose thought is swift as the lightning and subtle as the snake, one in whom passion burns like fire in the womb of the mountain, but who is filled with spirit that dances above the fire and who longs for things that are afar. Daughter of the Sun in whose blood run the moonbeams, thou shalt slip from the hated arms and the Sun shall be thy shelter, and in the beloved arms thou shalt sleep at last. Yet from the vengeance of the god betrayed fly fast and far!"

Again the voice ceased, and I thought that all was over. But it was not so, for after a little space the golden figure of the oracle glowed more fiercely than before and the emerald eyes shone more terribly, and in a kind of scream it spoke, saying:

"The snows of Tavantinsuyu shall be red with blood, the waters of her rivers shall be full of blood. Yes, ye three shall wade through blood, and in a rain of blood shall pluck the fruit of your desires. Still for a while the gods of Tavantinsuyu shall endure and its kings shall reign and its children shall be free. But in the end death for the gods and death for the kings and death for the people. Still, not yet—not yet! None who live shall see it, nor their children, nor their children's children. Rimac the Voice has spoken; treasure ye his words and interpret them as ye will."

****

The whistling voice died away like the thin cry of some starving child in a desert, and there was a great silence. Then in a moment the figure of gold ceased to glow and the eyes of emerald to burn, leaving the thing but a dead lump of metal. The priests prostrated themselves, and rising, led us from the place without a word, but in the light of the lamps I saw that their faces were full of terror—so full that I doubted whether it could be feigned.

As we had come, so we went, and at last found ourselves outside the glittering temple doors where the litters awaited us.

"What did it mean?" I whispered to Quilla, who was by my side.

"For you and the other I know not," she answered hurriedly; "but for me I think that it means death. Yet, not until—not until—" And she ceased.

At that moment the moon appeared from behind the rain-clouds and shone upon her upturned face, and in her eyes there was a glory.

****

Now, as I learned afterwards, these words of its most famous oracle went all through the land and caused great talk and wonder mixed with fear, for none of such import had been spoken by it for generations. More, they shaped my own fortunes, for, as I came to know, Quismancu and his people had determined that I should not be allowed to go from among them. Not every day did a white god rise from the sea, and they desired that having come to them, there he should bide to be their defence and boast, and with him that hermit named Zapana, to whom, as they believed, he had appeared upon the desert isle. But after Rimac had spoken all this was changed, and when I said it was my will to depart and accompany Quilla upon her journey home to her father, Huaracha, King of the Chancas, as by swift messenger this King invited me to do, Quismancu answered that if I so desired I must be obeyed as the god Rimac had commanded, but that nevertheless he was sure that we should meet again.

Now, thinking these things over, I wondered much whether that oracle came out of the golden Rimac or perchance from the heart of Quilla, or of Kari, or of both of them, who desired that I should leave the Yuncas and travel to the Chancas and further. I did not know, nor was I ever to learn, since about matters to do with their gods these people are as secret as the grave. I asked Kari and I asked Quilla, but both of them stared at me with innocent eyes, and replied who were they to inspire the golden tongue of Rimac? Nor, indeed, did I ever learn whether Rimac the Speaker was a spirit or but a lump of metal through which some priest talked. All I know is that from one end of Tavantinsuyu to the other he was believed to be a spirit who spoke the very will of God to those who could understand his words, though this as a Christian man I could not credit.

So it came about that some days later, with Quilla and Kari and certain old men who, I took it, were priests or ambassadors, or both, I departed on our journey. As we went the people wept around my litter for sorrow, real or feigned, for we travelled in litters guarded by some two hundred soldiers armed with axes of copper and bows, and cast flowers before the feet of the bearers. But I did not weep, for though I had been very kindly treated there and, indeed, worshipped, glad was I to see the last of that city and its people who wearied me.

Moreover, I felt that there I was in the midst of plots, though of what these were I knew nothing, save that Quilla, who to the outward eye was but a lovely, innocent maiden, had a hand in them. Plots there were indeed, for, as I came to understand in time, they were nothing less than the preparing of a great war which the Chancas and the Yuncas were to wage against their over-lord, the Inca, the king of the mighty nation of the Quichuas, who had his home at a city called Cuzco far inland. Indeed, there and then this alliance was arranged, and by Quilla—Quilla, who proposed to sacrifice herself and by the gift of her person to his heir, to throw dust in the eyes of the Inca, whose dominion her father planned to take and with it the imperial crown of Tavantinsuyu.

****

Leaving the coastland, we were borne forward through the passes of great mountains, upon a wonderful road so finely made that never had I seen its like in England. At times we crossed rivers, but over these were thrown bridges of stone. Or mayhap we came to swamps, yet there the road still ran, built upon deep foundations in the mud. Never did it turn aside; always it went on, conquering every hindrance, for this was one of the Inca's roads that pierced Tavantinsuyu from end to end. We came to many towns, for this land was thickly populated, and for the most part slept in one of them each night. But always my fame had gone before me, and the *Curacas*, or chiefs of the towns, waited upon me with offerings as though I were indeed divine.

For the first five days of that journey I saw little of Quilla, but at length one night we were forced to camp at a kind of rest-house upon the top of a high mountain pass, where it was very cold, for the deep snow lay all about. At this place, as here were no *Curacas* to trouble me, I went out alone when Kari was elsewhere, and climbed a certain peak which was not far from the rest-house, that thence I might see the sunset and think in quiet.

Very glorious was the scene from that high point. All round me stood the cold crests of snow-clad mountains towering to the very skies, while between them lay deep valleys where rivers ran like veins of silver. So immense was the landscape that it seemed to have no end, and so grand that it crushed the spirit, while above arched the perfect sky in whose rich blue the gorgeous lights of evening began to gather as the great sun sank behind the snowy peaks.

Far up in the heavens floated one wide-winged bird, the eagle of the mountains, which is larger than any other fowl that I have ever seen, and the red light playing on it turned it to a thing of fire. I watched that bird and wished that I too had pinions which could bear me far away to the sea and over it.

And yet did I wish to go who had no home left on all the earth and no kind heart that would welcome me? Awhile ago I should have answered, "Yes, anywhere out of this loneliness," but now I was not so sure. Here at least Kari was my friend if a jealous one, though of late, as I could see, he was thinking of other things than friendship—dark plottings and high ambitions of which as yet he said little to me.

Then there was that strange and beautiful woman, Quilla, to whom my heart went out and not only because she was beautiful, and who, as I thought, at times looked kindly on me. But if so, what did it avail; seeing that she was promised in marriage to some high-placed native man who would be a king? Surely I had known enough of women who were promised in marriage to other men, and should do well to let her be.

Thinking thus, desolation took hold of me and I sat myself down on a rock and covered my face with my hands that I might not see the tears, which I knew were gathering in my eyes, as they fell from them. Yes, there in the midst of that awful solitude, I, Hubert of Hastings, whose soul it filled, sat down like a lost child and wept.

Presently I felt a touch upon my shoulder and let fall my hands, thinking that Kari had found me out, to hear a soft voice, the voice of Quilla, say:

"So it seems that the gods can weep. Why do you weep, O God-from-the-Waves who here are named Hurachi?"

"I weep," I answered, "because I am a stranger in a strange land; I weep because I have not wings whereon I can fly away like that great bird above us."

She looked at me awhile, then said, most gently:

"And whither would you fly, O God-from-the-Sea? Back into the sea?"

"Cease to call me a god," I answered, "who, as you know well, am but a man though of another race than yours."

"I thought it but I did not know. But whither would you fly, O Lord Hurachi?"

"To the land where I was born, Lady Quilla; the land that I shall never see again."

"Ah! doubtless there you have wives and children for whom your heart is hungry."

"Nay, now I have neither wife nor child."

"Then once you had a wife. Tell me of that wife. Was she fair?"

"Why should I tell you a sad story? She is dead."

"Dead or living, you still love her, and where there is love there is no death."

"Nay, I only love what I thought she was."

"Was she false, then?"

"Yes, false and yet true. So true that she died because she was false."

"How can a woman be both false and true?"

"Woman can be all things. Ask the question of your own heart. Can you not perchance be both false and true?"

She thought awhile and, leaving this matter, said:

"So, having once loved, you can never love again."

"Why not? Perchance I can love too much. But what would be the use when more love would but mean more loss and pain?"

"Whom should you love, my lord Hurachi, seeing that the women of your own folk are far away?"

"I think one who is very near, if she would pay back love for love."

Quilla made no answer, and I thought that she was angry and would go away. But she did not; indeed, she sat herself down upon the stone at my side and covered her face with her hands as I had done and began to weep as I had done. Now in my turn I asked her:

"Why do you weep?"

"Because I, too, must know loneliness, and with it shame, Lord Hurachi."

At these words my heart beat and passion flamed up in me. Stretching out my hand I drew hers away and in the dying light gazed at the face beneath. Lo! on its loveliness there was a look which could not be misread.

"Do you, then, also love?" I whispered.

"Aye, more, I think, than ever woman loved before. From the moment when first I saw you sleeping in the moonbeams on the desert isle, I knew my fate had found me, and that I loved. I fought against it because I must, but that love has grown and grown, till now I am all love, and, having given everything, have no more left to give."

When I heard this, making no answer, I swept her into my arms and kissed her, and there she lay upon my breast and kissed me back.

"Let me go, and hear me," she murmured presently, "for you are strong and I am weak."

I obeyed, and she sank back upon the stone.

"My lord," she said, "our case is very sad, or at least my case is sad, since though you being a man may love often, I can love but once, and, my lord, it may not be."

"Why not?" I asked hoarsely. "Your people think me a god; cannot a god take whom he wills to wife?"

"Not when she is vowed to another god, he who will be Inca; not when on her, mayhap, hangs the fate of nations."

"We might fly, Quilla."

"Whither could the God-from-the-Sea fly and whither could fly the daughter of the Moon, who is vowed to the son of the Sun in marriage, save to death?"

"There are worse things than death, Quilla."

"Aye, but my life is in pawn. I must live that my people may not die. Myself I offered it to this cause and now, being royal, I cannot take it back again for my own joy. It is better to be shamed with honour than to be loved in the lap of shame."

"What then?" I asked hopelessly.

"Only this, that above us are the gods, and—heard you not the oracle of Rimac that declared to me that I should slip from the hated arms, that the Sun should be my shelter, and in the beloved arms I should sleep at last, though from the vengeance of the god betrayed I must fly fast and far? I think that this means death, but also it means life in death and—O arms beloved, you shall fold me yet. I know not how, but have faith—for you shall fold me yet. Meanwhile, tempt me not from the path of honour, since this I know, that it alone can lead me to my home. Yet who is the god betrayed from whom I must fly? Who, who?"

Thus she spoke and was silent, and I, too, was silent. Yes, there we sat, both silent in the darkness, searching the heavens for a guiding star. And as we sat, presently I heard the voice of Kari saying:

"Have I found you, Lord, and you also, Lady Quilla? Return, I pray you, for all search and are frightened."

"Why?" I answered. "The lady Quilla and I study this wondrous scene."

"Yes, Lord, though to those who are not god-born it would be difficult in this darkness. Suffer, now that I show you the path."

CHAPTER 5

Kari Goes

As it chanced during the remaining days of that journey, Quilla and I were not again alone together (that is to say, except once for a few minutes), for we were never out of eyeshot of someone in our company. Thus Kari clung to me very closely, indeed, and when I asked him why, told me bluntly that it was for my safety's sake. A god to remain a god, he said, should live alone in a temple. When he began to mix with others of the earth and to do those things they did, to eat and to drink, to laugh and to frown; even to slip in the mud or to stumble over the stones in the common path, those others would come to think that there was small difference between god and man. Especially would they think so if he were observed to love the company of women or to melt beneath their soft glances.

Now I grew sore at the sting of these arrows which of late he had loved to shoot at me, and without pretending to misunderstand him, said outright:

"The truth is, Kari, that you are jealous of the lady Quilla as once you were jealous of another."

He considered the matter in his grave fashion, and answered:

"Yes, Master, that is the truth, or part of it. You saved my life, and sheltered me when I was alone in a strange land, and for this and for yourself I came to love you very greatly, and love, if it be true, is always jealous and always hates a rival."

"There are different sorts of loves," I said; "that of a man for man is one, that of man for woman is another."

"Yes, Master, and that of woman for man is a third; moreover, there is this about it—it is the acid which turns all other loves sour. Where are a man's friends when a woman has him by the heart?—although perchance they love him better than ever will the woman who at bottom loves herself best of all. Still, let that be, for so Nature works, and who can fight against Nature? What Quilla takes, Kari loses, and Kari must be content to lose."

"Have you done?" I asked angrily, who wearied of his homilies.

"No, Master. The matter of jealousy is small and private; so is the matter of love. But, Master, you have not told me outright whether you love the lady Quilla, and, what is more important, whether she loves you."

"Then I will tell you now. I do and she does."

"You love the lady Quilla and she says that she loves you, which may or may not be true, or if true to-day may be false to-morrow. For your sake I hope that it is not true."

"Why?" I said in a rage.

"Because, Master, in this land there are many sorts of poison, as I have learned to my cost. Also there are knives, if not of steel, and many who might wish to discover whether a god who courts women like a man can be harmed by poisons or pierced by knives. Oh!" he added, in another tone, ceasing from his bitter jests, "believe me that I would shield, not mock you. This Lady Quilla is a queen in a great game of pieces such as you taught me to play far away in England, and without her perchance that game cannot be won, or so those who play it think. Now you would steal that queen and thereby, as they also think, bring death and destruction on a country. It is not safe, Master. There are plenty of fair women in this land; take your pick of them, but leave that one queen alone."

"Kari," I answered, "if there be such a game, are you not perchance one of the players on this side or on that?"

"It may be so, Master, and if you have not guessed it, perhaps one day I will tell you upon which side I play. It may even be that for my own sake I should be glad to see you lift this queen from off the board, and that what I tell you is for love of you and not of myself, also of the lady Quilla, who, if you fall, falls with you down through the black night into the arms of the Moon, her mother. But I have said enough, and indeed it is foolish to waste breath in such talk, since Fate will have its way with both of you, and the end of the game in which we play is already written in Pachacamac's book for every one of us. Did not Rimac speak of it the other night? So play on, play on, and let Destiny fulfil itself. If I dared to give counsel it was only because he who watches the battle with a general's eye sees more of it than he who fights."

Then he bowed in his stately fashion and left me, and it was long ere he spoke to me again of this matter of Quilla and our love for one another.

When he was gone my anger against him passed, since I saw that he was warning me of more than he dared to say, not for himself, but because he loved me. Moreover, I was afraid, for I felt that I was moving in the web of a great plot that I did not understand, of which Quilla and those cold-eyed lordlings of her company and the chief whose guest I had been, and Kari himself, and many others as yet unknown to me, spun the invisible threads. One day these might choke me. Well, if they did, what then? Only I feared for Quilla—greatly I feared for Quilla.

On the day following my talk with Kari at length we reached the great city of the Chancas, which, after them, was called Chanca—at least I always knew it by that name. From the dawn we had been passing through rich valleys where dwelt thousands of these Chancas who, I could see, were a mighty people that bore themselves proudly and like soldiers. In multitudes they gathered themselves together upon either side of the road, chiefly to catch a sight of me, the white god who had risen from the ocean, but also to greet their princess, the lady Quilla.

Indeed, now I learned for the first time how high a princess she was, since when her litter passed, these folk prostrated themselves, kissing the air and the dust. Moreover, as soon as she came among them Quilla's bearing changed, for her carriage grew more haughty and her words fewer. Now she seldom spoke save to issue a command, not even to myself, although I noted that she studied me with her eyes when she thought that I was not observing her.

During our midday halt I looked up and saw that an army was approaching us, five thousand men or more, and asked Kari its meaning.

"These," he answered, "are some of the troops of Huaracha, King of the Chancas, whom he sends out to greet his daughter and only child, also his guest, the White God."

"Some of the troops! Has he more, then?"

"Aye, Master, ten times as many, as I think. This is a great people; almost as great as that of the Incas who live at Cuzco. Come now into the tent and put on your armour, that you may be ready to meet them."

I did so, and, stepping forth clad in the shining steel, took my stand where Kari showed me, upon a rise of ground. On my right at a little distance stood Quilla, more splendidly arrayed than I had ever seen her, and behind her her maidens and the captains and counsellors of her following.

The army drew nearer, marshalled in regiments and halted on the plain some two hundred yards away. Presently from it advanced generals and old men, clad in white, whom I took to be priests and elders.

They approached to the number of twenty or more and bowed deeply, first to Quilla, who bent her head in acknowledgment and then to myself. After this they went to speak with Quilla and her following, but what they said I did not know. All the while, however, their eyes were fixed on me. Then Quilla brought them to me and one by one they bowed before me, saying something in a language which I did not understand well, for it was somewhat different from that which Kari had taught me.

After this we entered the litters, and, escorted by that great army, were borne forward down valleys and over ridges till about sunset we came to a large cup-like plain in the centre of which stood the city called Chanca. Of this city I did not see much except that it was very great as the darkness was falling when we entered, and afterwards I could not go out because of the crowds that pressed about me. I was borne down a wide street to a house that stood in a large garden which was walled about. Here in this fine house I found food prepared for me, and drink, all of it served in dishes and cups of gold and silver; also there were women who waited upon me, as did Kari who now was called Zapana and seemed to be my slave.

When I had eaten I went out alone into the garden, for on this plain the air was very warm and pleasant. It was a beautiful garden, and I wandered about among its avenues and flowering bushes, glad to be solitary and to have time to think. Amongst other things I wondered where Quilla might be, for of her I had seen nothing from the time that we entered the town. I hated to be parted from her, because in this vast strange land into which I had wandered she was the only one for whom I had come to care and without whom I felt I should die of loneliness.

There was Kari, it is true, who I knew loved me in his fashion, but between him and me there was a great gulf fixed, not only of race and faith, but of something now which I did not wholly understand. In London he had been my servant and his ends were my ends; on our wandering he had been my companion in great adventures. But now I knew that other interests and desires had taken a hold of him, and that he trod a road of which I could not see the goal; and no longer thought much of me save when what I did or desired to do came between him and that goal.

Therefore Quilla alone was left to me, and Quilla was about to be taken away. Oh! I wearied of this strange land with its snow-clad mountains and rich valleys, its hordes of dark-skinned people with large eyes, smiling faces, and secret hearts; its great cities, temples, and palaces filled with useless gold and silver; its brilliant sunshine and rushing rivers, its gods, kings, and policies. They were alien to me, every one of them, and if Quilla were taken away and I were left quite alone, then I thought that it would be well to die.

Something moved behind a palm trunk of the avenue in which I walked, and not knowing whether it were beast or man, I laid my hand upon my sword which I still wore, although I had taken off the armour. Before I could draw it my wrist was grasped and a soft voice whispered in my ear:

"Fear nothing; it is I—Quilla."

Quilla it was, wrapped in a long hooded cloak such as the peasant women wear in the cold country, for she threw back the hood and a beam of starlight fell upon her face.

"Hearken!" she said. "It is dangerous to both of us, but I have come to bid you farewell."

"Farewell! I feared it would be thus, but why so soon, Quilla?"

"For this reason, Love and Lord. I have seen my father the King, and made my report to him of the matter with which I was sent to deal among the Yuncas. It pleased him, and since his mood was gracious, I opened my heart to him and told him that no longer did I wish to be given in marriage to Urco, who will soon put on the Inca fringe, for, as you know, it is to him that I am promised!"

"What did he answer, Quilla?"

"He answered: 'This means, Daughter, that you have met some other man to whom you do wish to be given in marriage. I will not ask his name, since if I knew it it would be my duty to kill him, however high and noble he might be.'"

"Then he guesses, Quilla?"

"I think he guesses; I think that already some have whispered in his ear, but he does not wish to listen who desires to remain deaf and blind."

"Did he say no more, Quilla?"

"He said much more; he said this—now I tell you secrets, Lord, and place my honour in your keeping, for having given you all the rest, why should I not give you that also? He said: 'Daughter, you who have been my ambassador, you, my only child, who know all my counsel, know also that there is about to be the greatest war that the land of Tavantinsuyu has ever known, war between the two mighty nations of the Quichuas of Cuzco whereof the old Upanqui is king and god, and the Chancas whereof I am king and you, if you live, in a day to come will be the queen. No longer can these two lions dwell in the same forest; one of them must devour the other; nor shall I fight alone, since on our side are all the Yuncas of the coast who, as you report to me, are ripe for rebellion. But, as you also report, and as I have learned from others, they are not yet ready. Moons must go by before their armies are joined to mine and I throw off the mask. Is it not so?'

"I answered that it was so, and my father went on:

"'Then during that time, Daughter, a dust must be raised that will hide the shining of my spears, and, Daughter, you are that dust. To-morrow the old Inca Upanqui visits me here with a small army. I read your thought. It is—Why do you not kill him and his army? Daughter, for this reason. He is very aged and about to lay down his sceptre, who grows feeble of mind and body. If I killed him what would it serve me, seeing that he has left his son, Urco, who will be Inca, ruling at Cuzco, and that of his soldiers not one in fifty will be with him here? Moreover, he is my guest, and the gods frown on those who slay their guests, nor will men ever trust them more.'

"Now I answered: 'You spoke of me as a cloud of dust, Father; how, then, can this poor dust serve your ends and those of the Chanca people?'

"'Thus Daughter,' he answered. 'With your own consent you are promised in marriage to Urco. Upanqui the Inca has heard rumours that the Chancas prepare for war. Therefore, he who travels on his last journey through certain of his dominions comes to lead you away, to be Urco's bride, saying to himself, "If those rumours are true, King Huaracha will withhold his only child and heiress, since never will he make war upon Cuzco if she rules there as its queen." Therefore, if I refuse you to him, he will withdraw and begin the war, rolling down his thousands upon us before we are ready, and bringing the Chancas to destruction and enslavement. Therefore also not only my fate, but the fate of all your country lies in your hand.'

"'Father,' I said, 'tell me, who was ever dear to you that lack sons, is there no escape? Must I eat this bitter bread? Before you answer, learn that you have guessed aright, and that I who, when I made that promise, cared for no man, have come to feel the burning of love's fire!'

"Now he looked at me awhile, then said: 'Child of the Moon, there is but one escape, and it must be sought—in the moon. The dead cannot be given in marriage. If your strait is so sore, though it would cut me to the heart, perchance it is better that you should die and go whither doubtless he whom you love will soon follow you. Depart now and counsel with Heaven in your sleep. To-morrow, before Up-anqui comes, we will talk again.'

"So I knelt and kissed the hand of the King, my father, and left him, wondering at his nobleness who could show such a road to his only child, though its treading would mean woe to him and mayhap the ruin of his hopes. Still that road is an old one among the women of my people, and why should I not walk it, as thousands have done before me?"

"How came you here?" I asked hoarsely.

"Lord, I guessed that you would be walking in this garden which joins on to that of the palace, and—none were about, and—the door in the wall was open. Indeed, it was almost as though I were left alone and unwatched of set purpose. So I came and sought—and found, having a question to put to you."

"What question, Quilla?"

"This: Shall I live or shall I die? Speak the word and I obey. Yet ere you speak, remember that if I live we meet for the last time, since very soon I go hence to become the wife of Urco and play the part that is prepared for me?"

Now when I, Hubert, heard these words, I felt as though my heart would burst within my breast and knew not what to say. So to gain time I asked her:

"Which do you desire—to live or to die?"

She laughed a little as she answered:

"That is a strange question, Lord. Have I not told you that if I live I must do so befouled as one of Urco's women, whereas, if I die, I die clean and take my love with me to where Urco cannot come, but where, mayhap, another may follow at the appointed time."

"Which time would be very soon, I think, Quilla, seeing that he who had spoiled all this pretty plot would scarcely be left long upon the earth, even if he wished to stay there. Yet I say: Do not die—live on."

"To become Urco's woman! That is strange counsel from a lover's lips, Lord; such as would scarcely have been given by any of our nobles."

"Aye, Quilla, and it is given because I am not of your people and do not think as they think, who reject their customs. You are not yet Urco's wife, and may be rid of him by other paths than that of death, but from the grave there is no escape."

"And in the grave there is no more fear, Lord. Thither Urco cannot come; there are neither wars nor plottings; there honour does not beckon and love hold back. I say that I will die and make an end, as for like causes many of my blood have done, though not here and now. When I am about to be delivered to Urco then I will die, and perchance not alone. Perchance he will accompany me," she added slowly.

"And if this happens, what shall I do?"

"Live on, Lord, and find other women to love you, as a god should. There are many in this land fairer and wiser than I, and, save myself, you may take whom you will."

"Listen, Quilla. I have a story to tell you."

Then, as briefly as I could, I set out the tale of Blanche and of her end, while she hung upon my every word.

"Oh! I grieve for you," she said, when I had finished.

"You grieve for me, and yet, what she did for my sake you would do also, so that, as it were, both my hands must be dyed with blood. This first terror I have borne, but if a second falls upon me then I know that I shall go mad and perish in this way or in that, and you, Quilla, will be my murderess."

"No, no, not that!" she murmured.

"Then swear to me by your god and by your spirit, that you will do yourself no harm, whatever chances, and that if die you must, it shall be with me for company."

"Is your love so great that you would dare this for my sake, Lord?"

"I think so, though not till all else had failed. I think that if you were taken from me, Quilla, I could not live on here in loneliness and exile—however great the sin. But do you swear?"

"Aye, Love and Lord, I swear, for your sake. Moreover, I add to the oath. If perhaps we should escape these perils and come together, I will be such a wife to you as never man has had. I will wrap you round with love and lift you up to be a king, that you may live in glory forgetting your home across the sea, and all the sorrows that befell you there. Children you shall have also of whom you need not be ashamed, though my dark blood runs in them, and armies at command and palaces filled with gold, and all royal joys. And if perchance the gods declare against us, and we pass from the world together, then I think, oh! then I think that I shall give you finer gifts than these, though what they are I know not yet, since to the power of love there is no end—here on earth or yonder in the skies."

I stared at her face in the starlight, and oh! it had grown splendid. No longer was it that of a woman, since through it, like light through pearl, shone a soul divine. It might have been a goddess who stood beside me, for those eyes were holy and her embrace that wrapped me close was not that of the flesh alone.

"I must be gone," she whispered, "but now I go without fear. Perchance we may not speak again for long, but trust me always. Play your part and I will play mine. Follow me wherever I am taken and keep near to me, if you may, as ever my spirit shall be near to you.

Then what matters anything, even if we are slain? Farewell, beloved, kiss me and farewell."

Another moment and she had glided away and was lost in the shadows.

****

She was gone, and I stood amazed and overcome. Oh! what a love it was that this alien woman had given to me and how could I be worthy of it? Now I forgot my griefs; now I no longer mourned because I was an outcast who nevermore might look upon the land where I was born, nor see the face of one my own race or blood. All my loss was paid back to me again and yet again, in the coin of the glory of this woman whom I had won. Dangers rose about us, but I feared them no more, because I knew that her love's conquering feet would stamp them flat and lead me safe to a joyful treasure-house of splendour of spirit and of body where we should dwell side by side, triumphant and unafraid.

Whilst I thought thus, lost in a rapture such as I had not felt since Blanche kissed me at the mouth of the Hastings cave after I had killed the three Frenchmen with as many arrows from my black bow, I heard a sound and looked up to see a man standing before me.

"Who is it?" I asked, grasping my sword, for his face was hidden in the shadows.

"I," answered a voice which I knew to be that of Kari.

"Then how did you come here? I saw no one pass the open ground."

"Master, you are not the only one who loves to walk in gardens in the quiet of the night. I was here before yourself, behind yonder tree," and he pointed to a palm not three paces distant.

"Then, Kari, you must have seen—"

"Yes, Master, I saw and heard, not everything, because there came a point at which I shut my eyes and stopped my ears, but still much."

"I am minded to kill you, Kari," I said between my teeth, "who play the spy upon me."

"I guessed it would be so, Master," he replied in his gentlest voice, "and for that reason, as you will notice, I am standing out of reach of your sword. You wonder why I am here. I will tell you. It is not from any desire to watch your love-makings which weary me, who have seen such before, but rather that I might find secrets, of which love is always the loser, and those secrets I have learned. How could I have come by them otherwise, Master?"

145

"Surely you deserve to die," I exclaimed furiously.

"I think not, Master. But listen and judge for yourself. I have told you something of my story, now you shall hear more, after which we will talk of what I do or do not deserve. I am the eldest son of the Inca Upanqui, and Urco, of whom you have been talking is my younger brother. But Upanqui, our father, loved Urco's mother while mine he did not love, and swore to her before she died that against right and law, Urco, her son, should be Inca after him. Therefore he hated me because I stood in Urco's path; therefore too many troubles befell me, and I was given over into Urco's hand, so that he took my wife and tried to poison me, and the rest you know. Now it was needful to me to learn how things went, and for this reason I listened to the talk between you and a certain lady. It told me that Upanqui, my father, comes here to-morrow, which indeed I knew already, and much else that I had not heard. This being so I must vanish away, since doubtless Upanqui or his councillors would know me again, and as they are all of them friends of Urco, perhaps I should taste more poison and of a stronger sort."

"Whither will you vanish, Kari?"

"I know not, Master, or if I know, I will not say, who have but just been taught afresh how secrets can pass from ear to ear. I must lie hid, that is enough. Yet do not think that therefore I shall desert you—I, while I live, will watch over you, a stranger in my country, as you watched over me when I was a stranger in your England."

"I thank you," I answered, "and certainly you watch well—too well, sometimes, as I have found to-night."

"You think it pleases me to spy upon you and a certain lady," went on Kari with an unruffled voice, "but it is not so. What I do is for good reasons, amongst others that I may protect you both, and if I can, bring about what you desire. That lady has a great heart, as I learned but now, and after all you did well to love her, as she does well to love you. Therefore, although the dangers are so many, if I am able, I will help you in your love and bring you together, yes, and save her from the arms of Urco. Nay, ask me not how, for I do not know, and the case seems desperate."

"But if you go, what shall I do alone?" I asked, alarmed.

"Bide here, I think, Lord, giving it out that your servant Zapana has deserted you. Indeed it seems that this you must do, since the king of this country will scarcely suffer you to be the companion of his daughter upon her marriage journey to Cuzco, even if Upanqui so desires. Nor would it be wise, for if he did, misfortune might befall you on the road. There are some women, Lord, who cannot keep their love out of their eyes, and henceforward there will be plenty to watch the eyes and hearken to the most secret sighings of one of the greatest of them. Now farewell until I come to you again or send others on my behalf. Trust me, I pray you, since to whomever else I may seem false, to you I am true; yes, to you and to another because she has become a part of you."

Then before I could answer, Kari took my hand and touched it with his lips. Another moment and I had lost sight of him in the shadows.

CHAPTER 6
The Choice

That night I slept but ill who was overwhelmed with all that had befallen me of good and evil. I had gained a wondrous love, but she who gave it was, it seemed, about to be lost to me, aye, and to be thrown to another whom she hated, to forward the dark policies of a great and warlike people. I had spoken to her with high words of hope, but of it in my heart there was little. She would follow what she held to be her duty to the end, and that end, if she kept her promise and did not die as she desired to do—was—the arms of Urco. From these I could see no escape for her, and the thought maddened me. Moreover, Kari was gone leaving me utterly alone among these strangers, and whether he would return again I did not know. Oh! almost I wished that I were dead.

The morning broke at last and I arose and called for Zapana. Then came others who said that my servant, Zapana, could not be found, whereat I affected surprise and anger. Still these others waited on me well enough, and I rose and ate in pomp and luxury. Scarcely had I finished my meal than there appeared heralds who summoned me to the presence of the king Huaracha.

I went, borne in a litter, although an arrow from my black bow would have flown from door to door. At the portal of the palace, which was like others I had seen, only finer, I was met by soldiers and gaily dressed servants and led across a courtyard within, which I could see was prepared for some ceremony, to a small chamber on the further side. Here, when my eyes grew accustomed to the half-darkness, I perceived a man of some sixty years of age, and behind him two soldiers. At once I noted that everything about this man was plain and simple; the chamber, which was little more than four whitewashed walls with a floor of stone, the stool he sat on, even his apparel. Here were no gold or silver or broidered cloths, or gems, or other rich and costly things such as these people love, but rather those that are suited to a soldier. A soldier he looked indeed, being burly and broad and scarred upon his homely face, in which gleamed eyes that were steady and piercing.

As I entered, the king Huaracha, for it was he, rose from his stool and bowed to me, and I bowed back to him. Then he motioned to one of the soldiers to give me another stool, upon which I sat myself, and speaking in a strong, low voice, using that tongue which Kari had taught me, said:

"Greeting, White-God-from-the-Sea, or golden-bearded man named the lord Hurachi, I know not which, of whom I have heard so much and whom I am glad to behold in my poor city. Say, can you understand my talk?"

Thus he spoke, searching me with his eyes, though all the while I perceived that they rested rather on my armour and the great sword, Wave-Flame, than on my face.

I gave him back his greeting and answered that I understood the tongue he used though not so very well, whereon he began to speak about the armour and the sword, which puzzled him who had never seen steel.

"Make me some like them," he said, "and I will give you ten times their weight in gold, which, after all, is of no use since with it one cannot kill enemies."

"In my country with it one can corrupt them," I answered, "or buy them to be friends."

"So you have a country," he interrupted shrewdly. "I thought that the gods had none."

"Even the gods live somewhere," I replied.

He laughed, and turning to the two soldiers, who also were staring at my mail and sword, bade them go. When the heavy door had shut behind them and we were quite alone, he said:

"My lord Hurachi, I have heard from my daughter how she found you in the sea, a story indeed. I have also heard, or guessed, it matters not which, that her heart has turned towards you, as is not strange, seeing the manner of man you are, if indeed you be not more than man, and that women are ever prone to love those whom they think they have saved. Is this true, my lord Hurachi?"

"Ask of the Lady Quilla, O King."

"Mayhap I have asked and at last it seems that you make no denial. Now hearken, my lord Hurachi. You are my honoured guest and save one thing, all I have is yours, but you must talk no more alone with the lady Quilla in gardens at night."

Now, making no attempt to deny or explain which I saw would be useless, since he knew it all, I asked boldly: "Why not?"

"I thought that perchance my daughter had told you, Lord Hurachi, but if you desire to hear it from my own lips also, for this reason. The lady Quilla is promised in marriage and if she lives that promise must be fulfilled, since on it hangs the fate of nations. Therefore, it is, although to grieve to part such a pair, that you and she must meet no more in gardens or elsewhere. Know that if you do, you will bring about her death and your own, if gods can die."

Now I thought awhile and answered:

"These are heavy words, King Huaracha, seeing that I will not hide from you that I love your daughter well and that she, who is great-hearted, loves me well and desires me for her husband."

"I know it and I grieve for both of you," he said courteously.

"King Huaracha," I went on, "I see that you are a soldier and the lord of armies, and it has come into my mind that perchance you dream of war."

"The gods see far, White Lord."

"Now god or man, I also am a soldier, King, and I know arts of battle which perhaps are hidden from you and your people; also I cannot be harmed by weapons because of magic armour that I wear, and none can stand before me in fight because of this magic sword I carry, and I can direct battles with a general's mind. In a great war, King, I might be useful to you were I the husband of your daughter and therefore your son and friend, and perchance by my skill make the difference to you and your nation between victory and defeat."

"Doubtless this is so, O Son-of-the-Sea."

"In the same fashion, King, were I upon the side of your enemies, to them I might bring victory and to you defeat. Whom do you desire that I should serve, you or them?"

"I desire that you should serve me," he replied with eagerness. "Do so and all the wealth of this land shall be yours, with the rule of my armies under me. You shall have palaces and fields and gold and silver, and the fairest of its daughters for wives, and be worshipped as a god, and for aught I know, be king after me, not only of my country but mayhap of another that is even greater."

"It is a good offer, King, but not enough. Give me your daughter, Quilla, and you may keep all the rest."

"White Lord, I cannot, since to do so I must break my word."

"Then, King, I cannot serve you, and unless you kill me first—if you are able—I will be, not your friend, but your enemy."

"Can a god be killed, and if so can a guest be killed? Lord, you know that he cannot. Yet he can remain a guest. To my country you have come, Lord, and in my country you shall stay, unless you have wings beneath that silver coat. Quilla goes hence but here you bide, my lord Hurachi."

"Perchance I shall find the wings," I answered.

"Aye, Lord, for it is said that the dead fly, and if I may not kill you, others may. Therefore my counsel to you is to stay here, taking such things as my poor country can give you, and not to try to follow the moon (by this he meant Quilla) to the golden city of Cuzco, which henceforth must be her home."

Now having no more to say, since war had been declared between us, as it were, I rose to bid this king farewell. He also rose, then, as though struck by a sudden thought, said that he desired to speak with my servant, Zapana, he whom the lady Quilla had found with me in the island of the sea. I replied that he could not since Zapana had vanished, I knew not where.

At this intelligence he appeared to be disturbed and was beginning to question me somewhat sternly as to who Zapana might be and how I had first come into his company, when the door of the room opened and through it Quilla entered even more gorgeously robed and looking lovelier than ever I had seen her. She bowed, first to the King and then to me, saying: "Lord and Father, I come to tell you that the Inca Upanqui draws near with his princes and captains."

"Is it so, Daughter?" he answered. "Then make your farewell here and now to this White-Son-of-the-Sea, since it is my will that you depart with Upanqui who comes to escort you to Cuzco, the City of the Sun, there to be given as wife to the prince Urco, son of the Sun, who will sit on the Inca's throne."

"I make my farewell to the lord Hurachi as you command," she answered, curtseying, and in a very quiet voice, "but know, my father, that I love this White Lord as he loves me, and that therefore, although I may be given to the Prince Urco, as a gold cup is given, never shall he drink from the cup and never will I be his wife."

"You have courage, Daughter, and I like courage," said Huaracha. "For the rest, settle the matter as you will and if you can slip from the coils of this snake of an Urco unpoisoned, do so, since my bargain is fulfilled and my honour satisfied. Only hither you shall not return to the lord Hurachi, nor shall the lord Hurachi go to you at Cuzco."

"That shall be as the gods decree, my father, and meanwhile I play my part as *you* decree. Lord Hurachi, fare you well till in life or death we meet again."

Then she bowed to me, and went, and presently without more words we followed after her.

****

In front of the palace there was a great square of open ground surrounded by houses, except towards the east, and on this square was marshalled an army of men all splendidly arrayed and carrying copper-headed spears. In front of these was pitched a great pavilion made of cloths of various colours. Here King Huaracha, simply dressed in a robe of white cotton but wearing a little crown of gold and carrying a large spear, took his seat upon a throne, while to his right, on a smaller throne, sat Quilla, and on his left stood yet another throne ornamented with gold, that was empty. Between the throne of Huaracha and that which was empty stood a chair covered with silver on which I was bidden to take my seat, so placed that all could see me, while behind and around were lords and generals.

Scarcely were we arranged when from the dip beyond the open space appeared heralds who carried spears and were fantastically dressed. These shouted that the Inca Upanqui, the Child of the Sun, the god who ruled the earth, drew near.

"Let him approach!" said Huaracha briefly, and they departed.

Awhile later there arose a sound of barbarous music and of chanting and from the dip below emerged a glittering litter borne upon the shoulders of richly clothed men all of whom, I was told afterwards, were princes by blood, and surrounded by beautiful women who carried jewelled fans, and by councillors. It was the litter of the Inca Upanqui, and after it marched a guard of picked warriors, perhaps there were a hundred of them, not more.

The litter was set down in front of the throne; gilded curtains were drawn and out of it came a man whose attire dazzled the eyes. It seemed to consist of gold and precious stones sewn on to a mantle of crimson wool. He wore a head-dress also of as many colours as Joseph's coat, surmounted by two feathers, which he alone might bear, from which head-dress a scarlet fringe that was made of tasselled wool hung down upon his forehead. This was the Inca's crown, even to touch which was death, and its name was *Lautu*. He was a very old man for his white locks and beard hung down upon his splendid garments and he supported himself upon his royal staff that was headed by a great emerald. His fine-cut face also, though still kingly, was weak with age and his eyes were blear. At the sight of him all rose and Huaracha descended from his throne, saying in a loud voice:

"Welcome to the land of the Chancas, O Upanqui, Inca of the Quichuas."

The old monarch eyed him for a moment, then answered in a thin voice: "Greeting to Huaracha, *Curaca* of the Chancas."

Huaracha bowed and said:

"I thank you, but here among my own people my title is not *Curaca*, but King, O Inca."

Upanqui drew himself up to his full height and replied:

"The Incas know no kings throughout the land of Tavantinsuyu save themselves, O Huaracha."

"Be it so, O Inca; yet the Chancas, who are unconquered, know a king, and I am he. I pray you be seated, O Inca."

Upanqui stood still for a moment frowning, and, as I thought, was about to make some short answer, when suddenly his glance fell upon me and changed the current of his mind.

"Is that the White-god-from-the-Sea?" he asked, with an almost childish curiosity. "I heard that he was here, and to tell the truth that is why I came, just to look at him, not to bandy words with you, O Huaracha, who they say can only be talked to with a spear point. What a red beard he has and how his coat shines. Let him come and worship me."

"He will come, but I do not think that he will worship. They say he is a god himself, O Inca."

"Do they? Well, now I remember there are strange prophecies about a white god who should rise out of the sea, as did the forefather of the Incas. They say, too, that this god shall do much mischief to the land when he comes. So perhaps he had better not draw too near to me, for I like not the look of that great big sword of his. By the Sun, my father, he is tall and big and strong" (I had risen from my chair) "and his beard is like a fire; it will set the hearts of all the women burning, though perhaps if he is a god he does not care for women. I must consult my magicians about it, and the head priest of the Temple of the Sun. Tell the White God to make ready to return with me to Cuzco."

"The lord Hurachi is my guest, O Inca, and here he bides with me," said Huaracha.

"Nonsense, nonsense! When the Inca invites any one to his court, he must come. But enough of him for the present. I came here to talk of other matters. What were they? Let me sit down and think."

So he was conducted to his throne upon which he sat trying to collect his mind, which I saw was weak with age. The end of it was that he called to his aid a stern-faced, shifty-eyed, middle-aged minister, whom after I came to know as the High-priest Larico, the private Councillor of himself and of his son, Urco, and one of the most powerful men in the kingdom. This noble, I noted, was one who had the rank of an Earman, that is, he wore in his ear, which like that of Kari was stretched out to receive it, a golden disc of the size of an apple, whereon was embossed the image of the sun.

At a sign and a word from his dotard master this Larico began to speak for him as though he were the Inca himself, saying:

"Hearken, O Huaracha. I have undertaken this toilsome journey, the last I shall make as Inca, for be it known to you that I purpose to divest myself of the royal Fringe in favour of the prince, Urco, begotten to me in the body and of the Sun in spirit, and to retire to end my days in peace at my palace of Yucay, waiting there patiently until it pleases my father, the Sun, to take me to his bosom."

Here Larico paused to allow this great news to sink into the minds of his hearers, and I thought to myself that when I died I would choose to be gathered to any bosom rather than to that of the Sun, which put me in mind of hell. Then he went on:

"Rumours have reached me, the Inca, that you, Huaracha, Chief of the Chancas, are making ready to wage war upon my empire. It was to test these rumours, although I did not believe them, that awhile ago I sent an embassy to ask your only child, the lady Quilla, in marriage to the prince Urco, promising, since he has no sister whom he may wed and since on the mother's side she, your daughter, has the holy Inca blood in her veins, that she should become his *Coya*, or Queen, and the mother of him who shall succeed to the throne."

"The embassy came, and received my answer, O Inca," said Huaracha.

"Yes, and the answer was that the lady Quilla should be given in marriage to the Prince Urco, but as she was absent on a visit, this could not happen until she returned. But since then, O Huaracha, more rumours have reached me that you still prepare for war and seek to make alliances among my subjects, tempting them to rebel against me. Therefore I am here myself to lead away the lady Quilla and to deliver her to the Prince Urco."

"Why did not the Prince Urco come in person, O Inca?"

"For this reason, Huaracha, from whom I desire to hide nothing. If the Prince had come, you might have set a trap for him and killed him, who is the hope of the Empire."

"So I might for you, his father, O Inca."

"Aye, I know it, but what would that avail you while the Prince sits safe at Cuzco ready to assume the Fringe? Also I am old and care not when or how I die, whose work is done. Moreover, few would desire to anger the gods by the murder of an aged guest, and therefore I visit you sitting here in the midst of your armies with but a handful of followers, trusting to your honour and to my father the Sun to protect me. Now answer me—will you give the hand of your daughter to my son and thereby make alliance with me, or will you wage war upon my empire and be destroyed, you and your people together?"

Here Upanqui, who hitherto had been listening in silence to the words of Larico, spoken on his behalf, broke in, saying:

"Yes, yes, that is right, only make him understand that the Inca will be his over-lord, since the Inca can have no rivals in all the land."

"My answer is," said Huaracha, "that I will give my daughter in marriage as I have promised, but that the Chancas are a free people and accept no over-lord."

"Foolishness, foolishness!" said Upanqui. "As well might the tree say that it would not bend before the wind. However, you can settle that matter afterwards with Urco, and indeed with your daughter, who will be his queen and is your heiress, for I understand you have no other lawful child. Why talk of war and other troubles when thus your kingdom falls to us by marriage? Now let me see this lady Quilla who is to become my daughter."

Huaracha, who had listened to all this babble with a stern set face, turned to Quilla and made a sign. She descended from her chair and advancing, stood before the Inca, a vision of splendour and of beauty, and bowed to him. He stared at her awhile, as did all his company, then said:

"So you are the lady Quilla. A fair woman, a very fair woman, and a proud, one who ought to be able to lead Urco aright if any one can. Well named, too, after the moon, for the moonlight seems to shine in your eyes, Lady Quilla. Indeed and indeed were I but a score of years younger I should tell Urco to seek another queen and keep you for myself."

Then Quilla spoke for the first time, saying:

"Be it as you will, O Inca. I am promised in marriage to the Child of the Sun and which child is nothing to me."

"Well said, Lady Quilla, and why should I wonder? Though I grow old they tell me that I am still handsome, a great deal better looking than Urco, in fact, who is a rough man and of a coarser type. You ask my wives when you come to Cuzco; one of them told me the other day that there was no one so handsome in the whole city, and earned a beautiful present for her pretty speech. What is it you say, Larico? Why are you always interfering with me? Well, perhaps you are right, and, Lady Quilla, if you are ready, it is time to start. No, no, I thank you, Curaca, but I will not stop for any feasting who desire to be back at my camp before dark, since who knows what may happen to one in the dark in a strange country?"

Then at last Huaracha grew angry.

"Be it as you will, O Inca," he said, "but know that you offer me a threefold insult. First you refuse the feast that has been made ready for you whereat you were to meet all the notables of my kingdom. Secondly, you give me, who am a king, the title of a petty chief who owns your rule. Thirdly, you throw doubts upon my honour, hinting that I may cause you to be murdered in the dark. Now I am minded to say to you, 'Begone from my poor country, Lord Inca, in safety, but leave my daughter behind you.'"

Now at these words, I, Hubert, saw the fires of hope burn up in the large eyes of Quilla, as they did in my own heart, for might they not mean that she would escape from Urco after all? But, alas, they were extinguished like a brand that is dipped in water.

"*Tush, tush!*" said the old dotard, "what a fire-eater are you, friend Huaracha. Know that I never care to eat, except at night; also that the chill of the air after my father the Sun has set makes my bones ache, and as for titles—take any one you like, except that of Inca."

"Mayhap that is the one I shall take before all is done," broke in the furious Huaracha, who would not be quieted by the councillors whispering in his ears.

It was at this moment that the minister and high-priest, Larico, who had been noting all that passed with an impassive face, said coldly:

"Be not wroth, O King Huaracha, and lay not too much weight upon the idle words of the glorious Inca, since even the gods will doze at times when they are weighed down by the cares of empire. No affront was meant to you and least of all does the Inca or any one of us, dream that you would tarnish your honour by offering violence to your guests by day or by night. Yet know this, that if, after all that has been sworn, you withhold your daughter, the lady Quilla, from the house of Urco who is her lord to be, it will breed instant war, since as soon as word of it comes to Cuzco, which will be within twenty hours, for messengers wait all along the road, the great armies of the Inca that are gathered there will begin to move. Judge, then, if you have the strength to withstand them, and choose whether you will live on in glory and honour, or bring yourself to death and your people to slavery. Now, King Huaracha, speaking on behalf of Urco, who within some few moons will be Inca, I ask you—will you suffer the lady Quilla to journey with us to Cuzco and thereby proclaim peace between our peoples or will you keep her here against your oath and hers, and thereby declare war?"

Huaracha sat silent, lost in thought, and the old Inca Upanqui began to babble again, saying:

"Very well put, I could not have said it better myself; indeed, I did say it, for this coxcomb of a Larico, who thinks himself so clever just because I made him high-priest of the Sun under me and he is of my blood, is after all nothing but the tongue in my mouth. You don't really want to die, Huaracha, do you, after seeing most of your people killed and your country wasted? For you know that is what must happen. If you do not send your daughter as you promised, within a few hours a hundred thousand men will be marching on you and another hundred thousand gathering behind them. Anyhow, please make up your mind one way or another, as I wish to leave this place."

Huaracha thought on awhile. Then he descended from his throne and beckoned to Quilla. She came and he led her towards the back part of the pavilion behind and a little to the left of the chair on which I sat where none could hear their talk save me, of whom he seemed to take no note, perhaps because he had forgotten me, or perhaps because he desired that I should know all.

"Daughter," he said in a low voice, "what word? Before you answer remember that if I refuse to send you, now for the first time I break my oath."

"Of such oaths I think little," answered Quilla. "Yet of another thing I think much. Tell me, my father, if the Inca declares war and attacks us, can we withstand his armies?"

"No, Daughter, not until the Yuncas join us for we lack sufficient men. Moreover, we are not ready, nor shall be for another two moons, or more."

"Then it stands thus, Father. If I do not go the war will begin, and if I do go it seems that it will be staved off until you are ready, or perhaps for always, because I shall be the peace-offering and it will be thought that I, your heiress, take your kingdom as my marriage portion to be joined to that of the Incas at your death. Is it thus?"

"It is, Quilla. Only then you will work to bring it about that the Land of the Incas shall be joined to the Land of the Chancas, and not that of the Chancas to that of the Incas, so that in a day to come as

Queen of the Chancas you shall reign over both of them and your children after you."

Now I, Hubert, watching Quilla out of the corners of my eyes, saw her turn pale and tremble.

"Speak not to me of children," she said, "for I think that there will be none, and talk not of future glories, since for these I care nothing. It is for our people that I care. You swear to me that if I do not go your armies will be defeated and that those who escape the spear will be enslaved?"

"Aye, I swear it by the Moon your mother, also that I will die with my soldiers."

"Yet if I go I leave behind me that which I love," here she glanced towards me, "and give myself to shame, which is worse than death. Is that your desire, my father?"

"That is not my desire. Remember, Daughter, that you were party to this plan, aye, that it sprang from your far-seeing mind. Still, now that your heart has changed, I would not hold you to your bargain, who desire most of all things to see you happy at my side. Choose, therefore, and I obey. On your head be it."

"What shall I say, O Lord, whom I saved from the sea?" asked Quilla in a piercing whisper, but without turning her head towards me.

Now an agony took hold of me for I knew that what I bade her, that she would say, and that perchance upon my answer hung the fate of all this great Chanca people. If she went they would be saved, if she remained perchance she would be my wife if only for a while. For the Chancas I cared nothing and for the Quichuas I cared nothing, but Quilla was all that remained to me in the world and if she went, it was to another man. I would bid her bide. And yet—and yet if her case were mine and the fate of England hung upon my breath, what then?

"Be swift," she whispered again.

Then I spoke, or something spoke through me, saying:

"Do what honour bids you, O Daughter of the Moon, for what is love without honour? Perchance both shall still be yours at last."

"I thank you, Lord, whose heart speaks as my heart," she whispered for the third time, then lifting her head and looking Huaracha in the eyes, said:

"Father, I go, but that I will wed this Urco I do not promise."

Chapter 7

The Return of Kari

So Quilla, seated in a golden litter and accompanied by maidens as became her rank, soon was borne away in the train of the Inca Upanqui, leaving me desolate. Before she went, under pretence of bidding me farewell, none denying her, she gained private speech with me for a while.

"Lord and Lover," she said, "I go to what fate I know not, leaving you to what fate I know not, and as your lips have said, it is right that I should go. Now I have something to ask of you—that you will not follow me as it is in your heart to do. But last night I prayed of you to dog my steps and wherever I might go to keep close to me, that the knowledge of your presence might be my comfort. Now my mind is different. If I must be married to this Urco, I would not have you see me in my shame. And if I escape marriage you cannot help me, since I may only do so by death or by taking refuge where you cannot come. Also I have another reason."

"What reason, Quilla?" I asked.

"This: I ask that you will stop with my father and give him your help in the war that must come. I would see this Urco crushed, but without that help I am sure that the Chancas and the Yuncas are too weak to overthrow the Inca might. Remember that if I escape marriage thus only can you hope to win me, namely, by the defeat and death of Urco. Say, then, that you will stay here and help to lead the Chanca armies, and say it swiftly, since that dotard, Upanqui, frets to be gone. Hark! his messengers call and search; my women can hold them back no more."

"I will stay," I answered hoarsely.

"I thank you, and now farewell, till in life or death we meet again. Thoughts come to my mind which I have no time to utter."

"To mine also, Quilla, and here is one of them. You know the man who was with me on the island. Well, he is more than he seems."

159

"So I guessed, but where is he now?"

"In hiding, Quilla. If you should chance to find him, bear in mind that he is an enemy of Urco and one not friendless; also that he loves me after his fashion. Trust him, I pray you. Urco is not the only one of the Inca blood, Quilla."

She glanced at me quickly and nodded her head. Then without more words, for officers were pressing towards us, she drew a ring off her finger, a thick and ancient golden ring on which were cut what looked like flowers, or images of the sun, and gave it to me.

"Wear this for my sake. It is very old and has a story of true love that I have no time to tell," she said.

I took it and in exchange passed to her that ancient ring which my mother had given to me, the ring that had come down to her with the sword Wave-Flame, saying:

"This, too, is old and has a story; wear it in memory of me."

Then we parted and presently she was gone.

I stood watching her litter till it vanished in the evening haze. Then I turned to go to find myself face to face with Huaracha.

"Lord-from-the-Sea," he said, "you have played a man's—or a god's—part to-day. Had you bidden my daughter bide here, she would have done so for love of you and the Chanca people must have been destroyed, for as that old Inca or his spokesman told us, the breaking of my oath would have been taken as a declaration of instant war. Now we have breathing time, and in the end things may go otherwise."

"Yes," I answered, "but what of Quilla and what of me?"

"I know not your creed or what with you is honour, White Lord, but among us whom perhaps you think of small account, it is thought and held that there are times when a man or a woman, especially if they be highly placed, must do sacrifice for the good of the many who cling to them for guidance and for safety. This you and my daughter have done and therefore I honour both of you."

"To what end is the sacrifice made?" I asked bitterly. "That one people may struggle for dominion over another people, no more."

"You are mistaken, Lord. Not for victory or to increase my dominions do I desire to war upon the Incas, but because unless I strike I shall presently be struck, though for a little while this marriage might hold back the blow. Alone in the midst of the vast territories over which the Incas rule, the Chancas stem their tide of conquest and remain free amongst many nations of slaved. Therefore for ages these Incas, like those who ruled before them at Cuzco, have sworn to destroy us, and Urco has sworn it above all."

"Urco might die or be deposed, Huaracha."

"If so another would put on the Fringe and be vowed to the ancient policy that does not change from generation to generation. Therefore I must fight or perish with my people. Hearken, Lord-from-the-Sea! Stay here with me and become as my brother and a general of my armies, for where will they not follow when you lead, who are held to be a god? Then if we conquer, in reward, from a brother you shall become a son, and to you after me I swear shall pass the Chanca crown. Moreover, to you, if she can be saved, I will give in marriage her whom you love. Think before you refuse. I know not whence you come, but this I know: that you can return thither no more, unless, indeed, you are a spirit. Here your lot is cast till death. Therefore make it glorious. Perchance you might fly to the Inca and there become a marvel and a show, furnished with gold and palaces and lands, but always you would be a servant, while I offer to you a crown and the rule of a people great and free."

"I care nothing for crowns," I answered, sighing. "Still, such was Quilla's prayer, perchance the last that ever she will make to me. Therefore I accept and will serve you and your cause, that seems noble, faithfully to the end, O Huaracha."

Then I stretched out my hand to him and so our compact was sealed.

****

On the very next day my work began. Huaracha made me known to his captains, commanding them to obey me in all things, which, looking on me as half divine, they did readily enough.

Now, of soldiering I knew little who was a seaman bred, yet as I had learned, a man of the English race in however strange a country he finds himself can make a path there to his ends.

Moreover, in London I had heard much talk of armies and their ordering and often watched troops at their exercise; also I know how to handle bow and sword, and was accustomed to the management of men. So putting all these memories together, I set myself to the task of turning a mob of half-savage fellows with arms into an ordered host. I created regiments and officered them with the best captains that I could find, collecting in each regiment so far as possible the people of a certain town or district. These companies I drilled and exercised, teaching them to use such weapons as they had to the best purpose.

Also I caused them to shape stronger bows on the model of my own with which I had shot the three Frenchmen far away at Hastings that, as it was said, once had been the battle-bow of Thorgrimmer the Norseman my ancestor, as the sword Wave-Flame was his battle-sword. When these Chancas saw how far and with what a good aim I could shoot with this bow, they strove day and night to learn to equal me, though it is true they never did. Also I bettered their body-armour of quilting by settings sheets of leather (since in that country there is no iron) taken from the hides of wild animals and of their long-haired native sheep, between the layers of cotton. Other things I did also, too many and long to record.

The end of it was that within three months Huaracha had an army of some fifty thousand men who, if not well trained, still kept discipline, and could move in regiments; who knew also how to shoot with their bows and to use their copper-headed spears and axes of that metal, or of hard stone, to the best purpose.

Then at length came the Yuncas to join us, thirty or forty thousand of them, wild fellows and brave enough, but undisciplined. With these I could do little since time was lacking, save send some of the officers whom I had trained to teach their chiefs and captains what they were able.

Thus I was employed from dawn till dark and often after it, in talk with Huaracha and his generals, or in drawing plans with ink that I found a means to make, upon parchment of sheepskin and noting down numbers and other things, a sight at which these people who knew nothing of writing marvelled very much. Great were my labours, yet in them I found more happiness than I had known since that fatal day when I, the rich London merchant, Hubert of Hastings, had stood before the altar of St. Margaret's church with Blanche Aleys. Indeed, every cranny of my time and mind being thus filled with things finished or attempted, I forgot my great loneliness as an alien in a strange land, and once more became as I had been when I trafficked in the Cheap.

But toil as I would, I could not forget Quilla. During the day I might mask her memory in its urgent business, but when I lay down to rest she seemed to come to me as a ghost might do and to stand by my bed, looking at me with sad and longing eyes. So real was her presence that sometimes I began to believe that she must have died to the world and was in truth a ghost, or else that she had found the power to throw her soul afar, as it is said certain of these Indian folk, if so they should be called, can do. At least there she seemed to be while I remained awake and afterwards when I slept, and I know not whether her strange company joyed or pained me more. For alas! she could not talk to me, or tell me how it fared with her, and, to speak truth, now that she was the wife of another man, as I supposed, I desired to forget her if I could.

For of Quilla no word reached us. We heard that she had come safely to Cuzco and after that nothing more. Of her marriage there was no tidings; indeed she seemed to have vanished away. Certain of Huaracha's spies reported to him, however, that the great army which Urco had gathered to attack him had been partly disbanded, which seemed to show that the Inca no longer prepared for immediate war. Only then what had happened to Quilla, whose person was the price of peace? Perhaps she was hidden away during the preparations for her nuptials; at least I could think of nothing else, unless indeed she had chosen to kill herself or died naturally.

Soon, however, all news ceased, for Huaracha shut his frontiers, hoping that thus Urco might not learn that he was gathering armies.

At length, when our forces were almost ready to march, Kari came, Kari whom I thought lost.

One night when I was seated at my work by lamplight, writing down numbers upon a parchment, a shadow fell across it, and looking up I saw Kari standing before me, travel-worn and weary, but Kari without doubt, unless I dreamed.

"Have you food, Lord?" he asked while I stared at him. "I need it and would eat before I speak."

I found meat and native beer and brought them to him, for it was late and my servants were asleep, waiting till he had filled himself, for by this time I had learned something of the patience of these people. At length he spoke, saying:

"Huaracha's watch is good, and to pass it I must journey far into the mountains and sleep three nights without food amid their snows."

"Whence come you?" I asked.

"From Cuzco, Lord."

"Then what of the lady Quilla? Does she still live? Is she wed to Urco?"

"She lives, or lived fourteen days ago, and she is not wed. But where she is no man may ever come. You have looked your last upon the lady Quilla, Lord."

"If she lives and is unwed, why?" I asked, trembling.

"Because she is numbered among the Virgins of the Sun our Father, and therefore inviolate to man. Were I the Inca, though I love you and know all, should you attempt to take her, yes, even you, I would kill you if I could, and with my own sword. In our land, Lord, there is one crime which has no forgiveness, and that is to lay hands upon a Virgin of the Sun. We believe, Lord, that if this is done, great curses will fall upon our country, while as for the man who works the crime, before he passes to eternal vengeance he and all his house and the town whence he came must perish utterly, and that false virgin who has betrayed our father, the Sun, must die slowly and by fire."

"Has this ever chanced?" I asked.

"History does not tell it, Lord, since none have been so wicked, but such is the law."

I thought to myself that it was a very evil law, and cruel; also that I would break it if I found opportunity, but made no answer, knowing when to be silent and that I might as well strive to move a mountain from its base as to turn Kari from the blindness of his folly bred of false faith. After all, could I blame him, seeing that we held the same of the sacredness of nuns and, it was said, killed them if they broke their vows?

"What news, Kari?" I asked.

"Much, Lord. Hearken. Disguised as a peasant who had come into this country to barter wool from a village near to Cuzco, I joined myself to the train of the Inca Upanqui, among whose lords I found a friend who had loved me in past years and kept my secret as he was bound to do, having passed into the brotherhood of knights with me while we were lads. Through him, in place of a man who was sick, I became one of the bearers of the lady Quilla's litter and thus was always about her and at times had speech with her in secret, for she knew me again notwithstanding my disguise and uniform. So I became one of those who waited on her when she ate and noted all that passed.

"After the first day the Inca Upanqui, he who is my father and whose lawful heir I am, although he discarded me for Urco and believes me dead, made it a habit to take his food in the same tent or rest-house chamber as the lady Quilla. Lord, being very clever, she set herself to charm him, so that soon he began to dote upon her, as old, worn-out men sometimes do upon young and beautiful women. She, too, pretended to grow fond of him and at last told him in so many words that she grieved it was not he that she was to marry whose wisdom she hung upon, in place of a prince who, she heard, was not wise. This, she said, because she knew well that the Inca would never marry any more and indeed had lived alone for years. Still, being flattered, he told her it was hard that she should be forced to wed one to whom she had no mind, whereon she prayed him, even with tears, to save her from such a fate. At last he vowed that he would do so by setting her among the Virgins of the Sun on whom no man may look. She thanked him and said that she would consider the matter, since, for reasons that you may guess, Lord, she did not desire to become a Virgin of the Sun and to pass the rest of her days in prayer and the weaving of the Inca's garments.

"So it went on until when we were a day's march from Cuzco, Urco, my brother, came to meet his promised bride. Now, Urco is a huge man and hideous, one whom none would believe to have been born of the Inca blood. Coarse he is, and dissolute, given to drink also, though a great fighter and brave in battle, and quick-brained when he is sober. I was present when they met and I saw the lady Quilla shiver and turn pale at the sight of him, while he on his part devoured her beauty with his eyes. They spoke but few words together, yet before these were done, he told her it was his will that they should be wed at once on the day after she came to Cuzco, nor would he listen to the Inca Upanqui who said, being cunning and wishing to gain time, that due preparation must be made for so great a business.

"Thereupon Urco grew angry with his father, who both fears and loves him, and answered that, being almost Inca, this matter was one which he would settle for himself. So fierce was he that Upanqui became afraid and went away. When they were alone Urco strove to embrace Quilla, but she fled from him and hid with her maidens in a private place. After this, at the feast Urco took too much drink according to his custom and was led away to sleep by his lords. Then Quilla waited upon the Inca and said:

"'O Inca, I have seen the Prince and I claim your promise to save me from him. O Inca, abandoning all thought of marriage, I will become the bride of our Father the Sun.'

"Upanqui, who was wroth with Urco because he had crossed his will, swore by the Sun itself that he would not fail her, come what might, since Urco should learn that he was not yet Inca."

"What happened then?" I asked, staring him in the eyes.

"After this, Lord, when we were halted before making the state entry into Cuzco, for a moment the lady Quilla found opportunity for private speech with me. This is what she said:

"'Tell my father, King Huaracha, that I have fulfilled his oath, but that I cannot marry Urco. Therefore I seek refuge in the arms of the Sun, as the oracle Rimac foretold that I should do, having to choose between this fate and that of death. Tell my Lord-from-the-Sea what has befallen me and bid him farewell to me. Still say that he must keep a good heart, since I do not believe that all is ended between us.'

"Then we were parted and I saw her no more."

"And did you hear no more, Kari?"

"I heard much, Lord. I heard that when Urco learned that the lady Quilla had vanished away into the House of Virgins, whither he might not come, and that he was robbed of the bride whom he desired, he grew mad with rage. Indeed, of this I saw something myself. Two days later, with thousands of others I was in the great square in front of the Temple of the Sun, where the Inca Upanqui sat in state upon a golden throne to receive the praise of his people upon his safe return after his long and hard journey, and as some reported, to lay down his lordship in favour of Urco; also to tell the people that the danger of war with the Chancas had passed away. Scarcely had the ceremony begun when Urco appeared at the head of a number of lords and princes of the Inca blood, who are of his clan, and I noticed that he was drunk and furious. He advanced to the foot of the throne, almost without obeisance, and shouted:

"'Where is the lady Quilla, daughter of Huaracha, who is promised to me in marriage, Inca? Why have you hidden her away, Inca?'

"'Because the Sun, our Father, has claimed her as his bride and has taken her to dwell in his holy house, where never again may the eyes of man behold her, Prince!' answered Upanqui.

"'You mean that robbing me, you have taken her for yourself, Inca,' shouted Urco again.

"Then Upanqui stood up and swore by the Sun that this was not so and that what he had done was done by the decree of the god and at the prayer of the lady Quilla, who having seen Urco, had declared that either she would be wed to the god or die by her own hand, which would bring the vengeance of the Sun upon the people.

"Then Urco went mad. He raved at the Inca and while all present shivered with fear, he cursed the Sun our Father, yes, even when a cloud came up in the clear sky and veiled the face of the god, heedless of the omen, he continued his curses and blasphemy. Moreover, he said that soon he would be Inca and that then, if he must tear the House of Virgins stone from stone, as Inca he would drag forth the lady Quilla and make her his wife.

"Now at these words Upanqui stood up and rent his robes.

"'Must my ears be outraged with such blasphemies?' he cried. 'Know, Son Urco, that this day I was minded to take off the Royal Fringe and to set it on your head, crowning you Inca in my place while I withdrew to pass the remainder of my days at Yucay in peace and prayer. My will is changed. This I shall not do. My life is not done and strength returns to my mind and body. Here I stay as Inca. Now I see that I am punished for my sin.'

"'What sin?' shouted Urco.

"'The sin of setting you before my eldest lawful son, Kari, whose wife you stole; Kari, whom also it is said you poisoned and who at least has vanished and is doubtless dead.'

"Now, Lord, when I, Kari, heard this my heart melted in me and I was minded to declare myself to Upanqui my father. But while I weighed the matter for a moment, knowing that if I did so, such words as these might well be my last since Urco had many of is following present, who perhaps would fall upon and kill me, suddenly my father Upanqui fell forward in a swoon. His lords and physicians bore him away. Urco followed and presently the multitude departed this way and that. Afterwards we were told that the Inca had recovered but must not be disturbed for many days."

"Did you hear more of Quilla, Kari?"

"Yes, Lord," he answered gravely. "It was commonly reported that, through some priestess in his pay, Urco had poisoned her, saying that as she had chosen the Sun as husband, to the Sun she would go."

"Poisoned her!" I muttered, well-nigh falling to the ground. "Poisoned her!"

"Aye, Lord, but be comforted for this was added—that she who gave the poison was taken in the act by her who is named the Mother of the Virgins, and handed over to the women who cast her into the den of serpents, where she perished, screaming that it was Urco who had forced her to the deed."

"That does not comfort me, man. What of Quilla? Did she die?"

"Lord, it is said not. It is said that the Mother of the Virgins dashed away the cup as it touched her lips. But this is said also, that some of the poison flew into her eyes and blinded her."

I groaned, for the thought of Quilla blinded was horrible.

"Again take comfort, Lord, since perchance she may recover from this blindness. Also I was told, that although she can see nothing, her beauty is not marred; that the venom indeed has made her eyes seem larger and more lovely even than they were before."

I made no answer, who feared that Kari was deceiving me or perhaps was himself deceived and that Quilla was dead. Presently he continued his story in the same quiet, even voice, saying:

"Lord, after this I sought out certain of my friends who had loved me in my youth and my mother also while she lived, revealing myself to them. We made plans together, but before aught could be done in earnest, it was needful that I should see my father Upanqui. While I was waiting till he had recovered from the stroke that fell upon him, some spy betrayed me to Urco, who searched for me to kill me and well-nigh found me. The end of it was that I was forced to fly, though before I did so many swore themselves to my cause who would escape from the tyranny of Urco. Moreover, it was agreed that if I returned with soldiers at my back, they and their followers would come out to join me to the number of thousands, and help me to take my own again so that I may be Inca after Upanqui my father. Therefore I have come back here to talk with you and Huaracha.

"Such is my tale."

CHAPTER 8

The Field of Blood

When on the morrow Huaracha, King of the Chancas, heard all this story and that Urco had given poison to his daughter Quilla, who, if she still lived at all, did so, it was said, as a blind woman, a kind of madness took hold of him.

"Now let war come; I will not rest or stay," he cried, "till I see this hound, Urco, dead, and hang up his skin stuffed with straw as an offering to his own god, the Sun."

"Yet it was you, King Huaracha, who sent the lady Quilla to this Urco for your own purposes," said Kari in his quiet fashion.

"Who and what are you that reprove me?" asked Huaracha turning on him. "I only know you as the servant or slave of the White-Lord-from-the-Sea, though it is true I have heard stories concerning you," he added.

"I am Kari, the first-born lawful son of Upanqui and by right heir to the Inca throne, no less, O Huaracha. Urco my brother robbed me of my wife, as through the folly of my father, upon whose heart Urco's mother worked, he had already robbed me of my inheritance. Then, to make sure, he strove to poison me as he has poisoned your daughter, with a poison that would make me mad and incapable of rule, yet leave me living—because he feared lest the curse of the Sun should fall upon him if he murdered me. I recovered from that bane and wandered to a far land. Now I have returned to take my own, if I am able. All that I say I can prove to you."

For a while Huaracha stared at him astonished, then said:

"And if you prove it, what do you ask of me, O Kari?"

"The help of your armies to enable me to overthrow Urco, who is very strong, being the Commander of the Quichua hosts."

"And if your tale be true and Urco is overthrown, what do you promise me in return?"

"The independence of the Chanca people, who otherwise must soon be destroyed, and certain other added territories which you covet, while I am Inca."

"And with this my daughter, if she still lives?" asked Huaracha looking at him.

"Nay," replied Kari firmly. "As to the lady Quilla I promise nothing. She has vowed herself to my Father the Sun, and what I have already told the Lord Hurachi here, who loves her I tell you. Henceforward no man may look upon her, who is the Bride of the Sun, for if I suffered this, certainly the curse of the Sun would fall upon me and upon my people. He who lays a hand upon her I will strive to slay"—here he looked at me with meaning—"because I must or be accurst. Take all else, but let the lady Quilla be. What the Sun has, he holds forever."

"Perhaps the Moon, her mother, may have something to say in that matter," said Huaracha gloomily. "Still, let it lie for the while."

Then they fell to discussing the terms of their alliance and, when it came to battle, what help Kari could bring from among those who clung to him in Cuzco.

After this Huaracha took me to another chamber, where we debated the business.

"This Kari, if he be Kari himself, is a bigot," he said, "and if he has his way, neither you nor I will ever set eyes on Quilla again, because to him it is sacrilege. So, what say you?"

I answered that it would be best to make an alliance with Kari, whom I knew to be honest and no Pretender, since without his help I did not think that it would be possible to defeat the armies of the People of the Incas. For the rest, we must trust to chance, making no promises as to Quilla.

"If we did they would avail little," said Huaracha, "seeing that without doubt she is dead and only vengeance remains to us. There is more poison in Cuzco, White Lord!"

****

Eight days later we were marching on Cuzco, a great host of us, numbering at least forty thousand Chancas and twenty-five thousand of the rebellious Yuncas, who had joined our standard.

On we marched by the great road over mountains and across plains, driving with us numberless herds of the native sheep for food, but meeting no man, since so soon as we were out of the territory of the Chancas all fled at our approach. At length one night we camped upon a hill named Carmenca and saw beneath us at a distance the mighty city of Cuzco standing in a valley through which a river ran. There it was with its huge fortresses built of great blocks of stone, its temples, its palaces, its open squares, and its countless streets bordered by low houses. Moreover, beyond and around it we saw other things, namely, the camps of a vast army dotted with thousands of white tents.

"Urco is ready for us," said Kari to me grimly as he pointed to these tents.

We camped upon the hill Carmenca and that night there came to us an embassy which spoke in the names of Upanqui and Urco, as though they reigned jointly. This embassy of great lords who all wore discs of gold in their ears asked us what was our purpose. Huaracha answered—to avenge the murder of the lady Quilla, his daughter, that he heard had been poisoned by Urco.

"How know you that she is dead?" asked the spokesman.

"If she is not dead," replied Huaracha, "show her to us."

"That may not be," replied the spokesman, "since if she lives, it is in the House of the Virgins of the Sun, whence none come out and where none go in. Hearken, O Huaracha. Go back whence you came, or the countless army of the Incas will fall upon you and destroy you, you and your handful together."

"That is yet to be seen," answered Huaracha, and without more words the embassy withdrew.

That night also men crept into our camp secretly, who were of the party of Kari. Of Quilla they seemed to know nothing, for none spoke of those over whom the veil of the Sun had fallen. They told us, however, that the old Inca, Upanqui, was still in Cuzco and had recovered somewhat from his sickness. Also they said that now the feud between him and Urco was bitter, but that Urco had the upper hand and was still in command of the armies. These armies, they declared, were immense and would fight us on the morrow, adding, however, that certain regiments of them who were of the party of Kari would desert to us in the battle. Lastly, they said that there was great fear in Cuzco, since none knew how that battle would end, which was understood by all to be one for the dominion of Tavantinsuyu.

They had nothing more to say except that they prayed the Sun for our success to save them from the tyranny of Urco. This prince, it appeared, suspected their conspiracy, for now the rumour that Kari lived was everywhere, and having obtained the names of some who were connected with it through his spies, he pursued them with murder and sudden death. They were poisoned at their food; they were stabbed as they walked through the streets at night; their wives, if young and fair, vanished away, as they believed into the houses of those who desired them; even their children were kidnapped, doubtless to become the servants of whom they knew not. They had complained of these things to the old Inca Upanqui, but without avail, since in such matters he was powerless before Urco who had command of the armies. Therefore they would even welcome the triumph of Huaracha, which meant that Kari would become Inca if with lessened territory.

Before they parted to play their parts, Kari brought them before me, whom in their foolishness they worshipped, believing me to be in truth a god. Then he told them to have no fear, since I would command the armies of Huaracha in the battle.

Having surveyed the ground while the light lasted, for the most of that night, together with Huaracha and Kari, I toiled, making plans for the great fight that was to come. All being ready, I lay down to sleep awhile, wondering whether it were the last time I should do so upon the earth and, to tell the truth, not caring overmuch who, believing that Quilla was dead, had it not been for my sins which weighed upon me with none to whom I might confess them, should have been glad to leave the world and its troubles for whatever might lie beyond, even if it were but sleep.

There comes a time to most men when above everything they desire rest, and now that hour was with me, the exiled and the desolate. Here in this strange country and among these alien people I had found one soul which was akin to mine, that of a beautiful woman who loved me and whom I had come to love and desire. But what was the end of it? Owing to the necessities of statecraft and her own nobleness, she had been separated from me and although, as it would seem, she had as yet escaped defilement, was spirited away into the temple of some barbarous worship where I was almost sure death had found her.

At the best she was blinded, and where she lay in her darkness no man might come because of the superstitions of these folk. Even if Kari became Inca, it would not help me or her, should she still live, since he was the fiercest bigot of them all and swore that he would kill me, his friend, rather than that I should touch her, the vowed to his false gods.

Or perhaps, through the priests, to save himself such sorrow, he would kill her. At the least, dead or not, she was lost to me, while I—utterly alone—must fight for a cause in which I had but one concern, to bring some savage prince to his end because of his crime against

Quilla. And, if things went well and this chanced, what of the Future? Of what use to me were rewards that I did not want, and the worship of the vulgar which I hated? Rather would I have lived out my life as the humblest fisherman on Hastings beach, than be made a king over these glittering barbarians with their gold and gems which could buy nothing that I needed, not even a Book of Hours to feed my soul, or the sound of the English tongue to comfort my empty heart.

At length I fell asleep, and as it seemed but a few minutes later, though really six hours had gone by, was awakened by Kari, who told me that the dawn was not far off and came to help me to buckle on my armour. Then I went forth and together with Huaracha arranged our army for battle. Our plan was to advance from our rising ground across a great plain beneath us which was called Xaqui, but afterwards became known by the name of Yahuar-pampa, or Field of Blood.

This plain lay between us and the city of Cuzco, and my thought was that we would march or fight our way across it and rush into the city which was unwalled, and there amidst its streets and houses await the attack of the Inca hosts that were encamped upon its farther side, for thus protected by their walls we hoped that we should be more equal to them. Yet things happened otherwise, since with the first light, without which we did not dare to move over unknown ground, we perceived that during the darkness the Inca armies had moved round and through the town and were gathered by the ten thousand in dense battalions upon the farther side of the plain.

Now we took council together and in the end decided not to attack as we had proposed, but to await their onslaught on the rocky ridge up which they must climb. So we commanded that our army, which was marshalled in three divisions abreast and two wings with the Yuncas as a reserve behind, should eat and make ready. In the centre of our main division, which numbered some fifteen thousand of the Chanca troops, and a little in front of it, was a low long hill upon the highest point of which I took my place, standing upon a rock with a group of captains and messengers behind me and a guard of about a thousand picked men massed upon the slopes and around the hill. From this high point I could see everything, and in my glittering armour was visible to all, friends and foes together.

After a pause, during which the priests of the Chancas and of the Yuncas behind us sacrificed sheep to the moon and the many other gods they worshipped, and those of the Quichuas, as I could see from my rock, made prayers and offerings to the rising sun, with a mighty shouting the Inca hosts began to advance across the plain towards us.

Reckoning them with my eye I saw that they outnumbered us by two or three to one; indeed their hordes seemed to be countless, and always more of them came on behind from the dim recesses of the city. Divided into three great armies they crept across the plain, a wild and gorgeous spectacle, the sunlight shining upon the forest of their spears and on their rich barbaric uniforms.

A furlong or more away they halted and took counsel, pointing to me with their spears as though they feared me. We stood quite still, though some of our generals urged that we should charge, but this I counselled Huaracha not to do, who desired that the Quichuas should break their strength upon us. At length some word was given; the splendid "rainbow Banner" of the Incas was unfurled and, still divided into three armies with a wide stretch of plain between each of them they attacked, yelling like all the fiends of hell.

Now they had reached us and there began the most terrible battle that was told of in the history of that land. Wave after wave of them rolled up against us, but our battalions which I had not trained in vain stood like rocks and slew and slew and slew till the dead could be counted by the thousand. Again and again they strove to storm the hill on which I stood, hoping to kill me, and each time we beat them back. Picking out their generals I loosed shaft after shaft from my long bow, and seldom did I miss, nor could their cotton-quilted armour turn those bitter arrows.

"The shafts of the god! The shafts of the god!" they cried, and shrank back from before me.

There appeared a man with a yellow fillet on his head and a robe that was studded with precious stones; a huge man with great limbs and flaming eyes; a loose-mouthed, hideous man who wielded a big axe of copper and carried a bow longer than any I had seen in that land. Hooking the axe to his belt, he set an arrow on the bow and let drive at me. It sped true and struck me full upon the breast, only to shatter on the good French mail, which copper could not pierce.

Again he shot, and this time the arrow glanced from my helm. Then I drew on him and my shaft, that I had aimed at his head, cut away the fringe about his brow and carried it far away. At this sight a groan went up from the lords about him, and one cried:

"An omen, O Urco, an evil omen!"

"Aye," he shouted, "for the White Wizard who shot the arrow."

Dropping the bow, he rushed up the hill at me roaring, axe aloft, and followed by his company. He smote, and I caught the blow upon my shield, and striking back with Wave-Flame, shore through the shaft of the axe that he had lifted to guard his head as though it had been made of reed, aye, and through the quilted cotton on his shoulder strengthened with strips of gold, and to the bone beneath.

Then a man slipped past me. It was Kari, striking at Urco with Deleroy's sword. They closed and rolled down the slope locked in each other's arms. What chanced after this I do not know, for others rushed in and all grew confused, but presently Kari limped back somewhat shaken and bleeding, and I caught sight of Urco, little hurt, as it seemed, amidst his lords at the bottom of the slope.

At this moment I heard a great shouting and looking round, saw that the Quichuas had broken through our left and were slaughtering many, while the rest fled, also that our right was wavering. I sent messengers to Huaracha, bidding him call up the Yunca rear guard. They were slow in coming and I began to fear that all was lost for little by little the hordes of the men of Cuzco were surrounding us.

Then it was that Kari, or some with him, lifted a banner that had been wrapped upon a pole, a blue banner upon which was embroidered a golden sun. At the sight of it there was tumult in the Inca ranks, and presently a great body of men, five or six thousand of them that had seemed to be in reserve, ran forward shouting, *"Kari! Kari!"* and fell upon those who were pursuing our shattered left, breaking them up and dispersing them. Also at last the Yuncas came up and drove back the regiments that assailed our right, while from Urco's armies there rose a cry of "Treachery!"

Trumpets blew and the Inca host, gathering itself together and abandoning its dead and wounded, drew back sullenly on to the plain, and there halted in three bodies as before, though much lessened in number.

Huaracha appeared, saying:

"Strike, White Lord! It is our hour! The heart is out of them."

The signal was given, and roaring like a hurricane, presently the Chancas charged. Down the slope they went, I at the head of them with Huaracha on one side and Kari on the other. The swift-footed Chancas outran me who was hindered by my mail. We charged in three masses as we had stood on the ridge, following those open lanes of ground up which the foe had not come, because these were less cumbered with dead and wounded. Presently I saw why those of Cuzco had left these lanes untrod, for of a sudden some warriors, who had outstripped me, vanished. They had fallen into a pit covered over with earth laid upon canes, of which the bottom was set with sharp stakes. Others, who were running along the lanes of open ground to right and left, also fell into pits of which there were scores all carefully prepared against the day of battle. With trouble the Chancas were halted, but not before we had lost some hundreds of men. Then we advanced again across that ground over which the Inca host had retreated.

At length we reached their lines, passing through a storm of arrows, and there began such a battle as I had never heard of or even dreamed. With axes, stone-headed clubs and spears, both armies fought furiously, and though the Incas still outnumbered us by two to one, because of my training our regiments drove them back. Lord after lord rushed at me with glaring eyes, but my mail turned their copper spears and knives of flint. Oh! Wave-Flame fed full that day, and if Thorgrimmer my forefather could have seen us from his home in Valhalla, surely he must have sworn by Odin that never had he given it such a feast.

The Inca warriors grew afraid and shrank back.

"This Red-Beard from the sea is indeed a god. He cannot be slain!" I heard them cry.

Then Urco appeared, bloody and furious, shouting:

"Cowards! I will show you whether he cannot be slain."

He rushed onward to meet—not me, but Huaracha, who seeing that I was weary, had leapt in front of me. They fought, and Huaracha went down and was dragged away by some of his servants.

Now Urco and I were face to face, he wielding a huge copper-headed club with which, as my mail could not be pierced, he thought to batter out my life. I caught the blow upon my shield, but so great was the giant's strength that it brought me to my knees. Next second I was up and at him. Shouting, I smote with both hands, for my shield had fallen. The thick, turban-like headdress that Urco wore was severed, cut through as the axe had been, and Wave-Flame bit deep into the skull beneath.

Urco fell like a stunned ox and I sprang upon him to make an end. Then it was that a rope was flung about my shoulders, a noosed rope that was hauled tight. In vain I struggled. I was thrown down; I was seized by a score of hands and dragged away into the heart of Urco's host.

Waiting till a litter could be brought, they set me on my feet again, my arms still bound by the noose that these Indians call *laso*, which they know so well how to throw, the red sword Wave-Flame still hanging by its thong from my right wrist. Whilst I stood thus, like a bull in a net, they gathered round, staring at me, not with hate as it seemed to me, but in fear and with reverence. When at length the litter came they aided me to enter it quite gently.

As I did so I looked back. The battle still raged but it seemed to me with less fury than before. It was as though both sides were weary of slaughter, their leaders being fallen. The litter was borne forward, till at length the noise of shouting and tumult grew low. Twisting myself round I peered through the back curtains and saw that the Inca host and that of the Chancas were separating sullenly, neither of them broken since they carried their wounded away with them. It was plain that the battle remained drawn for there was no rout and no triumph.

I saw, too, that I was entering the great city of Cuzco, where women and children stood at the doors of the houses gazing, and some of them wringing their hands with tears upon their faces.

Passing down long streets and across a bridge, I came to a vast square round which stood mighty buildings, low, massive, and constructed of huge stones. At the door of one of these the litter halted and I was helped to descend. Men beautifully clad in broidered linen led me through a gateway and across a garden where I noted a marvellous thing, namely: that all the plants therein were fashioned of solid gold with silver flowers, or sometimes of silver with golden flowers. Also there were trees on which were perched birds of gold and silver. When I saw this I thought that I must be mad, but it was not so, for having no other use for the precious metals, of which they had so much abundance, thus did these Incas adorn their palaces.

Leaving the golden garden, I reached a courtyard surrounded by rooms, to one of which I was conducted. Passing its door, I found myself in a splendid chamber hung with tapestries fantastically wrought and having cushioned seats, and tables of rich woods incrusted with precious stones. Here servants or slaves appeared with a chamberlain who bowed deeply and welcomed me in the name of the Inca.

Then, as though I were something half divine, gently enough, they loosed the sword from my wrist, took the long bow from my back, with the few arrows that remained, also my dagger, and hid them away. They unbound me, and freeing me from my armour, as I told them how, and the garments beneath, laved me with warm, scented water, rubbed my bruised limbs, and clothed me in wonderful soft garments, also scented and fastened about my middle with a golden belt. This done, food and spiced drinks of their native wine were brought to me in golden vessels. I ate and drank and, being very weary, laid myself down upon one of the couches to sleep. For now I no longer took any thought as to what might befall me, but received all as it came, good and ill together, entrusting my body and soul to the care of God and St. Hubert. Indeed, what else could I do who was disarmed and a prisoner?

When I awoke again, very stiff and bruised, but much refreshed, night had fallen, for hanging lamps were lit about the room. By their light I saw the chamberlain of whom I have spoken standing before me. I asked him his errand. With many bows he said that if I were rested the Inca Upanqui desired my presence that he might speak with me.

I bade him lead on, and, with others who waited without, he conducted me through a maze of passages into a glorious chamber where everything seemed to be gold, for even the walls were panelled with it. Never had I dreamt of so much gold; indeed the sight of it wearied me till I could have welcomed that of humble brick or wood. At the end of this chamber that was also lit with lamps, were curtains. Presently these were drawn by two beautiful women in jewelled skirts and head-dresses, and behind them on a dais I saw a couch and on the couch the old Inca Upanqui looking feebler than when I had last beheld him in the Chanca city, and very simply clad in a white tunic. Only on his head he wore the red fringe from which I suppose he never parted day or night. He looked up and said:

"Greeting, White-Lord-from-the-Sea. So you have come to visit me after all, though you said that you would not."

"I have been brought to visit you, Inca," I answered.

"Yes, yes, they tell me they captured you in the battle, though I expect that was by your own will as you had wearied of those Chancas. For what *laso* can hold a god?"

"None," I answered boldly.

"Of course not, and that you are a kind of god there is no doubt because of the things you did in that battle. They say that the arrows and spears melted when they touched you and that you shot and cut down men by scores. Also that when the prince Urco tried to kill you, although he is the strongest man in my kingdom, you knocked him over as though he had been a little child and hacked his head open so that they do not know whether he will live or die. I think I hope he will die, for you see I have quarrelled with him."

I thought to myself that so did I, but I only asked:

"How did the battle end, Inca?"

"As it began, Lord Hurachi. A great many men have been killed on both sides, thousands and thousands of them, and neither army has the victory. They have drawn back and sit growling at each other like two angry lions which are afraid to fight again. Indeed, I do not want them to fight, and now that Urco cannot interfere, I shall put a stop to all this bloodshed if I am able. Tell me, for you were with him, why does this Huaracha, who I hear is also wounded, want to make war on me with those troublesome Chancas of his?"

"Because your son, the prince Urco, has poisoned, or tried to poison, his only child, Quilla."

"Yes, yes, I know, and it was a wicked thing to do. You see, Lord, what happened was this: That lovely Quilla, who is fairer than her mother the Moon, was to have married Urco. But, Lord, as it chanced on our journey together, although I am old—well, she became enamoured of me, and prayed me to protect her from Urco. Such things happen to women, Lord, whose hearts, when they behold the divine, are apt to carry them away from the vulgar," and he laughed in a silly fashion like the vain old fool that he was.

"Naturally. How could she help it, Inca? Who, after seeing you, would wish to turn to Urco?"

"No one, especially as Urco is a coarse and brutal fellow. Well, what was I to do? There are reasons why I do not wish to marry again at my age; indeed I am tired of the sight of women, who want time to pray and think of holy things; also if I had done what she wished, some might have thought that I had behaved badly to Urco. At the same time, a woman's heart is sacred and I could not do violence to that of one so sweet and understanding and lovely. So I put her into the House of the Virgins of the Sun where she will be quite safe."

"It seems that she was not safe, Inca."

"No, because that violent man, Urco, being disappointed and very jealous, through some low creature of his, who waited on the Virgins, tried to poison her with a drug which would have made her all swollen and hideous and covered her face with blotches, also perhaps have sent her mad. Luckily one of the matrons, whom we call *Mama-conas*, knocked the cup away before she drank, but some of the horrible poison went into her eyes and blinded her."

"So she lives, Inca."

"Certainly she lives. I have learnt that for myself, because in this country it is not wise to trust what they tell you. You know as Inca I have privileges, and although even I do not talk to them, I caused those Virgins of the Sun to be led in front of me, which in strictness even I ought not to have done. It was a dreary business, Lord Hurachi, for though those Virgins may be so holy, some of them are very old and hideous and of course Quilla as a novice came last in the line conducted by two *Mama-conas* who are cousins of my own. The odd thing is that the poison seems to have made her much more beautiful than before, for her eyes have grown bigger and are glorious, shining like stars seen when there is frost. Well, there she is safe from Urco and every other man, however wicked and impious. But what does this Huaracha want?"

179

"He wants his blinded daughter back, Inca."

"Impossible, impossible! Who ever heard of such a thing! Why, Heaven and Earth would come together and the Sun, my father, and her husband, would burn us all up. Still, perhaps, we could come to an agreement for Huaracha must have had enough fighting and very likely he will die. Now I am tired of talking about the lady Quilla and I want to ask you something."

"Speak on, Inca."

Suddenly the old dotard's manner changed: he became quick and shrewd, as doubtless he was in his prime, for this Upanqui had been a great king. At the beginning of our talk the two women of whom I have spoken and the chamberlain had withdrawn to the end of the chamber where they waited with their hands folded, like those who adore before an altar. Still he peered about him to make sure that none were within hearing, and in the end beckoned to me to ascend the dais and sit upon the couch beside him, saying:

"You see I trust you although you are a god from the sea who has been fighting against me. Now hearken. You had a servant with you, a very strange man, who is said also to have come out of the sea, though that I cannot believe since he is like one of our princes. Where is that man?"

"With the army of Huaracha, Inca."

"So I have heard. I heard also that in the battle he hoisted a banner with the sun blazoned on it, and that thereon certain regiments of mine deserted to Huaracha. Now, why did they do that?"

"I understand, O Inca, that the kings of this land have many children. Perhaps he might be one of them."

"Ah! You are clever as a god should be. Well, I am a god also and the same thought has come to me, although as a fact I have only had two legitimate sons and the others are of no account. The eldest of these was an able and beautiful prince named Kari, but we quarrelled, and to tell the truth there was a woman in the matter, or rather two women, for Kari's mother fought with Urco's mother whom I loved, because she never scolded me, which the other did. So Urco was named to be Inca after me. Yet that was not enough for him who remained jealous of his brother Kari who outpassed him in all things save strength of body. They wooed the same beautiful woman and Kari won her, whereon Urco seduced her from him, and afterwards he or someone killed her. At least she died, I forget how. Then the lords of the Inca blood began to turn towards Kari because he was royal and wise, which would have meant civil war when I had been gathered to the Sun. Therefore Urco poisoned him, or so it was rumoured; at any rate, he vanished away, and often since then I have mourned him."

"The dead come to life again sometimes, Inca."

"Yes, yes, Lord-from-the-Sea, that happens; the gods who took them away bring them back—and this servant of yours—they say he is so like to Kari that he might be the same man grown older. And—why did those regiments, all of them officered by men who used to love Kari, go over to Huaracha to-day, and why do rumours run through the land like the wind that springs up suddenly in fine weather? Tell me of this servant of yours and how you found him in the sea."

"Why should I tell you, Inca? Is it because you want to kill him who is so like to this lost Kari of yours?"

"No, no—gods can keep each other's counsel, can they not? It is because I would give—oh! half my godship to know that he is alive. Hark you, Urco wearies me so much that sometimes I wonder whether he really is my son. Who can tell? There was a certain lord of the coastlands, a hairy giant who, they said, could eat half a sheep at a sitting and break the backs of men in his hands, of whom Urco's mother used to think much. But who can tell? No one except my father, the Sun, and he guards his secrets—for the present. At least Urco wearies me with his coarse crimes and his drunkenness, though the army loves him because he is a butcher and liberal. We quarrelled the other day over the small matter of this lady Quilla, and he threatened me till I grew wrath and said that I would not hand him my crown as I had purposed to do. Yes, I grew wrath and hated him for whose sake I had sinned because his mother bewitched me. Lord-from-the-Sea," here his voice dropped to a whisper, "I am afraid of Urco. Even a god such as I am can be murdered, Lord-from-the-Sea. That is why I will not go to Yucay, for there I might die and none know it, whereas here I still am Inca and a god whom it is sacrilege to touch."

"I understand, but how can I help you, Inca, who am but a prisoner in your palace?"

"No, no, you are only a prisoner in name. At the worst Urco will be sick for a long while, since the physicians say that sword of yours has bitten deep, and during that time all power is mine. Messengers are at your service; you are free to come and go as you will. Bring this servant of yours to my presence, for doubtless he trusts you. I would speak with him, O Lord-from-the-Sea."

"If I should do this, Inca, will the lady Quilla be given back to her father?"

"Nay, it would be sacrilege. Ask what else you will, lands and rule

181

and palaces and wives—not that. Myself I should not dare to lay a finger on her who rests in the arms of the Sun. What does it matter about this Quilla who is but one fair woman among thousands?"

I thought awhile, then answered, "I think it matters much, Inca. Still, that this bloodshed may be stayed, I will do my best to bring him who was my servant to your presence if you can find me the means to come at him, and afterwards we will talk again."

"Yes, I am weary now. Afterwards we will talk again. Farewell, Lord-from-the-Sea."

CHAPTER 9

Kari Comes to His Own

When I awoke on the following morning in the splendid chamber of which I have spoken, it was to find that my armour and arms had been restored to me, and very glad was I to see Wave-Flame again. After I had eaten and, escorted by servants, walked in the gardens, for never could I be left alone, marvelling at the wondrous golden fruits and flowers, a messenger came to me, saying that the *Villaorna* desired speech with me. I wondered who this *Villaorna* might be, but when he entered I saw that he was Larico, that same stern-faced, cunning-eyed lord who had been the spokesman of the Inca when he visited the city of the Chancas. Also I learned that *Villaorna* was his title and meant "Chief priest."

We bowed to each other and all were sent from the chamber, leaving us quite alone.

"Lord-from-the-Sea," he said, "the Inca sends me, his Councillor and blood relative, who am head priest of the Sun, to desire that you will go on an embassy for him to the camp of the Chancas. First, however, it is needful that you should swear by the Sun that you will return thence to Cuzco. Will you do this?"

Now as there was nothing I desired more than to return to Cuzco where Quilla was, I answered that I would swear by my own god, by the Sun, and by my sword, unless the Chancas detained me by force. Further, I prayed him to set out his business.

He did so in these words:

"Lord, we have come to know, it matters not how, that the man who appeared with you in this land is no other than Kari, the elder son of the Inca, whom we thought dead. Now it is in the Inca's mind, and in the minds of us, his councillors, to proclaim the Prince Kari as heir to the throne which soon he would be called upon to fill. But the matter is very dangerous, seeing that Urco still commands the army and many of the great lords who are of his mother's House cling to him, hoping to receive advancement from him when he becomes Inca."

"But, Priest Larico, Urco, they say, is like to die, and if so all this trouble will melt like a cloud."

"Your sword bit deep, Lord, but I have it from his physicians that as the brain is uncut he will not die, although he will be sick for a long while. Therefore we must act while he is sick, since it is not lawful to bring about his end, even if he could be come at. Time presses, Lord, for as you have seen, the Inca is old and feeble and his mind is weak. Indeed at times he has no mind, though at others his strength returns to him."

"Which means that I deal with you who are the chief priest, and those behind you," I said, looking him in the eyes.

"That is what it means, Lord. Now hearken while I tell you the truth. After the Inca I am the most powerful man in Tavantinsuyu, indeed for the most part the Inca speaks with my voice although I seem to speak with his. Yet I am in a snare. Heretofore I have supported Urco because there was no other who could become Inca, although he is a brutal and an evil man. Of late, however, since my return from the City of the Chancas, I have quarrelled with Urco because he has lost that witch, the lady Quilla, whom he desires madly and lays the blame on me, and it has come to my knowledge that when he succeeds to the throne it is his purpose to kill me, which doubtless he will do if he can, or at the least to cast me from my place and power, which is as bad as death. Therefore, I desire to make my peace with Kari, if he will swear to continue me in my office, and this I can only do through you. Bring this peace about, Lord, and I will promise you anything you may wish, even perchance to the Incaship itself, should aught happen to Kari or should he refuse my offers. I think that the Quichuas might welcome a white god from the Sea who has shown himself so great a general and so brave in battle, and who has knowledge and wisdom more than theirs, to rule over them," he added reflectively. "Only then, Lord, it would be needful to be rid of Kari as well as of Urco."

"To which I would never consent," I replied, "seeing that he is my friend with whom I have shared many dangers. Moreover, I do not wish to be Inca."

"Is there then anything else that you wish very much, Lord? A thought came to me, yonder at the City of the Chancas. By the way, how lovely is that lady Quilla and how royal a woman. It is most strange that she should have turned her mind towards an aged man like Upanqui."

We looked at each other.

"Very strange," I said. "It seems to me sad also that this beauteous Quilla should be immured in a nunnery for life. To tell you the truth, High-priest, since it is not good for man to live alone, rather than that such a thing should have happened I would have married her myself, to which perchance she might have consented."

Again we looked at each other and I went on:

"I hinted as much to Kari after we heard she was numbered amongst the Virgins, and asked him whether, should he become Inca, he would take her thence and give her to me."

"What did he answer, Lord?"

"He said that though he loved me like a brother, first he would kill me with his own hand, since such a deed would be sacrilege against the Sun. Last night also the Inca himself said much the same."

"Is it so, Lord? Well, we priests bring up our Incas to think thus. If we did not, where would our power be, seeing that we are the Voice of the Sun upon earth and issue his decrees?"

"But do you always think thus yourselves, O High-priest?"

"Not quite always. There are loopholes in every law of gods and men. For example, I believe I see one in the instance of this lady Quilla. But before we waste more time in talking—tell me, White Lord, do you desire her, and if so, are you ready to pay me my price? It is that you shall assure to me the friendship of the prince Kari, should he become Inca, and the continuance of my power and office."

"My answer is that I do desire this lady, O High-priest, and that if I can I will obtain from Kari the promise of what you seek. And now where is the loophole?"

"I seem to remember, Lord, that there is an ancient law which says—that none who are maimed may be the wives of the Sun. It is true that this law applies to them *before* they contract the holy marriage. Still, if the point came up before me as high-priest, I might perhaps find that it applied also to those who were maimed *after* marriage. The case is rare, for which precedents cannot be found if the search be thorough. Now through the wickedness of Urco, as it happens, this lady Quilla has been blinded, and therefore is no longer perfect in her body. Do you understand?"

"Quite. But what would Upanqui or Kari say? The Incas you declare are always bigots and might interpret this law otherwise."

"I cannot tell, Lord, but let us cease from beating bushes. I will help you if I can, if you will help me if *you* can, though I daresay that in the end you, who are not a bigot, must take the law into your own hands, as perhaps the lady Quilla, who is a moon-worshipper, would be willing to do also."

The finish of it was that this cunning priest and statesman and I made a bargain. If I could win Kari over to his interests, then he swore by the Sun that he would gain me access to the lady Quilla and help me to fly with her, if so we both wished, while I on my part swore to plead his cause with Kari. Moreover, as he showed me, there was little fear that either of us would break these oaths since henceforth each lay in the power of the other.

After this we passed on to public matters. I was charged to offer an honourable truce to Huaracha and the Chancas with permission to them to camp their armies in certain valleys near to Cuzco where they would be fed until peace was declared, which peace would give them all they needed, namely, their freedom and safeguards from attack. For the rest I was to bring Kari and those who had deserted to him on the yesterday into Cuzco where none would molest them.

Then he went, leaving me happier than I had been since I bade farewell to Quilla. For now at last I saw light, a faint uncertain light, it was true, only to be reached, if reached at all, through many difficulties and dangers, but still light. At last I had found someone in this land of black superstition who was not a bigot, and who, being the High-priest of the Sun, knew too much of his god to fear him or to believe that he should come down to earth and burn it up should one of the hundreds of his brides seek another husband. Of course this Larico might betray me and Quilla, but I did not think he would, since he had nothing to gain thereby, and might have much to lose, for the reason that I was able, or he thought that I was able, to set Kari against him. At least I could only go forward and trust to fortune, though in fact hitherto she had never shown me favour where woman was concerned.

****

Awhile later I was being borne in one of the Inca's own litters back to the camp of the Chancas, accompanied by an embassy of great lords.

We passed over that dreadful, bloodstained plain where, under a flag of truce, both sides were engaged in burying the thousands of their dead, and came to the ridge whence we had charged on the yester morn. Here sentries stopped us and I descended from my litter. When the Chancas saw me in my armour come back to them alive, they set up a great shouting and presently I and the lords with me were led to the pavilion of King Huaracha.

We found him lying sick upon a couch, for though he showed no wound he had been badly bruised upon the body by a blow from Urco's club and, as I feared, was hurt in the bowels. He greeted me with delight, since he thought that I might have been killed after I was captured, and asked how I came to appear in his camp in the company of our enemies. I told him at once what had chanced and that I was sworn to return to Cuzco when I had done my business. Then the Inca's ambassadors set out their proposals for a truce, and retired, while Huaracha discussed them with his generals and Kari, who also was overjoyed to see me safe.

The end of it was that they were accepted on the terms offered, namely, that Huaracha and his army should withdraw to the valleys of which I have spoken, and there camp, receiving all the food they needed until a peace could be offered such as he would be willing to accept. Indeed, the Chancas were glad to agree to this plan for their losses in the battle had been very great and they were in no state to renew the attack upon Cuzco, which was still defended by such mighty hordes of brave warriors fighting for their homes, families, and freedom.

So all was agreed on the promise that peace should be made within thirty days or sooner, and that if it were not the war should re-commence.

Then privately, I told Huaracha all that I had learned about Quilla and that I had still hopes of saving her though what these were I did not tell him. When he had thought, he said that now the fate of Quilla must be left in the hands of the gods and mine, since not even for her could he neglect the opportunity of an honourable peace, seeing that another battle might mean destruction. Also he pointed out that he was hurt and I who had been general under him was a prisoner and bound by my oath to return to prison, so that the Chancas had lost their leaders.

After this we parted, I promising to work for his cause and to come to see him again, if I might.

These matters finished I went aside with Kari to a place where none could hear us, and there laid before him the offers of Larico, the high-priest, showing him how the case stood. Of Quilla, however, I said nothing to him, though it pained me to keep back part of the truth even from Kari. Yet, what was I to do, who knew that if I told him all and he became Inca, or the Inca's acknowledged heir, he would work against me because of his superstitious madness, and perhaps cause Quilla to be killed by the priests, as one whose feet were set in the path of sacrilege? So on this matter I held my peace, nor did he ask me anything concerning Quilla who, I think, wished to hear nothing of that lady and what had befallen her.

When he had learned all, he said:

"This may be a trap, Lord. I do not trust yonder Larico, who has always been my enemy and Urco's friend."

"I think he is his own friend first," I answered, "who knows that if Urco recovers he will kill him, because he has taken the part of your father, Upanqui, in their quarrels, and suspects him."

"I am not sure," said Kari. "Yet something must be risked. Did I not tell you when we were sailing down the English river that we must put faith in our gods, yes, afterwards also, and more than once? And did not the gods save us? Well, now again I trust to my god," and drawing out the image of Pachacamac, which he wore round his neck, he kissed it, then turning, bowed and prayed to the Sun.

"I will come with you," he said, when he had finished his devotions, "to live to be Inca, or to die, as the Sun decrees."

So he came and with him some of his friends, captains of those who had deserted to him in the battle. But the five thousand soldiers, or those who were left of them, did not come as yet because they feared lest they should be set upon and butchered by the regiments of Urco.

****

That night, when we were back safe in Cuzco, Kari and the high-priest, Larico talked together in secret. Of what passed between them he only told me that they had come to an agreement which satisfied them both. Larico said the same to me when next I saw him, adding:

"You have kept your word and served my turn, Lord-from-the-Sea, therefore I will keep mine and serve yours when the time comes. Yet be warned by me and say nothing of a certain lady to the prince Kari, since when I spoke a word to him on the matter, hinting that her surrender to her father Huaracha would make peace with him more easy and lasting, he answered that first would he fight Huaracha, and the Yuncas as well, to the last man in Cuzco.

"To the Sun she has gone," he said, "and with the Sun she must stay, lest the curse of the Sun and of Pachacamac, the Spirit above the sun, should fall on me and all of us."

Larico told me also that, fearing something, the great lords, who were of Urco's party, had borne him away in a litter to a strong city in the mountains about five leagues from Cuzco, escorted by thousands of picked men who would stay in and about that city.

On the next morning I was summoned to wait upon the Inca Upanqui, and went, wearing my armour. I found him in the same great chamber as before, only now he was more royally arrayed, and with him were sundry of his high lords of the Inca blood, also certain priests, among them the *Villaoma* Larico.

The old king, who on that day seemed clear in his mind and well, greeted me in his kindly fashion and bade me set out all that had passed between me and Huaracha in the Chanca camp. This I did, only I hid from him how great had been the Chanca losses in the battle and how glad they were to declare a truce and rest.

Upanqui said that the matter should be attended to, speaking in a royal fashion as though it were one of little moment, which showed me how great an emperor he must be. Great he was, indeed, seeing that all the broad land of England would have made but one province of his vast dominions, which in every part were filled with people who, unless they chanced to be in rebellion like the Yuncas, lived but to do his will.

After this, when I thought the audience was ended, a chamberlain advanced to the foot of the throne, and kneeling, said that a suppliant prayed speech with the Inca. Upanqui waved his sceptre, that long staff which I have described, in token that he should be admitted. Then presently up the chamber came Kari arrayed in the tunic and cloak of an Inca prince, wearing in his ear a disc carved with the image of the Sun, and a chain of emeralds and gold about his neck. Nor did he come alone, for he was attended by a brilliant band of those lords and captains who had deserted to him on the day of the great battle. He advanced and knelt before the throne.

"Who is this that carries the emblems of the Holy Blood and is clothed like a Prince of the Sun?" asked Upanqui, affecting ignorance and unconcern, though I saw the colour mount to his cheeks and the sceptre shake in his withered hand.

"One who is indeed of the holy Inca blood; one sprung from the purest lineage of the Sun," answered the stately Kari in his quiet voice.

"How then is he named?" asked the Inca again.

"He is named Kari, first-born son of Upanqui, O Inca."

"Such a son I had once, but he is long dead, or so they told me," said Upanqui in a trembling voice.

"He is not dead, O Inca. He lives and he kneels before you. Urco poisoned him, but the Sun his Father recovered him, and the Spirit that is above all gods supported him. The sea bore him to a far land, where he found a white god who befriended and cared for him," here he turned his head towards me. "With this god he returned to his own country and here he kneels before you, O Inca."

"It cannot be," said the Inca. "What sign do you bring who name yourself Kari? Show me the image of the Spirit above the gods that from his childhood for generations has been hung about the neck of the Inca's eldest son, born from the Queen."

Kari opened his robe and drew out that golden effigy of Pachacamac which he always wore.

Upanqui examined it, holding it close to his rheumy eyes.

"It seems to be the same," he said, "as I should know upon whose breast it lay until my first son was born. And yet who can be sure since such things may be copied?"

Then he handed back the image to Kari and after reflecting awhile, said: "Bring hither the Mother of the Royal Nurses."

Apparently this lady was in waiting, for in a minute she appeared before the throne, an old and withered woman with beady eyes.

"Mother," said the Inca, "you were with the *Coya* (that is the Queen) who has been gathered to the Sun, when her boy was born, and afterwards nursed him for years. If you saw it, would you know his body again after he has come to middle age?"

"Aye, O Inca."

"How, Mother?"

"By three moles, O Inca, which we women used to call *Yuti*, *Quilla*, and *Chasca*" (that is, the Sun, the Moon, and the planet Venus), "which were the marks of good fortune stamped by the gods upon the Prince's back between the shoulders, set one above the other."

"Man who call yourself Kari, are you willing that this old crone should see your flesh?" asked Upanqui.

By way of answer Kari with a little smile stripped himself of his broidered tunic and other garments and stood before us naked to the middle. Then he turned his back to the Mother of the Nurses. She hobbled up and searched it with her bright eyes.

"Many scars," she muttered, "scars in front and scars behind. This warrior has known battles and blows. But what have we here? Look, O Inca, *Yuti*, *Quilla*, and *Chasca*, set one above the other, though *Chasca* is almost hidden by a hurt. Oh! my fosterling, O my Prince whom I nursed at these withered breasts, are you come back from the dead to take your own again? O Kari of the Holy Blood; Kari the lost who is Kari the found!"

Then sobbing and muttering she threw her arms about him and kissed him. Nor did he shame to kiss her in return, there before them all.

"Restore his garments to the royal Prince," said Upanqui, "and bring hither the Fringe that is worn by the Inca's heir."

It was produced without delay by the high-priest Larico, which told me at once that all this scene had been prepared. Upanqui took it from Larico, and beckoning Kari to him, with the priest's help bound it about his brow, thereby acknowledging him and restoring him as heir-apparent to the Empire. Then he kissed him on the brow and Kari knelt down and did his father homage.

After this they went away together accompanied only by Larico and two or three of the councillors of Inca blood and as I learned from Larico afterwards, told each other their tales and made plans to outwit, and if need were to destroy, Urco and his faction.

On the following day Kari was established in a house of his own that was more of a fortress than a palace, for it was built of great stones with narrow gates, and surrounded by an open space. Upon this space, as a guard, were encamped all those who had deserted to him in the battle of the Field of Blood, who had returned to Cuzco from the camp of Huaracha now that Kari was accepted as the royal heir. Also other troops who were loyal to the Inca were stationed near by, while those who clung to Urco departed secretly to that town where he lay sick. Moreover, proclamation was made that on the day of the new moon, which the magicians declared to be auspicious, Kari would be publicly presented to the people in the Temple of the Sun as the Inca's lawful heir, in place of Urco disinherited for crimes that he had committed against the Sun, the Empire, and the Inca his father.

"Brother," said Kari to me, for so he called me now that he was an acknowledged Prince, when I went to meet him in his grandeur, "Brother, did I not tell you always that we must trust to our gods? See, I have not trusted in vain though it is true that dangers still lie ahead of me, and perhaps civil war."

"Yes," I answered, "your gods are in the way of giving you all you want, but it is not so with mine and me."

"What then do you desire, Brother, who can have even to the half of the kingdom?"

"Kari," I replied, "I cry not for the Earth, but for the Moon."

He understood, and his face grew stern.

"Brother, the Moon alone is beyond you, for she inhabits the sky while you still dwell upon the earth," he answered with a frown, and then began to talk of the peace with Huaracha.

191

CHAPTER 10

The Great Horror

The day of the new moon came and with it the great horror that caused all the Empire of Tavantinsuyu to tremble, fearing lest Heaven should be avenged upon it.

Since Upanqui had found his elder son again he began to dote upon him, as in such a case the old and weak-minded often do, and would walk about the gardens and palaces with his arm around his neck babbling to him of whatever was uppermost in his mind. Moreover, his soul was oppressed because he had done Kari wrong in the past, and preferred Urco to him under the urging of that prince's mother.

"The truth is, Son," I myself heard him say to Kari, "that we men who seem to rule the world do not rule it at all, because always women rule us. This they do through our passions which the gods planted in us for their own ends, also because they are more single in their minds. The man thinks of many things, the woman only thinks of what she desires. Therefore the man whom Nature already has bemused, only brings a little piece of his mind to fight against her whole mind, and so is conquered; he who was made for one thing only, to be the mate of the woman that she may mother more men in order to serve the wills of other women who yet seem to be those men's slaves."

"So I have learned, Father," answered the grave Kari, "and for this reason having suffered in the past, I am determined to have as little to do with women as is possible for one in my place. During my travels in other lands, as in this country, I have seen men great and noble brought to nothingness and ruin by their love for women; down into the dirt, indeed, when their hands were full of the world's wealth and glory. Moreover, I have noticed that they seldom learn wisdom, and that what they have done before, they are ready to do again, who believe anything that soft lips swear to them. Yes, even that they are loved for themselves alone, as I own to my sorrow, once I did myself. Urco could not have taken that fair wife of mine, Father, if she had not been willing to go when she saw that I had lost your favour and with it the hope of the Scarlet Fringe."

Here Kari looked at me, of whom I knew he was thinking all this time, and seeing that I could overhear his talk, began to speak of something else.

****

On the appointed day there was a great gathering of the nobles of the land, especially of those of the Inca blood, and of all that were "earmen," a class of the same rank as our peers in England, to hear the proclamation of Kari as the Inca's heir. It was made before this gorgeous company in the Great Temple of the Sun, which now I saw for the first time.

It was a huge and most wondrous place well named the "House of Gold." For here everything was gold. On the western wall hung an image of the Sun twenty feet or more across, an enormous graven plate of gold set about with gems and having eyes and teeth of great emeralds. The roof, too, and the walls were all panelled with gold, even the cornices and column heads were of solid gold.

Opening out of this temple also were others dedicated to the Moon and Stars, that of the Moon being clothed in silver, with her radiant face shaped in silver fixed to the western wall. So it was with the temple of the Stars, of the Lightnings and of the Rainbow, which perhaps with its many colours that sprang from jewels, was the most dazzling of them all.

The sight of so much glory overwhelmed me, and it came into my mind that if only it were known of in Europe, men would die by the ten thousand on the chance that they might conquer this country and make its wealth theirs. Yet here, save for these purposes of ornament and to be used as offerings to the gods and Incas, it was of no account at all.

But in this temple of the Sun was a marvel greater than its gold. For on either side of the carved likenesses of the sun, seated upon chairs of gold, sat the dead Incas and their queens. Yes, clothed in their royal robes and emblems, with the Fringe upon their brows, there they sat with their heads bent forward, so wonderfully preserved by the arts these people have, that except for the stamp of death upon their countenances, they might have been sleeping men and women. Thus in the dead face of the mother of Kari I could read her likeness to her son. Of these departed kings and queens there were many, since from the first Inca of whom history told all were gathered here in the holy

House and under the guardianship of the effigy of their god, the Sun, from whom they believed themselves to be descended. The sight was so solemn that it awed me, as it did all that congregation, for I noted that here men walked with unsandalled feet and that in speaking none raised their voices high.

The old Inca, Upanqui, entered, gloriously apparelled and accompanied by lords and priests, while after him came Kari with his retinue of great men. The Inca bowed to the company whereon everyone in the great temple, save myself alone whose British pride kept me on my feet, standing like one left living on a battlefield among a multitude of slain, prostrated himself before his divine majesty. At a sign they rose again and the Inca seated himself upon his jewelled golden throne beneath the effigy of the Sun, while Kari took his place upon a lesser throne to the Inca's right.

Looking at him there in his splendour on this day when he came into his own again, I bethought me of the wretched, starving Indian marked with blows and foul with filth whom I had rescued from the cruel mob upon the Thames-side wharf, and wondered at this enormous change of fortune and the chain of wonderful events by which it had been brought about.

My fortune also had changed, for then I was great in my own fashion, who now had become but a wanderer, welcomed indeed in this glittering new world of which yonder we knew nothing, because I was strange and different, also full of unheard-of learning and skilled in war, but still nothing but an outcast wanderer, and so doomed to live and die. And as I thought, so thought Kari, for our glances met, and I read it in his eyes.

Yonder sat my servant who had become my lord, and though he was still my friend, soon I felt he would be lost in the state matters of that great empire, leaving me more lonely than before. Also his mind was not as my mind, as his blood was not my blood, and he was the slave of a faith that to me was a hateful superstition doubtless begotten by the Devil, who under the name of *Cupay*, some worshipped in that land, though others declared that this *Cupay* was the God of the Dead.

Oh! that I could flee away with Quilla and at her side live out what was left to me of life, since of all these multitudes she alone understood and was akin to me, because the sacred fire of love had burned away our differences and opened her eyes. But Quilla was snatched from me by the law of their accursed faith, and whatever else Kari might give, he would never give me this lady of the Moon, since, as he had said, to him this would be sacrilege.

The ceremonies began. First Larico, the high-priest of the Sun, clothed in his white sacerdotal robes, made sacrifice upon a little altar which stood in front of the Inca's throne.

It was a very simple sacrifice of fruit and corn and flowers, with what seemed to be strange-shaped pieces of gold. At least I saw nothing else, and am sure that nothing that had life was laid upon that altar after the fashion of the bloody offerings of the Jews, and indeed of those of some of the other peoples of that great land.

Prayers, however, were spoken, very fine prayers and pure so far as I could understand them, for their language was more ancient and somewhat different to that which was used in common speech; also the priests moved about, bowing and bending the knees much as our own do in celebrating the mass, though whether these motions were in honour of the god or of the Inca, I am not sure.

When the sacrifice was over, and the little fire that burned upon the altar had sunk low, though I was told that for hundreds of years it had never been extinguished, suddenly the Inca began to speak. With many particulars that I had not heard before he told the tale of Kari and of his estrangement from him in past years through the plottings of the mother of Urco who now was dead, like the mother of Kari. This woman, it would appear, had persuaded him, the Inca, that Kari was conspiring against him, and therefore Urco was ordered to take him prisoner, but returned only with Kari's wife, saying that Kari had killed himself.

Here Upanqui became overcome with emotion as the aged are apt to do, and beat his breast, even shedding tears because most unjustly he had allowed these things to happen and the wicked triumph over the good, for which sin he said he felt sure his father the Sun would bring some punishment on him, as indeed was to chance sooner than he thought. Then he continued his story, setting out all Urco's iniquities and sacrileges against the gods, also his murders of people of high and low degree and his stealing of their wives and daughters. Lastly he told of the coming of Kari who was supposed to be dead, and all that story which I have set out.

Having finished his tale, with much solemn ceremonial he deposed Urco from his heirship to the Empire which he gave back to Kari to whom it belonged by right of birth and calling upon his dead forefathers, one by one, to be witness to the act, with great formality once more he bound the Prince's Fringe about his brow. As he did this, he said these words:

"Soon, O Prince Kari, you must change this yellow circlet for that which I wear, and take with it all the burden of empire, for know that as quickly as may be I purpose to withdraw to my palace at Yucay, there to make my peace with God before I am called hence to dwell in the Mansions of the Sun."

When he had finished Kari did homage to his father, and in that quiet, even voice of his, told his tale of the wrongs that he had suffered at the hands of Urco his brother and of how he had escaped, living but maddened, from his hate. He told also how he had wandered across the sea, though of England he said nothing, and been saved from misery and death by myself, a very great person in my own country. Still, since I had suffered wrong there, as he, Kari, had in his, he had persuaded me to accompany him back to his own land, that there my wisdom might shine upon its darkness, and owing to my divine and magical gifts hither we had come in safety. Lastly, he asked the assembled priests and lords if they were content to accept him as the Inca to be, and to stand by him in any war that Urco might wage against him.

To this they answered that they were content and would stand by him.

Then followed many other rites such as the informing of the dead Incas, one by one, of this solemn declaration, through the mouth of the high-priest, and the offering of many prayers to them and to the Sun their father. So long were these prayers with the chants from choirs hidden in side chapels by which they were interspersed, that the day drew towards its close before all was done.

Thus it came about that the dusk was gathering when the Inca, followed by Kari, myself, the priests, and all the congregation, left the temple to present Kari as the heir to the throne to the vast crowd which waited upon the open square outside its doors.

Here the ceremony went on. The Inca and most of us, for there was not space for all, although we were packed as closely together as Hastings herrings in a basket, took our stand upon a platform that was surrounded by a marvellous cable made of links of solid gold which, it was said, needed fifty men to lift it from the ground. Then Upanqui, whose strength seemed restored to him, perhaps because of some drug that he had eaten, or under the spur of this great event, stepped forward to the edge of the low platform and addressed the multitude in eloquent words, setting out the matter as he had done in the temple. He ended his speech by asking the formal question:

"Do you, Children of the Sun, accept the prince Kari, my first-born, to be Inca after me?"

There was a roar of assent, and as it died away Upanqui turned to call Kari to him that he might present him to the people.

At this very moment in the gathering twilight I saw a great fierce-faced man with a bandaged head, whom I knew to be Urco, leap over the golden chain. He sprang upon the platform and with a shout of "I do not accept him, and thus I pay back treachery," plunged a gleaming copper knife or sword into the Inca's breast.

In an instant, before any could stir in that packed crowd, Urco had leapt back over the golden chain, and from the edge of the platform, to vanish amongst those beneath, who doubtless were men of his following disguised as citizens or peasants.

Indeed all who beheld seemed frozen with horror. One great sigh went up and then there was silence, since no such deed as this was known in the annals of that empire. For a moment the aged Upanqui stood upon his feet, the blood pouring down his white beard and jewelled robe. Then he turned a little and said in a clear and gentle voice:

"Kari, you will be Inca sooner than I thought. Receive me, O God my Father, and pardon this murderer who, I think, can be no true son of mine."

Then he fell forward on his face and when we lifted him he was dead. Still the silence hung; it was as though the tongues of men were smitten with dumbness. At length Kari stepped forward and cried:

"The Inca is dead, but I, the Inca, live on to avenge him. I declare war upon Urco the murderer and all who cling to Urco!"

Now the spell was lifted, and from those dim hordes there went up a yell of hatred against Urco the butcher and parricide, while men rushed to and fro searching for him. In vain! for he had escaped in the darkness.

On the following day, with more ceremonies, though many of these were omitted because of the terror and trouble of the times, Kari was crowned Inca, exchanging the yellow for the crimson Fringe and taking the throne name of Upanqui after his father. In Cuzco there was none to say him nay for the whole city was horror-struck because of the sacrilege that had been committed. Also those who clung to Urco had fled away with him to a town named Huarina on the borders of the great lake called Titicaca, where was an island with marvellous temples full of gold, which town lay at a distance from Cuzco.

****

Then the civil war began and raged for three whole months, though of all that happened in that time because of the labour of it, I set down little, who would get forward with my story.

In this war I played a great part. The fear of Kari was that the Chancas, seeing the Inca realm thus rent in two, would once more attack Cuzco. This it became my business to prevent. As the ambassador of Kari I visited the camp of Huaracha, bearing offers of peace which gave to him more than he could ever hope to win by strength of arms. I found the old warrior-king still sick and wasted because of the hurt from Urco's club, though now he could walk upon crutches, and set out the case. He answered that he had no wish to fight against Kari who had offered him such honourable terms, especially when he was waging war against Urco whom he, Huaracha, hated, because he had striven to poison his daughter and dealt him a blow which he was sure would end in his death. Therefore he was ready to make a firm peace with the new Inca, if in addition to what he offered he would surrender to him Quilla who was his heiress and would be Queen of the Chancas after him.

With these words I went back to Kari, only to find that on this matter he was hard as a rock of the mountains. In vain did I plead with him, and in vain did the high-priest, Larico, by subtle hints and arguments, strive to gentle his mind.

"My brother," said Kari in that soft even voice of his, when he had heard me patiently to the end, "forgive me if I tell you that in advancing this prayer, for one word you say on behalf of King Huaracha, you say two for yourself, who having unhappily been bewitched by her, desire this Virgin of the Sun, the lady Quilla, to be your wife. My brother, take everything else that I have to give, but leave this lady alone. If I handed her over to Huaracha or to you, as I have told you before, I should bring upon myself and upon my people the curse of my father the Sun, and of Pachacamac, the Spirit who is above the Sun. It was because Upanqui, my father according to the flesh, dared to look upon her after she had entered the House of the Sun, as I have learned he did, that a bloody and a cruel death came upon him, for so the magicians and the wise men have assured me that the oracles declare. Therefore, rather than do this crime of crimes, I would choose that Huaracha should renew the war against us and that you should join yourself to him, or even to Urco, and strive to tear me from the Throne, for then even if I were slain, I should die with honour."

"That I could never do," I answered sadly.

"No, my brother Hubert (for now he called me by my English name again), that you could never do, being what you are, as I know well. So like the rest of us you must bear your burden. Mayhap it may please my gods, or your gods in the end, and in some way that I cannot foresee, to give you this woman whom you seek. But of my free will I will never give her to you. To me the deed would be as though in your land of England the King commanded the consecrated bread and cups of wine to be snatched from the hands of the priests of your temples and cast to the dogs, or given to cheer the infidels within your gates, or dragged away the nuns from your convents to become their lemans. What would you think of such a king in your own country? And what," he added with meaning, "would you have thought of me if there I had stolen one of these nuns because she was beautiful and I desired her as a wife?"

Now although Kari's words stung me because of the truth that was in them, I answered that to me this matter wore another face. Also that Quilla had become a Virgin of the Sun, not of her own free will, but to escape from Urco.

"Yes, my brother," he answered, "because you believe my religion to be idolatry, and do not understand that the Sun to me is the symbol and garment of God, and that when we of the Inca blood, or those of us who have the inner knowledge, talk of him as our Father, we mean that we are the children of God, though the common people are taught otherwise. For the rest, this lady took her vows of her own free will and of her secret reasons I know nothing, any more than I know why she offered herself in marriage to Urco before she found you upon the island. For you I grieve, and for her also; yet I would have you remember that, as your own priests teach, in every life that is not brutal there must be loss, sorrow, and sacrifice, since by these steps only man can climb towards the things of the spirit. Pluck then such flowers as you will from the garden that Fate gives you, but leave this one white bloom alone."

In such words as these he preached at me, till at length I could bear no more, and said roughly:

"To me it is a very evil thing, O Inca, to separate those who love each other, and one that cannot be pleasing to Heaven. Therefore, great as you are, and friend of mine as you are, I tell you to your face that if I can take the lady Quilla out of that golden grave of hers I shall do so."

"I know it, my brother," he answered, "and therefore, were I as some Incas have been, I should cause this holy Spouse to travel more quickly to the skies than Nature will take her. But this I will not do because I know also that Destiny is above all things and that which Destiny decrees will happen unhelped by man. Still I tell you that I will thwart you if I can and that should you succeed in your ends, I will kill you if I can and the lady also, because you have committed sacrilege. Yes, although I love you better than any other man, I will kill you. And if King Huaracha should be able to snatch her away by force I will make war on him until either I and my people or he and his people are destroyed. And now let us talk no more of this matter, but rather of our plans against Urco, since in these at least, where no woman is concerned, I know that you will be faithful to me and I sorely need your help."

****

So with a heavy heart I went back to the camp of Huaracha and told him Kari's words. He was very wroth when he heard them, since his gods were different to those of the Incas and he thought nothing of the holiness of the Virgins of the Sun, and once again talked of renewing the war. Still it came to nothing for sundry reasons of which the greatest was that his sickness increased on him as the days went by. Also I told him that much as I desired Quilla, I could not fight upon his side since I was sworn to aid Kari against Urco and my word might not be broken. Moreover, the Yuncas who had been our allies, wearying of their long absence from home and satisfied with the gentle forgiveness and the redress of their grievances which the new Inca had promised them, were gone, having departed on their long march to the coast, while many of the Chancas themselves were slipping back to their own country. Therefore Huaracha's hour had passed by.

So at length we agreed that it would be foolish to attack Cuzco in order to try to rescue Quilla, since even if Huaracha won in face of a desperate defence, probably it would be only to find that his daughter was dead or had vanished away to some unknown and distant convent. All that we could do was to trust to fortune to deliver her into our hands. We agreed further that, having obtained an honourable peace and all else that he desired, it would be well for Huaracha to return to his own land, leaving me a body of five thousand picked men who were willing to serve under me, to assist in the war against Urco, to be my guard and that of Quilla, if perchance I could deliver her from the House of the Sun.

When this was known five thousand of the best and bravest of the Chancas, young soldiers who sought adventure and battle and whom I had trained, stepped forward at once and swore themselves to my service. Bidding farewell to Huaracha, with these troops I returned to Cuzco, sending messengers ahead to explain the reason of their coming to Kari, who welcomed them well and gave them quarters round the palace which was allotted to me.

A few days later we advanced on the town Huarina, a great host of us, and outside of it met the yet greater host of Urco in a mighty battle that endured for a day and a night, and yet, like that of the Field of Blood, remained neither lost nor won. When the thousands of the dead had been buried and the wounded sent back to Cuzco, we attacked the city of Huarina, I leading the van with my Chancas, and stormed the place, driving Urco and his forces out on the farther side.

They retreated to the mountains and there followed a long and tedious war without great battles. At length, although the Inca's armies had suffered sorely, we forced those of Urco to the shores of the Lake Titicaca, where most of them melted away into the swamps and certain tree-clad, low-lying valleys. Urco himself, however, with a number of followers, escaped in boats to the holy island in the lake.

We built a fleet of *balsas* with reeds and blown-out sheepskins, and followed him. Landing on the isle we stormed the city of temples which were more wondrous and even fuller of gold and precious things than those of Cuzco. Here the men of Urco fought desperately, but driving them from street to street, at length we penned them in one of the largest of the temples of which by some mischance a reed roof was set on fire, so that there they perished miserably. It was a dreadful scene such as I never wish to behold again. Also, after all Urco and some of his captains, breaking out of the burning temple under cover of the smoke escaped, either in *balsas* or, as many declare, by swimming the lake. At least they were gone nor search as we might on the mainland could they be found.

So all being finished, except for the escape of Urco, we returned to Cuzco which Kari entered in triumph, I marching at his side, wearied out with war and bloodshed.

CHAPTER 11

The House of Death

Now at one time during this long war against Urco victory smiled upon him, though afterwards the scale went down against him. Kari was defeated in a pitched battle and I who commanded another army was almost surrounded in a valley. When everything seemed lost, afterwards I escaped by leading my soldiers round up the slope of a mountain and surprising Urco in the rear, but as it ended well for us I need not speak of that matter.

It was while all was at its blackest for us that a certain officer was brought to me who was captured while striving to desert, or at least to pass our outposts. As it happened I knew this man again having, unseen myself, noted him on the previous day talking earnestly to the high-priest Larico, who, with other priests, accompanied my army, perhaps to keep a watch on me. I took this captain apart and questioned him alone, threatening him with death by torment if he did not reveal his errand to me.

In the end, being very much afraid, he spoke. From him I learned that he was a messenger from Larico to Urco. Believing that our defeat was almost certain, Larico had sent him to make his peace with Urco by betraying all Kari's and my own plans to him and revealing how he might most easily destroy us. He said also that he, Larico, had only joined the party of Upanqui, and of Kari after him, under threats of death and that always in his heart he had been true to Urco, whom he acknowledged as his Lord and as the rightful Inca whom he would help to restore to the Throne with all the power of the Priesthood of the Sun. Further, he sent by this spy a secret message by means of little cords cunningly knotted, which knots served these people as writing, since they could read them as we read a book.

Now, being always desirous of knowledge, I had caused myself to be instructed in the plan of this knot-writing which by this time I could read well enough. Therefore I was able to spell out this message. It said shortly but plainly, that knowing he still desired her, he, Larico, as high-priest would hand over to Urco the lady Quilla, daughter to the King of the Chancas who unlawfully had been hidden away among the Virgins of the Sun, also that he would betray me, the White-God-from-the-Sea who sought to steal her away, into Urco's hands, that he might kill me if he could.

When I had mastered all this I was filled with rage and bethought me that I would cause Larico to be taken and suffer the fate of traitors. Soon, however, I changed this mind of mine and placing the spy in close keeping where none could come at him, I set a watch on Larico but said nothing to him or to Kari of all that I had learned.

A few days later our fortunes changed and Urco, defeated, was in full flight to the shores of Lake Titicaca. After this I knew we had nothing more to fear from this fox-hearted high-priest who above everything desired to be on the winning side and to continue in his place and power. So knowing that I held him fast I bided my time, because through him alone I could hope to come at Quilla. That time came after the war was over and we had returned to Cuzco in triumph. As soon as the rejoicings were over and Kari was firmly seated on his throne, I sent for Larico, which, as the greatest man in the kingdom after the Inca, I was able to do.

He appeared in answer to my summons and we bowed to each other, after which he began to praise me for my generalship, saying that had it not been for me, Urco would have won the war and that the Inca had done well to name me his Brother before the people and to say that to me he owed his throne.

"Yes, that is true," I answered, "and now, since through me, you, Larico, are the third greatest man in the kingdom and remain High-Priest of the Sun and Whisperer in the Inca's ear, I would put you in mind of a certain bargain that we made when I promised you all these things, Larico."

"What bargain, Lord-of-the-Sea."

"That you would bring me and a Virgin of the Sun, who while she was of the earth was named Quilla, together, Larico, and enable her to return from those of the Sun to my arms, Larico."

Now his face grew troubled and he answered:

"Lord, I have thought much of this matter, desiring above all things to fulfil my word and I grieve to tell you that it is impossible."

"Why, Larico?"

"Because I find that the law of my faith is against it, Lord."

"Is that all, Larico?" I asked with a smile.

"No, Lord. Because I find that the Inca would not suffer it and swears to kill all who attempt to touch the lady Quilla."

"Is that all, Larico?"

"No, Lord. Because I find that a woman who has been betrothed to one of the royal blood may never pass to another man."

"Now perhaps we come nearer to it, Larico. You mean that if this happened and perchance after all Urco should come to the throne, as he might do if Kari his brother died—as any man may die—he would hold you to account."

"Yes, Lord, if that chanced, as chance it may, since Urco still lives and I hear is gathering new armies among the mountains, certainly he would hold me to account for I have heard as much. Also our father the Sun would hold me to account and so would the Inca who wields his sceptre upon earth."

I asked him why he did not think of all these things before when he had much to gain instead of now when he had gained them through me, and he answered because he had not considered them enough. Then I pretended to grow angry and exclaimed:

"You are a rogue, Larico! You promise and take your pay and you do not perform. Henceforth I am your enemy and one to whom the Inca hearkens."

"He hearkens still more to this god the Sun and to me who am the voice of God, White Man," he answered, adding insolently, "You would strike too late; your power over me and my fortunes is gone, White Man."

"I fear it is so," I replied, pretending to be frightened, "so let us say no more of the matter. After all, there are other women in Cuzco besides this fair bride of the Sun. Now before you go, High-Priest, will you who are so learned help me who am ignorant? I have been striving to master your method of conveying thoughts by means of knots. Here I have a bundle of strings which I cannot altogether understand. Be pleased to interpret them to me, O most holy and upright High-Priest."

Then from my robe I drew out those knotted fibres that I had taken from his messenger and held them before Larico's eyes.

He stared at them and turned pale. His hand groped for his dagger till he saw that mine was on the hilt of Wave-Flame, whereon he let it fall. Next the thought took him that in truth I could not read the knots which he began to interpret falsely.

"Have done, Traitor," I laughed, "for I know them all. So Urco may wed Quilla and I may not. Also cease to fret as to that messenger of yours for whom you seek far and near, since he is safe in my keep-ing. To-morrow I take him to deliver his message not to Urco, but to Kari—and then, Traitor?"

Now Larico who, notwithstanding his stern face and proud man-ner, was a coward at heart, fell upon his knees before me trembling and prayed me to spare his life which lay in my hand. Well he knew that if once it came to Kari's ears, even a high priest of the Sun could not hope to escape the reward of such treachery as his.

"If I pardon you, what will you give me?" I asked.

"The only thing that you will take, Lord—the lady Quilla herself. Hearken, Lord. Outside the city is the palace of Upanqui whom Urco slew. There in the great hall the divine Inca sits embalmed and into that holy presence none dare enter save the Virgins of the Sun whose office it is to wait upon the mighty dead. To-morrow one hour before the dawn, when all men sleep, I will lead you to this hall disguised in the robes of a priest of the Sun, so that on the way thither none can know you. There you will find but one Virgin of the Sun, the lady whom you seek. Take her and begone. The rest I leave to you."

"How do I know that you will not set some trap for me, Larico?"

"Thus, Lord, that I shall be with you and share your sacrilege. Also my life will be in your hand."

"Aye, Larico," I answered grimly, "and if aught of ill befalls me, re-member that this," and I touched the knotted cords, "will find its way to Kari, and with it the man who was your messenger."

He nodded and answered:

"Be sure that I have but one desire, to know you, Lord, and this woman whom, being mad, you seek so madly, far from Cuzco and never to look upon your face again."

Then we made our plans as to when and where we should meet and other matters, after which he departed, bowing himself away with many smiles.

I thought to myself that there went as big a rogue as I had ever known, in London or elsewhere, and fell to wondering what snare he would set for me, since that he planned some snare I was sure. Why, then, did I prepare to fall into it? I asked myself. The answer was, for a double reason. First, although my whole heart was sick with long-ing for the sight of her, now, after months of seeking, I was no nearer to Quilla than when we had parted in the city of the Chancas, nor ever should be without Larico's aid. Secondly, some voice within me told me to go forward taking all hazards, since if I did not, our part-ing would be for always in this world. Yes, the voice warned me that unless I saved her soon, Quilla would be no more. As Huaracha had said, there was more poison in Cuzco, and murderers were not far to seek. Or despair might do its work with her. Or she might kill herself as once she had proposed to do. So I would go forward even though the path I walked should lead me to my doom.

That day I did many things. Now, being so great a general and man—or god—among these people, I had those about me who were sworn to my service and whom I could trust. For one of these, a prince of the Inca blood, of the House of Kari's mother, I sent and gave to him those knotted cords that were the proof of Larico's treachery, bidding him if aught of evil overtook me, or if I could not be found, to deliver them to the Inca on my behalf and with them the prisoned messenger who was in his keeping, but meanwhile to show them to no man. He bowed and swore by the Sun to do my bidding, thinking doubtless that, my work finished in this land, I purposed to return into the sea out of which I had risen, as doubtless a god could do.

Next I summoned the captains of the Chancas who had fought under me throughout the civil war, of whom about half remained alive, and bade them gather their men upon the ridge where I had stood at the beginning of the battle of the Field of Blood, and wait until I joined them there. If it chanced, however, that I did not appear within six days I commanded that they should march back to their own country and make report to King Huaracha that I had "returned into the sea" for reasons that he would guess. Also I commanded that eight famous warriors whom I named, men of my own bodyguard who had fought with me in all our battles and would have followed me through fire or water or the gates of Hell themselves, should come to the courtyard of my palace after nightfall, bringing a litter and disguised as its bearers, but having their arms hidden beneath their cloaks.

These matters settled, I waited upon the Inca Kari and craved of him leave to take a journey. I told him that I was weary with so much fighting and desired to rest amidst my friends the Chancas.

He gazed at me awhile, then stretched out his sceptre to me in token that my request was granted, and said in a sad voice:

"So you would leave me, my brother, because I cannot give you that which you desire. Bethink you. You will be no nearer to the Moon (by which he meant Quilla) at Chanca than you are at Cuzco and here, next to the Inca, you are the greatest in the Empire who by decree are named his brother and the general of his armies."

Now, though my gorge rose at it, I lied to him, saying:

"The Moon is set for me, so let her sleep whom I shall see no more. For the rest, learn, O Kari, that Huaracha has sworn to me that I shall be, not his brother but his son, and Huaracha is sick—they say to death."

"You mean that you would choose to be King over the Chancas rather than stand next to the throne among the Quichuas?" he said, scanning me sharply.

"Aye, Kari," I replied, still lying. "Since I must dwell in this strange land, I would do so as a king—no less."

"To that you have a right, Brother, who are far above us all. But when you are a king, what is your plan? Do you purpose to strive to conquer me and rule over Tavantinsuyu, as perchance you could do?"

"Nay, I shall never make war upon you, Kari, unless you break your treaty with the Chancas and strive to subdue them."

"Which I shall never do, Brother."

Then he paused awhile and spoke again with more passion that I had ever known in him, saying:

"Would that this woman who comes between us were dead. Would that she had never been born. In truth, I am minded to pray to my father, the Sun, that he will be pleased to take her to himself, for then perchance we two might be as we were in the old time yonder in your England, and when we faced perils side by side upon the ocean and in the forests. A curse on Woman the Divider, and all the curses of all the gods upon this woman whom I may not give to you. Had she been of my Household I would have bidden you to take her, yes, even if she were my wife, but she is the wife of the god and therefore I may not— alas! I may not," and he hid his face in his robe and groaned.

Now when I heard these words I grew afraid who knew well that she of whom the Inca prays the Sun that she may die, does die, and swiftly.

"Do not add to this lady's wrongs by robbing her of life as well as of sight and liberty, Kari," I said.

"Have no fear, Brother," he answered, "she is safe from me. No word shall pass my lips though it is true that in my heart I wish that she would die. Go your ways, Brother and Friend, and when you grow weary of kingship if it comes to you, as to tell truth already I grow weary, return to me. Perchance, forgetting that we had been kings, we might journey hence together over the world's edge."

Then he stood up on his throne and bowed towards me, kissing the air as though to a god, and taking the royal chain that every Inca wore from about his neck, set it upon mine. This done, turning, he left me without another word.

With a heavy heart I returned to my palace where I dwelt. At sundown I ate according to my custom, and dismissed those who waited upon me to the servants' quarters. There were but two of them for my private life was simple. Then I slept till past midnight and rising, went into the courtyard where I found the eight Chanca captains disguised as litter-bearers and with them the litter. I led them to an empty guard-house and bade them stay there in silence. After this I returned to my chamber and waited.

About two hours before the dawn Larico came, knocking on the side-door as we had planned. I opened to him and he entered disguised in a hooded cloak of sheep's wool which covered his robes and his face, such as priests wear when the weather is cold. He gave to me the garments of a priest of the Sun which he had brought with him in a cloth. I clothed myself in them though because of the fashion of them to do this I must be rid of my armour which would have betrayed me. Larico desired that I should take off the sword Wave-Flame also, but, mistrusting him, this I would not do, but made shift to hide it and my dagger beneath the priest's cloak. The armour I wrapped in a bundle and took with me.

Presently we went out, having spoken few words since the time for speech had gone by and peril or some fear of what might befall weighed upon our tongues. In the guard-house I found the Chancas at whom Larico looked curiously but said nothing. To them I gave the bundle of armour to be hidden in the litter and with it my long bow, having first revealed myself to them by lifting the hood of my cloak. Then I bade them follow me.

Larico and I walked in front and after us came the eight men, four of them bearing the empty litter, and the other four marching behind. This was well planned since if any saw us or if we met guards as once or twice we did, these thought that we were priests taking one who was sick or dead to be tended or to be made ready for burial. Once, however, we were challenged, but Larico spoke some word and we passed on without question.

At length in the darkness before the dawn we came to the private palace of dead Upanqui. At its garden gate Larico would have had me leave the litter with the eight Chanca warriors disguised as bearers. I refused, saying that they must come to the doors of the palace, and when he grew urgent, tapped my sword, whispering to him fiercely that he had best beware lest it should be he who stayed at the gate. Then he gave way and we advanced all of us across the garden to the door of the palace. Larico unlocked the door with a key and we entered, he and I alone, for here I bade the Chancas await my return.

We crept down a short passage that was curtained at its end. Passing the curtains I found myself in Upanqui's banqueting-hall. This hall was dimly lit with one hanging golden lamp. By its light I saw something more wondrous and of its sort more awful than ever I had seen in that strange land.

There, on a dais, in his chair of gold, sat dead Upanqui arrayed in all his gorgeous Inca robes and so marvellously preserved that he might have been a man asleep. With arms crossed and his sceptre at his side, he sat staring down the hall with fixed and empty eyes, a dreadful figure of life in death. About him and around the dais were set all his riches, vases and furniture of gold, and jewels piled in heaps, there to remain till the roof fell in and buried them, since on this hallowed wealth the boldest dared not lay a hand. In the centre of the hall, also, was a table prepared as though for feasters, for amid jewelled cups and platters stood the meats and wines which day by day were brought afresh by the Virgins of the Sun. Doubtless there were more wonders, but these I could not see because the light did not reach them, or to the doorways of the chambers that opened from the hall. Moreover, there was something else which caught my eye.

At the foot of the dais crouched a figure which at first I took to be that of some dead one also embalmed, perhaps a wife or daughter of the dead Inca who had been set with him in this place. While I stared at it the figure stirred, having heard our footsteps, rose and turned, standing so that the light from the hanging lamp fell full upon it. It was Quilla clad in white and purple with a golden likeness of the Sun blazoned upon her breast!

So beauteous did she look searching the darkness with great blind eyes and her rich flowing hair flowing from beneath her jewelled headdress, a diadem fashioned to resemble the Sun's rays, that my breath failed me and my heart stood still.

"There stands she whom you seek," muttered Larico in a mocking whisper, for here even he did not seem to dare to talk aloud. "Go take her, you whom men call a god, but I call a drunken fool ready to risk all for a woman's lips. Go take her and ask the blessing upon your kisses of yonder dead king whose holy rest you break."

"Be silent," I whispered back and passed round the table till I came face to face with Quilla. Then a strange dumbness fell upon me like a spell or dead Upanqui's curse, so that I could not speak.

I stood there staring at those beautiful blind eyes and the blind eyes stared back at me. Presently a look of understanding gathered on the face and Quilla spoke, or rather murmured to herself.

"Strange—but I could have sworn! Strange, but I seemed to feel!

Oh! I slept in my vigils upon that dead old man who in life was so foolish and in death appears to have become so wise, and sleeping I dreamed. I dreamed I heard a step I shall never hear again. I dreamed one was near me whom I shall never touch again. I will sleep once more, for in my darkness what are left to me save sleep and—death?"

Then at last I found my tongue and said hoarsely,

"Love is left, Quilla, and—life."

She heard and straightened herself. Her whole body seemed to become rigid as though with an agony of joy. Her blind eyes flashed, her lips quivered. She stretched out her hand, feeling at the darkness. Her fingers touched my forehead, and thence she ran them swiftly over my face.

"It is—dead or living—it is—" and she opened her arms.

Oh! was there ever anything more beautiful on the earth than this sight of the blind Quilla thus opening her arms to me there in the gorgeous house of death?

We clung and kissed. Then I thrust her away, saying:

"Come swiftly from this ill-omened place. All is ready. The Chancas wait."

She slipped her hand into mine and I turned to lead her away.

Then it was that I heard a low, mocking laugh, Larico's, I thought, heard also a sound of creeping footsteps around me. I looked. Out of the darkness that hid the doors of the chamber on the right appeared a giant form which I knew for that of Urco, and behind him others. I looked to the left and there were more of them, while in front beyond the gold-laid board stood the traitor, Larico, laughing.

"You have the first fruits, but it seems that another will reap the harvest, Lord-from-the-Sea," he jeered.

"Seize her," cried Urco in his guttural voice, pointing to Quilla with his mace, "and brain that white thief."

I drew Wave-Flame and strove to get at him, but from both sides men rushed in on me. One I cut down, but the others snatched Quilla away. I was surrounded, with no room to wield my sword, and already weapons flashed over me. A thought came to me. The Chancas were at the door. I must reach them, for perhaps so Quilla might be saved. In front was the table spread for the death feast. With a bound I leapt on to it, shouting aloud and scattering its golden furnishings this way and that. Beyond stood the traitor, Larico, who had trapped me—I sprang at him and lifting Wave-Flame with both hands I smote with all my strength. He fell, as it seemed to me, cloven to the middle. Then some spear cast at me struck the lamp.

It shattered and went out!

CHAPTER 12

The Fight to the Death

There was tumult in the hall; shoutings, groans from him whom I had first struck down, the sound of vases and vessels overthrown, and above all those of a woman's shrieks echoing from the walls and roof, so that I could not tell whence they came.

Through the gross darkness I went on towards the curtains, or so I hoped. Presently they were torn open, and by the faint light of the breaking dawn I saw my eight Chancas rushing towards me.

"Follow!" I cried, and at the head of them groped my way back up the hall, seeking for Quilla. I stumbled over the dead body of Larico and felt a path round the table. Then suddenly a door at the back of the hall was thrown open and by the grey light which came through the doorway I perceived the last of the ravishers departing. We scrambled across the dais where the golden chair was overthrown and the embalmed Upanqui lay, a stiff and huddled heap upon his back, staring at me with jewelled eyes.

We gained the door which, happily, none had remembered to close, and passed out into the park-like grounds beyond. A hundred paces or more ahead of us, by the glowing light, I saw a litter passing between the trees surrounded by armed men, and knew that in it was Quilla being borne to captivity and shame.

After it we sped. It passed the gate of the park wall, but when we reached that gate it was shut and barred and we must waste time breaking it down, which we did by help of a felled tree that lay at hand. We were through it, and now the rim of the sun had appeared so that through the morning mist, which clung to the hillside beyond the town, we could see the litter, the full half of a mile away. On we went up the hill, gaining as we ran, for we had no litter to bear, nor aught else save the sack of armour which one of the Chancas had thought to bring with him when he rushed into the hall, and with it my long bow and shaft.

Now, at a certain place between this hill and another there was a gorge such as are common in that country, a gorge so deep and narrow that in places the light of day scarcely struggles to the pathways at its bottom. Into this tunnel the litter vanished and when we drew near I saw that its mouth was held by armed men, six of them or more. Taking my bow from the Chanca I strung it and shot swiftly. The man at whom I aimed went down. Again I shot and another fell, whereon the rest of them took cover behind stones.

Throwing back the bow to the Chanca, for now it was useless, we charged. That business was soon over, for presently all those of Urco's men who remained there were dead, save one who, being cut off, fled down hill towards the city, taking with him the news of what had passed in the palace of dead Upanqui.

We entered the mouth of the gorge, plunging towards the gloom, though as it chanced this place faced towards the east, so that the low sun, which now was fully up, shone down it and gave us light that later would have been lacking.

I, who was very swift of foot and to whom rage and fear gave wings, outran my companions. Swinging myself round a rock which lay in the pathway, I saw the litter again not a hundred yards ahead. It halted because, as it seemed to me, one or more of the bearers stumbled and fell among the stones. I rushed at them, roaring. Perhaps it had been wiser to wait for my companions, but I was mad and feared nothing. They saw me and a cry went up of:

"The White God! The terrible White God!"

Then fear took hold of them and they fled, leaving the litter on the ground. Yes, all of them fled save one, Urco himself.

He stood there rolling his eyes and gnashing his teeth, looking huge and awful in those shadows, looking like a devil from hell. Suddenly a thought seemed to take him, and leaping at the litter he tore aside its curtains and dragged out Quilla, who fell prone upon the ground.

"If I may not have her, you shall not, White Thief. See! I give back his bride to the Sun," he shouted, and lifted his copper sword to pierce her through.

Now I was still ten paces or so away and saw that before I could reach him that sword would be in her heart. What could I do? Oh! St. Hubert must have helped me then for I knew in an instant. In my hand was Wave-Flame and with all my strength I hurled it at his head.

The great blade hurtled hissing through the air. I saw the sunlight shine on it. He strove to leap clear, but too late, for it caught him on the hand that he had lifted to protect his head, and shore off two of his fingers so that he dropped his sword. Next instant, still roaring, as doubtless old Thorgrimmer, my forefather, used to do when he fought to the death, for blood is very strong, I leapt on the giant, who like myself was swordless. There in the gulf we wrestled. He was a mighty man, but now my strength was as that of ten. I threw him to the ground by a Sussex trick I knew and there we rolled over and over each other. Once he had me undermost and I think would have choked me, had it not been that his right hand lacked two fingers.

With a mighty heave I lifted him so that now we lay side by side. He was groping for a knife—I did not see, but knew it. Near his head a sharp-edged stone rose in the path to the height of a man's hand or more. I saw it and bethought me what to do if I could. Again I heaved and as at length he found the knife and stabbed at me, scratching my face, I got his bull's neck upon that stone. Then I loosed my hand and caught him by the hair. Back I pressed his great head, back and back with all my might till something snapped.

Urco's neck was broken. Urco quivered and was dead!

I lay by his side, panting. A voice came from the white heap upon the ground by whom and for whom this dreadful combat had been fought, the voice of Quilla.

"One died, but who lives?" asked the voice.

I could not answer because I had no breath. All my strength was gone. Still I sat up, supporting myself with my hand and hoping that it would come back. Quilla turned her face towards me, or rather towards the sound that I had made in moving, and I thought to myself how sad it was that she should be blind. Presently she spoke again and now her voice quavered:

"I *see* who it is that lives," she said. "Something has broken in my eyes and, Lord and Love, I see that it is *you* who live. You, you, and oh! you bleed."

Then the Chancas came bounding down the gorge and found us.

They looked at the dead giant and saw how he had died, killed by strength, not by the sword; they looked and bent the knee and praised me, saying that I was indeed a god, since no man could have done this deed, killing the huge Urco with his naked hands. Then they placed Quilla back in her litter and six of them bore her down that black gorge. The two who remained, for in that fight none of them had been hurt, supported me till my strength came back, for the cut in the face that I had received from Urco's dagger was but slight. We reached the mouth of the gorge and took counsel.

To return to Cuzco after what I had done, would be to seek death. So we bore away to the right and, making a round, came about ten o'clock of the morning unmolested by any, to that ridge on which I had stood at the beginning of the battle of the Field of Blood. There I found the Chancas encamped, some three thousand of them, as I had commanded. When they saw me, living and but little hurt, they shouted for joy, and when they learned who was in that litter they went well-nigh mad.

Then the eight warriors with me told them all the tale of the saving of Quilla and the death of the giant Urco at my hands, whereon their captains came and kissed my feet, saying that I was in truth a god, though heretofore some of them had held me to be but a man.

"God or man," I answered, "I must rest. Let the women tend to lady Quilla, and give me food and drink, after which I will sleep. At sunset we march home to Huaracha, your king and mine, to give him back his daughter. Till then there is naught to fear, since Kari has no troops at hand with which to attack us. Still, set outposts."

So I ate and drank, but little of the former and much of the latter, I fear, and after that I slept as soundly as one who is dead, for I was outworn.

When the sun was within an hour of setting, captains awakened me and said that an embassy from Cuzco, ten men only, waited outside our lines, seeking speech with me. So I rose, and my face and wound having been dressed, caused water to be poured over my body, and was rubbed with oil; after which, clothed in the robes of a Chanca noble, but wearing no armour, I went out with nine Chanca captains to receive the embassy on the plain at the foot of the hill, at that very spot where first I had fought with Urco.

When we drew near, from out of the group of nobles advanced one man. I looked and saw that he was Kari, yes, the Inca himself.

I went forward to meet him and we spoke together just out of earshot of our followers.

"My brother," said Kari, "I have learned all that has passed and I give you praise who are the most daring among men and the first among warriors; you who slew the giant Urco with your naked hands."

"And thus made your throne safe for you, Kari."

"And thus made my throne safe for me. You also who clove Larico to the breast in the death-house of Upanqui, my father—"

"And thus delivered you from a traitor, Kari."

"And thus delivered me from a traitor, as I have learned also from your messenger who handed to me the knotted cord, and from the spy whom you had in your keeping. I repeat that you are the most daring among men and the first among warriors; almost a god as my people name you."

I bowed, and after a little silence he went on:

"Would that this were all that I have to say. But alas! it is not. You have committed the great sacrilege against the Sun, my father, of which I warned you, having robbed him of his bride, and, my brother, you have lied to me, who told me but yesterday that you had put all thought of her from your mind."

"To me that was no sacrilege, Kari, but rather a righteous deed, to free one from the bonds of a faith in which neither she nor I believe, and to lead her from a living tomb back to life and love."

"And was the lie righteous also, Brother?"

"Aye," I answered boldly, "if ever a lie can be. Bethink you. You prayed that this lady might die because she came between you and me, and those that kings pray may die, do die, if not with their knowledge or by their express command. Therefore I said that I had put her from my mind in order that she might go on living."

"To cherish you in her arms, Brother. Now hearken. Because of this deed of yours, we who were more than friends have become more than foes. You have declared war upon my god and me; therefore I declare war upon you. Yet hearken again. I do not wish that thousands of men should perish because of our quarrel. Therefore I make an offer to you. It is that you should fight me here and now, man to man, and let the Sun, or Pachacamac beyond the Sun, decide the matter as may be decreed."

"Fight *you!* Fight *you* Kari, the Inca," I gasped.

"Aye, fight me to the death, since between us all is over and done. In England you nurtured me. Here in the land of Tavantinsuyu, which I rule to-day, I have nurtured you, and in my shadow you have grown great, though it is true that had it not been for your generalship, perchance I should no longer be here to throw the shadow. Let us therefore set the one thing against the other and, forgetting all between us that is past, stand face to face as foes. Mayhap you will conquer me, being so mighty a man of war. Mayhap, also, if that chances, my people who look upon you as half a god will raise you up to be Inca after me, should such be your desire."

"It is not," I broke in.

"I believe you," he answered, bowing his head, "but will it not be the desire of that fair-faced harlot who has betrayed our Lord the Sun?"

At this word I started and bit my lip.

"Ah! that stings you," he went on, "as the truth always stings, and it is well. Understand, White Lord who were once my brother, that either you must fight me to the death, or I declare war upon you and upon the Chanca people, which war I will wage from month to month and from year to year until you are all destroyed, as destroyed you shall be. But should you fight and should the Sun give me the victory, then justice will be accomplished and I will keep the peace that I have sworn with the Chanca people. Further, should you conquer me, in the name of my people I swear that there shall still be peace between them and the Chancas, since I shall have atoned your sacrilege with my blood. Now summon those lords of yours and I will summon mine, and set out the matter to them."

So I turned and beckoned to my captains, and Kari beckoned to his. They came, and in the hearing of all, very clearly and quietly as was his fashion, he repeated every word that he had said to me, adding to them others of like meaning. While he spoke I thought, not listening over-much.

This thing was hateful to me, yet I was in a snare, since according to the customs of all these peoples I could not refuse such a challenge and remain unshamed. Moreover, it was to the advantage of the Chancas, aye, and of the Quichuas also, that I should not refuse it seeing that whether I lived or died, peace would then reign between them who otherwise must both be destroyed by war. I remembered how once Quilla had sacrificed herself to prevent such a war, though in the end that war had come; and what Quilla had done, should I not do also? Weary though I was I did not fear Kari, brave and swift as he might be, indeed I thought that I could kill him and perhaps take his throne, since the Quichuas worshipped me, who so often had led their armies to triumph, almost as much as did the Chancas. But—I could not kill Kari. As soon would I kill one born of my own mother. Was there then no escape?

The answer rose in my mind. There was an escape. I could suffer Kari to kill me. Only if I did this, what of Quilla! After all that had come and gone, must I lose Quilla thus, and must Quilla lose me? Surely she would break her heart and die. My plight was desperate. I knew not what to do. Then of a sudden, while I wavered, some voice seemed to whisper in my ear; I thought it must be that of St. Hubert. It seemed to say to me, "Kari trusts to his god, cannot you trust to yours, Hubert of Hastings, you who are a Christian man? Go forward, and trust to yours, Hubert of Hastings."

Kari's gentle voice died away; he had finished his speech and all men looked at me.

"What word?" I said roughly to my captains.

"Only this, Lord," answered their spokesman, "Fight you must, of that there can be no doubt, but we would fight with you, the ten of the Chancas against the ten of the Quichuas."

"Aye, that is good," replied the first of Kari's nobles. "This business is too great to set upon one man's skill and strength."

"Have done!" I said. "It lies between the Inca and myself," while Kari nodded, and repeated "Have done!" after me.

Then I sent one of the captains back to the camp for my sword and Kari commanded that his should be brought to him, since according to the custom of these people when ambassadors meet, neither of us was armed. Presently, the captain holding my sword returned, and with him servants who brought my armour. Also after them streamed all the army of the Chancas among whom the news had spread like wind-driven fire, and lined themselves upon the ridge to watch. As he came, too, I noticed that this captain sharpened Wave-Flame with a certain kind of stone that was used to give a keen edge to weapons.

He brought the ancient weapon and handed it to me on his knee. The Inca's man also brought his sword and handed it to him, as he did so, bowing his forehead to the dust. Well I knew that weapon, since once before I had faced it in desperate battle for my life. It was the ivory-handled sword of the lord Deleroy which Kari had taken from his dead hand after I slew him in the Solar of my house in the Cheap at London. Then the servant came to me with the armour, but I sent him away, saying that as the Inca had none, I would not wear it, at which my people murmured.

Kari saw and heard.

"Noble as ever," he said aloud. "Oh! that such bright honour should have been tarnished by a woman's breath."

Our lords discussed the manner of our fighting, but to them I paid little heed.

At length all was ready and we stepped forward to face each other at a given word, clad much alike. I had thrown off my outer garment and stood bareheaded in a jerkin of soft sheepskin. Kari, too, was stripped of his splendid dress and clad in a tunic of sheepskin. Also, that we might be quite equal, he had taken off his turban-like headgear and even the royal Fringe, whereat his lords stared at each other for they thought this a bad omen.

It was just then I heard a sound behind me, and turning my head I saw Quilla stumbling towards us down the stony slope as best her half-blind eyes would let her, and crying as she came:

"Oh! my Lord, fight not. Inca, I will return to the House of the Sun!"

"Silence, accursed woman!" said Kari, frowning. "Does the Sun take back such as you? Silence until the woe that you have wrought is finished, and then wail on forever."

She shrank back at his bitter, unjust words, and guided by the women who had followed her, sank upon a stone, where she sat still as a statue or as dead Upanqui in his hall.

Now one called aloud the pledges of the fight which were as Kari had spoken them. He listened and added:

"Be it known, also, that this battle is to the death of one or both of us, since if we live I take back my oaths and I will burn yonder witch as a sacrifice to the Sun whom she has betrayed, and destroy her people and her city according to the ancient law of Vengeance on the House of those who have deceived the Sun."

I heard but made no answer, who did not wish to waste my breath in bandying words with a great man, whose brain had been turned by bigotry and woman-hatred.

A moment later the signal was given and we were at it. Kari leapt at me like the tree-lion of his own forests, but I avoided and parried. Thrice he leapt and thrice I did this; yes, even when I saw an opening and might have cut him down. Almost I struck, then could not. The Chancas watched me, wondering what game I played who was not wont to fight in this fashion, and I also wondered, who still knew not what to do. Something I must do, or presently I should be slain, since soon my guard would fail and Deleroy's sword get home at last.

I think that Kari grew perplexed at this patient defence of mine, and never a blow struck back. At least he withdraw a little, then came for me with a rush, holding his sword high above his head with the purpose of striking me above that guard, or so I supposed. Then, of a sudden, I knew what to do. Wheeling Wave-Flame with all my strength in both hands, I smote, not at Kari but at the ivory handle of his sword. The keen and ancient steel that might well have been some of that which, as legend told, was forged by the dwarfs in Norseland, fell upon the ivory between his hand-grip and the cross-piece and shore through it as I had hoped that it would do, so that the blade of Kari's sword, severed just above the hilt, fell to the ground and the hilt itself was jarred from his hand.

His nobles saw and groaned while the Chancas shouted with joy, for now Kari was defenceless and save for the death itself, this fight to the death was ended.

Kari folded his arms upon his breast and bent his head.

"It is the decree of my god," he said, "and I did ill to trust to the sword of a villain whom you slew. Strike, Conqueror, and make an end."

I rested myself upon Wave-Flame and answered:

"If I strike not, O Inca, will you take back your words and let peace reign between your people and the Chancas?"

"Nay," he answered. "What I have said, I have said. If yonder false woman is given up to suffer the fate of those who have betrayed the Sun, then there shall be peace between the peoples, but not otherwise, since while I live I will wage war upon her and you, and upon the Chancas who shelter both of you."

Now rage took hold of me, who remembered that while this woman-hater lived blood must flow in streams, but that if he died there would be peace and Quilla would be safe. So I lifted my sword a little, and as I did so Quilla rose from her stone and stumbled forward, crying:

"O Lord, shed not the Inca's holy blood for me. Let me be given up! Let me be given up!"

Then some spirit entered into me and I spoke, saying:

"Lady, half of your prayer I grant and half I deny. I will not shed the Inca's blood; as soon would I shed yours. Nor will I suffer you to be given up who have done no wrong, since it was I who took you away by force, as Urco would have done. Kari, hearken to me. Not once only when we were in danger together in past days have you said to me that we must put our faith in the gods we worship, and thus we did. Now again I hearken to that counsel of yours and put my faith in the God I worship. You threaten to gather all the strength of your mighty empire, and because of what I hold to be your superstitions, to destroy the Chanca people to the last babe and to level their city to the last stone. I do not believe that the God I worship will suffer this to come about, though how he will stay your vengeance I do not know. Kari, great Inca of Tavantinsuyu, Lord of all this strange new world, I, the White Wanderer-from-the-Sea, give you your life and save you as once before I saved you in a far land, and with your life I give you my blessing in all matters but this one alone. Kari, my brother, look your last on me and go in peace."

The Inca heard, and raising his head, stared at me with his fine, melancholy eyes. Then suddenly from those eyes there came a gush of tears. More, he knelt before me and kissed the ground, as the humblest of his slaves might do before his own majesty.

"Most noble of men," he said, lifting himself up again, "I worship you. Yes, I, the Inca, worship you. Would that I might take back my oath, but this I cannot do because my god hardens my heart and then would decree destruction on my people. Mayhap he whom you serve will bring things to pass as you foretell, as it would seem he has brought it to pass that I should eat the dust before you. I hope that it may be so who love not the sight of blood, but who like the shot arrow must yet follow my course, driven by the strength that loosed me. Brother, honoured and beloved, fare you well! May happiness be yours in life and death, and there in death may we meet again and once more be brothers where no women come to part us."

****

Then Kari turned and went with bowed head, together with his nobles, who followed him as sadly as those who surround a corpse, but not until they had given to me that royal salute which is only rendered to the Inca in his glory.

CHAPTER 13

The Kiss of Quilla

Her women bore Quilla swooning from that ill-fated field, and sick and sad she remained until once more we saw the City of the Chancas. Yet all this while strength and sight were returning to her eyes, so that in the end she could see as well as ever she had done, for which I thanked Heaven.

Messengers had gone before us, so that when we drew near all the people of the Chancas came out to meet us, a mighty multitude, who spread flowers before us and sang songs of joy. On the same evening I was summoned by Huaracha and found him dying. There in the presence of his chief captains Quilla and I told him all our story, to which he listened, answering nothing. When it was finished he said:

"I thank you, Lord-from-the-Sea, who through great perils have saved my daughter and brought her home to bid farewell to me, untarnished as she went. I understand now that it was an evil policy which led me to promise her in marriage to the prince Urco. Through your valour it has come to naught and I am glad. Great dangers still lie ahead of you and of my people. Deal with them as you will and can, for henceforward, Lord-from-the-Sea, they are your people, yours and my daughter's together, since it is my desire and command that you two should wed so soon as I am laid with my fathers. Perchance it had been better if you had slain the Inca when he was in your hand, but man goes where his spirit leads him. My blessing and the blessing of my gods be on you both and on your children. Leave me, for I can say no more."

That night King Huaracha died.

Three days later he was buried with great pomp beneath the floor of the Temple of the Moon, not being preserved and kept above ground after the fashion of the Incas.

On the last day of the mourning a council was summoned of all the great ones in the country to the number of several hundreds, to which I was bidden. This was done in the name of Quilla, who was now named by a title which meant, "High Lady," or "Queen." I went to it eagerly enough who had seen nothing of her since that night of her father's death, for, according to the custom of this people, she had spent the time of mourning alone with her women.

To my surprise I was led by an officer, not into the great hall where I knew the notables were assembling, but to that same little chamber where first I had talked with Huaracha, Quilla's father. Here the officer left me wondering. Presently I heard a sound and looking up, saw Quilla herself standing between the curtains, like to a picture in its frame. She was royally arrayed and wore upon her brow and breast the emblem of the moon, so that she seemed to glitter in that dusky place, though nothing about her shone with such a light as did her large and doe-like eyes.

"Greeting, my Lord," she said in her soft voice, curtseying to me as she spoke. "Has my Lord aught to say to me? If so, it must be quick, since the Great Council waits."

Now I grew foolish and tongue-tied, but at length stammered out:

"Nothing, except what I have said before—that I love you."

She smiled a little in her slow fashion, then asked:

"Is there naught to add?"

"What can there be to add to love, Quilla?"

"I know not," she answered, still smiling. "Yet in what does the love of man and woman end?"

I shook my head and answered:

"In many things, all of them different. In hell sometimes, and more rarely in heaven."

"And on earth which lies between the two, should those who love escape death and separation?"

"Well, on earth—in marriage."

She looked at me again and this time a new light shone in her eyes which I could not misinterpret.

"Do you mean that you will marry me, Quilla?" I muttered.

"Such was my father's wish, Lord, but what is yours? Oh! have done," she went on in a changed voice. "For what have we suffered all these things and gone through such long partings and dangers so dreadful? Was it not that if Fate should spare us we might come together at last? And has not Fate spared us—for a while? What said the prophecy of me in the Temple of Rimac? Was it not that the Sun should be my refuge and—I forget the rest."

"I remember it," I said. "That in the beloved arms you should sleep at last."

"Yes," she went on, the blood mounting to her cheeks, "that in the beloved arms I should sleep at last. So, the first part of the prophecy has come true."

"As the rest shall come true," I broke in, awaking, and swept her to my breast.

"Are you sure," she murmured presently, "that you love me, a woman whom you think savage, well enough to wed me?"

"Aye, more than sure," I answered.

"Hearken, Lord. I knew it always, but being woman I desired to hear it from your own lips. Of this be certain: that though I am but what I am, a maiden, wild-hearted and untaught, no man shall ever have a truer and more loving wife. It is my hope, even that my love will be such that in it at last you may learn to forget that other lady far away who once was yours, if only for an hour."

Now I shrank as from a sword prick, since first loves, whatever the tale of them, as Quilla guessed or Nature taught her, are not easily forgot, and even when they are dead their ghosts will rise and haunt us.

"And my hope, most dear, is that you will be mine, not for an hour but for all our life's days," I answered.

"Aye," she said, sighing, "but who knows how many these will be? Therefore let us pluck the flowers before they wither. I hear steps. The lords come to summon us. Be pleased to enter the Council at my side and holding me by the hand. There I have somewhat to say to the people. The shadow of the Inca Kari, whom you spared, still lies cold upon us and them."

Before I could ask her meaning the lords entered, three of them, and glancing at us curiously, said that all were gathered. Then they turned and went before us to the great hall where every place was filled. Hand in hand we mounted the dais, and as we came all the audience rose and greeted us with a roar of welcome.

Quilla seated herself upon a throne and motioned to me to take my place upon another throne at her side, which I noted stood a little higher than that on which she sat, and this, as I learned afterwards, not by chance. It was planned so to tell the people, of the Chancas that henceforth I was their king while she was but my wife.

When the shouting had died away Quilla rose from her throne and began to speak, which like many of the higher class of this people she could do well enough.

"Lords and Captains of the Chanca nation," she said, "my father, the king Huaracha, being dead, leaving no lawful son, I have succeeded to his dignities, and summoned you here to take counsel with me.

"First, learn this, that I, your Queen and Lady, have been chosen as wife by him who sits at my side."

Here the company shouted again, thus announcing that this tidings pleased them. For though by now only the common people still believed me to be a god risen from the sea, all held that I was a great general and a great man, one who knew much that they did not know, and who could both lead and fight better than the best of them. Indeed, since I had slain Urco with my hands and overcome Kari, who as Inca was believed to be clothed with the strength of the Sun and therefore unconquerable, I was held to be unmatched throughout Tavantinsuyu. Moreover, the army that had fought under my command loved me as though I were their father as well as their general. Therefore all greeted this tidings well enough without astonishment, for they knew it was their dead king's wish that I should wed his daughter and that to win her I had gone through much.

In answer to their shoutings I, too, rose from my seat, and drawing the sword Wave-Flame, which I wore girt about my dinted armour, with it I saluted first Quilla and then the gathered nobles, saying:

"Lords of the Chancas, when on an island in the sea, my eyes fell upon this lady who to-day is your queen, I loved her and swore that I would wed her if I might. Between that day and this much has befallen. She was snatched away to be made the wife of Urco, heir to the Inca throne, and afterwards, to escape him whom she hated, she took refuge in the House of the Inca god. Then, people of the Chancas, came the great war which we shared together, and in the end I rescued her from that house of bondage, and slew Urco while he strove to steal or stab her. This done, I conquered Kari the Inca, who was as my brother, yet because I saved your lady from his god the Sun, became my enemy, and together she and I returned to this, her land. Now it is her will to wed me, as it has always been mine to wed her, and here in front of all of you I take her to wife, as she takes me to husband, hoping that for many years it may be given to us to rule over you, and to our children after us. Yet I warn you that although in the great war that has been, if with much loss, we have held our own against all the hosts of Cuzco and won an honourable peace, by this marriage of ours, which robs the Inca god of one of a thousand brides, that peace is broken. Therefore in the future, as in the past, there will be war between the Quichua and the Chanca peoples."

"We know it," shouted the nobles. "War is decreed, let war come!"

"What would you have had me do?" I went on. "Leave your queen to languish in the House of the Sun, wed to nothingness, or suffer her to be dragged away to be one of Urco's women, or hand her back to Kari to be slain as a sacrifice to a god whom you do not accept?"

"Nay!" they cried. "We would have her wed you, White Lord-from-the-Sea, that she may become a mother of kings."

"So I thought, Chancas. Yet I warn you that there is trouble near. The storm gathers and soon it will burst, since Kari is not one who breaks his oaths."

"Why did you not kill him when he was in your hand, and take his throne?" asked one.

"Because I could not. Because it would not have been pleasing to Heaven that I should slay a man who for years had been as my brother. Because in this way or in that the deed would have fallen back upon my head, upon the head of the lady Quilla, and upon your heads also, O people of the Chancas, because—"

At this moment there was disturbance at the end of the hall, and a herald cried: "An embassy! An embassy from Kari, the Inca."

"Let it be admitted," said Quilla.

Presently up the central passage marched the embassy with pomp, great lords and "earmen," every man of them, and bowed before us.

"Your words?" said Quilla quietly.

"They are these, Lady," answered the spokesman of the party. "For the last time the Inca demands that you should surrender yourself to be sacrificed as one who has betrayed the Sun. He asks it of you since he has learned that your father Huaracha is no more."

"And if I refuse to surrender myself, what then, O Ambassador?"

"Then in the name of the Empire and in his own name the Inca declares war upon you, war to the end, until not one of Chanca blood is left living beneath the sun and not one stone marks where your city stood. It may be that a while will pass before this sword of war falls upon your head, since the Inca must gather his armies and give a breathing space to his peoples after all the troubles that have been. Yet if not this year, then next year, and if not next year, then the year after, that sword shall fall."

Quilla listened and turned pale, though more, I think, with wrath than fear. Then she said:

"You have heard, Chancas, and know how stands this case. If I surrender myself to be sacrificed, the Inca in his mercy will spare you; if I do not surrender myself, soon or late he will destroy you—if he can. Say, then, shall I surrender myself?"

Now every man in that great hall leapt up and from every throat there arose a shout of,

"Never!"

When it had died away an aged chief and councillor, an uncle of Huaracha, the dead King, came forward and stared at the envoys with his horny eyes.

"Go back to the Inca," he said, "and tell him that the threats of the mouth are one thing and the deeds of the hand are another. In the late war that has been he has learned something of our quality, both as foes and friends, and perchance more remains for him to learn. Yonder is one"—and he pointed to myself—"who is about to become our King and the husband of our Queen. By the help of that one and of some of us the Inca won his throne. From the mercy of that one, also, but a little while ago the Inca won his life. Let him be careful lest through the might of that one, behind whom stands every Chanca that breathes, the Inca Kari Upanqui should yet lose both throne and life, and with them the ancient empire of the Sun. Thus say we all."

"Thus say we all!" repeated the great company with a roar that shook the walls.

In the silence that followed Quilla asked:

"Have you aught to add, O Ambassadors?"

"Ay, this," said the first of them.

"The Chanca tree is about to be cut down, but the Inca still offers a refuge to the Lion that hides among its branches because he has loved that Lion from of old. Let the White Lord-from-the-Sea over whom you have cast the net of your witcheries return with us and he shall be saved and given place and power, and with them a brother's love."

Now Quilla looked at me, and I rose to speak but could not, since all that came from my lips was laughter. At length I said:

"But the other day when I gave him his life, the Inca named me noble. What would he think of me if I said yes to this offer? Would he call me noble then and the Lion that dwells in the Chanca tree? Or, whatever his lips might speak, would not his heart name me the basest of slaves and no lion of the tree, but rather a snake that creeps at its roots? Get you gone, my lords, and say that here I bide happy with her whom I have won, and that the ancient sword Wave-Flame, on which Kari has looked of late, is still sharp and the arm that wields it is still strong, and that he will do well now that it has served his turn, to look on it no more," and again I drew the great blade and flashed it before their eyes there in that dusky hall.

Then, bowing courteously, for every man of them knew me and some of them loved me well, they turned and went. That was the last that ever I, Hubert of Hastings, saw of nobles of the Inca blood, though perchance, ere long, I shall meet them again in war.

"Let them be escorted safely from the city," commanded Quilla, and soldiers went to do her bidding.

When they had gone she issued another order, that the door should be closed and watchmen set about the hall, so that none could approach it unseen. Then after a pause she rose and spoke:

"My Lord," she said, "who soon, as I trust, will be my husband and my king, and you, the chosen of my people, hearken to me for I have a matter to lay before you. You have heard the Inca's message and you know that his words are not vain. He who is great in many ways, in one is small and narrow. He sets his god before his honour, and to satisfy his god, whom he thinks that I have outraged, is prepared to sacrifice his honour, and even to kill one to whom he owes all," and she touched me with her hand. "Moreover, these things he can do, not at once but in time to come, because for every man of ours he is able to gather ten. Therefore we stand thus; death and destruction stare us in the face."

She paused, and that old chief of whom I have spoken, asked in the midst of a silence, as I think was planned that he should ask:

"You have set our teeth in the bitter rind of truth. Is there no sweet fruit within? Can you not show us a way of escape, O Quilla, Daughter of the Moon, whose heart is fed with the wisdom of the Moon?"

"I believe that I can show you such a way," she answered. "You know the legend of our people—that in the old days, a thousand years ago—we came to this country out of the forests.

"You know, too, the legend tells that once far away, beyond the forest, there was a mighty empire of which the king sat in a City of Gold hidden within a ring of mountains. That king, it is said, had two sons, and when he died these sons made war upon each other, and one of them, my forefather, was defeated and driven away into the forests by those who clung to him. By boats he descended the river that runs through the forest, and at length with those who remained to him came to this land and there once more grew to be a king. Is it not so?"

"It is so," answered the aged chief. "The tale has come down to me through ten generations, and with it the prophecy that in a day to come the Chancas would return to that City of Gold whence they came and be welcomed of its people."

"I have heard that prophecy," said Quilla. "Moreover, of it I have

227

something to tell you. While I sat in despair and blindness in the Convent of the Sun at Cuzco it came into my mind and I brooded upon it much, who was always sure that the war between the Chancas and the armies of the Incas was but begun. In my darkness I prayed to my Mother, the Moon, for light and help. Long and often I prayed, and at length an answer came. One night the Spirit of the Moon appeared to my soul as a beautiful and shining goddess, and spoke to me.

""Be brave, Daughter,' she said, 'for all that seems to be lost shall yet be found again, and the light of a certain flashing sword shall pierce the blackness and give back vision to your eyes.' This, indeed, happened, my people, since it was when the sword of my Lord saved me from death at the hands of Urco that the first gleam of light returned to my darkened eyes.

""Be not afraid, moreover, for the Children of the Chancas who bow to me,' went on the shining Spirit of the Moon, 'since in the day of their danger I will show them a path towards my place of resting in the west. Yea, I will lead them far from wars and tyrannies back to that ancient city whence they came, and there they shall sleep in peace till all things are accomplished. Moreover, you shall be their ruler during your appointed days, you and another whom I led to you out of the deeps of the sea and showed to you sleeping in my beams.'

"Thus that Spirit spoke to me, Councillors, though at the time I did not know whether the vision were more than a happy dream. But now I do know that it was no dream, but the truth.

"For did not my sight begin to return to me in the flashing of the sword that is named Flame-of-the-Wave? And if this were true, why should not the rest be true also? People of the Chancas, I am your Queen to-day and my counsel to you is that we flee from this land before the Inca's net closes round us and the Inca's spears pierce our heart, to seek our ancient home far in the depths of the western forest where, as I trust, his armies cannot come. Is that your will, O my People? If so, by the tongues of your Lords and Captains declare it here and now before it be too late."

Back thundered the answer:

"It is our will, O Daughter of the Moon!"

When its echoes had died away Quilla turned to me, lovely to look on as the evening star and with eyes that shone like stars, and asked:

"Is it your will also, O Lord-from-the-Sea?"

"Your will is my will, Quilla," I answered, "and your heart is my home. Lead on; where you go I follow, even to the edge of the world and beyond the world."

"So be it!" she cried in a triumphant voice. "Now the evil past is finished with its fears and battles and before our feet, lit by moon-beams, stretches the Future's shining road leading us to the mystery in which all roads begin and for an hour are lost again. Now, too, our separations end in a perfect unity that perchance we have known before and shall know again in ages to be born and lands revisited. Now, Lord-from-the-Sea, at whose coming my sleeping heart awoke to love and whose sword saved me from shame and death, giving me back to life and light, here, before this company of our people, I, the Daughter of the Moon, defying the Sun who held me captive, and all his servants, take you to husband with this kiss," and leaning forward Quilla pressed her lips upon my own. . . .

****

The remaining parchment sheets of the ancient Manuscript are rotted with the damp of the tomb in which it lay for centuries and quite undecipherable. *Editor.*

Fair Margaret

CHAPTER 1

How Peter Met the Spaniard

It was a spring afternoon in the sixth year of the reign of King Henry VII. of England. There had been a great show in London, for that day his Grace opened the newly convened Parliament, and announced to his faithful people—who received the news with much cheering, since war is ever popular at first—his intention of invading France, and of leading the English armies in person. In Parliament itself, it is true, the general enthusiasm was somewhat dashed when allusion was made to the finding of the needful funds; but the crowds without, formed for the most part of persons who would not be called upon to pay the money, did not suffer that side of the question to trouble them. So when their gracious liege appeared, surrounded by his glittering escort of nobles and men-at-arms, they threw their caps into the air, and shouted themselves hoarse.

The king himself, although he was still young in years, already a weary-looking man with a fine, pinched face, smiled a little sarcastically at their clamour; but, remembering how glad he should be to hear it who still sat upon a somewhat doubtful throne, said a few soft words, and sending for two or three of the leaders of the people, gave them his royal hand, and suffered certain children to touch his robe that they might be cured of the Evil. Then, having paused a while to receive petitions from poor folk, which he handed to one of his officers to be read, amidst renewed shouting he passed on to the great feast that was made ready in his palace of Westminster.

Among those who rode near to him was the ambassador, de Ayala, accredited to the English Court by the Spanish sovereigns, Ferdinand and Isabella, and his following of splendidly attired lords and secretaries. That Spain was much in favour there was evident from his place in the procession. How could it be otherwise, indeed, seeing that already, four years or more before, at the age of twelve months, Prince Arthur, the eldest son of the king, had been formally affianced to the Infanta Catherine, daughter of Ferdinand and Isabella, aged one year and nine months? For in those days it was thought well that the affections of princes and princesses should be directed early into such paths as their royal parents and governors considered likely to prove most profitable to themselves.

At the ambassador's left hand, mounted on a fine black horse, and dressed richly, but simply, in black velvet, with a cap of the same material in which was fastened a single pearl, rode a tall cavalier. He was about five-and-thirty years of age, and very handsome, having piercing black eyes and a stern, clean-cut face.

In every man, it is said, there can be found a resemblance, often far off and fanciful enough, to some beast or bird or other creature, and certainly in this case it was not hard to discover. The man resembled an eagle, which, whether by chance or design, was the crest he bore upon his servants' livery, and the trappings of his horse. The unflinching eyes, the hooked nose, the air of pride and mastery, the thin, long hand, the quick grace of movement, all suggested that king of birds, suggested also, as his motto said, that what he sought he would find, and what he found he would keep. Just now he was watching the interview between the English king and the leaders of the crowd whom his Grace had been pleased to summon, with an air of mingled amusement and contempt.

"You find the scene strange, Marquis," said the ambassador, glancing at him shrewdly.

"*Señor*, here in England, if it pleases your Excellency," he answered gravely, "Señor d'Aguilar. The marquis you mentioned lives in Spain—an accredited envoy to the Moors of Granada; the Señor d'Aguilar, a humble servant of Holy Church," and he crossed himself, "travels abroad—upon the Church's business, and that of their Majesties'."

"And his own too, sometimes, I believe," answered the ambassador drily. "But to be frank, what I do not understand about you, Señor d'Aguilar, as I know that you have abandoned political ambitions, is why you do not enter my profession, and put on the black robe once and for all. What did I say—black? With your opportunities and connections it might be red by now, with a hat to match."

The Señor d'Aguilar smiled a little as he replied.

"You said, I think, that sometimes I travel on my own business. Well, there is your answer. You are right, I have abandoned worldly ambitions—most of them. They are troublesome, and for some people, if they be born too high and yet not altogether rightly, very dangerous. The acorn of ambition often grows into an oak from which men hang."

"Or into a log upon which men's heads can be cut off. Señor, I congratulate you. You have the wisdom that grasps the substance and lets the shadows flit. It is really very rare."

"You asked why I do not change the cut of my garments," went on d'Aguilar, without noticing the interruption. "Excellency, to be frank, because of my own business. I have failings like other men. For instance, wealth is that substance of which you spoke, rule is the shadow; he who has the wealth has the real rule. Again, bright eyes may draw me, or a hate may seek its slaking, and these things do not suit robes, black or red."

"Yet many such things have been done by those who wore them," replied the ambassador with meaning.

"Aye, Excellency, to the discredit of Holy Church, as you, a priest, know better than most men. Let the earth be evil as it must; but let the Church be like heaven above it, pure, unstained, the vault of prayer, the house of mercy and of righteous judgment, wherein walks no sinner such as I," and again he crossed himself.

There was a ring of earnestness in the speaker's voice that caused de Ayala, who knew something of his private reputation, to look at him curiously.

"A true fanatic, and therefore to us a useful man," he thought to himself, "though one who knows how to make the best of two worlds as well as most of them;" but aloud he said, "No wonder that our Church rejoices in such a son, and that her enemies tremble when he lifts her sword. But, Señor, you have not told me what you think of all this ceremony and people."

"The people I know well, Excellency, for I dwelt among them in past years and speak their language; and that is why I have left Granada to look after itself for a while, and am here to-day, to watch and make report—" He checked himself, then added, "As for the ceremony, were I a king I would have it otherwise. Why, in that house just now those vulgar Commons—for so they call them, do they not?—almost threatened their royal master when he humbly craved a tithe of the country's wealth to fight the country's war. Yes, and I saw him turn pale and tremble at the rough voices, as though their echoes shook his throne. I tell you, Excellency, that the time will come in this land when those Commons will be king. Look now at that fellow whom his Grace holds by the hand, calling him 'sir' and 'master,' and yet whom he knows to be, as I do, a heretic, a Jew in disguise, whose sins, if he had his rights, should be purged by fire. Why, to my knowledge last night, that Israelite said things against the Church—"

"Whereof the Church, or its servant, doubtless made notes to be used when the time comes," broke in de Ayala. "But the audience is done, and his Highness beckons us forward to the feast, where there will be no heretics to vex us, and, as it is Lent, not much to eat. Come, Señor! for we stop the way."

Three hours had gone by, and the sun sank redly, for even at that spring season it was cold upon the marshy lands of Westminster, and there was frost in the air. On the open space opposite to the banqueting-hall, in front of which were gathered squires and grooms with horses, stood and walked many citizens of London, who, their day's work done, came to see the king pass by in state. Among these were a man and a lady, the latter attended by a handsome young woman, who were all three sufficiently striking in appearance to attract some notice in the throng.

The man, a person of about thirty years of age, dressed in a merchant's robe of cloth, and wearing a knife in his girdle, seemed over six feet in height, while his companion, in her flowing, fur-trimmed cloak, was, for a woman, also of unusual stature. He was not, strictly speaking, a handsome man, being somewhat too high of forehead and prominent of feature; moreover, one of his clean-shaven cheeks, the right, was marred by the long, red scar of a sword-cut which stretched from the temple to the strong chin. His face, however, was open and manly, if rather stern, and the grey eyes were steady and frank. It was not the face of a merchant, but rather that of one of good degree, accustomed to camps and war. For the rest, his figure was well-built and active, and his voice when he spoke, which was seldom, clear and distinct to loudness, but cultivated and pleasant—again, not the voice of a merchant.

Of the lady's figure little could be seen because of the long cloak that hid it, but the face, which appeared within its hood when she turned and the dying sunlight filled her eyes, was lovely indeed, for from her birth to her death-day Margaret Castell—fair Margaret, as she was called—had this gift to a degree that is rarely granted to woman. Rounded and flower-like was that face, most delicately tinted also, with rich and curving lips and a broad, snow-white brow. But the wonder of it, what distinguished her above everything else from other beautiful women of her time, was to be found in her eyes, for these were not blue or grey, as might have been expected from her general colouring, but large, black, and lustrous; soft, too, as the eyes of a deer, and overhung by curling lashes of an ebon black. The effect of these eyes of hers shining above those tinted cheeks and beneath the brow of ivory whiteness was so strange as to be almost startling. They caught the beholder and held him, as might the sudden sight of a rose in snow, or the morning star hanging luminous among the mists of dawn. Also, although they were so gentle and modest, if that beholder chanced to be a man on the good side of fifty it was often long before he could forget them, especially if he were privileged to see how well they matched the hair of chestnut, shading into black, that waved above them and fell, tress upon tress, upon the shapely shoulders and down to the slender waist.

Peter Brome, for he was so named, looked a little anxiously about him at the crowd, then, turning, addressed Margaret in his strong, clear voice.

"There are rough folk around," he said; "do you think you should stop here? Your father might be angered, Cousin."

Here it may be explained that in reality their kinship was of the slightest, a mere dash of blood that came to her through her mother. Still they called each other thus, since it is a convenient title that may mean much or nothing.

"Oh! why not?" she answered in her rich, slow tones, that had in them some foreign quality, something soft and sweet as the caress of a southern wind at night. "With you, Cousin," and she glanced approvingly at his stalwart, soldier-like form, "I have nothing to fear from men, however rough, and I do greatly want to see the king close by, and so does Betty. Don't you, Betty?" and she turned to her companion.

Betty Dene, whom she addressed, was also a cousin of Margaret, though only a distant connection of Peter Brome. She was of very good blood, but her father, a wild and dissolute man, had broken her mother's heart, and, like that mother, died early, leaving Betty dependent upon Margaret's mother, in whose house she had been brought up. This Betty was in her way remarkable, both in body and mind. Fair, splendidly formed, strong, with wide, bold, blue eyes and ripe red lips, such was the fashion of her. In speech she was careless and vigorous. Fond of the society of men, and fonder still of their admiration, for she was romantic and vain, Betty at the age of five-and-twenty was yet an honest girl, and well able to take care of herself, as more than one of her admirers had discovered. Although her position was humble, at heart she was very proud of her lineage, ambitious also, her great desire being to raise herself by marriage back to the station from which her father's folly had cast her down—no easy business for one who passed as a waiting-woman and was without fortune.

For the rest, she loved and admired her cousin Margaret more than any one on earth, while Peter she liked and respected, none the less perhaps because, try as she would—and, being nettled, she did try hard enough—her beauty and other charms left him quite unmoved.

In answer to Margaret's question she laughed and answered:

"Of course. We are all too busy up in Holborn to get the chance of so many shows that I should wish to miss one. Still, Master Peter is very wise, and I am always counselled to obey him. Also, it will soon be dark."

"Well, well," said Margaret with a sigh and a little shrug of her shoulders, "as you are both against me, perhaps we had best be going. Next time I come out walking, cousin Peter, it shall be with some one who is more kind."

Then she turned and began to make her way as quickly as she could through the thickening crowd. Finding this difficult, before Peter could stop her, for she was very swift in her movements, Margaret bore to the right, entering the space immediately in front of the banqueting-hall where the grooms with horses and soldiers were assembled awaiting their lords, for here there was more room to walk. For a few moments Peter and Betty were unable to escape from the mob which closed in behind her, and thus it came about that Margaret found herself alone among these people, in the midst, indeed, of the guard of the Spanish ambassador de Ayala, men who were notorious for their lawlessness, for they reckoned upon their master's privilege to protect them. Also, for the most part, they were just then more or less in liquor.

One of these fellows, a great, red-haired Scotchman, whom the priest-diplomatist had brought with him from that country, where he had also been ambassador, suddenly perceiving before him a woman who appeared to be young and pretty, determined to examine her more closely, and to this end made use of a rude stratagem. Pretending to stumble, he grasped at Margaret's cloak as though to save himself, and with a wrench tore it open, revealing her beautiful face and graceful figure.

"A dove, comrades!—a dove!" he shouted in a voice thick with drink, "who has flown here to give me a kiss." And, casting his long arms about her, he strove to draw her to him.

"Peter! Help me, Peter!" cried Margaret as she struggled fiercely in his grip.

"No, no, if you want a saint, my bonny lass," said the drunken Scotchman, "Andrew is as good as Peter," at which witticism those of the others who understood him laughed, for the man's name was Andrew.

Next instant they laughed again, and to the ruffian Andrew it seemed as though suddenly he had fallen into the power of a whirlwind. At least Margaret was wrenched away from him, while he spun round and round to fall violently upon his face.

"That's Peter!" exclaimed one of the soldiers in Spanish.

"Yes," answered another, "and a patron saint worth having"; while a third pulled the recumbent Andrew to his feet.

The man looked like a devil. His cap had gone, and his fiery red hair was smeared with mud. Moreover, his nose had been broken on a cobble stone, and blood from it poured all over him, while his little red eyes glared like a ferret's, and his face turned a dirty white with pain and rage. Howling out something in Scotch, of a sudden he drew his sword and rushed straight at his adversary, purposing to kill him.

Now, Peter had no sword, but only his short knife, which he found no time to draw. In his hand, however, he carried a stout holly staff shod with iron, and, while Margaret clasped her hands and Betty screamed, on this he caught the descending blow, and, furious as it was, parried and turned it. Then, before the man could strike again, that staff was up, and Peter had leapt upon him. It fell with fearful force, breaking the Scotchman's shoulder and sending him reeling back.

"Shrewdly struck, Peter! Well done, Peter!" shouted the spectators.

But Peter neither saw nor heard them, for he was mad with rage at the insult that had been offered to Margaret. Up flew the iron-tipped staff again, and down it came, this time full on Andrew's head, which it shattered like an egg-shell, so that the brute fell backwards, dead.

For a moment there was silence, for the joke had taken a tragic turn. Then one of the Spaniards said, glancing at the prostrate form:

"Name of God! our mate is done for. That merchant hits hard."

Instantly there arose a murmur among the dead man's comrades, and one of them cried:

"Cut him down!"

Understanding that he was to be set on, Peter sprang forward and snatched the Scotchman's sword from the ground where it had fallen, at the same time dropping his staff and drawing his dagger with the left hand. Now he was well armed, and looked so fierce and soldier-like as he faced his foes, that, although four or five blades were out, they held back. Then Peter spoke for the first time, for he knew that against so many he had no chance.

"Englishmen," he cried in ringing tones, but without shifting his head or glance, "will you see me murdered by these Spanish dogs?"

There was a moment's pause, then a voice behind cried:

"By God! not I," and a brawny Kentish man-at-arms ranged up beside him, his cloak thrown over his left arm, and his sword in his right hand.

"Nor I," said another. "Peter Brome and I have fought together before."

"Nor I," shouted a third, "for we were born in the same Essex hundred."

And so it went on, until there were as many stout Englishmen at his side as there were Spaniards and Scotchmen before him.

"That will do," said Peter, "we want no more than man to man. Look to the women, comrades behind there. Now, you murderers, if you would see English sword-play, come on, or, if you are afraid, let us go in peace."

"Yes, come on, you foreign cowards," shouted the mob, who did not love these turbulent and privileged guards.

By now the Spanish blood was up, and the old race-hatred awake. In broken English the sergeant of the guard shouted out some filthy insult about Margaret, and called upon his followers to "cut the throats of the London swine." Swords shone red in the red sunset light, men shifted their feet and bent forward, and in another instant a great and bloody fray would have begun.

But it did not begin, for at that moment a tall *señor*, who had been standing in the shadow and watching all that passed, walked between the opposing lines, as he went striking up the swords with his arm.

"Have done," said d'Aguilar quietly, for it was he, speaking in Spanish. "You fools! do you want to see every Spaniard in London torn to pieces? As for that drunken brute," and he touched the corpse of Andrew with his foot, "he brought his death upon himself. Moreover, he was not a Spaniard, there is no blood quarrel. Come, obey me! or must I tell you who I am?"

"We know you, Marquis," said the leader in a cowed voice. "Sheath your swords, comrades; after all, it is no affair of ours."

The men obeyed somewhat unwillingly; but at this moment arrived the ambassador de Ayala, very angry, for he had heard of the death of his servant, demanding, in a loud voice, that the man who had killed him should be given up.

"We will not give him up to a Spanish priest," shouted the mob. "Come and take him if you want him," and once more the tumult grew, while Peter and his companions made ready to fight.

Fighting there would have been also, notwithstanding all that d'Aguilar could do to prevent it; but of a sudden the noise began to die away, and a hush fell upon the place. Then between the uplifted weapons walked a short, richly clad man, who turned suddenly and faced the mob. It was King Henry himself.

"Who dare to draw swords in my streets, before my very palace doors?" he asked in a cold voice.

A dozen hands pointed at Peter.

"Speak," said the king to him.

"Margaret, come here," cried Peter; and the girl was thrust forward to him.

"Sire," he said, "that man," and he pointed to the corpse of Andrew, "tried to do wrong to this maiden, John Castell's child. I, her cousin, threw him down. He drew his sword and came at me, and I killed him with my staff. See, it lies there. Then the Spaniards—his comrades—would have cut me down, and I called for English help. Sire, that is all."

The king looked him up and down.

"A merchant by your dress," he said; "but a soldier by your mien. How are you named?"

"Peter Brome, Sire."

"Ah! There was a certain Sir Peter Brome who fell at Bosworth Field—not fighting for me," and he smiled. "Did you know him perchance?"

"He was my father, Sire, and I saw him slain—aye, and slew the slayer."

"Well can I believe it," answered Henry, considering him. "But how comes it that Peter Brome's son, who wears that battle scar across his face, is clad in merchant's woollen?"

"Sire," said Peter coolly, "my father sold his lands, lent his all to the Crown, and I have never rendered the account. Therefore I must live as I can."

The king laughed outright as he replied:

"I like you, Peter Brome, though doubtless you hate me."

"Not so, Sire. While Richard lived I fought for Richard. Richard is gone; and, if need be, I would fight for Henry, who am an Englishman, and serve England's king."

"Well said, and I may have need of you yet, nor do I bear you any grudge. But, I forgot, is it thus that you would fight for me, by causing riot in my streets, and bringing me into trouble with my good friends the Spaniards?"

"Sire, you know the story."

"I know your story, but who bears witness to it? Do you, maiden, Castell the merchant's daughter?"

"Aye, Sire. The man whom my cousin killed maltreated me, whose only wrong was that I waited to see your Grace pass by. Look on my torn cloak."

"Little wonder that he killed him for the sake of those eyes of yours, maiden. But this witness may be tainted." And again he smiled, adding, "Is there no other?"

Betty advanced to speak, but d'Aguilar, stepping forward, lifted his bonnet from his head, bowed and said in English:

"Your Grace, there is; I saw it all. This gallant gentleman had no blame. It was the servants of my countryman de Ayala who were to blame, at any rate at first, and afterwards came the trouble."

Now the ambassador de Ayala broke in, claiming satisfaction for the killing of his man, for he was still very angry, and saying that if it were not given, he would report the matter to their Majesties of Spain, and let them know how their servants were treated in London.

At these words Henry grew grave, who, above all things, wished to give no offence to Ferdinand and Isabella.

"You have done an ill day's work, Peter Brome," he said, "and one of which my attorney must consider. Meanwhile, you will be best in safe keeping," and he turned as though to order his arrest.

"Sire," exclaimed Peter, "I live at Master Castell's house in Holborn, nor shall I run away."

"Who will answer for that," asked the king, "or that you will not make more riots on your road thither?"

"I will answer, your Grace," said d'Aguilar quietly, "if this lady will permit that I escort her and her cousin home. Also," he added in a low voice, "it seems to me that to hale him to a prison would be more like to breed a riot than to let him go."

Henry glanced round him at the great crowd who were gathered watching this scene, and saw something in their faces which caused him to agree with d'Aguilar.

"So be it, Marquis," he said. "I have your word, and that of Peter Brome, that he will be forthcoming if called upon. Let that dead man be laid in the Abbey till to-morrow, when this matter shall be inquired of. Excellency, give me your arm; I have greater questions of which I wish to speak with you ere we sleep."

CHAPTER 2

John Castell

When the king was gone, Peter turned to those men who had stood by him and thanked them very heartily. Then he said to Margaret:

"Come, Cousin, that is over for this time, and you have had your wish and seen his Grace. Now, the sooner you are safe at home, the better I shall be pleased."

"Certainly," she replied. "I have seen more than I desire to see again. But before we go let us thank this Spanish *señor—*" and she paused.

"D'Aguilar, Lady, or at least that name will serve," said the Spaniard in his cultured voice, bowing low before her, his eyes fixed all the while upon her beautiful face.

"Señor d'Aguilar, I thank you, and so does my cousin, Peter Brome, whose life perhaps you saved—don't you, Peter? Oh! and so will my father."

"Yes," answered Peter somewhat sulkily, "I thank him very much; though as for my life, I trusted to my own arm and to those of my friends there. Good night, Sir."

"I fear, Señor," answered d'Aguilar with a smile, "that we cannot part just yet. You forget, I have become bond for you, and must therefore accompany you to where you live, that I may certify the place. Also, perhaps, it is safest, for these countrymen of mine are revengeful, and, were I not with you, might waylay you."

Now, seeing from his face that Peter was still bent upon declining this escort, Margaret interposed quickly.

"Yes, that is wisest, also my father would wish it. Señor, I will show you the way," and, accompanied by d'Aguilar, who gallantly offered her his arm, she stepped forward briskly, leaving Peter to follow with her cousin Betty.

Thus they walked in the twilight across the fields and through the narrow streets beyond that lay between Westminster and Holborn.

In front tripped Margaret beside her stately cavalier, with whom she was soon talking fast enough in Spanish, a tongue which, for reasons that shall be explained, she knew well, while behind, the Scotchman's sword still in his hand, and the handsome Betty on his arm, came Peter Brome in the worst of humours.

John Castell lived in a large, rambling, many-gabled, house, just off the main thoroughfare of Holborn, that had at the back of it a garden surrounded by a high wall. Of this ancient place the front part served as a shop, a store for merchandise, and an office, for Castell was a very wealthy trader—how wealthy none quite knew—who exported woollen and other goods to Spain under the royal licence, bringing thence in his own ships fine, raw Spanish wool to be manufactured in England, and with it velvet, silks, and wine from Granada; also beautiful inlaid armour of Toledo steel. Sometimes, too, he dealt in silver and copper from the mountain mines, for Castell was a banker as well as a merchant, or rather what answered to that description in those days.

It was said that beneath his shop were dungeon-like store-vaults, built of thick cemented stone, with iron doors through which no thief could break, and filled with precious things. However this might be, certainly in that great house, which in the time of the Plantagenets had been the fortified palace of a noble, existed chambers whereof he alone knew the secret, since no one else, not even his daughter or Peter, ever crossed their threshold. Also, there slept in it a number of men-servants, very stout fellows, who wore knives or swords beneath their cloaks, and watched at night to see that all was well. For the rest, the living-rooms of this house where Castell, Margaret his daughter, and Peter dwelt, were large and comfortable, being new panelled with oak after the Tudor fashion, and having deep windows that looked out upon the garden.

When Peter and Betty reached the door, not that which led into the shop, but another, it was to find that Margaret and d'Aguilar, who were walking very quickly, must have already passed it, since it was shut, and they had vanished. At his knock—a hard one—a serving-man opened, and Peter strode through the vestibule, or ante-chamber, into the hall, where for the most part they ate and sat, for thence he heard the sound of voices. It was a fine room, lit by hanging lamps of olive oil, and having a large, open hearth where a fire burned pleasantly, while the oaken table in front of it was set for supper. Margaret, who had thrown off her cloak, stood warming herself at the fire, and the Señor d'Aguilar, comfortably seated in a big chair, which he seemed to have known for years, leaned back, his bonnet in his hand, and watched her idly.

Facing them stood John Castell, a stout, dark-bearded man of between fifty and sixty years of age, with a clever, clean-cut face and piercing black eyes. Now, in the privacy of his home, he was very richly attired in a robe trimmed with the costliest fur, and fastened with a gold chain that had a jewel on its clasp. When Castell served in his shop or sat in his counting-house no merchant in London was more plainly dressed; but at night, loving magnificence at heart, it was his custom thus to indulge in it, even when there were none to see him. From the way in which he stood, and the look upon his face, Peter knew at once that he was much disturbed. Hearing his step, Castell wheeled round and addressed him at once in the clear, decided voice which was his characteristic.

"What is this I am told, Peter? A man killed by you before the palace gates? A broil! A public riot in which things went near to great bloodshed between the English, with you at the head of them, and the bodyguard of his Excellency, de Ayala. You arrested by the king, and bailed out by this *señor*. Is all this true?"

"Quite," answered Peter calmly.

"Then I am ruined; we are all ruined. Oh! it was an evil hour when I took one of your bloodthirsty trade into my house. What have you to say?"

"Only that I want my supper," said Peter. "Those who began the story can finish it, for I think their tongues are nimbler than my own," and he glanced wrathfully at Margaret, who laughed outright, while even the solemn d'Aguilar smiled.

"Father," broke in Margaret, "do not be angry with cousin Peter, whose only fault is that he hits too hard. It is I who am to blame, for I wished to stop to see the king against his will and Betty's, and then— then that brute," and her eyes filled with tears of shame and anger, "caught hold of me, and Peter threw him down, and afterwards, when he attacked him with a sword, Peter killed him with his staff, and—all the rest happened."

"It was beautifully done," said d'Aguilar in his soft voice and foreign accent. "I saw it all, and made sure that you were dead. The parry I understood, but the way you got your smashing blow in before he could thrust again—ah! that—"

"Well, well," said Castell, "let us eat first and talk afterwards. Señor d'Aguilar, you will honour my poor board, will you not, though it is hard to come from a king's feast to a merchant's fare?"

"It is I who am honoured," answered d'Aguilar; "and as for the feast, his Grace is sparing in this Lenten season. At least, I could get little to eat, and, therefore, like the *señor* Peter, I am starved."

Castell rang a silver bell which stood near by, whereon servants brought in the meal, which was excellent and plentiful. While they were setting it on the table, the merchant went to a cupboard in the wainscoting, and took thence two flasks, which he uncorked himself with care, saying that he would give the *señor* some wine of his own country. This done, he said a Latin grace and crossed himself, an example which d'Aguilar followed, remarking that he was glad to find that he was in the house of a good Christian.

"What else did you think that I should be?" asked Castell, glancing at him shrewdly.

"I did not think at all, Señor," he answered; "but alas! every one is not a Christian. In Spain, for instance, we have many Moors and—Jews."

"I know," said Castell, "for I trade with them both."

"Then you have never visited Spain?"

"No; I am an English merchant. But try that wine, Señor; it came from Granada, and they say that it is good."

D'Aguilar tasted it, then drank off his glass.

"It is good, indeed," he said; "I have not its equal in my own cellars there."

"Do you, then, live in Granada, Señor d'Aguilar?" asked Castell.

"Sometimes, when I am not travelling. I have a house there which my mother left me. She loved the town, and bought an old palace from the Moors. Would you not like to see Granada, Señora?" he asked, turning to Margaret as though to change the subject. "There is a wonderful building there called the Alhambra; it overlooks my house."

"My daughter is never likely to see it," broke in Castell; "I do not purpose that she should visit Spain."

"Ah! you do not purpose; but who knows? God and His saints alone," and again he crossed himself, then fell to describing the beauties of Granada.

He was a fine and ready talker, and his voice was very pleasant, so Margaret listened attentively enough, watching his face, and forgetting to eat, while her father and Peter watched them both. At length the meal came to an end, and when the serving-men had cleared away the dishes, and they were alone, Castell said:

"Now, kinsman Peter, tell me your story."

So Peter told him, in few words, yet omitting nothing.

"I find no blame in you," said the merchant when he had done, "nor do I see how you could have acted otherwise than you did. It is Margaret whom I blame, for I only gave her leave to walk with you and Betty by the river, and bade her beware of crowds."

"Yes, father, the fault is mine, and for it I pray your pardon," said Margaret, so meekly that her father could not find the heart to scold her as he had meant to do.

"You should ask Peter's pardon," he muttered, "seeing that he is like to be laid by the heels in a dungeon over this business, yes, and put upon his trial for causing the man's death. Remember, he was in the service of de Ayala, with whom our liege wishes to stand well, and de Ayala, it seems, is very angry."

Now Margaret grew frightened, for the thought that harm might come to Peter cut her heart. The colour left her cheek, and once again her eyes swam with tears.

"Oh! say not so," she exclaimed. "Peter, will you not fly at once?"

"By no means," he answered decidedly. "Did I not say it to the king, and is not this foreign lord bond for me?"

"What can be done?" she went on; then, as a thought struck her, turned to d'Aguilar, and, clasping her slender hands, looked pleadingly into his face and asked: "Señor, you who are so powerful, and the friend of great people, will you not help us?"

"Am I not here to do so, Señora? Although I think that a man who can call half London to his back, as I saw your cousin do, needs little help from me. But listen, my country has two ambassadors at this Court—de Ayala, whom he has offended, and Doctor de Puebla, the friend of the king; and, strangely enough, de Puebla does not love de Ayala. Yet he does love money, which perhaps will be forthcoming. Now, if a charge is to be laid over this brawl, it will probably be done, not by the churchman, de Ayala, but through de Puebla, who knows your laws and Court, and—do you understand me, Señor Castell?"

"Yes," answered the merchant; "but how am I to get at de Puebla? If I were to offer him money, he would only ask more."

"I see that you know his Excellency," remarked d'Aguilar drily. "You are right, no money should be offered; a present must be made after the pardon is delivered—not before. Oh! de Puebla knows that John Castell's word is as good in London as it is among the Jews and infidels of Granada and the merchants of Seville, at both of which places I have heard it spoken."

At this speech Castell's eyes flickered, but he only answered:

"May be; but how shall I approach him, Señor?"

"If you will permit me, that is my task. Now, to what amount will you go to save our friend here from inconvenience? Fifty gold angels?"

"It is too much," said Castell; "a knave like that is not worth ten. Indeed, he was the assailant, and nothing should be paid at all."

"Ah! Señor, the merchant is coming out in you; also the dangerous man who thinks that right should rule the world, not kings—I mean might. The knave is worth nothing, but de Puebla's word in Henry's ear is worth much."

"Fifty angels be it then," said Castell, "and I thank you, Señor, for your good offices. Will you take the money now?"

"By no means; not till I bring the debt discharged. Señor, I will come again and let you know how matters stand. Farewell, fair maiden; may the saints intercede for that dead rogue who brought me into your company, and that of your father and your cousin of the quick eye and the stalwart arm! Till we meet again," and, still murmuring compliments, he bowed himself out of the room in charge of a manservant.

"Thomas," said Castell to this servant when he returned, "you are a discreet fellow; put on your cap and cloak, follow that Spaniard, see where he lodges, and find out all you can about him. Go now, swiftly."

The man bowed and went, and presently Castell, listening, heard a side door shut behind him. Then he turned and said to the other two:

"I do not like this business. I smell trouble in it, and I do not like the Spaniard either."

"He seems a very gallant gentleman, and high-born," said Margaret.

"Aye, very gallant—too gallant, and high-born—too high-born, unless I am mistaken. So gallant and so high-born—" And he checked himself, then added, "Daughter, in your wilfulness you have stirred a great rock. Go to your bed and pray God that it may not fall upon your house and crush it and us."

So Margaret crept away frightened, a little indignant also, for after all, what wrong had she done? And why should her father mistrust this splendid-looking Spanish cavalier?

When she was gone, Peter, who all this while had said little, looked up and asked straight out:

"What are you afraid of, Sir?"

"Many things, Peter. First, that use will be made of this matter to extort much money from me, who am known to be rich, which is a sin best absolved by angels. Secondly, that if I make trouble about paying, other questions will be set afoot."

"What questions?"

"Have you ever heard of the new Christians, Peter, whom the Spaniards call Maranos?"

He nodded.

"Then you know that a Marano is a converted Jew. Now, as it chances—I tell you who do not break secrets—my father was a Marano. His name does not matter—it is best forgotten; but he fled from Spain to England for reasons of his own, and took that of the country whence he came—Castile, or Castell. Also, as it is not lawful for Jews to live in England, he became converted to the Christian faith—seek not to know his motives, they are buried with him. Moreover, he converted me, his only child, who was but ten years old, and cared little whether I swore by 'Father Abraham' or by the 'Blessed Mary.' The paper of my baptism lies in my strong box still. Well, he was clever, and built up this business, and died unharmed five-and-twenty years ago, leaving me already rich. That same year I married an Englishwoman, your mother's second cousin, and loved her and lived happily with her, and gave her all her heart could wish. But after Margaret's birth, three-and-twenty years gone by, she never had her health, and eight years ago she died. You remember her, since she brought you here when you were a stout lad, and made me promise afterwards that I would always be your friend, for except your father, Sir Peter, none other of your well-born and ancient family were left. So when Sir Peter—against my counsel, staking his all upon that usurping rogue Richard, who had promised to advance him, and meanwhile took his money—was killed at Bosworth, leaving you landless, penniless, and out of favour, I offered you a home, and you, being a wise man, put off your mail and put on woollen and became a merchant's partner, though your share of profit was but small. Now, again you have changed staff for steel," and he glanced at the Scotchman's sword that still lay upon a side table, "and Margaret has loosed that rock of which I spoke to her."

"What is the rock, Sir?"

"That Spaniard whom she brought home and found so fine."

"What of the Spaniard?"

"Wait a while and I will tell you." And, taking a lamp, he left the room, returning presently with a letter which was written in cipher, and translated upon another sheet in John Castell's own hand.

"This," he said, "is from my partner and connection, Juan Bernaldez, a Marano, who lives at Seville, where Ferdinand and Isabella have their court. Among other matters he writes this: 'I warn all brethren in England to be careful. I have it that a certain one whose name I will not mention even in cipher, a very powerful and high-born man, and, although he appears to be a pleasure-seeker only, and is certainly of a dissolute life, among the greatest bigots in all Spain, has been sent, or is shortly to be sent, from Granada, where he is stationed to watch the Moors, as an envoy to the Court of England to conclude a secret treaty with its king. Under this treaty the names of rich Maranos that

249

are already well known here are to be recorded, so that when the time comes, and the active persecution of Jews and Maranos begins, they may be given up and brought to Spain for trial before the Inquisition. Also he is to arrange that no Jew or Marano may be allowed to take refuge in England. This is for your information, that you may warn any whom it concerns.'"

"You think that d'Aguilar is this man?" asked Peter, while Castell folded up the letter and hid it in the pocket of his robe.

"I do; indeed I have heard already that a fox was on the prowl, and that men should look to their hen-houses. Moreover, did you note how he crossed himself like a priest, and what he said about being among good Christians? Also, it is Lent and a fast-day, and by ill-fortune, although none of us ate of it, there was meat upon the table, for as you know," he added hurriedly, "I am not strict in such matters, who give little weight to forms and ceremonies. Well, he observed it, and touched fish only, although he drank enough of the sweet wine. Doubtless a report of that meat will go to Spain by the next courier."

"And if it does, what matter? We are in England, and Englishmen will not suffer their Spanish laws and ways. Perhaps the *señor* d'Aguilar learned as much as that to-night outside the banqueting-hall. There is something to be feared from this brawl at home; but while we are safe in London, no more from Spain."

"I am no coward, but I think there is much more to be feared, Peter. The arm of the Pope is long, and the arm of the crafty Ferdinand is longer, and both of them grope for the throats and moneybags of heretics."

"Well, Sir, we are not heretics."

"No, perhaps not heretics; but we are rich, and the father of one of us was a Jew, and there is something else in this house which even a true son of Holy Church might desire," and he looked at the door through which Margaret had passed to her chamber.

Peter understood, for his long arms moved uneasily, and his grey eyes flashed.

"I will go to bed," he said; "I wish to think."

"Nay, lad," answered Castell, "fill your glass and stay awhile. I have words to say to you, and there is no time like the present. Who knows what may happen to-morrow?"

Chapter 3

Peter Gathers Violets

Peter obeyed, sat down in a big oak chair by the dying fire, and waited in his silent fashion.

"Listen," said Castell. "Fifteen months ago you told me something, did you not?"

Peter nodded.

"What was it, then?"

"That I loved my cousin Margaret, and asked your leave to tell her so."

"And what did I answer?"

"That you forbade me because you had not proved me enough, and she had not proved herself enough; because, moreover, she would be very wealthy, and with her beauty might look high in marriage, although but a merchant's daughter."

"Well, and then?"

"And then—nothing," and Peter sipped his wine deliberately and put it down upon the table.

"You are a very silent man, even where your courting is concerned," said Castell, searching him with his sharp eyes.

"I am silent because there is no more to say. You bade me be silent, and I have remained so."

"What! Even when you saw those gay lords making their addresses to Margaret, and when she grew angry because you gave no sign, and was minded to yield to one or the other of them?"

"Yes, even then—it was hard, but even then. Do I not eat your bread? and shall I take advantage of you when you have forbid me?"

Castell looked at him again, and this time there were respect and affection in his glance.

"Silent and stern, but honest," he said as though to himself, then added, "A hard trial, but I saw it, and helped you in the best way by sending those suitors—who were worthless fellows—about their business. Now, say, are you still of the same mind towards Margaret?"

"I seldom change my mind, Sir, and on such a business, never."

"Good! Then I give you my leave to find out what her mind may be."

In the joy which he could not control, Peter's face flushed. Then, as though he were ashamed of showing emotion, even at such a moment, he took up his glass and drank a little of the wine before he answered.

"I thank you; it is more than I dared to hope. But it is right that I should say, Sir, that I am no match for my cousin Margaret. The lands which should have been mine are gone, and I have nothing save what you pay me for my poor help in this trade; whereas she has, or will have, much."

Castell's eyes twinkled; the answer amused him.

"At least you have an upright heart," he said, "for what other man in such a case would argue against himself? Also, you are of good blood, and not ill to look on, or so some maids might think; whilst as for wealth, what said the wise king of my people?—that ofttimes riches make themselves wings and fly away. Moreover, man, I have learned to love and honour you, and sooner would I leave my only child in your hands than in those of any lord in England."

"I know not what to say," broke in Peter.

"Then say nothing. It is your custom, and a good one—only listen. Just now you spoke of your Essex lands in the fair Vale of Dedham as gone. Well, they have come back, for last month I bought them all, and more, at a price larger than I wished to give because others sought them, and but this day I have paid in gold and taken delivery of the title. It is made out in your name, Peter Brome, and whether you marry my daughter, or whether you marry her not, yours they shall be when I am gone, since I promised my dead wife to befriend you, and as a child she lived there in your Hall."

Now moved out of his calm, the young man sprang from his seat, and, after the pious fashion of the time, addressed his patron saint, on whose feast-day he was born.

"Saint Peter, I thank thee—"

"I asked you to be silent," interrupted Castell, breaking him short. "Moreover, after God, it is one John who should be thanked, not St. Peter, who has no more to do with these lands than Father Abraham or the patient Job. Well, thanks or no thanks, those estates are yours, though I had not meant to tell you of them yet. But now I have something to propose to you. Say, first, does Margaret think aught of that wooden face and those shut lips of yours?"

"How can I know? I have never asked her; you forbade me."

"Pshaw! Living in one house as you do, at your age I would have known all there was to know on such a matter, and yet kept my word. But there, the blood is different, and you are somewhat over-honest for a lover. Was she frightened for you, now, when that knave made at you with the sword?"

Peter considered the question, then answered:

"I know not. I did not look to see; I looked at the Scotchman with his sword, for if I had not, I should have been dead, not he. But she was certainly frightened when the fellow caught hold of her, for then she called for me loud enough."

"And what is that? What woman in London would not call for such a one as Peter Brome in her trouble? Well, you must ask her, and that soon, if you can find the words. Take a lesson from that Spanish don, and scrape and bow and flatter and tell stories of the war and turn verses to her eyes and hair. Oh, Peter! are you a fool, that I at my age should have to teach you how to court a woman?"

"Mayhap, Sir. At least I can do none of these things, and poesy wearies me to read, much more to write. But I can ask a question and take an answer."

Castell shook his head impatiently.

"Ask the question, man, if you will, but never take the answer if it is against you. Wait rather, and ask it again—"

"And," went on Peter without noticing, his grey eyes lighting with a sudden fire, "if need be, I can break that fine Spaniard's bones as though he were a twig."

"Ah!" said Castell, "perhaps you will be called upon to make your words good before all is done. For my part, I think his bones will take some breaking. Well, ask in your own way—only ask and let me hear the answer before to-morrow night. Now it grows late, and I have still something to say. I am in danger here. My wealth is noised abroad, and many covet it, some in high places, I think. Peter, it is in my mind to have done with all this trading, and to withdraw me to spend my old age where none will take any notice of me, down at that Hall of yours in Dedham, if you will give me lodging. Indeed for a year and more, ever since you spoke to me on the subject of Margaret, I have been calling in my moneys from Spain and England, and placing them out at safe interest in small sums, or buying jewels with them, or lending them to other merchants whom I trust, and who will not rob me or

253

mine. Peter, you have worked well for me, but you are no chapman; it is not in your blood. Therefore, since there is enough for all of us and more, I shall pass this business and its goodwill over to others, to be managed in their name, but on shares, and if it please God we will keep next Yule at Dedham."

As he spoke the door at the far end of the hall opened, and through it came that serving-man who had been bidden to follow the Spaniard.

"Well," said Castell, "what tidings?"

The man bowed and said:

"I followed the Don as you bade me to his lodging, which I reached without his seeing me, though from time to time he stopped to look about him. He rests near the palace of Westminster, in the same big house where dwells the ambassador de Ayala, and those who stood round lifted their bonnets to him.

"Watching I saw some of these go to a tavern, a low place that is open all night, and, following them there, called for a drink and listened to their talk, who know the Spanish tongue well, having worked for five years in your worship's house at Seville. They spoke of the fray to-night, and said that if they could catch that long-legged fellow, meaning Master Brome yonder, they would put a knife into him, since he had shamed them by killing the Scotch knave, who was their officer and the best swordsman in their company, with a staff, and then setting his British bulldogs on them. I fell into talk with them, saying that I was an English sailor from Spain, which they were too drunk to question, and asked who might be the tall don who had interfered in the fray before the king came. They told me he is a rich *señor* named d'Aguilar, but ill to serve in Lent because he is so strict a churchman, although not strict in other matters. I answered that to me he looked like a great noble, whereon one of them said that I was right, that there was no blood in Spain higher than his, but unfortunately, there was a bend in its stream, also an inkpot had been upset into it."

"What does that mean?" asked Peter.

"It is a Spanish saying," answered Castell, "which signifies that a man is born illegitimate, and has Moorish blood in his veins."

"Then I asked what he was doing here, and the man answered that I had best put that question to the Holy Father and to the Queen of Spain. Lastly, after I had given the soldier another cup, I asked where the don lived, and whether he had any other name. He replied that he lived at Granada for the most part, and that if I called on him there I should see some pretty ladies and other nice things. As for his name, it was the Marquis of Nichel. I said that meant Marquis of Nothing, whereon the soldier answered that I seemed very curious, and that was just what he meant to tell me—nothing. Also he called to his comrades that he believed I was a spy, so I thought it time to be going, as they were drunk enough to do me a mischief."

"Good," said Castell. "You are watchman tonight, Thomas, are you not? See that all doors are barred so that we may sleep without fear of Spanish thieves. Rest you well, Peter. Nay, I do not come yet; I have letters to send to Spain by the ship which sails to-morrow night."

When Peter had gone, John Castell extinguished all the lamps save one. This he took in his hand and passed from the hall into an apartment that in old days, when this was a noble's house, had been the private chapel. There was an altar in it, and over the altar a crucifix. For a few moments Castell knelt before the altar, for even now, at dead of night, how knew he what eyes might watch him? Then he rose and, lamp in hand, glided behind it, lifted some tapestry, and pressed a spring in the panelling beneath. It opened, revealing a small secret chamber built in the thickness of the wall and without windows; a mere cupboard that once perhaps had been a place where a priest might robe or keep the sacred vessels.

In this chamber was a plain oak table on which stood candles and an ark of wood, also some rolls of parchment. Before this table he knelt down, and put up earnest prayers to the God of Abraham, for, although his father had caused him to be baptized into the Christian Church as a child, John Castell remained a Jew. For this good reason, then, he was so much afraid, knowing that, although his daughter and Peter knew nothing of his secret, there were others who did, and that were it revealed ruin and perhaps death would be his portion and that of his house, since in those days there was no greater crime than to adore God otherwise than Holy Church allowed. Yet for many years he had taken the risk, and worshipped on as his fathers did before him.

His prayer finished, he left the place, closing the spring-door behind him, and passed to his office, where he sat till the morning light, first writing a letter to his correspondent at Seville, and then painfully translating it into cipher by aid of a secret key. His task done, and the cipher letter sealed and directed, he burned the draft, extinguished his lamp, and, going to the window, watched the rising of the sun. In the garden beneath blackbirds sang, and the pale primroses were abloom.

"I wonder," he said aloud, "whether when those flowers come again I shall live to see them. Almost I feel as though the rope were tightening about my throat at last; it came upon me while that accursed Spaniard crossed himself at my table. Well, so be it; I will hide the truth while I can, but if they catch me I'll not deny it. The money is safe, most of it; my wealth they shall never get, and now I will make my daughter safe also, as with Peter she must be. I would I had not put it off so long; but I hankered after a great marriage for her, which, being a Christian, she well might make. I'll mend that fault; before to-morrow's morn she shall be plighted to him, and before May-day his wife. God of my fathers, give us one month more of peace and safety, and then, because I have denied Thee openly, take my life in payment if Thou wilt."

Before John Castell went to bed Peter was already awake—indeed, he had slept but little that night. How could he sleep whose fortunes had changed thus wondrously between sun set and rise? Yesterday he was but a merchant's assistant—a poor trade for one who had been trained to arms, and borne them bravely. To-day he was a gentleman again, owner of the broad lands where he was bred, and that had been his forefathers' for many a generation. Yesterday he was a lover without hope, for in himself he had never believed that the rich John Castell would suffer him, a landless man, to pay court to his daughter, one of the loveliest and wealthiest maids in London. He had asked his leave in past days, and been refused, as he had expected that he would be refused, and thenceforward, being on his honour as it were, he had said no tender word to Margaret, nor pressed her hand, nor even looked into her eyes and sighed. Yet at times it had seemed to him that she would not have been ill-pleased if he had done one of these things, or all; that she wondered, indeed, that he did not, and thought none the better of him for his abstinence. Moreover, now he learned that her father wondered also, and this was a strange reward of virtue.

For Peter loved Margaret with heart and soul and body. Since he, a lad, had played with her, a child, he loved her, and no other woman. She was his thought by day and his dream by night, his hope, his eternal star. Heaven he pictured as a place where for ever he would be with Margaret, earth without her could be nothing but a hell. That was why he had stayed on in Castell's shop, bending his proud neck to this tradesman's yoke, doing the bidding and taking the rough words of chapmen and of lordly customers, filling in bills of exchange, and cheapening bargains, all without a sign or murmur, though oftentimes he felt as though his gorge would burst with loathing of the life. Indeed, that was why he had come there at all, who otherwise would have been far away, hewing a road to fame and fortune, or digging out a grave with his broadsword. For here at least he could be near to

Margaret, could touch her hand at morn and evening, could watch the light shine in her beauteous eyes, and sometimes, as she bent over him, feel her breath upon his hair. And now his purgatory was at an end, and of a sudden the gates of joy were open.

But what if Margaret should prove the angel with the flaming sword who forbade him entrance to his paradise? He trembled at the thought. Well, if so, so it must be; he was not the man to force her fancy, or call her father to his aid. He would do his best to win her, and if he failed, why then he would bless her, and let her go.

Peter could lie abed no longer, but rose and dressed himself, although the dawn was not fully come. By his open window he said his prayers, thanking God for mercies past, and praying that He would bless him in his great emprise. Presently the sun rose, and there came a great longing on him to be alone in the countryside, he who was country-born and hated towns, with only the sky and the birds and the trees for company.

But here in London was no country, wherever he went he would meet men; moreover, he remembered that it might be best that just now he should not wander through the streets unguarded, lest he should find Spaniards watching to take him unawares. Well, there was the garden; he would go thither, and walk a while. So he descended the broad oak stairs, and, unbolting a door, entered this garden, which, though not too well kept, was large for London, covering an acre of ground perhaps, surrounded by a high wall, and having walks, and at the end of it a group of ancient elms, beneath which was a seat hidden from the house. In summer this was Margaret's favourite bower, for she too loved Nature and the land, and all the things it bore. Indeed, this garden was her joy, and the flowers that grew there were for the most part of her own planting—primroses, snowdrops, violets, and, in the shadow of the trees, long hartstongue ferns.

For a while Peter walked up and down the central path, and, as it chanced, Margaret, who also had risen early and not slept too well, looking through her window curtains, saw him wandering there, and wondered what he did at this hour; also, why he was dressed in the clothes he wore on Sundays and holidays. Perhaps, she thought, his weekday garments had been torn or muddied in last night's fray. Then she fell to thinking how bravely he had borne him in that fray. She saw it all again; the great red-headed rascal tossed up and whirled to the earth by his strong arms; saw Peter face that gleaming steel with nothing but a staff; saw the straight blows fall, and the fellow go reeling to the earth, slain with a single stroke.

Ah! her cousin, Peter Brome, was a man indeed, though a strange one, and remembering certain things that did not please her, she shrugged her ivory shoulders, turned red, and pouted. Why, that Spaniard had said more civil words to her in an hour than had Peter in two years, and he was handsome and noble-looking also; but then the Spaniard was—a Spaniard, and other men were—other men, whereas Peter was—Peter, a creature apart, one who cared as little for women as he did for trade.

Why, then, if he cared for neither women nor trade, did he stop here? she wondered. To gather wealth? She did not think it; he seemed to have no leanings that way either. It was a mystery. Still, she could wish to get to the bottom of Peter's heart, just to see what was hid there, since no man has a right to be a riddle to his loving cousin. Yes, and one day she would do it, cost what it might.

Meanwhile, she remembered that she had never thanked Peter for the brave part which he had played, and, indeed, had left him to walk home with Betty, a journey that, as she gathered from her sprightly cousin's talk while she undressed her, neither of them had much enjoyed. For Betty, be it said here, was angry with Peter, who, it seemed, once had told her that she was a handsome, silly fool, who thought too much of men and too little of her business. Well, since after the day's work had begun she would find no opportunity, she would go down and thank Peter now, and see if she could make him talk for once.

So Margaret threw her fur-trimmed cloak about her, drawing its hood over her head, for the April air was cold, and followed Peter into the garden. When she reached it, however, there was no Peter to be seen, whereon she reproached herself for having come to that damp place so early and meditated return. Then, thinking that it would look foolish if any had chanced to see her, she walked down the path pretending to seek for violets, and found none. Thus she came to the group of great elms at the end, and, glancing between their ancient boles, saw Peter standing there. Now, too, she understood why she could find no violets, for Peter had gathered them all, and was engaged, awkwardly enough, in trying to tie them and some leaves into a little posy by the help of a stem of grass. With his left hand he held the violets, with his right one end of the grass, and since he lacked fingers to clasp the other, this he attempted with his teeth. Now he drew it tight, and now the brittle grass stem broke, the violets were scattered, and Peter used words that he should not have uttered even when alone.

"I knew you would break it, but I never thought you could lose your temper over so small a thing, Peter," said Margaret; and he in the shadow looked up to see her standing there in the sunlight, fresh and lovely as the spring itself.

Solemnly, in severe reproof, she shook her head, from which the hood had fallen back, but there was a smile upon her lips, and laughter in her eyes. Oh! she was beautiful, and at the sight of her Peter's heart stood still. Then, remembering what he had just said, and certain other things that Master Castell had said, he blushed so deeply that her own cheeks went red in sympathy. It was foolish, but she could not help it, for about Peter this morning there was something strange, something that bred blushes.

"For whom are you gathering violets so early," she asked, "when you ought to be praying for that Scotchman's soul?"

"I care nothing for his soul," answered Peter testily. "If the brute had one, he can look after it himself; and I was gathering the violets— for you."

She stared. Peter was not in the habit of making her presents of flowers. No wonder he had looked strange.

"Then I will help you to tie them. Do you know why I am up so early? It is for your sake. I behaved badly to you last night, for I was cross because you wanted to thwart me about seeing the king. I never thanked you for all you did, you brave Peter, though I thanked you enough in my heart. Do you know that when you stood there with that sword, in the middle of those Englishmen, you looked quite no-ble? Come out into the sunlight, and I will thank you properly."

In his agitation Peter let the remainder of the flowers fall. Then an idea struck him, and he answered:

"Look! I can't; if you are really grateful for nothing at all, come in here and help me to pick up these violets—a pest on their short stalks!"

She hesitated a little, then by degrees drew nearer, and, bending down, began to find the flowers one by one. Peter had scattered them wide, so that at first the pair were some way apart, but when only a few remained, they drew close. Now there was but one violet left, and, both stretching for it, their hands met. Margaret held the violet, and Peter held Margaret's fingers. Thus linked they straightened them-selves, and as they rose their faces were very near together and oh! most sweet were Margaret's wonderful eyes; while in the eyes of Peter there shone a flame. For a second they looked at each other, and then of a sudden he kissed her on the lips.

CHAPTER 4

Lovers Dear

"Peter!" gasped Margaret—"*Peter!*"

But Peter made no answer, only he who had been red of face went white, so that the mark of the sword-cut across his cheek showed like a scarlet line upon a cloth.

"Peter!" repeated Margaret, pulling at her hand which he still held, "do you know what you have done?"

"It seems that you do, so what need is there for me to tell you?" he muttered.

"Then it was not an accident; you really meant it, and you are not ashamed."

"If it was, I hope that I may meet with more such accidents."

"Peter, leave go of me. I am going to tell my father, at once."

His face brightened.

"Tell him by all means," he said; "he won't mind. He told me—"

"Peter, how dare you add falsehood to—to—you know what. Do you mean to say that my father told you to kiss me, and at six o'clock in the morning, too?"

"He said nothing about kissing, but I suppose he meant it. He said that I might ask you to marry me."

"That," replied Margaret, "is a very different thing. If you had asked me to marry you, and, after thinking it over for a long while, I had answered Yes, which of course I should not have done, then, perhaps, before we were married you might have—Well, Peter, you have begun at the wrong end, which is very shameless and wicked of you, and I shall never speak to you again."

"I daresay," said Peter resignedly; "all the more reason why I should speak to you while I have the chance. No, you shan't go till you have heard me. Listen. I have been in love with you since you were twelve years old—"

"That must be another falsehood, Peter, or you have gone mad. If you had been in love with me for eleven years, you would have said so."

"I wanted to, always, but your father refused me leave. I asked him fifteen months ago, but he put me on my word to say nothing."

"To say nothing—yes, but he could not make you promise to show nothing."

"I thought that the one thing meant the other; I see now that I have been a fool, and, I suppose, have overstayed my market," and he looked so depressed that Margaret relented a little.

"Well," she said, "at any rate it was honest, and of course I am glad that you were honest."

"You said just now that I told falsehoods—twice; if I am honest, how can I tell falsehoods?"

"I don't know. Why do you ask me riddles? Let me go and try to forget all this."

"Not till you have answered me outright. Will you marry me, Margaret? If you won't, there will be no need for you to go, for I shall go and trouble you no more. You know what I am, and all about me, and I have nothing more to say except that, although you may find many finer husbands, you won't find one who would love and care for you better. I know that you are very beautiful and very rich, while I am neither one nor the other, and often I have wished to Heaven that you were not so beautiful, for sometimes that brings trouble on women who are honest and only have one heart to give, or so rich either. But thus things are, and I cannot change them, and, however poor my chance of hitting the dove, I determined to shoot my bolt and make way for the next archer. Is there any chance at all, Margaret? Tell me, and put me out of pain, for I am not good at so much talking."

Now Margaret began to grow disturbed; her wayward assurance departed from her.

"It is not fitting," she murmured, "and I do not wish—I will speak to my father; he shall give you your answer."

"No need to trouble him, Margaret. He has given it already. His great desire is that we should marry, for he seeks to leave this trade and to live with us in the Vale of Dedham, in Essex, where he has bought back my father's land."

"You are full of strange tidings this morning, Peter."

"Yes, Margaret, our wheel of life that went so slow turns fast enough to-day, for God above has laid His whip upon the horses of our Fate, and they begin to gallop, whither I know not. Must they run side by side, or separate? It is for you to say."

"Peter," she said, "will you not give me a little time?"

"Aye, Margaret, ten whole minutes by the clock, and then if it is nay, all your life, for I pack my chest and go. It will be said that I feared to be taken for that soldier's death."

"You are unkind to press me so."

"Nay, it is kindest to both of us. Do you then love some other man?"

"I must confess I do," she murmured, looking at him out of the corners of her eyes.

Now Peter, strong as he was, turned faint, and in his agitation let go her hand which she lifted, the violets still between her fingers, considering it as though it were a new thing to her.

"I have no right to ask you who he is," he muttered, striving to control himself.

"Nay, but, Peter, I will tell you. It is my father—what other man should I love?"

"Margaret!" he said in wrath, "you are fooling me."

"How so? What other man should I love—unless, indeed, it were yourself?"

"I can bear no more of this play," he said. "Mistress Margaret, I bid you farewell. God go with you!" And he brushed past her.

"Peter," she said when he had gone a few yards, "would you have these violets as a farewell gift?"

He turned and hesitated.

"Come, then, and take them."

So back he came, and with little trembling fingers she began to fasten the flowers to his doublet, bending ever nearer as she fastened, until her breath played upon his face, and her hair brushed his bonnet. Then, it matters not how, once more the violets fell to earth, and she sighed, and her hands fell also, and he put his strong arms round her and drew her to him and kissed her again and yet again on the hair and eyes and lips; nor did Margaret forbid him.

At length she thrust him from her and, taking him by the hand, led him to the seat beneath the elms, and bade him sit at one end of it, while she sat at the other.

"Peter," she whispered, "I wish to speak with you when I can get my breath. Peter, you think poorly of me, do you not? No—be silent; it is my turn to talk. You think that I am heartless, and have been play-ing with you. Well, I only did it to make sure that you really do love me, since, after that—accident of a while ago (when we were picking

262

up the violets, I mean), you would have been in honour bound to say it, would you not? Well, now I am quite sure, so I will tell you something. I love you many times as well as you love me, and have done so for quite as long. Otherwise, should I not have married some other suitor, of whom there have been plenty? Aye, and I will tell you this to my sin and shame, that once I grew so angry with you because you would not speak or give some little sign, that I went near to it. But at the last I could not, and sent him about his business also. Peter, when I saw you last night facing that swordsman with but a staff, and thought that you must die, oh! then I knew all the truth, and my heart was nigh to bursting, as, had you died, it would have burst. But now it is all done with, and we know each other's secret, and nothing shall ever part us more till death comes to one or both."

Thus Margaret spoke, while he drank in her words as desert sands, parched by years of drought, drink in the rain—and watched her face, out of which all mischief and mockery had departed, leaving it that of a most beauteous and most earnest woman, to whom a sense of the weight of life, with its mingled joys and sorrows, had come home suddenly. When she had finished, this silent man, to whom even his great happiness brought few words, said only:

"God has been very good to us. Let us thank God."

So they did, then, even there, seated side by side upon the bench, because the grass was too wet for them to kneel on, praying in their simple, childlike faith that the Power which had brought them together, and taught them to love each other, would bless them in that love and protect them from all harms, enemies, and evils through many a long year of life.

Their prayer finished, they sat together on the seat, now talking, and now silent in their joy, while all too fast the time wore on. At length—it was after one of these spells of blissful silence—a change came over them, such a change as falls upon some peaceful scene when, unexpected and complete, a black storm cloud sweeps across the sun, and, in place of its warm light, pours down gloom full of the promise of tempest and of rain. Apprehension got a hold of them. They were both afraid of what they could not guess.

"Come," she said, "it is time to go in. My father will miss us."

So without more words or endearments they rose and walked side by side out of the shelter of the elms into the open garden. Their heads were bent, for they were lost in thought, and thus it came about that Margaret saw her feet pass suddenly into the shadow of a man, and, looking up, perceived standing in front of her, grave, alert, amused, none other than the Señor d'Aguilar. She uttered a little stifled scream, while Peter, with the impulse that causes a brave and startled hound to rush at that which frightens it, gave a leap forward towards the Spaniard.

"Mother of God! do you take me for a thief?" he asked in a laughing voice, as he stepped to one side to avoid him.

"Your pardon," said Peter, shaking himself together; "but you surprised us appearing so suddenly where we never thought to see you."

"Any more than I thought to see you here, for this seems a strange place to linger on so cold a morning," and he looked at them again with his curious, mocking eyes that appeared to read the secret of their souls, while they grew red as roses beneath his scrutiny. "Permit me to explain," he went on. "I came here thus early on your service, to warn you, Master Peter, not to go abroad to-day, since a writ is out for your arrest, and as yet I have had no time to quash it by friendly settlement. Well, as it chanced, I met that handsome lady who was with you yesterday, returning from her marketing—a friendly soul—she says she is your cousin. She brought me to the house, and having learned that your father, whom I wished to see, was at his prayers, good man, in the old chapel, led me to its door and left me to seek him. I entered, but could not find him, so, having waited a while, strayed into this garden through the open door, purposing to walk here till some one should appear, and, you see, I have been fortunate beyond my expectations or deserts."

"So!" said Peter shortly, for the man's manner and elaborated explanations filled him with disgust. "Let us seek Master Castell that he may hear the story."

"And we thank you much for coming to warn us," murmured Margaret. "I will go find my father," and she slipped past him towards the door.

D'Aguilar watched her enter it, then turned to Peter and said:

"You English are a hardy folk who take the spring air so early. Well, in such company I would do the same. Truly she is a beauteous maiden. I have some experience of the sex, but never do I remember one so fair."

"My cousin is well enough," answered Peter coldly, for this Spaniard's very evident admiration of Margaret did not please him.

"Yes," answered d'Aguilar, taking no notice of his tone, "she is well enough to fill the place, not of a merchant's daughter, but of a great lady—a countess reigning over towns and lands, or a queen even; the royal robes and ornaments would become that carriage and that brow."

"My cousin seeks no such state who is happy in her quiet lot,"

264

answered Peter again; then added quickly, "See, here comes Master Castell seeking you."

D'Aguilar advanced and greeted the merchant courteously, noticing as he did so that, notwithstanding his efforts to appear unconcerned, Castell seemed ill at ease.

"I am an early visitor," he said, "but I knew that you business folk rise with the lark, and I wished to catch our friend here before he went out," and he repeated to him the reason of his coming.

"I thank you, Señor," answered Castell. "You are very good to me and mine. I am sorry that you have been kept waiting. They tell me that you looked for me in the chapel, but I was not there, who had already left it for my office."

"So I found. It is a quaint place, that old chapel of yours, and while I waited I went to the altar and told my beads there, which I had no time to do before I left my lodgings."

Castell started almost imperceptibly, and glanced at d'Aguilar with his quick eyes, then turned the subject and asked if he would not breakfast with them. He declined, however, saying that he must be about their business and his own, then promptly proposed that he should come to supper on the following night that was—Sunday—and make report how things had gone, a suggestion that Castell could not but accept.

So he bowed and smiled himself out of the house, and walked thoughtfully into Holborn, for it had pleased him to pay this visit on foot, and unattended. At the corner whom should he meet again but the tall, fair-haired Betty, returning from some errand which she had found it convenient to fulfil just then.

"What," he said, "you once more! The saints are very kind to me this morning. Come, Señora, walk a little way with me, for I would ask you a few questions."

Betty hesitated, then gave way. It was seldom that she found the chance of walking through Holborn with such a noble-looking cavalier.

"Never look at your working-dress," he said.

"With such a shape, what matters the robe that covers it?"—a compliment at which Betty blushed, for she was proud of her fine figure.

"Would you like a mantilla of real Spanish lace for your head and shoulders? Well, you shall have one that I brought from Spain with me, for I know no other lady in the land whom it would become better. But, Mistress Betty, you told me wrong about your master. I went to the chapel and he was not there."

"He was there, Señor," she answered, eager to set herself right with this most agreeable and discriminating foreigner, "for I saw him go in a moment before, and he did not come out again."

"Then, Señora, where could he have hidden himself? Has the place a crypt?"

"None that I have heard of; but," she added, "there is a kind of little room behind the altar."

"Indeed. How do you know that? I saw no room."

"Because one day I heard a voice behind the tapestry, Señor, and, lifting it, saw a sliding door left open, and Master Castell kneeling before a table and saying his prayers aloud."

"How strange! And what was there on the table?"

"Only a queer-shaped box of wood like a little house, and two candlesticks, and some rolls of parchment. But I forgot, Señor; I promised Master Castell to say nothing about that place, for he turned and saw me, and came at me like a watchdog out of its kennel. You won't say that I told you, will you, Señor?"

"Not I; your good master's private cupboard does not interest me. Now I want to know something more. Why is that beautiful cousin of yours not married? Has she no suitors?"

"Suitors, Señor? Yes, plenty of them, but she sends them all about their business, and seems to have no mind that way."

"Perhaps she is in love with her cousin, that long-legged, strong-armed, wooden-headed Master Brome."

"Oh! no, Señor, I don't think so; no lady could be in love with him—he is too stern and silent."

"I agree with you, Señora. Then perhaps he is in love with her."

Betty shook her head, and replied: "Peter Brome doesn't think anything of women, Señor. At least he never speaks to or of them."

"Which shows that probably he thinks about them all the more. Well, well, it is no affair of ours, is it? Only I am glad to hear that there is nothing between them, since your mistress ought to marry high, and be a great lady, not a mere merchant's wife."

"Yes, Señor. Though Peter Brome is not a merchant, at least by birth, he is high-born, and should be Sir Peter Brome if his father had not fought on the wrong side and sold his land. He is a soldier, and a very brave one, they say, as all might see last night."

"No doubt, and perhaps would make a great captain, if he had the chance, with his stern face and silent tongue. But, Señora Betty, say, how comes it that, being so handsome," and he bowed, "you are not married either? I am sure it can be from no lack of suitors."

Again Betty, foolish girl, flushed with pleasure at the compliment.

"You are right, Señor," she answered. "I have plenty of them; but I am like my cousin—they do not please me. Although my father lost his fortune, I come of good blood, and I suppose that is why I do not care for these low-born men, and would rather remain as I am than marry one of them."

"You are quite right," said d'Aguilar in his sympathetic voice. "Do not stain your blood. Marry in your own class, or not at all, which, indeed, should not be difficult for one so beautiful and charming." And he looked into her large eyes with tender admiration.

This quality, indeed, soon began to demonstrate itself so actively, for they were now in the fields where few people wandered, that Betty, who although vain was proud and upright, thought it wise to recollect that she must be turning homewards. So, in spite of his protests, she left him and departed, walking upon air.

How splendid and handsome this foreign gentleman was, she thought to herself, really a great cavalier, and surely he admired her truly. Why should he not? Such things had often been. Many a rich lady whom she knew was not half so handsome or so well born as herself, and would make him a worse wife—that is, and the thought chilled her somewhat—if he were not already married. From all of which it will be seen that d'Aguilar had quickly succeeded in the plan which only presented itself to him a few hours before. Betty was already half in love with him. Not that he had any desire to possess this beautiful but foolish woman's heart, who saw in her only a useful tool, a stepping-stone by means of which he might draw near to Margaret.

For with Margaret, it may be said at once, he was quite in love. At the sight of her sweet yet imperial beauty, as he saw her first, dishevelled, angry, frightened, in the crowd outside the king's banqueting-hall, his southern blood had taken sudden fire. Finished voluptuary though he was, the sensation he experienced then was quite new to him. He longed for this woman as he had never longed for any other, and, what is more, he desired to make her his wife. Why not? Although there was a flaw in it, his rank was high, and therefore she was beneath him; but for this her loveliness would atone, and she had wit and learning enough to fill any place that he could give her. Also, great as was his wealth, his wanton, spendthrift way of life had brought him many debts, and she was the only child of one of the richest merchants in England, whose dower, doubtless, would be a fortune that many a royal princess might envy. Why not again? He would turn Inez and those others adrift—at any rate, for a while—and make her mistress of his palace there in Granada. Instantly, as is often the fashion of those who have Eastern blood in their veins, d'Aguilar had made up his mind, yes, before he left her father's table on the previous night. He would marry Margaret and no other woman.

Yet at once he had seen many difficulties in his path. To begin with, he mistrusted him of Peter, that strong, quiet man who could kill a great armed knave with his stick, and at a word call half London to his side. Peter, he was sure, being human, must be in love with Margaret, and he was a rival to be feared. Well, if Margaret had no thoughts of Peter, this mattered nothing, and if she had—and what were they doing together in the garden that morning?—Peter must be got rid of, that was all. It was easy enough if he chose to adopt certain means; there were many of those Spanish fellows who would not mind sticking a knife into his back in the dark.

But sinful as he was, at such steps his conscience halted. Whatever d'Aguilar had done, he had never caused a man to be actually murdered, he who was a bigot, who atoned for his misdoings by periods of remorse and prayer, in which he placed his purse and talents at the service of the Church, as he was doing at this moment. No, murder must not be thought of; for how could any absolution wash him clean of that stain? But there were other ways. For instance, had not this Peter, in self-defence it is true, killed one of the servants of an ambassador of Spain? Perhaps, however, it would not be necessary to make use of them. It had seemed to him that the lady was not ill pleased with him, and, after all, he had much to offer. He would court her fairly, and if he were rejected by her, or by her father, then it would be time enough to act. Meanwhile, he would keep the sword hanging over the head of Peter, pretending that it was he alone who had prevented it from falling, and learn all that he could as to Castell and his history.

Here, indeed, Fortune, in the shape of the foolish Betty, had favoured him. Without a doubt, as he had heard in Spain, and been sure from the moment that he first saw him, Castell was still secretly a Jew. Mistress Betty's story of the room behind the altar, with the ark and the candles and the rolls of the Law, proved as much. At least here was evidence enough to send him to the fires of the Inquisition in Spain, and, perhaps, to drive him out of England. Now, if John Castell, the Spanish Jew, should not wish, for any reason, to give him his daughter in marriage, would not a hint and an extract from the Commissions of their Majesties of Spain and the Holy Father suffice to make him change his mind?

Thus pondering, d'Aguilar regained his lodgings, where his first task was to enter in a book all that Betty had told him, and all that he had observed in the house of John Castell.

CHAPTER 5

Castell's Secret

In John Castell's house it was the habit, as in most others in those days, for his dependents, clerks, and shopmen to eat their morning and mid-day meals with him in the hall, seated at two lower tables, all of them save Betty, his daughter's cousin and companion, who sat with them at the upper board. This morning Betty's place was empty, and presently Castell, lifting his eyes, for he was lost in thought, noted it, and asked where she might be—a question that neither Margaret nor Peter could answer.

One of the servants at the lower table, however—it was that man who had been sent to follow d'Aguilar on the previous night—said that as he came down Holborn a while before he had seen her walking with the Spanish don, a saying at which his master looked grave.

Just as they were finishing their meal, a very silent one, for none of them seemed to have anything to say, and after the servants had left the hall, Betty arrived, flushed as though with running.

"Where have you been that you are so late?" asked Castell.

"To seek the linen for the new sheets, but it was not ready," she answered glibly. "The mercer kept you waiting long," remarked Castell quietly. "Did you meet any one?"

"Only the folk in the street."

"I will ask you no more questions, lest I should cause you to lie and bring you into sin," said Castell sternly. "Girl, how far did you walk with the Señor d'Aguilar, and what was your business with him?"

Now Betty knew that she had been seen, and that it was useless to deny the truth.

"Only a little way," she answered, "and that because he prayed me to show him his path."

"Listen, Betty," went on Castell, taking no notice of her words. "You are old enough to guard yourself, therefore as to your walking abroad with gallants who can mean you no good I say nothing. But know this—no one who has knowledge of the matters of my house," and he looked at her keenly, "shall mix with any Spaniard. If you are found alone with this *señor* any more, that hour I have done with you, and you never pass my door again. Nay, no words. Take your food and eat it elsewhere."

So she departed half weeping, but very angry, for Betty was strong and obstinate by nature. When she had gone, Margaret, who was fond of her cousin, tried to say some words on her behalf; but her father stopped her.

"Pshaw!" he said, "I know the girl; she is vain as a peacock, and, remembering her gentle birth and good looks, seeks to marry above her station; while for some purpose of his own—an ill one, I'll warrant—that Spaniard plays upon her weakness, which, if it be not curbed, may bring trouble on us all. Now, enough of Betty Dene; I must to my work."

"Sir," said Peter, speaking for the first time, "we would have a private word with you."

"A private word," he said, looking up anxiously. "Well, speak on. No, this place is not private; I think its walls have ears. Follow me," and he led the way into the old chapel, whereof, when they had all passed it, he bolted the door. "Now," he said, "what is it?"

"Sir," answered Peter, standing before him, "having your leave at last, I asked your daughter in marriage this morning."

"At least you lose no time, friend Peter; unless you had called her from her bed and made your offer through the door you could not have done it quicker. Well, well, you ever were a man of deeds, not words, and what says my Margaret?"

"An hour ago she said she was content," answered Peter.

"A cautious man also," went on Castell with a twinkle in his eye, "who remembers that women have been known to change their minds within an hour. After such long thought, what say you now, Margaret?"

"That I am angry with Peter," she answered, stamping her small foot, "for if he does not trust me for an hour, how can he trust me for his life and mine?"

"Nay, Margaret, you do not understand me," said Peter. "I wished not to bind you, that is all, in case—"

"Now you are saying it again," she broke in vexed, and yet amused. "Do so a third time, and I will you at your word."

"It seems best that I should remain silent. Speak you," said Peter humbly.

"Aye, for truly you are a master of silence, as I should know, if any do," replied Margaret, bethinking her of the weary months and years of waiting. "Well, I will answer for you.—Father, Peter was right; I am content to marry him, though to do so will be to enter the Order of the Silent Brothers. Yes, I am content; not for himself, indeed, who has so many faults, but for myself, who chance to love him," and she smiled sweetly enough.

"Do not jest on such matters, Margaret."

"Why not, father? Peter is solemn enough for both of us—look at him. Let us laugh while we may, for who knows when tears may come?"

"A good saying," answered Castell with a sigh. "So you two have plighted your troth, and, my children, I am glad of it, for who knows when those tears of which Margaret spoke may come, and then you can wipe away each other's? Take now her hand, Peter, and swear by the Rood, that symbol which you worship"—here Peter glanced at him, but he went on—"swear, both of you that come what may, together or separate, through good report or evil report, through poverty or wealth, through peace or persecutions, through temptation or through blood, through every good or ill that can befall you in this world of bittersweet, you will remain faithful to your troth until you be wed, and after you are wed, faithful to each other till death do part you."

These words he spoke to them in a voice that was earnest almost to passion, searching their faces the while with his quick eyes as though he would read their very hearts. His mood crept from him to them; once again they felt something of that fear which had fallen on them in the garden when they passed into the shadow of the Spaniard. Very solemnly then, and with little of true lovers' joy, did they take each other's hands and swear by the Cross and Him Who hung on it, that through these things, and all others they could not foretell, they would, if need were, be faithful to the death.

"And beyond it also," added Peter; while Margaret bowed her stately head in sweet assent.

"Children," said Castell, "you will be rich—few richer in this land— though mayhap it would be wise that you should not show all your wealth at once, or ape the place of a great house, lest envy should fall upon your heads and crush you. Be content to wait, and rank will find you in its season, or if not you, your children. Peter, I tell you now, lest I should forget it, that the list of all my moneys and other possessions in chattels or lands or ships or merchandise is buried beneath the floor of my office, just under where my chair stands. Lift the boards and dig away a foot of rubbish, and you will find a stone trap, and below an iron box with the deeds, inventories, and some very precious jewels. Also, if by any mischance that box should be lost, duplicates of nearly all these papers are in the hands of my good friend and partner in our inland British trade, Simon Levett, whom you know. Remember my words, both of you."

"Father," broke in Margaret in an anxious voice, "why do you speak of the future thus?—I mean, as though you had no share in it? Do you fear aught?"

"Yes, daughter, much, or rather I expect, I do not fear, who am prepared and desire to meet all things as they come. You have sworn that oath, have you not? And you will keep it, will you not?"

"Aye!" they answered with one breath.

"Then prepare you to feel the weight of the first of those trials whereof it speaks, for I will no longer hold back the truth from you. Children, I, whom for all these years you have thought of your own faith, am a Jew as my forefathers were before me, back to the days of Abraham."

The effect of this declaration upon its hearers was remarkable. Peter's jaw dropped, and for the second time that day his face went white; while Margaret sank down into a chair that stood near by, and stared at him helplessly. In those times it was a very terrible thing to be a Jew. Castell looked from one to the other, and, feeling the insult of their silence, grew angry.

"What!" he exclaimed in a bitter voice, "are you like all the others? Do you scorn me also because I am of a race more ancient and honourable than those of any of your mushroom lords and kings? You know my life: say, what have I done wrong? Have I caught Christian children and crucified them to death? Have I defrauded my neighbour or oppressed the poor? Have I mocked your symbol of the Host? Have I conspired against the rulers of this land? Have I been a false friend or a cruel father? You shake your heads; then why do you stare at me as though I were a thing accursed and unclean? Have I not a right to the faith of my fathers? May I not worship God in my own fashion?" And he looked at Peter, a challenge in his eyes. "Sir," answered Peter, "without a doubt you may, or so it seems to me. But then, why for all these years have you appeared to worship Him in ours?"

At this blunt question, so characteristic of the speaker, Castell seemed to shrink like a pin-pricked bladder, or some bold fighter who has suddenly received a sword-thrust in his vitals. All courage went out of the man, his fiery eyes grew tame, he appeared to become visibly smaller, and to put on something of the air of those mendicants of his own race, who whine out their woes and beg alms of the passer-by. When next he spoke, it was as a suppliant for merciful judgment at the hands of his own child and her lover.

"Judge me not harshly," he said. "Think what it is to be a Jew—an outcast, a thing that the lowest may spurn and spit at, one beyond the law, one who can be hunted from land to land like a mad wolf, and tortured to death, when caught, for the sport of gentle Christians, who first have stripped him of his gains and very garments. And then think what it means to escape all these woes and terrors, and, by the doffing of a bonnet, and the mumbling of certain prayers with the lips in public, to find sanctuary, peace, and protection within the walls of Mother Church, and thus fostered, to grow rich and great."

He paused as though for a reply, but as they did not speak, went on:

"Moreover, as a child, I was baptized into your Church; but my heart, like that of my father, remained with the Jews, and where the heart goes the feet follow."

"That makes it worse," said Peter, as though speaking to himself.

"My father taught me thus," Castell went on, as though pleading his case before a court of law.

"We must answer for our own sins," said Peter again.

Then at length Castell took fire.

"You young folk, who as yet know little of the terrors of the world, reproach me with cold looks and colder words," he said; "but I wonder, should you ever come to such a pass as mine, whether you will find the heart to meet it half as bravely? Why do you think that I have told you this secret, that I might have kept from you as I kept it from your mother, Margaret? I say because it is a part of my penance for the sin which I have sinned. Aye, I know well that my God is a jealous God, and that this sin will fall back on my head, and that I shall pay its price to the last groat, though when and how the blow will strike me I know not. Go you, Peter, or you, Margaret, and denounce me if you will. Your priests will speak well of you for the deed, and open to you a shorter road to Heaven, and I shall not blame you, nor lessen your wealth by a single golden noble."

"Do not speak so madly, Sir," said Peter; "these matters are between you and God. What have we to do with them, and who made us judges over you? We only pray that your fears may come to nothing, and that you may reach your grave in peace and honour."

"I thank you for your generous words, which are such as befit your nature," said Castell gently; "but what says Margaret?"

"I, father?" she answered, wildly. "Oh! I have nothing to say. He is right. It is between you and God; but it is hard that I must lose my love so soon." Peter looked up, and Castell answered:

"Lose him! Why, what did he swear but now?"

"I care not what he swore; but how can I ask him, who is of noble, Christian birth, to marry the daughter of a Jew who all his life has passed himself off as a worshipper of that Jesus Whom he denies?"

Now Peter held up his hand.

"Have done with such talk," he said. "Were your father Judas himself, what is that to you and me? You are mine and I am yours till death part us, nor shall the faith of another man stand between us for an hour. Sir, we thank you for your confidence, and of this be sure, that although it makes us sorrowful, we do not love or honour you the less because now we know the truth."

Margaret rose from her chair, looked a while at her father, then with a sob threw herself suddenly upon his breast.

"Forgive me if I spoke bitterly," she said, "who, not knowing that I was half a Jewess, have been taught to hate their race. What is it to me of what faith you are, who think of you only as my dearest father?"

"Why weep then?" asked Castell, stroking her hair tenderly.

"Because you are in danger, or so you say, and if anything happened to you—oh! what shall I do then?"

"Accept it as the will of God, and bear the blow bravely, as I hope to do, should it fall," he answered, and, kissing her, left the chapel.

"It seems that joy and trouble go hand in hand," said Margaret, looking up presently.

"Yes, Sweet, they were ever twins; but provided we have our share of the first, do not let us quarrel with the second. A pest on the priests and all their bigotry, say I! Christ sought to convert the Jews, not to kill them; and for my part I can honour the man who clings to his own faith, aye, and forgive him because they forced him to feign to belong to ours. Pray then that neither of us may live to commit a greater sin, and that we may soon be wed and dwell in peace away from London, where we can shelter him."

"I do—I do," she answered, drawing close to Peter, and soon they forgot their fears and doubts in each other's arms.

On the following morning, that of Sunday, Peter, Margaret, and Betty went together to Mass at St. Paul's church; but Castell said that he was ill, and did not come. Indeed, now that his conscience was stirred as to the double life he had led so long, he purposed, if he could avoid it, to worship in a Christian church no more. Therefore he said that he was sick; and they, knowing that this sickness was of the heart, answered nothing. But privately they wondered what he would do who could not always remain sick, since not to go to church and partake of its Sacraments was to be published as a heretic.

But if he did not accompany them himself, Castell, without their knowledge, sent two of his stoutest servants, bidding these keep near to them and see that they came home safe.

Now, when they left the church, Peter saw two Spaniards, whose faces he thought he knew, who seemed to be watching them, but, as he lost sight of them presently in the throng, said nothing. Their shortest way home ran across some fields and gardens where there were few houses. This lane, then, they followed, talking earnestly to each other, and noting nothing till Betty behind called out to them to beware. Then Peter looked up and saw the two Spaniards scrambling through a gap in the fence not six paces ahead of them, saw also that they laid their hands upon their sword-hilts.

"Let us pass them boldly," he muttered to Margaret; "I'll not turn my back on a brace of Spaniards," but he also laid his hand upon the hilt of the sword he wore beneath his cloak, and bade her get behind him.

Thus, then, they came face to face. Now, the Spaniards, who were evil-looking fellows, bowed courteously enough, and asked if he were not Master Peter Brome. They spoke in Spanish; but, like Margaret Peter knew this tongue, if not too well, having been taught it as a child, and practised it much since he came into the service of John Castell, who used it largely in his trade.

"Yes," he answered. "What is your business with me?"

"We have a message for you, Señor, from a certain comrade of ours, one Andrew, a Scotchman, whom you met a few nights ago," replied the spokesman of the pair. "He is dead, but still he sends his message, and it is that we should ask you to join him at once. Now, all of us brothers have sworn to deliver that message, and to see that you keep the tryst. If some of us should chance to fail, then others will meet you with the message until you keep that tryst."

"You mean that you wish to murder me," said Peter, setting his mouth and drawing the sword from beneath his cloak. "Well, come on, cowards, and we will see whom Andrew gets for company in hell to-day. Run back, Margaret and Betty—run." And he tore off his cloak and threw it over his left arm.

So for a moment they stood, for he looked fierce and ill to deal with. Then, just as they began to feint in front of him, there came a rush of feet, and on either side of Peter appeared the two stout serving-men, also sword in hand.

"I am glad of your company," he said, catching sight of them out of the corners of his eyes. "Now, Señors Cut-throats, do you still wish to deliver that message?"

The answer of the Spaniards, who saw themselves thus unexpectedly out-matched, was to turn and run, whereon one of the serving-men, picking up a big stone that lay in the path, hurled it after them with all his force. It struck the hindmost Spaniard full in the back, and so heavy was the blow that he fell on to his face in the mud, whence he rose and limped away, cursing them with strange, Spanish oaths, and vowing vengeance.

"Now," said Peter, "I think that we may go home in safety, for no more messengers will come from Andrew to-day."

"No," gasped Margaret, "not to-day, but to-morrow or the next day they will come, and oh! how will it end?"

"That God knows alone," answered Peter gravely as he sheathed his sword.

When the story of this attempt was told to Castell he seemed much disturbed.

"It is clear that they have a blood-feud against you on account of that Scotchman whom you killed in self-defence," he said anxiously. "Also these Spaniards are very revengeful, nor have they forgiven you for calling the English to your aid against them. Peter, I fear that if you go abroad they will murder you."

"Well, I cannot stay indoors always, like a rat in a drain," said Peter crossly, "so what is to be done? Appeal to the law?"

"No; for you have just broken the law by killing a man. I think you had best go away for a while till this storm blows over."

"Go away! Peter go away?" broke in Margaret, dismayed.

"Yes," answered her father. "Listen, daughter. You cannot be married at once. It is not seemly; moreover, notice must be given and arrangement made. A month hence will be soon enough, and that is not long for you to wait who only became affianced yesterday. Also, until you are wed, no word must be said to any one of this betrothal of yours, lest those Spaniards should lay their feud at your door also, and work you some mischief. Let none know of it, I charge you, and in company be distant to each other, as though there were nothing between you."

"As you will, Sir," replied Peter; "but for my part I do not like all these hidings of the truth, which ever lead to future trouble. I say, let me bide here and take my chance, and let us be wed as soon as may be."

"That your wife may be made a widow before the week is out, or the house burnt about our ears by these rascals and their following? No, no, Peter; walk softly that you may walk safely. We will hear the report of the Spaniard d'Aguilar, and afterwards take counsel."

CHAPTER 6

Farewell

D'Aguilar came to supper that night as he had promised, and this time not on foot and unattended, but with pomp and circumstance as befitted a great lord. First appeared two running footmen to clear the way; then followed D'Aguilar, mounted on a fine white horse, and splendidly apparelled in a velvet cloak and a hat with nodding ostrich plumes, while after him rode four men-at-arms in his livery.

"We asked one guest, or rather he asked himself, and we have got seven, to say nothing of their horses," grumbled Castell, watching their approach from an upper window. "Well, we must make the best of it. Peter, go, see that man and beast are fed, and fully, that they may not grumble at our hospitality. The guard can eat in the little hall with our own folk. Margaret, put on your richest robe and your jewels, those which you wore when I took you to that city feast last summer. We will show these fine, foreign birds that we London merchants have brave feathers also."

Peter hesitated, misdoubting him of the wisdom of this display, who, if he could have his will, would have sent the Spaniard's following to the tavern, and received him in sober garments to a simple meal.

But Castell, who seemed somewhat disturbed that night, who loved, moreover, to show his wealth at times after the fashion of a Jew, began to fume and ask if he must go himself. So the end of it was that Peter went, shaking his head, while, urged to it by her father, Margaret departed also to array herself.

A few minutes later Castell, in his costliest feast-day robe, greeted d'Aguilar in the ante-hall, and, the two of them being alone, asked him how matters went as regarded de Ayala and the man who had been killed.

"Well and ill," answered d'Aguilar. "Doctor de Puebla, with whom I hoped to deal, has left London in a huff, for he says that there is not room for two Spanish ambassadors at Court, so I had to fall back upon de Ayala after all. Indeed, twice have I seen that exalted priest upon the subject of the well-deserved death of his villainous servant, and, after much difficulty, for having lost several men in such brawls, he thought his honour touched, he took the fifty gold angels—to be transmitted to the fellow's family, of course, or so he said—and gave a receipt. Here it is," and he handed a paper to Castell, who read it carefully.

It was to the effect that Peter Brome, having paid a sum of fifty angels to the relatives of Andrew Pherson, a servant of the Spanish ambassador, which Andrew the said Peter had killed in a brawl, the said ambassador undertook not to prosecute or otherwise molest the said Peter on account of the manslaughter which he had committed.

"But no money has been paid," said Castell.

"Indeed yes, I paid it. De Ayala gives no receipts against promises."

"I thank you for your courtesy, Señor. You shall have the gold before you leave this house. Few would have trusted a stranger thus far."

D'Aguilar waved his hand.

"Make no mention of such a trifle. I would ask you to accept it as a token of my regard for your family, only that would be to affront so wealthy a man. But listen, I have more to say. You are, or rather your kinsman Peter, is still in the wood. De Ayala has pardoned him; but there remains the King of England, whose law he has broken. Well, this day I have seen the King, who, by the way, talked of you as a worthy man, saying that he had always thought only a Jew could be so wealthy, and that he knew you were not, since you had been reported to him as a good son of the Church," and he paused, looking at Castell.

"I fear his Grace magnifies my wealth, which is but small," answered Castell coolly, leaving the rest of his speech unnoticed. "But what said his Grace?"

"I showed him de Ayala's receipt, and he answered that if his Excellency was satisfied, he was satisfied, and for his part would not order any process to issue; but he bade me tell you and Peter Brome that if he caused more tumult in his streets, whatever the provocation, and especially if that tumult were between English and Spaniards, he would hang him at once with trial or without it. All of which he said very angrily, for the last thing which his Highness desires just now is any noise between Spain and England."

"That is bad," answered Castell, "for this very morning there was near to being such a tumult," and he told the story of how the two Spaniards had waylaid Peter, and one of them been knocked down by the serving-man with a stone. At this news d'Aguilar shook his head.

"Then that is just where the trouble lies," he exclaimed. "I know it from my people, who keep me well informed, that all those servants of de Ayala, and there are more than twenty of them, have sworn an oath by the Virgin of Seville that before they leave this land they will have your kinsman's blood in payment for that of Andrew Pherson, who, although a Scotchman, was their officer, and a brave man whom they loved much. Now, if they attack him, as they will, there must be a brawl, for Peter fights well, and if there is a brawl, though Peter and the English get the best of it, as very likely they may, Peter will certainly be hanged, for so the King has promised."

"Before they leave the land? When do they leave it?"

"De Ayala sails within a month, and his folk with him, for his co-ambassador, the Doctor de Puebla, will bear with him no more, and has written from the country house where he is sulking that one of them must go."

"Then I think it is best, Señor, that Peter should travel for a month."

"Friend Castell, you are wise; I think so too, and, I counsel you, arrange it at once. Hush! here comes the lady, your daughter."

As he spoke, Margaret appeared descending the broad oak stairs which led into the ante-room. Holding a lamp in her hand, she was in full light, whereas the two men stood in the shadow. She wore a low-cut dress of crimson velvet, embroidered about the bodice with dead gold, which enhanced the dazzling whiteness of her shapely neck and bosom. Round her throat hung a string of great pearls, and on her head was a net of gold, studded with smaller pearls, from beneath which her glorious, chestnut-black hair flowed down in rippling waves almost to her knees. Having her father's bidding so to do, she had adorned herself thus that she might look her fairest, not in the eyes of their guest, but in those of her new-affianced husband. So fair was she seen thus that d'Aguilar, the artist, the adorer of loveliness, caught his breath and shivered at the sight of her.

"By the eleven thousand virgins!" he said, "your daughter is more beautiful than all of them put together. She should be crowned a queen, and bewitch the world."

"Nay, nay, Señor," answered Castell hurriedly; "let her remain humble and honest, and bewitch her husband."

"So I should say if I were the husband," he muttered, then stepped forward, bowing, to meet her.

Now the light of the silver lamp she held on high flowed over the two of them, d'Aguilar and Margaret, and certainly they seemed a well-matched pair. Both were tall and cast by Nature in a rich and splendid mould; both had that high air of breeding which comes with ancient blood—for what bloods are more ancient than those of the Jew and the Eastern?—both were slow and stately of movement, low-voiced, and dignified of speech. Castell noted it and was afraid, he knew not of what.

Peter, entering the room by another door, clad only in his grey clothes, for he would not put on gay garments for the Spaniard, noted it also, and with the quick instinct of love knew this magnificent foreigner for a rival and an enemy. But he was not afraid, only jealous and angry. Indeed, nothing would have pleased him better then than that the Spaniard should have struck him in the face, so that within five minutes it might be shown which of them was the better man. It must come to this, he felt, and very glad would he have been if it could come at the beginning and not at the end, so that one or the other of them might be saved much trouble. Then he remembered that he had promised to say or show nothing of how things stood between him and Margaret, and, coming forward, he greeted d'Aguilar quietly but coldly, telling him that his horses had been stabled, and his retinue accommodated.

The Spaniard thanked him very heartily, and they passed in to supper. It was a strange meal for all four of them, yet outwardly pleasant enough. Forgetting his cares, Castell drank gaily, and began to talk of the many changes which he had seen in his life, and of the rise and fall of kings. D'Aguilar talked also, of the Spanish wars and policy, for in the first he had seen much service, and of the other he knew every turn. It was easy to see that he was one of those who mixed with courts, and had the ear of ministers and majesty. Margaret also, being keen-witted and anxious to learn of the great world that lay beyond Holborn and London town, asked questions, seeking to know, amongst other things, what were the true characters of Ferdinand, King of Aragon, and Isabella his wife, the famous queen.

"I will tell you in few words, Señora. Ferdinand is the most ambitious man in Europe, false also if it serves his purpose. He lives for self and gain—that money and power. These are his gods, for he has no true religion. He is not clever but, being very cunning, he will succeed and leave a famous name behind him."

"An ugly picture," said Margaret. "And what of his queen?"

"She," answered d'Aguilar, "is a great woman, who knows how to use the temper of her time and so attain her ends. To the world she shows a tender heart, but beneath it lies hid an iron resolution."

"What are those ends?" asked Margaret again.

"To bring all Spain under her rule; utterly to crush the Moors and take their territories; to make the Church of Christ triumphant upon earth; to stamp out heresy; to convert or destroy the Jews," he added slowly, and as he spoke the words, Peter, watching, saw his eyes open and glitter like a snake's—"to bring their bodies to the purifying flames, and their vast wealth into her treasury, and thus earn the praise of the faithful upon earth, and for herself a throne in heaven."

For a while there was silence after this speech, then Margaret said boldly: "If heavenly thrones are built of human blood and tears, what stone and mortar do they use in hell, I wonder?" Then, without pausing for an answer, she rose, saying that she was weary, curtseyed to d'Aguilar, her father and Peter, each in turn, and left the hall.

When she had gone the talk flagged, and presently d'Aguilar asked for his men and horses and departed also, saying as he went:

"Friend Castell, you will repeat my news to your good kinsman here. I pray for all your sakes that he may bow his head to what cannot be helped, and thus keep it safe upon his shoulders."

"What meant the man?" asked Peter, when the sound of the horses' hoofs had died away.

Castell told him of what had passed between him and d'Aguilar before supper, and showed him de Ayala's receipt, adding in a vexed voice: "I have forgotten to repay him the gold; it shall be sent to-morrow."

"Have no fear; he will come for it," answered Peter coldly. "Now, if I have my way, I will take the risk of these Spaniards' swords and King Henry's rope, and bide here."

"That you must not do," said Castell earnestly, "for my sake and Margaret's, if not for yours. Would you make her a widow before she is a wife? Listen: it is my wish that you travel down to Essex to take delivery of your father's land in the Vale of Dedham and see to the repairing of the mansion house, which, I am told, needs it much. Then, when these Spaniards are gone, you can return and at once be married, say one short month hence."

"Will not you and Margaret come with me to Dedham?"

Castell shook his head.

"It is not possible. I must wind up my affairs, and Margaret cannot go with you alone. Moreover, there is no place for her to lodge. I will keep her here till you return."

"Yes, Sir; but will you keep her safe? The cozening words of Spaniards are sometimes more deadly than their swords."

"I think that Margaret has a medicine against all such arts," answered her father with a little smile, and left him.

281

On the morrow when Castell told Margaret that her lover must leave her for a while that night—for this Peter would not do himself—she prayed him even with tears that he would not send him so far from her, or that they might all go together. But he reasoned with her kindly, showing her that the latter was impossible, and that if Peter did not go at once it was probable that Peter would soon be dead, whereas, if he went, there would be but one short month of waiting till the Spaniards had sailed, after which they might be married and live in peace and safety.

So she came to see that this was best and wisest, and gave way; but oh! heavy were those hours, and sore was their parting. Essex was no far journey, and to enter into lands which only two days before Peter believed he had lost for ever, no sad errand, while the promise that at the end of a single month he should return to claim his bride hung before them like a star. Yet they were sad-hearted, both of them, and that star seemed very far away.

Margaret was afraid lest Peter might be waylaid upon the road, but he laughed at her, saying that her father was sending six stout men with him as an escort, and thus companioned he feared no Spaniards. Peter, for his part, was afraid lest d'Aguilar might make love to her while he was away. But now she laughed at him, saying that all her heart was his, and that she had none to give to d'Aguilar or any other man. Moreover, that England was a free land in which women, who were no king's wards, could not be led whither they did not wish to go. So it seemed that they had naught to fear, save the daily chance of life and death. And yet they were afraid.

"Dear love," said Margaret to him after she had thought a while, "our road looks straight and easy, and yet there may be pitfalls in it that we cannot guess. Therefore you must swear one thing to me: That whatever you shall hear or whatever may happen, you will never doubt me as I shall never doubt you. If, for instance, you should be told that I have discarded you, and given myself to some other husband; if even you should believe that you see it signed by my hand, or if you think that you hear it told to you by my voice—still, I say, believe it not."

"How could such a thing be?" asked Peter anxiously.

"I do not suppose that it could be; I only paint the worst that might happen as a lesson for us both. Heretofore my life has been calm as a summer's day; but who knows when winter storms may rise, and often I have thought that I was born to know wind and rain and lightning as well as peace and sunshine. Remember that my father is a Jew, and that to the Jews and their children terrible things chance at times. Why, all this wealth might vanish in an hour, and you might find me in a prison, or clad in rags begging my bread. Now do you swear?" and she held towards him the gold crucifix that hung upon her bosom.

"Aye," he said, "I swear it by this holy token and by your lips," and he kissed first the cross and then her mouth, adding, "Shall I ask the same oath of you?"

She laughed.

"If you will; but it is not needful. Peter, I think that I know you too well; I think that your heart will never stir even if I be dead and you married to another. And yet men are men, and women have wiles, so I will swear this: That should you slip, perchance, and I live to learn it, I will try not to judge you harshly." And again she laughed, she who was so certain of her empire over this man's heart and body.

"Thank you," said Peter; "but for my part I will try to stand straight upon my feet, so should any tales be brought to you of me, sift them well, I pray you."

Then, forgetting their doubts and dreads, they talked of their marriage, which they fixed for that day month, and of how they would dwell happily in Dedham Vale. Also Margaret, who well knew the house, named the Old Hall, where they should live, for she had stayed there as a child, gave him many commands as to the new arrangement of its chambers and its furnishing, which, as there was money and to spare, could be as costly as they willed, saying that she would send him down all things by wain so soon as he was ready for them.

Thus, then, the hours wore away, until at length night came and they took their last meal together, the three of them, for it was arranged that Peter should start at moonrise, when none were about to see him go. It was not a very happy meal, and, though they made a brave show of eating, but little food passed their lips. Now the horses were ready, and Margaret buckled on Peter's sword and threw his cloak about his shoulders, and he, having shaken Castell by the hand and bade him guard their jewel safely, without more words kissed her in farewell, and went.

Taking the silver lamp in her hand, she followed him to the anteroom. At the door he turned and saw her standing there gazing after him with wide eyes and a strained, white face. At the sight of her silent pain almost his heart failed him, almost he refused to go. Then he remembered, and went.

For a while Margaret still stood thus, until the sound of the horses' hoofs had died away indeed. Then she turned and said:

"Father, I know not how it is, but it seems to me that when Peter and I meet again it will be far off, yes, far off upon the stormy sea—but what sea I know not." And without waiting for an answer she climbed the stairs to her chamber, and there wept herself to sleep.

Castell watched her depart, then muttered to himself:

"Pray God she is not foresighted like so many of our race; and yet why is my own heart so heavy? Well, according to my judgment, I have done my best for him and her, and for myself I care nothing."

CHAPTER 7

News From Spain

Peter Brome was a very quiet man, whose voice was not often heard about the place, and yet it was strange how dull and different the big, old house in Holborn seemed without him. Even the handsome Betty, with whom he was never on the best of terms, since there was much about her of which he disapproved, missed him, and said so to her cousin, who only answered with a sigh. For in the bottom of her heart Betty both feared and respected Peter. The fear was of his observant eyes and caustic words, which she knew were always words of truth, and the respect for the general uprightness of his character, especially where her own sex was concerned.

In fact, as has been hinted, some little time before, when Peter had first come to live with the Castells, Betty, thinking him a proper man of gentle birth, such a one indeed as she would wish to marry, had made advances to him, which, as he did not seem to notice them, became by degrees more and more marked. What happened at last they two knew alone, but it was something that caused Betty to become very angry, and to speak of Peter to her friends as a cold-blooded lout who thought only of work and gain. The episode was passing, and soon forgotten by the lady in the press of other affairs; but the respect remained. Moreover, on one or two occasions, when the love of admiration had led her into griefs, Peter had proved a good friend, and what was better, a friend who did not talk. Therefore she wished him back again, especially now, when something that was more than mere vanity and desire for excitement had taken hold of her, and Betty found herself being swept off her feet into very deep and doubtful waters.

The shopmen and the servants missed him also, for to him all disputes were brought for settlement, nor, provided it had not come about through lack of honesty, were any pains too great for him to take to help them in a trouble. Most of all Castell missed him, since until Peter had gone he did not know how much he had learned to rely upon him, both in his business and as a friend. As for Margaret, her life without him was one long, empty night.

Thus it chanced that in such a house any change was welcome, and, though she liked him little enough, Margaret was not even displeased when one morning Betty told her that the lord d'Aguilar was coming to call on her that day, and purposed to bring her a present.

"I do not seek his presents," said Margaret indifferently; then added, "But how do you know that, Betty?"

The young woman coloured, and tossed her head as she answered:

"I know it, Cousin, because, as I was going to visit my old aunt yesterday, who lives on the wharf at Westminster, I met him riding, and he called out to me, saying that he had a gift for you and one for me also."

"Be careful you do not meet him too often, Betty, when you chance to be visiting your aunt. These Spaniards are not always over-honest, as you may learn to your sorrow."

"I thank you for your good counsel," said Betty, shortly, "but I, who am older than you, know enough of men to be able to guard myself, and can keep them at a distance."

"I am glad of it, Betty, only sometimes I have thought that the distance was scarcely wide enough," answered Margaret, and left the subject, for she was thinking of other things.

That afternoon, when Margaret was walking in the garden, Betty, whose face seemed somewhat flushed, ran up to her and said that the lord d'Aguilar was waiting in the hall.

"Very good," answered Margaret, "I will come. Go, tell my father, that he may join us. But why are you so disturbed and hurried?" she added wonderingly.

"Oh!" answered Betty, "he has brought me a present, so fine a present—a mantle of the most wonderful lace that ever I saw, and a comb of mottled shell mounted in gold to keep it off the hair. He made me wait while he showed me how to put it on, and that was why I ran."

Margaret did not quite see the connection; but she answered slowly:

"Perhaps it would have been wiser if you had run first. I do not understand why this fine lord brings you presents."

"But he has brought one for you also, Cousin, although he would not say what it was."

"That I understand still less. Go, tell my father that the Señor d'Aguilar awaits him."

Then she went into the hall, and found d'Aguilar looking at an illuminated Book of Hours in which she had been reading, that was written in Spanish in one column and in Latin in that opposite. He greeted her in his usual graceful way, that, where Margaret was concerned, was easy and well-bred without being bold, and said at once:

"So you read Spanish, Señora?"

"A little. Not very well, I fear."

"And Latin also?"

"A little again. I have been taught that tongue. By studying them thus I try to improve myself in both."

"I perceive that you are learned as you are beautiful," and he bowed courteously.

"I thank you, Señor; but I lay claim to neither grace."

"What need is there to claim that which is evident?" replied d'Aguilar; then added, "But I forgot, I have brought you a present, if you will be pleased to accept it. Or, rather, I bring you what is your own, or at the least your father's. I bargained with his Excellency Don de Ayala, pointing out that fifty gold angels were too much to pay for that dead rogue of his; but he would give me nothing back in money, since with gold he never parts. Yet I won some change from him, and it stands without your door. It is a Spanish jennet of the true Moorish blood, which, hundreds of years ago, that people brought with them from the East. He needs it no longer, as he returns to Spain, and it is trained to bear a lady." Margaret did not know what to answer, but, fortunately, at that moment her father appeared, and to him d'Aguilar repeated his tale, adding that he had heard his daughter say that the horse she rode had fallen with her, so that she could use it no more.

Now, Castell did not wish to accept this gift, for such he felt it to be; but d'Aguilar assured him that if he did not he must sell it and return him the price in money, as it did not belong to him. So, there being no help for it, he thanked him in his daughter's name and his own, and they went into the stable-yard, whither it had been taken, to look at this horse.

The moment that Castell saw it he knew that it was a creature of great value, pure white in colour, with a long, low body, small head, gentle eyes, round hoofs, and flowing mane and tail, such a horse, indeed, as a queen might have ridden. Now again he was confused, being sure that this beast had never been given back as a luck-penny, since it would have fetched more than the fifty angels on the market; moreover, it was harnessed with a woman's saddle and bridle of the most beautifully worked red Cordova leather, to which were attached a silver bit and stirrup. But d'Aguilar smiled, and vowed that things were as he had told them, so there was nothing more to be said. Margaret, too, was so pleased with the mare, which she longed to ride, that she forgot her scruples, and tried to believe that this was so. Noting her delight, which she could not conceal as she patted the beautiful beast, d'Aguilar said:

"Now I will ask one thing in return for the bargain that I have made—that I may see you mount this horse for the first time. You told me that you and your father were wont to go out together in the morning. Have I your leave, Sir," and he turned to Castell, "to ride with you before breakfast, say, at seven of the clock, for I would show the lady, your daughter, how she should manage a horse of this blood, which is something of a trick?"

"If you will," answered Castell—"that is, if the weather is fine," for the offer was made so courteously that it could scarcely be refused.

D'Aguilar bowed, and they re-entered the house, talking of other matters. When they were in the hall again, he asked whether their kinsman Peter had reached his destination safely, adding:

"I pray you, do not tell me where it is, for I wish to be able to put my hand upon my heart and swear to all concerned, and especially to certain fellows who are still seeking for him, that I know nothing of his hiding-place."

Castell answered that he had, since but a few minutes before a letter had come from him announcing his safe arrival, tidings at which Margaret looked up, then, remembering her promise, said that she was glad to hear of it, as the roads were none too safe, and spoke indifferently of something else. D'Aguilar added that he also was glad, then, rising, took his leave "till seven on the morrow."

When he had gone, Castell gave Margaret a letter, addressed to her in Peter's stiff, upright hand, which she read eagerly. It began and ended with sweet words, but, like his speech, was brief and to the point, saying only that he had accomplished his journey without adventure, and was very glad to find himself again in the old house where he was born, and amongst familiar fields and faces. On the morrow he was to see the tradesmen as to alterations and repairs which were much needed, even the moat being choked with mud and weeds. His last sentence was: "I much mistrust me of that fine Spaniard, and I am jealous to think that he should be near to you while I am far away. Beware of him, I say—beware of him. May the Mother of God and all the saints have you in their keeping! Your most true affianced lover."

This letter Margaret answered before she slept, for the messenger was to return at dawn, telling Peter, amongst other things, of the gift which d'Aguilar had brought her, and how she and her father were forced to accept it, but bidding him not be jealous, since, although the gift was welcome, she liked the giver little, who did but count the hours till her true lover should come back again and take her to himself.

Next morning she was up early, clothed in her riding-dress, for the day was very fine, and by seven o'clock d'Aguilar appeared, mounted on a great horse. Then the Spanish jennet was brought out, and deftly he lifted her to the saddle, showing her how she must pull but lightly on the reins, and urge or check her steed with her voice alone, using no whip or spur.

A perfect beast it proved to be, indeed, gentle as a lamb, and easy, yet very spirited and swift.

D'Aguilar was a pleasant cavalier also, talking of many things grave and gay, until at length even Castell forgot his thoughts, and grew cheerful as they cantered forward through the fresh spring morning by heath and hill and woodland, listening to the singing of the birds, and watching the husbandmen at their labour. This ride was but the first of several that they took, since d'Aguilar knew their hours of exercise, even when they changed them, and whether they asked him or not, joined or met them in such a natural fashion that they could not refuse his company. Indeed, they were much puzzled to know how he came to be so well acquainted with their movements, and even with the direction in which they proposed to ride, but supposed that he must have it from the grooms, although these were commanded to say nothing, and always denied having spoken with him. That Betty should speak of such matters, or even find opportunity of doing so, never chanced to cross their minds, who did not guess that if they rode with d'Aguilar in the morning, Betty often walked with him in the evening when she was supposed to be at church, or sewing, or visiting her aunt upon the wharf at Westminster. But of these walks the foolish girl said nothing, for her own reasons.

Now, as they rode together, although he remained very courteous and respectful, the manner of d'Aguilar towards Margaret grew ever more close and intimate. Thus he began to tell her stories, true or false, of his past life, which seemed to have been strange and eventful enough; to hint, too, of a certain hidden greatness that pertained to him which he did not dare to show, and of high ambitions which he had. He spoke also of his loneliness, and his desire to lose it in the companionship of a kindred heart, if he could find one to share his wealth, his station, and his hopes; while all the time his dark eyes, fixed on Margaret, seemed to say, "The heart I seek is such a one as yours." At length, at some murmured word or touch, she took affright, and, since she could not avoid him abroad, determined to stay at home, and, much as she loved the sport, to ride no more till Peter should return. So she gave out that she had hurt her knee, which made the saddle painful to her, and the beautiful Spanish mare was left idle in the stable, or mounted only by the groom.

Thus for some days she was rid of d'Aguilar, and employed herself in reading and working, or in writing long letters to Peter, who was busy enough at Dedham, and sent her thence many commissions to fulfil.

One afternoon Castell was seated in his office deciphering letters which had just reached him. The night before his best ship, of over two hundred tons burden, which was named the *Margaret*, after his daughter, had come safely into the mouth of the Thames from Spain. That evening she was to reach her berth at Gravesend with the tide, when Castell proposed to go aboard of her to see to the unloading of her cargo. This was the last of his ships which remained unsold, and it was his plan to re-load and victual her at once with goods that were waiting, and send her back to the port of Seville, where his Spanish partners, in whose name she was already registered, had agreed to take her over at a fixed price. This done, it was only left for him to hand over his business to the merchants who had purchased it in London, after which he would be free to depart, a very wealthy man, and spend the evening of his days at peace in Essex, with his daughter and her husband, as now he so greatly longed to do. So soon as they were within the river banks the captain of this ship, Smith by name, had landed the cargo-master with letters and a manifest of cargo, bidding him hire a horse and bring them to Master Castell's house in Holborn. This the man had done safely, and it was these letters that Castell read.

One of them was from his partner Bernaldez in Seville; not in answer to that which he had written on the night of the opening of this history—for this there had been no time—yet dealing with matters whereof it treated. In it was this passage:

"You will remember what I wrote to you of a certain envoy who has been sent to the Court of London, who is called d'Aguilar, for as our cipher is so secret, and it is important that you should be warned, I take the risk of writing his name. Since that letter I have learned more concerning this grandee, for such he is. Although he calls himself plain Don d'Aguilar, in truth he is the Marquis of Morella, and on one side, it is said, of royal blood, if not on both, since he is reported to be the son born out of wedlock of Prince Carlos of Viana, the half-brother of the king. The tale runs that Carlos, the learned and gentle, fell in love with a Moorish lady of Aguilar of high birth and great wealth, for she had rich estates at Granada and elsewhere, and, as he might not marry her because of the difference of their rank and faiths, lived with her without marriage, of which union one son was born. Before Prince Carlos died, or was poisoned, and while he was still a prisoner at Morella, he gave to, or procured for this boy the title of marquis, choosing from some fancy the name of Morella, that place where he had suffered so much. Also he settled some private lands upon him. After the prince died, the Moorish lady, his lover, who had secretly become a Christian, took her son to live at her palace in Granada, where she died also some ten years ago, leaving all her great wealth to him, for she never married. At this time it is said that his life was in danger, for the reason that, although he was half a Moor, too much of the blood-royal ran in his veins. But the Marquis was clever, and persuaded the king and queen that he had no ambition beyond his pleasures. Also the Church interceded for him, since to it he proved himself a faithful son, persecuting all heretics, especially the Jews, and even Moors, although they are of his own blood. So in the end he was confirmed in his possessions and left alone, although he refused to become a priest.

"Since then he has been made an agent of the Crown at Granada, and employed upon various embassies to London, Rome, and else-where, on matters connected with the faith and the establishment of the Holy Inquisition. That is why he is again in England at this moment, being charged to obtain the names and particulars concerning all Maranos settled there, especially if they trade with Spain. I have seen the names of those of whom he must inquire most closely, and that is why I write to you so fully, since yours is first upon the list. I think, therefore, that you do wisely to wind up your business with this country, and especially to sell your ships to us outright and quickly, since otherwise they might be seized—like yourself, if you came here. My counsel to you is—hide your wealth, which will be great when we have paid you all we owe, and go to some place where you will be forgotten for a while, since that bloodhound d'Aguilar, for so he calls himself, after his mother's birthplace, has not tracked you to London for nothing. As yet, thanks be to God, no suspicion has fallen on any of us; perhaps because we have many in our pay."

When Castell had finished transcribing all this passage he read it through carefully. Then he went into the hall, where a fire burned, for the day was cold, and threw the translation on to it, watching until it was consumed, after which he returned to his office, and hid away the letter in a secret cupboard behind the panelling of the wall. This done, he sat himself in his chair to think.

"My good friend Juan Bernaldez is right," he said to himself; "d'Aguilar, or the Marquis Morella, does not nose me and the others out for nothing. Well, I shall not trust myself in Spain, and the money, most of it, except what is still to come from Spain, is put out where it will never be found by him, at good interest too. All seems safe enough—and yet I would to God that Peter and Margaret were fast married, and that we three sat together, out of sight and mind, in the Old Hall at Dedham. I have carried on this game too long. I should have closed my books a year ago; but the trade was so good that I could not. I was wise also, who in this one lucky year have nearly doubled my fortune. And yet it would have been safer, before they guessed that I was so rich. Greed—mere greed—for I do not need this money which may destroy us all! Greed! The ancient pitfall of my race."

As he thought thus there came a knock upon his door. Snatching up a pen he dipped it in the ink-horn and, calling "Enter," began to add a column of figures on a paper before him.

The door opened; but he seemed to take no heed, so diligently did he count his figures. Yet, although his eyes were fixed upon the paper, in some way that he could not understand he was well aware that d'Aguilar and no other stood in the room behind him, the truth being, no doubt, that unconsciously he had recognised his footstep. For a moment the knowledge turned him cold—he who had just been reading of the mission of this man—and feared what was to come. Yet he acted well.

"Why do you disturb me, Daughter?" he said testily, and without looking round. "Have not things gone ill enough with half the cargo destroyed by sea-water, and the rest, that you must trouble me while I sum up my losses?" And, casting the pen down, he turned his stool round impatiently.

Yes! there sure enough stood d'Aguilar, very handsomely arrayed, and smiling and bowing as was his custom.

CHAPTER 8

D'Aguilar Speaks

"Losses?" said d'Aguilar. "Do I hear the wealthy John Castell, who holds half the trade with Spain in the hollow of his hand, talk of losses?"

"Yes, Señor, you do. Things have gone ill with this ship of mine that has barely lived through the spring gales. But be seated."

"Indeed, is that so?" said d'Aguilar as he sat down. "What a lying jade is rumour! For I was told that they had gone very well. Doubtless, however, what is loss to you would be priceless gain to one like me."

Castell made no answer, but waited, feeling that his visitor had not come to speak with him of his trading ventures.

"Señor Castell," said d'Aguilar, with a note of nervousness in his voice, "I am here to ask you for something."

"If it be a loan, Señor, I fear that the time is not opportune." And he nodded towards the sheet of figures.

"It is not a loan; it is a gift."

"Anything in my poor house is yours," answered Castell courteously, and in Oriental form.

"I rejoice to hear it, Señor, for I seek something from your house."

Castell looked a question at him with his quick black eyes.

"I seek your daughter, the Señora Margaret, in marriage."

Castell stared at him, then a single word broke from his lips.

"Impossible."

"Why impossible?" asked d'Aguilar slowly, yet as one who expected some such answer. "In age we are not unsuited, nor perhaps in fortune, while of rank I have enough, more than you guess perhaps. I vaunt not myself, yet women have thought me not uncomely. I should be a good friend to the house whence I took a wife, where perchance a day may come when friends will be needed; and lastly, I desire her not for what she may bring with her, though wealth is always welcome, but—I pray you to believe it—because I love her."

"I have heard that the Señor d'Aguilar loves many women, yonder in Granada."

"As I have heard that the *Margaret* had a prosperous voyage, Señor Castell. Rumour, as I said but now, is a lying jade. Yet I will not copy her. I have been no saint. Now I would become one, for Margaret's sake. I will be true to your daughter, Señor. What say you now?"

Castell only shook his head.

"Listen," went on d'Aguilar. "I am more than I seem to be; she who weds me will not lack for rank and titles."

"Yes, you are the Marquis de Morella, the reputed son of Prince Carlos of Viana by a Moorish mother, and therefore nephew to his Majesty of Spain."

D'Aguilar looked at him, then bowed and said:

"Your information is good—as good as mine, almost. Doubtless you do not like that bar in the blood. Well, if it were not there, I should be where Ferdinand is, should I not? So I do not like it either, though it is good blood and ancient—that of those high-bred Moors. Now, may not the nephew of a king and the son of a princess of Granada be fit to mate with the daughter of—a Jew, yes, a Marano, and of a Christian English lady, of good family, but no more?"

Castell lifted his hand as though to speak; but d'Aguilar went on:

"Deny it not, friend; it is not worth while here in private. Was there not a certain Isaac of Toledo who, hard on fifty years ago, left Spain, for his own reasons, with a little son, and in London became known as Joseph Castell, having, with his son, been baptized into the Holy Church? Ah! you see you are not the only one who studies genealogies."

"Well, Señor, if so, what of it?"

"What of it? Nothing at all, friend Castell. It is an old story, is it not, and, as that Isaac is long dead and his son has been a good Christian for nearly fifty years and had a Christian wife and child, who will trouble himself about such a matter? If he were openly a Hebrew now, or worse still, if pretending to be a Christian, he in secret practised the rites of the accursed Jews, why then—"

"Then what?"

"Then, of course, he would be expelled this land, where no Jew may live, his wealth would be forfeit to its king, whose ward his daughter would become, to be given in marriage where he willed, while he himself, being Spanish born, might perhaps be handed over to the power of Spain, there to make answer to these charges. But we wander to strange matters. Is that alliance still impossible, Señor?"

Castell looked him straight in the eyes and answered:

"Yes."

There was something so bold and direct in his utterance of the word that for a moment d'Aguilar seemed to be taken aback. He had not expected this sharp denial.

"It would be courteous to give a reason," he said presently.

"The reason is simple, Marquis. My daughter is already betrothed, and will ere long be wedded."

D'Aguilar did not seem surprised at this intelligence.

"To that brawler, your kinsman, Peter Brome, I suppose?" he said interrogatively. "I guessed as much, and by the saints I am sorry for her, for he must be a dull lover to one so fair and bright; while as a husband—" And he shrugged his shoulders. "Friend Castell, for her sake you will break off this match."

"And if I will not, Marquis?"

"Then I must break it off for you in the interest of all of us, including, of course, myself, who love her, and wish to lift her to a great place, and of yourself, whom I desire should pass your old age in peace and wealth, and not be hunted to your death like a mad dog."

"How will you break it, Marquis? by—"

"Oh no, Señor!" answered d'Aguilar, "not by other men's swords— if that is what you mean. The worthy Peter is safe from them so far as I am concerned, though if he should come face to face with mine, then let the best man win. Have no fear, friend, I do not practise murder, who value my own soul too much to soak it in blood, nor would I marry a woman except of her own free will. Still, Peter may die, and the fair Margaret may still place her hand in mine and say, 'I choose you as my husband.'"

"All these things, and many others, may happen, Marquis; but I do not think it likely that they will happen, and for my part, whilst thanking you for it, I decline your honourable offer, believing that my daughter will be more happy in her present humble state with the man she has chosen. Have I your leave to return to my accounts?" And he rose.

"Yes, Señor," answered d'Aguilar, rising also; "but add an item to those losses of which you spoke, that of the friendship of Carlos, Marquis de Morella, and on the other side enter again that of his hate. Man!" he added, and his dark, handsome face turned very evil as he spoke, "are you mad? Think of the little tabernacle behind the altar in your chapel, and what it contains."

Castell stared at him, then said:

"Come, let us see. Nay, fear no trick; like you I remember my soul, and do not stain my hands with blood. Follow me, so you will be safe."

Curiosity, or some other reason, prompted d'Aguilar to obey, and presently they stood behind the altar.

"Now," said Castell, as he drew the tapestry and opened the secret door, "look!" D'Aguilar peered into the place; but where should have been the table, the ark, the candlesticks, and the roll of the law of which Betty had told him, were only old dusty boxes filled with parchments and some broken furniture.

"What do you see?" asked Castell.

"I see, friend, that you are even a cleverer Jew than I thought. But this is a matter that you must explain to others in due season. Believe me, I am no inquisitor." Then without more words he turned and left him.

When Castell, having shut the secret door and drawn the tapestry, hurried from the chapel, it was to find that the marquis had departed.

He went back to his office much disturbed, and sat himself down there to think. Truly Fate, that had so long been his friend, was turning its face against him. Things could not have gone worse. D'Aguilar had discovered the secret of his faith through his spies, and, having by some accursed mischance fallen in love with his daughter's beauty, was become his bitter enemy because he must refuse her to him. Why must he refuse her? The man was of great position and noble blood; she would become the wife of one of the first grandees of Spain, one who stood nearest to the throne. Perhaps—such a thing was possible—she might live herself to be queen, or the mother of kings. Moreover, that marriage meant safety for himself; it meant a quiet age, a peaceable death in his own bed—for, were he fifty times a Marano, who would touch the father-in-law of the Marquis de Morella? Why? Just because he had promised her in marriage to Peter Brome, and through all his life as a merchant he had never yet broken with a bargain because it went against himself. That was the answer. Yet almost he could find it in his heart to wish that he had never made that bargain; that he had kept Peter, who had waited so long, waiting for another month. Well, it was too late now. He had passed his word, and he would keep it, whatever the cost might be.

Rising, he called one of the servants, and bade her summon Margaret. Presently she returned, saying that her mistress had gone out walking with Betty, adding also that his horse was at the door for him to ride to the river, where he was to pass the night on board his ship.

Taking paper, he bethought him that he would write to Margaret, warning her against the Spaniard. Then, remembering that she had nothing to fear from him, at any rate at present, and that it was not wise to set down such matters, he told her only to take good care of herself, and that he would be back in the morning.

That evening, when Margaret was in her own little sitting-chamber which adjoined the great hall, the door opened, and she looked up from the work upon which she was engaged, to see d'Aguilar standing before her.

"Señor!" she said, amazed, "how came you here?"

"Señora," he answered, closing the door and bowing, "my feet brought me. Had I any other means of coming I think that I should not often be absent from our side."

"Spare me your fine words, I pray you, Señor," answered Margaret, frowning. "It is not fitting that I should receive you thus alone at night, my father being absent from the house." And she made as though she would pass him and reach the door.

D'Aguilar, who stood in front of it, did not move, so perforce she stopped half way.

"I found that he was absent," he said courteously, "and that is why I venture to address you upon a matter of some importance. Give me a few minutes of your time, therefore, I beseech you."

Now, at once the thought entered Margaret's mind that he had some news of Peter to communicate to her—bad news perhaps.

"Be seated, and speak on, Señor," she said, sinking into a chair, while he too sat down, but still in front of the door.

"Señora," he said, "my business in this country is finished, and in a few days I sail hence for Spain." And he hesitated a moment.

"I trust that your voyage will be pleasant," said Margaret, not knowing what else to answer.

"I trust so also, Señora, since I have come to ask you if you will share it. Listen, before you refuse. To-day I saw your father, and begged your hand of him. He would give me no answer, neither yea nor nay, saying that you were your own mistress, and that I must seek it from your lips."

"My father said that?" gasped Margaret, astonished, then bethought her that he might have had reasons for speaking so, and went on rapidly, "Well, it is short and simple. I thank you, Señor; but stay in England."

"Even that I would be willing to do for your sake Señora, though, in truth, I find it a cold and barbarous country."

"If so, Señor d'Aguilar, I think that I should go to Spain. I pray you let me pass."

"Not till you have heard me out, Señora, when I trust that your words will be more gentle. See now I am a great man in my own country. Although it suits me to pass here incognito as plain Señor d'Aguilar I am the Marquis of Morella, the nephew of Ferdinand the King, with some wealth and station, official and private. If you disbelieve me, I can prove it to you."

"I do not disbelieve," answered Margaret indifferently, "it may well be so; but what is that to me?"

"Then is it not something, Lady, that I, who have blood-royal in my veins, should seek the daughter of a merchant to be my wife?"

"Nothing at all—to me, who am satisfied with my humble lot."

"Is it nothing to you that I should love as I do, with all my heart and soul? Marry me, and I tell you that I will lift you high, yes, perhaps even to the throne."

She thought a moment, then asked:

"The bribe is great, but how would you do that? Many a maid has been deceived with false jewels, Señor."

"How has it been done before? Not every one loves Ferdinand. I have many friends who remember that my father was poisoned by his father and Ferdinand's, he being the elder son. Also, my mother was a princess of the Moors, and if I, who dwell among them as the envoy of their Majesties, threw in my sword with theirs—or there are other ways. But I am speaking things that have never passed my lips before, which, were they known, would cost me my head—let it serve to show how much I trust you."

"I thank you, Señor, for your trust; but this crown seems to me set upon a peak that it is dangerous to climb, and I had sooner sit in safety on the plain."

"You reject the pomp," went on d'Aguilar in his passionate, pleading voice, "then will not the love move you? Oh! you shall be worshipped as never woman was. I swear to you that in your eyes there is a light which has set my heart on fire, so that it burns night and day, and will not be quenched. Your voice is my sweetest music, your hair is a cord that binds me to you faster than the prisoner's chain, and, when you pass, for me Venus walks the earth. More, your mind is pure and noble as your beauty, and by the aid of it I shall be lifted up through the high places of the earth to some white throne in heaven. I love you, my lady, my fair Margaret; because of you, all other women are become coarse and hateful in my sight. See how much I love you, that I, one of the first grandees of Spain, do this for your sweet sake," and suddenly he cast himself upon his knees before her, and lifting the hem of her dress pressed it to his lips.

Margaret looked down at him, and the anger that was rising in her breast melted, while with it went her fear. This man was much in earnest; she could not doubt it. The hand that held her robe trembled like shaken water, his face was ashen, and in his dark eyes swam tears. What cause had she to be afraid of one who was so much her slave?

"Señor," she said very gently, "rise, I pray you. Do not waste all this love upon one who chances to have caught your fancy, but who is quite unworthy of it, and far beneath you; one, moreover, by whom it may not be returned. Señor, I am already affianced. Therefore, put me out of your mind and find some other love."

He rose and stood in front of her.

"Affianced," he said, "I knew it. Nay, I will say no ill of the man; to revile one more fortunate is poor argument. But what is it to me if you are affianced? What to me if you were wed? I should seek you all the same, who have no choice. Beneath me? You are as far above me as a star, and it would seem as hard to reach. Seek some other love? I tell you, lady, that I have sought many, for not all are so hard to win, and I hate them every one. You I desire alone, and shall desire till I be dead, aye, and you I will win or die. No, I will not die till you are my own. Have no fear, I will not kill your lover, save perhaps in fair fight; I will not force you to give yourself to me, should I find the chance, but with your own lips I will yet listen to you asking me to be your husband. I swear it by Him Who died for us. I swear that, laying aside all other ends, to that sole purpose I will devote my days. Yes, and should you chance to pass from earth before me, then I will follow you to the very gates of death and clasp you there."

Now again Margaret's fear returned to her. This man's passion was terrible, yet there was a grandeur in it; Peter had never spoken to her in so high a fashion.

"Señor," she said almost pleadingly, "corpses are poor brides; have done with such sick fancies, which surely must be born of your Eastern blood."

"It is your blood also, who are half a Jew, and, therefore, at least you should understand them."

"Mayhap I do understand, mayhap I think them great in their own fashion, yes, noble even, and admire, if it can be noble to seek to win away another man's betrothed. But, Señor, I am that man's betrothed, and all of me, my body and my soul, is his, nor would I go back upon my word, and so break his heart, to win the empire of the earth. Señor, once more I implore you to leave this poor maid to the humble life that she has chosen, and to forget her."

"Lady," answered d'Aguilar, "your words are wise and gentle, and I thank you for them. But I cannot forget you, and that oath I swore just now I swear again, thus." And before she could prevent him, or even guess what he was about to do, he lifted the gold crucifix that hung by a chain about her neck, kissed it, and let it fall gently back upon her breast, saying, "See, I might have kissed your lips before you could have stayed me, but that I will never do until you give me leave, so in place of them I kiss the cross, which till then we both must carry. Lady, my lady Margaret, within a day or two I sail for Spain, but your image shall sail with me, and I believe that ere long our paths must cross again. How can it be otherwise since the threads of your life and mine were intertwined on that night outside the Palace of Westminster—intertwined never to be separated till one of us has ceased to be, and then only for a little while. Lady, for the present, farewell."

Then swiftly and silently as he had come, d'Aguilar went.

It was Betty who let him out at the side door, as she had let him in. More, glancing round to see that she was not observed—for it chanced now that Peter was away with some of the best men, and the master was out with others, no one was on watch this night—leaving the door ajar that she might re-enter, she followed him a little way, till they came to an old arch, which in some bygone time had led to a house now pulled down. Into this dark place Betty slipped, touching d'Aguilar on the arm as she did so. For a moment he hesitated, then, muttering some Spanish oath between his teeth, followed her.

"Well, most fair Betty," he said, "what word have you for me now?"

"The question is, Señor Carlos," answered Betty with scarcely suppressed indignation, "what word you have for me, who dared so much for you to-night? That you have plenty for my cousin, I know, since standing in the cold garden I could hear you talk, talk, talk, through the shutters, as though for your very life."

"I pray that those shutters had no hole in them," reflected d'Aguilar to himself. "No, there was a curtain also; she can have seen nothing." But aloud he answered: "Mistress Betty, you should not stand about in this bitter wind; you might fall ill, and then what should I suffer?"

"I don't know, nothing perhaps; that would be left to me. What I want to understand is, why you plan to come to see me, and then spend an hour with Margaret?"

"To avert suspicion, most dear Betty. Also I had to talk to her of this Peter, in whom she seems so greatly interested. You are very shrewd, Betty—tell me, is that to be a match?"

"I think so; I have been told nothing, but I have noticed many things, and almost every day she is writing to him, though why she should care for that owl of a man I cannot guess."

"Doubtless because she appreciates solid worth, Betty, as I do in you. Who can account for the impulses of the heart, which come, say some of the learned, from heaven, and others, from hell? At least it is no affair of ours, so let us wish them happiness, and, after they are married, a large and healthy family. Meanwhile, dear Betty, are you making ready for your voyage to Spain?"

"I don't know," answered Betty gloomily. "I am not sure that I trust you and your fine words. If you want to marry me, as you swear, and be sure I look for nothing less, why cannot it be before we start, and how am I to know that you will do so when we get there?"

"You ask many questions, Betty, all of which I have answered before. I have told you that I cannot marry you here because of that permission which is necessary on account of the difference in our ranks. Here, where your place is known, it is not to be had; there, where you will pass as a great English lady—as of course you are by birth—I can obtain it in an hour. But if you have any doubts, although it cuts me to the heart to say it, it would be best that we should part at once. I will take no wife who does not trust me fully and alone. Say then, cruel Betty, do you wish to leave me?"

"You know I don't; you know it would kill me," she answered in a voice that was thick with passion, "you know I worship the ground you tread on, and hate every woman you go near, yes, even my cousin who has been so good to me, and whom I love. I will take the risk and come with you, believing you to be an honest gentleman, who would not deceive a girl who trusts him; and if you do, may God deal with you as I shall, for I am no toy to be broken and thrown away, as you would find out. Yes, I will take the risk because you have made me love you so that I cannot live without you."

"Betty, your words fill me with rapture, showing me that I have not misread your noble mind; but speak a little lower—there are echoes in this hole. Now for the plans, for time is short, and you may be missed. When I am about to sail I will invite Mistress Margaret and yourself to come aboard my ship."

"Why not invite me without my cousin Margaret?" asked Betty.

"Because it would excite suspicion which we must avoid—do not interrupt me. I will invite you both or get you there upon some other pretext, and then I will arrange that she shall be brought ashore again and you taken on. Leave it all to me, only swear that you will obey any instructions I may send you for if you do not, I tell you that we have enemies in high places who may part us for ever. Betty, I will be frank, there is a great lady who is jealous, and watches you very closely. Do you swear?"

"Yes, yes, I swear. But about the great lady?"

"Not a word about her—on your life—and mine. You shall hear from me shortly. And now, sweetheart—good-night."

"Good-night," said Betty, but still she did not stir.

Then, understanding that she expected something more, d'Aguilar nerved himself to the task, and touched her hair with his lips.

Next moment he regretted it, for even that tempered salute fanned her passion into flame.

Throwing her arms about his neck Betty drew his face to hers and kissed him many times, till at length he broke, half choking, from her embrace, and escaped into the street.

"Mother of Heaven!" he muttered to himself, "the woman is a volcano in eruption. I shall feel her kisses for a week," and he rubbed his face ruefully with his hand. "I wish I had made some other plan; but it is too late to change it now—she would betray everything. Well, I will be rid of her somehow, if I have to drown her. A hard fate to love the mistress and be loved of the maid!"

CHAPTER 9

The Snare

On the following morning, when Castell returned, Margaret told him of the visit of d'Aguilar, and of all that had passed between them, told him also that he was acquainted with their secret, since he had spoken of her as half a Jew.

"I know it, I know it," answered her father, who was much disturbed and very angry, "for yesterday he threatened me also. But let that go, I can take my chance; now I would learn who brought this man into my house when I was absent, and without my leave."

"I fear that it was Betty," said Margaret, "who swears that she thought she did no wrong."

"Send for her," said Castell. Presently Betty came, and, being questioned, told a long story.

She said she was standing by the side door, taking the air, when Señor d'Aguilar appeared, and, having greeted her, without more words walked into the house, saying that he had an appointment with the master.

"With me?" broke in Castell. "I was absent."

"I did not know that you were absent, for I was out when you rode away in the afternoon, and no one had spoken of it to me, so, thinking that he was your friend, I let him in, and let him out again afterwards. That is all I have to say."

"Then I have to say that you are a hussy and a liar, and that, in one way or the other, this Spaniard has bribed you," answered Castell fiercely. "Now, girl, although you are my wife's cousin, and therefore my daughter's kin, I am minded to turn you out on to the street to starve."

At this Betty first grew angry, then began to weep; while Margaret pleaded with her father, saying that it would mean the girl's ruin, and that he must not take such a sin upon him. So the end of it was, that, being a kind-hearted man, remembering also that Betty Dene was of his wife's blood, and that she had favoured her as her daughter did, he relented, taking measures to see that she went abroad no more save in the company of Margaret, and that the doors were opened only by men-servants.

So this matter ended.

That day Margaret wrote to Peter, telling him of all that had happened, and how the Spaniard had asked her in marriage, though the words that he used she did not tell. At the end of her letter, also, she bade him have no fear of the Señor d'Aguilar or of any other man, as he knew where her heart was.

When Peter received this writing he was much vexed to learn that both Master Castell and Margaret had incurred the enmity of d'Aguilar, for so he guessed it must be, also that Margaret should have been troubled with his love-making; but for the rest he thought little of the matter, who trusted her as he trusted heaven. Still it made him anxious to return to London as soon as might he, even though he must take the risk of the Spaniards' daggers. Within three days, however, he received other letters both from Castell and from Margaret, which set his fears at rest.

These told him that d'Aguilar had sailed for Spain indeed, Castell said that he had seen him standing on the poop of the Ambassador de Ayala's vessel as it dropped down the Thames towards the sea. Moreover, Margaret had a note of farewell from his hand, which ran:

Adieu, sweet lady, till that predestined hour when we meet again.
I go, as I must, but, as I told you, your image goes with me.
Your worshipper till death,
Morella

"He may take her image so long as I keep herself and if he comes back with his worship, I promise him that death and he shall not be far apart," was Peter's grim comment as he laid the paper down. Then he went on with his letters, which told that now, when the Spaniards had gone, and there was nothing more to fear, he was awaited in London. Indeed, Castell fixed a day when he should arrive—May 31st—that was within a week, adding that on its morrow—namely, June 1st, for Margaret would not be wed in May, the Virgin Mary's month, since she held it to be unlucky—their marriage might take place as quietly as they would.

Margaret wrote the same news, and in such sweet words that he kissed her letter, then hastened to answer it, shortly, after his custom, for Peter was no great scribe, saying, that if the saints willed it he would be with them by nightfall on the last day of May, and that in all England there was no happier man than he.

****

Now all that week Margaret was very busy preparing her marriage robe, and other garments also, for it was settled that on the next day they should ride together down to Dedham, in Essex, whither her father would follow them shortly. The Old Hall was not ready, indeed, nor would it be for some time; but Peter had furnished certain rooms in it which might serve them for the summer season, and by winter time the house would be finished and open.

Castell was busy also, for now, having worked very hard at the task, his ship the *Margaret* was almost refitted and laden, so that he hoped to get her to sea on this same May 31st, and thus be clear of the last of his business, except the handing over of his warehouses and stock to those who had bought them. These great affairs kept him much at Gravesend, where the ship lay, but, as he had no dread of further trouble now that d'Aguilar and the other Spaniards, among them that band of de Ayala's servants who had vowed to take Peter's life, were gone, this did not disturb him.

Oh! happy, happy was Margaret during those sweet spring days, when her heart was bright and clear as the skies from which all winter storms had passed. So happy was she indeed, and so full of a hundred joyful cares, that she found no time to take note of her cousin Betty, who worked with her at her wedding broideries, and helped to make preparations for the journey which should follow after. Had she done so, she might have seen that Betty was anxious and distressed, like one who waited for some tidings that did not come, and from hour to hour fought against anguish and despair But she took no note, whose heart was too full of her own matters, and who did but count the hours till she should see her lover back and pass to his arms, a wife.

Thus the time went on until the appointed day of Peter's return, the morrow of her marriage, for which all things were now prepared, down to Peter's wedding garments, that were finer than any she had yet seen him wear, and the decking of the neighbouring church with flowers. In the early morning her father rode away to Gravesend with the most of his men-servants for the ship *Margaret* was to sail at the following dawn and there was yet much to be done before she could lift anchor. Still, he had promised to be back by nightfall in time to meet Peter who, leaving Dedham that morning, could not reach them before then.

At length it was past four of the afternoon, and everything being finished, Margaret went to her room to dress herself anew, that she might look fine in Peter's eyes when he should come. Betty she did not take with her, for there were things to which her cousin must attend; moreover, her heart was so full that she wished to be alone a while.

Betty's heart was full also, but not with joy. She had been deceived. The fine Spanish Don, who had made her love him so desperately, had sailed away and left her without a word. She could not doubt it, he had been seen standing on the ship—and not one word. It was cruel, cruel, and now she must help another woman to be made a happy wife, she who was beggared of hope and love. Moodily, full of bitterness, she went about her tasks, biting her lips and wiping her fine eyes with the sleeve of her robe, when suddenly the door opened, and a servant, not one of their own, but a strange man who had been brought in to help at the morrow's feast, called out that a sailor wished to speak with her.

"Then let him enter here; I have no time to go out to listen to his talk," snapped Betty.

Presently the sailor was shown in, the man who brought him leaving the room at once. He was a dark fellow, with sly black eyes, who, had he not spoken English so well, might have been taken for a Spaniard.

"Who are you, and what is your business?" asked Betty sharply.

"I am the carpenter of the ship *Margaret*," he answered, "and I am here to say that our master Castell has met with an accident there, and desires that Mistress Margaret, his daughter, should come to him at once."

"What accident?" asked Betty.

"In seeing to the stowage of cargo he slipped and fell down the hold, hurting his back and breaking his right arm, and that is why he cannot write. He is in great pain; but the physician whom we summoned bade me tell Mistress Margaret that at present he has no fear for his life. Are you Mistress Margaret?"

"No," answered Betty; "but I will go to her at once; do you bide here."

"Then are you her cousin, Mistress Betty Dene, for if so I have something for you?"

"I am. What is it?"

"This," said the man, drawing out a letter which he handed to her.

"Who gave you this?" asked Betty suspiciously. "I do not know his name, but he was a noble-looking Spanish Don, and a liberal one too. He had heard of the accident on the *Margaret*, and, knowing my errand, asked me if I would deliver this letter to you, for the fee of a gold *ducat*, and promise to say nothing of it to any one else."

"Some rude gallant, doubtless," said Betty, tossing her head; "they are ever writing to me. Bide here; I go to Mistress Margaret."

Once she was outside the door Betty broke the seal of the letter eagerly enough, for she had been taught with Margaret, and could read well. It ran:

Beloved,

You thought me faithless and gone, but it is not so. I was silent only because I knew you could not come alone who are watched; but now the God of Love gives us our chance. Doubtless your cousin will bring you with her to visit her father, who lies on his ship sadly hurt. While she is with him I have made a plan to rescue you, and then we can be wed and sail at once—yes, to-night or to-morrow, for with much trouble, knowing that you wished it, I have even succeeded in bringing that about, and a priest will be waiting to marry us. Be silent, and show no doubt or fear, whatever happens, lest we should be parted for always. Be sure then that your cousin comes that you may accompany her. Remember that your true love waits you.
C. d'A.

When Betty had mastered the contents of this amorous effusion she went pale with joy, and turned so faint that she was like to fall. Then a doubt struck her that it might be some trick. No, she knew the writing—it was d'Aguilar's, and he was true to her, and would marry her as he had promised, and take her to be a great lady in Spain. If she hesitated now she might lose him for ever—him whom she would follow to the end of the world. In an instant her mind was made up, for Betty had plenty of courage. She would go, even though she must desert the cousin whom she loved.

Thrusting the letter into her bosom she ran to Margaret's room, and, bursting into it, told her of the man and his sad message. But of that letter she said nothing. Margaret turned white at the news, then, recovering herself, said:

"I will come and speak with him at once." And together they went down the stairs.

To Margaret the sailor repeated his story, nor could all her questions shake it. He told her how the mischance had happened, for he had seen it, so he said, and where her father's hurts were, adding, that although the physician held that as yet he was in no danger of his life,

Master Castell thought otherwise, and did nothing but cry that his daughter should be brought to him at once.

Still Margaret doubted and hesitated, for she feared she knew not what.

"Peter should be here within two hours at most," she said to Betty. "Would it not be best to wait for him?"

"Oh! Margaret, and what if your father should die in the meanwhile? Perhaps he knows better how deep his hurts are than does this leech. If so, you would have a sore heart for all your life. Sure you had better go, or at the least I will."

Still Margaret wavered, till the sailor said:

"Lady, if it is your will to come, I can guide you to where a boat waits to take you across the river. If not, I must be gone, for the ship sails with the moonrise, and they only wait your coming to carry the master, your father, to the warehouse on shore thinking it best that you should be present. If you do not come, this will be done as gently as possible, and there you must seek him to-morrow, alive or dead." And the man took up his cap as though to leave.

"I will come with you," said Margaret. "Betty you are right; order the two horses to be saddled mine and the groom's, with a pillion on which you can ride, for I will not send you or go alone, understand that this sailor has his own horse."

The man nodded, and accompanied Betty to the stable. Then Margaret took pen and wrote hastily to Peter, telling him of their evil chance, and bidding him follow her at once to the ship, or, if it had sailed to the warehouse. "I am loth to go," she added "alone with a girl and a strange man, yet I must since my heart is torn with fear for my beloved father. Sweetheart, follow me quickly."

This done, she gave the letter to that servant who had shown in the sailor, bidding him hand it, without fail, to Master Peter Brome when he came, which the man promised to do.

Then she fetched plain dark cloaks for herself and Betty, with hoods to them, that their faces might not be seen, and presently they were mounted.

"Stay!" said Margaret to the sailor as they were about to start. "How comes it that my father did not send one of his own men instead of you, and why did none write to me?"

The man looked surprised; he was a very good actor.

"His people were tending him," he said, "and he bade me to go because I knew the way, and had a good, hired horse ashore which I have used when riding with messages to London about new timbers and other matters. As for writing, the physician began a letter, but he was so slow and long that Master Castell ordered me to be off without it. It seems," the man added, addressing Betty with some irritation, "that Mistress Margaret misdoubts me. If so, let her find some other guide, or bide at home. It is naught to me, who have only done as I was bidden."

Thus did this cunning fellow persuade Margaret that her fears were nothing, though, remembering the letter from d'Aguilar, Betty was somewhat troubled. The thing had a strange look, but, poor, vain fool, she thought to herself that, even if there were some trick, it was certainly arranged only that she might seem to be taken, who could not come alone. In truth she was blind and mad, and cared not what she did, though, let this be said for her, she never dreamed that any harm was meant towards her cousin Margaret, or that a lie had been told as to Master Castell and his hurts.

Soon they were out of London, and riding swiftly by the road that followed the north bank of the river, for their guide did not take them over the bridge, as he said the ship was lying in mid-stream and that the boat would be waiting on the Tilbury shore. But there was more than twenty miles to travel, and, push on as they would, night had fallen ere ever they came there. At length, when they were weary of the dark and the rough road, the sailor pulled up at a spot upon the river's brink—where there was a little wharf, but no houses that they could see—saying that this was the place. Dismounting, he gave his horse to the groom to hold, and, going to the wharf, asked in a loud voice if the boat from the *Margaret* was there, to which a voice answered, "Aye." Then he talked for a minute to those in the boat, though what he said they could not hear, and ran back again, bidding them dismount, and adding that they had done well to come, as Master Castell was much worse, and did nothing but cry for his daughter.

The groom he told to lead the horses a little way along the bank till he found an inn that stood there, where he must await their return or further orders, and to Betty he suggested that she should go with him, as there was but little place left in the boat. This she was willing enough to do, thinking it all part of the plan for her carrying off; but Margaret would have none of it, saying that unless her cousin came with her she would not stir another step. So grumbling a little the sailor gave way, and hurried them both to some wooden steps and down these into a boat, of which they could but dimly see the outline.

So soon as ever they were seated side by side in the stern it was pushed off, and rowed away rapidly into the darkness, while one of the sailors lit a lantern which he fastened to the bow, and far out on the river, as though in answer to the signal, another star of light appeared, towards which they headed. Now Margaret, speaking through the gloom, asked the rowers of her father's state; but the sailor, their guide, prayed her not to trouble them, as the tide ran very swiftly and they must give all their mind to their business lest they should overset. So she was silent, and, racked with doubts and fears, watched that star of light growing ever nearer, till at length it hung above them.

"Is that the ship *Margaret*?" cried their guide, and again a voice answered "Aye."

"Then tell Master Castell that his daughter has come at last," he shouted again, and in another minute a rope had been thrown to them, and they were fast alongside a ladder on to which Betty, who was nearest to it, was pushed the first, except for their guide, who had run up the wooden steps very swiftly.

Betty, who was active and strong, followed him, Margaret coming next. As she reached the deck Betty thought she heard a voice say in Spanish, of which she understood something, "Fool! Why have you brought both?" but the answer she could not catch. Then she turned and gave her hand to Margaret, and together they walked forward to the foot of the mast.

"Lead me to my father," said Margaret.

Whereon the guide answered:

"Yes, this way, Mistress, but come alone, for the sight of two of you at once may disturb him."

"Nay," she answered, "my cousin comes with me." And she took Betty's hand and clung to it.

Shrugging his shoulders the sailor led them forwards, and as they went she noted that men were hauling on a sail, while other men, who sang a strange, wild song, worked on what seemed to be a windlass. Now they reached a cabin, and entered it, the door being shut behind them. In the cabin a man sat at a table with a lamp hanging over his head. He rose and turned towards them, bowing, and Margaret saw that it was—*d'Aguilar*!

Betty stood silent; she had expected to meet him, though not here and thus. Her foolish heart bounded so at the sight of him that she seemed to choke, and could only wonder dimly what mistake had been made, and how he would explain to Margaret and get her away, leaving herself and him together to be married. Indeed, she searched the cabin with her eyes to see where the priest was waiting, then noting a door beyond, thought that doubtless he must be hidden there. As for Margaret, she uttered a little stifled cry, then, being a brave woman, one of that high nature which grows strong in the face of trouble, straightened herself to her full height and said in a low, fierce voice:

"What do you here? Where is my father?"

"Señora," he answered humbly, "I am on board my ship, the *San Antonio*, and as for your father, he is either on his ship, the *Margaret*, or more likely, by now, at his house in Holborn."

At these words Margaret reeled back till the wall of the cabin stayed her, and there she rested.

"Spare me your reproaches," went on d'Aguilar hurriedly. "I will tell you all the truth. First, be not anxious as to your father; no accident has happened to him; he is sound and well. Forgive me if you have suffered pain and doubt; but there was no other way. That tale was only one of love's snares and tricks—" He paused, overcome, fascinated by Margaret's face, which of a sudden had grown awful—that of a goddess of vengeance, of a Medusa, which seemed to chill his blood to ice.

"A snare! A trick!" she muttered hoarsely, while her eyes flamed on him like burning stars. "Thus then I pay you for your tricks." And in an instant he became aware that she had snatched a dagger from her bosom and was springing on him.

He could not move; those fearful eyes held him fast. In another moment that steel would have pierced his heart. But Betty had seen also, and, thrusting her strong arms about Margaret, held her back, crying:

"Listen, you do not understand. It is I he wants—not you; I whom he loves, and who love him, and am about to marry him. You he will send back home."

"Loose me," said Margaret, in such a voice that Betty's arms fell from her, and she stood there, the dagger still in her hand. "Now," she said to d'Aguilar, "the truth, and be swift with it. What means this woman?"

"She knows best," answered d'Aguilar uneasily. "It has pleased her to wrap herself in this web of conceits."

"Which it has pleased you to spin, perchance. Speak, girl!"

"He made love to me," gasped Betty; "and I love him. He promised to marry me. He sent me a letter but to-day—here it is," and she drew it out.

"Read," said Margaret; and Betty read.

"So *you* have betrayed me," said Margaret, "you, my cousin, whom I have sheltered and cherished."

"No," cried Betty. "I never thought to betray you; sooner would I have died. I believed that your father was hurt, and that while you were visiting him that man would take me."

"What have you to say?" asked Margaret of d'Aguilar in the same dreadful voice. "You offered your accursed love to me—and to her, and you have snared us both. Man, what have you to say?"

"Only this," he answered bravely, "that woman is a fool, whose vanity I played on that I might make use of her to keep near to you."

"Do you hear, Betty? do you hear?" cried Margaret with a terrible little laugh; but Betty only groaned as though she were dying.

"I love you, and you only," went on d'Aguilar "As for your cousin, I will send her ashore. I have committed this sin because I could not help myself. The thought that you were to be married to another man to-morrow drove me mad, and I dared all to take you from his arms, even though you should never come to mine. Did I not swear to you," he said with an attempt at his old gallantry, "that your image should accompany me to Spain, whither we are sailing now?" And as he spoke the words the ship lurched a little in the wind.

Margaret made no answer, only toyed with the dagger blade, and watched him with eyes that glittered more coldly than its steel.

"Kill me, if you will, and have done," he went on in a voice that was desperate with love and shame. "So shall I be rid of all this torment."

Then Margaret seemed to awake, for she spoke to him in a new voice—a measured, frozen voice. "No," she answered, "I will not stain my hands even with your blood, for why should I rob God of His own vengeance? If you attempt to touch me, or even to separate me from this poor woman whom you have fooled, then I will kill—not you, but myself, and I swear to you that my ghost shall accompany you to Spain, and from Spain down to the hell that awaits you. Listen, Carlos d'Aguilar, Marquis of Morella, this I know about you, that you believe in God and hear His anger. Well, I call down upon you the vengeance of Almighty God. I see it hang above your head. I say that it shall fall upon you, waking and sleeping, loving and hating, in life and in death to all eternity. Do your worst, for you shall do it all in vain. Whether I die or whether I live, every pang that you cause me to suffer, every misery that you have brought, or shall bring, upon the head of my betrothed, my father, and this woman, shall be repaid to you a million-fold in this world and the next. Now do you still wish that I should accompany you to Spain, or will you let me go?"

"I cannot," he answered hoarsely; "it is too late."

"So be it, I will accompany you to Spain, I and Betty Dene, and the vengeance of Almighty God that hovers over you. Of this at least be sure—I hate you, I despise you, but I fear you not at all. Go." Then d'Aguilar stumbled from that cabin, and the two women heard the door bolted behind him.

CHAPTER 10

The Chase

About the time that Margaret and Betty were being rowed aboard the *San Antonio*, Peter Brome and his servants, who had been delayed an hour or more by the muddy state of the roads, pulled rein at the door of the house in Holborn. For over a month he had been dreaming of this moment of return, as a man does who expects such a welcome as he knew awaited him, and who on the morrow was to be wed to a lovely and beloved bride. He had thought how Margaret would be watching at the window, how, spying him advancing down the street, she would speed to the door, how he would leap from his horse and take her to his arms in front of every one if need be—for why should they be ashamed who were to be wed upon the morrow?

But there was no Margaret at the window, or at any rate he could not see her, for it was dark. There was not even a light; indeed the whole face of the old house seemed to frown at him through the gloom. Still, Peter played his part according to the plan; that is, he leapt from his horse, ran to the door and tried to enter, but could not for it was locked, so he hammered on it with the handle of his sword, till at length some one came and unbolted. It was the hired man with whom Margaret had left the letter, and he held a lantern in his hand.

The sight of him frightened Peter, striking a chill to his heart.

"Who are you?" he asked; then, without waiting for an answer, went on, "Where are Master Castell and Mistress Margaret?"

The man answered that the master was not yet back from his ship, and that the Lady Margaret had gone out nearly three hours before with her cousin Betty and a sailor—all of them on horseback.

"She must have ridden to meet me, and missed us in the dark," said Peter aloud, whereon the man asked whether he spoke to Master Brome, since, if so, he had a letter for him.

"Yes," answered Peter, and snatched it from his hand, bidding him close the door and hold up the lantern while he read, for he could see that the writing was that of Margaret.

"A strange story," he muttered, as he finished it. "Well, I must away," and he turned to the door again.

As he stretched out his hand to the key, it opened, and through it came Castell, as sound as ever he had been.

"Welcome, Peter!" he cried in a jolly voice. "I knew you were here, for I saw the horses; but why are you not with Margaret?"

"Because Margaret has gone to be with you, who should be hurt almost to death, or so says this letter."

"To be with me—hurt to the death! Give it me—nay, read it, I cannot see." So Peter read.

"I scent a plot," said Castell in a strained voice as he finished, "and I think that hound of a Spaniard is at the bottom of it, or Betty, or both. Here, you fellow, tell us what you know, and be swift if you would keep a sound skin."

"That would I, why not?" answered the man, and told all the tale of the coming of the sailor.

"Go, bid the men bring back the horses, all of them," said Castell almost before he had done; "and, Peter, look not so dazed, but come, drink a cup of wine. We shall need it, both of us, before this night is over. What! is there never a fellow of all my servants in the house?" So he shouted till his folk, who had returned with him from the ship, came running from the kitchen.

He bade them bring food and liquor, and while they gulped down the wine, for they could not eat, Castell told how their Mistress Margaret had been tricked away, and must be followed. Then, hearing the horses being led back from the stables, they ran to the door and mounted, and, followed by their men, a dozen or more of them, in all, galloped off into the darkness, taking another road for Tilbury, that by which Margaret went, not because they were sure of this, but because it was the shortest.

But the horses were tired, and the night was dark and rainy, so it came about that the clock of some church struck three of the morning before ever they drew near to Tilbury. Now they were passing the little quay where Margaret and Betty had entered the boat, Castell and Peter riding side by side ahead of the others in stern silence, for they had nothing to say, when a familiar voice hailed them—that of Thomas the groom.

"I saw your horses' heads against the sky," he explained, "and knew them."

"Where is your mistress?" they asked both in a breath.

"Gone, gone with Betty Dene in a boat, from this quay, to be rowed to the *Margaret*, or so I thought. Having stabled the horses as I was bidden, I came back here to await them. But that was hours ago, and I have seen no soul, and heard nothing except the wind and the water, till I heard the galloping of your horses."

"On to Tilbury, and get boats," said Castell. "We must catch the *Margaret* ere she sails at dawn. Perhaps the women are aboard of her."

"If so, I think Spaniards took them there, for I am sure they were not English in that craft," said Thomas, as he ran by the side of Castell's horse, holding to the stirrup leather.

His master made no answer, only Peter groaned aloud, for he too was sure that they were Spaniards.

An hour later, just as the dawn broke, they with their men climbed to the deck of the *Margaret* while she was hauling up her anchor. A few words with her captain, Jacob Smith, told them the worst. No boat had left the ship, no Margaret had come aboard her. But some six hours before they had watched the Spanish vessel, *San Antonio*, that had been berthed above them, pass down the river. Moreover, two watermen in a skiff, who brought them fresh meat, had told them that while they were delivering three sheep and some fowls to the *San Antonio*, just before she sailed, they had seen two tall women helped up her ladder, and heard one of them say in English, "Lead me to my father."

Now they knew all the awful truth, and stared at each other like dumb men.

It was Peter who found his tongue the first, and said slowly:

"I must away to Spain to find my bride, if she still lives, and to kill that fox. Get you home, Master Castell."

"My home is where my daughter is," answered Castell fiercely. "I go a-sailing also."

"There is danger for you in that land of Spaniards, if ever we get yonder," said Peter meaningly.

"If it were the mouth of hell, still I would go," replied Castell. "Why should I not who seek a devil?"

"That we do both," said Peter, and stretching out his hand he took that of Castell. It was the pledge of the father and the lover to follow her who was all to them, till death stayed their quest.

Castell thought a little while, then gave orders that all the crew should be called together on deck in the waist of the ship, which was a *carack* of about two hundred tons burden, round fashioned, and sitting deep in the water, but very strongly built of oak, and a swift sailer. When they were gathered, and with them the officers and their own servants, accompanied by Peter, he went and addressed them just as the sun was rising. In few and earnest words he told them of the great outrage that had been done, and how it was his purpose and that of Peter Brome who had been wickedly robbed of the maid who this day should have become his wife, to follow the thieves across the sea to Spain, in the hope that by the help of God, they might rescue Margaret and Betty. He added that he knew well this was a service of danger, since it might chance that there would be fighting, and he was loth to ask any man to risk life or limb against his will, especially as they came out to trade and not to fight. Still, to those who chose to accompany them, should they win through safely, he promised double wage, and a present charged upon his estate, and would give them writings to that effect. As for those who did not, they could leave the ship now before she sailed.

When he had finished, the sailormen, of whom there were about thirty, with the stout-hearted captain, Jacob Smith, a sturdy-built man of fifty years of age, at the head of them, conferred together, and at last, with one exception—that of a young new-married man, whose heart failed him—they accepted the offer, swearing that they would see the thing through to the end, were it good or ill, for they were all Englishmen, and no lovers of the Spaniards. Moreover, so bitter a wrong stirred their blood. Indeed, although for the most part they were not sailors, six of the twelve men who had ridden with them from London prayed that they might come too, for the love they had to Margaret, their master, and Peter; and they took them. The other six they sent ashore again, bearing letters to Castell's friends, agents, and reeves, as to the transfer of his business and the care of his lands, houses, and other properties during his absence. Also, they took a short will duly signed by Castell and witnessed, wherein he left all his goods of whatever sort that remained unsettled or undevised, to Margaret and Peter, or the survivor of them, or their heirs, or failing these, for the purpose of founding a hospital for the poor. Then these men bade them farewell and departed, very heavy at heart, just as the anchor was hauled home, and the sails began to draw in the stiff morning breeze.

About ten o'clock they rounded the Nore bank safely, and here spoke a fishing-boat, who told them that more than six hours before they had seen the *San Antonio* sail past them down Channel, and noted two women standing on her deck, holding each other's hands and gazing shorewards. Then, knowing that there was no mistake, there being nothing more that they could do, worn out with grief and journeying, they ate some food and went to their cabin to sleep.

As he laid him down Peter remembered that at this very hour he should have been in church taking Margaret as his bride—Margaret, who was now in the power of the Spaniard—and swore a great and bitter oath that d'Aguilar should pay him back for all this shame and agony. Indeed, could his enemy have seen the look on Peter's face he might well have been afraid, for this Peter was an ill man to cross, and had no forgiving heart; also, his wrong was deep.

For four days the wind held, and they ran down Channel before it, hoping to catch sight of the Spaniard; but the *San Antonio* was a swift caravel of 250 tons with much canvas, for she carried four masts, and although the *Margaret* was also a good sailer, she had but two masts, and could not come up with her. Or, for anything they knew, they might have missed her on the seas. On the afternoon of the fourth day, when they were off the Lizard, and creeping along very slowly under a light breeze, the look-out man reported a ship lying becalmed ahead. Peter, who had the eyes of a hawk, climbed up the mast to look at her, and presently called down that he believed from her shape and rig she must be the caravel, though of this he could not be sure as he had never seen her. Then the captain, Smith, went up also, and a few minutes later returned saying that without doubt it was the *San Antonio*.

Now there was a great and joyful stir on board the *Margaret*, every man seeing to his sword and their long or cross bows, of which there were plenty, although they had no bombards or cannon, that as yet were rare on merchant ships. Their plan was to run alongside the *San Antonio* and board her, for thus they hoped to recover Margaret. As for the anger of the king, which might well fall on them for this deed, since he would think little of the stealing of a pair of Englishwomen, of that they must take their chance.

Within half an hour everything was ready, and Peter, pacing to and fro, looked happier than he had done since he rode away to Dedham. The light breeze still held, although, if it reached the *San Antonio*, it did not seem to move her, and, with the help of it, by degrees they came to within half a mile of the caravel. Then the wind dropped altogether, and there the two ships lay. Still the set of the tide, or some current, seemed to be drawing them towards each other, so that when the night closed in they were not more than four hundred paces apart, and the Englishmen had great hopes that before morning they would close, and be able to board by the light of the moon.

But this was not to be, since about nine o'clock thick clouds rose up which covered the heavens, while with the clouds came strong winds blowing off the land, and, when at length the dawn broke, all they could see of the *San Antonio* was her topmasts as she rose upon the seas, flying southwards swiftly. This, indeed, was the last sight they had of her for two long weeks.

From Ushant all across the Bay the airs were very light and variable, but when at length they came off Finisterre a gale sprang up from the north-east which drove them forward very fast. It was on the second night of this gale, as the sun set, that, running out of some mist and rain, suddenly they saw the *San Antonio* not a mile away, and rejoiced, for now they knew that she had not made for any port in the north of Spain, as, although she was bound for Cadiz, they feared she might have done to trick them. Then the rain came on again, and they saw her no more.

All down the coast of Portugal the weather grew more heavy day by day, and when they reached St. Vincent's Cape and bore round for Cadiz, it blew a great gale. Now it was that for the third time they viewed the *San Antonio* labouring ahead of them, nor, except at night, did they lose sight of her any more until the end of that voyage. Indeed, on the next day they nearly came up with her, for she tried to beat in to Cadiz, but, losing one of her masts in a fierce squall, and seeing that the *Margaret*, which sailed better in this tempest, would soon be aboard of her, abandoned her plan, and ran for the Straits of Gibraltar.

Past Tarifa Point they went, having the coast of Africa on their right; past the bay of Algeciras, where the *San Antonio* did not try to harbour; past Gibraltar's grey old rock, where the signal fires were burning, and so at nightfall, with not a mile between them, out into the Mediterranean Sea.

Here the gale was furious, so that they could scarcely carry a rag of canvas, and before morning lost one of their topmasts. It was an anxious night, for they knew not if they would live through it; moreover, the hearts of Castell and of Peter were torn with fear lest the Spaniard should founder and take Margaret with her to the bottom of the sea. When at length the wild, stormy dawn broke, however, they saw her, apparently in an evil case, labouring away upon their starboard bow, and by noon came to within a furlong of her, so that they could see the sailors crawling about on her high poop and stern. Yes, and they saw more than this, for presently two women ran from some cabin waving a white cloth to them; then were hustled back, whereby they learned that Margaret and Betty still lived and knew that they followed, and thanked God. Presently, also, there was a flash, and, before ever they heard the report, a great iron bullet fell upon their decks and, rebounding, struck a sailor, who stood by Peter, on the breast, and dashed him away into the sea. The *San Antonio* had fired the bombard which she carried, but as no more shots came they judged that the cannon had broke its lashings or burst.

A while after the *San Antonio*, two of whose masts were gone, tried to put about and run for Malaga, which they could see far away beneath the snow-capped mountains of the Sierra. But this the Spaniard could not do, for while she hung in the wind the *Margaret* came right atop of her, and as her men laboured at the sails, every one of the Englishmen who could be spared, under the command of Peter, let loose on them with their long shafts and crossbows, and, though the heaving deck of the *Margaret* was no good platform, and the wind bent the arrows from their line, they killed and wounded eight or ten of them, causing them to loose the ropes so that the *San Antonio* swung round into the gale again. On the high tower of the caravel, his arm round the stern-most mast, stood d'Aguilar, shouting commands to his crew. Peter fitted an arrow to his string and, waiting until the *Margaret* was poised for a moment on the crest of a great sea, aimed and loosed, making allowance for the wind.

True to line sped that shaft of his, yet, alas! a span too high, for when a moment later d'Aguilar leapt from the mast, the arrow quivered in its wood, and pinned to it was the velvet cap he wore. Peter ground his teeth in rage and disappointment; almost he could have wept, for the vessels swung apart again, and his chance was gone.

"Five times out of seven," he said bitterly, "can I send a shaft through a bull's ring at fifty paces to win a village badge, and now I cannot hit a man to save my love from shame. Surely God has forsaken me!"

Through all that afternoon they held on, shooting with their bows whenever a Spaniard showed himself, and being shot at in return, though little damage was done to either side. But this they noted—that the *San Antonio* had sprung a leak in the gale, for she was sinking deeper in the water. The Spaniards knew it also, and, being aware that they must either run ashore or founder, for the second time put about, and, under the rain of English arrows, came right across the bows of the *Margaret*, heading for the little bay of Calahonda, that is the port of Motril, for here the shore was not much more than a league away.

"Now," said Jacob Smith, the captain of the *Margaret*, who stood under the shelter of the bulwarks with Castell and Peter, "up that bay lies a Spanish town. I know it, for I have anchored there, and if once the *San Antonio* reaches it, good-bye to our lady, for they will take her to Granada, not thirty miles away across the mountains, where this Marquis of Morella is a mighty man, for there is his palace. Say then, master, what shall we do? In five more minutes the Spaniard will be across our bows again. Shall we run her down, which will be easy, and take our chance of picking up the women, or shall we let them be taken captive to Granada and give up the chase?"

"Never," said Peter. "There is another thing that we can do—follow them into the bay, and attack them there on shore."

"To find ourselves among hundreds of the Spaniards, and have our throats cut," answered Smith, the captain, coolly.

"If we ran them down," asked Castell, who had been thinking deeply all this while, "should we not sink also?"

"It might be so," answered Smith; "but we are built of English oak, and very stout forward, and I think not. But she would sink at once, being near to it already, and the odds are that the women are locked in the cabin or between decks out of reach of the arrows, and must go with her."

"There is another plan," said Peter sternly, "and that is to grapple with her and board her, and this I will do."

The captain, a stout man with a flat face that never changed, lifted his eyebrows, which was his only way of showing surprise.

"What!" he said. "In this sea? I have fought in some wars, but never have I known such a thing."

"Then, friend, you shall know it now, if I can but find a dozen men to follow me," answered Peter with a savage laugh. "What? Shall I see my mistress carried off before my eyes and strike no blow to save her? Rather will I trust in God and do it, and if I die, then die I must, as a man should. There is no other way."

Then he turned and called in a loud voice to those who stood around or loosed arrows at the Spaniard:

"Who will come with me aboard yonder ship? Those who live shall spend their days in ease thereafter, that I promise, and those who fall will win great fame and Heaven's glory."

The crew looked at the waves running hill high, and the water-logged Spaniard labouring in the trough of them as she came round slowly in a wide circle, very doubtfully, as well they might, and made no answer. Then Peter spoke again.

"There is no choice," he said. "If we give that ship our stem we can sink her, but then how will the women be saved? If we leave her alone, mayhap she will founder, and then how will the women be saved? Or she may win ashore, and they will be carried away to Granada, and how can we snatch them out of the hand of the Moors or of the power of Spain? But if we can take the ship, we may rescue them before they go down or reach land. Will none back me at this inch?"

"Aye, son," said old Castell, "I will."

Peter stared at him in surprise. "You—at your years!" he said.

"Yes, at my years. Why not? I have the fewer to risk."

Then, as though he were ashamed of his doubts, one brawny sailorman stepped forward and said that he was ready for a cut at the Spanish thieves in foul weather as in fair. Next all Castell's household servants came out in a body for love of him and Peter and their lady, and after them more sailors, till nearly half of those aboard, something over twenty in all, declared that they were ready for the venture, wherein Peter cried, "Enough." Smith would have come also; but Castell said No, he must stop with the ship.

Then, while the *carack's* head was laid so as to cut the path of the *San Antonio* circling round them slowly like a wounded swan, and the boarders made ready their swords and knives, for here archery would not avail them, Castell gave some orders to the captain. He bade him, if they were cut down or taken, to put about and run for Seville, and there deliver over the ship and her cargo to his partners and correspondents, praying them in his name to do their best by means of gold, for which the sale value of the vessel and her goods should be chargeable, or otherwise, to procure the release of Margaret and Betty, if they still lived, and to bring d'Aguilar, the Marquis of Morella, to account for his crime. This done, he called to one of his servants to buckle on him a light steel breastplate from the ship's stores. But Peter would wear no iron because it was too heavy, only an archer's jerkin of bull-hide, stout enough to turn a sword-cut, such as the other boarders put on also with steel caps, of both of which they had a plenty in the cabin.

Now the *San Antonio*, having come round, was steering for the mouth of the bay in such fashion that she would pass them within fifty yards. Hoisting a small sail to give his ship way, the captain, Smith, took the helm of the *Margaret* and steered straight at her so as to cut her path, while the boarders, headed by Peter and Castell, gathered near the bowsprit, lay down there under shelter of the bulwarks, and waited.

CHAPTER 11

The Meeting on the Sea

For another minute or more the *San Antonio* held on until she divined the desperate purpose of her foe. Then, seeing that soon the *carack*'s prow must crash into her frail side, she shifted her helm and came round several points, so that in the end the *Margaret* ran, not into her, but alongside of her, grinding against her planking, and shearing away a great length of her bulwark. For a few seconds they hung together thus, and, before the seas bore them apart, grapnels were thrown from the *Margaret* whereof one forward got hold and brought them bow to bow. Thus the end of the bowsprit of the *Margaret* projected over the high deck of the *San Antonio*.

"Now for it," said Peter. "Follow me, all." And springing up, he ran to the bowsprit and began to swarm along it.

It was a fearful task. One moment the great seas lifted him high into the air, and the next down he came again till the massive spar crashed on to the deck of the *San Antonio* with such a shock that he nearly flew from it like a stone from a sling. Yet he hung on, and, biding his chance, seized a broken stay-rope that dangled from the end of the bowsprit like a lash from a whip, and began to slide down it. The gale caught him and blew him to and fro; the vessel, pitching wildly, jerked him into the air; the deck of the *San Antonio* rose up and receded like a thing alive. It was near—not a dozen feet beneath him—and loosing his hold he fell upon the forward tower without being hurt then, gaining his feet, ran to the broken mast and flinging his left arm about it, with the other drew his sword.

Next instant—how, he never knew—Castell was at his side, and after him came two more men, but one of these rolled from the deck into the sea and was lost. As he vanished, the chain of the grappling iron parted, and the *Margaret* swung away from them, leaving those three alone in the power of their foes, nor, do what she would, could she make fast again. As yet, however, there were no Spaniards to be seen, for the reason that none had dared to stand upon this high tower whereof the bulwarks were all gone, while the bowsprit of the *Margaret* crashed down upon it like a giant's club, and, as she rolled, swept it with its point.

So there they stood, clinging to the mast and waiting for the end, for now their friends were a hundred yards away, and they knew that their case was desperate. A shower of arrows came, loosed from other parts of the ship, and one of these struck the man with them through the throat, so that he fell to the deck clasping at it, and presently rolled into the sea also. Another pierced Castell through his right forearm, causing his sword to drop and slide away from him. Peter seized the arrow, snapped it in two, and drew it out; but Castell's right arm was now helpless, and with his left he could do no more than cling to the broken mast.

"We have done our best, son," he said, "and failed. Margaret will learn that we would have saved her if we could, but we shall not meet her here."

Peter ground his teeth, and looked about him desperately, for he had no words to say. What should he do? Leave Castell and rush for the waist of the ship and so perish, or stay and die there? Nay, he would not be butchered like a bird on a bough, he would fall fighting.

"Farewell," he called through the gale. "God rest our souls!" Then, waiting till the ship steadied herself, he ran aft, and reaching the ladder that led to her tower, staggered down it to the waist of the vessel, and at its foot halted, holding to the rail.

The scene before him was strange enough, for there, ranged round the bulwarks, were the Spanish men, who watched him curiously, whilst a few paces away, resting against the mast, stood d'Aguilar, who lifted his hand, in which there was no weapon, and addressed him.

"Señor Brome," he shouted, "do not move another step or you are a dead man. Listen to me first, and then do what you will. Am I safe from your sword while I speak?"

Peter nodded his head in assent, and d'Aguilar drew nearer, for even in that more sheltered place it was hard to hear because of the howling of the tempest.

"Señor," he said to Peter, "you are a very brave man, and have done a deed such as none of us have seen before; therefore, I wish to spare you if I may. Also, I have worked you bitter wrong, driven to it by the might of love and jealousy, for which reason also I wish to spare you. To set upon you now would be but murder, and, whatever else I do,

I will not murder. First, let me ease your mind. Your lady and mine is aboard here; but fear not, she has come and will come to no harm from me, or from any man while I live. If for no other reason, I do not desire to affront one who, I hope, will be my wife by her own free will, and whom I have brought to Spain that she might not make this impossible by becoming yours. Señor, believe me, I would no more force a woman's will than I would do murder on her lover."

"What did you, then, when you snatched her from her home by some foul trick?" asked Peter fiercely.

"Señor, I did wrong to her and all of you, for which I would make amends."

"What amends? Will you give her back to me?"

"No, that I cannot do, even if she should wish it, of which I am not sure; no—never while I live."

"Bring her forth, and let us hear whether she wishes it or no," shouted Peter, hoping that his words would reach Margaret.

But d'Aguilar only smiled and shook his head, then went on:

"That I cannot either, for it would give her pain. Still, Señor, I will repay the heavy debt that I owe to you, and to you also, Señor." And he bowed towards Castell who, unseen by Peter, had crept down the ladder, and now stood behind him staring at d'Aguilar with cold rage and indignation. "You have wrought us much damage, have you not? hunting us across the seas, and killing sundry of us with your arrows, and now you have striven to board our ship and put us to the sword, a design in which God has frustrated you. Therefore your lives are justly forfeit, and none would blame us if we slew you. Yet I spare you both. If it is possible I will put you back aboard the *Margaret*, and if it is not possible you shall be set free ashore to go unmolested whither you will. Thus I will wipe out my debt and be free of all reproach."

"Do you take me for such a man as yourself?" asked Peter, with a bitter laugh. "I do not leave this ship alive unless my affianced wife, Mistress Margaret, goes with me."

"Then, Señor Brome, I fear that you will leave it dead, as indeed we may all of us, unless we make land soon, for the vessel is filling fast with water. Still, knowing your metal, I looked for some such words from you, and am prepared with another offer which I am sure you will not refuse. Señor, our swords are much of the same length, shall we measure them against each other? I am a grandee of Spain, the Marquis of Morella, and it will, therefore, be no dishonour for you to fight with me."

"I am not so sure," said Peter, "for I am more than that—an honest man of England, who never practised woman-stealing. Still, I will fight you gladly, at sea or on shore, wherever and whenever we meet, till one or both are dead. But what is the stake, and how do I know that some of these," and he pointed to the crew, who were listening intently, "will not stab me from behind?"

"Señor, I have told you that I do not murder, and that would be the foulest murder. As for the stake, it is Margaret to the victor. If you kill me, on behalf of all my company, I swear by our Saviour's Blood that you shall depart with her and her father unharmed, and if I kill you, then you both shall swear that she shall be left with me, and no suit or question raised but to her woman I give liberty, who have seen more than enough of her."

"Nay," broke in Castell, speaking for the first time "I demand the right to fight with you also when my arm is healed."

"I refuse it," answered d'Aguilar haughtily. "I cannot lift my sword against an old man who is the father of the maid who shall be my wife, and, moreover, a merchant and a Jew. Nay, answer me not, lest all these should remember your ill words. I will be generous, and leave you out of the oath. Do your worst against me, Master Castell, and then leave me to do my worst against you. Señor Brome, the light grows bad, and the water gains upon us. Say, are you ready?"

Peter nodded his head, and they stepped forward.

"One more word," said d'Aguilar, dropping his sword-point. "My friends, you have heard our compact. Do you swear to abide by it, and, if I fall, to set these two men and the two ladies free on their own ship or on the land, for the honour of chivalry and of Spain?"

The captain of the *San Antonio* and his lieutenants answered that they swore on behalf of all the crew.

"You hear, Señor Brome. Now these are the conditions—that we fight to the death, but, if both of us should be hurt or wounded, so that we cannot despatch each other, then no further harm shall be done to either of us, who shall be tended till we recover or die by the will of God."

"You mean that we must die on each other's swords or not at all, and if any foul chance should overtake either, other than by his adversary's hand, that adversary shall not despatch him?"

"Yes, Señor, for in our case such things may happen," and he pointed to the huge seas that towered over them, threatening to engulf the water-logged caravel. "We will take no advantage of each other, who wish to fight this quarrel out with our own right arms."

"So be it," said Peter, "and Master Castell here is the witness to our bargain."

D'Aguilar nodded, kissed the cross-hilt of his sword in confirmation of the pact, bowed courteously, and put himself on his defence.

For a moment they stood facing each other, a well-matched pair—Peter, lean, fierce-faced, long-armed, a terrible man to see in the fiery light that broke upon him from beneath the edge of a black cloud; the Spaniard tall also, and agile, but to all appearance as unconcerned as though this were but a pleasure bout, and not a duel to the death with a woman's fate hanging on the hazard. D'Aguilar wore a breastplate of gold-inlaid black steel and a helmet, while Peter had but his tunic of bull's hide and iron-lined cap, though his straight cut-and-thrust sword was heavier and mayhap half an inch longer than that of his foe.

Thus, then, they stood while Castell and all the ship's company, save the helmsman who steered her to the harbour's mouth, clung to the bulwarks and the cordage of the mainmast, and, forgetful of their own peril, watched in utter silence.

It was Peter who thrust the first, straight at the throat, but d'Aguilar parried deftly, so that the sword point went past his neck, and before it could be drawn back again, struck at Peter. The blow fell upon the side of his steel cap, and glanced thence to his left shoulder, but, being light, did him no harm. Swiftly came the answer, which was not light, for it fell so heavily upon d'Aguilar's breastplate, that he staggered back. After him sprang Peter, thinking that the game was his, but at that moment the ship, which had entered the breakers of the harbour bar, rolled terribly, and sent them both reeling to the bulwarks. Nor did she cease her rolling, so that, smiting and thrusting wildly, they staggered backwards and forwards across the deck, gripping with their left hands at anything they could find to steady them, till at length, bruised and breathless, they fell apart unwounded, and rested awhile.

"An ill field this to fight on, Señor," gasped d'Aguilar.

"I think that it will serve our turn," said Peter grimly, and rushed at him like a bull. It was just then that a great sea came aboard the ship, a mass of green water which struck them both and washed them like straws into the scuppers, where they rolled half drowned. Peter rose the first, coughing out salt water, and rubbing it from his eyes, to see d'Aguilar still upon the deck, his sword lying beside him, and holding his right wrist with his left hand.

"Who gave you the hurt?" he asked, "I or your fall?"

"The fall, Señor," answered d'Aguilar; "I think that it has broken my wrist. But I have still my left hand. Suffer me to arise, and we will finish this fray."

As the words passed his lips a gust of wind, more furious than any that had gone before, concentrated as it was through a gorge in the mountains, struck the caravel at the very mouth of the harbour, and laid her over on her beam ends. For a while it seemed as though she must capsize and sink, till suddenly her mainmast snapped like a stick and went overboard, when, relieved of its weight, by slow degrees she righted herself. Down upon the deck came the cross yard, one end of it crashing through the roof of the cabin in which Margaret and Betty were confined, splitting it in two, while a block attached to the other fell upon the side of Peter's head and, glancing from the steel cap, struck him on the neck and shoulder, hurling him senseless to the deck, where, still grasping his sword, he lay with arms outstretched.

Out of the ruin of the cabin appeared Margaret and Betty, the former very pale and frightened, and the latter muttering prayers, but, as it chanced, both uninjured. Clinging to the tangled ropes they crept forward, seeking refuge in the waist of the ship, for the heavy spar still worked and rolled above them, resting on the wreck of the cabin and the bulwarks, whence presently it slid into the sea. By the stump of the broken mainmast they halted, their long locks streaming in the gale, and here it was that Margaret caught sight of Peter lying upon his back, his face red with blood, and sliding to and fro as the vessel rolled.

She could not speak, but in mute appeal pointed first to him and then to d'Aguilar, who stood near, remembering as she did so her vision in the house at Holborn, which was thus terribly fulfilled. Holding to a rope, d'Aguilar drew near to her and spoke into her ear. "Lady," he said, "this is no deed of mine. We were fighting a fair fight, for he had boarded the ship when the mast fell and killed him. Blame me not for his death, but seek comfort from God."

She heard, and, looking round her wildly, perceived her father struggling towards her; then, with a bitter cry, fell senseless on his breast.

CHAPTER 12

Father Henriques

The night came down swiftly, for a great storm cloud, in which jagged lightning played, blotted out the last rays of the sunk sun. Then, with rolling thunder and torrents of rain, the tempest burst over the sinking ship. The mariners could no longer see to steer, they knew not whither they were going, only the lessened seas told them that they had entered the harbour mouth. Presently the *San Antonio* struck upon a rock, and the shock of it threw Castell, who was bending over the senseless shape of Margaret, against the bulwarks and dazed him.

There arose a great cry of "The vessel founders!" and water seemed to be pouring on the deck, though whether this were from the sea or from the deluge of the falling rain he did not know. Then came another cry of "Get out the boat, or we perish!" and a sound of men working in the darkness. The ship swung round and round and set-tled down. There was a flash of lightning, and by it Castell saw Betty holding the unconscious Margaret in her strong arms. She saw him also, and screamed to him to come to the boat. He started to obey, then remembered Peter. Peter might not be dead; what should he say to Margaret if he left him there to drown? He crept to where he lay upon the deck, and called to a sailor who rushed by to help him. The man answered with a curse, and vanished into the deep gloom. So, unaided, Castell essayed the task of lifting this heavy body, but his right arm being almost useless, could do no more than drag it into a sitting posture, and thus, by slow degrees, across the deck to where he imagined the boat to be.

But here there was no boat, and now the sound of voices came from the other side of the ship, so he must drag it back again. By the time he reached the starboard bulwarks all was silent, and another flash of lightning showed him the boat, crowded with people, upon the crest of a wave, fifty yards or more from him, whilst others, who had not been able to enter, clung to its stern and gunwale. He shouted aloud, but no answer came, either because none were left living on the ship, or because in all that turmoil they could not hear him.

Then Castell, knowing that he had done everything that he could, dragged Peter under the overhanging deck of the forward tower, which gave some little shelter from the rain, and, laying his bleeding head upon his knees so that it might be lifted above the wash of the waters, sat himself down and began to say prayers after the Jewish fashion whilst awaiting his end.

That he was about to die he had no doubt, for the waist of the ship, as he could perceive by the lightning, was almost level with the sea, which, however, here in the harbour was now much calmer than it had been. This he knew, for although the rain still fell steadily and the wind howled above, no spray broke over them. Deeper and deeper sank the caravel as she drifted onwards, till at length the water washed over her deck from side to side, so that Castell was obliged to seat himself on the second step of the ladder down which Peter had charged up on the Spaniards. A while passed, and he became aware that the *San Antonio* had ceased to move, and wondered what this might mean. The storm had rolled away now, and he could see the stars; also with it went the wind. The night grew warmer, too, which was well for him, for otherwise, wet as he was, he must have perished. Still it was a long night, the longest that ever he had spent, nor did any sleep come to relieve his misery or make his end easier, for the pain from the arrow wound in his arm kept him awake.

So there he sat, wondering if Margaret was dead, as Peter seemed to be dead, and if so, whether their spirits were watching him now, watching and waiting till he joined them. He thought, too, of the days of his prosperity until he had seen the accursed face of d'Aguilar, and of all the worthless wealth that was his, and what would become of it. He hoped even that Margaret was gone; better that she should be dead than live on in shame and misery. If there were a God, how came it that He could allow such things to happen in the world? Then he remembered how, when Job sat in just such an evil case, his wife had invited him to curse God and die, and how the patriarch had answered to her, "What! shall we receive good at the hand of God, and shall we not receive evil?" Remembered, too, after all his troubles, what had been the end of that just man, and therefrom took some little comfort. After this a stupor crept over him, and his last thought was that the vessel had sunk and he was departing into the deeps of death.

****

Listen! A voice called, and Castell awoke to see that it was growing light, and that before him supporting himself on the rail of the ladder, stood the tall form of Peter—Peter with a ghastly, blood-stained countenance, chattering teeth, and glazed, unnatural eyes.

"Do you live, John Castell?" said that hollow voice, "or are we both dead and in hell?"

"Nay," he answered, "I live yet; we are still this side of doom."

"What has chanced?" asked Peter. "I have been lost in a great blackness."

Castell told him briefly.

Peter listened till he had done, then staggered to the bulwark rail and looked about him, making no comment.

"I can see nothing," he said presently—"the mist is too deep; but I think we must lie near the shore. Come, help me. Let us try to find victuals; I am faint."

Castell rose, stretched his cramped limbs, and going to him, placed his uninjured arm round Peter's middle, and thus supported him towards the stern of the ship, where he guessed that the main cabin would be. They found and entered it, a small place, but richly furnished, with a carved crucifix screwed to its stern-most wall. A piece of pickled meat and some of the hard wheaten cakes such as sailors use, lay upon the floor where they had been cast from the table, while in a swinging rack above stood flagons of wine and of water. Castell found a horn mug, and filling it with wine gave it to Peter, who drank greedily, then handed it back to him, who also drank. Afterwards they cut off portions of the meat with their knives, and swallowed them, though Peter did this with great difficulty because of the hurt to his head and neck. Then they drank more wine, and, somewhat refreshed, left the place.

The mist was still so thick that they could see nothing, and therefore they went into the wreck of that cabin which had been occupied by Margaret and Betty, sat themselves down upon the bed wherein they had slept, and waited. Resting thus, Peter noted that this cabin had been fitted sumptuously as though for the occupation of a great lady, for even the vessels were of silver, and in a wardrobe, whereof the doors were open, hung beautiful gowns. Also, there were a few written books, on the outer leaves of one of which Margaret had set down some notes and a prayer of her own making, petitioning that Heaven would protect her; that Peter and her father might be living and learn

330

the truth of what had befallen, and that it would please the saints to deliver her, and to bring them together again. This book Peter thrust away within his jerkin to study at his leisure.

Now the sun rose suddenly above the eastern range of the mountains wherewith they were surrounded. Leaving the cabin, they climbed to the forecastle tower and gazed about them, to find that they were in a land-locked harbour, and stranded not more than a hundred yards from the shore. By tying a piece of iron to a rope and letting it down into the sea, they discovered that they lay upon a ridge, and that there were but four feet of water beneath their bow, and, having learned this, determined to wade to the beach. First, however, they went back to the cabin and filled a leather bag they found with food and wine. Then, by an afterthought, they searched for the place where d'Aguilar slept, and discovered it between decks; also a strong-box which they made shift to break open with an iron bar.

In it was a great store of gold, placed there, no doubt, for the payment of the crew, and with it some jewels. The jewels they left, but the money they divided and stowed it about them to serve their needs should they come safe ashore. Then they washed each other's wounds and bound them up, and descending the ladder which had been thrown over the ship's side when the Spaniards escaped in the boat, let themselves down into the sea and bade farewell to the *San Antonio*.

By now the wind had fallen and the sun shone brightly, warming their chilled blood; also the water, which was quite calm, did not rise much above their middles, so that they were able—the bottom being smooth and sandy—to wade without trouble to the shore. As they drew near to it they saw people gathering there, and guessed that they came from the little town of Motril, which lay up the river that here ran into the bay. Also they saw other things—namely, the boat of the *San Antonio* upon the shore, and rejoiced to know that it had come safe to land, for it rested upon its keel with but little water in its bottom. Lying here and there also were the corpses of drowned men, five or six of them: no doubt those sailors who had swum after the boat or clung to its gunwale, but among these bodies none were those of women.

When at length they reached the shore, very few people were left there, for of the rest some had begun to wade out towards the ship to plunder her, whilst others had gone to fetch boats for the same purpose. Therefore, the company who awaited them consisted only of women, children, three old men, and a priest. The last, a hungry-eyed, smooth-faced, sly-looking man, advanced to greet them courteously, bidding them thank God for their escape.

"That we do indeed," said Castell; "but tell us, Father, where are our companions?"

"There are some of them," answered the priest, pointing to the dead bodies; "the rest, with the two *señoras*, started two hours ago for Granada. The Marquis of Morella, from whom I hold this cure, told us that his ship had sunk, and that no one else was left alive, and, as the mist hid everything, we believed him. That is why we were not here before, for," he added significantly, "we are poor folk, to whom the saints send few wrecks."

"How did they go to Granada, Father?" asked Castell. "On foot?"

"Nay, Señor, they took all the horses and mules in the village by force, though the marquis promised that he would return them and pay for their hire later, and we trusted him because we must. The ladies wept much, and prayed us to take them in and keep them; but this the marquis would not allow, although they seemed so sad and weary. God send that we see our good beasts back again," he added piously.

"Have you any left for us? We have a little money, and can pay for them if they be not too dear."

"Not one, Señor—not one; the place has been cleared even down to the mares in foal. But, indeed you seem scarcely fit to ride at present, who have undergone so much," and he pointed to Peter's wounded head and Castell's bandaged arm. "Why do you not stay and rest awhile?"

"Because I am the father of one of the *señoras*, and doubtless she thinks me drowned, and this *señor* is her affianced husband," answered Castell briefly.

"Ah!" said the priest, looking at them with interest, "then what relation to her is the marquis? Well, perhaps I had better not ask, for this is no confessional, is it? I understand that you are anxious, for that great grandee has the reputation of being gay—an excellent son of the Church, but without doubt very gay," and he shook his shaven head and smiled. "But come up to the village, Señors, where you can rest and have your hurts attended to; afterwards we will talk."

"We had best go," said Castell in English to Peter. "There are no horses on this beach, and we cannot walk to Granada in our state."

Peter nodded, and, led by the priest, whose name they discovered to be Henriques, they started.

On the crest of the hill a few hundred paces away they turned and looked back, to see that every able-bodied inhabitant of the village seemed by now to be engaged in plundering the stranded vessel.

"They are paying themselves for the mules and horses," said Fray Henriques with a shrug. "So I see," answered Castell, "but you—" and he stopped.

"Oh, do not be afraid for me," replied the priest with a cunning little smile. "The Church does not loot; but in the end the Church gets her share. These are a pious folk. Only when he learns that the caravel did not sink after all, I fear the marquis will demand an account of us."

Then they limped on over the hill, and presently saw the white-walled and red-roofed village beneath them on the banks of the river.

Five minutes later their guide stopped at a door in a roughly paved street, which he opened with a key.

"My humble dwelling, when I am in residence here, and not at Granada," he said, "in which I shall be honoured to receive you. Look, near by is the church."

Then they entered a patio, or courtyard, where some orange-trees grew round a fountain of water, and a life-sized crucifix stood against the wall. As he passed this sacred emblem Peter bowed and crossed himself, an example that Castell did not follow. The priest looked at him sharply.

"Surely, Señor," he said, "you should do reverence to the symbol of our Saviour, who, by His mercy, have just been saved from the death which the marquis told me had overtaken both of you."

"My right arm is hurt," answered Castell readily, "so I must do that reverence in my heart."

"I understand, Señor; but if you are a stranger to this country, which you do not seem to be, who speak its tongue so well, with your permission I will warn you that here it is wise not to confine your reverences to the heart. Of late the directors of the Inquisition have become somewhat strict, and expect that the outward forms should be observed as well. Indeed, when I was a familiar of the Holy Office at Seville, I have seen men burned for the neglect of them. You have two arms and a head, Señor, also a knee that can be bent."

"Pardon me," answered Castell to this lecture. "I was thinking of other matters. The carrying off of my daughter at the hands of your patron, the Marquis of Morella, for instance."

Then, making no reply, the priest led them through his sitting-room to a bed-chamber with high barred windows, that, although it was large and lofty, reminded them somehow of a prison cell. Here he left them, saying that he would go to find the local surgeon, who, it seemed, was a barber also, if, indeed, he were not engaged in "lightening the ship," recommending them meanwhile to take off their wet clothes and lie down to rest.

A woman having brought hot water and some loose garments in which to wrap themselves while their own were drying, they undressed and washed and afterwards, utterly worn out, threw themselves down and fell asleep upon the beds, having first hidden away their gold in the food bag, which Peter placed beneath his pillow. Two hours later or more they were awakened by the arrival of Father Henriques and the barber-surgeon, accompanied by the woman-servant, and who brought them back their clothes cleaned and dried.

When the surgeon saw Peter's hurt to the left side of his neck and shoulder, which now were black, swollen, and very stiff, he shook his head, and said that time and rest alone could cure it, and that he must have been born under a fortunate star to have escaped with his life, which, save for his steel cap and leather jerkin, he would never have done. As no bones were broken, however, all that he could do was to dress the parts with some soothing ointment and cover them with clean cloths. This finished, he turned to Castell's wound, that was through the fleshy part of the right forearm, and, having syringed it out with warm water and oil, bound it up, saying that he would be well in a week. He added drily that the gale must have been fiercer even than he thought, since it could blow an arrow through a man's arm—a saying at which the priest pricked up his ears.

To this Castell made no answer, but producing a piece of Morella's gold, offered it to him for his services, asking him at the same time to procure them mules or horses, if he could. The barber promised to try to do so, and being well pleased with his fee, which was a great one for Motril, said that he would see them again in the evening, and if he could hear of any beasts would tell them of it then. Also he promised to bring them some clothes and cloaks of Spanish make, since those they had were not fit to travel in through that country, being soiled and blood-stained.

After he had gone, and the priest with him, who was busy seeing to the division of the spoils from the ship and making sure of his own share, the servant, a good soul, brought them soup, which they drank. Then they lay down again upon the beds and talked together as to what they should do.

Castell was downhearted, pointing out that they were still as far from Margaret as ever, who was now once more lost to them, and in the hand of Morella, whence they could scarcely hope to snatch her. It would seem also that she was being taken to the Moorish city of Granada, if she were not already there, where Christian law and justice had no power.

When he had heard him out, Peter, whose heart was always stout, answered:

"God has as much power in Granada as in London, or on the seas whence He has saved us. I think, Sir, that we have great reason to be thankful to God, seeing that we are both alive to-day, who might so well have been dead, and that Margaret is alive also, and, as we believe, unharmed. Further, this Spanish thief of women is, it would seem, a strange man, that is, if there be any truth in his words, for although he could steal her, it appears that he cannot find it in his heart to do her violence, but is determined to win her only with her own consent, which I think will not be had readily. Also, he shrinks from murder, who, when he could have butchered us, did not do so."

"I have known such men before," said Castell, "who hold some sins venial, but others deadly to their souls. It is a fruit of superstition."

"Then, Sir, let us pray that Morella's superstitions may remain strong, and get us to Granada as quickly as we can, for there, remember, you have friends, both among the Jews and Moors, who have traded with the place for many years, and these may give us shelter. Therefore, though things are bad, still they might be worse."

"That is so," answered Castell more cheerfully, "if, indeed, she has been taken to Granada; and as to this, we will try to learn something from the barber or the Father Henriques."

"I put no faith in that priest, a sly fellow who is in the pay of Morella," answered Peter.

Then they were silent, being still very weary, and having nothing more to say, but much to think about.

About sundown the doctor came back and dressed their wounds. He brought with him a stock of clothes of Spanish make, hats and two heavy cloaks fit to travel in, which they bought from him at a good price. Also, he said that he had two fine mules in the courtyard, and Castell went out to look at them. They were sorry beasts enough, being poor and wayworn, but as no others were to be had they returned to the room to talk as to the price of them and their saddles. The chaffering was long, for he asked twice their value, which Castell said poor shipwrecked men could not pay; but in the end they struck a bargain, under which the barber was to keep and feed the mules for the night, and bring them round next morning with a guide who would show them the road to Granada. Meanwhile, they paid him for the clothes, but not for the beasts.

Also they tried to learn something from him about the Marquis of Morella, but, like the Fray Henriques, the man was cunning, and kept his mouth shut, saying that it was ill for poor men like himself to chatter of the great, and that at Granada they could hear everything. So he went away, leaving some medicine for them to drink, and shortly afterwards the priest appeared.

He was in high good-humour, having secured those jewels which they had left behind in the iron coffer as his share of the spoil of the ship. Taking note of him as he showed and fondled them, Castell added up the man, and concluded that he was very avaricious; one who hated the poverty in which he had been reared, and would do much for money. Indeed, when he spoke bitterly of the thieves who had been at the ship's strong-box and taken nearly all the gold, Castell determined that he must never know who those thieves were, lest they should meet with some accident on their journey.

At length the trinkets were put away, and the priest said that they must sup with him, but lamented that he had no wine to give them, who was forced to drink water; whereon Castell prayed him to procure a few flasks of the best at their charges, which, nothing loth, he sent his servant out to do.

So, dressed in their new Spanish clothes, and having all the gold hidden about them in two money-belts that they had bought from the barber at the same time, they went in to supper, which consisted of a Spanish dish called *olla podrida*—a kind of rich stew—bread, cheese, and fruit. Also the wine that they had bought was there, very good and strong, and, whilst taking but little of it themselves for fear they should fever their wounds, they persuaded Father Henriques to drink heartily, so that in the end he forgot his cunning, and spoke with freedom. Then, seeing that he was in a ripe humour, Castell asked him about the Marquis of Morella, and how it happened that he had a house in the Moorish capital of Granada.

"Because he is half a Moor," answered the priest. "His father, it is said, was the Prince of Viana, and his mother a lady of royal Moorish blood, from whom he inherited great wealth, and his lands and palace in Granada. There, too, he loves to dwell, who, although he is so good a Christian by faith, has many heathen tastes, and, like the Moors, surrounds himself with a seraglio of beautiful women, as I know, for often I act as his chaplain, as in Granada there are no priests. Moreover, there is a purpose in all this, for, being partly of their blood, he is accredited to the court of their sultan, Boabdil, by Ferdinand and Isabella in whose interests he works in secret. For, strangers, you should know, if you do not know it already, that their Majesties have for long been at war against the Moor, and purpose to take what remains of his kingdom from him, and make it Christian, as they have already taken Malaga, and purified it by blood and fire from the accursed stain of infidelity."

"Yes," said Castell, "we heard that in England, for I am a merchant who have dealings with Granada, whither I am going on my affairs."

"On what affairs then goes the *señora*, who you say is your daughter, and what is that story that the sailors told of, about a fight between the *San Antonio* and an English ship, which indeed we saw in the offing yesterday? And why did the wind blow an arrow through your arm, friend Merchant? And how came it that you two were left aboard the caravel when the marquis and his people escaped?"

"You ask many questions, holy Father. Peter, fill the glass of his reverence; he drinks nothing who thinks that it is always Lent. Your health, Father. Ah! well emptied. Fill it again, Peter, and pass me the flask. Now I will begin to answer you with the story of the shipwreck." And he commenced an endless tale of the winds and sails and rocks and masts carried away, and of the English ship that tried to help the Spanish ship, and so forth, till at length the priest, whose glass Peter filled whenever his head was turned, fell back in his chair asleep.

"Now," whispered Peter in English across the table to Castell— "now I think that we had best go to bed, for we have learned much from this holy spy—as I take him to be—and told little."

So they crept away quietly to their chamber, and, having swallowed the draught that the doctor had given them, said their prayers each in his own fashion, locked the door, and lay down to rest as well as their wounds and sore anxieties would allow them.

CHAPTER 13

The Adventure of the Inn

Peter did not sleep well, for, notwithstanding all the barber's dressing, his hurt pained him much. Moreover, he was troubled by the thought that Margaret must be sure that both he and her father were dead, and of the sufferings of her sore heart. Whenever he dozed off he seemed to see her awake and weeping, yes, and to hear her sobs and murmurings of his name. When the first light of dawn crept through the high-barred windows, he arose and called Castell, for they could not dress without each other's help. Then they waited until they heard the sound of men talking and of beasts stamping in the courtyard without. Guessing that this was the barber with the mules, they unlocked their door and, finding the servant yawning in the passage, persuaded her to let them out of the house.

The barber it was, sure enough, and with him a one-eyed youth mounted on a pony, who, he said, would guide them to Granada. So they returned with him into the house, where he looked at their wounds, shaking his head over that of Peter, who, he said, ought not to travel so soon. After this came more haggling as to the price of the mules, saddlery, saddle-bags in which they packed their few spare clothes, hire of the guide and his horse, and so forth, since, anxious as they were to get away, they did not dare to seem to have money to spare.

At length everything was settled, and as their host, Father Henriques, had not yet appeared, they determined to depart without bidding him farewell, leaving some money in acknowledgment of his hospitality and as a gift to his church. Whilst they were handing it over to the servant, however, together with a fee for herself, the priest joined them, unshaven, and holding his hand to his tonsured head whilst he explained, what was not true, that he had been celebrating some early Mass in the church; then asked whither they were going.

They told him, and pressed their gift upon him, which he accepted, nothing loth, though its liberality seemed to make him more urgent to delay their departure. They were not fit to travel; the roads were most unsafe; they would be taken captive by the Moors, and thrown into a dungeon with the Christian prisoners; no one could enter Granada without a passport, he declared, and so forth, to all of which they answered that they must go.

Now he appeared to be much disturbed, and said finally that they would bring him into trouble with the Marquis of Morella—how or why, he would not explain, though Peter guessed that it might be lest the marquis should learn from them that this priest, his chaplain, had been plundering the ship which he thought sunk, and possessing himself of his jewels. At length, seeing that the man meant mischief and would stop them in some fashion if they delayed, they bade him farewell hastily, and, pushing past him, mounted the mules that stood outside and rode away with their guide.

As they went they heard the priest, who now was in a rage, abusing the barber who had sold them the beasts, and caught the words "Spies," "English *señoras*," and "Commands of the Marquis," so that they were glad when at length they found themselves outside the town, where as yet few were stirring, and riding unmolested on the road to Granada.

This road proved to be no good one, and very hilly; moreover, the mules were even worse than they had thought, that which Peter rode stumbling continually. Now they asked the youth, their guide, how long it would take them to reach Granada; but all he answered them was:

"*Quien sabe?*" (Who knows?) "It depends upon the will of God."

An hour later they asked him again, whereon he replied:

Perhaps to-night, perhaps to-morrow, perhaps never, as there were many thieves about, and if they escaped the thieves they would probably be captured by the Moors.

"I think there is one thief very near to us," said Peter in English, looking at this ill-favoured young man, then added in his broken Spanish, "Friend, if we fall in with robbers or Moors, the first one who dies will be yourself," and he tapped the hilt of his sword.

The lad uttered a Spanish curse, and turned the head of his pony round as though he would ride back to Motril, then changed his mind and pushed on a long way in front of them, nor could they come near him again for hours. So hard was the road and so feeble were the mules that, notwithstanding a midday halt to rest them, it was nightfall before they reached the top of the Sierra, and in the last sunset glow, separated from them by the rich *vega* or plain, saw the minarets and palaces of Granada. Now they wished to push on, but their guide swore that it was impossible, as in the dark they would fall over precipices while descending to the plain. There was a *venta* or inn near by, he said, where they could sleep, starting again at dawn.

When Castell said that they did not wish to go to an inn, he answered that they must, since they had eaten what food they had, and here on the road there was no fodder for the beasts. So, reluctantly enough, they consented, knowing that unless they were fed the mules would never carry them to Granada, whereon the guide, pointing out the house to them, a lonely place in a valley about a hundred yards from the road, said that he would go on to make arrangements, and galloped off.

As they approached this hostelry, which was surrounded by a rough wall for purposes of defence, they saw the one-eyed youth engaged in earnest conversation with a fat, ill-favoured man who had a great knife stuck in his girdle. Advancing to them, bowing, this man said that he was the host, and, in reply to their request for food and a room, told them that they could have both.

They rode into the courtyard, whereon the inn-keeper locked the door in the wall behind them, explaining that it was to keep out robbers, and adding that they were fortunate to be where they could sleep quite safely. Then a Moor came and led away their mule to the stable, and they accompanied the landlord into the sitting-room, a long, low apartment furnished with tables and benches, on which sat several rough-looking fellows, drinking wine. Here the host suddenly demanded payment in advance, saying that he did not trust strangers. Peter would have argued with him; but Castell, thinking it best to comply, unbuttoned his garments to get at his money, for he had no loose coin in his pocket, having paid away the last at Motril.

His right hand being still helpless, this he did with his left, and so awkwardly that the small doubloon he took hold of slipped from his fingers and fell on to the floor. Forgetting that he had not re-fastened the belt, he bent down to pick it up, whereon a number of gold pieces of various sorts, perhaps twenty of them, fell out and rolled hither and thither on the ground. Peter, watching, saw the landlord and the other men in the room exchange a quick and significant glance. They rose, however, and assisted to find the money, which the host returned to Castell, remarking with an unpleasant smile, that if he had known that his guests were so rich he would have charged them more for their accommodation.

"Of your good heart I pray you not," answered Castell, "for that is all our worldly goods," and even as he spoke another gold piece, this time a large doubloon, which had remained in his clothing, slipped to the floor.

"Of course, Señor," the host replied as he picked this up also and handed it back politely, "but shake yourself, there may still be a coin or two in your doublet." Castell did so, whereon the gold in his belt, loosened by what had fallen out, rattled audibly, and the audience smiled again, while the host congratulated him on the fact that he was in an honest house, and not wandering on the mountains, which were the home of so many bad men. Having pocketed his money with the best grace he could, and buckled his belt beneath his robe, Castell and Peter sat down at a table a little apart, and asked if they could have some supper. The host assented, and called to the Moorish servant to bring food, then sat down also, and began to put questions to them, of a sort which showed that their guide had already told all their story.

"How did you learn of our shipwreck?" asked Castell by way of answer.

"How? Why, from the people of the marquis, who stopped here to drink a cup of wine when he passed to Granada yesterday with his company and two *señoras*. He said that the *San Antonio* had sunk, but told us nothing of your being left aboard of her."

"Then forgive us, friend, if we, whose business is of no interest to you, copy his discretion, as we are weary and would rest."

"Certainly, Señors—certainly," replied the man; "I go to hasten your supper, and to fetch you a flask of the wine of Granada worthy of your degree," and he left them.

A while later their food came—good meat enough of its sort— and with it the wine in an earthenware jug, which, as he filled their horn mugs, the host said he had poured out of the flask himself that the crust of it might not slip. Castell thanked him, and asked him to drink a cup to their good journey; but he declined, answering that it was a fast day with him, on which he was sworn to touch only water. Now Peter, who had said nothing all this time, but noted much, just touched the wine with his lips, and smacked them as though in approbation while he whispered in English to Castell:

"Drink it not; it is drugged!"

"What says your son?" asked the host.

"He says that it is delicious, but suddenly he has remembered what I too forgot, that the doctor at Motril forbade us to touch wine for fear lest we should worsen the hurts that we had in the shipwreck. Well, let it not be wasted. Give it to your friends. We must be content with thinner stuff." And taking up a jug of water that stood upon the table, he filled an empty cup with it and drank, then passed it to Peter, while the host looked at them sourly.

Then, as though by an afterthought, Castell rose and politely presented the jug of wine and the two filled mugs to the men who were
sitting at a table close by, saying that it was a pity that they should
not have the benefit of such fine liquor. One of these fellows, as it
chanced, was their own guide, who had come in from tending the
mules. They took the mugs readily enough, and two of them tossed off
their contents, whereon, with a smothered oath, the landlord snatched
away the jug and vanished with it.

Castell and Peter went on with their meal, for they saw their
neighbours eating of the same dish, as did the landlord also, who had
returned, and, it seemed to Peter, was watching the two men who had
drunk the wine with an anxious eye. Presently one of these rose from
the table and, going to a bench on the other side of the room, flung
himself down upon it and became quite silent, while their one-eyed
guide stretched out his arms and fell face forward so that his head
rested on an empty plate, where he remained apparently insensible.
The host sprang up and stood irresolute, and Castell, rising, said that
evidently the poor lad was sleepy after his long ride, and as they were
the same, would he be so courteous as to show them to their room?

He assented readily, indeed it was clear that he wished to be rid of
them, for the other men were staring at the guide and their companion, and muttering amongst themselves.

"This way, Señors," he said, and led them to the end of the place
where a broad step-ladder stood. Going up it, a lamp in his hand, he
opened a trap-door and called to them to follow him, which Castell
did. Peter, however, first turned and said good-night to the company
who were watching them; at the same moment, as though by accident
or thoughtlessly, half drawing his sword from its scabbard. Then he too
went up the ladder, and found himself with the others in an attic.

It was a bare place, the only furniture in it being two chairs and
two rough wooden bedsteads without heads to them, mere trestles
indeed, that stood about three feet apart against a boarded partition
which appeared to divide this room from some other attic beyond.
Also, there was a hole in the wall immediately beneath the eaves of
the house that served the purpose of a window, over which a sack was
nailed. "We are poor folk," said the landlord as they glanced round
this comfortless garret, "but many great people have slept well here, as
doubtless you will also," and he turned to descend the ladder.

"It will serve," answered Castell; "but, friend, tell your men to leave
the stable open, as we start at dawn, and be so good as to give me that
lamp."

"I cannot spare the lamp," he grunted sulkily, with his foot already on the first step.

Peter strode to him and grasped his arm with one hand, while with the other he seized the lamp. The man cursed, and began to fumble at his belt, as though for a knife, whereon Peter, putting out his strength, twisted his arm so fiercely that in his pain he loosed the lamp, which remained in Peter's hand. The inn-keeper made a grab at it, missed his footing and rolled down the ladder, falling heavily on the floor below.

Watching from above, to their relief they saw him pick himself up, and heard him begin to revile them, shaking his fist and vowing vengeance. Then Peter shut down the trap-door. It was ill fitted, so that the edge of it stood up above the flooring, also the bolt that fastened it had been removed, although the staples in which it used to work remained. Peter looked round for some stick or piece of wood to pass through these staples, but could find nothing. Then he bethought him of a short length of cord that he had in his pocket, which served to tie one of the saddle-bags in its place on his mule. This he fastened from one staple to the other, so that the trap-door could not be lifted more than an inch or two.

Reflecting that this might be done, and the cord cut with a knife passed through the opening, he took one of the chairs and stood it so that two of its legs rested on the edge of the trap-door and the other two upon the boarding of the floor. Then he said to Castell:

"We are snared birds; but they must get into the cage before they wring our necks. That wine was poisoned, and, if they can, they will murder us for our money—or because they have been told to do so by the guide. We had best keep awake to-night."

"I think so," answered Castell anxiously. "Listen, they are talking down below."

Talking they were, as though they debated something, but after a while the sound of voices died away. When all was silent they hunted round the attic, but could find nothing that was unusual to such places. Peter looked at the window-hole, and, as it was large enough for a man to pass through, tried to drag one of the beds beneath it, thinking that if any such attempt were made, he who lay thereon would have the thief at his mercy, only to find, however, that these were screwed to the floor and immovable. As there was nothing more that they could do, they went and sat upon these beds, their bare swords in their hands, and waited a long while, but nothing happened.

At length the lamp, which had been flickering feebly for some time, went out, lacking oil, and except for the light which crept through the window-place, for now they had torn away the sacking that hung over it, they were in darkness.

A little while later they heard the sound of a horse's hoofs, and the door of the house open and shut, after which there was more talking below, and mingling with it a new voice which Peter seemed to remember.

"I have it," he whispered to Castell. "Here is our late host, Father Henriques, come to see how his guests are faring."

Another half-hour and the waning moon rose, throwing a beam of light into their chamber; also they heard horse's hoofs again. Going to the window, Peter looked out of it and saw the horse, a fine beast, being held by the landlord, then a man came and mounted it and, at some remark of his, turned his face upwards towards their window. It was that of Father Henriques.

The two whispered together for a while till the priest blessed the landlord in Latin words and rode away, and again they heard the door of the house close.

"He is off to Granada, to warn Morella his master of our coming," said Castell, as they reseated themselves upon the beds.

"To warn Morella that we shall never come, perhaps; but we will beat him yet," replied Peter.

The night wore on, and Castell, who was very weary, sank back upon the bolster and began to doze, when suddenly the chair that was set upon the trap-door fell over with a great clatter, and he sprang up, asking what that noise might be.

"Only a rat," answered Peter, who saw no good in telling him the truth—namely, that thieves or murderers had tried to open the trap-door. Then he crept down the room, felt the cord, to find that it was still uncut, and replaced the chair where it had been. This done, Peter came back to the bed and threw himself down upon it as though he would slumber, though never was he more wide awake. The weariness of Castell had overcome him again, however, for he snored at his side.

For a long while nothing further happened, although once the ray of moonlight was cut off, and for an instant Peter thought that he saw a face at the window. If so, it vanished and returned no more. Now from behind their heads came faint sounds, like those of stifled breathing, like those of naked feet; then a slight creaking and scratching in the wall—a mouse's tooth might have caused it—and suddenly, right in that ray of moonlight, a cruel-looking knife and a naked arm projected through the panelling.

The knife flickered for a second over the breast of the sleeping Castell as though it were a living thing that chose the spot where it would strike. One second—only one—for the next Peter had drawn himself up, and with a sweep of the sword which lay unscabbarded at his side, had shorn that arm off above the elbow, just where it projected from the panelling.

"What was that?" asked Castell again, as something fell upon him.

"A snake," answered Peter, "a poisonous snake. Wake up now, and look."

Castell obeyed, staring in silence at the horrible arm which still clasped the great knife, while from beyond the panelling there came a stifled groan, then a sound as of a heavy body stumbling away.

"Come," said Peter, "let us be going, unless we would stop here for ever. That fellow will soon be back to seek his arm."

"Going! How?" asked Castell.

"There seems to be but one road, and that a rough one, through the window and over the wall," answered Peter. "Ah! there they come; I thought so." And as he spoke they heard the sound of men scrambling up the ladder.

They ran to the window-place and looked out, but there seemed to be no one below, and it was not more than twelve feet from the ground. Peter helped Castell through it, then, holding his sound arm with both his own, lowered him as far as he could, and let go. He dropped on to his feet, fell to the ground, then rose again, unhurt. Peter was about to follow him when he heard the chair tumble over again, and, looking round, saw the trap-door open, to fall back with a crash. They had cut the cord!

The figure of a man holding a knife appeared in the faint light, followed by the head of another man. Now it was too late for him to get through the window-place safely; if he attempted it he would be stabbed in the back. So, grasping his sword with both hands, Peter leapt at that man, aiming a great stroke at his shadowy mass. It fell upon him somewhere, for down he went and lay quite still. By now the second man had his knee upon the edge of flooring. Peter thrust him through, and he sank backwards on to the heads of others who were following him, sweeping the ladder with his weight, so that all of them tumbled in a heap at its foot, save one who hung to the edge of the trap frame by his hands. Peter slammed its door to, crushing them so that he loosed his grip, with a howl. Then, as he had nothing else, he dragged the body of the dead man on to it and left him there.

Next he rushed to the window, sheathing his sword as he ran, scrambled through it, and, hanging by his arms, let himself drop, coming to the ground safely, for he was very agile, and in the excitement of the fray forgot the hurt to his head and shoulder.

"Where now?" asked Castell, as he stood by him panting.

"To the stable for the mules. No, it is useless; we have no time to saddle them, and the outer gate is locked. The wall—the wall—we must climb it! They will be after us in a minute."

They ran thither and found that, though ten feet high, fortunately this wall was built of rough stone, which gave an easy foothold. Peter scrambled up first, then, lying across its top, stretched down his hand to Castell, and with difficulty—for the man was heavy and crippled—dragged him to his side. Just then they heard a voice from their garret shout:

"The English devils have gone! Get to the door and cut them off."

"Come on," said Peter. So together they climbed, or rather fell, down the wall on to a mass of prickly-pear bush, which broke the shock but tore them so sorely in a score of places that they could have shrieked with the pain. Somehow they freed themselves, and, bleeding all over, broke from that accursed bush, struggling up the bank of the ditch in which it grew, ran for the road, and along it towards Granada.

Before they had gone a hundred yards they heard shoutings, and guessed that they were being followed. Just here the road crossed a ravine full of boulders and rough scrubby growth, whereas beyond it was bare and open. Peter seized Castell and dragged him up this ravine till they came to a place where, behind a great stone, there was a kind of hole, filled with bushes and tall, dead grass, into which they plunged and hid themselves.

"Draw your sword," he said to Castell. "If they find us, we will die as well as we can."

He obeyed, holding it in his left hand.

They heard the robbers run along the road; then, seeing that they had missed their victims, these returned again, five or six of them, and fell to searching the ravine. But the light was very bad, for here the rays of the moon did not penetrate, and they could find nothing. Presently two of them halted within five paces of them and began to talk, saying that the swine must still be hidden in the yard, or perhaps had doubled back for Motril.

"I don't know where they are hidden," answered the other man; "but this is a poor business. Fat Pedro's arm is cut clean off, and I expect he will bleed to death, while two of the other fellows are dead or dying, for that long-legged Englishman hits hard, to say nothing of those who drank the drugged wine, and look as though they would never wake. Yes, a poor business to get a few doubloons and please a priest, but oh! if I had the hogs here I—"And he hissed out a horrible threat. "Meanwhile we had best lie up at the mouth of this place in case they should still be hidden here."

Peter heard him and listened. All the other men had gone, running back along the road. His blood was up, and the thorn pricks stung him sorely. Saying no word, out of his lair he came with that terrible sword of his aloft.

The men caught sight of him, and gave a gasp of fear. It was the last sound that one of them ever made. Then the other turned and ran like a hare. This was he who had uttered the threat.

"Stop!" whispered Peter, as he overtook him—"stop, and do what you promised."

The brute turned, and asked for mercy, but got none.

"It was needful," said Peter to Castell presently; "you heard—they were going to wait for us."

"I do not think that they will try to murder any more Englishmen at that inn," panted Castell, as he ran along beside him.

CHAPTER 14

Inez and Her Garden

For two hours or more John Castell and Peter travelled on the Granada road, running when it was smooth, walking when it was rough, and stopping from time to time to get their breath and listen. But the night was quite silent, no one seemed to be pursuing them. Evidently the remaining cut-throats had either taken another way or, having their fill of this adventure, wanted to see no more of Peter and his sword.

At length the dawn broke over the great misty plain, for now they were crossing the *vega*. Then the sun rose and dispelled the vapours, and a dozen miles or more away they saw Granada on its hill. They saw each other also, and a sorry sight they were, torn by the sharp thorns, and stained with blood from their scratches. Peter was bare-headed too, for he had lost his cap, and almost beside himself now that the excitement had left him, from lack of sleep, pain, and weariness. Moreover, as the sun rose, it grew fearfully hot upon that plain, and its fierce rays, striking full upon his head, seemed to stupefy him, so that at last they were obliged to halt and weave a kind of hat out of corn and grasses, which gave him so strange an appearance that some Moors, whom they met going to their toil, thought that he must be a madman, and ran away.

Still they crawled forward, refreshing themselves with water whenever they could find any in the irrigation ditches that these people used for their crops, but covering little more than a mile an hour. Towards noon the heat grew so dreadful that they were obliged to lie down to rest under the shade of some palm-like trees, and here, absolutely outworn, they sank into a kind of sleep.

They were awakened by a sound of voices, and staggered to their feet, drawing their swords, for they thought that the thieves from the inn had overtaken them. Instead of these ruffianly murderers, however, they saw before them a body of eight Moors, beautifully mounted upon white horses, and clad in turbans and flowing robes, the like of which Peter had never yet beheld, who sat there regarding them gravely with their quiet eyes, and, as it seemed, not without pity.

"Put up your swords, Señors," said the leader of these Moors in excellent Spanish—indeed, he seemed to be a Spaniard dressed in Eastern garments—"for we are many and fresh; and you are but two and wounded."

They obeyed, who could do nothing else.

"Now tell us, though there is little need to ask," went on the captain, "you are those men of England who boarded the *San Antonio* and escaped when she was sinking, are you not?"

Castell nodded, then answered:

"We boarded her to seek——"

"Never mind what you sought," the captain answered; "the names of exalted ladies should not be mentioned before strange men. But you have been in trouble again since then, at the inn yonder, where this tall *señor* bore himself very bravely. Oh! we have heard all the story, and give him honour who can wield a sword so well in the dark."

"We thank you," said Castell, "but what is your business with us?"

"Señor, we are sent by our master, his Excellency, the high Lord and Marquis of Morella, to find you and bring you to be his guests at Granada."

"So the priest has told. I thought as much," muttered Peter.

"We pray you to come without trouble, as we do not wish to do any violence to such gallant men," went on the captain. "Be pleased to mount two of these horses, and ride with us."

"I am a merchant, with friends of my own at Granada," answered Castell. "Cannot we go to them, who do not seek the hospitality of the marquis?"

"Señor, our orders are otherwise, and here the word of our master, the marquis, is a law that may not be broken."

"I thought that Boabdil was king of Granada," said Castell.

"Without doubt he is king, Señor, and by the grace of Allah will remain so, but the marquis is allied to him in blood; also, while the truce lasts, he is a representative of their Majesties of Spain in our city," and, at a sign, two of the Moors dismounted and led forward their horses, holding the stirrups, and offering to help them to the saddle.

"There is nothing for it," said Peter; "we must go." So, awkwardly enough, for they were very stiff, they climbed on to the beasts and rode away with their captors.

The sun was sinking now, for they had slept long, and by the time they reached the gates of Granada the muezzins were calling to the sunset prayer from the minarets of the mosques.

It was but a very dim and confused idea that Peter gathered of the great city of the Moors, as, surrounded by their white-robed escort, he rode he knew not whither. Narrow winding streets, white houses, shuttered windows, crowds of courteous, somewhat silent people, all men, and all clad in those same strange, flowing dresses, who looked at them curiously, and murmured words which afterwards he came to learn meant "Christian prisoners," or sometimes "Christian dogs"; fretted and pointed arches, and a vast fairy-like building set upon a hill. He was dazed with pain and fatigue as, a long-legged, blood-stained figure, crowned with his quaint hat of grasses, he rode through that wondrous and imperial place.

Yet no man laughed at him, absurd as he must have seemed; but perhaps this was because under the grotesqueness of his appearance they recognised something of his quality. Or they might have heard rumours of his sword-play at the inn and on the ship. At any rate, their attitude was that of courteous dislike of the Christian, mingled with respect for the brave man in misfortune.

At length, after mounting a long rise, they came to a palace on a mount, facing the vast, red-walled fortress which seemed to dominate the place, which he afterwards knew as the Alhambra, but separated from it by a valley. This palace was a very great building, set on three sides of a square, and surrounded by gardens, wherein tall cypress-trees pointed to the tender sky. They rode through the gardens and sundry gateways till they came to a courtyard where servants, with torches in their hands, ran out to meet them. Somebody helped him off his horse, somebody supported him up a flight of marble steps, beneath which a fountain splashed, into a great, cool room with an ornamented roof. Then Peter remembered no more.

****

A time went by, a long, long time—in fact it was nearly a month—before Peter really opened his eyes to the world again. Not that he had been insensible for all this while—that is, quite—for at intervals he had become aware of that large, cool room, and of people talking about him—especially of a dark-eyed, light-footed, and pretty woman with a white wimple round her face, who appeared to be in charge of him. Occasionally he thought that this must be Margaret, and yet knew that it could not, for she was different. Also, he remembered that once or twice he had seemed to see the haughty, handsome face of

Morella bending over him, as though he watched curiously to learn whether he would live or not, and then had striven to rise to fight him, and been pressed back by the soft, white hands of the woman that yet were so terribly strong.

Now, when he awoke at last, it was to see her sitting there with a ray of sunlight from some upper window falling on her face, sitting with her chin resting on her hand and her elbow on her knee, and contemplating him with a pretty, puzzled look. She made a sweet picture thus, he thought. Then he spoke to her in his slow Spanish, for somehow he knew that she would not understand his own tongue.

"You are not Margaret," he said.

At once the dream went out of the woman's soft eyes; she became intensely interested, and, rising, advanced towards him, a very gracious figure, who seemed to sway as she walked.

"No, no," she said, bending over him and touching his forehead with her taper fingers; "my name is Inez. You wander still, Señor."

"Inez what?" he asked.

"Inez only," she answered, "Inez, a woman of Granada, the rest is lost. Inez, the nurse of sick men, Señor."

"Where then is Margaret—the English Margaret?"

A veil of secrecy seemed to fall over the woman's face, and her voice changed as she answered, no longer ringing true, or so it struck his senses made quick and subtle by the fires of fever:

"I know no English Margaret. Do you then love her—this English Margaret?"

"Aye," he answered, "she was stolen from me; I have followed her from far, and suffered much. Is she dead or living?"

"I have told you, Señor, I know nothing, although"—and again the voice became natural—"it is true that I thought you loved somebody from your talk in your illness."

Peter pondered a while, then he began to remember, and asked again: "Where is Castell?"

"Castell? Was he your companion, the man with a hurt arm who looked like a Jew? I do not know where he is. In another part of the city, perhaps. I think that he was sent to his friends. Question me not of such matters, who am but your sick-nurse. You have been very ill, Señor. Look!" And she handed him a little mirror made of polished silver, then, seeing that he was too weak to take it, held it before him.

Peter saw his face, and groaned, for, except the red scar upon his cheek, it was ivory white and wasted to nothing.

"I am glad Margaret did not see me like this," he said, with an at-

351

tempt at a smile, "bearded too, and what a beard! Lady, how could you have nursed one so hideous?"

"I have not found you hideous," she answered softly; "besides, that is my trade. But you must not talk, you must rest. Drink this, and rest," and she gave him soup in a silver bowl, which he swallowed readily enough, and went to sleep again.

Some days afterwards, when Peter was well on the road to convalescence, his beautiful nurse came and sat by him, a look of pity in her tender, Eastern eyes.

"What is it now, Inez?" he asked, noting her changed face.

"Señor Pedro, you spoke to me a while ago, when you woke up from your long sleep, of a certain Margaret, did you not? Well, I have been inquiring of this Dona Margaret, and have no good news to tell of her."

Peter set his teeth, and said:

"Go on, tell me the worst."

"This Margaret was travelling with the Marquis of Morella, was she not?"

"She had been stolen by him," answered Peter.

"Alas! it may be so; but here in Spain, and especially here in Granada, that will scarcely screen the name of one who has been known to travel with the Marquis of Morella."

"So much the worse for the Marquis of Morella when I meet him again," answered Peter sternly. "What is your story, Nurse Inez?"

She looked with interest at his grim, thin face, but, as it seemed to him, with no displeasure.

"A sad one. As I have told you, a sad one. It seems that the other day this *señora* was found dead at the foot of the tallest tower of the marquis's palace, though whether she fell from it, or was thrown from it, none know."

Peter gasped, and was silent for a while; then asked:

"Did you see her dead?"

"No, Señor; others saw her."

"And told you to tell me? Nurse Inez, I do not believe your tale. If the Dona Margaret, my betrothed, were dead I should know it; but my heart tells me that she is alive."

"You have great faith, Señor," said the woman, with a note of admiration in her voice which she could not suppress, but, as he observed, without contradicting him.

"I have faith," he answered. "Nothing else is left; but so far it has been a good crutch."

Peter made no further allusion to the subject, only presently he asked: "Tell me, where am I?"

"In a prison, Señor."

"Oh! a prison, with a beautiful woman for jailer, and other beautiful women"—and he pointed to a fair creature who had brought something into the room—"as servants. A very fine prison also," and he looked about him at the marbles and arches and lovely carving.

"There are men without the gate, not women," she replied, smiling.

"I daresay; captives can be tied with ropes of silk, can they not? Well, whose is this prison?"

She shook her head.

"I do not know, Señor. The Moorish king's perhaps—you yourself have said that I am only the jailer."

"Then who pays you?"

"Perhaps I am not paid, Señor; perhaps I work for love," and she glanced at him swiftly, "or hate," and her face changed.

"Not hate of me, I think," said Peter.

"No, Señor, not hate of you. Why should I hate you who have been so helpless and so courteous to me?" and she bent the knee to him a little.

"Why indeed? especially as I am also grateful to you who have nursed me back to life. But then, why hide the truth from a helpless man?"

Inez glanced about her; the room was empty now. She bent over him and whispered:

"Have you never been forced to hide the truth? No, I read it in your face, and you are not a woman—an erring woman."

They looked into each other's eyes a while, then Peter asked: "Is the Dona Margaret really dead?"

"I do not know," she answered; "I was told so." And as though she feared lest she should betray herself, Inez turned and left him quickly.

The days went by, and through the slow degrees of convalescence Peter grew strong again. But they brought him no added knowledge. He did not know where he dwelt or why he was there. All he knew was that he lived a prisoner in a sumptuous palace, or as he suspected, for of this he could not be sure, since the arched windows of one side of the building were walled up, in the wing of a palace. Nobody came near to him except the fair Inez, and a Moor who either was deaf or could understand nothing that he said to him in Spanish. There were other women about, it is true, very pretty women all of them, who acted as servants, but none of these were allowed to approach him; he only saw them at a distance.

Therefore Inez was his sole companion, and with her he grew very intimate, to a certain extent, but no further. On the occasion that has been described she had lifted a corner of her veil which hid her true self, but a long while passed before she enlarged her confidence. The veil was kept down very close indeed. Day by day he questioned her, and day by day, without the slightest show of irritation, or even annoyance, she parried his questions. They knew perfectly well that they were matching their wits against each other; but as yet Inez had the best of the game, which, indeed, she seemed to enjoy. He would talk to her also of all sorts of things—the state of Spain, the Moorish court, the danger that threatened Granada, whereof the great siege now drew near, and so forth—and of these matters she would discourse most intelligently, with the result that he learned much of the state of politics in Castile and Granada, and greatly improved his knowledge of the Spanish tongue.

But when of a sudden, as he did again and again, he sprang some question on her about Morella, or Margaret, or John Castell, that same subtle change would come over her face, and the same silence would seal her lips.

"Señor," she said to him one day with a laugh, "you ask me of secrets which I might reveal to you—perhaps—if you were my husband or my love, but which you cannot expect a nurse, whose life hangs on it, to answer. Not that I wish you to become my husband or my lover," she added, with a little nervous laugh.

Peter looked at her with his grave eyes.

"I know that you do not wish that," he said, "for how could I attract one so gay and beautiful as you are?"

"You seem to attract the English Margaret," she replied quickly in a nettled voice.

"To have attracted, you mean, as you tell me that she is dead," he answered; and, seeing her mistake, Inez bit her lip. "But," he went on, "I was going to add, though it may have no value for you, that you have attracted me as your true friend."

"Friend!" she said, opening her large eyes, "what talk is this? Can the woman Inez find a friend in a man who is under sixty?"

"It would appear so," he answered. And again with that graceful little curtsey of hers she went away, leaving him very puzzled. Two days later she appeared in his room, evidently much disturbed.

"I thought that you had left me altogether, and I am glad to see you, for I tire of that deaf Moor and of this fine room. I want fresh air."

"I know it," she answered; "so I have come to take you to walk in a garden."

He leapt for joy at her words, and snatching at his sword, which had been left to him, buckled it on.

"You will not need that," she said.

"I thought that I should not need it in yonder inn, but I did," he answered. Whereat she laughed, then turned, put her hand upon his shoulder and spoke to him earnestly.

"See, friend," she whispered, "you want to walk in the fresh air—do you not?—and to learn certain things—and I wish to tell you them. But I dare not do it here, where we may at any moment be surrounded by spies, for these walls have ears indeed. Well, when we walk in that garden, would it be too great a penance for you to put your arm about my waist—you who still need support?"

"No penance at all, I assure you," answered Peter with something like a smile. For after all he was a man, and young; while the waist of Inez was as pretty as all the rest of her. "But," he added, "it might be misunderstood."

"Quite so, I wish it to be misunderstood: not by me, who know that you care nothing for me and would as soon place your arm round that marble column."

Peter opened his lips to speak, but she stopped him at once.

"Oh! do not waste falsehoods on me, in which of a truth you have no art," she said with evident irritation. "Why, if you had the money, you would offer to pay me for my nursing, and who knows, I might take it! Understand, you must either do this, seeming to play the lover to me, or we cannot walk together in that garden."

Peter hesitated a little, guessing a plot, while she bent forward till her lips almost touched his ear and said in a still lower voice:

"And I cannot tell you how, perhaps—I say perhaps—you may come to see the remains of the Dona Margaret, and certain other matters. Ah!" she added after a pause, with a little bitter laugh, "now you will kiss me from one end of the garden to the other, will you not? Foolish man! Doubt no more; take your chance, it may be the last."

"Of what? Kissing you? Or the other things?"

"That you will find out," she said, with a shrug of her shoulders. "Come!"

Then, while he followed dubiously, she led him down the length of the great room to a door with a spy-hole in the top of it, that was set in a Moorish archway at the corner.

This door she opened, and there beyond it, a drawn scimitar in his hand, stood a tall Moor on guard. Inez spoke a word to him, whereon he saluted with his scimitar and let them pass across the landing to a turret stair that lay beyond, which they descended. At its foot was another door, whereon she knocked four times. Bolts shot back, keys turned, and it was opened by a black porter, beyond whom stood a second Moor, also with drawn sword. They passed him as they had passed the first, turned down a little passage to the right, ending in some steps, and came to a third door, in front of which she halted.

"Now," she said, "nerve yourself for the trial."

"What trial?" he asked, supporting himself against the wall, for he found his legs still weak.

"This," she answered, pointing to her waist, "and these," and she touched her rich, red lips with her taper finger-points. "Would you like to practise a little, my innocent English knight, before we go out? You look as though you might seem awkward and unconvincing."

"I think," answered Peter drily, for the humour of the situation moved him, "that such practice is somewhat dangerous for me. It might annoy you before I had done. I will postpone my happiness until we are in the garden."

"I thought so," she answered; "but look now, you must play the part, or I shall suffer, who am bearing much for you."

"I think that I may suffer also," he murmured, but not so low that she did not catch his words.

"No, friend Pedro," she said, turning on him, "it is the woman who suffers in this kind of farce. She pays; the man rides away to play another," and without more ado she opened the door, which proved to be unlocked and unguarded.

Beyond the foot of some steps lay a most lovely garden. Great, tapering cypresses grew about it, with many orange-trees and flowering shrubs that filled the soft, southern air with odours. Also there were marble fountains into which water splashed from the mouths of carven lions, and here and there arbours with stone seats, whereon were laid soft cushions of many colours. It was a veritable place of Eastern delight and dreams, such as Peter had never known before he looked upon it on that languorous eve—he who had not seen the sky or flowers for so many weary weeks of sickness. It was secluded also, being surrounded by a high wall, but at one place the tall, windowless tower of some other building of red stone soared up between and beyond two lofty cypress-trees.

"This is the harem garden," Inez whispered, "where many a painted favourite has flitted for a few happy, summer hours, till winter came and the butterfly was broken," and, as she spoke, she dropped her veil over her face and began to descend the stairs.

Peter Plays a Part

"Stop," said Peter from the shadow of the doorway, "I fear this business, Inez, and I do not understand why it is needful. Why cannot you say what you have to say here?"

"Are you mad?" she answered almost fiercely through her veil. "Do you think that it can be any pleasure for me to seem to make love to a stone shaped like a man, for whom I care nothing at all—except as a friend?" she added quickly. "I tell you, Señor Peter, that if you do not do as I tell you, you will never hear what I have to say, for I shall be held to have failed in my business, and within a few minutes shall vanish from you for ever—to my death perhaps; but what does that matter to you? Choose now, and quickly, for I cannot stand thus for long."

"I obey you, God forgive me!" said the distraught Peter from the darkness of the doorway; "but must I really—?"

"Yes, you must," she answered with energy, "and some would not think that so great a penance."

Then she lifted the corner of her veil coyly and, peeping out beneath it, called in a soft, clear voice, "Oh! forgive me, dear friend, if I have run too fast for you, forgetting that you are still so very weak. Here, lean upon me; I am frail, but it may serve." And she passed up the steps again, to reappear in another moment with Peter's hand resting on her shoulder.

"Be careful of these steps," she said, "they are so slippery"—a statement to which Peter, whose pale face had grown suddenly red, murmured a hearty assent. "Do not be afraid," she went on in her flute-like voice; "this is the secret garden, where none can hear words, however sweet, and none can see even a caress, no, not the most jealous woman. That is why in old days it was called the Sultana's Chamber, for there at the end of it was where she bathed in the summer season. What say you of spies? Oh! yes, in the palace there are many, but to look towards this place, even for the Guardian of the Women, was always death. Here there are no witnesses, save the flowers and the birds."

As she spoke thus they reached the central path, and passed up it slowly, Peter's hand still upon the shoulder of Inez, and her white arm about him, while she looked up into his eyes.

"Bend closer over me," she whispered, "for truly your face is like that of a wooden saint," and he bent. "Now," she went on, "listen. Your lady lives, and is well—kiss me on the lips, please, that news is worth it. If you shut your eyes you can imagine that I am she."

Again Peter obeyed, and with a better grace than might have been expected.

"She is a prisoner in this same palace," she went on, "and the marquis, who is mad for love of her, seeks by all means, fair or foul, to make her his wife!"

"Curse him!" exclaimed Peter with another embrace.

"Till a few days ago she thought you dead; but now she knows that you are alive and recovering. Her father, Castell, escaped from the place where he was put, and is in hiding among his friends, the Jews, where even Morella cannot find him; indeed, he believes him fled from the city. But he is not fled, and, having much gold, has opened a door between himself and his daughter."

Here she stopped to return the embrace with much warmth. Then they passed under some trees, and came to the marble baths where the sultanas were supposed to have bathed in summer, for this place had been one of the palaces of the Kings of Granada before they lived in the Alhambra. Here Inez sat down upon a seat and loosened some garment about her throat, for the evening was very hot.

"What are you doing?" Peter asked doubtfully, for he was filled with many fears.

"Cooling myself," she answered; "your arm was warm, and we may sit here for a few minutes."

"Well, go on with your tale," he said.

"I have little more to say, friend, except that if you wish to send any message, I might perhaps be able to take it."

"You are an angel," he exclaimed.

"That is another word for messenger, is it not? Continue."

"Tell her—that if she hears anything of all this business, it isn't true."

"On that point she may form her own opinion," replied Inez demurely. "If I were in her place I know what mine would be. Don't waste time; we must soon begin to walk again."

Peter stared at her, for he could understand nothing of all this play. Apparently she read his look, for she answered it in a quiet, serious voice: You are wondering what everything means, and why I am doing what I do. I will tell you, Señor, and you can believe me or not as you like. Perhaps you think that I am in love with you. It would not be wonderful, would it? Besides, in the old tales, that always happens—the lady who nurses the Christian knight and worships him and so forth."

"I don't think anything of the sort; I am not so vain."

"I know it, Señor, you are too good a man to be vain. Well, I do all these things, not for love of you, or any one, but for hate—for hate. Yes, for hate of Morella," and she clenched her little hand, hissing the words out between her teeth.

"I understand the feeling," said Peter. "But—but what has he done to *you*?"

"Do not ask me, Señor. Enough that once I loved him—that accursed priest Henriques sold me into his power—oh! a long while ago, and he ruined me, making me what I am, and—I bore his child, and—and it is dead. Oh! Mother of God, my boy is dead, and since then I have been an outcast and his slave—they have slaves here in Granada, Señor—dependent on him for my bread, forced to do his bidding, forced to wait upon his other loves; I, who once was the sultana; I, of whom he has wearied. Only to-day—but why should I tell you of it? Well, he has driven me even to this, that I must kiss an unwilling stranger in a garden," and she sobbed aloud.

"Poor girl!—poor girl!" said Peter, patting her hand kindly with his thin fingers. "Henceforth I have another score against Morella, and I will pay it too."

"Will you?" she asked quickly. "Ah! if so, I would die for you, who now live only to be revenged upon him. And it shall be my first vengeance to rob him of that noble-looking mistress of yours, whom he has stolen away and has set his heart upon wholly, because she is the first woman who ever resisted him—him, who thinks that he is invincible."

"Have you any plan?" asked Peter.

"As yet, none. The thing is very difficult. I go in danger of my life, for if he thought that I betrayed him he would kill me like a rat, and think no harm of it. Such things can be done in Granada without sin, Señor, and no questions asked—at least if the victim be a woman of the murderer's household. I have told you already that if I had refused to do what I have done this evening I should certainly have been got rid of in this way or that, and another set on at the work. No, I have no plan yet, only it is I through whom the Señor Castell communicates with his daughter, and I will see him again, and see her, and we will make some plan. No, do not thank me. He pays me for my services, and I am glad to take his money, who hope to escape from this hell and live on it elsewhere. Yet, not for all the money in the world would I risk what I am risking, though in truth it matters not to me whether I live or die. Señor, I will not disguise it from you, all this scene will come to the Dona Margaret's ears, but I will explain it to her."

"I pray you, do," said Peter earnestly—"explain it fully."

"I will—I will. I will work for you and her and her father, and if I cease to work, know that I am dead or in a dungeon, and fend for yourselves as best you may. One thing I can tell you for your comfort— no harm has been done to this lady of yours. Morella loves her too well for that. He wishes to make her his wife. Or perhaps he has sworn some oath, as I know that he has sworn that he will not murder you—which he might have done a score of times while you have lain a prisoner in his power. Why, once when you were senseless he came and stood over you, a dagger in his hand, and reasoned out the case with me. I said, 'Why do you not kill him?' knowing that thus I could best help to save your life. He answered, 'Because I will not take my wife with her lover's blood upon my hands, unless I slay him in fair fight. I swore it yonder in London. It was the offering which I made to God and to my patron saint that so I might win her fairly, and if I break that oath, God will be avenged upon me here and hereafter. Do my bidding, Inez. Nurse him well, so that if he dies, he dies without sin of mine.' No, he will not murder you or harm her. Friend Pedro, he dare not."

"Can you think of nothing?" asked Peter.

"Nothing—as yet nothing. These walls are high, guards watch them day and night, and outside is the great city of Granada where Morella has much power, and whence no Christian may escape. But he would marry her. And there is that handsome fool-woman, her servant, who is in love with him—oh! she told me all about it in the worst Spanish I ever heard, but the story is too long to repeat; and the priest, Father Henriques—he who wished that you might be killed at the inn, and who loves money so much. Ah! now I think I see some light. But we have no more time to talk, and I must have time to think. Friend Pedro, make ready your kisses, we must go on with our game, and, in truth, you play but badly. Come now, your arm. There is a seat prepared for us yonder. Smile and look loving. I have not art enough for both. Come!— come!" And together they walked out of the dense shadow of the trees and past the marble bath of the sultanas to a certain seat beneath a bower on which were cushions, and lying among them a lute.

"Seat yourself at my feet," she said, as she sank on to the bench. "Can you sing?"

"No more than a crow," he answered.

"Then I must sing to you. Well, it will be better than the love-making." Then in a very sweet voice she began to warble amorous Moorish ditties that she accompanied upon the lute, whilst Peter, who was weary in body and disturbed in mind, played a lover's part to the best of his ability, and by degrees the darkness gathered.

At length, when they could no longer see across the garden, Inez ceased singing and rose with a sigh.

"The play is finished and the curtain down," she said; "also it is time that you went in out of this damp. Señor Pedro, you are a very bad actor; but let us pray that the audience was compassionate, and took the will for the deed."

"I did not see any audience," answered Peter.

"But it saw you, as I dare say you will find out by-and-by. Follow me now back to your room, for I must be going about your business—and my own. Have you any message for the Señor Castell?"

"None, save my love and duty. Tell him that, thanks to you, although still somewhat feeble, I am recovered of my hurt upon the ship and the fever which I took from the sun, and that if he can make any plan to get us all out of this accursed city and the grip of Morella I will bless his name and yours."

"Good, I will not forget. Now be silent. Tomorrow we will walk here again; but be not afraid, then there will be no more need for love-making."

Margaret sat by the open window-place of her beautiful chamber in Morella's palace. She was splendidly arrayed in a rich, Spanish dress, whereof the collar was stiff with pearls, she who must wear what it pleased her captor to give her. Her long tresses, fastened with a jewelled band, flowed down about her shoulders, and, her hand resting on her knee, from her high tower prison she gazed out across the valley at the dim and mighty mass of the Alhambra and the ten thousand lights of Granada which sparkled far below. Near to her, seated beneath a silver hanging-lamp, and also clad in rich array, was Betty.

"What is it, Cousin?" asked the girl, looking at her anxiously. "At least you should be happier than you were, for now you know that Peter is not dead, but almost recovered from his sickness and in this very palace; also, that your father is well and hidden away, plotting for our escape. Why, then, are you so sad, who should be more joyful than you were?"

"Would you learn, Betty? Then I will tell you. I am betrayed. Peter Brome, the man whom I looked upon almost as my husband, is false to me."

"Master Peter false!" exclaimed Betty, staring at her open-mouthed. "No, it is not possible. I know him; he could not be, who will not even look at another woman, if that is what you mean."

"You say so. Then, Betty, listen and judge. You remember this afternoon, when the marquis took us to see the wonders of this palace, and I went thinking that perhaps I might find some path by which afterwards we could escape?"

"Of course I remember, Margaret. We do not leave this cage so often that I am likely to forget."

"Then you will remember also that high-walled garden in which we walked, where the great tower is, and how the marquis and that hateful priest Father Henriques and I went up the tower to study the prospect from its roof, I thinking that you were following me."

"The waiting-women would not let me," said Betty. "So soon as you had passed in they shut the door and told me to bide where I was till you returned. I went near to pulling the hair out of the head of one of them over it, since I was afraid for you alone with those two men. But she drew her knife, the cat, and I had none."

"You must be careful, Betty," said Margaret, "lest some of these heathen folk should do you a mischief."

"Not they," she answered; "they are afraid of me. Why, the other day I bundled one of them, whom I found listening at the door, head first down the stairs. She complained to the marquis, but he only laughed at her, and now she lies abed with a plaster on her nose. But tell me your tale."

"We climbed the tower," said Margaret, "and from its topmost room looked out through the windows that face south at all the mountains and the plain over which they dragged us from Motril. Presently the priest, who had gone to the north wall, in which there are no windows, and entered some recess there, came out with an evil smile upon his face, and whispered something to the marquis, who turned to me and said:

"'The father tells me of an even prettier scene which we can view yonder. Come, Señora, and look.'

"So I went, who wished to learn all that I could of the building. They led me into a little chamber cut in the thickness of the stonework, in the wall of which are slits like loop-holes for the shooting of arrows, wide within, but very narrow without, so that I think they cannot be seen from below, hidden as they are between the rough stones of the tower.

"'This is the place,' said the marquis, 'where in the old days the kings of Granada, who were always jealous, used to sit to watch their women in the secret garden. It is told that thus one of them discovered his sultana making love to an astrologer, and drowned them both in the marble bath at the end of the garden. Look now, beneath us walk a couple who do not guess that we are the witnesses of their vows.'

"So I looked idly enough to pass the time, and there I saw a tall man in a Moorish dress, and with him, for their arms were about each other, a woman. As I was turning my head away who did not wish to spy upon them thus, the woman lifted her face to kiss the man, and I knew her for that beautiful Inez who has visited us here at times, as a spy I think. Presently, too, the man, after paying her back her embrace, glanced about him guiltily, and I saw his face also, and knew it."

"Who was it?" asked Betty, for this gossip of lovers interested her.

"Peter Brome, no other," Margaret answered calmly, but with a note of despair in her voice. "Peter Brome, pale with recent sickness, but no other man."

"The saints save us! I did not think he had it in him!" gasped Betty with astonishment.

"They would not let me go," went on Margaret; "they forced me to see it all. The pair tarried for a while beneath some trees by the bath and were hidden there. Then they came out again and sat them down upon a marble seat, while the woman sang songs and the man leaned against her lovingly. So it went on until the darkness fell, and we went, leaving them there. Now," she added, with a little sob, "what say you?"

"I say," answered Betty, "that it was not Master Peter, who has no liking for strange ladies and secret gardens."

"It was he, and no other man, Betty."

"Then, Cousin, he was drugged or drunk or bewitched, not the Peter whom we know."

"Bewitched, perchance, by that bad woman, which is no excuse for him."

Betty thought a while. She could not doubt the evidence, but from her face it was clear that she took no severe view of the offence.

"Well, at the worst," she said, "men, as I have known them, are men. He has been shut up for a long while with that minx, who is very fair and witching, and it was scarcely right to watch him through a slit in a tower. If he were my lover, I should say nothing about it."

"I will say nothing to him about that or any other matter," replied Margaret sternly. "I have done with Peter Brome."

Again Betty thought, and spoke.

"I seem to see a trick. Cousin Margaret, they told you he was dead, did they not? And then that news came to us that he was not dead, only sick, and here. So the lie failed. Now they tell you, and seem to show you, that he is faithless. May not all this have been some part played for a purpose by the woman?"

"It takes two to play such parts, Betty. If you had seen—"

"If I had seen, I should have known whether it was but a part or love made in good earnest; but you are too innocent to judge. What said the marquis all this while, and the priest?"

"Little or nothing, only smiled at each other, and at length, when it grew dark and we could see no more, asked me if I did not think that it was time to go—me! whom they had kept there all that while to be the witness of my own shame."

"Yes, they kept you there—did they not?—and brought you there just at the right time—did they not?—and shut me out of the tower so that I might not be with you—oh! and all the rest. Now, if you have any justice in you, Cousin, you will hear Peter's side of this story before you judge him."

"I have judged him," answered Margaret coldly, "and, oh! I wish that I were dead."

Margaret rose from her seat and, stepping to the window-place in the tower which was built upon the edge of a hill, searched the giddy depth beneath with her eyes, where, two hundred feet below, the white line of a roadway showed faintly in the moonlight.

"It would be easy, would it not," she said, with a strained laugh, "just to lean out a little too far upon this stone, and then one swift rush and darkness—or light—for ever—which, I wonder?"

"Light, I think," said Betty, jerking her back from the window—"the light of hell fire, and plenty of it, for that would be self-murder, nothing else, and besides, what would one look like on that road? Cousin, don't be a fool. If you are right, it isn't you who ought to go out of that window; and if you are wrong, then you would only make a bad business worse. Time enough to die when one must, say I—which, perhaps, will be soon enough. Meanwhile, if I were you, I would try to speak to Master Peter first, if only to let him know what I thought of him."

"Mayhap," answered Margaret, sinking back into a chair, "but I suffer—how can you know what I suffer?"

"Why should I not know?" asked Betty. "Are you the only woman in the world who has been fool enough to fall in love? Can I not be as much in love as you are? You smile, and think to yourself that the poor relation, Betty, cannot feel like her rich cousin. But I do—I do. I know that he is a villain, but I love this marquis as much as you hate him, or as much as you love Peter, because I can't help myself; it is my luck, that's all. But I am not going to throw myself out of a window; I would rather throw him out and square our reckoning, and that I swear I'll do, in this way or the other, even if it should cost me what I don't want to lose—my life." And Betty drew herself up beneath the silver lamp with a look upon her handsome, determined face, which was so like Margaret's and yet so different, that, could he have seen it, might well have made Morella regret that he had chosen this woman for a tool.

While Margaret studied her wonderingly she heard a sound, and glanced up to see, standing before them, none other than the beautiful Spaniard, or Moor, for she knew not which she was, Inez, that same woman whom, from her hiding-place in the tower, she had watched with Peter in the garden.

"How did you come here?" she asked coldly.

"Through the door, Señora, that was left unlocked, which is not wise of those who wish to talk privately in such a place as this," she answered with a humble curtsey.

"The door is still unlocked," said Margaret, pointing towards it.

"Nay, Señora, you are mistaken; here is its key in my hand. I pray you do not tell your lady to put me out, which, being so strong, she well can do, for I have words to say to you, and if you are wise you will listen to them."

Margaret thought a moment, then answered:

"Say on, and be brief."

Betty Shows Her Teeth

"Señora," said Inez, "you think that you have something against me."

"No," answered Margaret, "you are—what you are; why should I blame you?"

"Well, against the Señor Brome then?"

"Perhaps, but that is between me and him. I will not discuss it with you."

"Señora," went on Inez, with a slow smile, "we are both innocent of what you thought you saw."

"Indeed; then who is guilty?"

"The Marquis of Morella."

Margaret made no answer, but her eyes said much.

"Señora, you do not believe me, nor is it wonderful. Yet I speak the truth. What you saw from the tower was a play in which the Señor Brome took his part badly enough, as you may have noticed, because I told him that my life hung on it. I have nursed him through a sore sickness, Señora, and he is not ungrateful."

"So I judged; but I do not understand you."

"Señora, I am a slave in this house, a discarded slave. Perhaps you can guess the rest, it is a common story here. I was offered my freedom at a price, that I should weave myself into this man's heart, I who am held fair, and make him my lover. If I failed, then perhaps I should be sold as a slave—perhaps worse. I accepted—why should I not? It was a small thing to me. On the one hand, life, freedom, and wealth, an hidalgo of good blood and a gallant friend for a little while, and, on the other, the last shame or blackness which doubtless await me now—if I am found out. Señora, I failed, who in truth did not try hard to succeed. The man looked on me as his nurse, no more, and to me he was one very sick, no more. Also, we grew to be true friends, and in this way or in that I learned all his story, learned also why the trap was baited thus—that you might be deceived and fall into a deeper trap. Señora, I could not explain it all to him, indeed, in that chamber where we were spied on, I had but little chance. Still, it was necessary that he should seem to be what he is not, so I took him into the garden and, knowing well who watched us, made him act his part, well enough to deceive you it would seem."

"Still I do not understand," said Margaret more softly. "You say that your life or welfare hung on this shameful business. Then why do you reveal it to me now?"

"To save you from yourself, Señora, to save my friend the Señor Brome, and to pay back Morella in his own coin."

"How will you do these things?"

"The first two are done, I think, but the third is difficult. It is of that I come to speak with you, at great risk. Indeed, had not my master been summoned to the court of the Moorish king I could not have come, and he may return at any time."

"Have you some plan?" asked Margaret, leaning towards her eagerly.

"No plan as yet, only an idea." She turned and looked at Betty, adding, "This lady is your cousin, is she not, though of a different station, and somewhat far away?"

Margaret nodded.

"You are not unlike," went on Inez, "of much the same height and shape, although the Señora Betty is stronger built, and her eyes are blue and her hair golden, whereas your eyes are black and your hair chestnut. Beneath a veil, or at night, it would not be easy to tell you apart if your hands were gloved and neither of you spoke above a whisper."

"Yes," said Margaret, "what then?"

"Now the Señora Betty comes into the play," replied Inez. "Señora Betty, have you understood our talk?"

"Something, not quite all," answered Betty.

"Then what you do not understand your lady must interpret, and be not angry with me, I pray you, if I seem to know more of you and your affairs than you have ever told me. Render my words now, Dona Margaret."

Then, after this was done, and she had thought awhile, Inez continued slowly, Margaret translating from Spanish into English whenever Betty could not understand:

"Morella made love to you in England, Señora Betty—did he not?—and won your heart as he has won that of many another woman, so that you came to believe that he was carrying you off to marry you, and not your cousin?"

"What affair is that of yours, woman?" asked Betty, flushing angrily.

"None at all, save that I could tell much such another story, if you cared to listen. But hear me out, and then answer me a question, or rather, answer the question first. Would you like to be avenged upon this high-born knave?"

"Avenged?" answered Betty, clenching her hands and hissing the words through her firm, white teeth. "I would risk my life for it."

"As I do. It seems that we are of one mind there. Then I think that perhaps I can show you a way. Look now, your cousin has seen certain things which women placed as she is do not like to see. She is jealous, she is angry—or was until I told her the truth. Well, to-night or to-morrow, Morella will come to her and say, 'Are you satisfied? Do you still refuse me in favour of a man who yields his heart to the first light-of-love who tempts him? Will you not be my wife?' What if she answer, 'Yes, I will.' Nay, be silent both of you, and hear me out. What if then there should be a secret marriage, *and the Señora Betty should chance to wear the bride's veil*, while the Dona Margaret, in the robe of Betty, was let go with the Señor Brome and her father?"

Inez paused, watching them both, and playing with the fan she held, while, the rendering of her words finished, Margaret and Betty stared at her and at each other, for the audacity and fearfulness of this plot took their breath away. It was Margaret who spoke the first.

"You must not do it, Betty," she said. "Why, when the man found you out, he would kill you." But Betty took no heed of her, and thought on. At length she looked up and answered:

"Cousin, it was my vain folly that brought you all into this trouble, therefore I owe something to you, do I not? I am not afraid of the man—he is afraid of me; and if it came to killing—why, let Inez lend me that knife of hers, and I think that perhaps I should give the first blow. And—well, I think I love him, rascal though he is, and, afterwards, perhaps we might make it up, who can say?—while, if not—But tell me, you, Inez, should I be his legal wife according to the law of this land?"

"Assuredly," answered Inez, "if a priest married you and he placed the ring upon your hand and named you wife. Then, when once the words of blessing have been said, the Pope alone can loose that knot, which may be risked, for there would be much to explain, and is this a tale that Morella, a good servant of the Church, would care to take to Rome?"

"It would be a trick," broke in Margaret—"a very ugly trick."

"And what was it he played on me and you?" asked Betty. "Nay, I'll chance it, and his rage, if only I can be sure that you and Peter will go free, and your father with you."

"But what of this Inez?" asked Margaret, bewildered.

"She will look after herself," answered Inez. "Perchance, if all goes well, you will let me ride with you. And now I dare stop no longer, I go to see your father, the Señor Castell, and if anything can be arranged, we will talk again. Meanwhile, Dona Margaret, your affianced is nearly well again at last and sends his heart's love to you, and, I counsel you, when Morella speaks turn a gentle ear to him."

Then with another deep curtsey she glided to the door, unlocked it, and left the room.

****

An hour later Inez was being led by an old Jew, dressed in a Moslem robe and turban, through one of the most tortuous and crowded parts of Granada. It would seem that this Jew was known there, for his appearance, accompanied by a veiled woman, apparently caused no surprise to those followers of the Prophet that he met, some of whom, indeed, saluted him with humility.

"These children of Mahomet seem to love you, Father Israel," said Inez.

"Yes, yes, my dear," answered the old fellow with a chuckle; "they owe me money, that is why, and I am getting it in before the great war comes with the Spaniards, so they would sweep the streets for me with their beards—all of which is very good for the plans of our friend yonder. Ah! he who has crowns in his pocket can put a crown upon his head; there is nothing that money will not do in Granada. Give me enough of it, and I will buy his sultana from the king."

"This Castell has plenty?" asked Inez shortly.

"Plenty, and more credit. He is one of the richest men in England. But why do you ask? He would not think of you, who is too troubled about other things."

Inez only laughed bitterly, but did not resent the words. Why should she? It was not worth while.

"I know," she answered, "but I mean to earn some of it all the same, and I want to be sure that there is enough for all of us."

"There is enough, I have told you there is enough and to spare," answered the Hebrew Israel as he tapped on a door in a dirty-looking wall.

It opened as though by magic, and they crossed a paved patio, or courtyard, to a house beyond, a tumble-down place of Moorish architecture.

"Our friend Castell, being in seclusion just now, has hired the cellar floor," said Israel with a chuckle to Inez, "so be pleased to follow me, and take care of the rats and beetles."

Then he led her down a rickety stair which opened out of the courtyard into vaults filled with vats of wine, and, having lit a taper, through these, shutting and locking sundry doors behind him, to what appeared to be a very damp wall covered with cobwebs, and situated in a dark corner of a wine-cave. Here he stopped and tapped again in his peculiar fashion, whereon a portion of the wall turned outwards on a pivot, leaving an opening through which they could pass.

"Well managed, isn't it?" chuckled Israel. "Who would think of looking for an entrance here, especially if he owed the old Jew money? Come in, my pretty, come in."

Inez followed him into this darksome hole, and the wall closed behind them. Then, taking her by the arm, he turned first to the right, next to the left, opened a door with a key which he carried, and, behold, they stood in a beautifully furnished room well lighted with lamps, for it seemed to have no windows. "Wait here," he said to Inez, pointing to a couch on which she sat herself down, "while I fetch my lodger," and he vanished through some curtains at the end of the room.

Presently these opened again, and Israel reappeared through them with Castell, dressed now in Moorish robes, and looking somewhat pale from his confinement underground, but otherwise well enough. Inez rose and stood before him, throwing back her veil that he might see her face. Castell searched her for a while with his keen eyes that noted everything, then said: "You are the lady with whom I have been in communication through our friend here, are you not? Prove it to me now by repeating my messages."

Inez obeyed, telling him everything.

"That is right," he said, "but how do I know that I can trust you? I understand you are, or have been, the lover of this man Morella, and such an one he might well employ as a spy to bring us all to ruin."

"Is it not too late to ask such questions, Señor? If I am not to be trusted, already you and your people are in the hollow of my hand?"

"Not at all, not at all, my dear," said Israel. "If we see the slightest cause to doubt you, why, there are many great vats in this place, one of which, at a pinch, would serve you as a coffin, though it would be a pity to spoil the good wine."

Inez laughed as she answered: "Save your wine, and your time too. Morella has cast me off, and I hate him, and wish to escape from him and rob him of his prize. Also, I desire money to live on afterwards, and this you must give to me or I do not stir, or rather the promise of it, for you Jews keep your word, and I do not ask a *maravedi* from you until I have played my part."

"And then how many *maravedis* do you ask, young woman?"

Inez named a sum, at the mention of which both of them opened their eyes, and old Israel exclaimed drily:

"Surely—surely you must be one of us."

"No," she answered, "but I try to follow your example, and, if I am to live at all, it shall be in comfort."

"Quite so," said Castell, "we understand. But now tell us, what do you propose to do for this money?"

"I propose to set you, your daughter, the Dona Margaret, and her lover, the Señor Brome, safe and free outside the walls of Granada, and to leave the Marquis of Morella married to another woman."

"What other woman? Yourself?" asked Castell, fixing on this last point in the programme.

"No, Señor, not for all the wealth of both of you. To your dependent and your daughter's relative, the handsome Betty."

"How will you manage that?" exclaimed Castell, amazed.

"These cousins are not unlike, Señor, although the link of blood between them is so thin. Listen now, I will tell you." And she explained the outlines of her plan.

"A bold scheme enough," said Castell, when she had finished, "but even if it can be done, would that marriage hold?"

"I think so," answered Inez, "if the priest knew—and he could be bribed—and the bride knows. But if not, what would it matter, since Rome alone can decide the question, and long before that is done the fates of all of us will be settled."

"Rome—or death," said Castell; and Inez read what he was afraid of in his eyes.

"Your Betty takes her chance," she replied slowly, "as many a one has done before her with less cause. She is a woman with a mind as strong as her body. Morella made her love him and promised to marry her. Then he used her to steal your daughter, and she learned that she had been no more than a stalking-heifer, from behind which he would net the white swan. Do you not think, therefore, that she has something to pay him back, she through whom her beloved mistress and cousin has been brought into all this trouble? If she wins, she becomes the wife of a grandee of Spain, a marchioness; and if she loses, well, she has had her fling for a high stake, and perhaps her revenge. At least she is willing to take her chance, and, meanwhile, all of you can be gone."

Castell looked doubtfully at the Jew Israel, who stroked his white beard and said:

"Let the woman set out her scheme. At any rate she is no fool, and it is worth our hearing, though I fear that at the best it must be costly."

"I can pay," said Castell, and motioned to Inez to proceed.

As yet, however, she had not much more to say, save that they must have good horses at hand, and send a messenger to Seville, whither the *Margaret* had been ordered to proceed, bidding her captain hold his ship ready to sail at any hour, should they succeed in reaching him.

These things, then, they arranged, and a while later Inez and Israel departed, the former carrying with her a bag of gold.

That same night Inez sought the priest, Henriques of Motril, in that hall of Morella's palace which was used as a private chapel, saying that she desired to speak with him under pretence of making confession, for they were old friends—or rather enemies.

As it chanced she found the holy father in a very ill humour. It appeared that Morella also was in a bad humour with Henriques, having heard that it was he who had possessed himself of the jewels in his strong-box on the *San Antonio*. Now he insisted upon his surrendering everything, and swore, moreover, that he would hold him responsible for all that his people had stolen from the ship, and this because he said that it was his fault that Peter Brome had escaped the sea and come on to Granada.

"So, Father," said Inez, "you, who thought yourself rich, are poor again."

"Yes, my daughter, and that is what chances to those who put their faith in princes. I have served this marquis well for many years—to my soul's hurt, I fear me—hoping that he who stands so high in the favour of the Church would advance me to some great preferment. But instead, what does he do? He robs me of a few trinkets that, had I not found them, the sea would have swallowed or some thief would have taken, and declares me his debtor for the rest, of which I know nothing."

"What preferment did you want, Father? I see that you have one in your mind."

"Daughter, a friend had written to me from Seville that if I have a hundred gold doubloons to pay for it, he can secure me the place of a secretary in the Holy Office where I served before as a familiar until the marquis made me his chaplain, and gave the benefice of Motril, which proved worth nothing, and many promises that are worth less. Now those trinkets would fetch thirty, and I have saved twenty, and came here to borrow the other fifty from the marquis, to whom I have done so many good turns—as *you* know well, Inez. You see the end of that quest," and he groaned angrily.

"It is a pity," said Inez thoughtfully, "since those who serve the Inquisition save many souls, do they not, including their own? For instance," she added, and the priest winced at the words, "I remember that they saved the soul of my own sister and would have saved mine, had I been—what shall I say?—more—more prejudiced. Also, they get a percentage of the goods of wicked heretics, and so become rich and able to advance themselves."

"That is so, Inez. It was the chance of a lifetime, especially to one who, like myself, hates heretics. But why speak of it now when that cursed, dissolute marquis—" and he checked himself.

Inez looked at him.

"Father," she asked, "if I happen to be able to find you those hundred gold doubloons, would you do something for me?"

The priest's foxy face lit up.

"I wonder what there is that I would not do, my daughter!"

"Even if it brought you into a quarrel with the marquis?

"Once I was a secretary to the Inquisition of Seville, he would have more reason to fear me than I him. Aye, and fear me he should, who bear him no love," answered the priest with a snarl.

"Then listen, Father. I have not made my confession yet; I have not told you, for instance, that I also hate this marquis, and with good cause—though perhaps you know that already. But remember that if you betray me, you will never see those hundred gold doubloons, and some other holy priest will be appointed secretary at Seville. Also worse things may happen to you."

"Proceed, my daughter," he said unctuously; "are we not in the confessional—or near it?"

So she told him all the plot, trusting to the man's avarice and other matters to protect her, for Inez hated Fray Henriques bitterly, and knew him from the crown of his shaven head to the soles of his erring feet, as she had good cause to do. Only she did not tell him whence the money was to come.

"That does not seem a very difficult matter," he said, when she had finished. "If a man and a woman, unwed and outside the prohibited degrees, appear before me to be married, I marry them, and once the ring has passed and the office is said, married they are till death or the Pope part them."

"And suppose that the man thinks he is marrying another woman, Father?"

The priest shrugged his shoulders.

"He should know whom he is marrying; that is his affair, not the

Church's or mine. The names need not be spoken too loudly, my daughter."

"But you would give me a writing of the marriage with them set out plain?"

"Certainly. To you or to anybody else; why should I not?—that is, if I were sure of this wedding fee."

Inez lifted her hand, and showed beneath it a little pile of ten doubloons.

"Take them, Father," she said; "they will not be counted in the contract. There are others where they came from, whereof twenty will be paid before the marriage, and eighty when I have that writing at Seville."

He swept up the coins and pocketed them, saying:

"I will trust you, Inez."

"Yes," she answered as she left him, "we must trust each other now—must we not?—seeing that you have the money, and both our necks are in the same noose. Be here, Father, to-morrow at the same time, in case I have more confessions to make, for, alas! this is a sinful world, as you should know very well."

CHAPTER 17

The Plot

On the morning following these conversations, just after Margaret and Betty had breakfasted, Inez appeared, and, as before, locked the door behind her.

"Señoras," she said calmly, "I have arranged that little business of which I spoke to you yesterday, or at least the first act of the play, since it remains for you to write the rest. Now I am sent to say that the noble Marquis of Morella craves leave to see you, Dona Margaret, and within an hour. So there is no time to lose."

"Tell us what you have done, Inez?" said Margaret.

"I have seen your worshipful father, Dona Margaret; here is the token of it, which you will do well to destroy when you have read." And she handed her a slip of paper, whereon was written in her father's writing, and in English:

Beloved Daughter,
This messenger, who I think may be trusted by you, has made arrangements with me which she will explain. I approve, though the risk is great. Your cousin is a brave girl, but, understand, I do not force her to this dangerous enterprise. She must choose her own road, only I promise that if she escapes and we live I will not forget her deed. The messenger will bring me your answer. God be with us all, and farewell.
J.C.

Margaret read this letter first to herself and then aloud to Betty, and, having read, tore it into tiny fragments and threw them from the turret window.

"Speak now," she said; and Inez told her everything.

"Can you trust the priest?" asked Margaret, when she had finished.

375

"He is a great villain, as I have reason to know; still, I think I can," she answered, "while the cabbage is in front of the donkey's nose—I mean until he has got all the money. Also, he has committed himself by taking some on account. But before we go further, the question is—does this lady play?" and she pointed to Betty.

"Yes, I play," said Betty, when she understood everything. "I won't go back upon my word; there is too much at stake. It is an ugly business for me, I know well enough, but," she added slowly, setting her firm mouth, "I have debts to pay all round, and I am no Spanish putty to be squeezed flat—like some people," and she glanced at the humble-looking Inez. "So, before all is done, it may be uglier for him."

When she had mastered the meaning of this speech the soft-voiced Inez lifted her gentle eyes in admiration, and murmured a Spanish proverb as to what is supposed to occur when Satan encounters Beelzebub in a high-walled lane. Then, being a lady of resource and experience, the plot having been finally decided upon, not altogether with Margaret's approval, who feared for Betty's fate when it should be discovered, Inez began to instruct them both in various practical expedients, by means of which the undoubted general resemblance of these cousins might be heightened and their differences toned down. To this end she promised to furnish them with certain hair-washes, pigments, and articles of apparel.

"It is of small use," said Betty, glancing first at herself and then at the lovely Margaret, "for even if they change skins, who can make the calf look like the fawn, though they chance to feed in the same meadow? Still, bring your stuffs and I will do my best; but I think that a thick veil and a shut mouth will help me more than any of them, also a long gown to hide my feet."

"Surely they are charming feet," said Inez politely, adding to herself, "to carry you whither you wish to go." Then she turned to Margaret and reminded her that the marquis desired to see her, and waited for her answer.

"I will not meet him alone," said Margaret decidedly.

"That is awkward," answered Inez, "as I think he has words to say to you which he does not wish others to hear, especially the *señora* yonder," and she nodded towards Betty.

"I will not meet him alone," repeated Margaret.

"Yet, if things are to go forward as we have arranged, you must meet him, Dona Margaret, and give him that answer which he desires. Well, I think it can be arranged. The court below is large. Now, while you and the marquis talk at one end of it, the Señora Betty and I might walk out of earshot at the other. She needs more instruction in our Spanish tongue; it would be a good opportunity to begin our lessons."

"But what am I to say to him?" asked Margaret nervously.

"I think," answered Inez, "that you must copy the example of that wonderful actor, the Señor Peter, and play a part as well as you saw him do, or even better, if possible."

"It must be a very different part then," replied Margaret, stiffening visibly at certain recollections.

The gentle Inez smiled as she said:

"Yes, but surely you can seem jealous, for that is natural to us all, and you can yield by degrees, and you can make a bargain as the price of yourself in marriage."

"What exact bargain should I make?"

"I think that you shall be securely wed by a priest of your own Church, and that letters, signed by that priest and announcing the marriage, shall be delivered to the Archbishop of Seville, and to their Majesties King Ferdinand and Queen Isabella. Also, of course, you must arrange that the Señor Brome and your father, the Señor Castell, and your cousin Betty here shall be escorted safe out of Granada before your marriage, and that you shall see them pass through the gate beneath your turret window, swearing that thereafter, at nightfall of the same day, you will suffer the priest to do his office and make you Morella's wife. By that time they should be well upon their road, and, after the rite is celebrated, I will receive the signed papers from the priest and follow them, leaving the false bride to play her part as best she can."

Again Margaret hesitated; the thing seemed too complicated and full of danger. But while she thought, a knock came on the door.

"That is to tell me that Morella awaits your answer in the court," said Inez. "Now, which is it to be? Remember that there is no other chance of escape for you, or the others, from this guarded town—at least I can see none."

"I accept," said Margaret hurriedly, "and God help us all, for we shall need Him."

"And you, Señora Betty?"

"Oh! I made up my mind long ago," answered Betty coolly. "We can only fail, when we shall be no worse off than before."

"Good. Then play your parts well, both of you. After all, they should not be so difficult, for the priest is safe, and the marquis will never scent such a trick as this. Fix the marriage for this day week, as I have much to think of and make ready," and she went.

****

Half an hour later Margaret sat under the cool arcade of the marble court, and with her, Morella, while upon the further side of its splashing fountain and out of earshot, Betty and Inez walked to and fro in the shadow.

"You sent for me, Marquis," said Margaret presently, "and, being your prisoner, I have come because I must. What is your pleasure with me?"

"Dona Margaret," he answered gravely, "can you not guess? Well, I will tell you, lest you should guess wrong. First, it is to ask your forgiveness as I have done before, for the many crimes to which my love, my true love, for you has driven me. This time yesterday I knew well that I could expect none. To-day I dare to hope that it may be otherwise."

"Why so, Marquis?"

"Last evening you looked into a certain garden and saw two people walking there—yonder is one of them," and he nodded towards Inez. "Shall I go on?"

"No," she answered in a low voice, and passing her hands before her face. "Only tell me who and what is that woman?" and in her turn she looked towards Inez.

"Is it necessary?" he asked. "Well, if you wish to know, she is a Spaniard of good blood who with her sister was taken captive by the Moors. A certain priest, who took an interest in the sister, brought her to my notice and I bought her from them; so, as her parents were dead and she had nowhere else to go, she elected to stay in my house. You must not judge such things too harshly; they are common here. Also, she has been very useful to me, being clever, for through her I have intelligence of many things. Of late, however, she has grown tired of this life, and wishes to earn her freedom, which I have promised her in return for certain services, and to leave Granada."

"Was the nursing of my betrothed one of those services, Marquis?"

He shrugged his shoulders.

"As you will, Señora. Certainly I forgive her this indiscretion, if at last she has shown you the truth about that man for whose sake you have endured so much. Margaret, now that you know him for what he is, say, do you still cling to him?"

She rose and walked a few steps down the arcade, then came back and asked:

"Are you any better than this fallen man?"

"I think so, Margaret, for since I knew you I am a risen man; all my old self is left behind me, I am a new creature, and my sins have been for you, not against you. Hear me, I beseech you. I stole you away, it is true, but I have done you no harm, and will do you none. For your sake also I have spared your father when I had but to make a sign to remove him from my path. I suffered him to escape from the prison where he was confined, and I know the place where he thinks himself hidden to-day among the Jews of Granada. Also, I nursed Peter Brome back to life, when at any hour I could have let him die, lest afterwards I might have it on my conscience that, but for my love for you, he might perhaps still be living. Well, you have seen him as he is, and what say you now? Will you still reject me? Look on me," and he drew up his tall and stately shape, "and tell me, am I such a man as a woman should be ashamed to own as husband? Remember, too, that I have much to give you in this land of Spain, whereof you shall become one of the greatest ladies, or perhaps in the future," he added significantly, "even more. War draws near, Margaret; this city and all its rich territories will fall into the hands of Spain, and afterwards I shall be their governor, almost their king."

"And if I refuse?" asked Margaret.

"Then," he answered sternly, "you bide here, and that false lover of yours bides here, and your father bides here to take the chance of war as Christian captives with a thousand others who languish in the dungeons of the Alhambra, while, my mission ended, I go hence to play my part in battle amongst my peers, as one of the first captains of their Most Catholic Majesties. Yet it is not to your fears that I would appeal, but to your heart, for I seek your love and your dear companionship through life, and, if I can help it, desire to work you and yours no harm."

"You desire to work them no harm. Then, if I were to fall in with your humour, would you let them go in safety?—I mean my father and the Señor Brome and my cousin Betty, whom, if you were as honest as you pretend to be, you should ask to bide with you as your wife, and not myself."

"The last I cannot do," he answered, flushing. "God knows I meant her no hurt, and only used her to keep near to and win news of you, thinking her, to tell truth, somewhat other than she is."

"Are no women honest here in Spain, then, my lord Marquis?"

"A few, a very few, Dona Margaret. But I erred about Betty, whom I took for a simple serving-girl, and to whom, if need be, I am ready to make all amends."

"Except that which is due to a woman you have asked to be your wife, and who in our country could claim the fulfilment of your promise, or declare you shamed. But you have not answered. Would they go free?"

"As free as air—especially the Señora Betty," he added with a little smile, "for to speak truth, there is something in that woman's eyes which frightens me at times. I think that she has a long memory. Within an hour of our marriage you shall look down from your window and see them depart under escort, every one, to go whither they will."

"Nay," answered Margaret, "it is not enough. I should need to see them go before, and then, if I consented, not till the sun had set would I pay the price of their ransom."

"Then do you consent? he asked eagerly.

"My lord Marquis, it would seem that I must. My betrothed has played me false. For a month or more I have been prisoner in your palace, which I understand has no good name, and, if I refuse, you tell me that all of us will be cast into yonder dungeons to be sold as slaves or die prisoners of the Moors. My lord Marquis, fate and you leave me but little choice. On this day week I will marry you, but blame me not if you find me other than you think, as you have found my cousin whom you befooled. Till then, also, I pray you that you will leave me quite untroubled. If you have arrangements to make or commands to send, the woman Inez yonder will serve as messenger, for of her I know the worst."

"I will obey you in all things, Dona Margaret," he answered humbly. "Do you desire to see your father or—" and he paused.

"Neither of them," she answered. "I will write to them and send my letters by this Inez. Why should I see them," she added passionately, "who have done with the old days when I was free and happy, and am about to become the wife of the most noble Marquis of Morella, that honourable grandee of Spain, who tricked a poor girl by a false promise of marriage, and used her blind and loving folly to trap and steal me from my home? My lord, till this day week I bid you farewell," and, walking from the arcade to the fountain, she called aloud to Betty to accompany her to their rooms.

The week for which Margaret had bargained had gone by. All was prepared. Inez had shown to Morella the letters that his bride to be wrote to her father and to Peter Brome; also the answers, imploring and passionate, to the same. But there were other letters and other answers which she had not shown. It was afternoon, swift horses were ready in the courtyard, and with them an escort, while, disguised as

Moors, Castell and Peter waited under guard in a chamber close at hand. Betty, dressed in the robes of a Moorish woman, and thickly veiled, stood before Morella, to whom Inez had led her.

"I come to tell you," she said, "that at sundown, three hours after we have passed beneath her window, my cousin and mistress will wait to be made your wife, but if you try to disturb her before then she will be no wife of yours, or any man's."

"I obey," answered Morella; "and, Señora Betty, I pray your pardon, and that you will accept this gift from me in token of your forgiveness." And with a low bow he handed to her a beautiful necklace of pearls.

"I take them," said Betty, with a bitter laugh, "as they may serve to buy me a passage back to England. But forgive you I do not, Marquis of Morella, and I warn you that there is a score between us which I may yet live to settle. You seem to have won, but God in Heaven takes note of the wickedness of men, and in this way or in that He always pays His debts. Now I go to bid farewell to my cousin Margaret, but to you I do not bid farewell, for I think that we shall meet again," and with a sob she let fall the veil which she had lifted above her lips to speak and departed with Inez, to whom she whispered as they went, "He will not linger for any more good-byes with Betty Dene."

They entered Margaret's room and locked the door behind them. She was seated on a low divan wrapped in a loose robe, and by her side, glittering with silver and with gems, lay her bridal veil and garments.

"Be swift," said Inez to Betty, who stripped off her Moorish dress and the long, flowing veil that was wrapped about her head, whereon it was seen that her hair had changed greatly in colour, from yellow to dark chestnut indeed, while her eyes, ringed about with pigments, and made lustrous by drugs dropped into them, looked no longer blue, but black like Margaret's. Yes, and wonder of wonders, on the right side of the chin and on the back of the neck were moles, or beauty-spots, just such as Margaret had borne there from her birth! In short, their stature being much the same, though Betty was more thickly built, except in the strongest light it would not have been easy to distinguish them apart, even unveiled, for at all such arts of the altering of the looks of women, Inez was an adept, and she had done her best.

Now Margaret clothed herself in the white robes and the thick head-dress that hid her face, all except a little crack left for the eyes to peep through, whilst Betty, with the help of Inez, arrayed herself in the wondrous wedding robe beset with jewels that was Morella's bridal gift, and hid her dyed tresses beneath the pearl-sewn veil.

Within ten minutes all was finished, even to the dagger that Betty had tied about her beneath her robe, and the two transformed women stood staring at each other.

"It is time to go," said Inez.

Then Margaret broke out:

"I do not like this business; I never did. When he discovers all, that man's rage will be terrible, and he will kill her. I repent that I have consented to the plot."

"It is too late to repent now, Señora," said Inez.

"Cannot Betty be got away also?" asked Margaret desperately.

"It is just possible," answered Inez; "thus, before the marriage, according to the old custom here, I hand the cups of wine to the bridegroom and the bride. That for the marquis will be drugged, since he must not see too clear to-night. Well, I might brew it stronger so that within half an hour he would not know whether he were married or single, and then, perhaps, she might escape with me and come to join you. But it is very risky, and, of course, if we were discovered—the stitch would be out of the wineskin, and the cellar floor might be stained!"

Now Betty interrupted:

"Keep your stitches whole, Cousin; if any skins are to be pricked it can't be helped, and at least you won't have to wipe up the mess. I am not going to run away from the man, more likely he will run away from me. I look well in this fine dress of yours, and I mean to wear it out. Now begone—begone, before some of them come to seek me. Don't you grieve for me; I'll lie in the bed that I have made, and if the worst comes to the worst, I have money in my pocket—or its worth—and we will meet again in England. Come, give my love and duty to Master Peter and your father, and if I should see them no more, bid them think kindly of Betty Dene, who was such a plague to them."

Then, taking Margaret in her strong arms, she kissed her again and again, and fairly thrust her from the room.

But when they were gone, poor Betty sat down and cried a little, till she remembered that hot tears might melt the paint upon her face, and, drying them, went to the window and watched.

A while later, from her lofty niche, she saw six Moorish horsemen riding along the white road to the embattled gate. After them came two men and a woman, all splendidly mounted, also dressed as Moors, and then six other horsemen. They passed the gate which was opened for them and began to mount the slope beyond. At the crest of it the woman halted and, turning, waved a handkerchief. Betty answered the signal, and in another minute they had vanished, and she was alone.

Never did she spend a more weary afternoon. Two hours later, still watching at her window, she saw the Moorish escort return, and knew that all was well, and that by now, Margaret, her lover, and her father were safely started on their journey. So she had not risked her life in vain.

The Holy Hermandad

Down the long passages, through the great, fretted halls, across the cool marble courts, flitted Inez and Margaret. It was like a dream. They went through a room where women, idling or working at tapestries, looked at them curiously. Margaret heard one of them say to another:

"Why does the Dona Margaret's cousin leave her?" And the answer, "Because she is in love with the marquis herself, and cannot bear to stay."

"What a fool!" said the first woman. "She is good looking, and would only have had to wait a few weeks."

They passed an open door, that of Morella's own chambers. Within it he stood and watched them go by. When they were opposite to him some doubt or idea seemed to strike his mind, for he looked at them keenly, stepped forward, then, thinking better of it, or perhaps remembering Betty's bitter tongue, halted and turned aside. That danger had gone by!

At length, none hindering them, they reached the yard where the escort and the horses waited. Here, standing under an archway, were Castell and Peter. Castell greeted Margaret in English and kissed her through her veil, while Peter, who had not seen her close since months before he rode away to Dedham, stared at her with all his eyes, and began to draw near to her, designing to find out, as he was sure he could do if once he touched her, whether indeed this were Margaret, or only Betty after all. Guessing what was in his mind, and that he might reveal everything, Inez, who held a long pin in her hand with which she was fastening her veil that had come loose, pretended to knock against him, and ran the point deep into his arm, muttering, "Fool!" as she did so. He sprang back with an oath, the guard smiled, and she began to pray his pardon.

Castell helped Margaret on to her horse, then mounted his own, as did Peter, still rubbing his arm, but not daring to look towards Margaret, whose hand Inez shook familiarly in farewell as though she were her equal, addressing her the while in terms of endearment such as Spanish women use to each other. An officer of Morella's household came and counted them, saying:

"Two men and a woman. That is right, though I cannot see the woman's face."

For a moment he seemed to be about to order her to unveil, but Inez called to him that it was not decent before all these Moors, whereon he nodded and ordered the captain to proceed.

They rode through the arch of the castle along the roadway, through the great gate of the wall also, where the guard questioned their escort, stared at them, and, after receiving a present from Castell, let them go, telling them they were lucky Christians to get alive out of Granada, as indeed they were.

At the brow of the rise Margaret turned and waved her handkerchief towards that high window which she knew so well. Another handkerchief was waved in answer, and, thinking of the lonely Betty watching them there while she awaited the issue of her desperate venture, Margaret went on, weeping beneath her veil. For an hour they rode forward, speaking few words to each other, till at length they came to the cross-roads, one of which ran to Malaga, and the other towards Seville.

Here the escort halted, saying that their orders were to leave them at this point, and asking which road they intended to take. Castell answered that to Malaga, whereon the captain replied that they were wise, as they were less likely to meet bands of marauding thieves who called themselves Christian soldiers, and murdered or robbed all travellers who fell into their hands. Then Castell offered him a present, which he accepted gravely, as though he did him a great favour, and, after bows and salutations, they departed.

As soon as the Moors were gone the three rode a little way towards Malaga. Then, when there was nobody in sight, they turned across country and gained the Seville road. At last they were alone and, halting beneath the walls of a house that had been burnt in some Christian raid, they spoke together freely for the first time, and oh! what a moment was that for all of them!

Peter pushed his horse alongside that of Margaret, crying:

"Speak, beloved. Is it truly you?"

But Margaret, taking no heed of him, leant over and, throwing her arm around her father's neck, kissed him again and again through her veil, blessing God that they had lived to meet in safety. Peter tried to kiss her also; but she caused her horse to move so that he nearly fell from his saddle.

"Have a care, Peter," she said to him, "or your love of kissing will lead you into more trouble." Whereon, guessing of what she spoke, he coloured furiously, and began to explain at length.

"Cease," she said—"cease. I know all that story, for I saw you," then, relenting, with some brief, sweet words of greeting and gratitude, gave him her hand, which he kissed often enough.

"Come," said Castell, "we must push on, who have twenty miles to cover before we reach that inn where Israel has arranged that we should sleep to-night. We will talk as we go." And talk they did, as well as the roughness of the road and the speed at which they must travel would allow.

Riding as hard as they were able, at length they came to the *venta*, or rough hostelry, just as the darkness closed in. At the sight of it they thanked God aloud, for this place was across the Moorish border, and now they had little to fear from Granada. The host, a half-bred Spaniard and a Christian, expected them, having received a message from Israel, with whom he had had dealings, and gave them two rooms, rude enough, but sufficient, and good food and wine, also stabling and barley for their horses, bidding them sleep well and have no fear, as he and his people would watch and warn them of any danger.

Yet it was late before they slept, who had so much to say to each other—especially Peter and Margaret—and were so happy at their escape, if only for a little while. Yet across their joy, like the sound of a funeral bell at a merry feast, came the thought of Betty and that fateful marriage in which ere now she must have played her part. Indeed, at last Margaret knelt down and offered up prayers to Heaven that the saints might protect her cousin in the great peril which she had incurred for them, nor was Peter ashamed to join her in that prayer. Then they embraced—especially Peter and Margaret—and laid them down, Castell and his daughter in one room, and Peter in the other, and slept as best they could.

Half an hour before dawn Peter was up seeing to the horses while the others breakfasted and packed the food that the landlord had made ready for their journey. Then he also swallowed some meat and wine, and at the first break of day, having discharged their reckoning and taken a letter from their host to those of other inns upon the road, they pressed on towards Seville, very thankful to find that as yet there were no signs of their being pursued.

All that day, with short pauses to rest themselves and their horses, they rode on without accident, for the most part over a fertile plain watered by several rivers which they crossed at fords or over bridges. As night fell they reached the old town of Oxuna, which for many hours they had seen set upon its hill before them, and, notwithstanding their Moorish dress, made their way almost unobserved in the darkness to that inn to which they had been recommended. Here, although he stared at their garments, on finding that they had plenty of money, the landlord received them well enough, and again they were fortunate in securing rooms to themselves. It had been their purpose to buy Spanish clothes in this town, but, as it happened, it was a feast day, and at night every shop in the place was closed, so they could get none. Now, as they greatly desired to reach Seville by the following nightfall, hoping under cover of the darkness to find and come aboard of their ship, the *Margaret*, which they knew lay safely in the river, and had been advised by messenger of their intended journey, it was necessary for them to leave Oxuna before the dawn. So, unfortunately enough as it proved, it was impossible for them to put off their Moorish robes and clothe themselves as Christians.

They had hoped, too, that here at Oxuna Inez might overtake them, as she had promised to do if she could, and give them tidings of what had happened since they left Granada. But no Inez came. So, comforting themselves with the thought that however hard she rode it would be difficult for her to reach them, who had some hours' start, they left Oxuna in the darkness before any one was astir.

Having crossed some miles of plain, they passed up through olive groves into hills where cork-trees grew, and here stopped to eat and let the horses feed. Just as they were starting on again, Peter, looking round, saw mounted men—a dozen or more of them of very wild aspect—cantering through the trees evidently with the object of cutting them off.

"Thieves!" he said shortly. "Ride for it."

So they began to gallop, and their horses, although somewhat jaded, being very swift, passed in front of these men before they could regain the road. The band shouted to them to surrender, and, as they did not stop, loosed a few arrows and pursued them, while they galloped down the hillside on to a plain which separated them from more hills also clothed with cork-trees. This plain was about three miles wide and boggy in places. Still they kept well ahead of the brigands, as they took them to be, hoping that they would give up the pursuit or lose sight of them amongst the trees. As they entered these, however, to their dismay they saw, drawn up in front of them and right across the road, another band of rough-looking men, perhaps twelve in all.

"Trap!" said Peter. "We must ride through them—it is our only chance," at the same time spurring his horse to the front and drawing his sword.

Choosing the spot where their line was weakest he dashed through it easily enough but next second heard a cry from Margaret, and pulled his horse round to see that her mare had fallen, and that she and Castell were in the hands of the thieves. Indeed, already rough men had hold of her, and one of them was trying to tear the veil from her face. With a shout of rage Peter charged them, and struck so fierce a blow that his sword cut through the fellow's helmet into his skull, so that he fell down, dying or dead, Margaret's veil still in his hand.

Then they rushed at him, five or six of them, and, although he wounded another man, dragged him from his horse, and, as he lay upon his back, sprang at him to finish him before he could rise. Already their knives and swords were over him, and he was making his farewells to life, when he heard a voice command them to desist and bind his arms. This was quickly done, and he was suffered to rise from the ground to see before him, not Morella, as he half expected, but a man clad in fine armour beneath his rough cloak, evidently an officer of rank. "What kind of a Moor are you," he asked, "who dare to kill the soldiers of the Holy Hermandad in the heart of the King's country?" and he pointed to the dead man.

"I am not a Moor," answered Peter in his rough Spanish. "I am a Christian escaped from Granada, and I cut down that man because he was trying to insult my betrothed, as you would have done, Señor. I did not know that he was a soldier of the Hermandad; I thought him a common thief of the hills."

This speech, or as much as he could understand of it, seemed to please the officer, but before he could answer, Castell said: "Sir Officer, the *señor* is an Englishman, and does not speak your language well—"

"He uses his sword well, anyhow," interrupted the captain, glancing at the dead soldier's cloven helm and head.

"Yes, Sir, he is of your trade and, as the scar upon his face shows, has fought in many wars. Sir, what he tells you is true. We are Christian captives escaped from Granada and flying to Seville with my daughter, to whom I pray you to do no harm, to ask for the protection of their gracious Majesties, and to find a passage back to England."

"You do not look like an Englishman," answered the captain; "you look like a Marano."

"Sir, I cannot help my looks. I am a merchant of London, Castell by name. It is one well known in Seville and throughout this land, where I have large dealings, as, if I can but see him, your king himself will acknowledge. Be not deceived by our dress, which we had to put on in order to escape from Granada, but, I beseech you, let us go on to Seville."

"Señor Castell," answered the officer, "I am the Captain Arrano of Puebla, and, since you would not stop when we called to you, and have killed one of my best soldiers, to Seville you must certainly go, but with me, not by yourselves. You are my prisoners, but have no fear. No violence shall be done to you or the lady, who must take your trials for your deeds before the King's court, and there tell your story, true or false."

So, having been disarmed of their swords, they were allowed to remount their horses and taken on towards Seville as prisoners.

"At least," said Margaret to Peter, "we have nothing more to fear from highwaymen, and have escaped these soldiers' swords unhurt."

"Yes," answered Peter with a groan, "but I hoped that to-night we should have slept upon the *Margaret* while she slipped down the river towards the open sea, and not in a Spanish jail. Now, as fate will have it, for the second time I have killed a man on your behalf, and all the business will begin again. Truly our luck is bad!"

"I think it might be worse, and I cannot blame you for that deed," answered Margaret, remembering the rough hands of the dead soldier, whom some of his comrades had stopped behind to bury.

During all the remainder of that long day they rode on through the burning heat, across the rich, cultivated plain, towards the great city of Seville, whereof the Giralda, which once had been the minaret of a Moorish mosque, towered hundreds of feet into the air before them. At length, towards evening, they entered the eastern suburbs of the vast city and, passing through them and a great gate beyond, began to thread its tortuous streets.

"Whither go we, Captain Arrano?" asked Castell presently.

"To the prison of the Holy Hermandad to await your trial for the slaying of one of its soldiers," answered the officer.

"I pray that we may get there soon then," said Peter, looking at Margaret, who, overcome with fatigue, swayed upon her saddle like a flower in the wind.

"So do I," muttered Castell, glancing round at the dark faces of the people, who, having discovered that they had killed a Spanish soldier, and taking them to be Moors, were marching alongside of them in great numbers, staring sullenly, or cursing them for infidels. Indeed, once when they passed a square, a priest in the mob cried out, "Kill them!" whereon a number of rough fellows made a rush to pull them off their horses, and were with difficulty beaten back by the soldiers.

Foiled in this attempt they began to pelt them with garbage, so that soon their white robes were stained and filthy. One fellow, too, threw a stone which struck Margaret on the wrist, causing her to cry out and drop her rein. This was too much for the hot-blooded Peter, who, spurring his horse alongside of him, before the soldiers could interfere, hit him such a buffet in the face that the man rolled upon the ground. Now Castell thought that they would certainly be killed, but to his surprise the mob only laughed and shouted such things as "Well hit, Moor!" "That infidel has a strong arm," and so forth.

Nor was the officer angry, for when the man rose, a knife in his hand, he drew his sword and struck him down again with the flat of it, saying to Peter:

"Do not sully your hand with such street swine, Señor."

Then he turned and commanded his men to charge the crowd ahead of them.

So they got through these people and, after many twists and turns down side streets to avoid the main avenues, came to a great and gloomy building and into a courtyard through barred gates that were opened at their approach and shut after them. Here they were ordered to dismount and their horses led away, while the officer, Arrano, entered into conversation with the governor of the prison, a man with a stern but not unkindly face, who surveyed them with much curiosity. Presently he approached and asked them if they could pay for good rooms, as if not he must put them in the common cells.

Castell answered, "Yes," and, by way of earnest of it, produced five pieces of gold, and giving them to the Captain Arrano, begged him to distribute them among his soldiers as a thanks offering for their protection of them through the streets. Also, he said loudly enough for every one to hear, that he would be willing to compensate the relatives of the man whom Peter had killed by accident—an announcement that evidently impressed his comrades very favourably. Indeed one of them said he would bear the message to his widow, and, on behalf of the rest, thanked him for his gift. Then having bade farewell to the officer, who told them that they would meet again before the judges, they were led through the various passages of the prison to two rooms, one small and one of a fair size with heavily barred windows, given water to wash in, and told that food would be brought to them.

In due course it came, carried by jailers—meat, eggs, and wine, and glad enough were they to see it. While they ate, also the governor appeared with a notary, and, having waited till their meal was finished, began to question them.

"Our story is long," said Castell, "but with your leave I will tell it you, only, I pray you, suffer my daughter, the Dona Margaret, to go to rest, for she is quite outworn, and if you will you can question her to-morrow."

The governor assenting, Margaret threw off her veil to embrace her father, thus showing her beauty for the first time, whereat the governor and the notary stared amazed. Then having given Peter her hand to kiss, and curtseyed to the governor and the notary, she went to her bed in the next room, which opened out of that in which they were.

When she had gone, Castell told his story of how his daughter had been kidnapped by the Marquis of Morella, a name that caused the governor to open his eyes very wide, and brought from London to Granada, whither they, her father and her betrothed, had followed her and escaped. But of Betty and all the business of the changed bride he said nothing. Also, knowing that these must come out in any case, he told them his name and business, and those of his partners and correspondents in Seville, the firm of Bernaldez, which was one that the governor knew well enough, and prayed that the head of that firm, the Señor Juan Bernaldez, might be communicated with and allowed to visit them on the next morning. Lastly, he explained that they were no thieves or adventurers, but English subjects in misfortune, and again hinted that they were both able and willing to pay for any kindness or consideration that was shown to them, of all of which sayings the governor took note.

Also this officer said that he would communicate with his superiors, and, if no objection were made, send a messenger to ask the Señor Bernaldez to attend at the prison on the following day. Then at length he and the notary departed, and, the jailers having cleared away the food and locked the door, Castell and Peter lay down on the beds that they had made ready for them, thankful enough to find themselves at Seville, even though in a prison, where indeed they slept very well that night.

On the following morning they woke much refreshed, and, after they had breakfasted, the governor appeared, and with him none other than the Señor Juan Bernaldez, Castell's secret correspondent and Spanish partner, whom he had last seen some years before in England, a stout man with a quiet, clever face, not over given to words.

Greeting them with a deference that was not lost upon the governor, he asked whether he had leave to speak with them alone. The governor assented and went, saying he would return within an hour. As soon as the door was closed behind him, Bernaldez said:

"This is a strange place to meet you in, John Castell, yet I am not altogether surprised, since some of your messages reached me through our friends the Jews; also your ship, the *Margaret*, lies refitted in the river, and to avoid suspicion I have been lading her slowly with a cargo for England, though how you will come aboard that ship is more than I can say. But we have no time to waste. Tell me all your story, keeping nothing back."

So they told him everything as quickly as they could, while he listened silently. When they had done, he said, addressing Peter:

"It is a thousand pities, young sir, that you could not keep your hands off that soldier, for now the trouble that was nearly done with has begun anew, and in a worse shape. The Marquis of Morella is a very powerful man in this kingdom, as you may know from the fact that he was sent to London by their Majesties to negotiate a treaty with your English King Henry as to the Jews and their treatment, should any of them escape thither after they have been expelled from Spain. For nothing less is in the wind, and I would have you know that their Majesties hate the Jews, and especially the Maranos, whom already they burn by dozens here in Seville," and he glanced meaningly at Castell.

"I am very sorry," said Peter, "but the fellow handled her roughly, and I was maddened at the sight and could not help myself. This is the second time that I have come into trouble from the same cause. Also, I thought that he was but a bandit."

"Love is a bad diplomatist," replied Bernaldez, with a little smile, "and who can count last year's clouds? What is done, is done. Now I will try to arrange that the three of you shall be brought straight before their Majesties when they sit to hear cases on the day after to-morrow. With the Queen you will have a better chance than at the hands of any *alcalde*. She has a heart, if only one can get at it—that is, except where Jews and Maranos are concerned," and again he glanced at Castell. "Meanwhile, there is money in plenty, and in Spain we ride to heaven on gold angels," he added, alluding to that coin and the national corruption.

Before they could say more the governor returned, saying that the Señor Bernaldez' time was up, and asking if they had finished their talk.

"Not altogether," said Margaret. "Noble Governor, is it permitted that the Señor Bernaldez should send me some Christian clothes to wear, for I would not appear before your judges in this soiled heathen garb, nor, I think, would my father or the Señor Brome?"

The governor laughed, and said he thought that might be arranged, and even allowed them another five minutes, while they talked of what these clothes should be. Then he departed with Bernaldez, leaving them alone.

It was not until the latter had gone, however, that they remembered that they had forgotten to ask him whether he had heard anything of the woman Inez, who had been furnished with his address, but, as he had said nothing of her, they felt sure that she could not have arrived in Seville, and once more were much afraid as to what might have happened after they had left Granada.

That night, to their grief and alarm, a new trouble fell on them. Just as they finished their supper the governor appeared and said that, by order of the Court before which they must be tried, the Señor Brome, who was accused of murder, must be separated from them. So, in spite of all they could say or do, Peter was led away to a separate cell, leaving Margaret weeping.

CHAPTER 19

Betty Pays Her Debts

Betty Dene was not a woman afflicted with fears or apprehensions. Born of good parents, but in poverty, for six-and-twenty years she had fought her own way in a rough world and made the best of circumstances. Healthy, full-blooded, tough, affectionate, romantic, but honest in her way, she was well fitted to meet the ups and downs of life, to keep her head above the waters of a turbulent age, and to pay back as much as she received from man or woman.

Yet those long hours which she passed alone in the high turret chamber, waiting till they summoned her to play the part of a false bride, were the worst that she had ever spent. She knew that her position was, in a sense, shameful, and like to end in tragedy, and, now that she faced it in cold blood, began to wonder why she had chosen so to do. She had fallen in love with the Spaniard almost at first sight, though it is true that something like this had happened to her before with other men. Then he had played his part with her, till, quite deceived, she gave all her heart to him in good earnest, believing in her infatuation that, notwithstanding the difference of their place and rank, he desired to make her his wife for her own sake.

Afterwards came that bitter day of disillusion when she learned, as Inez had said to Castell, that she was but a stalking heifer used for the taking of the white swan, her cousin and mistress—that day when she had been beguiled by the letter which was still hid in her garments, and for her pains heard herself called a fool to her face. In her heart she had sworn to be avenged upon Morella then, and now the hour had come in which to fulfil her oath and play him back trick for cruel trick.

Did she still love the man? She could not say. He was pleasing to her as he had always been, and when that is so women forgive much. This was certain, however—love was not her guide to-night. Was it vengeance then that led her on? Perhaps; at least she longed to be able to say to him, "See what craft lies hid even in the bosom of an outwitted fool."

Yet she would not have done it for vengeance' sake alone, or rather she would have paid herself in some other fashion. No, her real reason was that she must discharge the debt due to Margaret and Peter, and to Castell who had sheltered her for years. She it was who had brought them into all this woe, and it seemed but just that she should bring them out again, even at the cost of her own life and womanly dignity. Or, perchance, all three of these powers drove her on,—love for the man if it still lingered, the desire to be avenged upon him, and the desire to snatch his prey from out his maw. At least she had set the game, and she would play it out to its end, however awful that might be.

The sun sank, the darkness closed about her, and she wondered whether ever again she would see the dawn. Her brave heart quailed a little, and she gripped the dagger hilt beneath her splendid, borrowed robe, thinking to herself that perhaps it might be wisest to drive it into her own breast, and not wait until a balked madman did that office for her. Yet not so, for it is always time to die when one must.

A knock came at the door, and her courage, which had sunk so low, burned up again within her. Oh! she would teach this Spaniard that the Englishwoman, whom he had made believe was his desired mistress, could be his master. At any rate, he should hear the truth before the end.

She unlocked the door, and Inez entered bearing a lamp, by the light of which she scanned her with her quiet eyes.

"The bridegroom is ready," she said slowly that Betty might understand, "and sends me to lead you to him. Are you afraid?"

"Not I," answered Betty. "But tell me, how will the thing be done?"

"The marquis meets us in the ante-room to that hall which is used as a chapel, and there on behalf of the household I, as the first of the women, give you both the cups of wine. Be sure that you drink of that which I hold in my left hand, passing the cup up beneath your veil so as not to show your face, and speak no word, lest he should recognise your voice. Then we shall go into the chapel, where the priest Henriques waits, also all the household. But that hall is great, and the lamps are feeble, so none will know you there. By this time also the drugged wine will have begun to work upon Morella's brain, wherefore, provided that you use a low voice, you may safely say, 'I, Betty, wed thee, Carlos,' not 'I, Margaret, wed thee.' Then, when it is over, he will lead you away to the chambers prepared for you, where, if there is any virtue in my wine, he will sleep sound to-night, that is, as soon as the priest has given me the marriage-lines, whereof I will hand you one copy and keep the others. Afterwards—" and she shrugged her shoulders.

"What becomes of you?" asked Betty, when she had fully mastered these instructions.

"Oh! I and the priest start to-night for a ride together to Seville, where his money awaits him; ill company for a woman who means henceforth to be honest and rich, but better than none. Perhaps we shall meet again there, or perhaps we shall not; at least, you know where to seek me and the others, at the house of the Señor Bernaldez. Now it is time. Are you ready to be made a marchioness of Spain?"

"Of course," answered Betty coolly, and they started.

Through the empty halls and corridors they went, and oh! surely no Eastern plot that had been conceived in them was quite so bold and desperate as theirs. They reached the ante-chamber to the chapel, and took their stand outside of the circle of light that fell from its hanging lamps. Presently a door opened, and through it came Morella, attended by two of his secretaries. He was splendidly arrayed in his usual garb of black velvet, and about his neck hung chains of gold and jewels, and to his breast were fastened the glittering stars and orders pertaining to his rank. Never, or so thought Betty, had Morella seemed more magnificent and handsome. He was happy also, who was about to drink of that cup of joy which he so earnestly desired. Yes, his face showed that he was happy, and Betty, noting it, felt remorse stirring in her breast. Low he bowed before her, while she curtseyed to him, bending her tall and graceful form till her knee almost touched the ground. Then he came to her and whispered in her ear:

"Most sweet, most beloved," he said, "I thank heaven that has led me to this joyous hour by many a rough and dangerous path. Most dear, again I beseech you to forgive all the sorrow and the ill that I have brought upon you, remembering that it was done for your adored sake, that I love you as woman has been seldom loved, you and you only, and that to you, and you only, will I cling until my death's day. Oh! do not tremble and shrink, for I swear that no woman in Spain shall have a better or a more loyal lord. You I will cherish alone, for you I will strive by night and day to lift you to great honour and satisfy your every wish. Many and pleasant may the years be that we shall spend side by side, and peaceful our ends when at last we lay us down side by side to sleep awhile and wake again in heaven, whereof the shadow lies on me to-night. Remembering the past, I do not ask much of you—as yet; still, if you are minded to give me a bridal gift that I shall prize above crowns or empires, say that you forgive me all that I have done amiss, and in token, lift that veil of yours and kiss me on the lips."

Betty heard this speech, whereof she only fully understood the end, and trembled. This was a trial that she had not foreseen. Yet it must be faced, for speak she dared not. Therefore, gathering up her courage, and remembering that the light was at her back, after a little pause, as though of modesty and reluctance, she raised the pearl-embroidered veil, and, bending forward beneath its shadow, suffered Morella to kiss her on the lips.

It was over, the veil had fallen again, and the man suspected nothing.

"I am a good artist," thought Inez to herself, "and that woman acts better than the wooden Peter. Scarcely could I have done it so well myself."

Then, the jealousy and hate that she could not control glittering in her soft eyes, for she too had loved this man, and well, Inez lifted the golden cups that had been prepared, and, gliding forward, beautiful in her broidered, Eastern robe, fell upon her knee and held them to the bridegroom and the bride. Morella took that from her right hand, and Betty that from her left, nor, intoxicated as he was already with that first kiss of love, did he pause to note the evil purpose which was written on the face of his discarded slave. Betty, passing the cup beneath her veil, touched it with her lips and returned it to Inez; but Morella, exclaiming, "I drink to you, sweet bride, most fair and adored of women," drained his to the dregs, and cast it back to Inez as a gift in such fashion that the red wine which clung to its rim stained her white robes like a splash of blood.

Humbly she bowed, humbly she gathered the precious vessel from the floor; but when she rose again there was triumph in her eyes—not hate.

Now Morella took his bride's hand and, followed by his gentlemen and Inez, walked to the curtains that were drawn as they came into the great hall beyond, where had mustered all his household, perhaps a hundred of them. Between their bowing ranks they passed, a stately pair, and, whilst sweet voices sang behind some hidden screen, walked onward to the altar, where stood the waiting priest. They kneeled down upon the gold-embroidered cushions while the office of the Church was read over them. The ring was set upon Betty's hand— scarce, it would seem, could he find her finger—the man took the woman to wife, the woman took the man for husband. His voice was thick, and hers was very low; of all that listening crowd none could hear the names they spoke.

It was over. The priest bowed and blessed them. They signed some papers, there by the light of the altar candles. Father Henriques filled in certain names and signed them also, then, casting sand upon them, placed them in the outstretched hand of Inez, who, although Morella never seemed to notice, gave one to the bride, and thrust the other two into the bosom of her robe. Then both she and the priest kissed the hands of the marquis and his wife, and asked his leave to be gone. He bowed his head vaguely, and—if any had been there to listen—within ten short minutes they might have heard two horses galloping hard towards the Seville gate.

Now, escorted by pages and torch-bearers, the new-wed pair re-passed those dim and stately halls, the bride, veiled, mysterious, fateful; the bridegroom, empty-eyed, like one who wanders in his sleep. Thus they reached their chamber, and its carved doors shut behind them.

****

It was early morning, and the serving-women who waited without that room were summoned to it by the sound of a silver gong. Two of them entered and were met by Betty, no longer veiled, but wrapped in a loose robe, who said to them:

"My lord the marquis still sleeps. Come, help me dress and make ready his bath and food."

The women stared at her, for now that she had washed the paint from her face they knew well that this was the Señora Betty and not the Dona Margaret, whom, they had understood, the marquis was to marry. But she chid them sharply in her bad Spanish, bidding them be swift, as she would be robed before her husband should awake. So they obeyed her, and when she was ready she went with them into the great hall where many of the household were gathered, waiting to do homage to the new-wed pair, and greeted them all, blushing and smiling, saying that doubtless the marquis would be among them soon, and commanding them meanwhile to go about their several tasks.

So well did Betty play her part indeed, that, although they also were bewildered, none questioned her place or authority, who remembered that after all they had not been told by their lord himself which of these two English ladies he meant to marry. Also, she distributed among the meaner of them a present of money on her husband's behalf and her own, and then ate food and drank some wine before them all, pledging them, and receiving their salutations and good wishes.

When all this was done, still smiling, Betty returned to the marriage-chamber, closing its door behind her, sat her down on a chair near the bed, and waited for the worst struggle of all—that struggle on which hung her life. See! Morella stirred. He sat up, gazing about him and rubbing his brow. Presently his eyes lit upon Betty, seated stern and upright in her high chair. She rose and, coming to him, kissed him and called him "Husband," and, still half-asleep, he kissed her back. Then she sat down again in her chair and watched his face.

It changed, and changed again. Wonder, fear, amaze, bewilderment, flitted over it, till at last he said in English:

"Betty, where is my wife?"

"Here," answered Betty.

He stared at her. "Nay, I mean the Dona Margaret, your cousin and my lady, whom I wed last night. And how come you here? I thought that you had left Granada."

Betty looked astonished.

"I do not understand you," she answered. "It was my cousin Margaret who left Granada. I stayed here to be married to you, as you arranged with me through Inez."

His jaw dropped.

"Arranged with you through Inez! Mother of Heaven! what do you mean?"

"Mean?" she answered—"I mean what I say. Surely"—and she rose in indignation—"you have never dared to try to play some new trick upon me?"

"Trick!" muttered Morella. "What says the woman? Is all this a dream, or am I mad?"

"A dream, I think. Yes, it must be a dream, since certainly it was to no madman that I was wed last night. Look," and she held before him that writing of marriage signed by the priest, by him, and by herself, which stated that Carlos, Marquis of Morella, was on such a date, at Granada, duly married to the Señora Elizabeth Dene of London in England.

He read it twice, then sank back gasping; while Betty hid away the parchment in her bosom.

Then presently he seemed to go mad indeed. He raved, he cursed, he ground his teeth, he looked round for a sword to kill her or himself, but could find none. And all the while Betty sat still and gazed at him like some living fate.

At length he was weary, and her turn came.

"Listen," she said. "Yonder in London you promised to marry me; I have it hidden away, and in your own writing. By agreement I fled with you to Spain. By the mouth of your messenger and former love this marriage was arranged between us, I receiving your messages to me, and sending back mine to you, since you explained that for reasons of your own you did not wish to speak of these matters before my cousin Margaret, and could not wed me until she and her father and her lover were gone from Granada. So I bade them farewell, and stayed here alone for love of you, as I fled from London for love of you, and last night we were united, as all your household know, for but now I have eaten with them and received their good wishes. And now you dare—you dare to tell me, that I, your wife—I, who have sacrificed everything for you, I, the Marchioness of Morella, am *not* your wife. Well, go, say it outside this chamber, and hear your very slaves cry 'Shame' upon you. Go, say it to your king and your bishops, aye, and to his Holiness the Pope himself, and listen to their answer. Why, great as you are, and rich as you are, they will hale you to a mad-house or a prison."

Morella listened, rocking himself to and fro upon the bed, then with an oath sprang towards her, to be met by a dagger-point glinting in his eyes.

"Hear me again," she said as he shrank back from that cold steel. "I am no slave and no weakling; you shall not murder me or thrust me away. I am your wife and your equal, aye, and stronger than you in body and in mind, and I will have my rights in the face of God and man."

"Certainly," he said with a kind of unwilling admiration—"certainly you are no weakling. Certainly, also, you have paid back all you owe me with a Jew's interest. Or, mayhap, you are not so clever as I think, but just a strong-minded fool, and it is that accursed Inez who has settled her debts. Oh! to think of it," and he shook his fist in the air, "to think that I believed myself married to the Dona Margaret, and find you in her place—*you!*"

"Be silent," she said, "you man without shame, who first fly at the throat of your new-wedded wife and then insult her by saying that you wish you were wedded to another woman. Be silent, or I will unlock the door and call your own people and repeat your monstrous talk to them." And she drew herself to her full height and stood over him on the bed.

Morella, his first rage spent, looked at her reflectively, and not without a certain measure of homage.

"I think," he remarked, "that if he did not happen to be in love with another woman and to believe that he had married her, you, my good Betty, would make a useful wife to any man who wished to get on in the world. I understood you to say that the door is locked, and if I might hazard a guess, you have the key, as also you happen to have a dagger. Well, I find the air in this place close, and I want to go *out.*"

"Where to?" asked Betty.

"Let us say, to join Inez."

"What," she asked, "would you already be running after that woman again? Do you already forget that you are married?"

"It seems that I am not to be allowed to forget it. Now, let us bargain. I wish to leave Granada for a while, and without scandal. What are your terms? Remember that there are two to which I will not consent. I will not stop here with you, and you shall not accompany me. Remember also, that, although you hold the dagger at present, it is not wise of you to try to push this jest too far."

"As you did when you decoyed me on board the *San Antonio*," said Betty. "Well, our honeymoon has not begun too sweetly, and I do not mind if you go away for a while—to look for Inez. Swear now that you mean me no harm, and that you will not plot my death or disgrace, or in any way interfere with my liberty or position here in Granada. Swear it on the Rood." And she took down a silver crucifix that hung upon the wall over the bed and handed it to him. For she knew Morella's superstitions, and that if once he swore upon this symbol he dare not break his oath.

"And if I will not swear?" he asked sullenly.

"Then," she answered, "you stop here until you do, you who are anxious to be gone. I have eaten food this morning, you have not; I have a dagger, you have none; and, being as we are, I am sure that no one will venture to disturb us until Inez and your friend the priest have gone further than you can follow."

"Very well, I will swear," he said, and he kissed the crucifix and threw it down, "You can stop here and rule my house in Granada, and I will do you no mischief, nor trouble you in any way. But if you come out of Granada, then we cross swords."

"You mean that you intend to leave this city? Then, here is paper and ink. Be so good as to sign an order to the stewards of your estates, within the territories of the Moorish king, to pay all their revenue to me during your absence, and to your servants to obey me in everything."

"It is easy to see that you were brought up in the house of a Jew merchant," said Morella, biting the pen and considering this woman who, whether she were hawk or pigeon, knew so well how to feather her nest. "Well, if I grant you this position and these revenues, will you leave me alone and cease to press other claims upon me?"

Now Betty, bethinking her of those papers that Inez had carried away with her, and that Castell and Margaret would know well how to use them if there were need, bethinking her also that if she pushed him too far at the beginning she might die suddenly as folk sometimes did in Granada, answered:

"It is much to ask of a deluded woman, but I still have some pride, and will not thrust myself in where it seems I am not wanted. Therefore, so be it. Till you seek me or send for me, I will not seek you so long as you keep your bargain. Now write the paper, sign it, and call in your secretaries to witness the signature."

"In whose favour must I word it?" he asked.

"In that of the Marquessa of Morella," she answered, and he, seeing a loophole in the words, obeyed her, since if she were not his wife this writing would have no value.

Somehow he must be rid of this woman. Of course he might cause her to be killed; but even in Granada people could not kill one to whom they had seemed to be just married without questions being asked. Moreover, Betty had friends, and he had enemies who would certainly ask them if she vanished away. No, he would sign the paper and fight the case afterwards, for he had no time to lose. Margaret had slipped away from him, and if once she escaped from Spain he knew that he would never see her more. For aught he knew, she might already have escaped or be married to Peter Brome. The very thought of it filled him with madness. There had been a conspiracy against him; he was outwitted, robbed, befooled. Well, hope still remained—and vengeance. He could still fight Peter, and perhaps kill him. He could hand over Castell, the Jew, to the Inquisition. He could find a way to deal with the priest Henriques and the woman Inez, and, perhaps, if fortune favoured him he could get Margaret back into his power.

Oh! yes, he would sign anything if only thereby he was set at liberty and freed for a while from this servant who called herself his wife, this strong-minded, strong-bodied, clever Englishwoman, of whom he had thought to make a tool, and who had made a tool of him.

So Betty dictated and he wrote: yes, it had come to this—she dictated and he wrote, and signed too. The order was comprehensive. It gave power to the most honourable Marquessa of Morella to act for him, her husband, in all things during his absence from Granada. It commanded that all rents and profits due to him should be paid to her, and that all his servants and dependants should obey her as though she were himself, and that her receipt should be as good as his receipt.

When the paper was written, and Betty had spelt it over carefully to see that there was no omission or mistake, she unlocked the door, struck upon the gong, and summoned the secretaries to witness their lord's signature to a settlement. Presently they came, bowing, and offering many felicitations, which to himself Morella vowed he would remember against them.

"I have to go a journey," he said. "Witness my signature to this document, which provides for the carrying on of my household and the disposal of my property during my absence."

They stared and bowed.

"Read it aloud first," said Betty, "so that my lord and husband may be sure that there is no mistake."

One of them obeyed, but before ever he had finished the furious Morella shouted to them from the bed:

"Have done and witness, then go, order me horses and an escort, for I ride at once."

So they witnessed in a great hurry, and left the room. Betty left with them, holding the paper in her hand, and when she reached the large hall where the household were gathered waiting to greet their lord, she commanded one of the secretaries to read it out to all of them, also to translate it into the Moorish tongue that every one might understand. Then she hid it away with the marriage lines, and, seating herself in the midst of the household, ordered them to prepare to receive the most noble marquis.

They had not long to wait, for presently he came out of the room like a bull into the arena, whereon Betty rose and curtseyed to him, and at her word all his servants bowed themselves down in the Eastern fashion. For a moment he paused, again like the bull when he sees the picadors and is about to charge. Then he thought better of it, and, with a muttered curse, strode past them.

Ten minutes later, for the third time within twenty-four hours, horses galloped from the palace and through the Seville gate.

"Friends," said Betty in her awkward Spanish, when she knew that he had gone, "a sad thing has happened to my husband, the marquis. The woman Inez, whom it seems he trusted very much, has departed, stealing a treasure that he valued above everything on earth, and so I, his new-made wife, am left desolate while he tries to find her."

Isabella of Spain

On the afternoon following his first visit, Castell's agent, Bernaldez, arrived again at the prison of the Hermandad at Seville accompanied by a tailor, a woman, and a chest full of clothes. The governor ordered these two persons to wait while the garments were searched under his own eye, but Bernaldez he permitted to be led at once to the prisoners. As soon as he was with them he said:

"Your marquis has been married fast enough."

"How do you know that?" asked Castell.

"From the woman Inez, who arrived with the priest last night, and gave me the certificates of his union with Betty Dene signed by himself. I have not brought them with me lest I should be searched, when they might have been taken away; but Inez has come disguised as a sempstress, so show no surprise when you see her, if she is admitted. Perhaps she will be able to tell the Dona Margaret something of what passed if she is allowed to fit her robes alone. After that she must lie hidden for fear of the vengeance of Morella; but I shall know where to put my hand upon her if she is wanted. You will all of you be brought before the queen to-morrow, and then I, who shall be there, will produce the writings." Scarcely were the words out of his mouth when the governor appeared, and with him the tailor and Inez, who curtseyed and glanced at Margaret out of the corners of her soft eyes, looking at them all as though with curiosity, like one who had never seen or heard of them before.

When the dresses had been produced, Margaret asked whether she might be allowed to try them on with the woman in her own chamber, as she had not been measured for them.

The governor answered that as both the sempstress and the robes had been searched, there was no objection, so the two of them retired—Inez, with her arms full of garments.

"Tell me all about it," whispered Margaret as soon as the door was closed. "I die to hear your story."

So, while she fitted the clothes, since in that place they could never be sure but that they were watched through some secret loophole, Inez, with her mouth full of aloe thorns, which those of the trade used as pins, told her everything down to the time of her escape from Granada. When she came to that part of the tale where the false bride had lifted her veil and kissed the bridegroom, Margaret gasped in her amaze.

"Oh! how could she do it?" she said, "I should have fainted first."

"She has a good courage, that Betty—turn to the light, please, Señora—I could not have acted better myself—I think it is a little high on the left shoulder. He never guessed a thing, the besotted fool, and that was before I gave him the wine, for he wasn't likely to guess much afterwards. Did the *señora* say it was tight under the arm? Well, perhaps a little, but this stuff stretches. What I want to know is, what happened afterwards? Your cousin is the bull that I put my money on: I believe she will clear the ring. A woman with a nerve of steel; had I as much I should have been the Marchioness of Morella long ago, or there would be another marquis by now. There, the sit of the skirt is perfect; the *señora's* beautiful figure looks more beautiful in it than ever. Well, whoever lives will learn all about it, and it is no use worrying. Meanwhile, Bernaldez has paid me the money—and a handsome sum too—so you needn't thank me. I only worked for hire—and hate. Now I am going to lie low, as I don't want to get my throat cut, but he can find me if I am really needed.

"The priest? Oh, he is safe enough. We made him sign a receipt for his cash. Also, I believe that he has got his post as a secretary to the Inquisition, and began his duties at once as they were short-handed, torturing Jews and heretics, you know, and stealing their goods, both of which occupations will exactly suit him. I rode with him all the way to Seville, and he tried to make love to me, the slimy knave, but I paid him out," and Inez smiled at some pleasant recollection. "Still, I did not quarrel with him outright, as he may come in useful. Who knows? There's the governor calling me. One moment, Excellency, only one moment!

"Yes, Señora, with those few alterations the dress will be perfect. You shall have it back tonight without fail, and I can cut the others that you have been pleased to order from the same pattern. Oh! I thank you, Señora, you are too good to a poor girl, and," in a whisper, "the Mother of God have you in her guard, and send that Peter has improved in his love making!" and, half hidden in garments, Inez

405

bowed herself out of the room through the door which the governor had already opened.

About nine o'clock on the following morning one of the jailers
came to summon Margaret and her father to be led before the court.
Margaret asked anxiously if the Señor Brome was coming too, but the
man replied that he knew nothing of the Señor Brome, as he was in
one of the cells for dangerous criminals, which he did not serve.

So forth they went, dressed in their new clothes, which were as
fine as money could buy, and in the latest Seville fashion, and were
conducted to the courtyard. Here, to her joy, Margaret saw Peter waiting for them under guard, and dressed also in the Christian garments
which they had begged might be supplied to him at their cost. She
sprang to his side, none hindering her, and, forgetting her bashfulness,
suffered him to embrace her before them all, asking him how he had
fared since they were parted.

"None too well," answered Peter gloomily, "who did not know if
we should ever meet again; also, my prison is underground, where but
little light comes through a grating, and there are rats in it which will
not let a man sleep, so I must lie awake the most of the night thinking
of you. But where go we now?"

"To be put upon our trial before the queen, I think. Hold my hand
and walk close beside me, but do not stare at me so hard. Is aught
wrong with my dress?"

"Nothing," answered Peter. "I stare because you look so beautiful
in it. Could you not have worn a veil? Doubtless there are more mar-
quises about this court."

"Only the Moors wear veils, Peter, and now we are Christians
again. Listen—I think that none of them understand English. I have
seen Inez, who asked after you very tenderly—nay, do not blush, it is
unseemly in a man. Have you seen her also? No—well, she escaped
from Granada as she planned, and Betty is married to the marquis."

"It will never hold good," answered Peter shaking his head, "being
but a trick, and I fear that she will pay for it, poor woman! Still, she
gave us a start, though, so far as prisons go, I was better off in Granada
than in that rat-trap."

"Yes," answered Margaret innocently, "you had a garden to walk in
there, had you not? No, don't be angry with me. Do you know what
Betty did?" And she told him of how she had lifted her veil and kissed
Morella without being discovered.

"That isn't so wonderful," said Peter, "since if they are painted up
young women look very much alike in a half-lit room—"

"Or garden?" suggested Margaret.

"What is wonderful," went on Peter, scorning to take note of this interruption, "is that she could consent to kiss the man at all. The double-dealing scoundrel! Has Inez told you how he treated her? The very thought of it makes me ill."

"Well, Peter, he didn't ask you to kiss him, did he? And as for the wrongs of Inez, though doubtless you know more about them than I do, I think she has given him an orange for his pomegranate. But look, there is the Alcazar in front of us. Is it not a splendid castle? You know, it was built by the Moors."

"I don't care who it was built by," said Peter, "and it looks to me like any other castle, only larger. All I know about it is that I am to be tried there for knocking that ruffian on the head—and that perhaps this is the last we shall see of each other, as probably they will send me to the galleys, if they don't do worse."

"Oh! say no such thing. I never thought of it; it is not possible!" answered Margaret, her dark eyes filling with tears.

"Wait till your marquis appears, pleading the case against us, and you will see what is or is not possible," replied Peter with conviction. "Still, we have come through some storms, so let us hope for the best."

At that moment they reached the gate of the Alcazar, which they had approached from their prison through gardens of orange-trees, and soldiers came up and separated them. Next they were led across a court, where many people hurried to and fro, into a great marble-columned room glittering with gold, which was called the Hall of Justice. At the far end of this place, seated on a throne set upon a richly carpeted dais and surrounded by lords and counsellors, sat a magnificently attired lady of middle age. She was blue-eyed and red-haired, with a fair-skinned, open countenance, but very reserved and quiet in her demeanour.

"The Queen," muttered the guard, saluting, as did Castell and Peter, while Margaret curtseyed.

A case had just been tried, and the queen Isabella, after consultation with her assessors, was delivering judgment in few words and a gentle voice. As she spoke, her mild blue eyes fell upon Margaret, and, held it would seem by her beauty, rested on her till they wandered off to the tall form of Peter and the dark, Jewish-looking Castell by him, at the sight of whom she frowned a little.

That case was finished, and other suitors stood up in their turn, but the queen, waving her hand and still looking at Margaret, bent down and asked a question of one of the officers of the court, then gave an order, whereon the officer rising, summoned "John Castell, Margaret Castell, and Peter Brome, all of England," to appear at the bar and answer to the charge of murder of one Luiz of Basa, a soldier of the Holy Hermandad.

At once they were brought forward, and stood in a line in front of the dais, while the officer began to read the charge against them.

"Stay, friend," interposed the queen, "these accused are the subjects of our good brother, Henry of England, and may not understand our language, though one of them, I think"—and she glanced at Castell—"was not born in England, or at any rate of English blood. Ask them if they need an interpreter."

The question was put, and all of them answered that they could speak Spanish, though Peter added that he did so but indifferently.

"You are the knight, I think, who is charged with the commission of this crime," said Isabella, looking at him.

"Your Majesty, I am not a knight, only a plain esquire, Peter Brome of Dedham in England. My father was a knight, Sir Peter Brome, but he fell at my side, fighting for Richard, on Bosworth Field, where I had this wound," and he pointed to the scar upon his face, "but was not knighted for my pains."

Isabella smiled a little, then asked:

"And how came you to Spain, Señor Peter Brome?"

"Your Majesty," answered Peter, Margaret helping from time to time when he did not know the Spanish words, "this lady at my side, the daughter of the merchant John Castell who stands by her, is my affianced—"

"Then you have won the love of a very beautiful maiden, Señor," interrupted the queen; "but proceed."

"She and her cousin, the Señora Dene, were kidnapped in London by one who I understand is the nephew of the King Ferdinand, and an envoy to the English court, who passed there as the Señor d'Aguilar, but who in Spain is the Marquis of Morella."

"Kidnapped! and by Morella!" exclaimed the queen.

"Yes, your Majesty, cozened on board his ship and kidnapped. The Señor Castell and I followed them, and, boarding their vessel, tried to rescue them, but were shipwrecked at Motril. The marquis carried them away to Granada, whither we followed also, I being sorely hurt in the shipwreck. There, in the palace of the marquis, we have lain prisoners many weeks, but at length escaped, purposing to come to Seville and seek the protection of your Majesties. On the road, while we were dressed as Moors, in which garb we compassed our escape, we were attacked by men that we thought were bandits, for we had been warned against such evil people. One of them rudely molested the Dona Margaret, and I cut him down, and by misfortune killed him, for which manslaughter I am here before you to-day. Your Majesty, I did not know that he was a soldier of the Holy Hermandad, and I pray you pardon my offence, which was done in ignorance, fear, and anger, for we are willing to pay compensation for this unhappy death."

Now some in the court exclaimed:

"Well spoken, Englishman!"

Then the queen said:

"If all this tale be true, I am not sure that we should blame you over much, Señor Brome; but how know we that it is true? For instance, you said that the noble marquis stole two ladies, a deed of which I can scarcely think him capable. Where then is the other?"

"I believe," answered Peter, "that she is now the wife of the Marquis of Morella."

"The wife! Who bears witness that she is the wife? He has not advised us that he was about to marry, as is usual."

Then Bernaldez stood forward, stating his name and occupation, and that he was a correspondent of the English merchant, John Castell, and producing the certificate of marriage signed by Morella, Betty, and the priest Henriques, handed it up to the queen saying that he had received them in duplicate by a messenger from Granada, and had delivered the other to the Archbishop of Seville.

The queen, having looked at the paper, passed it to her assessors, who examined it very carefully, one of them saying that the form was not usual, and that it might be forged.

The queen thought a little while, then said:

"That is so, and in one way only can we know the truth. Let our warrant issue summoning before us our cousin, the noble Marquis of Morella, the Señora Dene, who is said to be his wife, and the priest Henriques of Motril, who is said to have married them. When they have arrived, all of them, the king my husband and I will examine into the matter, and, until then, we will not suffer our minds to be prejudiced by hearing any more of this cause."

Now the governor of the prison stood forward, and asked what was to be done with the captives until the witnesses could be brought from Granada. The queen answered that they must remain in his charge, and be well treated, whereon Peter prayed that he might be given a better cell with fewer rats and more light. The queen smiled, and said that it should be so, but added that it would be proper that he should still be kept apart from the lady to whom he was affianced, who could dwell with her father. Then, noting the sadness on their faces, she added:

"Yet I think they may meet daily in the garden of the prison."

Margaret curtseyed and thanked her, whereon she said very graciously:

"Come here, Señora, and sit by me a little," and she pointed to a footstool at her side. "When I have done this business I desire a few words with you."

So Margaret was brought up upon the dais, and sat down at her Majesty's left hand upon the broidered footstool, and very fair indeed she looked placed thus above the crowd, she whose beauty and whose bearing were so royal; but Castell and Peter were led away back to the prison, though, seeing so many gay lords about, the latter went unwillingly enough. A while later, when the cases were finished, the queen dismissed the court save for certain officers, who stood at a distance, and, turning to Margaret, said:

"Now, fair maiden, tell me your story, as one woman to another, and do not fear that anything you say will be made use of at the trial of your lover, since against you, at any rate at present, no charge is laid. Say, first, are you really the affianced of that tall gentleman, and has he really your heart?"

"All of it, your Majesty," answered Margaret, "and we have suffered much for each other's sake." Then in as few words as she could she told their tale, while the queen listened earnestly.

"A strange story indeed, and if it be all true, a shameful," she said when Margaret had finished. "But how comes it that if Morella desired to force you into marriage, he is now wed to your companion and cousin? What are you keeping back from me?" and she glanced at her shrewdly.

"Your Majesty," answered Margaret, "I was ashamed to speak the rest, yet I will trust you and do so, praying your royal forgiveness if you hold that we, who were in desperate straits, have done what is wrong. My cousin, Betty Dene, has paid back Morella in his own false gold. He won her heart and promised to marry her, and at the risk of her own life she took my place at the altar, thereby securing our escape."

"A brave deed, if a doubtful," said the queen, "though I question whether such a marriage will be upheld. But that is a matter for the Church to judge of, and I must speak of it no more. Certainly it is hard to be angry with any of you. What did you say that Morella promised you when he asked you to marry him in London?"

410

"Your Majesty, he promised that he would lift me high, perhaps even"—and she hesitated—"to that seat in which you sit."

Isabella frowned, then laughed, and said, as she looked her up and down: "You would fit it well, better than I do in truth. But what else did he say?"

"Your Majesty, he said that not every one loves the king, his uncle; that he had many friends who remembered that his father was poisoned by the father of the king, who was Morella's grandfather; also, that his mother was a princess of the Moors, and that he might throw in his lot with theirs, or that there were other ways in which he could gain his end."

"So, so," said the queen. "Well, though he is such a good son of the Church, and my lord is so fond of him, I never loved Morella, and I thank you for your warning. But I must not speak to you of such high matters, though it seems that some have thought otherwise. Fair Margaret, have you aught to ask of me?"

"Yes, your Majesty—that you will deal gently with my true love when he comes before you for trial, remembering that he is hot of head and strong of arm, and that such knights as he—for knightly is his blood—cannot brook to see their ladies mishandled by rough men, and the wrappings that shield them torn from off their bosoms. Also, I pray that I may be protected from Morella, that he may not be allowed to touch or even to speak to me, who, for all his rank and splendour, hate him as though he were some poisoned snake."

"I have said that I must not prejudge your case, you beautiful English Margaret," the queen answered with a smile, "yet I think that neither of those things you ask will cause justice to slip the bandage that is about her eyes. Go, and be at peace. If you have spoken truth to me, as I am sure you have, and Isabella of Spain can prevent it, the Señor Brome's punishment shall not be heavy, nor shall the shadow of the Marquis of Morella, the base-born son of a prince and of some royal infidel"—these words she spoke with much bitterness—"so much as fall upon you, though I warn you that my lord the king loves the man, as is but natural, and will not condemn him lightly. Tell me one thing. This lover of yours is brave, is he not?"

"Very brave," answered Margaret, smiling.

"And he can ride a horse and hold a lance, can he not, at any rate in your quarrel?"

"Aye, your Majesty, and wield a sword too, as well as most knights, though he has been but lately sick. Some learned that on Bosworth Field."

411

"Good. Now farewell," and she gave Margaret her hand to kiss. Then, calling two of her officers, she bade them conduct her back to the prison, and say that she should have liberty to send messages or to write to her, the queen, if she should so desire.

On the night of that same day Morella galloped into Seville. Indeed he should have been there long before, but misled by the story of the Moors who had escorted Peter, Margaret, and her father out of Granada and seen them take the Malaga road, he travelled thither first, only to find no trace of them in that city. Then he returned and tracked them to Seville, where he was soon made acquainted with all that had happened. Amongst other things, he discovered that ten hours before swift messengers had been despatched to Granada, commanding his attendance and that of Betty, with whom he had gone through the form of marriage.

On the following morning he asked an audience with the queen, but it was refused to him, and the king, his uncle, was away. Next he tried to win admission into the prison and see Margaret, only to find that neither his high rank and authority nor any bribe would suffice to unlock its doors. The queen had commanded otherwise, he was informed, and knew therefrom that in this matter he must reckon with Isabella as an enemy. Then he bethought him of revenge, and began a search for Inez and the priest Henriques of Motril, only to find that the former had vanished, none knew whither, and the holy father was safe within the walls of the Inquisition, whence he was careful not to emerge, and where no layman, however highly placed, could enter to lay a hand upon one of its officers. So, full of rage and disappointment, he took counsel of lawyers and friends, and prepared to defend the suit which he saw would be brought against him, hoping that chance might yet deliver Margaret into his hands. One good card he held, which now he determined to play. Castell, as he knew, was a Jew who for years had posed as a Christian, and for such there was no mercy in Seville. Perhaps for her father's sake he might yet be able to work upon Margaret, whom now he desired to win more fiercely than ever before.

At least it was certain that he would try this, or any other means, however base, rather than see her married to his rival, Peter Brome. Also there was the chance that this Peter might be condemned to imprisonment, or even to death, for the killing of a soldier of the Hermandad.

So Morella made him ready for the great struggle as best he could, and, since he could not stop her coming, awaited the arrival of Betty in Seville.

CHAPTER 21

Betty States Her Case

Seven days had passed, during which time Margaret and her father had rested quietly in the prison, where, indeed, they dwelt more as guests than as captives. Thus they were allowed to receive what visitors they would, and among them Juan Bernaldez, Castell's connection and agent, who told them of all that passed without. Through him they sent messengers to meet Betty on her road and apprise her of how things stood, and of the trial in which her cause would be judged.

Soon the messengers returned, stating that the "Marchioness of Morella" was travelling in state, accompanied by a great retinue, that she thanked them for their tidings, and hoped to be able to defend herself at all points.

At this news Castell stared and Margaret laughed, for, although she did not know all the story, she was sure that in some way Betty had the mastery of Morella, and would not be easily defeated, though how she came to be travelling with a great retinue she could not imagine. Still, fearing lest she should be attacked or otherwise injured, she wrote a humble letter to the queen, praying that her cousin might be defended from all danger at the hands of any one whomsoever until she had an opportunity of giving evidence before their Majesties.

Within an hour came the answer that the lady was under the royal protection, and that a guard had been sent to escort her and her party and to keep her safe from interference of any sort; also, that for her greater comfort, quarters had been prepared for her in a fortress outside of Seville, which would be watched night and day, and whence she would be brought to the court.

Peter was still kept apart from them, but each day at noon they were allowed to meet him in the walled garden of the prison, where they talked together to their heart's content. Here, too, he exercised himself daily at all manly games, and especially at sword-play with some of the other prisoners, using sticks for swords. Further, he was allowed the use of his horse that he had ridden from Granada, on which he jousted in the yard of the castle with the governor and certain other gentlemen, proving himself better at that play than any of them. These things he did vigorously and with ardour, for Margaret had told him of the hint which the queen gave her, and he desired to get back his full strength, and to perfect himself in the handling of every arm which was used in Spain.

So the time went by, until one afternoon the governor informed them that Peter's trial was fixed for the morrow, and that they must accompany him to the court to be examined also upon all these matters. A little later came Bernaldez, who said that the king had returned and would sit with the queen, and that already this affair had made much stir in Seville, where there was much curiosity as to the story of Morella's marriage, of which many different tales were told. That Margaret and her father would be discharged he had little doubt, in which case their ship was ready for them; but of Peter's chances he could say nothing, for they depended upon what view the king took of his offence, and, though unacknowledged, Morella was the king's nephew and had his ear.

Afterwards they went down into the garden, and there found Peter, who had just returned from his jousting, flushed with exercise, and looking very manly and handsome. Margaret took his hand and, walking aside, told him the news.

"I am glad," he answered, "for the sooner this business is begun the sooner it will be done. But, Sweet," and here his face grew very earnest, "Morella has much power in this land, and I have broken its law, so none know what the end will be. I may be condemned to death or imprisoned, or perhaps, if I am given the chance, with better luck I may fall fighting, in any of which cases we shall be separated for a while, or altogether. Should this be so, I pray that you will not stay here, either in the hope of rescuing me, or for other reasons; since, while you are in Spain, Morella will not cease from his attempts to get hold of you, whereas in England you will be safe from him."

When Margaret heard these words she sobbed aloud, for the thought that harm might come to Peter seemed to choke her.

"In all things I will do your bidding," she said, "yet how can I leave you, dear, while you are alive, and if, perchance, you should die, which may God prevent, how can I live on without you? Rather shall I seek to follow you very swiftly."

"I do not desire that," said Peter. "I desire that you should endure your days till the end, and come to meet me where I am in due season, and not before. I will add this, that if in after-years you should meet any worthy man, and have a mind to marry him, you should do so, for I know well that you will never forget me, your first love, and that beyond this world lie others where there are no marryings or giving in marriage. Let not my dead hand lie heavy upon you, Margaret."

"Yet," she replied in gentle indignation, "heavy must it always lie, since it is about my heart. Be sure of this, Peter, that if such dreadful ill should fall upon us, as you left me so shall you find me, here or hereafter."

"So be it," he said with a sigh of relief, for he could not bear to think of Margaret as the wife of some other man, even after he was gone, although his honest, simple nature, and fear lest her life might be made empty of all joy, caused him to say what he had said.

Then behind the shelter of a flowering bush they embraced each other as do those who know not whether they will ever kiss again, and, the hour of sunset having come, parted as they must.

On the following morning once more Castell and Margaret were led to the Hall of Justice in the Alcazar; but this time Peter did not go with them. The great court was already full of counsellors, officers, gentlemen, and ladies who had come from curiosity, and other folk connected with or interested in the case. As yet, however, Margaret could not see Morella or Betty, nor had the king and queen taken their seats upon the throne. Peter was already there, standing before the bar with guards on either side of him, and greeted them with a smile and a nod as they were ushered to their chairs near by. Just as they reached them also trumpets were blown, and from the back of the hall, walking hand in hand, appeared their Majesties of Spain, Ferdinand and Isabella, whereat all the audience rose and bowed, remaining standing till they were seated on the thrones.

The king, whom they now saw for the first time, was a thickset, active man with pleasant eyes, a fair skin, and a broad forehead, but, as Margaret thought, somewhat sly-faced—the face of a man who never forgot his own interests in those of another. Like the queen, he was magnificently attired in garments broidered with gold and the arms of Aragon, while in his hand he held a golden sceptre surmounted by a jewel, and about his waist, to show that he was a warlike king, he wore his long, cross-handled sword. Smilingly he acknowledged the homage of his subjects by lifting his hand to his cap and bowing. Then his eye fell upon the beautiful Margaret, and, turning, he put a question to the queen in a light, sharp voice, asking if that were the lady whom Morella had married, and, if so, why in the name of heaven he wished to be rid of her.

Isabella answered that she understood that this was the *señora* whom he had desired to marry when he married some one else, as he alleged by mistake, but who was in fact affianced to the prisoner before them; a reply at which all who heard it laughed.

At this moment the Marquis of Morella, accompanied by his gentlemen and some long-gowned lawyers, appeared walking up the court, dressed in the black velvet that he always wore, and glittering with orders. Upon his head was a cap, also of black velvet, from which hung a great pearl, and this cap he did not remove even when he bowed to the king and queen, for he was one of the few grandees of Spain who had the right to remain covered before their Majesties. They acknowledged his salutation, Ferdinand with a friendly nod and Isabella with a cold bow, and he, too, took the seat that had been prepared for him. Just then there was a disturbance at the far end of the court, where one of its officers could be heard calling:

"Way! Make way for the Marchioness of Morella!" At the sound of this name the marquis, whose eyes were fixed on Margaret, frowned fiercely, rising from his seat as though to protest, then, at some whispered word from a lawyer behind him, sat down again.

Now the crowd of spectators separated, and Margaret, turning to look down the long hall, saw a procession advancing up the lane between them, some clad in armour and some in white Moorish robes blazoned with the scarlet eagle, the cognisance of Morella. In the midst of them, her train supported by two Moorish women, walked a tall and beautiful lady, a coronet upon her brow, her fair hair outspread, a purple cloak hanging from her shoulders, half hiding that same splendid robe sewn with pearls which had been Morella's gift to Margaret, and about her white bosom the chain of pearls which he had presented to Betty in compensation for her injuries.

Margaret stared and stared again, and her father at her side murmured: "It is our Betty! Truly fine feathers make fine birds." Yes, Betty it was without a doubt, though, remembering her in her humble woollen dress at the old house in Holborn, it was hard to recognise the poor companion in this proud and magnificent lady, who looked as though all her life she had trodden the marble floors of courts, and consorted with nobles and with queens. Up the great hall she came, stately, imperturbable, looking neither to the right nor to the left, taking no note of the whisperings about her, no, nor even of Morella or of Margaret, till she reached the open space in front of the bar where Peter and his guards, gazing with all their eyes, hastened to make place for her. There she curtseyed thrice, twice to the queen, and once to the king, her consort; then, turning, bowed to the marquis, who fixed his eyes upon the ground and took no note, bowed to Castell and Peter, and lastly, advancing to Margaret, gave her her cheek to kiss. This Margaret did with becoming humility, whispering in her ear:

"How fares your Grace?"

"Better than you would in my shoes," whispered Betty back with ever so slight a trembling of her left eyelid; while Margaret heard the king mutter to the queen: "A fine peacock of a woman. Look at her figure and those big eyes. Morella must be hard to please."

"Perhaps he prefers swans to peacocks," answered the queen in the same voice with a glance at Margaret, whose quieter and more refined beauty seemed to gain by contrast with that of her nobly built and dazzling-skinned cousin. Then she motioned to Betty to take the seat prepared for her, which she did, with her suite standing behind her and an interpreter at her side.

"I am somewhat bewildered," said the king, glancing from Morella to Betty and from Margaret to Peter, for evidently the humour of the situation did not escape him. "What is the exact case that we have to try?"

Then one of the legal assessors, or *alcaldes*, rose and said that the matter before their Majesties was a charge against the Englishman at the bar of killing a certain soldier of the Holy Hermandad, but that there seemed to be other matters mixed up with it.

"So I gather," answered the king; "for instance, an accusation of the carrying off of subjects of a friendly Power out of the territory of that Power; a suit for nullity of a marriage, and a cross-suit for the declaration of the validity of the said marriage—and the holy saints know what besides. Well, one thing at a time. Let us try this tall Englishman."

So the case was opened against Peter by a public prosecutor, who restated it as it had been laid before the queen. The Captain Arrano gave his evidence as to the killing of the soldier, but, in cross-examination by Peter's advocate, admitted, for evidently he bore no malice against the prisoner, that the said soldier had roughly handled the Dona Margaret, and that the said Peter, being a stranger to the country, might very well have taken them for a troop of bandits or even Moors. Also, he added, that he could not say that the Englishman had intended to kill the soldier.

Then Castell and Margaret gave their evidence, the latter with much modest sweetness. Indeed, when she explained that Peter was her affianced husband, to whom she was to have been wed on the day after she had been stolen away from England, and that she had cried out to him for help when the dead soldier caught hold of her and rent away her veil, there was a murmur of sympathy, and the king and queen began to talk with each other without paying much heed to her further words.

Next they spoke to two of the judges who sat with them, after which the king held up his hand and announced that they had come to a decision on the case. It was, that, under the circumstances, the Englishman was justified in cutting down the soldier, especially as there was nothing to show that he meant to kill him, or that he knew that he belonged to the Holy Hermandad. He would, therefore, be discharged on the condition that he paid a sum of money, which, indeed, it appeared had already been paid to the man's widow, in compensation for the man's death, and a further small sum for Masses to be said for the welfare of his soul.

Peter began to give thanks for this judgment; but while he was still speaking the king asked if any of those present wished to proceed in further suits. Instantly Betty rose and said that she did. Then, through her interpreter, she stated that she had received the royal commands to attend before their Majesties, and was now prepared to answer any questions or charges that might be laid against her.

"What is your name, Señora?" asked the king.

"Elizabeth, Marchioness of Morella, born Elizabeth Dene, of the ancient and gentle family of Dene, a native of England," answered Betty in a clear and decided voice.

The king bowed, then asked:

"Does any one dispute this title and description?"

"I do," answered the Marquis of Morella, speaking for the first time.

"On what grounds, Marquis?"

"On every ground," he answered. "She is not the Marchioness of Morella, inasmuch as I went through the ceremony of marriage with her believing her to be another woman. She is not of ancient and gentle family, since she was a servant in the house of the merchant Castell yonder, in London."

"That proves nothing, Marquis," interrupted the king. "My family may, I think, be called ancient and gentle, which you will be the last to deny, yet I have played the part of a servant on an occasion which I think the queen here will remember"—an allusion at which the audience, who knew well enough to what it referred, laughed audibly, as did her Majesty[1]. "The marriage and rank are matters for proof," went

---

1. When travelling from Saragossa to Valladolid to be married to Isabella, Ferdinand was obliged to pass himself off as a valet. Prescott says: "The greatest circumspection, therefore, was necessary. The party journeyed chiefly in the night; Ferdinand assumed the disguise of a servant and, when they halted on the road, took care of the mules and served his companions at table."

on the king, "if they are questioned; but is it alleged that this lady has committed any crime which prevents her from pleading?"

"None," answered Betty quickly, "except that of being poor, and the crime, if it is one, as it may be, of having married that man, the Marquis of Morella," whereat the audience laughed again.

"Well, Madam, you do not seem to be poor now," remarked the king, looking at her gorgeous and bejewelled apparel; "and here we are more apt to think marriage a folly than a crime," a light saying at which the queen frowned a little. "But," he added quickly, "set out your case, Madam, and forgive me if, until you have done so, I do not call you Marchioness."

"Here is my case, Sire," said Betty, producing the certificate of marriage and handing it up for inspection.

The judges and their Majesties inspected it, the queen remarking that a duplicate of this document had already been submitted to her and passed on to the proper authorities.

"Is the priest who solemnised the marriage present?" asked the king; whereon Bernaldez, Castell's agent, rose and said that he was, though he neglected to add that his presence had been secured for no mean sum.

One of the judges ordered that he should be called, and presently the foxy-faced Father Henriques, at whom the marquis glared angrily, appeared bowing, and was sworn in the usual form, and, on being questioned, stated that he had been priest at Motril, and chaplain to the Marquis of Morella, but was now a secretary of the Holy Office at Seville. In answer to further questions he said that, apparently by the bridegroom's own wish, and with his full consent, on a certain date at Granada, he had married the marquis to the lady who stood before them, and whom he knew to be named Betty Dene; also, that at her request, since she was anxious that proper record should be kept of her marriage, he had written the certificates which the court had seen, which certificates the marquis and others had signed immediately after the ceremony in his private chapel at Granada. Subsequently he had left Granada to take up his appointment as a secretary to the Inquisition at Seville, which had been conferred on him by the ecclesiastical authorities in reward of a treatise which he had written upon heresy. That was all he knew about the affair.

Now Morella's advocate rose to cross-examine, asking him who had made the arrangements for the marriage. He answered that the marquis had never spoken to him directly on the subject—at least he had never mentioned to him the name of the lady; the Señora Inez arranged everything.

Now the queen broke in, asking where was the Señora Inez, and who she was. The priest replied that the Señora Inez was a Spanish woman, one of the marquis's household at Granada, whom he made use of in all confidential affairs. She was young and beautiful, but he could say no more about her. As to where she was now he did not know, although they had ridden together to Seville. Perhaps the marquis knew.

Now the priest was ordered to stand down, and Betty tendered herself as a witness, and through her interpreter told the court the story of her connection with Morella. She said that she had met him in London when she was a member of the household of the Señor Castell, and that at once he began to make love to her and won her heart. Subsequently he suggested that she should elope with him to Spain, promising to marry her at once, in proof of which she produced the letter he had written, which was translated and handed up for the inspection of the court—a very awkward letter, as they evidently thought, although it was not signed with the writer's real name. Next Betty explained the trick by which she and her cousin Margaret were brought on board his ship, and that when they arrived there the marquis refused to marry her, alleging that he was in love with her cousin and not with her—a statement which she took to be an excuse to avoid the fulfilment of his promise. She could not say why he had carried off her cousin Margaret also, but supposed that it was because, having once brought her upon the ship, he did not know how to be rid of her.

Then she described the voyage to Spain, saying that during that voyage she kept the marquis at a distance, since there was no priest to marry them; also, she was sick and much ashamed, who had involved her cousin and mistress in this trouble. She told how the Señors Castell and Brome had followed in another vessel, and boarded the caravel in a storm; also of the shipwreck and their journey to Granada as prisoners, and of their subsequent life there. Finally she described how Inez came to her with proposals of marriage, and how she bargained that if she consented, her cousin, the Señor Castell, and the Señor Brome should go free. They went accordingly, and the marriage took place as arranged, the marquis first embracing her publicly in the presence of various people—namely, Inez and his two secretaries, who, except Inez, were present, and could bear witness to the truth of what she said.

After the marriage and the signing of the certificates she had accompanied him to his own apartments, which she had never entered before, and there, to her astonishment, in the morning, he announced that he must go a journey upon their Majesties' business. Before he went, however, he gave her a written authority, which she produced, to receive his rents and manage his matters in Granada during his absence, which authority she read to the gathered household before he left. She had obeyed him accordingly until she had received the royal command, receiving moneys, giving her receipt for the same, and generally occupying the unquestioned position of mistress of his house.

"We can well believe it," said the king drily. "And now, Marquis, what have you to answer to all this?"

"I will answer presently," replied Morella, who trembled with rage. "First suffer that my advocate cross-examine this woman."

So the advocate cross-examined, though it cannot be said that he had the better of Betty. First he questioned her as to her statement that she was of ancient and gentle family, whereon Betty overwhelmed the court with a list of her ancestors, the first of whom, a certain Sieur Dene de Dene, had come to England with the Norman Duke, William the Conqueror. After him, so she still swore, the said Denes de Dene had risen to great rank and power, having been the favourites of the kings of England, and fought for them generation after generation.

By slow degrees she came down to the Wars of the Roses, in which she said her grandfather had been attainted for his loyalty, and lost his land and titles, so that her father, whose only child she was—being now the representative of the noble family, Dene de Dene—fell into poverty and a humble place in life. However, he married a lady of even more distinguished race than his own, a direct descendant of a noble Saxon family, far more ancient in blood than the upstart Normans. At this point, while Peter and Margaret listened amazed, at a hint from the queen, the bewildered court interfered through the head *alcalde*, praying her to cease from the history of her descent, which they took for granted was as noble as any in England.

Next she was examined as to her relations with Morella in London, and told the tale of his wooing with so much detail and imaginative power that in the end that also was left unfinished. So it was with everything. Clever as Morella's advocate might be, sometimes in English and sometimes in the Spanish tongue, Betty overwhelmed him with words and apt answers, until, able to make nothing of her, the poor man sat down wiping his brow and cursing her beneath his breath.

Then the secretaries were sworn, and after them various members of Morella's household, who, although somewhat unwillingly, confirmed all that Betty had said as to his embracing her with lifted veil and the rest. So at length Betty closed her case, reserving the right to address the court after she had heard that of the marquis.

Now the king, queen, and their assessors consulted for a little while, for evidently there was a division of opinion among them, some thinking that the case should be stopped at once and referred to another tribunal, and others that it should go on. At length the queen was heard to say that at least the Marquis of Morella should be allowed to make his statement, as he might be able to prove that all this story was a fabrication, and that he was not even at Granada at the time when the marriage was alleged to have taken place.

The king and the *alcaldes* assenting, the marquis was sworn and told his story, admitting that it was not one which he was proud to repeat in public. He narrated how he had first met Margaret, Betty, and Peter at a public ceremony in London, and had then and there fallen in love with Margaret, and accompanied her home to the house of her father, the merchant John Castell.

Subsequently he discovered that this Castell, who had fled from Spain with his father in childhood, was that lowest of mankind, an unconverted Jew who posed as a Christian (at this statement there was a great sensation in court, and the queen's face hardened), although it is true that he had married a Christian lady, and that his daughter had been baptized and brought up as a Christian, of which faith she was a loyal member. Nor did she know—as he believed—that her father remained a Jew, since, otherwise, he would not have continued to seek her as his wife. Their Majesties would be aware, he went on, that, owing to reasons with which they were acquainted, he had means of getting at the truth of these matters concerning the Jews in England, as to which, indeed, he had already written to them, although, owing to his shipwreck and to the pressure of his private affairs, he had not yet made his report on his embassy in person.

Continuing, he said that he admitted that he had made love to the serving-woman, Betty, in order to gain access to Margaret, whose father mistrusted him, knowing something of his mission. She was a person of no character.

Here Betty rose and said in a clear voice:

"I declare the Marquis of Morella to be a knave and a liar. There is more good character in my little finger than in his whole body, and," she added, "than in that of his mother before him"—an allusion at which the marquis flushed, while, satisfied for the present with this home-thrust, Betty sat down.

He had proposed to Margaret, but she was not willing to marry him, as he found that she was affianced to a distant cousin of hers, the Señor Peter Brome, a swashbuckler who was in trouble for the killing of a man in London, as he had killed the soldier of the Holy Hermandad in Spain. Therefore, in his despair, being deeply enamoured of her, and knowing that he could offer her great place and fortune, he conceived the idea of carrying her off, and to do so was obliged, much against his will, to abduct Betty also.

So after many adventures they came to Granada, where he was able to show the Dona Margaret that the Señor Peter Brome was employing his imprisonment in making love to that member of his household, Inez, who had been spoken of, but now could not be found.

Here Peter, who could bear this no longer, also rose and called him a liar to his face, saying that if he had the opportunity he would prove it on his body, but was ordered by the king to sit down and be silent.

Having been convinced of her lover's unfaithfulness, the marquis went on, the Dona Margaret had at length consented to become his wife on condition that her father, the Señor Brome, and her servant, Betty Dene, were allowed to escape from Granada—

"Where," remarked the queen, "you had no right to detain them, Marquis. Except, perhaps, the father, John Castell," she added significantly.

Where, he admitted with sorrow, he had no right to detain them.

"Therefore," went on the queen acutely, "there was no legal or moral consideration for this alleged promise of marriage,"—a point at which the lawyers nodded approvingly.

The marquis submitted that there was a consideration; that at any rate the Dona Margaret wished it. On the day arranged for the wedding the prisoners were let go, disguised as Moors, but he now knew that through the trickery of the woman Inez, whom he believed had been bribed by Castell and his fellow-Jews, the Dona Margaret escaped in place of her servant, Betty, with whom he subsequently went through the form of marriage, believing her to be Margaret.

As regards the embrace before the ceremony, it took place in a shadowed room, and he thought that Betty's face and hair must have been painted and dyed to resemble those of Margaret. For the rest, he was certain that the ceremonial cup of wine that he drank before he led the woman to the altar was drugged, since he only remembered the marriage itself very dimly, and after that nothing at all until he woke upon the following morning with an aching brow to see Betty sitting by him. As for the power of administration which she produced, being perfectly mad at the time with rage and disappointment, and sure that if he stopped there any longer he should commit the crime of killing this woman who had deceived him so cruelly, he gave it that he might escape from her. Their Majesties would notice also that it was in favour of the Marchioness of Morella. As this marriage was null and void, there was no Marchioness of Morella. Therefore, the document was null and void also. That was the truth, and all he had to say.

The Doom of John Castell

His evidence finished, the Marquis of Morella sat down, whereon, the king and queen having whispered together, the head *alcalde* asked Betty if she had any questions to put to him. She rose with much dignity, and through her interpreter said in a quiet voice:

"Yes, a great many. Yet she would not debase herself by asking a single one until the stain which he had cast upon her was washed away, which she thought could only be done in blood. He had alleged that she was a woman of no character, and he had further alleged that their marriage was null and void. Being of the sex she was, she could not ask him to make good his assertions at the sword's point, therefore, as she believed she had the right to do according to all the laws of honour, she asked leave to seek a champion—if an unfriended woman could find one in a strange land—to uphold her fair name against this base and cruel slander."

Now, in the silence that followed her speech, Peter rose and said:

"I ask the permission of your Majesties to be that champion. Your Majesties will note that according to his own story I have suffered from this marquis the bitterest wrong that one man can receive at the hands of another. Also, he has lied in saying that I am not true to my affianced lady, the Dona Margaret, and surely I have a right to avenge the lie upon him. Lastly, I declare that I believe the Señora Betty to be a good and upright woman, upon whom no shadow of shame has ever fallen, and, as her countryman and relative, I desire to uphold her good name before all the world. I am a foreigner here with few friends, or none, yet I cannot believe that your Majesties will withhold from me the right of battle which all over the world in such a case one gentleman may demand of another. I challenge the Marquis of Morella to mortal combat without mercy to the fallen, and here is the proof of it."

Then, stepping across the open space before the bar, he drew the leathern gauntlet off his hand and threw it straight into Morella's face, thinking that after such an insult he could not choose but fight.

With an oath Morella snatched at his sword; but, before he could draw it, officers of the court threw themselves on him, and the king's stern voice was heard commanding them to cease their brawling in the royal presences.

"I ask your pardon, Sire," gasped Morella, "but you have seen what this Englishman did to me, a grandee of Spain."

"Yes," broke in the queen, "but we have also heard what you, a grandee of Spain, did to this gentleman of England, and the charge you brought against him, which, it seems, the Dona Margaret does not believe."

"In truth, no, your Majesty," said Margaret. "Let me be sworn also, and I can explain much of what the marquis has told to you. I never wished to marry him or any man, save this one," and she touched Peter on the arm, "and anything that he or I may have done, we did to escape the evil net in which we were snared."

"We believe it," answered the queen with a smile, then fell to consulting with the king and the *alcaldes*.

For a long time they debated in voices so low that none could hear what they said, looking now at one and now at another of the parties to this strange suit. Also, some priest was called into their council, which Margaret thought a bad omen. At length they made up their minds, and in a low, quiet voice and measured words her Majesty, as Queen of Castile, gave the judgment of them all. Addressing herself first to Morella, she said:

"My lord Marquis, you have brought very grave charges against the lady who claims to be your wife, and the Englishman whose affianced bride you admit you snatched away by fraud and force. This gentleman, on his own behalf and on behalf of these ladies, has challenged you to a combat to the death in a fashion that none can mistake. Do you accept his challenge?"

"I would accept it readily enough, your Majesty," answered Morella in sullen tones, "since heretofore none have doubted my courage; but I must remember that I am"—and he paused, then added—"what your Majesties know me to be, a grandee of Spain, and something more, wherefore it is scarcely lawful for me to cross swords with a Jew-merchant's clerk, for that was this man's high rank and office in England."

"You could cross them with me on your ship, the *San Antonio*," exclaimed Peter bitterly, "why then are you ashamed to finish what you were not ashamed to begin? Moreover, I tell you that in love or war I hold myself the equal of any woman-thief and bastard in this kingdom, who am one of a name that has been honoured in my own."

Now again the king and queen spoke together of this question of rank—no small one in that age and country. Then Isabella said:

"It is true that a grandee of Spain cannot be asked to meet a simple foreign gentleman in single combat. Therefore, since he has thought fit to raise it, we uphold the objection of the Marquis of Morella, and declare that this challenge is not binding on his honour. Yet we note his willingness to accept the same, and are prepared to do what we can to make the matter easy, so that it may not be said that a Spaniard, who has wrought wrong to an Englishman, and been asked openly to make the amend of arms in the presence of his sovereigns, was debarred from so doing by the accident of his rank. Señor Peter Brome, if you will receive it at our hands, as others of your nation have been proud to do, we propose, believing you to be a brave and loyal man of gentle birth, to confer upon you the knighthood of the Order of St. James, and thereby and therein the right to consort with as equal, or to fight as equal, any noble of Spain, unless he should be of the right blood-royal, to which place we think the most puissant and excellent Marquis of Morella lays no claim."

"I thank your Majesties," said Peter, astonished, "for the honour that you would do to me, which, had it not been for the fact that my father chose the wrong side on Bosworth Field, being of a race somewhat obstinate in the matter of loyalty, I should not have needed to accept from your Majesties. As it is I am very grateful, since now the noble marquis need not feel debased in settling our long quarrel as he would desire to do."

"Come hither and kneel down, Señor Peter Brome," said the queen when he had finished speaking.

He obeyed, and Isabella, borrowing his sword from the king, gave him the accolade by striking him thrice upon the right shoulder and saying: "Rise, Sir Peter Brome, Knight of the most noble Order of Saint Iago, and by creation a Don of Spain."

He rose, he bowed, retreating backwards as was the custom, and thereby nearly falling off the dais, which some people thought a good omen for Morella. As he went the king said:

"Our Marshal, Sir Peter, will arrange the time and manner of your combat with the marquis as shall be most convenient to you both. Meanwhile, we command you both that no unseemly word or deed should pass between you, who must soon meet face to face to abide the judgment of God in battle *à l'outrance*. Rather, since one of you must die so shortly, do we entreat you to prepare your souls to appear before His judgment-seat. We have spoken."

Now the audience appeared to think that the court was ended, for many of them began to rise; but the queen held up her hand and said:

"There remain other matters on which we must give judgment. The *señora* here," and she pointed to Betty, "asks that her marriage should be declared valid, or so we understand, and the Marquis of Morella asks that his marriage with the said *señora* should be declared void, or so we understand. Now this is a question over which we claim no power, it having to do with a sacrament of the Church. Therefore we leave it to his Holiness the Pope in person, or by his legate, to decide according to his wisdom in such manner as may seem best to him, if the parties concerned should choose to lay their suit before him. Meanwhile, we declare and decree that the *señora*, born Elizabeth Dene, shall everywhere throughout our dominions, until or unless his Holiness the Pope shall decide to the contrary, be received and acknowledged as the Marchioness of Morella, and that during his lifetime her reputed husband shall make due provision for her mainte-nance, and that after his death, should no decision have been come to by the court of Rome upon her suit, she shall inherit and enjoy that proportion of his lands and property which belongs to a wife under the laws of this realm."

Now, while Betty bowed her thanks to their Majesties till the jew-els on her bodice rattled, and Morella scowled till his face looked as black as a thunder-cloud above the mountains, the audience, whisper-ing to each other, once more rose to disperse. Again the queen held up her hand, for the judgment was not yet finished.

"We have a question to ask of the gallant Sir Peter Brome and the Dona Margaret, his affianced. Is it still their desire to take each other in marriage?"

Now Peter looked at Margaret, and Margaret looked at Peter, and there was that in their eyes which both of them understood, for he answered in a clear voice:

"Your Majesty, that is the dearest wish of both of us."

The queen smiled a little, then asked: "And do you, Señor John Castell, consent and allow your daughter's marriage to this knight?"

"I do, indeed," he answered gravely. "Had it not been for this man here," and he glanced with bitter hatred at Morella, "they would have been united long ago, and to that end," he added with meaning, "such little property as I possessed has been made over to trustees in England for their benefit and that of their children. Therefore I am hencefor-ward dependent upon their charity."

"Good," said the queen. "Then one question remains to be put, and only one. Is it your wish, both of you, that you should be wed before the single combat between the Marquis of Morella and Sir Peter Brome? Remember, Dona Margaret, before you answer, that in this event you may soon be made a widow, and that if you postpone the ceremony you may never be a wife."

Now Margaret and Peter spoke a few words together, then the former answered for them both.

"Should my lord fall," she said in her sweet voice that trembled as she uttered the words, "in either case my heart will be widowed and broken. Let me live out my days, therefore, bearing his name, that, knowing my deathless grief, none may thenceforth trouble me with their love, who desire to remain his bride in heaven."

"Well spoken," said the queen. "We decree that here in our cathedral of Seville you twain shall be wed on the same day, but before the Marquis of Morella and you, Sir Peter Brome, meet in single combat. Further, lest harm should be attempted against either of you," and she looked sideways at Morella, "you, Señora Margaret, shall be my guest until you leave my care to become a bride, and you, Sir Peter, shall return to lodge in the prison whence you came, but with liberty to see whom you will, and to go when and where you will, but under our protection, lest some attempt should be made on you."

She ceased, whereon suddenly the king began speaking in his sharp, thin voice.

"Having settled these matters of chivalry and marriage," he said, "there remains another, which I will not leave to the gentle lips of our sovereign Lady, that has to do with something higher than either of them—namely, the eternal welfare of men's souls, and of the Church of Christ on earth. It has been declared to us that the man yonder, John Castell, merchant of London, is that accursed thing, a Jew, who for the sake of gain has all his life feigned to be a Christian, and, as such, deceived a Christian woman into marriage; that he is, moreover, of our subjects, having been born in Spain, and therefore amenable to the civil and spiritual jurisdiction of this realm."

He paused, while Margaret and Peter stared at each other affright-ed. Only Castell stood silent and unmoved, though he guessed what must follow better than either of them.

"We judge him not," went on the king, "who claim no authority in such high matters, but we do what we must do—we commit him to the Holy Inquisition, there to take his trial!"

Now Margaret cried aloud. Peter stared about him as though for help, which he knew could never come, feeling more afraid than ever he had been in all his life, and for the first time that day Morella smiled. At least he would be rid of one enemy. But Castell went to Margaret and kissed her tenderly. Then he shook Peter by the hand, saying:

"Kill that thief," and he looked at Morella, "as I know you will, and would if there were ten as bad at his back. And be a good husband to my girl, as I know you will also, for I shall ask an account of you of these matters when we meet where there is neither Jew nor Christian, priest nor king. Now be silent, and bear what must be borne as I do, for I have a word to say before I leave you and the world.

"Your Majesties, I make no plea for myself, and when I am questioned before your Inquisition the task will be easy, for I desire to hide nothing, and will tell the truth, though not from fear or because I shrink from pain. Your Majesties, you have told us that these two, who, at least, are good enough Christians from their birth, shall be wed. I would ask you if any spiritual crime, or supposed crime, of mine will be allowed to work their separation, or to their detriment in any way whatsoever."

"On that point," answered the queen quickly, as though she wished to get in her words before the king or any one else could speak, "you have our royal word, John Castell. Your case is apart from their case, and nothing of which you may be convicted shall affect them in person or," she added slowly, "in property."

"A large promise," muttered the king.

"It is my promise," she answered decidedly, "and it shall be kept at any cost. These two shall marry, and if Sir Peter lives through the fray they shall depart from Spain unharmed, nor shall any fresh charge be brought against them in any court of the realm, nor shall they be persecuted or proceeded against in any other realm or on the high seas at our instance or that of our officers. Let my words be written down, and one copy of them signed and filed and another copy given to the Dona Margaret."

"Your Majesty," said Castell, "I thank you, and now, if die I must, I shall die happy. Yet I make bold to tell you that had you not spoken them it was my purpose to kill myself, here before your eyes, since that is a sin for which none can be asked to suffer save the sinner. Also, I say that this Inquisition which you have set up shall eat out the heart of Spain and bring her greatness to the dust of death. The torture and the misery of those Jews, than whom you have no better or more faithful subjects, shall be avenged on the heads of your children's children for so long as their blood endures."

He finished speaking, and, while something that sounded like a gasp of fear rose from that crowded court as the meaning of Castell's bold words came home to his auditors, the crowd behind him separated, and there appeared, walking two by two, a file of masked and hooded monks and a guard of soldiers, all of whom doubtless were in waiting. They came to John Castell, they touched him on the shoulder, they closed around him, hiding him as it were from the world, and in the midst of them he vanished away.

Peter's memories of that strange day in the Alcazar at Seville always remained somewhat dim and blurred. It was not wonderful. Within the space of a few hours he had been tried for his life and acquitted. He had seen Betty, transformed from a humble companion into a magnificent and glittering marchioness, as a chrysalis is transformed into a butterfly, urge her strange suit against the husband who had tricked her, and whom she had tricked, and, for the while at any rate, more than hold her own, thanks to her ready wit and native strength of character.

As her champion, and that of Margaret, he had challenged Morella to a single combat, and when his defiance was refused on the ground of his lack of rank, by the favour of the great Isabella, who wished to use him as her instrument, doubtless because of those secret ambitions of Morella's which Margaret had revealed to her, he had been suddenly advanced to the high station of a Knight of the Order of St. James of Spain, to which, although he cared little for it, otherwise he might vainly have striven to come.

More, and better far, the desire of his heart would at length be attained, for now it was granted to him to meet his enemy, the man whom he hated with just cause, upon a fair field, without favour shown to one or the other, and to fight him to the death. He had been promised, further, that within some few days Margaret should be given to him as wife, although it well might be that she would keep that name but for a single hour, and that until then they both should dwell safe from Morella's violence and treachery; also that, whatever chanced, no suit should lie against them in any land for aught that they did or had done in Spain.

Lastly, when all seemed safe save for that chance of war, whereof, having been bred to such things, he took but little count; when his cup, emptied at length of mire and sand, was brimming full with the good red wine of battle and of love, when it was at his very lips indeed,

Fate had turned it to poison and to gall. Castell, his bride's father, and the man he loved, had been haled to the vaults of the Inquisition, whence he knew well he would come forth but once more, dressed in a yellow robe "relaxed to the civil arm," to perish slowly in the fires of the Quemadero, the place of burning of heretics.

What would his conquest over Morella avail if Heaven should give him power to conquer? What kind of a bridal would that be which was sealed and consecrated by the death of the bride's father in the torturing fires of the Inquisition? How would they ever get the smell of the smoke of that sacrifice out of their nostrils? Castell was a brave man; no torments would make him recant. It was doubtful even if he would be at the pains to deny his faith, he who had only been baptized a Christian by his father for the sake of policy, and suffered the fraud to continue for the purposes of his business, and that he might win and keep a Christian wife. No, Castell was doomed, and he could no more protect him from priest and king than a dove can protect its nest from a pair of hungry peregrines.

Oh that last scene! Never could Peter forget it while he lived—the vast, fretted hall with its painted arches and marble columns; the rays of the afternoon sun piercing the window-places, and streaming like blood on to the black robes of the monks as, with their prey, they vanished back into the arcade where they had lurked; Margaret's wild cry and ashen face as her father was torn away from her, and she sank fainting on to Betty's bejewelled bosom; the cruel sneer on Morella's lips; the king's hard smile; the pity in the queen's eye; the excited murmurings of the crowd; the quick, brief comments of the lawyers; the scratching of the clerk's quill as, careless of everything save his work, he recorded the various decrees; and above it all as it were, upright, defiant, unmoved, Castell, surrounded by the ministers of death, vanishing into the blackness of the arcade, vanishing into the jaws of the tomb.

CHAPTER 23

Father Henriques and
the Baker's Oven

A week had gone by. Margaret was in the palace, where Peter had
been to see her twice, and found her broken-hearted. Even the fact
that they were to be wed upon the following Saturday, the day fixed
also for the combat between Peter and Morella, brought her no joy or
consolation. For on the next day, the Sunday, there was to be an "Act
of Faith," an *auto-da-fé* in Seville, when wicked heretics, such as Jews,
Moors, and persons who had spoken blasphemy, were to suffer for
their crimes—some by fire on the Quemadero, or place of burning,
outside the city; some by making public confession of their grievous
sin before they were carried off to perpetual and solitary imprisonment; some by being garrotted before their bodies were given to the
flames, and so forth. In this ceremony it was known that John Castell
had been doomed to play a leading part.

On her knees, with tears and beseechings, Margaret had prayed
the queen for mercy. But in this matter those tears produced no
more effect upon the heart of Isabella than does water dripping on a
diamond. Gentle enough in other ways, where questions of the Faith
were concerned she had the craft of a fox and the cruelty of a tiger.
She was even indignant with Margaret. Had not enough been done
for her? she asked. Had she not even passed her royal word that no
steps should be taken to deprive the accused of such property as he
might own in Spain if he were found guilty, and that none of those
penalties which, according to law and custom fell upon the children
of such infamous persons, should attach to her, Margaret? Was she
not to be publicly married to her lover, and, should he survive the
combat, allowed to depart with him in honour without even being asked to see her father expiate his iniquity? Surely, as a good
Christian she should rejoice that he was given this opportunity of

433

reconciling his soul with God and be made an example to others of his accursed faith. Was she then a heretic also?

So she stormed on, till Margaret crept from her presence wondering whether this creed could be right that would force the child to inform against and bring the parent to torment. Where were such things written in the sayings of the Saviour and His Apostles? And if they were not written, who had invented them?

"Save him!—save him!" Margaret had gasped to Peter in despair. "Save him, or I swear to you, however much I may love you, however much we may seem to be married, never shall you be a husband to me."

"That seems hard," replied Peter, shaking his head mournfully, "since it was not I who gave him over to these devils, and probably the end of it would be that I should share his fate. Still, I will do what a man can."

"No, no," she cried in despair; "do nothing that will bring you into danger." But he had gone without waiting for her answer.

It was night, and Peter sat in a secret room in a certain baker's shop in Seville. There were present there besides himself the Fray Henriques—now a secretary to the Holy Inquisition, but disguised as a layman—the woman Inez, the agent Bernaldez, and the old Jew, Israel of Granada.

"I have brought him here, never mind how," Inez was saying, pointing to Henriques. "A risky and disagreeable business enough. And now what is the use of it?"

"No use at all," answered the Fray coolly, "except to me who pocket my ten gold pieces."

"A thousand doubloons if our friend escapes safe and sound," put in the old Jew Israel. "God in Heaven! think of it, a thousand doubloons."

The secretary's eyes gleamed hungrily.

"I could do with them well enough," he answered, "and hell could spare one filthy Jew for ten years or so, but I see no way. What I do see, is that probably all of you will join him. It is a great crime to try to tamper with a servant of the Holy Office."

Bernaldez turned white, and the old Jew bit his nails; but Inez tapped the priest upon the shoulder.

"Are you thinking of betraying us?" she asked in her gentle voice. "Look here, friend, I have some knowledge of poisons, and I swear to you that if you attempt it, you shall die within a week, tied in a double knot, and never know whence the dose came. Or I can bewitch you, I, who have not lived a dozen years among the Moors for nothing, so that your head swells and your body wastes, and you utter blasphemies, not knowing what you say, until for very shame's sake they toast you among the faggots also."

"Bewitch me!" answered Henriques with a shiver. "You have done that already, or I should not be here."

"Then, if you do not wish to be in another place before your time," went on Inez, still tapping his shoulder gently, "think, think! and find a way, worthy servant of the Holy Office."

"A thousand doubloons!—a thousand gold doubloons!" croaked old Israel, "or if you fail, sooner or later, this month or next, this year or next, death—death as slow and cruel as we can make it. There are two Inquisitions in Spain, holy Father; but one of them does its business in the dark, and your name is on its ledger."

Now Henriques was very frightened, as well he might be with all those eyes glaring at him.

"You need fear nothing," he said, "I know the devilish power of your league too well, and that, if I kill you all, a hundred others I have never seen or heard of would dog me to my death, who have taken your accursed money."

"I am glad that you understand at last, dear friend," said the soft, mocking voice of Inez, who stood behind the monk like an evil genius, and again tapped him affectionately on the shoulder, this time with the bare blade of a poniard. "Now be quick with that plan of yours. It grows late, and all holy people should be abed."

"I have none. I defy you," he answered furiously.

"Very well, friend—very well; then I will say good night, or rather farewell, since I am not likely to meet you again in this world."

"Where are you going?" he asked anxiously.

"Oh! to the palace to meet the Marquis of Morella and a friend of his, a relation indeed. Look you here. I have had an offer of pardon for my part in that marriage if I can prove that a certain base priest knew that he was perpetrating a fraud. Well, I *can* prove it—you may remember that you wrote me a note—and, if I do, what happens to such a priest who chances to have incurred the hatred of a grandee of Spain and of his noble relation?"

"I am an officer of the Holy Inquisition; no one dare touch me," he gasped.

"Oh! I think that there are some who would take the risk. For instance—the king."

Fray Henriques sank back in his chair. Now he understood whom Inez meant by the noble relative of Morella, understood also that he had been trapped. "On Sunday morning," he began in a hollow whisper, "the procession will be formed, and wind through the streets of the city to the theatre, where the sermon will be preached before those who are relaxed proceed to the Quemadero. About eight o'clock it turns on to the quay for a little way only, and here will be but few spectators, since the view of the pageant is bad, nor is the road guarded there. Now, if a dozen determined men were waiting disguised as peasants with a boat at hand, perhaps they might—" and he paused.

Then Peter, who had been watching and listening to all this play, spoke for the first time, asking:

"In such an event, reverend Sir, how would those determined men know which was the victim that they sought?"

"The heretic John Castell," he answered, "will be seated on an ass, clad in a *zamarra* of sheepskin painted with fiends and a likeness of his own head burning—very well done, for I, who can draw, had a hand in it. Also, he alone will have a rope round his neck, by which he may be known."

"Why will he be seated on an ass?" asked Peter savagely. "Because you have tortured him so that he cannot walk?"

"Not so—not so," said the Dominican, shrinking from those fierce eyes. "He has never been questioned at all, not a single turn of the *mancuerda*, I swear to you, Sir Knight. What was the use, since he openly avows himself an accursed Jew?"

"Be more gentle in your talk, friend," broke in Inez, with her familiar tap upon the shoulder. "There are those here who do not think so ill of Jews as you do in your Holy House, but who understand how to apply the *mancuerda*, and can make a very serviceable rack out of a plank and a pulley or two such as lie in the next room. Cultivate courtesy, most learned priest, lest before you leave this place you should add a cubit to your stature."

"Go on," growled Peter.

"Moreover," added Fray Henriques shakily, "orders came that it was not to be done. The Inquisitors thought otherwise, as they believed—doubtless in error—that he might have accomplices whose names he would give up; but the orders said that as he had lived so long in England, and only recently travelled to Spain, he could have none. Therefore he is sound—sound as a bell; never before, I am told, has an impenitent Jew gone to the stake in such good case, however worthy and worshipful he might be."

"So much the better for you, if you do not lie," answered Peter. "Continue!"

"There is nothing more to say, except that I shall be walking near to him with the two guards, and, of course, if he were snatched away from us, and there were no boats handy in which to pursue, we could not help it, could we? Indeed, we priests, who are men of peace, might even fly at the sight of cruel violence."

"I should advise you to fly fast and far," said Peter. "But, Inez, what hold have you on this friend of yours? He will trick everybody."

"A thousand doubloons—a thousand doubloons!" muttered old Israel like a sleepy parrot.

"He may think to screw more than that out of the carcases of some of us, old man. Come, Inez, you are quick at this game. How can we best hold him to his word?"

"Dead, I think," broke in Bernaldez, who knew his danger as the partner and relative of Castell, and the nominal owner of the ship *Margaret* in which it was purposed that he should escape. "We know all that he can tell, and if we let him go he will betray us soon or late. Kill him out of the way, I say, and burn his body in the oven."

Now Henriques fell upon his knees, and with groans and tears began to implore mercy.

"Why do you complain so?" asked Inez, watching him with reflective eyes. "The end would be much gentler than that which you righteous folk mete out to many more honest men, yes, and women too. For my part, I think that the Señor Bernaldez gives good counsel. Better that you should die, who are but one, than all of us and others, for you will understand that we cannot trust you. Has any one got a rope?"

Now Henriques grovelled on the ground before her, kissing the hem of her robe, and praying her in the name of all the saints to show pity on one who had been betrayed into this danger by love of her.

"Of money you mean, Toad," she answered, kicking him with her slippered foot. "I had to listen to your talk of love while we journeyed together, and before, but here I need not, and if you speak of it again you shall go living into that baker's oven. Oh! you have forgotten it, but I have a long score to settle with you. You were a familiar of the Holy Office here at Seville—were you not?—before Morella promoted you to Motril for your zeal, and made you one of his chaplains? Well, I had a sister," And she knelt down and whispered a name into his ear.

He uttered a sound—it was more of a scream than a gasp.

"I had nothing to do with her death," he protested. "She was brought within the walls of the Holy House by some one who had a grudge against her and bore false witness."

"Yes, I know. It was you who had the grudge, you snake-souled rogue, and it was you who gave the false witness. It was you, also,

437

who but the other day volunteered the corroborative evidence that was necessary against Castell, saying that he had passed the Rood at your house in Motril without doing it reverence, and other things. It was you, too, who urged your superiors to put him to the question, because you said he was rich and had rich friends, and much money could be wrung out of him and them, whereof you were to get your share. Oh! yes, my information is good, is it not? Even what passes in the dungeons of the Holy House comes to the ears of the woman Inez. Well, do you still think that baker's oven too hot for you?"

By this time Henriques was speechless with terror. There he knelt upon the floor, glaring at this soft-voiced, remorseless woman who had made a tool and a fool of him; who had beguiled him there that night, and who hated him so bitterly and with so just a cause. Peter was speaking now.

"It would be better not to stain our hands with the creature's blood," he said. "Caged rats give little sport, and he might be tracked. For my part, I would leave his judgment to God. Have you no other way, Inez?"

She thought a while, then prodded the Fray Henriques with her foot, saying:

"Get up, sainted secretary to the Holy Office, and do a little writing, which will be easy to you. See, here are pens and paper. Now I'll dictate:

"'Most Adorable Inez,

"'Your dear message has reached me safely here in this accursed Holy House, where we lighten heretics of their sins to the benefit of their souls, and of their goods to the benefit of our own bodies—'"

"I cannot write it," groaned Henriques; "it is rank heresy."

"No, only the truth," answered Inez.

"Heresy and the truth—well, they are often the same thing. They would burn me for it."

"That is just what many heretics have urged. They have died gloriously for what they hold to be the truth, why should not you? Listen," she went on more sternly. "Will you take your chance of burning on the Quemadero, which you will not do unless you betray us, or will you certainly burn more privately, but better, in a baker's oven, and within half an hour? Ah! I thought you would not hesitate. Continue your letter, most learned scribe. Are those words down? Yes. Now add these:

"'I note all you tell me about the trial at the Alcazar before their Majesties. I believe that the Englishwoman will win her case. That was a very pretty trick that I played on the most noble marquis at Granada.

Nothing neater was ever done, even in this place. Well, I owed him a long score, and I have paid him off in full. I should like to have seen his exalted countenance when he surveyed the features of his bride, the waiting-woman, and knew that the mistress was safe away with another man. The nephew of the king, who would like himself to be king some day, married to an English waiting-woman! Good, very good, dear Inez.

"'Now, as regards the Jew, John Castell. I think that the matter may possibly be managed, provided that the money is all right, for, as you know, I do not work for nothing. Thus—'" And Inez dictated with admirable lucidity those suggestions as to the rescue of Castell, with which the reader is already acquainted, ending the letter as follows:

These Inquisitors here are cruel beasts, though fonder of money than of blood; for all their talk about zeal for the Faith is so much wind behind the mountains. They care as much for the Faith as the mountain cares for the wind, or, let us say, as I do. They wanted to torture the poor devil, thinking that he would rain *maravedis*; but I gave a hint in the right quarter, and their fun was stopped. Carissima, I must stop also; it is my hour for duty, but I hope to meet you as arranged, and we will have a merry evening. Love to the newly married marquis, if you meet him, and to yourself you know how much.
Your
Henriques
Postscriptum.—This position will scarcely be as remunerative as I hoped, so I am glad to be able to earn a little outside, enough to buy you a present that will make your pretty eyes shine.

"There!" said Inez mildly, "I think that covers everything, and would burn you three or four times over. Let me read it to see that it is plainly written and properly signed, for in such matters a good deal turns on handwriting. Yes, that will do. Now you understand, don't you, if anything goes wrong about the matter we have been talking of—that is, if the worthy John Castell is not rescued, or a smell of our little plot should get into the wind—this letter goes at once to the right quarter, and a certain secretary will wish that he had never been born. Man!" she added in a hissing whisper, "you shall die by inches as my sister did."

"A thousand doubloons if the thing succeeds, and you live to claim them," croaked old Israel. "I do not go back upon my word. Death and shame and torture or a thousand doubloons. Now he knows our terms, blindfold him again, Señor Bernaldez, and away with him, for he poisons the air. But first you, Inez, be gone and lodge that letter where you know."

****

That same night two cloaked figures, Peter and Bernaldez, were rowed in a little boat out to where the *Margaret* lay in the river, and, making her fast, slipped up the ship's side into the cabin. Here the stout English captain, Smith, was waiting for them, and so glad was the honest fellow to see Peter that he cast his arms about him and hugged him, for they had not met since that desperate adventure of the boarding of the *San Antonio*.

"Is your ship fit for sea, Captain?" asked Peter.

"She will never be fitter," he answered. "When shall I get sailing orders?"

"When the owner comes aboard," answered Peter.

"Then we shall stop here until we rot; they have trapped him in their Inquisition. What is in your mind, Peter Brome?—what is in your mind? Is there a chance?"

"Aye, Captain, I think so, if you have a dozen fellows of the right English stuff between decks."

"We have got that number, and one or two more. But what's the plan?"

Peter told him.

"Not so bad," said Smith, slapping his heavy hand upon his knee; "but risky—very risky. That Inez must be a good girl. I should like to marry her, notwithstanding her bygones."

Peter laughed, thinking what an odd couple they would make. "Hear the rest, then talk," he said. "See now! On Saturday next Mistress Margaret and I are to be married in the cathedral; then, towards sunset, the Marquis of Morella and I run our course in the great bull-ring yonder, and you and half a dozen of your men will be present. Now, I may conquer or I may fail—"

"Never!—never!" said the captain. "I wouldn't give a pair of old boots for that fine Spaniard's chance when you get at him. Why, you will crimp him like a cod-fish!"

"God knows!" answered Peter. "If I win, my wife and I make our adieux to their Majesties, and ride away to the quay, where the boat will be waiting, and you will row us on board the *Margaret*. If I fail, you will take up my body, and, accompanied by my widow, bring it in the same fashion on board the *Margaret*, for I shall give it out that in

440

this case I wish to be embalmed in wine and taken back to England for burial. In either event, you will drop your ship a little way down the river round the bend, so that folk may think that you have sailed. In the darkness you must work her back with the tide and lay her behind those old hulks, and if any ask you why, say that three of your men have not yet come aboard, and that you have dropped back for them, and whatever else you like. Then, in case I should not be alive to guide you, you and ten or twelve of the best sailors will land at the spot that this gentleman will show you to-morrow, wearing Spanish cloaks so as not to attract attention, but being well armed underneath them, like idlers from some ship who had come ashore to see the show. I have told you how you may know Master Castell. When you see him make a rush for him, cut down any that try to stop you, tumble him into the boat, and row for your lives to the ship, which will slip her moorings and get up her canvas as soon as she sees you coming, and begin to drop down the river with the tide and wind, if there is one. That is the plot, but God alone knows the end of it! which depends upon Him and the sailors. Will you play this game for the love of a good man and the rest of us? If you succeed, you shall be rich for life, all of you."

"Aye," answered the captain, "and there's my hand on it. So sure as my name is Smith, we will hook him out of that hell if men can do it, and not for the money either. Why, Peter, we have sat here idle so long, waiting for you and our lady, that we shall be glad of the fun. At any rate, there will be some dead Spaniards before they have done with us, and, if we are worsted, I'll leave the mate and enough hands upon the ship to bring her safe to Tilbury. But we won't be—we won't be. By this day week we will all be rolling homewards across the Bay with never a Spaniard within three hundred miles, you and your lady and Master Castell, too. I know it! I tell you, lad, I know it!"

"How do you know it?" asked Peter curiously.

"Because I dreamed it last night. I saw you and Mistress Margaret sitting sweet as sugar, with your arms around each other's middles, while I talked to the master, and the sun went down with the wind blowing stiff from sou-sou-west, and a gale threatening. I tell you that I dreamed it—I who am not given to dreams."

The Falcon Stoops

It was the marriage day of Margaret and Peter. Clad in white armour that had been sent to him as a present from the queen, a sign and a token of her good wishes for his success in his combat with Morella, wearing the insignia of a Knight of St. James hanging by a ribbon from his neck, his shield emblazoned with his coat of the stooping falcon, which appeared also upon the white cloak that hung from his shoulders, behind him a squire of high degree, who carried his plumed *casque* and lance, and accompanied by an escort of the royal guards, Peter rode from his quarters in the prison to the palace gates, and waited there as he had been bidden. Presently they opened, and through them, seated on a palfrey, appeared Margaret, wonderfully attired in white and silver, but with her veil lifted so that her face could be seen. She was companioned by a troop of maidens mounted, all of them, on white horses, and at her side, almost outshining her in glory of apparel, and attended by all her household, rode Betty, Marchioness of Morella—at any rate for that present time.

Although she could never be less than beautiful, it was a worn and pale Margaret who bowed her greetings to the bridegroom without those palace gates. What wonder, since she knew that within a few hours his life must be set upon the hazard of a desperate fray. What wonder, since she knew that to-morrow her father was doomed to be burnt living upon the Quemadero.

They met, they greeted; then, with silver trumpets blowing before them, the glittering procession wound its way through the narrow streets of Seville. But few words passed between them, whose hearts were too full for words, who had said all they had to say, and now abided the issue of events. Betty, however, whom many of the populace took for the bride, because her air was so much the happier of the two, would not be silent. Indeed she chid Margaret for her lack of gaiety upon such an occasion.

"Oh, Betty!—Betty!" answered Margaret, "how can I be gay, upon whose heart lies the burden of to-morrow?"

"A pest upon the burden of to-morrow!" exclaimed Betty. "The burden of to-day is enough for me, and that is not so bad to bear. Never shall we have another such ride as this, with all the world staring at us, and every woman in Seville envying us and our good looks and the favour of the queen."

"I think it is you they stare at and envy," said Margaret, glancing at the splendid woman at her side, whose beauty she knew well overshadowed her own rarer loveliness, at any rate in a street pageant, as in the sunshine the rose overshadows the lily.

"Well," answered Betty, "if so, it is because I put the better face on things, and smile even if my heart bleeds. At least, your lot is more hopeful than mine. If your husband has to fight to the death presently, so has mine, and between ourselves I favour Peter's chances. He is a very stubborn fighter, Peter, and wonderfully strong—too stubborn and strong for any Spaniard."

"Well, that is as it should be," said Margaret, smiling faintly, "seeing that Peter is your champion, and if he loses, you are stamped as a serving-girl, and a woman of no character."

"A serving-girl I was, or something not far different," replied Betty in a reflective voice, "and my character is a matter between me and Heaven, though, after all, it might scrape through where others fail to pass. So these things do not trouble me over much. What troubles me is that if my champion wins he kills my husband."

"You don't want him to be killed then?" asked Margaret, glancing at her.

"No, I think not," answered Betty with a little shake in her voice, and turning her head aside for a moment. "I know he is a scoundrel, but, you see, I always liked this scoundrel, just as you always hated him, so I cannot help wishing that he was going to meet some one who hits a little less hard than Peter. Also, if he dies, without doubt his heirs will raise suits against me."

"At any rate your father is not going to be burnt to-morrow," said Margaret to change the subject, which, to tell the truth, was an awkward one.

"No, Cousin, if my father had his deserts, according to all accounts, although the lineage that I gave of him is true enough, doubtless he was burnt long ago, and still goes on burning—in Purgatory, I mean—

though God knows I would never bring a faggot to his fire. But Master Castell will not be burnt, so why fret about it."

"What makes you say that?" asked Margaret, who had not confided the details of a certain plot to Betty.

"I don't know, but I am sure that Peter will get him out somehow. He is a very good stick to lean on, Peter, although he seems so hard and stupid and silent, which, after all, is in the nature of sticks. But look, there is the cathedral—is it not a fine place?—and a great crowd of people waiting round the gate. Now smile, Cousin. Bow and smile as I do."

They rode up to the great doors, where Peter, springing to the ground, assisted his bride from her palfrey. Then the procession formed, and they entered the wonderful place, preceded by vergers with staves, and by acolytes. Margaret had never visited it before, and never saw it again, but all her life the memory of it remained clear and vivid in her mind. The cold chill of the air within, the semi-darkness after the glare of the sunshine, the seven great naves, or aisles, stretching endlessly to right and left, the dim and towering roof, the pillars that sprang to it everywhere like huge forest trees aspiring to the skies, the solemn shadows pierced by lines of light from the high-cut windows, the golden glory of the altars, the sounds of chanting, the sepulchres of the dead—a sense of all these things rushed in upon her, overpowering her and stamping the picture of them for ever on her memory.

Slowly they passed onward to the choir, and round it to the steps of the great altar of the chief chapel. Here, between the choir and the chapel, was gathered the congregation—no small one—and here, side by side to the right and without the rails, in chairs of state, sat their Majesties of Spain, who had chosen to grace this ceremony with their presence. More, as the bride came, the queen Isabella, as a special act of grace, rose from her seat and, bending forward, kissed her on the cheek, while the choir sang and the noble music rolled. It was a splendid spectacle, this marriage of hers, celebrated in perhaps the most glorious fane in Europe. But even as Margaret noted it and watched the bishops and priests decked with glittering embroideries, summoned there to do her honour, as they moved to and fro in the mysterious ceremonial of the Mass, she bethought her of other rites equally glorious that would take place on the morrow in the greatest square of Seville, where these same dignitaries would condemn fellow human beings—perhaps among them her own father—to be married to the cruel flame.

Side by side they knelt before the wondrous altar, while the incense-clouds from the censers floated up one by one till they were lost in the gloom above, as the smoke of to-morrow's sacrifice would lose itself in the heavens, she and her husband, won at last, won after so many perils, perhaps to be lost again for ever before night fell upon the world. The priests chanted, the gorgeous bishop bowed over them and muttered the marriage service of their faith, the ring was set upon her hand, the troths were plighted, the benediction spoken, and they were man and wife till death should them part, that death which stood so near to them in this hour of life fulfilled. Then they two, who already that morning had made confession of their sins, kneeling alone before the altar, ate of the holy Bread, sealing a mystery with a mystery.

All was done and over, and rising, they turned and stayed a moment hand in hand while the sweet-voiced choir sang some wondrous chant. Margaret's eyes wandered over the congregation till presently they lighted upon the dark face of Morella, who stood apart a little way, surrounded by his squires and gentlemen, and watched her. More, he came to her, and bowing low, whispered to her:

"We are players in a strange game, my lady Margaret, and what will be its end, I wonder? Shall I be dead to-night, or you a widow? Aye, and where was its beginning? Not here, I think. And where, oh where shall this seed we sow bear fruit? Well, think as kindly of me as you can, since I loved you who love me not."

And again bowing, first to her, then to Peter, he passed on, taking no note of Betty, who stood near, considering him with her large eyes, as though she also wondered what would be the end of all this play.

Surrounded by their courtiers, the king and queen left the cathedral, and after them came the bridegroom and the bride. They mounted their horses and in the glory of the southern sunlight rode through the cheering crowd back to the palace and to the marriage feast, where their table was set but just below that of their Majesties. It was long and magnificent; but little could they eat, and, save to pledge each other in the ceremonial cup, no wine passed their lips. At length some trumpets blew, and their Majesties rose, the king saying in his thin, clear voice that he would not bid his guests farewell, since very shortly they would all meet again in another place, where the gallant bridegroom, a gentleman of England, would champion the cause of his relative and countrywoman against one of the first grandees of Spain whom she alleged had done her wrong. That fray, alas! would be no pleasure joust, but to the death, for the feud between these knights was deep and bitter, and such were the conditions of their combat. He could not wish success to the one or to the other; but of this he was sure, that in all Seville there was no heart that would not give equal honour to the conqueror and the conquered, sure also that both would bear themselves as became brave knights of Spain and England.

Then the trumpets blew again, and the squires and gentlemen who were chosen to attend him came bowing to Peter, and saying that it was time for him to arm. Bride and bridegroom rose and, while all the spectators fell back out of hearing, but watching them with curious eyes, spoke some few words together.

"We part," said Peter, "and I know not what to say."

"Say nothing, husband," she answered him, "lest your words should weaken me. Go now, and bear you bravely, as you will for your own honour and that of England, and for mine. Dead or living you are my darling, and dead or living we shall meet once more and be at rest for aye. My prayers be with you, Sir Peter, my prayers and my eternal love, and may they bring strength to your arm and comfort to your heart."

Then she, who would not embrace him before all those folk, curtseyed till her knee almost touched the ground, while low he bent before her, a strange and stately parting, or so thought that company; and taking the hand of Betty, Margaret left him.

****

Two hours had gone by. The Plaza de Toros, for the great square where tournaments were wont to be held was in the hands of those who prepared it for the *auto-da-fé* of the morrow, was crowded as it had seldom been before. This place was a huge amphitheatre—perchance the Romans built it—where all sorts of games were celebrated, among them the baiting of bulls as it was practised in those days, and other semi-savage sports. Twelve thousand people could sit upon the benches that rose tier upon tier around the vast theatre, and scarce a seat was empty. The arena itself, that was long enough for horses starting at either end of it to come to their full speed, was strewn with white sand, as it may have been in the days when gladiators fought there. Over the main entrance and opposite to the centre of the ring were placed the king and queen with their lords and ladies, and between them, but a little behind, her face hid by her bridal veil, sat Margaret, upright and silent as a statue. Exactly in front of them, on the further side of the ring in a pavilion, and attended by her household, appeared Betty, glittering with gold and jewels, since she was the lady in whose cause, at least in name, this combat was to be fought *à l'outrance*. Quite unmoved she sat, and her presence seemed to draw every eye in that vast assembly which talked of her while it waited, with a sound like the sound of the sea as it murmurs on a beach at night.

Now the trumpets blew, and silence fell, and then, preceded by heralds in golden tabards, Carlos, Marquis of Morella, followed by his squires, rode into the ring through the great entrance. He bestrode a splendid black horse, and was arrayed in coal-black armour, while from his *casque* rose black ostrich plumes. On his shield, however, painted in scarlet, appeared the eagle crowned with the coronet of his rank, and beneath, the proud motto—"What I seize I tear." A splendid figure, he pressed his horse into the centre of the arena, then causing it to wheel round, pawing the air with its forelegs, saluted their Majesties by raising his long, steel-tipped lance, while the multitude greeted him with a shout. This done, he and his company rode away to their station at the north end of the ring.

Again the trumpets sounded, and a herald appeared, while after him, mounted on a white horse, and clad in his white armour that glistened in the sun, with white plumes rising from his *casque*, and on his shield the stooping falcon blazoned in gold with the motto of "For love and honour" beneath it, appeared the tall, grim shape of Sir Peter Brome. He, too, rode out into the centre of the arena, and, turning his horse quite soberly, as though it were on a road, lifted his lance in salute. Now there was no cheering, for this knight was a foreigner, yet soldiers who were there said to each other that he looked like one who would not easily be overthrown.

A third time the trumpets sounded, and the two champions, advancing from their respective stations, drew rein side by side in front of their Majesties, where the conditions of the combat were read aloud to them by the chief herald. They were short. That the fray should be to the death unless the king and queen willed otherwise and the victor consented; that it should be on horse or on foot, with lance or sword or dagger, but that no broken weapon might be replaced and no horse or armour changed; that the victor should be escorted from the place of combat with all honour, and allowed to depart whither he would, in the kingdom or out of it, and no suit or blood-feud raised against him; and that the body of the fallen be handed over to his friends for burial, also with all honour. That the issue of this fray should in no way affect any cause pleaded in Courts ecclesiastical or civil, by the lady who asserted herself to be the Marchioness of Morella, or by the most noble Marquis of Morella, whom she claimed as her husband.

These conditions having been read, the champions were asked if they assented to them, whereon each of them answered, "Aye!" in a clear voice. Then the herald, speaking on behalf of Sir Peter Brome, by creation a knight of St. Iago and a Don of Spain, solemnly challenged the noble Marquis of Morella to single combat to the death, in that he, the said marquis, had aspersed the name of his relative, the English lady, Elizabeth Dene, who claimed to be his wife, duly united to him in holy wedlock, and for sundry other causes and injuries worked towards him, the said Sir Peter Brome, and his wife, Dame Margaret Brome, and in token thereof, threw down a gauntlet, which gauntlet the Marquis of Morella lifted upon the point of his lance and cast over his shoulder, thus accepting the challenge.

Now the combatants dropped their visors, which heretofore had been raised, and their squires, coming forward, examined the fastenings of their armour, their weapons, and the girths and bridles of their horses. These being pronounced sound and good, pursuivants took the steeds by the bridles and led them to the far ends of the lists. At a signal from the king a single clarion blew, whereon the pursuivants loosed their hold of the bridles and sprang back. Another clarion blew, and the knights gathered up their reins, settled their shields, and set their lances in rest, bending forward over their horses' necks.

An intense silence fell upon all the watching multitude as that of night upon the sea, and in the midst of it the third clarion blew—to Margaret it sounded like the trump of doom. From twelve thousand throats one great sigh went up, like the sigh of wind upon the sea, and ere it died away, from either end of the arena, like arrows from the bow, like levens from a cloud, the champions started forth, their stallions gathering speed at every stride. Look, they met! Fair on each shield struck a lance, and backward reeled their holders. The keen points glanced aside or up, and the knights, recovering themselves, rushed past each other, shaken but unhurt. At the ends of the lists the squires caught the horses by the bridles and turned them. The first course was run.

Again the clarions blew, and again they started forward, and presently again they met in mid career. As before, the lances struck upon the shields; but so fearful was the impact, that Peter's shivered, while that of Morella, sliding from the topmost rim of his foe's buckler, got hold in his visor bars. Back went Peter beneath the blow, back and still back, till almost he lay upon his horse's crupper. Then, when it seemed that he must fall, the lacings of his helm burst. It was torn from his head, and Morella passed on bearing it transfixed upon his spear point.

"The Falcon falls," screamed the spectators; "he is unhorsed."

But Peter was not unhorsed. Freed from that awful pressure, he let drop the shattered shaft and, grasping at his saddle strap, dragged

448

himself back into the *selle*. Morella tried to stay his charger, that he might come about and fall upon the Englishman before he could recover himself; but the brute was heady, and would not be turned till he saw the wall of faces in front of him. Now they were round, both of them, but Peter had no spear and no helm, while the lance of Morella was cumbered with his adversary's *casque* that he strove to shake free from it, but in vain.

"Draw your sword," shouted voices to Peter—the English voices of Smith and his sailors—and he put his hand down to do so, then bethought him of some other counsel, for he let it lie within its scabbard, and, spurring the white horse, came at Morella like a storm.

"The Falcon will be spiked," they screamed. "The Eagle wins!—the Eagle wins!" And indeed it seemed that it must be so. Straight at Peter's undefended face drove Morella's lance, but lo! as it came he let fall his reins and with his shield he struck at the white plumes about its point, the plumes torn from his own head. He had judged well, for up flew those plumes, a little, a very little, yet far enough to give him space, crouching on his saddle-bow, to pass beneath the deadly spear. Then, as they swept past each other, out shot that long, right arm of his and, gripping Morella like a hook of steel, tore him from his saddle, so that the black horse rushed forward riderless, and the white sped on bearing a double burden.

Grasping desperately, Morella threw his arms about his neck, and intertwined, black armour mixed with white, they swayed to and fro, while the frightened horse beneath rushed this way and that till, swerving suddenly, together they fell upon the sand, and for a moment lay there stunned.

"Who conquers?" gasped the crowd; while others answered, "Both are sped!" And, leaning forward in her chair, Margaret tore off her veil and watched with a face like the face of death.

See! As they had fallen together, so together they stirred and rose—rose unharmed. Now they sprang back, out flashed the long swords, and, while the squires caught the horses and, running in, seized the broken spears, they faced each other. Having no helm, Peter held his buckler above his head to shelter it, and, ever calm, awaited the onslaught.

At him came Morella, and with a light, grating sound his sword fell upon the steel. Before he could recover himself Peter struck back; but Morella bent his knees, and the stroke only shore the black plumes from his *casque*. Quick as light he drove at Peter's face with his point; but the Englishman leapt to one side, and the thrust went past him. Again Morella came at him, and struck so mighty a blow that, although Peter caught it on his buckler, it sliced through the edge of it and fell upon his unprotected neck and shoulder, wounding him, for now red blood showed on the white armour, and Peter reeled back beneath the stroke.

"The Eagle wins!—the Eagle wins! Spain and the Eagle" shouted ten thousand throats. In the momentary silence that followed, a single voice, a clear woman's voice, which even then Margaret knew for that of Inez, cried from among the crowd:

"Nay, the Falcon stoops!"

Before the sound of her words died away, maddened it would seem, by the pain of his wound, or the fear of defeat, Peter shouted out his war-cry of *"A Brome! A Brome"*! and, gathering himself together, sprang straight at Morella as springs a starving wolf. The blue steel flickered in the sunlight, then down it fell, and lo! half the Spaniard's helm lay on the sand, while it was Morella's turn to reel backward—and more, as he did so, he let fall his shield.

"A stroke!—a good stroke!" roared the crowd. "The Falcon!—the Falcon!"

Peter saw that fallen shield, and whether for chivalry's sake, as thought the cheering multitude, or to free his left arm, he cast away his own, and grasping the sword with both hands rushed on the Spaniard. From that moment, helmless though he was, the issue lay in doubt no longer. Betty had spoken of Peter as a stubborn swordsman and a hard hitter, and both of these he now showed himself to be. As fresh to all appearance as when he ran the first course, he rained blow after blow upon the hapless Spaniard, till the sound of his sword smiting on the good Toledo steel was like the sound of a hammer falling continually on the smith's red iron. They were fearful blows, yet still the tough steel held, and still Morella, doing what he might, staggered back beneath them, till at length he came in front of the tribune, in which sat their Majesties and Margaret. Out of the corner of his eye Peter saw the place, and determined in his stout heart that then and there he would end the thing. Parrying a cut which the desperate Spaniard made at his head, he thrust at him so heavily that his blade bent like a bow, and, although he could not pierce the black mail, almost lifted Morella from his feet. Then, as he reeled backwards, Peter whirled his sword on high, and, shouting *"Margaret!"* struck downwards with all his strength. It fell as lightning falls, swift, keen, dazzling the eyes of all who watched. Morella raised his arm to break the blow. In vain! The weapon that he held was shattered, the *casque* beneath was cloven, and, throwing his arms wide, he fell heavily to the ground and lay there moving feebly.

For an instant there was silence, and in it a shrill woman's voice that cried: "The Falcon has stooped. The English hawk *has stooped!*"

Then there arose a tumult of shouting. "He is dead!" "Nay, he stirs." "Kill him!" "Spare him; he fought well!"

Peter leaned upon his sword, looking at the fallen foe. Then he glanced upwards at their Majesties, but these sat silent, making no sign, only he saw Margaret try to rise from her seat and speak, to be pulled back to it again by the hands of women. A deep hush fell upon the watching thousands who waited for the end. Peter looked at Morella. Alas! he still lived, his sword and the stout helmet had broken the weight of that stroke, mighty though it had been. The man was but wounded in three places and stunned. "What must I do?" asked Peter in a hollow voice to the royal pair above him.

Now the king, who seemed moved, was about to speak; but the queen bent forward and whispered something to him, and he remained silent. They both were silent. All the intent multitude was silent. Knowing what this dreadful silence meant, Peter cast down his sword and drew his dagger, wherewith to cut the lashings of Morella's *gorget* and give the *coup de grâce*.

Just then it was that for the first time he heard a sound, far away upon the other side of the arena, and, looking thither, saw the strangest sight that ever his eyes beheld. Over the railing of the pavilion opposite to him a woman climbed nimbly as a cat, and from it, like a cat, dropped to the ground full ten feet below, then, gathering up her dress about her knees, ran swiftly towards him. It was Betty! Betty without a doubt! Betty in her gorgeous garb, with pearls and braided hair flying loose behind her. He stared amazed. All stared amazed, and in half a minute she was on them, and, standing over the fallen Morella, gasped out:

"Let him be! I bid you let him be."

Peter knew not what to do or say, so advanced to speak with her, whereon with a swoop like that of a swallow she pounced upon his sword that lay in the sand and, leaping back to Morella, shook it on high, shouting:

"You will have to fight me first, Peter."

Indeed, she did more, striking at him so shrewdly with his own sword that he was forced to spring sideways to avoid the stroke. Now a great roar of laughter went up to heaven. Yes, even Peter laughed, for no such thing as this had ever before been seen in Spain. It died away, and again Betty, who had no low voice, shouted in her villainous Spanish:

"He shall kill me before he kills my husband. Give me my husband!"

"Take him, for my part," answered Peter, whereon, letting fall the sword, Betty, filled with the strength of despair, lifted the senseless Spaniard in her strong white arms as though he were a child, and his bleeding head lying on her shoulder, strove to carry him away, but could not.

Then, while all that audience cheered frantically, Peter with a gesture of despair threw down his dagger and once more appealed to their Majesties. The king rose and held up his hand, at the same time motioning to Morella's squires to take him from the woman, which, seeing their cognizance, Betty allowed them to do.

"Marchioness of Morella," said the king, for the first time giving her that title, "your honour is cleared, your champion has conquered, and this fierce fray was to the death. What have you to say?"

"Nothing," answered Betty, "except that I love the man, though he has treated me and others ill, and, as I knew he would if he crossed swords with Peter, has got his deserts for his deeds. I say I love him, and if Peter wishes to kill him, he must kill me first."

"Sir Peter Brome," said the king, "the judgment lies in your hand. We give you the man's life, to grant or to take."

Peter thought a while, then answered: "I grant him his life if he will acknowledge this lady to be his true and lawful wife, and live with her as such, now and for ever, staying all suits against her."

"How can he do that, you fool," asked Betty, "when you have knocked all his senses out of him with that great sword of yours?"

"Perhaps," suggested Peter humbly, "some one will do it for him."

"Yes," said Isabella, speaking for the first time, "I will. On behalf of the Marquis of Morella I promise these things, Don Peter Brome, before all these people here gathered. I add this: that if he should live, and it pleases him to break this promise made on his behalf to save him from death, then let his name be shamed, yes, let it become a byword and a scorn. Proclaim it, heralds."

So the heralds blew their trumpets and one of them called out the queen's decree, whereat the spectators cheered again, shouting that it was good, and they bore witness to that promise.

Then Morella, still senseless, was borne away by his squires, Betty in her blood-stained robe marching at his side, and his horse having been brought to him again, Peter, wounded though he was, mounted and galloped round the arena amidst plaudits such as that place had never heard, till, lifting his sword in salutation, suddenly he and his gentlemen vanished by the gate through which he had appeared.

Thus strangely enough ended that combat which thereafter was always known as the Fray of the Eagle and the English Hawk.

How the Margaret Won Out to Sea

It was night. Peter, faint with loss of blood and stiff with bruises, had bade his farewell to their Majesties of Spain, who spoke many soft words to him, calling him the Flower of Knighthood, and offering him high place and rank if he would abide in their service. But he thanked them and said No, for in Spain he had suffered too much to dwell there. So they kissed his bride, the fair Margaret, who clung to her wounded husband like ivy to an oak, and would not be separated from him, even for a moment, that husband whom living she had scarcely hoped to clasp again. Yes, they kissed her, and the queen threw about her a chain from her own neck as a parting gift, and wished her joy of so gallant a lord.

"Alas! your Majesty," said Margaret, her dark eyes filling with tears, "how can I be joyous, who must think of to-morrow?"

Thereon Isabella set her face and answered:

"Dona Margaret Brome, be thankful for what to-day has brought you, and forget to-morrow and that which it must justly take away. Go now, and God be with you both!"

So they went, the little knot of English sailormen, who, wrapped in Spanish cloaks, had sat together in the amphitheatre and groaned when the Eagle struck, and cheered when the Falcon swooped, leading, or rather carrying Peter under cover of the falling night to a boat not far from this Place of Bulls. In this they embarked unobserved, for the multitude, and even Peter's own squires believed that he had returned with his wife to the palace, as he had given out that he would do. So they were rowed to the *Margaret*, which straightway made as though she were about to sail, and indeed dropped a little way down stream. Here she anchored again, just round a bend of the river, and lay there for the night.

It was a heavy night, and in it there was no place for love or lovers' tenderness. How could there be between these two, who for so long had been tormented by doubts and fears, and on this day had endured such extremity of terror and such agony of joy? Peter's wound also was deep and wide, though his shield had broken the weight of Morella's sword, and its edge had caught upon his shoulder-piece, so that by good chance it had not reached down to the arteries, or shorn into the bone; yet he had lost much blood, and Smith, the captain, who was a better surgeon than might have been guessed from his thick hands, found it needful to wash out the cut with spirit that gave much pain, and to stitch it up with silk. Also Peter had great bruises on his arms and thighs, and his back was hurt by that fall from the white charger with Morella in his arms.

So it came about that most of that night he lay outworn, half-sleeping and half-waking, and when at sunrise he struggled from his berth, it was but to kneel by the side of Margaret and join her in her prayers that her father might be rescued from the hands of these cruel priests of Spain.

Now during the night Smith had brought his ship back with the tide, and laid her under the shelter of those hulks whereof Peter had spoken, having first painted out her name of *Margaret*, and in its place set that of the *Santa Maria*, a vessel of about the same build and tonnage, which, as they had heard, was expected in port. For this reason, or because there were at that time many ships in the river, it happened that none in authority noted her return, or if they did, neglected to report the matter as one of no moment. Therefore, so far all went well.

According to the tale of Henriques, confirmed by what they had learned otherwise, the great procession of the Act of Faith would turn on to the quay at about eight o'clock, and pass along it for a hundred yards or so only, before it wound away down a street leading to the *plaza* where the theatre was prepared, the sermon would be preached, the Mass celebrated, and the "relaxed" placed in cages to be carried to the Quemadero.

At six in the morning Smith mustered those twelve men whom he had chosen to help him in the enterprise, and Peter, with Margaret at his side, addressed them in the cabin, telling them all the plan, and praying them for the sake of their master and of the Lady Margaret, his daughter, to do what men might to save one whom they loved and honoured from so horrible a death.

They swore that they would, every one of them, for their English blood was up, nor did they so much as speak of the great rewards that had been promised to those who lived through this adventure, and to the families of those who fell. Then they breakfasted, girded their swords and knives about them, and put on their Spanish cloaks, though, to speak truth, these lads of Essex and of London made but poor Spaniards. Now, at length the boat was ready, and Peter, although he could scarcely stand, desired to be carried into it that he might accompany them. But the captain, Smith, to whom perhaps Margaret had been speaking, set down his flat foot on the deck and said that he, who commanded there, would suffer no such thing. A wounded man, he declared, would but cumber them who had little room to spare in that small boat, and could be of no service, either on land or water. Moreover, Master Peter's face was known to thousands who had watched it yesterday, and would certainly be recognised, whereas none would take note at such a time of a dozen common sailors landed from some ship to see the show. Lastly, he would do best to stop on board the vessel, where, if anything went wrong, they must be short-handed enough, who, if they could, ought to get her away to sea and across it with all speed.

Still Peter would have gone, till Margaret, throwing her arms about him, asked him if he thought that she would be the better if she lost both her father and her husband, as, if things miscarried, well might happen. Then, being in pain and very weak, he yielded, and Smith, having given his last directions to the mate, and shaken Peter and Margaret by the hand, asking their prayers for all of them, descended with his twelve men into the boat, and dropping down under shelter of the hulks, rowed to the shore as though they came from some other vessel. Now the quay was not more than a bowshot from them, and from a certain spot upon the *Margaret* there was a good view of it between the stern of one hulk and the bow of another. Here, then, Peter and Margaret sat themselves down behind the bulwark, and watched with fears such as cannot be told, while a sharp-eyed seaman climbed to the crow's-nest on the mast, whence he could see over much of the city, and even the old Moorish castle that was then the Holy House of the Inquisition. Presently this man reported that the procession had started, for he saw its banners and the people crowding to the windows and to the roof-tops; also the cathedral bell began to toll slowly. Then came a long, long wait, during which their little knot of sailors, wearing the Spanish cloaks, appeared upon the quay and mingled with the few folk that were gathered there, since the most of the people were collected by thousands on the great *plaza* or in the adjacent streets.

At length, just as the cathedral clock struck eight, the "triumphant" march, as it was called, began to appear upon the quay. First came a body of soldiers with lances; then a crucifix, borne by a priest and veiled in black crape; then a number of other priests, clad in snow-white robes to symbolise their perfect purity. Next followed men carrying wood or leather images of some man or woman who, by flight to a foreign land or into the realms of Death, had escaped the clutches of the Inquisition. After these marched other men in fours, each four of them bearing a coffin that contained the body or bones of some dead heretic, which, in the absence of his living person, like the effigies, were to be committed to the flames as a token of what the Inquisition would have done to him if it could—to enable it also to seize his property.

Then came many penitents, their heads shaven, their feet bare, and clad, some in dark-coloured cloaks, some in yellow robes, called the *sanbenito*, which were adorned with a red cross. These were followed by a melancholy band of "relaxed" heretics, doomed to the fire or strangulation at the stake, and clothed in *zamarras* of sheepskin, painted all over with devils and the portraits of their own faces surrounded by flames. These poor creatures wore also flame-adorned caps called *corozas*, shaped like bishops' mitres, and were gagged with blocks of wood, lest they should contaminate the populace by some declaration of their heresy, while in their hands they bore tapers, which the monks who accompanied them relighted from time to time if they became extinguished.

Now the hearts of Peter and Margaret leaped within them, for at the end of this hideous troop rode a man mounted on an ass, clothed in a *zamarra* and *coroza*, but with a noose about his neck. So the Fray Henriques had told the truth, for without doubt this was John Castell. Like people in a dream, they saw him advance in his garb of shame, and after him, gorgeously attired, civil officers, inquisitors, and familiars of noble rank, members of the Council of Inquisition, behind whom was borne a flaunting banner, called the Holy Standard of the Faith.

Now Castell was opposite to the little group of seamen, and, or so it seemed, something went wrong with the harness of the ass on which he sat, for it stopped, and a man in the garb of a secretary stepped to it, apparently to attend to a strap, thus bringing all the procession behind to a halt, while that in front proceeded off the quay and round the corner of a street. Whatever it might be that had happened, it necessitated the dismounting of the heretic, who was pulled roughly off the brute's back, which, as though in joy at this riddance of its burden, lifted its head and brayed loudly.

Men from the thin line of crowd that edged the quay came forward as though to help, and among them were several in capes, such as were worn by the sailors of the *Margaret*. The officers and grandees behind shouted, "Forward!—forward!" whereon those attending to the ass hustled it and its rider a little nearer to the water's edge, while the guards ran back to explain what had happened. Then suddenly a confusion arose, of which it was impossible to distinguish the cause, and next instant Margaret and Peter, still gripping each other, saw the man who had been seated on the ass being dragged rapidly down the steps of the quay, at the foot of which lay the boat of the *Margaret*.

The mate at the helm saw also, for he blew his whistle, a sign at which the anchor was slipped—there was no time to lift it—and men who were waiting on the yards loosed the lashings of certain sails, so that almost immediately the ship began to move.

Now they were fighting on the quay. The heretic was in the boat, and most of the sailors; but others held back the crowd of priests and armed familiars who strove to get at him. One, a priest with a sword in his hand, slipped past them and tumbled into the boat also. At last all were in save a single man, who was attacked by three adversaries—John Smith, the captain. The oars were out, but his mates waited for him. He struck with his sword, and some one fell. Then he turned to run. Two masked familiars sprang at him, one landing on his back, one clinging to his neck. With a desperate effort he cast himself into the water, dragging them with him. One they saw no more, for Smith had stabbed him, the other floated up near the boat, which already was some yards from the quay, and a sailor battered him on the head with an oar, so that he sank.

Smith had vanished also, and they thought he must be drowned. The sailors thought it too, for they began to give way, when suddenly a great brown hand appeared and clasped the stern-sheets, while a bull-voice roared:

"Row on, lads, I'm right enough."

Row they did indeed, till the ashen oars bent like bows, only two of them seized the officer who had sprung into the boat and flung him screaming into the river, where he struggled a while, for he could not swim, gripping at the air with his hands, then disappeared. The boat was in mid-stream now, and shaping her course round the bow of the first hulk beyond which the prow of the *Margaret* began to appear, for the wind was fresh, and she gathered way every moment.

"Let down the ladder, and make ready ropes," shouted Peter.

It was done, but not too soon, for next instant the boat was bumping on their side. The sailors in her caught the ropes and hung on, while the captain, Smith, half-drowned, clung to the stern-sheets, for the water washed over his head.

"Save him first," cried Peter. A man, running down the ladder, threw a noose to him, which Smith seized with one hand and by degrees worked beneath his arms. Then they tackled on to it, and dragged him bodily from the river to the deck, where he lay gasping and spitting out foam and water. By now the ship was travelling swiftly, so swiftly that Margaret was in an agony of fear lest the boat should be towed under and sink.

But these sailor men knew their trade. By degrees they let the boat drop back till her bow was abreast of the ladder. Then they helped Castell forward. He gripped its rungs, and eager hands gripped him. Up he staggered, step by step, till at length his hideous, fiend-painted cap, his white face, whence the beard had been shaved, and his open mouth, in which still was fixed the wooden gag, appeared above the bulwarks, as the mate said afterwards, like that of a devil escaped from hell. They lifted him over, and he sank fainting in his daughter's arms. Then one by one the sailors came up after him—none were missing, though two had been wounded, and were covered with blood. No, none were missing—God had brought them, every one, safe back to the deck of the *Margaret*.

Smith, the captain, spat up the last of his river water and called for a cup of wine, which he drank; while Peter and Margaret drew the accursed gag from her father's mouth, and poured spirit down his throat. Shaking the water from him like a great dog, but saying never a word, Smith rolled to the helm and took it from the mate, for the navigation of the river was difficult, and none knew it so well as he. Now they were abreast the famous Golden Tower, and a big gun was fired at them; but the shot went wide. "Look!" said Margaret, pointing to horsemen galloping southwards along the river's bank.

"Yes," said Peter, "they go to warn the ports. God send that the wind holds, for we must fight our way to sea."

The wind did hold, indeed it blew ever more strongly from the north; but oh! that was a long, evil day. Hour after hour they sped forward down the widening river; now past villages, where knots of people waved weapons at them as they went; now by desolate marshes, plains, and banks clothed with pine.

When they reached Bonanza the sun was low, and when they were off San Lucar it had begun to sink. Out into the wide river

458

mouth, where the white waters tumbled on the narrow bar, rowed two great galleys to cut them off, very swift galleys, which it seemed impossible to escape.

Margaret and Castell were sent below, the crew went to quarters, and Peter crept stiffly aft to where the sturdy Smith stood at the helm, which he would suffer no other man to touch. Smith looked at the sky, he looked at the shore, and the safe, open sea beyond. Then he bade them hoist more sail, all that she could carry, and looked grimly at the two galleys lurking like deerhounds in a pass, that hung on their oars in the strait channel, with the tumbling breakers on either side, through which no ship could sail. "What will you do?" asked Peter. "Master Peter," he answered between his teeth, "when you fought the Spaniard yesterday I did not ask you what *you* were going to do. Hold your tongue, and leave me to my own trade."

The *Margaret* was a swift ship, but never yet had she moved so swiftly. Behind her shrilled the gale, for now it was no less. Her stout masts bent like fishing poles, her rigging creaked and groaned beneath the weight of the bellying canvas, her port bulwarks slipped along almost level with the water, so that Peter must lie down on the deck, for stand he could not, and watch it running by within three feet of him.

The galleys drew up right across her path. Half a mile away they lay bow by bow, knowing well that no ship could pass the foaming shallows; lay bow by bow, waiting to board and cut down this little English crew when the *Margaret* shortened sail, as shorten sail she must. Smith yelled an order to the mate, and presently, red in the setting sun, out burst the flag of England upon the mainmast top, a sight at which the sailors cheered. He shouted another order, and up ran the last jib, so that now from time to time the port bulwarks dipped beneath the sea, and Peter felt salt water stinging his sore back.

Thus did the *Margaret* shorten sail, and thus did she yield her to the great galleys of Spain.

The captains of the galleys hung on. Was this foreigner mad, or ignorant of the river channel, they wondered, that he would sink with every soul there upon the bar? They hung on, waiting for that leopard flag and those bursting sails to come down; but they never stirred; only straight at them rushed the *Margaret* like a bull. She was not two furlongs away, and she held dead upon her course, till at last those galleys saw *that she would not sink alone.* Like a bull with shut eyes she held dead upon her furious course!

Confusion arose upon the Spanish ships, whistles were blown, men shouted, overseers ran down the planks flogging the slaves, lifted oars shone red in the light of the dying sun as they beat the water wildly. The prows began to back and separate, five feet, ten feet, a dozen feet perhaps; then straight into that tiny streak of open water, like a stone from the hand of the slinger, like an arrow from a bow, rushed the wind-flung *Margaret*.

What happened? Go ask it of the fishers of San Lucar and the pirates of Bonanza, where the tale has been told for generations. The great oars snapped like reeds, the slaves were thrown in crushed and mangled heaps, the tall deck of the port galley was ripped out of her like rent paper by the stout yards of the stooping *Margaret*, the side of the starboard galley rolled up like a shaving before a plane, and the *Margaret* rushed through.

Smith, the captain, looked aft to where, ere they sank, the two great ships, like wounded swans, rolled and fluttered on the foaming bar. Then he put his helm about, called the carpenter, and asked what water she made.

"None, Sir," he answered; "but she will want new tarring. It was oak against eggshells, and we had the speed."

"Good!" said Smith, "shallows on either side; life or death, and I thought I could make room. Send the mate to the helm. I'll have a sleep."

Then the sun vanished beneath the roaring open sea, and, escaped from all the power of Spain, the *Margaret* turned her scarred and splintered bow for Ushant and for England.

Envoi

Ten years had gone by since Captain Smith took the good ship *Margaret* across the bar of the Guadalquiver in a very notable fashion. It was late May in Essex, and all the woods were green, and all the birds sang, and all the meadows were bright with flowers. Down in the lovely vale of Dedham there was a long, low house with many gables—a charming old house of red brick and timbers already black with age. It stood upon a little hill, backed with woods, and from it a long avenue of ancient oaks ran across the park to the road which led to Colchester and London. Down that avenue on this May afternoon an aged, white-haired man, with quick black eyes, was walking, and with him three children—very beautiful children—a boy of about nine and two little girls, who clung to his hand and garments and pestered him with questions.

"Where are we going, Grandfather?" asked one little girl.

"To see Captain Smith, my dear," he answered.

"I don't like Captain Smith," said the other little girl; "he is so fat, and says nothing."

"I do," broke in the boy, "he gave me a fine knife to use when I am a sailor, and Mother does, and Father, yes, and Grandad too, because he saved him when the cruel Spaniards wanted to put him in the fire. Don't you, Grandad?"

"Yes, my dear," answered the old man. "Look! there is a squirrel running over the grass; see if you can catch it before it reaches that tree."

Off went the children at full pelt, and the tree being a low one, began to climb it after the squirrel. Meanwhile John Castell, for it was he, turned through the park gate and walked to a little house by the roadside, where a stout man sat upon a bench contemplating nothing in particular. Evidently he expected his visitor, for he pointed to the place beside him, and, as Castell sat down, said:

"Why didn't you come yesterday, Master?"

"Because of my rheumatism, friend," he answered. "I got it first in the vaults of that accursed Holy House at Seville, and it grows on me year by year. They were very damp and cold, those vaults," he added reflectively.

"Many people found them hot enough," grunted Smith, "also, there was generally a good fire at the end of them. Strange thing that we should never have heard any more of that business. I suppose it was because our Margaret was such a favourite with Queen Isabella who didn't want to raise questions with England, or stir up dirty water."

"Perhaps," answered Castell. "The water *was* dirty, wasn't it?"

"Dirty as a Thames mud-bank at low tide. Clever woman, Isabella. No one else would have thought of making a man ridiculous as she did by Morella when she gave his life to Betty, and promised and vowed on his behalf that he would acknowledge her as his lady. No fear of any trouble from him after that, in the way of plots for the Crown, or things of that sort. Why, he must have been the laughing-stock of the whole land—and a laughing-stock never does anything. You remember the Spanish saying, 'King's swords cut and priests' fires burn, but street-songs kill quickest!' I should like to learn more of what has become of them all, though, wouldn't you, Master? Except Bernaldez, of course, for he's been safe in Paris these many years, and doing well there, they say."

"Yes," answered Castell, with a little smile—"that is, unless I had to go to Spain to find out."

Just then the three children came running up, bursting through the gate all together.

"Mind my flower-bed, you little rogues," shouted Captain Smith, shaking his stick at them, whereat they got behind him and made faces.

"Where's the squirrel, Peter?" asked Castell.

"We hunted it out of the tree, Grandad, and right across the grass, and got round it by the edge of the brook, and then—"

"Then what? Did you catch it?"

"No, Grandad, for when we thought we had it sure, it jumped into the water and swam away."

"Other people in a fix have done that before," said Castell, laughing, and bethinking him of a certain river quay.

"It wasn't fair," cried the boy indignantly. "Squirrels shouldn't swim, and if I can catch it I will put it in a cage."

"I think that squirrel will stop in the woods for the rest of its life, Peter."

"Grandad!—Grandad!" called out the youngest child from the gate, whither she had wandered, being weary of the tale of the squirrel, "there are a lot of people coming down the road on horses, such fine people. Come and see."

This news excited the curiosity of the old gentlemen, for not many fine people came to Dedham. At any rate both of them rose, somewhat stiffly, and walked to the gate to look. Yes, the child was right, for there, sure enough, about two hundred yards away, advanced an imposing cavalcade. In front of it, mounted on a fine horse, sat a still finer lady, a very large and handsome lady, dressed in black silks, and wearing a black lace veil that hung from her head. At her side was another lady, much muffled up as though she found the climate cold, and riding between them, on a pony, a gallant looking little boy. After these came servants, male and female, six or eight of them, and last of all a great wain, laden with baggage, drawn by four big Flemish horses.

"Now, whom have we here?" ejaculated Castell, staring at them.

Captain Smith stared too, and sniffed at the wind as he had often done upon his deck on a foggy morning.

"I seem to smell Spaniards," he said, "which is a smell I don't like. Look at their rigging. Now, Master Castell, of whom does that barque with all her sails set remind you?"

Castell shook his head doubtfully.

"I seem to remember," went on Smith, "a great girl decked out like a maypole running across white sand in that Place of Bulls at Seville—but I forgot, you weren't there, were you?"

Now a loud, ringing voice was heard speaking in Spanish, and commanding some one to go to yonder house and inquire where was the gate to the Old Hall. Then Castell knew at once.

"It is Betty," he said. "By the beard of Abraham, it is Betty."

"I think so too; but don't talk of Abraham, Master. He is a dangerous man, Abraham, in these very Christian lands; say, 'By the Keys of St. Peter,' or, 'By St. Paul's infirmities.'"

"Child," broke in Castell, turning to one of the little girls, "run up to the Hall and tell your father and mother that Betty has come, and brought half Spain with her. Quickly now, and remember the name, *Betty!*"

The child departed, wondering, by the back way; while Castell and Smith walked towards the strangers.

"Can we assist you, Señora?" asked the former in Spanish.

"Marchioness of Morella, *if* you please—" she began in the same language, then suddenly added in English, "Why, bless my eyes! If it isn't my old master, John Castell, with white wool instead of black!"

"It came white after my shaving by a sainted barber in the Holy House," said Castell. "But come off that tall horse of yours, Betty, my dear—I beg your pardon—most noble and highly born Marchioness of Morella, and give me a kiss."

"That I will, twenty, if you like," she answered, arriving in his arms so suddenly from on high, that had it not been for the sturdy support of Smith behind, they would both of them have rolled upon the ground.

"Whose are those children?" she asked, when she had kissed Castell and shaken Smith by the hand. "But no need to ask, they have got my cousin Margaret's eyes and Peter's long nose. How are they?" she added anxiously.

"You will see for yourself in a minute or two. Come, send on your people and baggage to the Hall, though where they will stow them all I don't know, and walk with us."

Betty hesitated, for she had been calculating upon the effect of a triumphal entry in full state. But at that moment there appeared Margaret and Peter themselves—Margaret, a beautiful matron with a child in her arms, running, and Peter, looking much as he had always been, spare, long of limb, stern but for the kindly eyes, striding away behind, and after him sundry servants and the little girl Margaret.

Then there arose a veritable babble of tongues, punctuated by embracings; but in the end the retinue and the baggage were got off up the drive, followed by the children and the little Spanish-looking boy, with whom they had already made friends, leaving only Betty and her closely muffled-up attendant. This attendant Peter contemplated for a while, as though there were something familiar to him in her general air.

Apparently she observed his interest, for as though by accident she moved some of the wrappings that hid her face, revealing a single soft and lustrous eye and a few square inches of olive-coloured cheek. Then Peter knew her at once.

"How are you, Inez?" he said, stretching out his hand with a smile, for really he was delighted to see her.

"As well as a poor wanderer in a strange and very damp country can be, Don Peter," she answered in her languorous voice, "and certainly somewhat the better for seeing an old friend whom last she met in a certain baker's shop. Do you remember?"

"Remember!" answered Peter. "It is not a thing I am likely to forget. Inez, what became of Fray Henriques? I have heard several different stories."

"One never can be sure," she answered as she uncovered her smiling red lips; "there are so many dungeons in that old Moorish Holy

House, and elsewhere, that it is impossible to keep count of their occupants, however good your information. All I know is that he got into trouble over that business, poor man. Suspicions arose about his conduct in the procession which the captain here will recall," and she pointed to Smith. "Also, it is very dangerous for men in such positions to visit Jewish quarters and to write incautious letters—no, not the one you think of; I kept faith—but others, afterwards, begging for it back again, some of which miscarried."

"Is he dead then?" asked Peter.

"Worse, I think," she answered—"a living death, the 'Punishment of the Wall.'"

"Poor wretch!" said Peter, with a shudder.

"Yes," remarked Inez reflectively, "few doctors like their own medicine."

"I say, Inez," said Peter, nodding his head towards Betty, "that marquis isn't coming here, is he?"

"In the spirit, perhaps, Don Peter, not otherwise."

"So he is really dead? What killed him?"

"Laughter, I think, or, rather, being laughed at. He got quite well of the hurts you gave him, and then, of course, he had to keep the queen's gage, and take the most noble lady yonder, late Betty, as his marchioness. He couldn't do less, after she beat you off him with your own sword and nursed him back to life. But he never heard the last of it. They made songs about him in the streets, and would ask him how his godmother, Isabella, was, because she had promised and vowed on his behalf; also, whether the marchioness had broken any lances for his sake lately, and so forth."

"Poor man!" said Peter again, in tones of the deepest sympathy. "A cruel fate; I should have done better to kill him."

"Much; but don't say so to the noble Betty, who thinks that he had a very happy married life under her protecting care. Really, he ate his heart out till even I, who hated him, was sorry. Think of it! One of the proudest men in Spain, and the most gallant, a nephew of the king, a pillar of the Church, his sovereigns' plenipotentiary to the Moors, and on secret matters—the common mock of the vulgar, yes, and of the great too!"

"The great! Which of them?"

"Nearly all, for the queen set the fashion—I wonder why she hated him so?" Inez added, looking shrewdly at Peter; then without waiting for an answer, went on: "She did it very cleverly, by always making the most of the most honourable Betty in public, calling her near to her, talking with her, admiring her English beauty, and so forth, and what her

Majesty did, everybody else did, until my exalted mistress nearly went off her head, so full was she of pride and glory. As for the marquis, he fell ill, and after the taking of Granada went to live there quietly. Betty went with him, for she was a good wife, and saved lots of money. She buried him a year ago, for he died slow, and gave him one of the finest tombs in Spain—it isn't finished yet. That is all the story. Now she has brought her boy, the young marquis, to England for a year or two, for she has a very warm heart, and longed to see you all. Also, she thought she had better go away a while, for her son's sake. As for me, now that Morella is dead, I am head of the household—secretary, general purveyor of intelligence, and anything else you like at a good salary."

"You are not married, I suppose?" asked Peter.

"No," Inez answered; "I saw so much of men when I was younger that I seem to have had enough of them. Or perhaps," she went on, fixing that mild and lustrous eye upon him, "there was one of them whom I liked too well to wish—"

She paused, for they had crossed the drawbridge and arrived opposite to the Old Hall. The gorgeous Betty and the fair Margaret, accompanied by the others, and talking rapidly, had passed through the wide doorway into its spacious vestibule. Inez looked after them, and perceived, standing like a guard at the foot of the open stair, that scarred suit of white armour and riven shield blazoned with the golden falcon, Isabella's gift, in which Peter had fought and conquered the Marquis of Morella. Then she stepped back and contemplated the house critically.

At each end of it rose a stone tower, built for the purposes of defence, and all around ran a deep moat. Within the circle of this moat, and surrounded by poplars and ancient yews, on the south side of the Hall lay a walled *pleasaunce*, or garden, of turf pierced by paths and planted with flowering hawthorns and other shrubs, and at the end of it, almost hidden in drooping willows, a stone basin of water. Looking at it, Inez saw at once that so far as the circumstances of climate and situation would allow, Peter, in the laying out of this place, had copied another in the far-off, southern city of Granada, even down to the details of the steps and seats. She turned to him and said innocently:

"Sir Peter, are you minded to walk with me in that garden this pleasant evening? I do not see any window in yonder tower."

Peter turned red as the scar across his face, and laughed as he answered: "There may be one for all that. Get you into the house, dear Inez, for none can be more welcome there; but I walk no more alone with you in gardens."